D1035090

BURTON
and
SPEKE

BURTON
and
SPEKE

WILLIAM HARRISON

ST. MARTIN'S / MAREK
NEW YORK

Harrison, William, 1933–
  Burton and Speke.

  "A St. Martin's Press/Marek book."
   1. Burton, Richard Francis, Sir, 1821–1890—Fiction.
2. Speke, John Hanning, 1827–1864—Fiction. I. Title.
PS3558.A672B8   813'.54   82-5620
ISBN 0-312-10873-7   AACR2

First Edition
10 9 8 7 6 5 4 3 2 1

for Merlee again
and for
the
friendship
of
Dr. William Floyd Harrison

My thanks to

Lady Gerald Fuller, Neston Park, Wiltshire; Mrs. A. Kelly, Archivist of the Royal Geographical Society, London; Dr. Clive Quennel of the Mineral Water Hospital, Bath; Mr. Peter Reid of the British Department of the Environment, London; Mr. Peter Gerald Hanning Speke, Rowlands, Ilmin ster; and to the many biographers, historians, students, and contemporaries of the explorers from whom I drew insights and inspiration, especially to Fawn Brodie, Isabel Burton, Byron Farwell, Humphrey Hare, James Pope Hennessey, Alexander Maitland, Dorothy Middleton, T. Wemyss Reid, Georgiana Stisted, Algernon Charles Swinburne and Cecil Woodham-Smith.

Contents

1854–1855 *The First Meeting, East African Journeys, the Disaster at Berbera, Wounds and Hard Feelings*   1

1855–1856 *Victorian Society, the War in the Crimea, the Return to Africa*   49

1857–1859 *The Great Journey and the Betrayal*   87

1859–1860 *Controversy Begins*   209

1860–1861 *Down the Nile and Across the Mississippi*   259

1862–1863 *Success and Exile*   319

1863–1864 *The Last Year: Dahomey, Paris, London, Bath*   365

Afterword   417

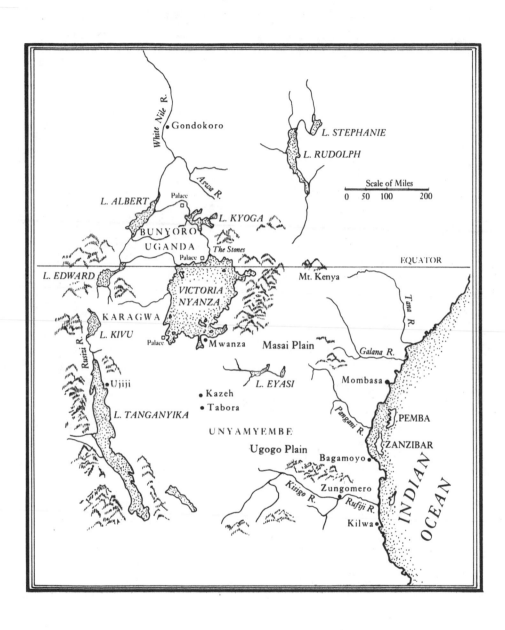

1854–1855

—————)◖(—————

The First Meeting,
East African Journeys,
the Disaster at Berbera,
Wounds and Hard Feelings

*O*N A TWO-MASTED BRIG NEARING THE PORT OF ADEN A CLUSTER OF ENGLISH gentlemen stood watching a handsome young Army officer shoot the gulls which had begun to trail the ship's wake. Standing around the taffrail they leaned on their canes, their top hats tied to their heads with scarves against the steady eastern breeze of the Indian Ocean, their cigars and pipes sending up small white puffs to accompany the discharge of the young officer's matchlock.

The young officer stood haughty and aloof as he carefully loaded his weapon, then shot the gulls. When he blew another one out of the sky and watched it drop into the sea, his audience—very impressed—tapped their canes on the deck in appreciation.

"Har!" the eldest of them cried. He was an elderly official of the East India Company, en route back to England on this company vessel. Beside him stood Samuel White Baker, the well-known British outdoorsman and traveler.

"Damn nice shooting," Baker assured everyone. He was clearly the leader of this audience, which grunted its approval.

"Har!" the old man added again, as if the meaning of this syllable were perfectly clear.

The gulls had come out to meet the ship. They rode with the wind behind the sails, occasionally swooping down toward the foaming sea. The young officer, his gaze steady and revealing a slight disdain for things around him, shot the gulls as they glided at the apex of their flight before they swooped and dived. His audience continued to look on with grunts, coughs, and taps of their canes; they noted that the young officer used a musket, not a scattergun, so made difficult shots, yet they also noted that he wasn't very sporting.

They considered themselves the best of sports. They had transformed this dull merchant brig with its cargo of tea and hemp into a tolerable gaming and social club during its journey westward from Bombay. In the evenings they drank, played cards, and smoked a little opium. During the days they told endless stories about the rajahs, shooting tigers, making money, and taking the pleasures of women at tropical latitudes. Most of them had traveled around the edges of Africa for the East India Company or the British government—largely the same in this September of 1854—and many of them had put ashore at Aden previously. The port guarded the entrance to the Red Sea en route up to Cairo and frequently served as a point of departure for excursions along the African coast and into the unmapped interiors.

Another gull hovered on the wind, its wings extended. The young officer fired again and the shot created an explosion of feathers. The men murmured their appreciation.

Baker, however, in a loud basso voice, called out, "Next time wait till a bird dives and see if you can hit 'im in full flight!"

The men grunted approval at this suggestion.

"Har!" the old official snorted.

The young officer, not turning his eyes toward his audience, slowly and carefully loaded powder into his old matchlock. He rammed the ball into place.

Then, again, he aimed and shot a gull that was a perfect target, poised in place on the breeze.

The young officer didn't explain himself, but it was clear that he meant to slaughter as many gulls as he could.

In the last hours of the voyage tables were set up on the aft deck and covered with bright strips of Somali cloth. Stewards hurried around the tables with bottles of gin and warm beer.

"Please, come join me," Baker said to the young officer.

A cool east wind sent them toward the harbor, but the sun was glowing overhead. At the horizon an arid coastline was in constant sight, and beyond its green surf the Arabian desert kept its silence. The young officer stood at the rail gazing out, striking a melancholy pose. Like the distant land beyond, he possessed an exotic solitude: many who saw him were attracted to him, but few would ever know him. John Hanning Speke practiced aloofness like an art.

"Sit with me, Lieutenant," Baker repeated. All during the trip he had tried to engage the young man in conversation.

At last, Speke did come and sit at Baker's table.

Samuel White Baker was a robust man of private means who spent his money and time on personally financed explorations. But as this last lunch began, it was Baker who asked the questions, as if his young companion with his fierce indifference were the more important man.

"No, I'm not going back to England," Speke said in answer to a question. "I'm stopping at the garrison in Aden, where I plan to get permits for Africa. I want to travel into Somaliland and Berbera."

"Really?" Baker asked. "What for?"

"Hunting," Speke said. "I want to kill a lion. I've killed one of each specimen in India and now I mean to do the same in Africa."

"Damn me, that's ambition."

"I have the trophies of all my hunts sent back to Jordans—our family estate. My mother intends to establish a museum collection."

"Africa's a hard country," Baker told him. "Been there before?"

"No, I've been in the army in India for ten years—since I was just seventeen years old. Haven't even taken leave until now. Fought in the Punjab campaign. Went on a few hunts and walked into the Himalayas a few times. But I've mostly saved my wages for this African activity."

"Always wanted to travel in Africa myself," Baker admitted. "But there's always a war, or the seasons aren't right. Tell the truth, I've always wanted to go search for the sources of the Nile. You know, the fabled inland lakes. Except they're not fables. I don't think so—and neither does the Royal Geographical Society."

"Inland lakes?"

"The ones Ptolemy wrote about."

"Ah, those," Speke said, covering his uncertainty.

"Always wanted to go on some first-rate expedition," Baker said, drinking off a beer. "Swear if I still don't! Once, I petitioned the Society, but they turned me down. They think I should spend my own fortune and none of theirs."

"It takes a lot of money, I suppose," Speke said.

"Damn, yes, a man's whole purse. But if the Society and the government keep their funds to themselves, the Nile will never be traced, don't you see?"

"I've got beads, some copper wire, and the wages I've saved up. Think that will do for a year's hunting?" Speke asked.

"If you stay along the coast. But any penetration inland is a great quartermastering task: a caravan must always carry enough to go in, then enough to come out again. That's why the Nile is so terrible. One can travel three thousand miles upriver from Cairo without seeing anything except desert."

"I walked into the Himalayas above Katmandu," Speke said, becoming slightly haughty. "So I know about long journeys."

"But there are mountain villages in the Himalayas. And monasteries on top where a man can buy a bit of goat's cheese, right?"

"Yes, true."

"But what's in the middle of Africa? I mean, we don't have the foggiest, do we?"

The stewards brought plates of curry. Baker ate hurriedly, his face growing redder as he forked hot morsels of meat into his mouth and drank more beer. Baker's upper arms stretched against the fabric. He looked like a wrestler, but like a clubman, too: dressed in an expensive tropical suit, whiskered, and with an air of professional authority about him.

As they finished lunch—Speke had only a few bites of curry and a twist of bread—the crew began to trim the sails. Passengers began moving to the rails to look for the distant minarets of the city.

In this last hour before docking Speke and Baker exchanged some information about themselves. Speke's father, he told Baker, was a quiet farmer, a former captain with the 14th Dragoons. His mother, he said, actually ran the family estate and much of its business. She had arranged the interview with the Duke of Wellington, for instance, which resulted in her son's commission into the regiment in India.

"You didn't attend university?" Baker asked him.

"Cared nothing for school," Speke answered.

Baker himself was from a family of navy men, he told Speke, but his father had been a banker and shipowner with connections in the colonies. So Baker had grown up as a trader.

"Overseer of a plantation in Ceylon," Baker commented in his lilting basso. "But, damn, what an unsatisfying life! Sending out packets of tea, getting back packets of letters with orders for more! Taking money from one account and popping it into another! So I married and had children. But, damn me, that was boring, too! Family life back in England, I mean, is rot! So I sailed back to India and shot a tiger or two, but sport didn't help. So I went to Germany—where I was educated, actually—and helped build a railroad. Now my accounts are full, my children are growing up, my wife is religious, and I want a great adventure!"

Baker wiped his whiskers with a napkin.

Someone up top yelled down that harbor had been sighted. Speke stood up, shook Baker's hand, and announced that he had to go below to pack his gear. "Goodbye, sir," he said. He could achieve stiff formality in an instant.

"Perhaps we'll someday meet in Africa," Baker said as they parted. "I know that I intend to travel there. And I predict you'll find good hunting!"

"So goodbye," Speke repeated, pumping Baker's hand. Then, as if he were suddenly uncertain of everything, of who Ptolemy was and of who he was himself, as if he couldn't possibly talk longer, he pivoted and walked away.

Within the hour an Indian dhow appeared next to the ship, its crew of lepers begging for coins. Dolphins were sighted. Then the harbor and city appeared with their mirage of white walls, like flame: the light from which one jumped off into darkness.

On the afternoon of his arrival Speke went to see the British political resident at the garrison, Colonel James Outram. The young lieutenant stood before the colonel's desk dressed in uniform and saber.

"So what exactly are you asking of me?" the colonel wanted to know, staring into Speke's letters of introduction.

"To let me go over to Africa," Speke answered. "To hunt along the coast."

"Not possible," Outram replied, and he continued to peruse the letters without even glancing up. "The Somali are unfriendly and the Berbera tribesmen are feuding. And we've got too many problems at the garrison to worry over some young lieutenant on leave who wants to shoot animals over on the continent." The colonel rattled Speke's papers, signaling an end to argument.

The garrison, as Speke knew, had been a trouble spot for a long time. The colonel had been at this post only two months, having replaced a much more popular officer, Brigadier Haines, who had skillfully handled both the British troops and the troublesome Arabs. Unfortunately, Haines had been arrested by the East India Company for embezzlement and sent off to prison. This brought Outram—and a heavy hand—to Aden. The colonel seemed to dislike his troops, the blacks, the Arabs, and all who passed his way.

"Do we have any troops over on the coast?" Speke ventured to ask. "Perhaps I could join anyone who—"

Outram's red face grew redder. His white sideburns glistened. "I wouldn't put a British soldier anywhere along the Somali coast when there's danger, would I?" he snapped. "No, too much risk!"

Speke tried to keep his composure.

"Now there's Burton," the colonel said. "You might try him."

"Who?" Speke asked.

"Richard Francis Burton, the *hero*," the colonel said with sarcasm. "He came here on leave, same as you, but with the financing of the Royal Geographical Society. He's going to the coast, but out of our jurisdiction. If I had my way, he wouldn't even be in Aden."

"Burton the explorer?" Speke inquired.

"Yes, the *hero* who penetrated the forbidden cities in disguise! Mecca and Medina! Surely, you read about him in the press! Why, he's here! Studying the bloody language, so he can talk to the scorpions over on the coast!"

"Could I meet with him?" Speke asked.

"This is strictly out of my jurisdiction," Outram said, and he flicked his snowy sideburns, first one, then the other, with his thumb.

"Is he staying in the garrison?"

"Oh, no," the colonel said, looking up. "Not Captain Burton, the *hero*. No, he lives where he can study the language. Where he can be the true soldier and scholar. Captain Burton lives in the native quarter, Lieutenant, where he says he always lives—among the whores!"

That night Speke settled himself in one of those cramped little rooms that were assigned to young officers just off the courtyard and promenade of the garrison. He bathed in a small wooden tub that smelled of camphor. Then he dressed in one of his white uniforms, combed his thick blond hair, and prepared to go visit Dick Burton. Like everyone else in England and the Empire, he had heard of this adventurer. In the disguise of an Afghan pilgrim, Burton had joined a caravan to Mecca. Thought to be another Arab because of his renowned swarthy looks, he had managed to penetrate the holy shrine at the Grand Mosque. It was a feat that ranked somewhere between a schoolboy prank and a daring anthropological exploit, but many newspaper columnists had adored him and called for his knighthood. The Royal Geographical Society had entertained him. The army had granted him extended leave for more of such activities.

Speke strolled out into the hot, moonless night. He heard the sound of a distant lute and stood for a moment listening.

Perhaps Burton would take him along to the Somali coast, he was thinking. If gruff Colonel Outram disliked the man so much, perhaps Burton would turn out to be a good sort. And, surely, that was an exaggeration about the prostitutes. It was well known that Burton composed poetry. He had also published books on India (where, like Speke, he had served in the army), on the bayonet and its use and on falconry. The man was literary. He might prove to be eccentric, Speke concluded, but surely he wasn't common.

The town that encircled the garrison consisted of a dark maze of streets. Odors of cabbage and urine permeated the night air, and white dogs seemed to lurk everywhere, moving among the shadows as Speke made his way toward the address given to him. Doors stood open, so that as he went along he could see into rooms. In one, some children slept on straw mats around a candle. In another, old men smoked their long pipes, *chibouks*, and talked to one another. Then, at another open portal, Speke stopped to watch a strange dance: a plump woman, veiled except for the bulge of her naked stomach, moved across a rug and watched her own sensuous movements in a full-length mirror. Seated in a corner was a boy who kept rhythm on the strings of a *darabukeh* as the woman rotated her hips and shuffled softly over the rug. She danced for no one, just for herself, and Speke stood there watching, feeling her odd loneliness. He forgot for a moment his reason for passing by; his own curse attended him; sex was a sadness to the lieutenant and the source of his aloofness, and now he stood there, his face impassive, but his emotions suddenly caught in the dance.

He stumbled along the street once more.

Weary of foreign cities and weary of himself inside them, Speke wanted to get into the open country again and away from such sewers. Leaning against a wall, thinking this, he brushed himself off; his clothes were already sticky with perspiration, and he worried that he wouldn't make a good impression on the adventurer, that he might not be an acceptable companion and that he might never see Africa.

At a private hotel out on Steamer Point beyond the garrison, Speke found an old sleeping porter who wore a threadbare fez. Yes, the captain and the captain's manservant were there.

Goatskins of foul water hung from wooden pegs along the stairwell and landing. As he went up, Speke heard the sounds of a tambourine and a woman's laughter.

Rooms of pillows, couches and incense.

The whores' bodies were clean shaven, and each of them seemed to move —strolling here, lying there—to display this boldly. While all their limbs seemed loose and open and they lacked modesty about their nakedness, they kept their faces veiled and hidden. As the lieutenant paused in the doorway, watching them dumbfounded, their eyes behind those veils regarded him with amusement. One of them, a large black Somali, arched herself on her bed of pillows, her thighs slack and inviting.

The captain strolled the room with a tall, cinnamon-skinned woman who wore translucent green robes with a coral necklace—the only apparel worn by any of the whores. The two of them seemed to be arguing softly over a matter in a book they shared. Meanwhile, a little black man in baggy trousers trailed after them trying to light the captain's pipe.

Speke thought of clearing his throat or in some other delicate manner announcing himself. Captain Burton, he noticed, was a broad-shouldered gentleman, hairy, dark, and intense.

The windowseat where most of the whores lounged on pillows was in one of those shuttered bay windows of the east: a *moucharbieh*. Beyond its open panels lay the indigo waters of the Gulf of Aden. One girl, a white young thing with rosy cheeks who wore only veil, rings, and bracelets, poured scented water into a large brass basin. Another whore paced the room, her nubian skin gleaming in the candlelight.

As Burton accepted his pipe from the little manservant in baggy pants, he acknowledged Speke with a glance.

"Yes?" he inquired, his voice filled with authority. He blew a ring of blue smoke.

Speke found that he was unable to state his business.

Burton said something in Arabic, which made the woman in the translucent gown throw back her head in laughter.

Then he addressed the lieutenant as if he had been asked to lecture on his life. "I have seen a great deal," he said, sounding a little drunk, yet friendly and articulate. "I've heard the sounds in the desert at night of the slave traders mutilating their slaves, fitting them for service in the harems. I've seen the upper Nile with the golden sun of the pharaohs on it! I've seen minarets covered with birds of prey—at a strange oasis in the middle of nowhere! I've seen the priests shed their black robes and walk naked! And the dervishes! And now I want to see Zanzibar, the Mountains of the Moon, King Solomon's Mines, and the mystic inland cities! Where did you serve, Lieutenant? You're not from the garrison!"

Speke only just managed to reply, "In India."

"Ah!" Burton said. "The fire of the Indus! The shadows of the Himalayas! I made a report, you know, for the army. A written report which contained material on the existence of male brothels in India! You can imagine what I got for my trouble—scholarly work, all of it! I nearly got sacked and court-martialed! That damned report kept me out of battle in the only war we had! Here, come with me."

Speke followed the captain and the tall woman in robes into yet a larger room with more pillows and couches. A huge round *cafas* occupied the center

9

of the room: an upturned basket with a mattress inside, which served as a bed. The floor around it was strewn with ostrich fans. Each pillow and drape wore tassels of silk. Thrown across tables were colorful eastern rugs, and on these sat brass pots, bottles of *raki* and gin, cigarettes, books, and loose gold coins. Bottles of colored oils with burning wicks hung overhead. On the back of a couch a white Persian cat lay on a spray of discarded veils. Beside the bed—where the woman now stretched out—was a small table that held a boiling carafe of coffee, warmed by a candle, and pewter cups.

"I stole a young nun from some sisters out in India," the captain went on, pouring everyone a cup of coffee. "I won the army's language examinations every year. If it hadn't been for my eye infections, I would have been promoted, not that I cared a fig for it, but I would've gone up to battle, at least, and not ended up on that bloody survey crew. I met good men on that survey, mind you, and they're here with me now, good comrades who will go over to Africa with me, but, damn, what a waste of my talents out there! Better for you, I trust. Have some coffee."

Speke nodded his acceptance. Beside them, the woman turned herself and closed her eyes.

"Have they canceled my leave and sent for me?" Burton asked. "Are you from the Bombay office sent to tell me to go back on active duty and to forget the fountains of the Nile?"

"I'm on leave from the army, too," Speke said with a nervous shrug. "And I want to travel over to the Somali coast with you."

They drank coffee in silence, regarding one another over the rims of their cups. Burton's eyes were like nothing the lieutenant had ever seen; they burned with a dark, melodramatic flame. The captain's mustaches curved below his chin, giving him a kind of permanent scowl, yet when he smiled, as he did now, the whole room grew more pleasant. He had the look of a pirate and the voice of an actor.

Speke, on the other hand, was boyish. His blond hair flowed like a lion's mane and he had cold blue eyes. Burton's impression was that he was quite shy, very young, a bit stupid, and that he might try to cover his youth and shortcomings with arrogance.

In the far room the whores began to dance. The young white girl with rosy cheeks whirled around, that brass basin above her head, and this inspired the manservant to join her. Burton looked at Speke as though he were trying to think of something profound to say. In the ensuing pause, the woman on the *cafas* opened her eyes and asked for a cigarette, so Burton gave her one and held a candle to it.

The whores still danced, but mostly pushed each other, giggled, and staggered around. The manservant picked up the tambourine and kept a poor beat to the sound of the lute.

"The goal of every journey," Burton said to his young visitor, trying, it seemed, to impress, "is to explore oneself in new surroundings. Don't you agree?"

Speke nodded yes and shrugged, as if to say, of course, why not?

The Nubian with the gleaming skin walked on her fat knees, leaning backward and swaying with the music, rolling her breasts from side to side. The manservant, dizzy with all this suggestive activity, turned in a circle and slapped the tambourine against his backside.

"So tell me," Burton asked, measuring his words, "what exactly is it that you want from Africa?" He smiled, hardly expecting a romanticism to match his own.

"I want to go to Africa," Speke said, his eyes glazed with melancholy as he paused for effect himself, "to die."

Burton could only look at the lieutenant with stunned awe.

On the sunlit verandah of that ramshackle hotel on Steamer Point, the group spent the mornings discussing their proposed trip to Somaliland. The principal business of those morning sessions, as best as Speke could determine, was to drink quantities of cognac, coffee, beer, and the local wines while telling stories and flirting with the prostitutes; seldom did Burton or his companions actually say much about necessary preparations, so only with difficulty did Speke learn what was going on and why.

Most of it he learned from Dr. Steinhauser, who was the chief civil surgeon at Aden and Burton's close friend. The doctor's whitewashed little house and office was near the hotel, so every morning he appeared with loaves of bread for breakfast. He was a rotund little man, an energetic scholar, fond of his cognac, an expert on Arab matters, who considered Burton his superior in these things, and who wanted someday to translate *The Arabian Nights* into English. Pieces of bread or tobacco frequently lodged in the doctor's beard, and Burton always called attention to the fact, so that Steinhauser would say, "Ho, well then, we'll send the five after them!" and he would scratch his chin with his five fingers until the morsels were dislodged and he and the captain laughed hard at what Speke considered to be an old joke between them.

The other Westerners in the mornings were Lieutenants Stroyan and Herne. Stroyan was a quiet, unassuming chap who had been with Burton in India. Since he liked hunting, he and Speke found they had lots to talk about. Stroyan also admired Burton to the point of reverence and laughed loudest at their leader's bawdiness. Herne was competent and aloof. He was a photographer, a surveyor, and a mechanic who could fix the oldest and least promising of their rifles, chronometers, and sextants. He had served in India, too, but not with Burton, and had been selected for the trip on the basis of skill alone.

The manservant was called End of Time. He did little work, grinned to reveal a row of scattered teeth, and bragged that he was a complete coward who did not want to meet either lion or foe in Africa. Al-Hammal, the last of the group, was police chief of Aden. A big, bullnecked man who sweated and cursed profusely, he seemed to be just a muscular buffoon. Speke was surprised to discover that Al-Hammal would be manager of the whole expedition.

"Burton doesn't intend to hire the porters and tend to the caravan himself?" Speke asked the doctor.

"Oh, no," Steinhauser explained casually. "That's mere administration."

Slowly, then, Speke learned about their mission. Burton had originally planned to pierce inland from the Somali coast toward Zanzibar and to locate en route, if possible, the famed fountains of the Nile and the snow-capped Mountains of the Moon. These were, roughly, somewhere in the middle of Africa. But Colonel Outram's opposition, meager funds, and actual native hostilities among the Berbera tribesmen and others had caused plans to be modified.

Plans—modified or otherwise—still seemed haphazard. Speke finally asked Burton what exactly they might try to accomplish.

"We have four major goals," Burton said, looking out to sea and finding a deeper voice. "First, we want to discourage slavery by showing these tribes the British uniform and letting them know that we are high-minded and resolute on this matter. Second, we want to establish a camp for later departure in the search for the source of the Nile. There is a forbidden city in the high plateau country inland: Harar. I intend to go there, make friends, and see if we can arrange a later caravan from there toward Zanzibar."

"The human head, unlike the rose, does not grow back once it is struck off," Steinhauser said, eating his morning jam and bread. The men, especially End of Time, thought this very comical, but Burton continued.

"Third, we search for gold," he said. "It would be highly unpatriotic if we didn't. And there is supposed to be a dry stream, the Wadi Nogal, in which great nuggets lie around."

Again, laughter.

"And, finally, we closely examine the women," Burton said.

Laughter and applause. Al-Hammal slapped his thick knees and End of Time revealed his few teeth. Even the stoic Herne seemed amused.

"From an anthropological viewpoint, there are some interesting sexual practices over there in Africa," he said, lecturing as he sipped his coffee and gazed out on the sheen of the gulf. Stroyan laughed loudest of all the men. "Prostitutes, wives, and simple country girls alike, I understand, have the labia and clitoris cut off. Their men do them this favor to diminish the heat of passion and to keep the females home where they belong. But the mutilation produces a curious effect. Rumor has it that the women are hotter than ever. Using our every tool and device, we will investigate this. Are you interested, Speke?"

The lieutenant was clearly embarrassed.

Steinhauser tried to pat him on the shoulder, but Speke turned aside.

When the sun beat down warmly, they moved indoors. There, they gave up coffee for beer, so that breakfast became lunch.

Days passed this way. It seemed to Speke that the hours slowed and blent together, nothing ever getting accomplished.

In his time to himself, Speke prepared for the journey—even if no one else seemed interested in organized preparation. He went barefoot to toughen his feet. He took daily calesthenics. He also checked and counted his barter goods and personal belongings every day, worrying that he might not have sufficient beads and trinkets or that someone might steal from his room.

Before sundown one afternoon Speke walked barefoot over to the doctor's office. Over a cup of tea and a glass of cognac, Steinhauser insisted that the lieutenant should read a manuscript of Burton's *Personal Narrative of a Pilgrimmage to Al-Medinah and Meccah*.

"Oh, I'm not much for books," Speke told him.

"There are long footnotes, and the style isn't really all that wonderful, but you should read it," the doctor urged him.

"Will it make him famous?"

"Ah, fame," the doctor said, sipping his cognac. "Who knows? I think if he had gone directly back to England after the exploit, the queen would have knighted him. Men have been knighted for less. But he stayed in Cairo for months and didn't return."

"He wasn't interested in the honors?"

"Perhaps. But he was more interested in Cairo. And, now, perhaps all the newspapermen and geographers aren't in the mood to honor him. One should be present to accept honors and medals—I told him this—when others are in the mood to bestow them. All he got from his extra months in Cairo was syphilis."

"Contemptible," Speke said, the word rushing out of him and falling between him and the doctor like steel.

Yet the doctor, showing patience with the young lieutenant, decided against a strong response to such a judgment. Instead, he said, "Men want to be around Dick Burton. They want to watch him, listen to him, and do whatever he wants. So do women. And so do you. After all, you're using his energies and initiatives to get yourself to the Somali coast."

Somehow, too much had been said. Speke drank off his tea and got up abruptly to leave.

"Take the manuscript, please," Steinhauser urged him.

"Don't get me wrong," Speke said, standing barefoot in the doctor's doorway, his chin held high. "I like Burton well enough."

"I'm sure you do," Steinhauser said evenly.

"And thank you very much for tea."

"Don't mention it."

Although the manuscript gave him difficulty, Speke did take it and read it. There were notes on tribes, races, Moslem customs and rituals. With understatement, Burton played down the danger of his trip in disguise to the forbidden holy cities. The author also seemed to like Moslem ways and the Bedouin particularly ("the dignity of pride and dirt") and seemed proud that he had made the *hajj*—or sacred pilgrimage—and spoke with no real irony of it.

Cantankerous opinions lurked everywhere. Burton thought highly of veils on women, sunglasses in the desert, the use of the bayonet in warfare, and polygamy. He despised slavery, Germans ("none but Germans have ideas unexplainable by words"), the practice of spiritualism and the occult sciences, and sexual prudishness.

Most of the asides and footnotes in the thick manuscript were concerned with sex—and were not particularly fit, Speke felt, for publication. Burton, he decided, seemed to have an inordinate interest in the copulations of strangers in foreign lands.

Speke also made note that Burton had made an important friend: James Grant Lumsden, a senior member of the Bombay council of the East India Company. Burton had met his new friend and benefactor after the pilgrimage to Mecca, had traveled to Bombay to stay at Lumsden's house, and had written the manuscript while a guest there. The book was dedicated to Lumsden, who, in turn, had arranged with the Royal Geographical Society for this present expedition to the Somali coast.

Speke was a poor reader, tracing sentences with his index finger and moving his lips with the words as he struggled through the narrative. But he considered the effort part of his duty and preparation while in Aden, so plodded along—finishing, finally, in just over a fortnight.

At times, he recalled his own arduous schooling. Here was Burton's erudite work; and here he sat, attended by his curse, oafish and slow, somehow more dim-witted and unnatural than ever before.

Weeks went on, too, without Burton or anyone else actually saying outright that Speke was an acceptable and confirmed member of the expedition.

He did find out that he would be the replacement—if confirmed—for a favorite companion who had died.

"Burton loved Stocks. Everyone did," Herne confided to Speke one day as they strolled along the seawall. "We counted on his being with us."

"What did he die of?"

"Apoplexy. Just keeled over. Burton knew him longest and trusted him most of all those who were on the Sind survey with him. Stocks was a surgeon, you know, and, I say, you don't have any talent for medicine, do you?"

"None," Speke replied.

He walked barefoot, still trying to toughen his feet. Fishermen worked at their nets along the shore, and the sky was a pleasant cobalt blue, but Speke felt miserable.

"Harar won't be as easy as Mecca," Steinhauser warned Burton. "They're both forbidden cities, but Harar is the missionary training center for the whole Islamic religion—and a place where virtually no strangers go. No European has ever seen it. I think they'll lop off your head."

"That's why I'll use my Arab disguise," Burton said.

They were on the roof of the hotel, so that the burnoose Burton wore flowed in the breeze. He turned his profile toward a gust of wind and liked the effect.

"First they'll find you out, *then* they'll lop off your head," the doctor pointed out.

"Well, I've decided to go alone to Harar," Burton said, straightening his burnoose. "There, do you think I look like a man of the desert?"

"You look vain," the doctor said. "And what will the others do, if you save all the excitement for yourself?"

"I'm sending Herne and Stroyan to Berbera to investigate the slave caravans. They'll also make notes on the geography, the weather, commerce, and all such usual stuff of expeditions, but I think we have a responsibility to let the tribesmen know that England wants the slave traffic stopped. If we show a real presence, we might have some influence."

"What about Speke? Will he go?"

"I think I'll have him explore the Wadi Nogal. There's probably no gold, but he can stay outdoors and keep busy. You know what he told me? He said he wanted to go die in Africa! Curious. What do you make of that?"

"Very Byronic. The melancholy song of a young lieutenant."

"You don't trust Speke, do you?" Burton asked the doctor.

"No," Steinhauser said.

Burton adjusted his burnoose and once again turned his face to the wind.

On the night before setting off for the coast, the group held a party in the hotel. Half the garrison, assorted civil officials, the whores, and a number of local policemen in the company of Al-Hammal filled those upstairs rooms and the verandah. The tall woman in the coral necklace occupied the *cafas*, but never woke up. The entertainments were a pleasant mixture: soldiers in white uniforms sang familiar music-hall versions of "The Rat-Catcher's Daughter" and other songs; the whores strolled around with their navels bare; End of Time provided pipes of opium; toasts were raised with glasses of *raki* and beer. Stroyan stood by the upright piano, placed his hand inside his jacket like young Napoleon, and rendered a tenor solo: "I'm a Young Man from the Country, but You Won't Get over Me." It was the favorite song of the evening. Afterward, conversation turned to the Crimean War, the disastrous charge of the Light Brigade, the idiocy of the generals, and the evils of an army where aristocrats could purchase commissions and leadership. When arguments began, the men turned to other matters at home: the Epsom Races, the death of entertainer Henri Latour, whose hot-air balloon had fallen in Tottenham Marshes, and Prince Albert, who did well enough as a husband for Victoria, but was nobody's favorite.

Assignments for the next morning and afterward were now clear: Burton would sail for the coast with men and supplies; Speke would soon take another boat to the coast, to the harbor of Arz Al-Aman near the mouth of the Wadi Nogal; Herne and Stroyan would set up camp and begin reconnaissance at Berbera; and after Burton had gone to Harar they would all reunite in Berbera.

Toward the end of the evening a thin officer with a thinner mustache, Outram's secretary, showed up to sound the official warning again. "Major Gordon Laing was murdered in Harar thirty years ago," he reminded them. "And now, we fully expect the Amir of Harar to murder you, Captain, but you seem to be going to your death in high spirits, so farewell!"

Burton bristled, but managed to smile.

"You here in Aden have a simple duty," he said, raising his voice to the level of rhetoric. "Your duty is to keep the road to Yemen open, to keep ships sailing back and forth between here and Berbera, and to keep your heads stuck in the sand. This, I take it, is British policy in these parts. Furthermore, you don't like the Somalis and you don't understand the Arab chiefs. If a traveler trespasses anywhere and gets himself killed, your soldiers ride out of the garrison and burn villages in reprisal. All around you is a fierce, free race of people who want their own territory and their own ways. But the British will have nothing to do with them outside exploitation."

"I was speaking of Harar, not the whole of politics," the secretary put in.

"Harar is an ancient metropolis of a once mighty race, the only permanent settlement in East Africa, the seat of Moslem theology, a walled city with an unknown language, its own coinage, the headquarters of the slave trade, the emporium of the coffee and cotton trade, and the home of the kat plant—a fine narcotic," Burton replied. "Besides, all African cities are prisons into which you enter by your own will and leave by another's. I will go there, then return."

"Very brave," the thin secretary managed.

"It isn't a matter of bravery," Burton said, raising a toast to the whole room. "So let me say this to all gathered here tonight: in every corner of the world where fate drops him, a man must find a friend—or a beautiful woman, or, if lucky, both."

Everyone at the party, with the exception of the secretary, laughed and applauded. Glasses were filled.

"In Africa, especially," Burton continued, "shyness or pride or bravery or English phlegm won't work. You have to make friends fast. You have to walk up to a man, clasp his fist, talk—even if you don't understand each other—and make him your own."

"Hear, hear," someone said, and glasses were raised.

"I am sorry that the colonel, who was invited here tonight, cannot be here personally to drink with comrades. But let this be clear: I need no policy to confirm my journey. I need no sword. I need only friends—because I go in friendship. And as I've been shown friendship here in Aden among men of good and ancient races, so will I carry this spirit with me through the desert into the mountains around Harar!"

Stroyan and Al-Hammal led the cheers as the men drank.

After Burton sailed for Zayla, the little African coastal town where he hoped to buy camels and mules for his overland trip to Harar, Speke waited at the garrison for another ship. He felt odd, neither fully part of Burton's expedition nor fully on his own.

One evening he dined with Colonel Outram and told the colonel as much.

"Well, you're a young gentleman and Burton isn't," the colonel told him. "I mean, one can tell by *looking* at Burton: that complexion, those mustaches, eyes like a bloody gypsy. He reminds me of the Prince Consort: a foreigner. Something not quite right about either of them."

The accusation amused Speke, who thought of Burton as very English, yet he said nothing in reply.

Because the night was windless, they took supper on the roof of the officers' barracks at the garrison. Beyond the rooftops, stars announced themselves in the darkening sky.

"The man doesn't take tea," the colonel went on, sitting rigid and dabbing at his chin with his linen napkin. "Doesn't hunt—very much deplores it, so I'm told. Fraternizes with the natives. Especially the women—who have diseased him. And doesn't accept his rank. That's what I can't bear: he writes reports and sends them off to officials beyond his immediate superiors! He's an egotist, you see, who imagines that he's above army protocol, so you shouldn't feel part of any scheme of his. After all, you're the son of a good family."

Again, Speke said nothing.

"I like you," the colonel said. "By the time you return from the African coast—and I pray your safe return—I'll be retired from this post. My replacement will be Brigadier Coghlan, who I know will look forward to meeting you.

I intend to tell him that you're a good soldier, a fine young chap, and that your future should be much more promising apart from Burton."

"Very kind of you, sir," Speke responded.

The ruler of Zayla, that fortress town of fifteen hundred on the Somali coast, was Sharmakay. He was sixty years old, tall, fair of skin, red of beard, with a shaved head and lip. He lived without splendor in a compound of plaster houses and barns with reed walls; his weapons—rifles, spears, and sabers—adorned his rooms. In his Arab dress, bedecked with knives and pistols, he stood thick and imposing.

"You are known as a man who accepts no gifts or bribes," Burton said, meeting Sharmakay for the first time on the shore. Around them as they stood in the sandy gravel, Burton's men unloaded cargo which was heavily scrutinized by the governor's aides. "But I very much want to present you with my personal pistol," Burton went on, extending the weapon toward his host. "I carried this weapon on my hajj to the holy shrine at Mecca. And hereafter I would take pleasure, praise the Prophet, in knowing that it is pointed at your enemies."

"I have heard of you," the ruler said, moved by the speech and tucking the new pistol into his belt. "And I welcome you. But I must tell you that I am a man obsessed, who much annoys thy government in these times. By Allah's will, I shall conquer Berbera and Harar and rule this entire coast. I have served the British navy and carry a saber wound on my body. I am here by the leave of the British. But, lo, I am a man, like the British, of great and probably unworthy ambition."

Burton laughed. "An ambitious man should have women to console him and many allies," he said.

"Well spoken. I have seen the cities of Cairo and Bombay and know of men's ways. I am an able governor and warrior. But ambition is a curse."

"My own ambition," Burton announced, "is to visit Harar."

"I have closed the road to Harar," Sharmakay told him. "My son was killed on that road a year ago. Recently, brigands struck down a favorite slave. No one goes to Harar."

"It is my own curse that I wish to go," Burton admitted.

"Your room in my house is prepared," the ruler explained. "But you must put it from your mind that you can go to Harar."

Sharmakay's house was a rambling affair of added rooms, attached barns, courtyards, and outdoor kitchens; its walls were of coralline and mud, white-washed, and on its roof, in the evenings, the ruler liked to sit and gaze at the white moon over the sea and the distant Tajjurrah hills. From this roof, in daytime, he could see the width of the city, situated in the midst of nothing, and adorned by the single fat minaret where the muezzin sang his song. At the gates of the city were the savage Bedouin tents. The Bedu sat out there scowling, even the women, and oiled themselves with grease and butter to keep the flies away; they were a harsh, gypsy people, as different from the Somali as Burton and the English, yet from them the city had its existence. They brought ivory, hides, and slaves, so the male citizens of Zayla did no work, just lived off this Bedouin desert commerce, letting their wives run the households inside the walls while they went out in the mornings for their long chats, their endless coffees, and their games.

Burton's room was upstairs over a barn which served as the ruler's warehouse. Below were bales, boxes, rugs, animal skins, ivory, weapons, and ammunition. Above, Burton's bed was an assortment of pillows; he had a pleasant balcony which looked toward the sea.

Mornings, again, became busy times. By ten o'clock he would go downstairs for a breakfast of grain cakes and mutton. Afterward, he would take a pipe and coffee and watch Sharmakay, gigantic and friendly, as the ruler entertained the daily flow of visitors. Some wanted favors or jobs, but most of them came just to talk. As they did, Sharmakay placed a napkin underneath Burton's chin and scolded him for not eating more.

Clearly, Sharmakay liked the Englishman, but regarded him as a foolish son who should be shown hospitality and discouraged from thinking about Harar.

To the astonishment of the local visitors, Burton announced that he had made the hajj to Mecca and that he considered himself a true Moslem. He ordered his prayer rug that first morning and afterward recited the two-bow prayer, read from the Koran, and listened to the *khatib* who came around to preach every day. To Burton, it all seemed like a rural parish in England—some by-way church where all civic and social activities were conducted.

"It is part of our religion that we should seek converts," Sharmakay explained. "But, truth be told, we have never actually seen one. So you should not be offended if we gape at you."

"Not all Moslems are cousins," Burton told him.

On the third of these mornings Burton brought out of his luggage a copy of *The Arabian Nights*, written in Arabic, bound in handsome leather. No one present, not even the ruler himself, was equipped to read from it, though, so Burton, noting their illiteracy, opened it with care on his lap as he sat cross-legged. The men in the room—perhaps thirty, in all—sat quietly as he read to them the four hundred and forty-third night, the story in which a clever wife warned some unwanted guests, "Be careful of yourselves lest the wind come forth from your bellies, for with me dwelleth the wife of my father, who dieth if she hear a fart!" Reading these comic lines, Burton looked up to see if any of his audience smiled or laughed, but none did. They kept a hushed silence as he read on.

Three tales later his voice tired and he stopped.

The next morning wives and children were brought to the storyteller. Almost one hundred villagers crowded into the room, sitting on the bales and boxes, leaning forward to listen. Pipes were lit, coffee was poured for the honored few, and Burton read again—this time from a less offensive tale. After this, a little bright-eyed girl, no more than four years old, followed the captain everywhere he went, noting his stride and posture, and saying about him, "Oh, fine!" His reputation in Zayla was secure.

In the evenings, entertainments were more intimate. Although his hosts drank no liquor, they used opium in quantities. "Divorce is common here," Sharmakay explained to Burton. "Please, take your choice." Burton, then, began learning the coastal languages and dialects from ex-wives of the village. One afternoon, strolling outside the walls, he met a striking Eesa girl—a gaunt beauty from the troublesome tribe which for the last year had been robbing and killing travelers along the road to Harar. The girl had skin like soft ebony, and Burton could see into her wrap: her breasts stood up full and erect.

"You are like the moon in a dark sky here," he told her. "Why don't you come visit me at the house of Sharmakay?"

"I have a price," she said, and she laughed.

"And what would that be?"

"A necklace for myself and a present for my father."

"This is a small price, but my feeling for you is not small," he told her, and he rested his eyes in that gap of her cloak.

At sunset, when the gates of the city were locked and the keys brought to Sharmakay, the Eesa girl was also delivered to Burton. Naked in his rooms, she padded slowly over his floor like a panther. Grace and softness: she had those enormous breasts and that slender waist he liked so much. When he took her in his arms, she yielded without any emotion—neither fear nor desire—yet excited him. She was like an animal, some wild desert thing, he decided, for whom copulation meant little. Even so, her beauty—those arching ribs, those breasts, that perfect mound—brought him back to her time after time as the night went on. He promised her a whole coil of copper so that she could make ornaments for herself and her father, and, in turn, she agreed to stay with him until he left the city.

The lunch was greasy mutton, maize cakes, and curds, followed by coffee. Again the room was filled, and everyone smoked from a common hookah as the master of ordnance, a burly one-eyed creature from the port, came to shave Burton's head. It was a ritual that made him one of them: the razor scraped him clean, smoke and laughter ascended in the room, and serious discussion was the order of the day.

The topic was the spear versus the gun.

"Guns," announced one of the Somali elders, "allow the poltroon to slay the bravest."

"True," another agreed. "Guns are good weapons. But the use of one injures the soul. In my opinion, they are for cowards only."

"I agree," Burton said, and everyone nodded approval that their new friend had so much sense. "Yet the use of the pistol or rifle may be needed against cowards who also have them."

"No one throws the javelin so well as Sharmakay," the master of ordnance said, as he shaved around Burton's ear.

"Pay attention to your work and don't talk," Burton told him, and the room burst into laughter.

In midafternoon everyone went out into the hot sun of a courtyard that opened onto the beach. They tossed their spears—with Sharmakay easily winning—and shot for a mark on a wall with their pistols and rifles. Their debate over guns and spears still continued, so Burton went up to his room and brought down his saber.

The Eesa girl stood on his balcony and watched. Everyone in the courtyard admired the blade.

"When I was a boy practicing the foil with my brother," he told them, "I ran the blade into his mouth and stuck him in the back of the throat. We weren't wearing headgear."

Interpretations of his words spread around the courtyard. The men looked puzzled until finally an elder asked, "You killed your brother?"

"Oh, no, Edward was very tough," he said, and the villagers smiled and allowed themselves to be amused. "Now then, someone should attack me with a spear," he said, and he waved the saber so that it glinted in the sunlight.

"He wants someone to pretend to attack," Sharmakay told the audience.

"No, they should try to kill me," Burton corrected him.

"Truly, you are brave," said a man near the edge of the crowd. His voice was filled with sarcasm. He was a tall man whose shoulders seemed to ride high around his ears; his muscles were lean and hard and his fingers hung down like claws. His name was Gumal and he was well known as a mercenary.

"There's no risk to me," Burton said to Gumal. "Would you like to try the spear against me?"

"We want no bloodshed," Sharmakay said.

In minutes, though, the two men were squared off against one another. Gumal smiled before the first lunge. Pretending to look toward the beach, he whirled and came at the captain, but was turned aside with what seemed a mere flick of Burton's wrist. Caught by surprise, he stumbled and fell at the feet of his target; Burton could have slashed his head off.

They squared off again. Once more, the mercenary charged, but with a feint and a sidestep. Burton parried again, catching the spear and turning it downward so that it stuck in the sand.

Gumal had an abundance of energy. Nine times more he tried to stick this insolent foreigner, but Burton turned him away without effort, chatting with the audience, glancing up at the Eesa girl who smiled from the balcony, exchanging knowing smiles with Sharmakay. In the end, Gumal the mercenary went over and sat down beneath a scraggly palm tree; he looked more amazed than exhausted.

One day Burton and some of the villagers set sail for Saad al Din, a small island not far off the mainland which had once been the site of Zayla. He made notes as they steered a course for the island, speculating that some interesting ruins of an ancient civilization might still be found.

But there were no ruins, no people, and not even a good clump of trees for shade on the island.

He wondered at the origin of Zayla and these curious people. Did the Phoenicians pass here? Who? The notes in his diary were all questions.

One morning at the communal pipe and coffee Burton entertained his hosts by drawing horoscopes and, in turn, had his palm read by the seer of the city. As their individual fates were pondered and their personalities discussed, they also fell into a theological conversation about Allah's will, determinism, and man's free spirit. It was very much like the arguments, Burton felt, in the basement of some Presbyterian chapel in the midlands.

"Man trims the sail of his own destiny," Sharmakay told the listeners. "Allah is the wind that blows, but man trims his own sail."

"I would say it another way," Burton interjected. "Life deals each of us one great opportunity. We must have sense enough to seize it."

"All I say is that there is man's effort and Allah's whimsy," said the ruler of Zayla.

"So what do you see, wise one, in the palm of my hand?" Burton asked, turning to the seer. He was a withered old man who wore his cloak over his head and whose bony knees stuck out.

Those present sucked on their pipes. The seer squinted at Burton's palm, hissed as he laughed, shrugged, and squinted again. "You will accomplish more than twenty men!" he said in a cracked voice.

"Ah so!" said the audience.

"You will travel far and solve great mysteries!"

"Ah so!" they said in unison.

"And you will be honored by kings and sultans!"

"Ah so!"

"But you will be discontent."

The men in the room fell silent and watched for Burton's reaction. For the first time since his arrival they saw a weakness in his mouth.

"Discontent?" he asked softly.

"Not happy with yourself or your life," said the old man, staring into Burton's outstretched palm.

"But if I accomplish such a great lot, I find it difficult to believe that I'll be very upset," Burton countered, smiling and looking around the room as if to gain support.

"Discontent," the seer repeated. "No need to argue. It is written here in your own flesh."

Al-Hammal spent his days with his men at the rear of some stables while trying to secure camels, mules, and porters for the journey to Harar, a journey about which he could actually say little, since Sharmakay had not given consent.

One afternoon three weeks after their arrival in Zayla, the big policeman came to Burton's room. The Eesa girl was stretched out asleep on the pillows and beside her, his writing materials in use, Burton propped himself on an elbow and gave audience to his manager.

"I have five camels, mules, and have now hired two cooks who will surely please you," Al-Hammal said, grinning down on the sleeping form of the girl.

"As soon as my research is finished, we will go," Burton said.

That night Burton had six women—one widow and five ex-wives—brought upstairs for his inspection. He and the Eesa girl fell into an argument over the whole matter and she asked for her coil of copper wire, saying that she intended to leave immediately for her village. When Burton refused to pay, she tried to scratch his eyes, but he held her wrists and commanded her to go sit in a corner and behave.

"You will receive gifts more than I promised," he told her, as she slumped in a corner with her knees drawn up and her mouth fixed in a pout.

The women arranged themselves on the pillows, pulled their skirts over their heads, and spread their legs. Holding a lighted candle, Burton knelt down, went from one to another, examined them, and made notes. People of the desert, he knew, considered writing or note taking the activity of infidels and strangers, so he instructed them, "Keep your faces covered and don't look at me." Carefully, then, he made notes and drawings of their mutilations and all that lay before him.

The Eesa girl, who had been placated, peeked out from between her knees and began to laugh, infuriating the women who, in turn, began to scold her and call her names. While their female raging went on and on, Burton proceeded. One of the ex-wives, he noted, seemed to be in a state of special excitement, but he took no advantage of it.

Sharmakay heard of this scholarly escapade in the room above his warehouse and teased Burton about it.

"Truly, women are your downfall," he told his guest. "In all other matters, you are a prince."

"Allah made woman of a crooked rib," Burton replied, quoting the old desert truism. "He who would straighten her, breaketh her."

"You give me much pleasure," said the ruler, laughing and rubbing a rough hand over the top of his bald head.

"Zayla is an isolated and lonely place," Burton answered, "and you people here are too easily amused. I intend to go to Harar, so that I can see if I amuse them as much."

"I am sentimental about you, Burton, and I admit it. But if you go through the land of the Eesa, they will kill you. If you go along the coast, the Berbera tribesmen—who are at war among themselves—will also kill you. And if by some accident you should arrive in Harar, they will kill you. I have heard tales that the Amir drinks the blood of strangers. Remain here and we will import women for your scholarship."

Burton placed his hands on the ruler's shoulders and looked deep into his eyes. "I intend to go," he said, and Sharmakay looked at him, in return, as if he were doomed.

The next morning the five camels, complaining and spitting, were brought to their knees for loading. The elders, the master of ordnance, the mercenary, Sharmakay, the old seer, and dozens of others came to clasp hands, pray, and say goodbye.

By the time the sun was hot, the caravan started. Sharmakay himself walked for a mile into the desert with them, saying farewell and quoting the Koran.

They traveled along the coast toward Berbera with plans to turn toward Harar and to avoid as much of the hostile Eesa tribe as possible.

The two cooks hired by Al-Hammal were fat, strong females, whom Burton immediately named Shehrazade and Deenarzade. They drove the camels, adjusted the burdens, made tea, pitched camp, cooked, and slept apart from the men. That first night, when all of their chores were finished, they walked on each other's backs. This form of massage would continue every night after a long day's march.

Thorn trees and dry grass adorned the countryside. Walking within sight of the sea, they took every precaution. End of Time, to his great relief, was entrusted with a pistol, and Burton, bedded down in his blankets with the sound of the sea and the keening of jackals in his ears, rested his head on his rifle butt and kept two pistols loaded and ready.

As they went along they noticed stones piled high along the coast and inland toward the desert. Graves: they dotted the landscape. Men were buried where they fell—and many had fallen.

Burton began to feel alone and thought of the people of his life: his frail mother and family, Lumsden, friends in London and India. He thought of his men, too, and wondered how they fared. Speke, especially: there was a curious young man, deep and dark at the center of himself.

Speke's *abban*, or guide, in his trip to the Wadi Nogal was Sumunter, a Somali who lived in Aden, who had a wife there and another over in Africa, and who was besieged by creditors—some of whom actually followed the party over to the coast. Sumunter and Speke had no common language between them, and the interpreter was from Sumunter's tribe and worked for the *abban*, not for Speke.

After landing on the coast, the group stopped at Bunder Goray, a tiny hamlet, where Sumunter began working with the local sultan to rob Speke of all their goods. Good salt and rice were traded for poor grain. Money for mules was paid, but no mules appeared. And the sultan refused Speke permission to travel further, keeping the little expedition at the hamlet so that the robbery could continue.

Frustrated and not knowing what to do or how to communicate, Speke walked into the desert every day to hunt. Even this became a controversy.

"The Sultan says you are to hunt no more!" Sumunter yelled at the lieutenant one day out in the desert. Speke, paying no attention, aimed and dropped a partridge that was flying low among the windblown acacias.

Furious and cursing in his own language, Sumunter shook his fist at Speke, mounted his horse, and rode back to the hamlet.

One night there was an emotional dispute around the fireplace. Speke, who had been eating dates, his complete meal for the evening, tossed the pits into the fire. Immediately, some of the porters cried out that this was a sacrilege.

"We should kill you for this!" one of them shouted in Speke's face.

The lieutenant stood his ground, staring the angry men down.

Meanwhile, the interpreter and Sumunter arrived and entered into what seemed to Speke a furious and incomprehensible argument. Everyone glowered at Speke until he went off to sleep in the darkness. There, far from the fire, he wrapped himself in a blanket and went to sleep with his pistol in hand.

Finally, Speke and the interpreter went to the Sultan. Speke made it clear that he intended to leave the hamlet and to look for the dry stream called the Wadi Nogal.

"If you cross from here into the territory of the Dulbahanta tribe, they will certainly kill you," the Sultan informed Speke. "They will consider you my guest and friend and—since we are at war with the Dulbahanta—they will murder you."

"Well, I can't stay here any longer," Speke said firmly.

"It is also a matter of obtaining my permission," the Sultan said, smiling.

"I am sure," Speke told the interpreter, as he rested his hands on the pistols in his holsters, "that the Sultan would not wish to try and keep me here."

This initiated a long conversation between the Sultan and the interpreter. After ten minutes of it, Speke turned and walked out.

When Speke left the hamlet with his small group of camel drivers, Sumunter made excuses to remain behind.

Out in the desert, the camel drivers immediately went on strike for more rations of water and food.

"Tell them that I'm eating and drinking no more than any of them," Speke instructed the interpreter. But the interpreter—a little man who squinted one eye and who had obviously taken instructions from Sumunter—refused to talk to the drivers. "Tell them!" Speke shouted at him, but the man squinted and smiled without obeying.

The drivers circled Speke and jeered at him. One of them went from camel to camel taking the water bags. Seeing this, Speke moved over to the camel that carried the bags of rice, dates, and salt. As the men moved forward and a knife flashed, Speke drew his pistol and glared at them. Just then the Sultan and Sumunter rode up on horses asking what was the matter.

"They're on strike and insolent!" Speke said, his hand shaking as he returned the pistol to its holster.

"We will have a trial!" the Sultan announced, and witnesses were solicited. For an hour in the hot sun, they all stood around accusing each other. Speke's best argument included a threat to bring all of them before the British consul in Aden.

"English justice is not present here!" the Sultan shouted at him.

"You, especially," Speke said, pointing a finger at Sumunter. "You need to return to Aden. If anything happens to me, they will certainly hear of it. And even for your behavior so far you will be punished!"

The *abban* became visibly upset at this. "You will say nothing of me in Aden!" he told Speke, but uncertainty entered his tone.

When the mock trial was concluded, no wrongdoing was found. The Sultan said that the demands of the camel drivers were meager and that, if Speke were generous, they would be given larger rations.

Disgusted with their bickering, Speke went over to his camel and began to loosen the leather thongs that held his rifle. The Somali stiffened, and two of the camel drivers drew knives as if to protect their Sultan. But Speke, putting his rifle over his shoulder, simply walked off into the desert to hunt, and everyone else stood in silence watching him go.

As Burton and his caravan slowly made their way into the mountains toward the citadel of Harar, they were continually heckled by nomads. One scraggly group of Bedu, camped at a distance from where they stopped one evening, jeered and threw rocks. In spite of this, the two fat women cooks, Shehrazade and Deenarzade, had the courage to stroll toward the antagonists and to ask for goat's milk. Getting none, they strolled back toward their own caravan under a hail of curses.

Wrapped in his blanket that night beneath the canopy of whirling stars, instinct gave Burton an important truth: Africans were not truly fighters. Their long suits were bluff and noise. Perhaps because they walked a continent of superior beasts—the great cats, the invincible rhinos and elephants—their confidence was low. But the word for war in Africa was *barouf*, the Arab word for gunpowder, or, actually, the sound of powder as it harmlessly exploded. War was common in most tribes and peoples of the continent, but death in battle was rare. Warriors lurched forward, jabbed with their spears, cursed, but seldom risked injury; few were skilled with a weapon, as Gumal the pitiful mercenary proved; in this region a favorite tactic was to attack at night and to cut down a foe's tent with him inside, so that one could hurry forward, jab at the writhing folds of the tent, and escape without risk. They often sounded fierce, but they were cowards. Their muscles looked strong, but they had poor diets, so were often weak.

The next morning Burton saw two vultures—birds that the Bedouins particularly hated—between the two camps. He killed one of them on the ground with a shot that startled the Bedouins and started them cursing. Then, reloading with swan shot, he killed the other as it circled above.

"Protect us from such calamity!" an old Bedouin prayed to Allah so that all could hear. Around him, his companions exclaimed their wonder at Burton's powers.

The Bedouin leader came to Al-Hammal and begged for a charm for his sick camel. He was given a rag which Burton had used in cleaning the rifle, and in appreciation he spat on everything for luck.

Sitting around the fires at night, the men of his caravan constantly maligned women. All Moslems were misogynists.

Burton felt the immense loneliness of this foreign plain. More than a week had passed, and the hours were all much alike. Wrapped in his blanket, his thoughts set adrift, he thought of the Eesa girl, his mother, and a nameless beauty about whom he had written a poem in India. Women. All his energy, he sometimes felt, was sexual; his deepest associations were feminine.

From a hillside they could see the conelike hills of the white ants, thousands of them, so that, together, they looked like the ruins of a city on the landscape. The boiling thermometer measured their altitude at 3,350 feet.

As they advanced, groups of nomads watched them and drew as close as possible when the caravan stopped to make camp, so they could beg tobacco and food. At times, too, the nomads would offer their services and friendship, then turn suddenly hostile.

"I have seen no good and have received nothing from this caravan!" a burly nomad shouted one evening.

"What have you done for us?" Burton shouted back at him.

"Whose land is this?" the big man asked. "Why should we help you?"

No answer. Both groups quieted down.

"I will offer a camel for either of your fat women!" the big man shouted once again, as if giving an ultimatum.

Neither of the women replied, and once more the two groups kept silence with the stars.

"And I will wrestle your best man!" the nomad finally shouted in frustration.

It would have been prudent to have kept silence again, but Burton was in a restless mood, so he stepped forward and pulled off his shirt.

"No gouging," the big nomad said, slipping out of his cloak.

"And no knives!" said End of Time as the two men began to circle each other. The nomad, who, as it turned out, was a renegade from the Eesa tribe, charged with his head down, trying to butt his foe. This was his entire strategy, and Burton could have easily sidestepped each run, but instead, he met each charge with his fists, punishing the man with short, chopping blows to the side of the face. The nomad charged six times and received six brutal blows. Finally, he managed to tackle Burton, but by this time blood was like glue on his face, closing one eye, and as they grappled in the dirt, Burton struck him twice more until the man got up of his own will and staggered away. Then Burton went after him, fastening him with a headlock and making him cry out in pain. It was a short, dry shriek. The fight, suddenly, was no longer fair, as Burton's mood had grown foul. When he let go, the nomad dropped to his knees, raising a hand in the air, but Burton took the big man's fingers and with raw strength bent them backward until they cracked.

The audience groaned and the fight was finished.

Afterward, they gave tobacco to all the nomads and to the one whose hand was broken they gave half a bolt of cloth and a drink of brandy.

Toward morning Burton awakened to a strange, wondrous noise. He got up and walked among his sleeping companions, hoping to hear it again, until at last it came. The roar of a lion.

Staring out into the heavy gray of the wilderness before the first light, he saw that the nomads had quietly put out their fires during the night and had gone.

For a short distance the caravan passed through Eesa country, but that notorious tribe gave them no trouble. These people were blacker than most, Burton noted, and spent a great deal of time counting their cattle. By this time his reputation had gone before him, too, which helped to keep the journey without incident. The Somali Bedouins called him many names, including: King, Ruler of Aden, the Chief of Zayla, Sharmakay's Son, an Old Woman, a Man Painted White, a Warrior in Silver Armor, a Pilgrim, a Priest, a Turk, a Genii, Ahmad the Indian, a Banyan, a Frenchman, a Merchant, and The Calamity Sent down from Heaven to Weary out the Lives of the Somal.

At night, more and more Bedouins and villagers came out to sit around the fires of the caravan. A blind girl, celebrated for her skill in the Fal—or Omens —told Burton that he had "naught to fear except the wild beasts." Most of the evening conversations were the usual frenzy of theology.

One day the low hills turned greener. They had reached the Marar Prairie, and all around them lay a country which Burton likened to southern Italy or to Provence.

He still wore the wide trousers and loose shirt and burnoose of an Arab, but now he began to doubt his attire because of the constant assessment of all those who came around his fires. He asked one somewhat more prosperous-looking Bedouin what he thought about the Arab clothing, and the man smiled and answered, "Ah, they will spoil that white skin of thine at Harar."

In the last large village before the ascent into the mountains and up toward the citadel of Harar, Burton was greeted by the leader, called the Gerad, who stood in the street and held out his arms in welcome. The Gerad wore a blue silk robe—only slightly tattered around the hem—and in his belt was a jeweled scabbard containing his curved knife.

"I have ordered a sheep slaughtered," he said in greeting. "And I have sent to Harar for millet beer, which should arrive tomorrow. Many will come to see you, stranger, and so we will celebrate!"

The Gerad took Burton inside his house, which was like the interior of a pillow with all its rugs and cushions. They toasted each other with a bitter liqueur and exchanged every courtesy. The first conversation revealed that there were five hundred warriors in the village, most of them presently out in the hills chasing renegades.

"Our hills are filled with feuds," the Gerad explained. "And constant politics. If we had cannon, we would behave like Europe."

The next day the beer arrived and a feast was held. Burton, still concerned with his dress and the plan to enter Harar in Arab disguise, asked the advice of the Gerad, who stroked his short gray beard and smiled.

"They will kill you in the citadel," he said. "If you wear this clothing, they will call you a fool first."

"I thought of sending a letter to the Amir," Burton said. "But then I rejected the idea. If he sent a reply that he wouldn't see me, I would never penetrate the walls of the city. I do want to see what's there."

"At the price of your head?" the Gerad asked.

"I have come too far to turn back."

Among those who came during the feast day to see the Englishman was a group of hostile tribesmen on fine Arabian horses. Their animals snorted and raised dust in the streets, leaving dung everywhere they stopped, and the Gerad, who gave them the safety of the feast day, finally lost his temper and ordered them off. That night there were three dancers, and long kabobs of meat on brass trays. "Would you like more food?" the Gerad asked Burton, watching the foreigner's eyes and smiling at what he saw.

"No, thank you kindly."

"Would you like a dancer?"

"Yes, please, and thank you for the kindness."

"It is my pleasure," the Gerad said. "Wash carefully afterward."

The next morning, with the dancer lying asleep at his side, his body drained but his mind clear, Burton forged a letter. It was addressed to the Amir of Harar and purported to be from the consul at Aden, introducing Burton as an official ambassador from the British government. Having composed the document, Burton got up and dressed in his captain's uniform—replete with epaulets and saber. Then he went to breakfast to the astonishment of his host and to the dismay of his caravan.

"This is the only way," he explained to everyone.

"Oh, master," End of Time begged. "Please, allow me to stay in this hospitable village along with the women and cowards."

"Don't worry," Burton said. "From here on, I'll take only Al-Hammal and volunteers, my weapons, and presents for the Amir. You will be in charge, and if I'm not back in a month, send my gear—including my journals—back to Aden. Tell them at Berbera that we came this far."

Breakfast became a lengthy meal and an occasion of farewell. There were elaborate consolations, for Burton was considered a dead man. The Gerad kept exclaiming how much he admired bravery while looking at Burton, shaking his head slowly from side to side, and thinking, clearly, what an idiot he entertained at this last, sad meal.

Burton took out his notebook and made sketches of his host, the dancer, who wandered in sleepy-eyed looking for coffee, and those villagers who appeared at the window to gape at the wrinkled but highly dashing uniform. Conversations turned to Burton's wonderful hajj to Mecca and to points of Moslem theology. In the early afternoon, everyone stood up and embraced.

There was only a single volunteer apart from Burton and Al-Hammal, a former Aden criminal whose suicidal tendencies had won him the name Mad Sa'id. The three of them started walking into the mountains that afternoon. It was the first day of the New Year, 1855.

Speke, meanwhile, could not locate the Wadi Nogal.

They were deep in hostile Dulbahanta territory, Sumunter and the interpreter once again arrogantly refused the lieutenant's orders, and supplies—including the contents of the waterskins—were dangerously low.

"We're turning toward the sea," Speke finally said.

Thin smiles passed between Sumunter, the interpreter, and the camel drivers. "You surrender, do you not?" Sumunter asked, goading him. "You admit, now, that there is no such golden river?"

"It doesn't matter anymore," Speke said. "And you can answer to the Aden authorities for your actions."

"You will not prosecute!" Sumunter shouted. "I have my trade and my family! You will not prosecute!"

With stiff formality, Speke turned to the interpreter. "Tell my *abban,*" he said, "that he no longer has a trade unless he intends to be a thief full-time."

At the gates of the city of Harar the peasants filed out with their gourds filled with butter, ghee, and milk. As Burton and his two companions walked among them, they parted and marveled at this specimen about whom they had heard such horrors. A few of them spat—whether for luck or for insolence Burton couldn't tell.

The city sat on a hill surrounded by green fields, thistles, and wildflowers; the morning air was cool and invigorating. Two rude minarets rose above the rooftops. Orchards, a cemetery, battlements, grey walls: it wasn't all that much, Burton found himself thinking, but no white man had ever seen it and lived.

An old grandee, turbaned and wearing his fine tobe with an Abyssinian broadsword over his shoulder, appeared with his entourage. His seven footmen glared at Burton until their leader himself, riding a mule, handed a gourd of fresh water to Al-Hammal and bellowed his salutations. The language, Harari, was unknown to Burton, but he replied in Arabic and everyone seemed pleased enough.

The warder at the gate carried a long wand. As they approached, his eyes revealed his fright, and when Burton ordered him to announce their presence he stumbled off in a hurry. Al-Hammal and Mad Sa'id kept their hands on their knives and pistols, looking around nervously. Burton sat down to sketch the walls and gate. As they waited for the warder, the crowd grew bold and began to deride them. After fifteen minutes three tattered tribesmen arrived—visitors from a nearby village.

"We did not know that you meant to enter the sacred city," their leader cried, and the three of them pulled their daggers and danced around, urged on by the audience.

"Pay them no mind," Burton said calmly to Al-Hammal and Mad Sa'id.

"It is war to the knife!" the leader went on.

Burton and his companions ignored them until, at last, they faded into the crowd and seemed to be shouting and arguing among themselves.

Finally, the warder came back, shoved back the wooden bolts, and opened their way into a crude courtyard encompassed by reddish stucco walls. There, they removed their slippers, and everyone except Burton gave up his weapons.

"No, not these," Burton said with courtesy, not letting the guards have either his pistol or dagger. For a moment Al-Hammal, who had no weapon, looked as though he might faint, but the guards ushered them toward an inner corridor without insisting.

Along the corridor, Burton was separated from his companions. As they parted they exchanged glances, saying nothing, as the guards accompanied the captain through a door, into a series of anterooms, and at last into the comforts of the Amir's chamber.

The Amir, or Sultan Ahmad bin Sultan Abibakr, was a thin young man of some twenty-five years of age. His chamber was adorned with rusty matchlocks and fetters and his throne was a simple Indian *kursi*—a raised cot—where he sat dressed in a flowing crimson robe edged with snowy fur; his narrow white turban bore a single jewel, an emerald. Standing by the Amir's throne was an old man with a wisp of a smile showing from his beard: the Wazir, or counselor.

"Peace be upon ye!" Burton shouted, throwing up a hand in greeting as he entered the chamber. His words boomed out louder than he anticipated, and the Wazir's smile widened.

The guards, taking hold of Burton's shoulders, bent him forward to the outstretched hand of the young Amir, but Burton neglected to kiss it.

The Wazir went into a fit of coughing.

"My letter," Burton said, and he brought his forgery out of his tunic with a flourish, extending it to the Amir. The Wazir, however, intercepted it.

Nervous and uncertain, Burton began a speech. His voice, again, seemed louder than he wanted it, but the Amir and his counselor, curiosity getting the best of them, listened attentively as Burton announced that he had come from Aden with the compliments of the governor, that he had entered Harar to see the light of the Amir's countenance, that the English and the deceased chief Abibakr, the Amir's father, had sworn friendship, and that hope existed that this great city would be open to trade and communications with the great British Empire.

After a pause that seemed an eternity, the Amir smiled.

Burton allowed himself a sigh of relief.

After this he was shown out, the Amir never having uttered a word. When he reached the courtyard, though, all was different: servants and guards smiled and bowed. He was led to an open kitchen, where Al-Hammal and Mad Sa'id stood next to a boiling pot eating holcus cakes thickly powdered with red pepper. Everyone exchanged greetings with the eyes and smiled.

Eventually the Wazir arrived, coughing and spitting. Burton knew that he had consumption.

"You will have rooms in the palace," the old man said. "And you are free to come and go in the streets. But we have a strict curfew in the evenings."

"I understand," Burton said, removing his pistol and dagger. "This pistol is for the Amir and I will be pleased to show him how to use it. The dagger is for you. Both of these I carried with me on my own hajj, for I am a convert to the true faith and have seen the holy of holies."

"We have heard this," the Wazir said, accepting the gifts with a smile that was both wise and ironic. "And we have heard that you break the bones of strong men and bring down the birds from the sky."

At the banquet they ate fowl, mutton, coarse bread, and kat—the tender points of the leaves of the kat tree, which they rolled into balls, popped into their mouths, and washed down with water, millet beer, or mead. Burton stuffed himself with kat—which was reputed to be a wonderful narcotic—but felt no effect. "Subtle and wonderful," he kept exclaiming, smiling at his hosts and rolling another ball of leaves, but he supposed he was used to stronger stuff. The Somali around the low table claimed that this product exaggerated time and distance, enlivened the imagination, cleared the ideas, cheered the heart, diminished the need for sleep, and took the place of food. Quantities of it disappeared from their table.

The Amir, who had seated Burton at his right hand, seemed young and shy and pious. One of the elders recited a long blessing, reading from a huge book, and after each passage the guests, including Burton, intoned, "Allah bless our Lord Muhammad with his Progeny and his Companions, one and all!" The exercise lasted half an hour. Toward the end, the elder happened to say, "Angels, men, and geniis," in reciting a passage, but Burton corrected him—to everyone's astonishment.

"Men, angels, and then geniis," Burton said, waxing theological. "For in the creation of Allah, man ranks highest because prophets, apostles and saints derive from man whereas the others are mere connections between the Creator and his creatures."

The elders listened with satisfaction and the Wazir coughed and smiled.

After dinner, Burton received another short audience with the Amir, who, dressed in a sleeveless cloak over his cotton shirt, asked, "Did you come here to buy or sell?"

"No, only to see the Amir—praise be unto him—and to state our wishes for good relations between England and Harar."

"Do you come as the friend of Sharmakay—who wishes to conquer our city?" the Amir asked.

"No, please Allah, only to wish thee well," Burton insisted. "And when it pleases thee, we shall depart. Truly, this high mountain air is hard on the lungs of an Englishman."

"On that you shall have our answer," the Amir said, smiling slightly, but hiding his meaning. Burton was dismissed.

The mornings, as in Zayla, saw the palace filled with visitors—except here the eating of kat took the place of the drinking of coffee. Burton used the time in his room to make notes and sketches and to set about learning the language. His vocabulary list grew long.

Harar was at 5,500 feet, with an air like Tuscany, he noted, and its principal function was that of a trading town. The Bedouins came by the thousands, and the Amir taxed each camel and donkey that entered. Coffee was grown on the hillsides and cotton was planted in the surrounding valleys. Caravans were arranged for Berbera and Zayla. Cloth weaving had the proportion of an industry.

He was sitting in his nightshirt, still writing one morning at half past eight o'clock, when two slave girls arrived with his breakfast: lumps of boiled beef and holcus cakes. One of them drove out the cats, which filled every room and passageway in the palace, while the other set up his meal on a low table beside his elbow. Neither of the girls were veiled. They were slender and black, like ebony reeds, with shy smiles and graceful movements. Both wore a series of cloaks and robes, so that their thin arms emerged from folds of cloth.

"You are not veiled, but you are dressed in many clothes," he told them as they moved around him.

"Yes, true," one of them said, and her eyes met his. "But beneath these cloaks, sire, we are naked."

"Is this so?" he asked with a smile, looking at the other girl only to find that she, too, gave him a straight and arrogant stare.

The young Amir seemed in no particular hurry to let Burton and his companions leave the city, but the matter of the Wazir's cough prevailed. Burton wisely suggested that he should return to Aden and send back some of the new, helpful medicines.

"Truly, I am sometimes sick," the old man said, trying not to complain.

"In England there are many such coughs," Burton told him, "so that the people of my island are adept at medicines. If you wish, I could also arrange to send you a doctor."

The next day Al-Hammal and Mad Sa'id received their weapons. Burton heard them dancing with joy in the courtyard.

"We will get out alive!" Al-Hammal said in a loud stage whisper when Burton looked down on him from a balcony.

Messages, packages, and official letters accumulated, and they were given a mule on which to pack these items to Berbera. One of the Amir's trusted sheikhs, Jami, would accompany the party on its return to the coast: a tall, thin, serious fellow with fingers yellow and long like the talons of a kite. The Wazir, as if not to complain of his misery, never mentioned the medicine again, so that Burton had to seek him out.

"I will send you medicine, never fear," he told the old counselor.

"Do you think I will soon die?" the old man wanted to know.

"Allah willing, not until your service to the young Amir is finished," Burton told him, and the Wazir, looking as though he might weep at this sudden farewell, placed a hand on the captain's shoulder.

At the hour of their leaving there was loud salaaming at the city gate. The Bedouin peasants looked at the caravan of strangers as if a miracle had come to pass. Across the wide plain surrounding the citadel, giant columns of rain came down, blue and magnificent, and the scent of it filled the air.

In five hard days—the last one without water—Burton and his small caravan reached the outskirts of Berbera, the windswept slave market on the coast. Alongside an old, crumbling seawall Herne and Stroyan had pitched their tents. From their position they could see the town and watch the road as it curved beside the shore and could count the slaves who were brought into market. They were exhausted with this waiting and watching. The yard around their camp was strewn with rotting fish heads, broken chicken coops, and the litter of weeks of boredom. Once, Stroyan had gone into the desert with some drunken sailors and had managed to shoot an elephant; its tusks, dried but still stinking, lay among the debris.

When they heard of Burton's approach, they hurried along the road for a mile and met the caravan with a single waterskin—which wasn't enough for the thirsty travelers. Everyone embraced and talked at once.

"You made it! Everyone in the world will hear of this!" Stroyan said.

"Perhaps," Burton answered, and he smiled, thinking that everyone might.

In camp, he drank his fill, then collapsed on a cot.

"There are terrible rumors about how we intend to stop the slave trade," Herne said to him as he lay there. "And how we're allies of Zayla. And how your friend Sharmakay will soon attack. I'm glad you're here because things are getting sticky. We should probably go back to Aden right away."

"Yes, quite right," Burton replied, but he wasn't listening anymore. Closing his eyes, he tried to estimate his accomplishment. He definitely wanted to return to Harar with a large caravan capable of proceeding toward Zanzibar in search for the Nile.

Or have I already made history, he wondered, and will I be remembered for this odd visit to the citadel? Will fame bless me or pay me only a small nod?

As he tried to consider all this, he fell asleep.

Nothing was known of Speke, so on the day Burton, Herne, and Stroyan sailed into the harbor at Aden they were surprised to learn that their colleague had been back for a month.

"Jack," Burton said, putting out his hand. "Good to see you fit. Did you find the Wadi Nogal?"

"No, and it's worse than that: my *abban* deceived me and caused the end of the mission."

"Sumunter? I arranged for him myself. He was reputed to be one of the best men for hire."

"Yes, you arranged for him," Speke said sharply. "But now we'll have to put him on trial. I've already brought charges against him."

Burton looked at the young lieutenant carefully. He was understandably upset and defensive, so Burton determined to take care. As they talked, they stood in the officers' bar at the garrison. Others stood close enough to overhear any argument.

"Well, how did your time go?" Burton asked. "Was it all a waste?"

Sensing that they were at the edge of a public disagreement, Speke tried to smile. "I shot some fine specimens," he said. "Perhaps ninety different species of birds and a number of trophies. I understand that Stroyan shot an elephant, though, and I'm properly envious."

Annoyed even more, but trying to hide it, Burton asked, "If you don't speak the language, are you absolutely sure that Sumunter was deceiving you?"

"I won't be questioned about that," Speke replied.

In the week of their return from Africa, Steinhauser gave a party at the Steamer Point hotel. Speke, instead of attending the party, had dinner that night with William Coghlan, the new commander of the garrison.

It was a quiet party except for an incident on the verandah when Al-Hammal threatened to toss a male friend of one of the resident prostitutes off into the sea. And only once in the evening did Steinhauser and Burton discuss Speke and the upcoming trial of the *abban*.

"Naturally, I support my lieutenant," Burton said. "He's young, doesn't speak the languages, isn't a Moslem, and doesn't have much patience, but he's English and an officer."

"He should have dominated Sumunter," Steinhauser offered.

"He should have found the riverbed. He should have stayed longer. And he shouldn't have shot so damn many birds."

The two old friends looked at each other and laughed. It wasn't that they disliked Speke, but he was too stiff, too defensive, too young, and just not one of them.

The trial was brief.

Called as a witness—who had, in fact, witnessed nothing—Burton testified that the use of the *abban* was probably an unnecessary practice.

"A good soldier can do well enough without guides—especially inept or unscrupulous ones," he told the Aden police court.

"The economy of Aden requires the system," the judge pointed out.

"Unfortunate," Burton said. His remarks caused a stir in the courtroom. The natives were furious at his suggestion.

Sumunter was sentenced to two months in prison. He wailed when the verdict and sentence were passed, and Speke, looking justified, turned and walked out of the room without saying anything to anyone.

A week passed before Speke arrived at the hotel to give Burton some notes he had compiled while on the Somali coast.

"Notes? Good! Didn't know you had any!" Burton said, accepting them and gesturing toward a pile of cushions on which Speke declined to sit.

"When do you expect we'll go back?" Speke asked.

"I want a large caravan, plenty of foresight, and everything in order," Burton said.

"Weeks, then?"

"Yes, I'd say so."

"I want to train some men," the lieutenant said. "I've met a guide named

Balyuz whom I trust. We thought we'd train a dozen or so men with muskets and sabers. This all right with you?"

"Perfectly fine with me."

"I should have picked my own men last time," Speke said.

"I fully agree," Burton replied.

"It's exciting to go for the Nile."

"Yes," Burton agreed. "Very exciting."

For a time, Burton went into a flurry of writing and correspondence, so didn't join the men for breakfasts on the verandah. Also, he received word of his mother's death, so wore a black arm band, said little to anyone, and kept to himself, except for the hostess of those upstairs rooms at the Steamer Point hotel with whom, he claimed, he was still studying the Somali language.

Steinhauser was the only one who saw much of him. The doctor found him compiling notes on Harar, writing letters to his family about the mother's passing, making additional changes for his publisher in the manuscript of his volume on Medina and Mecca, writing letters and reports to Lumsden and the East India Company, applying for a new rank of major with the army, listing the genealogies of various Somali tribes, revising Speke's notes, and making notes on infibulation and other forms of sexual mutilation practiced on the native women.

"You'll get into trouble again with this," the doctor warned him.

"I'm always in trouble," Burton said proudly.

His troubles in India were well known to his friend. Burton had mastered six dialects, but the important jobs as an interpreter for which he applied always went to lesser scholars who knew only modest amounts of Hindustani. He had been assigned reports on the natives, but his work included notes on marriage, sexual eccentricities, and pederasty, which shocked the pious officers, including General Napier, who kept him out of action when the second Sikh war broke out and thereafter blocked his advancement in the army. He lived among the natives and kept mistresses—as others did—but although he viewed himself as a Victorian gentleman and officer, he became known to his critics as the White Nigger.

"Are you writing to the government again?" Steinhauser asked.

"I'm suggesting that we strengthen our force in Africa," he said. "They won't listen, but I'm writing anyway. I told them how we should run things in India, but they paid me no attention. Take my word for it, we'll have a mutiny there."

The doctor shook his head and smiled. "I enjoy watching you work," he said. "Everyone enjoys it. You're the one who always scolds the boss. Or talks about sex. Or criticizes official policies. It's wonderful being a spectator."

"I don't mean to be in trouble," Burton assured him. "To me, my research and opinions are always so *sound!*"

The doctor produced a flask of brandy as they laughed.

"Be careful with Speke's notes," Steinhauser warned, pouring them a glass each. "If you incorporate them in your report, he'll end up saying they weren't meant for your use."

"The notes of my junior officers belong to me," Burton said.

"Yes, but Speke doesn't exactly consider himself your junior officer."

"Who does he think he is?"

"Oh, a special attaché."

"Well, if he intends to go back to Africa with us, his status should be made clear," Burton said.

"Exactly my point," the doctor told him.

The winter passed, and in early March 1855 Burton held interviews with his group toward making final plans for their next trip.

"And how have you been spending your time?" he asked Stroyan.

"Getting drunk, sir."

"And you, Herne?"

"Watching Stroyan drink."

Everyone laughed and even Speke allowed himself a smile.

"Time to visit Africa again, then, and cease this degrading life in Aden," Burton said. "Give us the count, will you, Speke?"

"Well, Herne, Stroyan, and I go to the coast and you'll follow with the gunboat and the main body of men. We'll be forty-two altogether, with fifty-six camels. Balyuz and the sentries are ready. For as long as we stay around Berbera, we'll be under the protection of the gunboat."

"The coast is dangerous—more so than before," Burton warned them. "They've heard that we put Sumunter in jail and they're angry over that. They've also heard rumors that we intend to stop the slave trade. And they fear that I want to give Berbera to my friend Sharmakay. So we'll leave the coastal area as soon as possible and travel inland. Prepare your personal gear and write your letters home. I'll write to the Royal Geographical Society telling them we're on our way to see if there are actually snow-covered mountains at the equator."

When their breakfast conference ended and they were leaving the hotel verandah, Burton asked Herne to remain for a moment.

"What do you make of Balyuz and the sentries?" Burton asked him. "I want your honest appraisal."

"They're an odd lot," Herne said, his smile faintly indulgent. "Speke recruited an international platoon for us: Egyptians, Nubians, Somali, and all sorts. But Balyuz himself is a tough chap. In a skirmish, I think he might actually fight."

"Not the others?" Burton asked.

"Not a bloody chance," Herne said.

Burton sailed for the African coast again on April 7 on the gunboat *Mahi*. He wore his full uniform, neatly washed and pressed, with shiny boots and saber. If all passed well, he felt, he and his men would distinguish themselves in this expedition and be better off missing the war in the Crimea, where former Indian officers were being treated with disdain by Lord Raglan—who seemed to want no irregular horsemen, bashi-bazouks, or others mixing with his elegant British cavalry of blond young men from good families.

On shipboard, Burton learned from the sailors that a fair was being celebrated in Berbera. Traders and tribesmen from the whole coast were present, they said, and there were hundreds of whores, many of them young girls who had arrived from distant villages to ply the trade for the first time.

"We have cannonball, muskets, rifles, and ammunition of all sorts on board," Burton told the sailors, "but if we have to fuck our way out of Berbera, so be it!"

Their camp consisted of three tents set less than a mile from the town and near the beach under the protection of the *Mahi*'s guns. Burton and Herne occupied the large tent in the center, with Speke and Stroyan in the smaller tents on the flanks; in the large tent was a table, so that their maps could be spread out and Herne could check out their sextants, compasses, and other crude navigational instruments. Balyuz, the big black *abban* whom everyone respected, kept his men on the peripheries of the camp. They built up the fires at night and posted at least two sentries at all times.

After a few days Speke became impatient to move on and expressed his unrest to Herne.

"Isn't the equipment in order yet?" he asked.

"I think so. But you should ask Burton yourself," Herne told him.

"Perhaps I will soon," Speke said. "We can't linger around forever."

"We might stay until the fair closes," Herne mused. "Or until Balyuz' negotiations are finished. He has four or five volunteers from the local tribes and Burton wants others, especially women."

"Women on the caravan?"

"He had two women with him en route to Harar."

Speke looked incredulous and went back to his tent.

The next day the captain of the *Mahi* reported to Burton that the gunboat had been called to duty back in Aden.

"Then go back," Burton told him. "We'll be off soon enough."

"Sure you're all right?" the captain asked.

"A few Bedouins have yelled curses at us. A few days ago three horsemen rode up and looked us over—Balyuz thought they might be scouts for a raiding party. But the elders of the town also gave us ghee and honey, and some locals have volunteered to go with us. Have a safe voyage back."

That night Burton proposed to go into town for the festivities, but Balyuz argued against it. It was no longer a simple bazaar, he informed his leader; the residents were dizzy on mead and opium; warring tribes mingled in the streets, and there were stabbings and rapes; the mood was sullen at best, and usually openly hostile. Taking the *abban*'s advice, Burton stayed.

It rained that night and the next morning, and the streams flowing down to the sea were swollen. In town, mats were stripped down, camels laden, and caravans formed. By afternoon the roads were packed with Bedouins as the fair suddenly ended.

"I've sent messages ahead to Harar," Burton told the men. "We must finish distributing loads among the camels and porters and be off. You've checked the weapons, Speke?"

"I'm afraid they've been in the salt air too long and might rust," Speke said. "Best to be off as soon as possible."

"Hmm, yes, good point, Jack, it won't be long," Burton told him.

That night they ate fish again. The town was empty and quiet, so that out there on the dark flats near the dunes they seemed to talk in whispers to one another. Stroyan saw a falling star. A cool breeze blew up, so they stuck close to the fires until bedtime. At last, Burton went in, slipped on his rough flannel shirt, and placed his pistols and saber beside the pillow of his cot before lying down.

In the midst of a wild noise, Burton heard the voice of Balyuz crying out that the enemy was upon them. Quickly, he sprang up from his cot—it was just after three in the morning—slipped into his trousers, buckled his pistols and saber in place, and went out into the moonless dark. Herne was already outside, trying to determine the number of attackers, and toward the rear of the tent where the camels were tethered he fired two shots as a knife came whistling by his ear. Turning, he tripped over a tent rope, and as he fell a Somali came for him, club held high, so that Herne fired just in time to save himself.

"Where's the guard?" Burton yelled.

"Nowhere in sight!" Herne said, breathing heavily as he came back to the captain's side.

The strategy of these renegade Eesa was soon clear: they lurked out of sight around the camp, lunged forward occasionally, whooping and screaming, then retreated into the darkness again. They tried to rush in, at times, and cut the tents down. They jabbed out with their spears or threw stones.

"Stay close!" Burton cried out. "Close together! Where's Speke and Stroyan?"

"Here! I'm here!" Speke shouted, and Burton handed him a pistol, gave his other to Herne, and stood between his two lieutenants with only a saber. The Somali screamed and rushed in and out, trying to make an impression with their superior numbers, hurling stones, knives, and javelins. Herne called for Stroyan and Balyuz. Clearly, all the sentries and porters had fled.

Speke turned back toward his tent, going for more weapons and ammunition, but Burton called him back.

"Stand! They'll think you're retreating!" he snapped.

"Dammit!" Speke shouted at him, angry at being rebuked.

Stroyan, waking slowly, staggered forward into the darkness outside his tent trying to pull on a boot and cock his pistol. He heard the others calling his name, but couldn't see them. Suddenly, a figure rushed at him. He tried to make out the identity of the man, but it was too late. A spear was thrust into the lieutenant's chest, breaking through the sternum and piercing his heart. His killer dragged him out into the darkness by the shaft of the weapon, and there others quickly surrounded him and jabbed their spears and javelins into his lifeless form.

Two raiders advanced on Speke, jabbing their spears before them. Aiming, he fired twice—and heard the deep thud of the bullets entering their bodies as they fell back. Stung by Burton's order and feeling more confident, he stepped forward one pace, then another, firing as he went forward into the darkness. He would not be thought a coward. A man ran at him, but Speke whirled and smashed the butt of the pistol into his face. Darkness and sudden movement all around.

With Speke going forward, Burton stepped out, too, swinging his saber. He cut through a man's shoulder. All around him the raiders parted in fright and ran. Jumping at them, he grabbed one who ran by: Balyuz.

"Too many of them!" the *abban* cried. "We must retreat to the beach!"

"Good!" Burton shouted back at him. "Show us the way!"

Herne, who remained at his spot, stood tall and calm, loading and firing his two pistols at those who swerved toward the camels or tents. He could no longer see either Speke or Burton, but heard the captain's voice, so hoped for the best. One of the raiders staggered up to him, either drunk or wounded, armed with a club but not using it, and Herne shot him dead.

Balyuz moved among the raiders as though he were invincible, swinging his fists and knocking men down. He took a spear away from one man and a club from another, arming himself as he led Burton back toward Herne.

At that moment a raider stepped forward, lunged, and shoved a javelin through Burton's face. Its sharp point entered his left cheek and passed through to exit the other; Burton felt bone cracking inside his head, but didn't fall.

Instead, he swung at his attacker, but missed—almost striking Balyuz again.

He reeled in the darkness. While Balyuz managed to hold the attackers at bay, Burton broke off the shaft of the javelin. He almost fainted from this, but kept his feet. Blood was everywhere, and he could taste the metal in his mouth.

Speke had moved out too far. He found himself near the fires of the sentries and surrounded by figures who darted toward him, feinted, then darted away. Then he fired his last shot and was out of ammunition. Using the pistol butt as a club, he started back toward the tents, but a blow caught him across the chest and dropped him. As he gasped for breath, men fell on him and pinned his arms; one of them fumbled roughly at his crotch, and Speke thought, no, God, they're going to cut off my genitals. But one of his attackers actually fought off the others, claiming custody of a prisoner. Confused, Speke tried to get his breath, think, and see what was happening, while the big Somal held his arm, barked incomprehensible commands at him, and then, curiously, gave him a drink of water out of a goatskin. Around them, the others screamed and shook their spears; he was among his attackers now and had no idea where the tents stood.

Balyuz found Herne and turned him toward the beach, but now Burton had become separated. Weak with pain and lost in the darkness, the captain lay down and tried to gather his senses. It seemed odd to take a rest, but there he waited. A few feet away he saw a form—perhaps Stroyan. A dozen spears fanned out from some lifeless form on the sand.

Then one of Burton's own men appeared: Golab of the Yusuf tribe. He saw a glint of the captain's saber in the darkness and pulled Burton to his feet. "Here, this way, sire," the young porter cried in Arabic, and began to guide his master into the dry bed of a stream that led toward the beach. The stream zigzagged among dunes and high grass and they stumbled over rocks as they hurried along. Meanwhile, Herne and Balyuz ran toward the beach, too. Herne's ammunition was gone and he called for Speke as he ran, but his voice was lost among the shouts of the raiders, who tore down the tents and scattered the mules and camels.

By this time Speke was spread-eagled and tied loosely to stakes. His captor seemed almost kindly, but the lieutenant well knew his fate. He detected a change in the cries of the Somali now: the fighting, which had flared quickly, dwindled and would soon be over. They had found liquor and spoils. He felt that he could pull an arm free, but kept trying to see where he was. He looked for any sign of dawn's first grey light, so that he could determine the direction of the beach.

Herne and Balyuz turned toward town and discovered a merchant vessel leaving the harbor, lights aglow, so hailed it and asked to be taken aboard. As luck had it, the boat was commanded by some local sailors who had received courtesies in Burton's camp, so not only were Herne and Balyuz taken aboard but the sailors edged along the shore, staying as close in as possible, to look for other survivors. At the beach near the mouth of the dry stream, Golab put his captain into a rowboat and pushed out to sea. Minutes later when they hailed the merchant vessel, Herne's voice came back over the water.

Burton was pulled onto the deck where everyone saw his condition—the javelin still piercing his face. As they came toward him to help, he threw out his arms and thrust them back. In a single swift motion, he took hold of the metal tip and pulled it out of his face. When he fell to his knees, Herne and the sailors came to him with rags to stop the blood.

Tied down, Speke waited until dawn.

His captors moved around the broken tents now, looking for spoils and singing a solemn song. Five of their wounded groaned, and their attendants pressed dates into their open hands—the assumption being, as Speke guessed, that if they had no interest in this delicacy they were near death. The corpses were ignored. Cases of brandy lay open and the raiders were drunk and listless, except for occasional arguments about the spoils. Speke's own captor had left to join in an argument over a camel, and while he was gone another tribesman came up, stood over Speke, and asked in broken English if he was a Moslem or a Nazarene.

"If you a Christian, I kill you!" the man swore.

"Well, I am," Speke shouted at him. "So go ahead and kill me!"

But the man only laughed, happy to be tormenting the captive, and turned away. Before long, another tribesman appeared, brandishing Stroyan's sword. He made motions as if he meant to behead Speke, but then he left, too.

Speke waited. In only a minute or two more, he knew, the light would be enough so that he could possibly tear loose and sprint for the sea, finding his way among the brush and dunes. But as he prepared himself for this, a third native appeared. His sneer told Speke that this was his executioner. As the man hovered over him with a spear, Speke tore loose a hand, and when the first thrust came he was able to turn away a fatal effort to get at his heart.

In a series of quick movements, the man jabbed at Speke as the lieutenant began to untie himself. The spear went into Speke's shoulder. Another jab went through his hand. Another missed. Furiously, Speke worked at the ropes. The man jumped over Speke, cursing, and drove the spear through the lieutenant's thigh; it made a rough, sucking sound as the native pulled it out and kept trying. As his executioner bent low, still jabbing, Speke lashed out with his fist and caught the man flush on the face. To the native's horror, Speke was on his feet; he had eleven wounds by this time and blood covered him, but he was taller than the tribesman, wild-eyed, and looked dangerous even though unarmed. Before the raider could think what to do next, Speke turned and ran.

Wounded in the thigh so that he could only hobble along, Speke ran through the midst of the camp, where the renegades stood around among their spoils. They cursed him and lobbed a spear in his direction, but perhaps because he was on his feet and looking determined, no one attacked him as he hurried toward the dunes.

At the beach he turned toward town, but went only as far as some old wells that were surrounded by a crumbling stone wall on the outskirts. There, as dawn arrived, he slumped against the wall and tried to clear his thoughts. His bleeding had stopped, but folds of flesh hung from his thighs where the spear had gouged him, and his pierced hand throbbed. An old woman, robed in black and carrying her waterskins, came toward him.

"English," she said, pointing, and he was able to understand that his companions were in a boat offshore.

In spite of his wounds, he started back down the beach in the direction of camp, somehow unafraid now; pain drove out the fear, but he also knew that the Somali wanted no more fighting.

Near the mouth of the dry stream he saw Burton, Herne, Balyuz, Golab, and the sailors, all armed, coming ashore. Burton wore a kerchief around his bloody head and his face was swollen almost beyond recognition, but he looked fully in charge. Speke called to them, and Herne and the sailors ran to his aid.

The group made its way back to the littered camp—now abandoned by the renegades, who had driven the animals several hundred yards out into the desert. All was lost: personal effects, stores, even the tents themselves. They found Stroyan's stiff and cold body, which had been beaten and stabbed repeatedly after death. Out in the desert, circling his camel, an ostrich plume sticking up from his headband, a young raider waved his fist back at them. Seeing the ostrich feather, Burton told them that this was undoubtedly the one who had killed their companion. They watched him circle that camel, going around and around; they watched as if they were spellbound, none of them even bothering to lift a rifle to fire a shot, as if he were some faraway dervish, whirling in a swirl of sand like nature itself, cursing them and moving beyond their reach.

Speke, back in Aden, swerved toward death. His legs contracted painfully and he tossed in a delirium of fever and temporarily went blind. In a private room at a house just outside the garrison walls, he sweated through his sheets and cried out in unconscious pain; Brigadier Coghlan came to visit and stood at the foot of the bed, gripping the iron bedposts, and had tears in his eyes at the young man's suffering.

Steinhauser tended to Burton at the hotel. The javelin had knocked out two teeth and split the palate.

"You've got to leave this hot weather and return to England," the doctor told his patient. "You've had secondary syphilis and you're susceptible to infection. I'd say you should go quickly."

45

Burton gazed out the window from his bed, the jagged scar on his face accentuating his severity; the anger and disappointment in his face looked as though it had been set in stone.

The next day he was up, though, and moving about with energy. He wrote his full report to the government and had it sent over to Coghlan, to be forwarded to Bombay and London. Then he walked in the hotel gardens with the whores, worked at his language notes, and wrote letters. On the following morning the brigadier came to see him. Coghlan seemed shocked at first by the severity of Burton's wound, but the captain seemed so vigorous that not much sympathy continued.

"If we had received the smallest support from the garrison or the Aden police force, this wouldn't have occurred," Burton said. "As it was, Speke trained a few scatterbrained niggers—none of whom stayed to fight."

"Yes, you put all that in your report," Coghlan said. "Even so, I can't help feel you didn't exercise proper caution. And I've added this in a letter of my own to the government, which will accompany yours."

"There were so many contributions to the mess," Burton said, having difficulty speaking through his swollen mouth. "We waited for the Berbera fair to end and for the arrival of the mid-April mail. We could have left under the protection of some larger native caravans, but this seemed unnecessary. The rains were a factor. The gunboat had to depart. Rumors and threats came every day, but the Somali deal in these with each other, so we paid them no attention. We had sentries posted. Yet not one stayed to fight—not one!"

"Yes, but we want no blame for what happened," the brigadier said. "We warned you against going. And we did lend the gunboat and other encouragements."

"All my life," Burton said, "my government has been willing to employ my initiative and risk. If ever I succeed at anything, it will happily take the honors. If I fail, it will always blame me. And, meanwhile, it will only allow the most meager support. My government—like its people—is a parsimonious, stingy, tightwad little apparition. It leaves great undertakings like the mapping of Africa to a wretched committee like the Royal Geographical Society—which, if possible, is even more frugal and conservative."

"You're in pain and not completely yourself," Coghlan said, getting up stiffly to leave the interview.

"I am completely myself," Burton told him. "And I always am."

When Speke's fever passed and the spasms in his legs subsided, he tried the painful process of walking. Herne and an orderly carried him, sitting in a wicker chair, to the roof of the officer's mess, so that he could recuperate during long meals as he looked out over the city and harbor. Before dinner one evening, Burton came to see him.

"Your scar might be handsome—like a dueling scar," Speke told him.

"I'm sorry about our setback," Burton said softly. "And Stroyan. And your legs."

"I'll be fit soon," Speke replied. "Stay for dinner?"

"I don't eat English food," Burton told him. "My father was a retired army officer with asthma, you know, and we lived and traveled around the Mediterranean. I took an early fancy to continental food. Never liked boiled potatoes in the officers' mess and never will."

Speke sat straight in his chair, as if his upper torso were at attention. His mouth grew tight and he said, "I have to tell you that I suffered a terrible loss of property over in Berbera. All my savings and the barter goods with which I planned to travel in Africa. All my guns and instruments."

"I'm sorry for that, too," Burton answered.

"I mean to apply to the government for consideration."

"Good luck, my friend."

"You don't think they'll repay my loss?"

"Not likely."

"What of you, then?" Speke asked. "Can you restore it?"

"My own losses are bitter. I wish I could ensure yours."

"You headed the expedition," Speke reminded him. "So perhaps you can restore my loss or witness to others in my behalf. I can't afford idleness in the matter."

"I'll see what I can do," Burton promised, trying to overlook the lieutenant's tone.

The next day the commander came to Speke with the full report on the incident: Burton's explanations and his own additional notes. Speke read over the entries, including his own statements, and nodded his approval as Coghlan sat beside him and watched. Then, for the first time, Speke saw Burton's further reports: materials written after their first visit to the Somali coast, the trip to Harar, and the aborted attempt to find the Wadi Nogal. In these, Burton suggested a criticism of Lieutenant Speke, writing

. . . though the traveller suffered from the system of blackmail to which the inhospitable Somal subject all strangers, though he was delayed, persecuted by his protector and threatened with war, danger, and destruction, his life was never in real peril. Some allowance must be made for the people of the country. Lt. Speke was, of course, recognized as a servant of Government; and savages cannot believe that a man wastes his rice and cloth to collect dead beasts and to ascertain the direction of streams. He was known to be a Christian. He was ignorant of the Moslem faith; most fatal to his enterprise he was limited in time. Not knowing either the Arabic or Somali tongue, he was forced to communicate with the people through the medium of a dishonest interpreter and Abban.

Speke was furious. His hands gripped the sides of his wicker chair and he glared at the brigadier, asking, "Did you read this? Did you?"

"Yes," Coghlan admitted. "Afraid I did."

"He suggests that I was incompetent. And that I was never in danger!"

"He was making an official excuse for you," Coghlan said.

"Yes, but I'll never forgive him for this," Speke swore. "I never will! Never!"

1855–1856

—)0(—

Victorian Society,

the War in the Crimea,

the Return to Africa

SOON AFTER BURTON RETURNED TO LONDON, HE MADE AN OBLIGATORY ADDRESS at the Royal Geographical Society in rooms above the Burlington House. The dinner beforehand consisted of an inedible lamb chop, overcooked vegetables, and a soggy pudding. Then he stood up at the table, the scar on his cheek still bright red and forbidding, and gave an account of his journey to Harar and Berbera. Only a small crowd listened, and few of the truly distinguished members were present. They applauded warmly as he finished, then everyone stood around smoking cigars. He tried to cover his disappointment, but felt, somehow, that they weren't interested in Africa or in him or in the occasion. He even worried about his clothes, which were tweedy and out of style and season.

"Will you go on active service, Captain, and join the war?" the Secretary asked him, so that everyone in the room could hear the question and listen for the reply. "Or will you pursue your literary research?"

"I expect to be recovered and in the Crimea within a month," Burton answered, chewing on his cigar. Actually, his reply startled him somewhat, but he smiled and tried to see it through.

He had yielded to opinion. The war was popular.

That night he walked back to his new rooms in St. James Street. A heavy mist fell around him, but he wore no hat and didn't care. Little in England was his, he thought. Most of it was atrocious: the food, the weather, the political and social life. His intellectual contemporaries spoke of true freedom and pure knowledge, but they were conservative to the core and raging moralists in thin disguises: Ruskin, Dickens, Carlyle, Mill, Macaulay, all of them. There wasn't a genuine freethinker among them, for all their heavy reputations. And the institutions were pathetic: the government wouldn't govern, the Geographical Society wouldn't boldly explore, the schools wouldn't teach, the restaurants wouldn't even serve food. Neither was the army his. For those preening aristocrats who wanted to command others, the Purchase System existed—supported even by the late great Wellington. The lords bought themselves regiments and fancy staffs. And only those with money and influence became colonels or generals—never those officers with experience, skill, or accomplishment.

Back in his rooms he stood by the window of his study and gazed down into the rainy street. His scar itched.

Why not go on active service? The war with the Russians dragged on. He would get letters of introduction, travel to Constantinople, buy himself the gaudiest and most outlandish uniform he could afford, sharpen his saber, and give it a try. After all, Lord Cardigan had become a hero, even though he had misread his orders and had led the Light Brigade on a wild charge at the wrong objective—an impenetrable wall of Cossacks. Where else, except in war, could the adventurer find sufficient challenge? And so the Crimea with all its major battles probably in the past, with all its glories mostly gone, remained the only available action.

Speke, walking with the aid of two canes, went back to Jordans, his family home, where his brothers, sisters, mother and father looked after him in convalescence. He hardly knew his family and so became quiet in their company, listening to them talk, watching them, and learning their habits and affections as if they were strangers. Those rolling hills of Somerset had become a dream, too, in all his years away. His elder brother, William, drove him from village to village in the family carriage, and Speke felt that he should seal up each odor, each moment and image inside himself for the time when he would be leaving again; there were the old bridges, the hedgerows, the little stone church at Dowlish Wake, that long ridge of hillside where his mother's family lived, the velvet pastures, and in the towns those tarts and cakes in the bakery windows, those pewter pitchers of thick cream on the tables of the hotel dining room, the buildings made of grey stone that had been pried out of the fields. A beautiful, serene, restless place: ponies ran headlong in the high grass among the red cattle, the cobbled village streets gave off unsettling echoes, the streams flowed out of the hills with brooding whispers. At home, at the beginning of his stay, he enjoyed the pleasant lull. Then his uneasiness settled over the farm, those soft orchards, all the little hamlets and wooded groves where he traveled.

"When your strength comes back, we can certainly use you on the place," his father told him.

His mother with her great horsey face and knowing stare watched him, though, and knew: he was restive and discontent.

"Are you thinking of going to the war?" she asked him outright.

"Thinking of it," he admitted.

When he could walk again without his legs wobbling under him, he paced off short hunts, looking for partridge or rook or anything on the wing. His brother Ben went with him, often pausing to sit on the low stone walls so that Speke could rest. They talked very little, but occasionally commented on their plans for themselves. Since their elder brother, William, would carry on the family farm, they would have to find careers.

"I'll probably become a minister," Ben allowed. "Will you continue in the army?"

"Probably until I'm killed in battle," Speke told him.

Speke fretted over his wounds and his condition. He brought stones into his bedroom at Jordans, hefting them for an hour each morning until his arms and torso became powerful.

"The Somali are a sleek people, especially the men," he told the family at dinner. "I don't care for the fat, black Africans. But I do admire the good physique of the Somali warriors. They're very haughty hunters who carry their spears high and never seem to alter their expressions."

His wounds healed, his muscles grew strong, and in paying rigorous attention to his physique, he also became obsessed with his sexual longings. He dealt with his frustration in this by walking and hunting. Soon, Ben couldn't keep up with him. Speke made long daily circles, hiking through dappled forests, cutting across meadows adorned with foxglove and sunlight, taking back roads that ended in trails which exhausted themselves in broken paths and disappeared. He walked miles every day, and then, at night, allowing himself nakedness in the silence of his room, he tried to compose letters—principally to those who might help in recovering the price of his lost barter goods and personal effects stolen in the Berbera raid. But his hands would fall from his desk, touch his genitals, and fondle his thoughts away. Then, in the morning, he would dress and begin his hiking again, eating nothing before going out, saying little, carrying one of the old scatterguns over his shoulder. He preferred the antique weapons, which were carved and inlaid, if somewhat more dangerous and capable of a false discharge.

He had been born and raised at Jordans and knew its every step: the barns, the mossy stone walls, the sloping fields. His father treated the workers well, but demanded a military smoothness in operations. His mother had been Georgina Elizabeth Hanning, the daughter of wealthy local merchants and an emotional, willful family. In their early marriage she had supervised the estate almost by herself, but lately she concerned herself with the careers of her children. For her third son, Jack, she felt a special pain: he was the slow learner, the quiet and backward one, aloof and gentle. All his life, she knew, he would be away from her, yet more her own than any other.

Toward the end of his convalescence, he seemed particularly anxious. She began to detect so much about him—how, for instance, he seemed to have none of his brothers' simple and harmless vices. He neither drank nor smoked. His muscles seemed coiled and ready. He neither laughed too hard nor said too much, but seemed to measure every response, which put distance between him and the others. Yet this was clearly defensive, and his anguish, she sensed, might be deeper than he could tell, so that in hiding it he also hid too much of his more natural self. What pain, though, she wanted to ask him, and what anguish? Some secret? What?

"Why don't you marry and stay home?" his elder brother asked him one evening. It was a question that she, the mother, would never have posed.

"Who would have me?" Speke asked in reply. "An old, scarred soldier!"

After weeks had passed, he came to his mother for the favor he required. She was in her study, going over accounts.

"I want a good posting in the war," he told her. "It isn't likely, but could you help me make contacts again?"

"You have a wonderful military record," she said. "You'll get a fine regiment, I'm sure, if you want it. I'll write for you tomorrow."

He sat down on a sofa and looked across her desk, always more cluttered with work and less neat than his father's. She entered her accounts with a large black quill that looked wonderfully old-fashioned and official.

"Will we still have our museum?" he asked her.

"We certainly shall. Where are all your specimens?"

"At a native taxidermy in Aden. I have, let's see, twenty mammals, three dozen bird specimens, three reptiles, one fish, and one scorpion—all being stuffed! A very jolly lot from my trip in search of the Wadi Nogal. I'm sure Captain Burton didn't know how many items I shot and captured. My packs were full of creatures! The scorpion is this long!"

He held his hands apart as his mother laughed.

"We'll turn the old gazebo into the first room of the display," she promised. "Oh, Jack, we do love you. Stay at Jordans."

"You know I can't stay," he said quietly.

"Yes, I know," she answered, and they held hands across the corner of the desk.

Speke was posted to a Turkish regiment in the Crimea, an assignment that he took as a personal slight, but about which he could do nothing. Even in those last months of the war officers who had served in India received the less important positions. Speke felt that his army career was at an end: no chance of promotion, little chance of seeing battle so that he could merit one, and attachment to these foreigners. But he was promoted to captain and given time to recuperate and report; he decided to celebrate by stopping off at Athens en route to Constantinople and the war.

England and France had entered the war on the side of the Turks against Russia—not so much because of the invasion of the Crimea, but because that peninsula opened an access to the Mediterranean, where the Western powers hoped to keep naval superiority. It was a somewhat vague war, then, with its great distance from England making supply impossible, its officers arrogantly incompetent, its tactics suspicious. Yet, against staggering odds, the British had won at Alma—fording the river and storming what had seemed an impenetrable natural fortress of steep rock, a mountain in which the Cossacks had mounted heavy guns; against equally terrible odds, the cavalry, in spite of the loss of the Light Brigade, had also fought the Russians to a draw at Balaklava; now, through a whole winter and spring, the siege of Sevastopol continued as the British troops, a superior cavalry useless under the circumstances of siege, bombarded that seaside port. Cholera raged and the heroine was Florence Nightingale. Battle was sporadic and the heroes, on close examination, appeared too often to be fools. The officers constantly went off duty to attend dress balls, to take the sun around those Black Sea resorts, to whore in Constantinople, or to parade. Wives and girl friends were often present, and the men concerned themselves with bright uniforms or fancy horses. Duels were fought. Teatime was rigidly observed. Picnics, tours, and yacht parties were popular. The spirit of British entertainment dominated: it was all a foxhunt, a season at the races, and a long weekend at a somewhat exotic estate.

When Speke arrived in Athens, the hotels were crammed with tourists and army officers, but the mood was lighthearted and the air seemed filled with antiquity, jasmine, garlic, and brine. In the crowded dining salon that night he found himself seated next to a short, highly animated British diplomat, Sir Anthony, and his stylishly dressed, foppish dandy of a son. The son was Laurence Oliphant, who occasionally worked as a correspondent for *The Times*, but who seemed in no hurry to travel up to the front lines of the war. Both father and son spoke with all the hems and haws of fashionable school speech, so that Speke felt mildly uncomfortable, at first, in their presence.

"I say, the *wine*, haw, has so much *resin* in it that I'd stick to the beer," Sir Anthony warned, heavily pronouncing some of his words. "And, damn, we need another *glass* and some silverware, don't we? I say, *waiter!*"

The son, who sat there amused, his white gloves lying beside his plate, gave Speke a wink that somehow made them mutual allies and spectators as the old man carried on.

"Yes, I'm definitely on a *mission*," the father said in answer to Speke's polite question. "Have to see Lord Stratford, so we'll *eventually* take a steamer up the Bosporus to Therapia. Meanwhile, we'll sail around the *isles*. You should join us! Very educational and all *that!*"

"You really should consider it," said the son. "Where are you being posted?"

"Well, I've just been upgraded to captain and I'll be second in command of a Turkish regiment in a place called Kertch," Speke said.

"Sounds as if you've been posted to obscurity," young Oliphant said. "So why not take your time? With luck, the war will be finished before you arrive!"

"I want to do my part," Speke said.

"Yes, haw, naturally *so*," the father said. "But the Greek isles! I mean to say, no one could fault you for wanting a bit of that!"

Within two days the three of them booked a sailing vessel that set out for Rhodes, with stops along the way. The summer weather turned the sea to bluish silver; the winds were soft and perfect. Speke stripped off his shirt and allowed his body to tan while the Oliphants sat on deck sipping Pernod. They sailed from island to island, in and out of those picturesque rocky harbors, and at night rowed ashore to dine in little cafés situated below the olive groves.

Sir Anthony had been a jurist and attorney general at the Cape in South Africa, where Laurence Oliphant had been born. After they returned to the family home in Scotland, the father had been posted to Ceylon as a judge. Young Oliphant stayed home with his attentive mother, and together they attended parties, went riding, went to the ballet with the rich uncle who lived in Wimbledon, and visited the female cousin who wrote novels. At age nineteen, Oliphant went out to Ceylon to assist his father, and although he had always shunned schooling in favor of travel to Paris and the social life with his mother, he read law and was admitted to the Ceylon bar at only twenty-two years of age. To Speke, he seemed very quick-witted, very literary, intellectually superior—yet not as intimidating as Burton had been. It turned out, too, that Oliphant liked hunting, especially when he could be vicious at it.

"Yes," he admitted, "I used to hamstring the boars for fun. And shoot crocodiles! Gad, loved it!"

"Tell him about your elephant trophy," Sir Anthony insisted. They sunned themselves on deck. Along the shoreline were white beaches and enticing caves.

"You tell him, Papa!"

"When he was just seven years old, he shot a big male *elephant* who was keeping watch over a herd of *females*. We were out with a rajah drinking gin, hunting, and ordering the coolies about when the *group* of elephant strolled up to us. Well, *haw*, our tiny little one gets out his knife and goes forward to claim his prize. He was standing on the beast, you see, but then the big male wakes up, shakes its head, struggles to its feet, and *walks* off with the females—as if it had only meant to take a short *nap!*"

Speke laughed at the story, but it was the old man, telling it and remembering, who laughed loudest.

"It was a splendid little rag," Oliphant added. "I liked India. Wore a gold-braided turban when I was a boy!"

"I took my army leaves and walked into the Himalayas," Speke put in. "Did you ever go into the Himalayas?"

"Wrote a book on it," Oliphant said. "Called *Journey to Katmandu*. I thought surely I'd be a famous author, but fame—ah, piss on it. Anyway, I don't have much imagination."

"Nonsense, he's a *wonder* with words," the father said.

"I am fluent," Oliphant said. "But my great talent is flexibility of conscience. I find I can bend my morals around like a gifted sculptor bends clay."

"Nonsense again," the father told Speke. "He's an excellent man of law, a fine young journalist, and has a *delicate* sense of fairness in everything."

"I'm sure this is so," Speke replied.

"It is *certainly* so. And, Lowry, I detest hearing you belittle yourself—even if you do it just to advertise your wit."

"Sorry, Papa," Oliphant said, and they all managed to laugh.

Squandering their days among the tiny islands and villages, they did not go toward Rhodes, but turned toward Constantinople and their separate duties. The weather held; each day was a warm, brilliant jewel. On one of the last evenings Sir Anthony got drunk and joined a group of French officers at a local tavern. Speke and Oliphant decided to return to their ship, but their rowboat and oarsman were missing when they reached the quay. Oliphant was just tipsy enough to suggest that they swim for it.

"Or do your wounds prevent such foolishness?" he asked Speke.

"You're drunk and I'm crippled," Speke answered. "We're about even, I'd say. Let's have a go."

Leaving their clothing on the quay, they jumped down onto the beach and ran into the surf. Under a bright moon, they started swimming for the ship, which lay at anchor one hundred yards offshore. Although the sea was calm, they tired quickly. "Can you make it?" Speke called out, treading water.

"I refuse to drown during a prank," Oliphant answered, and they swam on.

Arriving at the ship, they were too tired to climb on deck. Hanging on some ropes below the gunwale, they shouted for help, but none of the crew had returned. Small, annoying waves bobbed them up and down and nudged them against the rough sides of the ship at its waterline. At last, they made an effort. But halfway up the rope, Oliphant began laughing, went limp, let go, and dropped back into the dark waters with a heavy splash.

"Steady!" Speke called from the deck. "I'll fetch a rope and haul you up!"

From the sea came the sound of Oliphant's high-pitched laughter.

Tired and miserable, Speke managed to pull Oliphant up the side. In a last bold heave, he jerked him over the rail and they sprawled on the wet deck, their bodies sliding into a sudden embrace as they bumped against the mast. They were laughing and groaning as Oliphant threw his arms around the young captain and pressed his lips on Speke's; it was a strange, awkward, impulsive, exhausted kiss, which Speke neither resisted nor took part in. He watched their mouths join; his wet beard seemed invaded by Oliphant's probing lips, and their teeth, once, lightly clicked together.

Then they got up without a word and went their separate ways, each to his own cabin to dress. By the time they reappeared on deck, the crew had returned, bearing Sir Anthony, who had passed out.

The war's presence in Constantinople seemed swallowed up in the city: its own corruptions overwhelmed soldiers, diplomats, and all who used it as the great staging center for the Crimean conflict. With its basic wares of sex and opium, it both aroused and extinguished the senses; with its parades and parties, it held out an illusion to the English officers that their careers would be well served if they lingered in its society.

Oliphant was all for staying on, and for a time it seemed they would, for

Lord Stratford was rumored to be in the city. But Sir Anthony soon learned that his contact had returned to Therapia, so booked a steamer for them.

"You'll come with us," he told Speke. "I've paid your passage."

"Very kind," Speke replied.

"Isn't Papa kind?" Oliphant asked with a sigh of admiration. "Generous. Enthusiastic. Very organized. I've been such a mama's boy, you know, but I do enjoy the judge! He makes me feel middle-aged!"

On the passage through the Black Sea going toward their destination, Speke tried to remain aloof, but Oliphant constantly flattered him, spoke of him, and drew him into conversations. Everyone talked of battle, of the siege, and of how the war was such a grand, exciting sport, and Oliphant often suggested that Speke would be a daring officer whose presence would make a difference.

"He wants to go back to Africa and discover the source of the Nile for our Geographical Society," Oliphant said to a group at lunch. "But he'll have a turn at Sevastopol first!"

"Please," Speke said to Oliphant later. "You mustn't talk about me."

"Can't help myself," Oliphant confided. "You're on my mind."

About the kiss, Speke naturally said nothing. Yet his thoughts about it were constant. Oliphant, meanwhile, made no suggestion of physical contact, but took another strategy: he spoke of how unique, how special Speke was. As the steamer neared the harbor at Therapia, Oliphant made a strong appeal.

"Our society is both liberal and very demanding of outsiders such as you and I," he said. "On one hand, it demands of us all the conservative values: honor, success, courage, seriousness, respect for money and power, responsibility to the home and family. But it also holds that there are other values: adventure, wit, freedom, exploration, scientific experimentation—and, even, if you will, sexual freedom and experimentation for the special few."

"I'm not sure I'm special," Speke argued weakly.

"You are very much so. And very much one of those free souls who must journey out to the boundaries of life, don't you see?"

"I have many uncertainties," Speke confessed.

"Quite so," Oliphant consoled him. "But many more extraordinary strengths. I expect great things of you. You'll not be held back because you're a man of true quest. You know it yourself! I can't tell you how I admire you."

The harbor at Therapia swarmed with French troops, bullock wagons, girls with bright parasols, flag bearers, horses, porters, and officers bedecked in braid and shiny buttons. Lord Stratford, paunchy and in high spirits, stepped out of his carriage and greeted them as they disembarked. Hailing them loudly, he grabbed Sir Anthony and embraced him while Oliphant stood there smiling and drawing on his white gloves.

"I'm going up to the front lines to confer medals on our gallant officers who have so well earned them!" Lord Stratford shouted, so that half those people crowding the docks could hear. "You must all come for the ceremony! Lowry, how are you? Join us! You'll have something to write for *The Times!*"

"Wouldn't miss it," Oliphant assured him.

Speke shook hands with Lord Stratford, but announced that he had to report immediately to his regiment.

"So it's goodbye for a time," he said to Oliphant. "I see my corporal waving for me."

"Soon again, dear friend," Oliphant answered as they gripped each other's hands. Around them, porters hefted Speke's bags onto their shoulders.

"Fine, fine young man!" Lord Stratford shouted above the din, the object of his admiration somewhat unclear.

Sir Anthony gave Speke a wrapped gift to be opened later.

"And did you hear?" Oliphant shouted at Speke as the crowd began to separate them. "I'm attending a costume ball tonight! Up at the front lines within earshot of the battlefield guns! I'll dress as a harlequin! Imagine!" Speke nodded and smiled, but the crowd closed around them, shoving and crying out, and the corporal ran up, saluting and cracking his heels together, insisting on showing the new captain toward his bivouac area. Oliphant went on chatting about his costume, laughing as he waved goodbye, and then noise was everywhere until Speke could hear him no more.

When Burton reached Constantinople his younger brother Edward was with him. Their mission to find a regiment became difficult, but they were happy in each other's company, glad to be together again after years apart. Edward, who was three years younger than his famous brother, had been out in Ceylon, another young officer attached to the needs and duties of the East India Company.

It was July and hot. General Raglan had died, but his replacement had no use for officers with Indian service, either, so Burton and his brother went from office to office with no luck. Since they had money from the publication of *Pilgrimmage to Al-Medinah and Meccah,* they languished in the bars and back streets of Constantinople at night, then each morning made their way to the officers' club, scrubbed and shaved, took breakfast in full uniform, and tried to look as crisp as possible in hopes that some colonel might offer them staff positions—or at least a company of recruits. It was aristocratic and freelance soldiering: one tried to appear important and hoped for the best. Edward liked the ritual, but his elder brother quickly grew cynical of it.

"Brace up," Edward told him. "I've brought you a gift! Remember DuPre, our tutor? Look, your first poem! It was about him!" With a smile, he pushed a crumpled scrap of paper across the breakfast table beside Burton's coffee. The poem read:

Stand, passenger! hang down thy head and weep,
A young man from Exeter here doth sleep;
If any one ask who that young man be,
'Tis the Devil's dear friend and companion—DuPre.

Reading the epitaph, Burton smiled. "How did you find this?" he asked.

"I've saved everything of yours," Edward told him, poking bread and jam into his mouth as he grinned. "You're a good poet. You're a wonderful writer and philosopher. You're a splendid adventurer and linguist. And a fine brother. Someone will see your talents in this goddamned land, too. You mark my words."

General W. F. Beatson had been a soldier of fortune in India, had served the Bengal Army for fifteen years, had commanded cavalry for several Indian princes, and had seen twenty victorious battles before arriving in the Crimea. At a higher level than almost anyone, he had sought a position, too, but Raglan, Lord Lucan, and others had turned him down before General James Scarlett of the Heavy Brigade finally accepted him as a staff member. Late in the war, now, it appeared that more cavalry was needed, so Beatson was granted permission to raise a group of irregular horsemen among the Turks. These were local men, brutal, almost incapable of being trained in British ways, but equally unstoppable in battle. They were popularly known as the Bashi Bazouks. They hated the Russians, rode their mounts like whirlwinds, and had reputations for torturing and mutilating their prisoners.

"I've heard of you," Beatson said to Burton when he presented himself. They were standing in the foyer of the officers' club—just before another breakfast.

"And I've heard of you, sir," Burton replied. "All to the good."

"Are you looking for a staff position?"

"Exactly so," Burton said, an amount of exasperation in his tone.

"And, let's see, didn't you make your trip to Mecca disguised as an Afghan Moslem? So you know these parts, eh?"

"That's right, I went as an Afghan merchant. But I also speak Turkish."

"You speak the language?" Beatson asked with amazement.

"Well enough to command the Bashi Bazouks," Burton said, and Beatson smiled. "Do you by any chance have a position for me?"

"How does chief of staff sound?"

"Rather nice," Burton said, and his own broad smile appeared.

Burton and his brother went into the city and paid tailors to fit them out with elaborate uniforms. Like Beatson himself, they decided to look gaudy—to impress the Turks. Braid, buttons, epaulets, stitching, and more braid: they looked extravagant.

"Damn me," Edward said, turning and admiring himself in the tailor's mirror. "I'm so beautiful!"

The training went on near the Dardanelles on the outskirts of Gallipoli. Every rape and murder in Constantinople was soon blamed on "Beatson's Horse," as his irregular force came to be called, and in the camp itself discipline was impossible. When drunk, the Turks fought wild duels: each man held a cocked pistol and a glass of *raki*. The one who finished his drink first, fired first —at close, deadly range. Burton found himself referee to these misunderstandings; he finally gave up trying to stop the inevitable and just insisted on fair fights —with no cheating on the drinking of that glass of *raki*.

General Beatson's house was located on a shady hillside overlooking the camp. He lived there with his wife and two daughters, one of whom was pretty enough to attract Edward. Burton urged caution in this.

Most of Burton's time came to be spent teaching the use of the saber— which the Turks used in an emotional way like a sharpened club. He could disarm any of his recruits and make them look foolish, but they wouldn't learn from him. Edward worked with the horsemen and also found that they were not interested in the finer points of riding; their plan was to go hell-bent at an objective, using their poor mounts as shields and battering rams.

Burton also found himself a go-between for General Beatson and the civilian locals, who generally tried to live off the army by cheating it and stealing from it. At one point, the general threatened to hang the local pasha. Later, the British consul came around to the camp to check on the behavior of the troops, and Beatson almost threw him out.

"My men will not be hampered by politicians!" he shouted at the consul.

"And my politics won't be hampered by your bandits," the consul shouted back.

Burton, who was usually the one to get into trouble, found himself calming the hotheaded Beatson. His days passed in correspondence with the British high command, the regional pashas, and his general. His private letters, meanwhile, went out to Dr. Norton Shaw of the Royal Geographical Society, with whom he had begun to discuss a trip to the Nile sources by way of Zanzibar. He also tried to recover his and Speke's personal losses at Berbera, but the letters in reply were filled with excuses. Finally, he used his desk to request promotion; he considered that he was the lowest-ranked chief of staff in the army.

His mood worsened and Edward couldn't console him. Every night they drank too much and raged against the system. As the summer passed into autumn, Burton was still a captain, still unsure if he could ever go back to Africa, and still kept busy by his wild Bashi Bazouks and his intemperate general.

One afternoon Beatson summoned Burton to his house. The general's sitting room was filled with Persian rugs and London bric-a-brac. His daughters glided in and out with tea and cakes, distracting Burton with each swish of their skirts.

"Lord Stratford has sent for you," Beatson said. "You think you can tell him we're ready to fight?"

"We can produce over two thousand Turkish sabers for the upcoming siege of Kars," Burton said, trying to focus his thoughts on military matters. "Think this is why he wants to see me?"

"No, not exactly," the general said. "I believe he wants you to go on a mission as a spy. He has a poor plan for someone to penetrate the Caucasus. Since you're the only one in our army who seems to speak the bloody languages, he thought of you. Stroke of genius on his part, eh?"

"They're all imbeciles," Burton said, meaning all the generals and politicians. The remark made one of the daughters jump and rattle the teacups.

"Quite so," General Beatson said. "But careful when you tell Lord Stratford this. He has a damned bad temper at times."

Clearly, the general wanted to employ Burton's foul mood and brash manners for his own purposes.

Lord Stratford de Redcliffe, who was the ambassador to Turkey and the most influential British diplomat in the war zone, entertained the generals and minor officials like Sir Anthony Oliphant, and regarded war as a great stage on which he could socialize with extraordinary men. He met Captain Richard Francis Burton at lunch at the consulate. From its opulent rooms, one could look out over the minarets of the city and see the shimmering waters of the Sea of Marmara. The ambassador was modestly fat, red in the face, and tended to spit out his words.

That noon in September was a pressing moment for the British cause. Kars, a medieval fortress in Armenia held by the Turks, had been under siege by thousands of Russian troops for weeks; its inhabitants were starving and lost unless regiments were sent to their relief, and Burton, trying to be as gently persuasive about this as he could, stated that his Bashi Bazouks could be added to the relief column.

"Don't be an ass," Lord Stratford spat at him. "Nobody wants that!"

"Beg pardon, sir," Burton replied, trying to smile, remain charming, and achieve his purpose. "We're short of men and supplies. It might be that—"

"No irregulars! Damn, man, that's it! The Foreign Office doesn't want them, the generals don't want them, and I don't want them!"

His rejection had the unmistakable tone of insult, so that Burton knew he couldn't eat, think, or continue to behave with courtesy.

"Now here's my . . . hmm, plan . . . about that spy mission," Lord Stratford began at last. "We will commission you in our intelligence forces. You will travel to the Caucasus, where you will contact . . . hmm, all those tribes who have fought for independence from Russia for so many years. If you can convince these tribes that they will gain independence by joining us in the Crimea, perhaps we can turn the tide of the war! What do you think of my plan?"

"Why me?" Burton asked.

"Jove, because—hmm, you're famous for getting in and out of tight places!"

"Well, I won't do it this time," Burton stated flatly.

"Why not?" The ambassador's face began to redden. "I've already spoken to General Simpson, and he agrees that it's a shrewd idea!"

"I'm to travel into Russia with no arms, troops, or support? No, thanks," Burton said. "If you want to help end the war, send relief to Kars immediately —and let the Bashi Bazouks fight."

"You are impudent!" Lord Stratford bellowed, sending out a fine mist of spittle.

"This war is conducted by incompetent generals and diplomats who know nothing of their enemy, even less of their allies, and who invariably choose the wrong strategies," Burton said, folding his hands on his empty plate.

"You are the most impudent man in the Bengal Army!" the ambassador shouted, his face crimson.

"And you are a man who has lived his life in the Eastern world without learning a word of Turkish, Persian, or Arabic," Burton told him. "And who has gained a prodigious reputation in Europe—by living away from it!"

"And you, sir, are a coward! We need a man with resourcefulness to visit those tribes!"

"They would find me out as a spy and flay me," Burton shouted. "I can't trot over into Russia and start a revolution among dissident tribes! My chances of returning to Constantinople would be small, indeed, and if I came back I might not have any skin! You do understand flaying, do you not? A man's skin is stripped from him—."

"A coward and virtually a deserter!"

"You *won't* call me that! By God, you're a fat politician sitting up here away from the war! You have only a few vague tactics in your head—like our idiotic generals! Don't you see there's no military advantage in such a spy mission at this late date because we have not a scrap of military intelligence! So this is just vague, hopeful, pitiful fumbling! Please, let the Bashi Bazouks into the war! They're mad to fight and hate the Russians! It doesn't take either intelligence or hope to see that!"

Lord Stratford, crimson and spitting, rose from the luncheon table and seemed to stagger above it as if he might fall into the dishes. His fingers trembled above the silver and porcelain. Yet the old diplomat managed to bite his lip and calm himself.

"You'll stay and dine with us tonight?" he asked. "There are . . . hmm, ladies . . . who wish to hear of your . . . hmm, famous pilgrimage to the . . . hmm, holy city of Mecca."

"Beg pardon, sir?" Burton whispered in reply.

"Dinner this evening. You are a mere subaltern, but . . . hmm, a coveted dinner guest, as you surely know and understand," the old man said, and his body teetered as if he still might fall over.

For a moment it was more than Burton could comprehend. This terrible war was all around them: clumsily managed, filled with death, riddled with misunderstanding and lack of communication, cursed with ineptitude, yet the social vanities managed to stay intact.

"No, very sorry," he said, shaking his head slowly in dismay. "I just can't dine with you and the ladies, Lord Stratford. I have to return to my troops."

"Naturally, I quite understand," the ambassador said, still gaining control over himself. He tried a smile, but spittle ran off his lip.

Burton hurried downstairs, walked through the consulate gardens, and entered the streets of the city, where the afternoon odors overpowered him: those fetid vegetable smells, urine, centuries of grime, the press of bodies. A raging independence took hold of him and he wanted to pull that silly braid from his shoulders. If ever he traveled to a foreign field again, he told himself, and if ever he left the shores of England, it would not be for glory or honor, but just to get away from Englishmen.

A week later the combined British and French forces drove the Russians out of Sevastopol. Losses were heavy, as no native regiments again took part.

As the Russians evacuated the fortress and city, they left behind their sick and dying in the hospital. When the allies inspected the site, they found men whose sores had blent into the rough canvas sheets on which they lay; flies and vermin swarmed over the bodies; blood, shit, maggots, and human flesh were one.

When Burton settled into camp at the Dardanelles again, his Bashi Ba-zouks got into a late-night brawl with some French regulars. Shots were fired, sabers were raised, curses were exchanged, but no one suffered injury. Yet by the time Burton and his sergeant major marched up to General Beatson's hillside house and knocked on his door at three in the morning, the offended Frenchmen had gone to reinforce themselves with Turkish regulars, who brought artillery and surrounded the camp.

"We came to report a bit of an intramural skirmish," Burton offered at the general's door. "But it seems we're surrounded and under siege."

"From whom?" Beatson wanted to know. "The Russians?"

"Sorry to say, sir, that it's the French and Turks."

"We're surrounded by our own men?"

"Precisely so," Burton said, and he almost laughed.

By the time the general had pulled on his trousers and buckled his saber in place, two steamers in the harbor near the camp had pointed their guns on the tents of the Bashi Bazouks. Beatson and Burton stalked down into camp, swearing and shouting orders for quiet, waving lanterns that threw harsh shadows on the confusion. Word came that William Howard Russell, the renowned war correspondent who had just come back from the battle zones, was on his way to file a report, and that residents and shopkeepers in the vicinity had fled because they expected a major battle. Both Burton and his general regarded everything as a mere outbreak of male hysteria, but couldn't get the men to their tents.

When the Turkish military pasha swept into camp, Beatson screamed at him to get his regulars home to bed. Someone sent up a red flare, bathing the darkness with light and revealing swarms of half-naked Turks, their eyes wide and their mouths agape, strolling around in aimless patterns.

Edward appeared and gave his brother a sip of *raki*. Illumined in red, they stood in the middle of the parade grounds and discussed the melee.

"Looks mildly humorous," Burton offered, "but I fear it isn't. Beatson's Horse may never get into battle because of this little rag."

"Surely," Edward said, taking a heavy swig, "morning will bring calm."

"I don't know. Look at that," Burton said, and he pointed across the way at Beatson, the pasha, and a French officer screaming at one another.

Some of the Bashi Bazouks were down at the shore heaving stones toward the steamers in the harbor, their tosses falling far short of the mark.

A horse pulled loose from its tether and sprang about wild-eyed, men chasing after it.

Up on the hillside, Beatson's wife and daughters had come out on the verandah to observe the excitement, and in the red glow of the dying flare their forms were outlined beneath their nightdresses. What a shame, Burton felt, to be in a place where one's talents were wasted—even one's simple desires.

At his camp in the Crimea, Speke lacked even the wild company of the Bashi Bazouks. His commander, Major Greene, ran everything according to orders, never veering from protocol, never asking the High Command for action, never seeking to interrupt the routine of life near the little village of Kertch. Speke, as second in command, had nothing to do. He did renew his friendship with Edmund Smyth, whom he had known in India, and they planned hunting excursions together, but even their plans came to little. They heard of bears, wolves, and large chamois and mountain sheep over in the nearby Caucasian forests, and they bought new rifles and outfitted themselves to go, but their requests for permission were denied.

"Yes, I understand that the forests are inside Russia," Speke argued with

Major Greene. "But they're virtually uninhabited. And we won't stay more than a week at most."

"You're an inventive fellow," Greene said, shaking his head wisely.

Major Greene was such a dullard, Speke thought, and, in the end, when he and Smyth knew they wouldn't go and his companion wanted to continue to talk about it, he felt that Smyth was a dullard, too. It was maddening: this bleak outpost so close to the war, yet so far away.

By turns, Speke became angry and depressed. Frequently sullen and aloof, he would sit in his tent for hours, remembering his school days and how he suffered fits of depression and temperament as a boy, especially after his so-called eye trouble, when study was impossible. The eye trouble: that was another matter to recall and brood over. His mother preferred to blame his problems on ophthalmia, but the truth was he couldn't read. Some odd disability made him see the words on a page backward. His mother assured him that he was as smart as other children, yet had this odd quirk. Even so, it frustrated him, made him short-tempered, and because of it he was forced to do without university and to leave home—and all his mother's understanding—to seek a place in the army.

Now, stuck in the Crimea, just another Indian officer who would not be permitted to serve in battle, he felt his frustrations, angers, and depressions returned. He couldn't even hunt.

The men stayed away from him, even Major Greene and Lieutenant Smyth. He had changed, physically, since Berbera, and although he was still tall and Scandinavian looking, he had put on weight and looked severe. His anger lacked the charm of youth and wasn't easily overlooked; the moods that had once seemed petulant and spirited had turned grim and deeply troubled.

"I hate saying this, Speke, but your mood has been so ugly lately that . . . well, the men are afraid of you," Major Greene told him.

"Afraid? Then let them be," Speke answered.

Occasionally, he became buoyant and hopeful, getting excited over rumors that they might be part of the relief column at Kars, for instance, or that prospects for a posting at a new camp might be good. But these brief, intense periods of cheer gave way, again, to depression and displays of irritation.

During this time he tried to write letters. Even these were painful exercises, as if he had to concoct every syllable with extreme effort. He wrote to the new secretary, Dr. Norton Simon, at the Royal Geographical Society, still asking about recovering his lost money and barter goods from the Berbera expedition. The secretary offered little encouragement. He also wrote to his mother, suggesting that he might have to come back to Jordans. Speke felt that he was smoldering; on fire with some fatal flame.

Kars fell to the Russians—unrelieved by British, French, or Turkish regulars. At the last, the inhabitants of the fortress dug up their dead horses for food. Neither the Bashi Bazouks nor any other group of irregulars were even considered and sat idle in their camps. Rumor had it that the British High Command decided to sacrifice the fortress for advantage elsewhere.

Beatson's Horse ended when the regiment's general was dismissed and recalled to England. Burton, who predicted complications from that night when trouble occurred between his men and the French troops, could not foresee the worst. It seemed that every diplomat and regular army officer testified against poor Beatson. Slander and hearsay were rampant. Everyone wrote reports and letters to the editors of *The Times* deploring the use of Indian officers, irregulars, and anything or anyone except standard military units.

"Brother dear, I'm going back to Boulogne," Edward said. "Then back to India, if I can arrange a new posting. To hell with all this."

"We'll never see action," Burton concurred. "So I plan to start packing myself. Do you suppose anyone would buy these silly secondhand uniforms of ours?"

In December 1855 Burton was back in his rooms in London, paying daily visits to the Royal Geographical Society in Whitehall Place. His author's royalties had expired, his army career was at a standstill, and he felt that his best bet was to display himself as an explorer. He paid his daily respects to Norton Shaw, the secretary, who was a pale little man who kept the maps, filed correspondence, and tended to the vanities of the lords and officers of the Society.

The secretary showed Burton one map drawn by two German missionaries, Rebmann and Erhardt, depicting a gigantic lake 800 miles long and 300 miles wide.

"This monster's supposed to be the source of the Nile?" Burton scoffed. "Ridiculous!"

"Yes, quite," the secretary replied. "The committee thought so, too, when they examined it."

"Oh, is that so?" Burton said, picking up a clue.

After that, he concentrated on trying to meet any of the distinguished committee members he could. With Christmas approaching, their weekly meetings were being postponed until the new year. But, diligently, he dropped by the dank stone building every day, hoping to find some congenial committee member present. In the meantime, he submitted a proposal for consideration: he would lead a caravan north from Zanzibar on the coast of East Africa, find the high lakes, possibly find those snow-covered Mountains of the Moon, and map the region. If possible, he would locate the source of the Nile and then follow its course toward Egypt. He hoped to take Dr. Steinhauser, his physician friend at Aden, he added, and a third in command approved by the Society.

"Has Sir Roderick seen my proposal yet?" he kept asking Shaw.

"Yes, he has it. I assure you there will be a meeting," the secretary continued to reply.

After Christmas and the New Year celebrations, there was still no meeting. Burton got into other matters. He wrote letters to *The Times*, supporting General Beatson, who was still in the news. He also wrote letters proposing new military schemes that would employ large regiments of irregular Kurdish cavalry. In addition, he popped in and out of Fleet Street offices, talking to solicitors about forming a company to be called The Hajilik, or Pilgrimage to Mecca Syndicate, Limited. He wrote an elaborate prospectus, but his company never got started. He also began writing his book about Harar, to be called *First Footsteps in East Africa*. In transforming his notes, he freely used those Speke had given him. Almost as an afterthought, he arranged for Speke's collection of mammals, birds, reptiles, and insects, which were still housed at the garrison in Aden, to be sent to an acquaintance in Calcutta, a zoologist named Edward Blyth, who would identify them and publish the results in the *Journal of the Royal Society of Bengal*, later to be reprinted in London under Burton's name. His rationale was consistent with army procedure: any junior officer's work belonged to his commanding officer.

Finally, just before noon one day in January, Burton went around to the Whitehall offices of the Society once more. There was snow on the streets and a cold wind blowing. He was hungry, without money for lunch, and wearing his heavy army boots underneath his flannel trousers when he met Monckton Milnes, Lord Houghton, in the map room.

"I say, Burton! Good seeing you! Have you seen this?" Milnes asked, pumping Burton's outstretched hand. Milnes was distinguished-looking, with white muttonchop whiskers, and had the most unusual expression on his face: he looked always as if someone had caught him by surprise, so that his mouth was shaped to form a surprised O! His expression, in fact, was rather jolly and made Burton feel lucky. And as this distinguished member of the Society's inner circle unfolded the Rebmann/Erhardt drawing of the huge African lake, he made Burton feel very much an insider, too.

"Yes, I've seen that damned map," Burton said. "Rubbish, I'd say!"

"Germans don't know a thing, do they?" Milnes said, laughing out loud through that little round O in his face.

"My proposal is with Sir Roderick Murchison," Burton ventured. "If we act, we'll have a caravan heading inland from Zanzibar within a year."

"Good spirit," Milnes said, and he clapped Burton on the shoulder. "And good meeting you at last! I've heard a lot about you!"

"Oh, something good?"

"Well, your exploits made good reading. But, I say, you have an interest in common with me—or so I'm told."

"Really?" Burton asked, pleasantly surprised. "What is that?"

"Pornography, of course!"

"I do have a few items from the East," Burton admitted.

"So you must come to my house soon!" Milnes said. "And bring your materials! I have another friend with very special interests! Got any photos?"

"A few," Burton said, hoping that he actually did. "And, meanwhile, perhaps you can see your way toward supporting my proposal to the Society. I do want to have a go at the Nile."

"Yes, yes! Thing to do," Milnes said, his face wearing that look of innocent astonishment, "is to get Vice-Admiral Back on our side! He's the man who sailed the Arctic, you know, and if he supports us I'm sure Murchison and the rest of the committee will agree!"

"Sounds fine," Burton said, excited and just able to control himself. He noted Milnes' use of the plural pronoun.

"So, good, is there anything I can do for you meanwhile?" Milnes asked.

"Buy me some lunch?" Burton suggested.

"Lunch, is it? Haw, well enough! You hungry?"

"Starved—and too poor these days to eat in restaurants," Burton confessed.

"Not today, you aren't!" Milnes said, and his mouth made its little round O once again before he laughed.

When the committee met that next week, Milnes saw to it that Vice-Admiral George Back, presently the Royal Geographical Society's brightest star, supported Burton's petition. Sir Roderick Murchison, the Society's current president, grumbled about Burton's name appearing so often in the press, but all was approved: Burton would go toward the Nile source when funds were raised.

On hearing the news, Burton immediately posted a note to Speke, inviting him to join the expedition. The war in the Crimea had ended and demobilization had begun, so as he sent the note off Burton realized that it might never find its way to Speke or his regiment. But he was excited about prospects and felt he owed something to the young officer for his losses and wounds in Berbera. Also, there was a more selfish and public motive: Coghlan and others in the army still blamed Burton for what had happened to the Berbera expedition, so Burton hoped that this gesture toward Speke would mend feelings—and perhaps even appear in any final judgments or reviews of *First Footsteps in East Africa* when it was published.

Finally, he felt that it didn't matter—apart from Steinhauser—who became his colleague on the caravan. Confident of himself, he always thought that anyone under his command, weak or strong, capable or inept, would be made sufficient by his own strong leadership.

On a bright Saturday that early spring, Burton went out to Fryston, Milnes' estate, for one of the weekend parties that frequently gathered together a number of rogues and congenial outsiders from conventional London society. He took lunch with Milnes, his pleasant and talkative wife, and Fred Hankey, an old friend who was also a fellow collector of pornography. After cakes and tea, Burton strolled in the gardens, then had a look at the rambling stone house. The bath suites with their marble and fine woodwork were larger than Burton's entire flat in St. James Street. In the wide, carpeted hallways were family portraits, fancy chairs with gilt and marquetry, silken wallpapers with floral designs, and tables adorned with Staffordshire pottery, decorative oil lamps, and bell jars. The parlors and sitting rooms, warmed by fires in the wide, stone hearths, contained bird cages, paintings by Landseer, Bechstein pianos, stacks of magazines, spangled fans, and embossed Valentines. An elegant, expensive mansion, the sort of place Burton would never possess himself, yet he measured his material ambitions by it: he would own something, someday, perhaps furnished with such good taste if more modest—and with, perhaps, touches of the exotic, such as African shields or spears on the walls of certain rooms.

A man who had no material ambitions was less a man, Burton felt. One lived for the new and interesting, but one also collected, built, and produced. Houses, books, companies, institutions, families: one's presence was in the physical world, so one wanted to take from it, add to it, and in the interchange define oneself.

In the late afternoon before dinner he went to his suite and sat on the wonderful Deluge Pull-Chain Toilet. Afterward, he washed, powdered, then dressed in his unstylish blend of silks, woolens, and forlorn army boots. He wished, still, for better clothes. Yet he was excited at being there, at being part of men doing important things, and not wanting to go downstairs early, he took hold of the heavy brass bedstead and lifted—pulling the whole bed up, mattress and all, to his chin. Three, four times: he felt his biceps strain. Blood boomed in his veins.

Dinner was late.

None other than Palmerston, the Prime Minister, stopped in for a sudden conference with Milnes. They went into one of the small drawing rooms while a carriage and guards waited on the front lawn.

"What's it about, do you suppose?" Burton asked Hankey.

"Oh, just money," Hankey guessed, offering Burton a whiskey. They stood in the main library, and from the distance came the sound of women's voices.

"Tell me," Burton asked in a confidential tone. "Do you suppose there's some young lady here for the weekend who would like a fuck?"

"Hm, I'll think on it," Hankey said. "There are one or two plump cousins, someone's wife, Mrs. Milnes, and surely a parlor maid or two. If you can wait until after we dine, perhaps I can help with a more scientific survey."

The two of them laughed and drank off their whiskeys.

Dinner was delayed by two hours, so that Burton had time to find out about the other guests. There was Charles Tennyson, the poet's brother; James MacQueen, one of the Royal Society's chief members, who had made known his enthusiasm for Burton's proposed search for the Nile source; and a young man with white gloves and a lace handkerchief, both of which constantly waved about as he entertained the ladies. This was Laurence Oliphant, called Lowry by everyone.

It was exciting to have Palmerston in the next room, and everyone got a bit tipsy and remarked on the importance of their host, who had, in fact, once been offered the post of head of Treasury when Palmerston first formed his government, but had refused on grounds that he had too many cultural and literary interests.

As a young man, Milnes had sailed the Greek isles with the great Wordsworth. According to MacQueen, the lord also had a good singing voice, wrote poetry, and could drink untold quantities of spirits of all sorts. He had once lost a university poetry competition in which Alfred Tennyson was also an entrant.

"Brother didn't win either," Charles Tennyson said, laughing, as they waited for those doors of the drawing room to open. "But the incident turned into literary advantage for our Milnes. There are still members of the press who consider him a genius who just hasn't got time for actual writing."

Milnes, Burton learned, with his pop eyes and pleasant wit, was always invited to each season's best gatherings. He had raised large sums for Florence Nightingale's efforts. Among his close friends were the Gladstones, Leigh Hunt, and Carlyle. He attended most major scientific and geographical meetings, wrote an occasional book review, and as Palmerston's lifelong friend and confidant was a great supporter of the Crimean War, the Whig Party, and the use of the press for political and liberal causes.

At last those drawing-room doors opened and out came the Prime Minister.

"Come on, Palmy, have a nip with us," Milnes insisted. No one else in England would have called him Palmy.

"Can't, just can't," Palmerston said in a voice so that everyone could hear. "I'd love to drink Irish whiskey and have your literary talk tonight, but can't. Which brings to mind your host's opinion of Coleridge's masterpiece! 'The Rime of the Ancient Mariner,' according to Milnes, is an epic poem meant to help prevent cruelty to animals!"

The guests dutifully laughed as Palmerston, satisfied with a good exit line, coughing and snorting into his handkerchief, waved again and was gone.

The dinner, mostly prepared by Mrs. Milnes herself, was roast lamb, truffles, delicate pastries, and selections of French wines. After dinner, the men

were provided with Greek smoking caps and woolen slippers studded with colored agates; filing into their parlor, they looked like figures at a foreign masque ball. Milnes passed around cigars and set up a hookah.

The evening discourse was about sex and travel. Hankey observed that he knew exactly why the Royal Geographical Society had been created: so that real explorers could bring back spicy stories to the old codgers sitting in the overstuffed chairs down at Whitehall Place.

Burton told the stories of how the Somali removed the clitorises of their poor women, and when questioned he related the events above Sharmakay's warehouse in Zayla—only half believed by his listeners—about how he inspected the local women by candlelight.

MacQueen talked about a few choice Mayfair brothels where more exotic pleasures were being imported. Yellow, he said, was the year's fashionable color. This started Oliphant on Far Eastern matters; he planned to be in China with Lord Elgin, he announced, within the year.

"Do they have items to suit your taste in China, Lowry?" Hankey inquired.

"All items suit my taste," Oliphant said, strolling around the room. "I can bugger lampposts, geese, page boys, or codfish when I'm in the mood. I've even been known to lie with an occasional woman."

In the ensuing laughter, Burton imagined a detection: Oliphant seemed witty in saying this, yet oddly candid. He watched this curious young man as he strolled around the room, idly dusting Milnes' books and stacks of magazines with his white gloves; Oliphant was tall, slim, handsome, and seemed to see everything with a keen, alert proficiency.

The evening wore down with foolish speculations concerning the color of progeny born between various races, the shape of the Asiatic cunt, and the use of contraceptives. (Casanova, Hankey reminded the gathering, used a half peel of a lime as a diaphragm.) MacQueen, who was not used to the potency of the hookah, took a heavy draw from its smoke, then slumped sideways in his chair.

After midnight, Burton, Oliphant, and their host strolled out on the terrace overlooking a moonlit formal garden and fountain.

"I know a colleague of yours," Oliphant revealed. "John Hanning Speke. He would give anything, I know, to go on your journey with you."

"I've written to Jack," Burton said. "He's invited."

"Oh?" Oliphant asked, brightening. "Has he accepted? Is he back in London?"

"Haven't heard from him," Burton said.

"I think Jack Speke . . . hmm, how shall I say this?" Oliphant mused. "I think that given the opportunity he could be a great man. A very great man."

"What's his talent?" Milnes asked, listening intently.

"Talent? Oh, not talent for anything so much," Oliphant said. "But he is so resolute. Stronger than anyone so far seems to know." This remark seemed aimed at Burton, who didn't respond. Instead, he grunted.

Milnes took that moment to state his admiration for Burton. "I'm sure that whomever Captain Burton chooses for the Nile trip will be extraordinary," he said. "I have to tell you, Lowry, that Burton is a special blend: a poet, a man of action and adventure, and all the things we men should be!"

"Hmm, yes," Oliphant replied. "I should very much like to read all that in your books sometime, Captain. Fascinating, I'm sure." The remark had an edge that Burton, again, let pass. Clearly, Oliphant didn't like him, but this made no conceivable difference; Burton now had such strong and influential friends —Milnes in London and Lumsden in Bombay—that the surly little antagonisms of such dandies as Oliphant could almost be taken as compliments.

That Sunday passed with the guests playing lawn games. Hankey, who noted that he detested croquet, sat in the shade of the marquee giving Burton a long testament for Warburg Drops.

"The perfect medicine for caravans and explorations," he stated, thrusting a package toward Burton, who juggled his glass of gin and accepted them. "Blend of quinine, sloes, and opium! Cures damn near everything! Take cases of these with you, Burton, when you hike off for Zanzibar!"

Burton popped one into his mouth. Not bad.

"Others will consult witch doctors, attach leeches to themselves, and go blind with fever, but not you if you have your Warburg Drops!"

"I like the ingredients," Burton agreed. "I probably won't care if I'm sick or not."

That evening, before the carriages took everyone back into London, Mrs. Milnes brought out trays of cold meats. She wore a layered taffeta dress, and her hair was done up in tubed ringlets, and Burton thought that she was especially lovely and wondered, for an instant, why he didn't have a competent wife such as this for himself. In those last hours the conversations had turned intellectual and literary: the forlorn theories of Marx, the mystery of the great book Charles Darwin was supposedly writing, and the wit of one of Milnes' poet friends, Swinburne, whom everyone wanted Burton to meet. Toward the end of the day Burton found that he was exhausted, but with enough Warburg Drops he did manage to get through.

Speke received Burton's note and went to see him the day he reached London. They sat in Burton's rooms, papers and writing materials strewn around like blown leaves, as Speke laughed, turned formal and stiff, broke into enthusiastic laughter again, recovered, and dissolved once more.

"I just can't believe it! But, mind, I can't afford to lose any personal property again! Can we possibly get enough money to ensure our losses if we suffer another disaster? I mean, we need a lot of money, don't we?"

"Yes, a lot," Burton answered, grinning. "I'm at work on that."

"My family can't be responsible."

"Yes, I understand."

"I pay my own way. Always have. But, damn, what a turn of good luck! I can't dream it! It doesn't matter now that we were Indian officers kept out of the war, does it? We'll be famous! We'll find the Nile sources and we'll be famous!"

"I think we will," Burton said, joining the laughter. "You must stop at the next meeting of the Society and introduce yourself. Then go home and rest. Are your wounds healed?"

"I think my legs are made of Indian rubber. I hardly have scars."

"Good. Do some hunting. Get your body ready."

"We'll have to write and ask the East India Company for leave, won't we?"

"Yes, I'll see to that," Burton said. "I'll ask permission for you—as well as for Steinhauser, who will be second in command behind me."

"Steinhauser?" Speke asked.

"The doctor, you remember! Yes, he'll require permission for leave, too."

"I thought this would just be the two of us."

"No, not at all," Burton said, gathering up some of Speke's sudden formality himself. "Having a physician along will be very important. But Steinhauser is uniquely qualified: he's a scholar, well organized, and speaks half the dialects on the continent. You do see the importance of all that, don't you?"

"Yes," Speke managed. "Of course."

At Jordans, the summer days of that bright, green, Somerset countryside kept Speke and his family in high spirits. He became their honored soldier—having served well, although without any particular distinction, in the Crimea, and having been chosen for this important and perilous mission into Africa. Occasionally, he enjoyed seizures of egotism.

"I think I made an impression at the Royal Society," he told them one afternoon when they were all drinking lemonade out at the gazebo. "Particularly on Murchison, who is really the ramrod of that whole little circle."

His brother William's clothes were dappled with grass stain, and since he was still sweating from his work that day in the fields he drank more than his share of the lemonade as he talked. "Don't you owe your choice to Burton?" the brother asked, looking over the rim of his glass.

"He had to choose me because of my qualifications," Speke told them. "And, besides, I think he had to save his own face after word spread around on how things were mishandled at Berbera."

"Burton is a maverick, isn't he?" Speke's mother added. "I'd imagine him very difficult to like."

"He has a good intellect and a good knowledge of languages," Speke admitted. "I think he probably knows African ways well enough. But, then, he hasn't done me any real favors, has he? I've got scars all over my body. He reduced my notes by half and published them for profit in his own book. He took the specimens I collected and took credit for some scholarship concerning them. He's not a gentleman, not even truly British, some say, and I think our trip together will show everyone's true colors."

"Well spoken, Jack, and here's to you," William concluded, and he drank off his third glass of lemonade as everyone agreed.

Speke put his guns and gear in order, took long hikes across the countryside and along the coast, and corresponded with both Burton and the Royal Society. His notes were short and practical, yet he often made errors of grammar or spelling, so that he copied them over carefully before posting them to London.

As the weeks passed, he grew worried about money. Both his father and William complained about finances at the estate. At last, Burton wrote to announce that the government had agreed to pay an additional £1000 toward the expedition. This lifted Speke's mood, but only for a little while. For reasons he couldn't explain he sank into days of depression and doubt, staying in his room.

"There's a mariners' tailor in town," his mother said. "Let's have him make you some canvas walking trousers for your caravan—something to resist thorns."

"They might be too hot down there in Africa."

"Perhaps. But you might find I'm right about them. If you find I'm wrong, toss them away."

"You're probably right, Mama," he said. "You usually are. We'll have some proper trousers sewn up—stiff ones!"

She invented other distractions for him, but his moods came and went. In the end there was only one solace: hunting. The cupboards and smokehouses filled up with dead birds, rabbit, and deer. Each morning he and the gamekeeper prepared the day's ammunition, and each night they cleaned their kill in a weary frenzy of feathers, blood, hide, and sinew.

The day Oliphant's letter arrived his mood soared, then plummeted. It was a short, witty note, inviting Speke to London for a round of parties, but he couldn't bring himself to reply. His curse, suddenly, seemed to wall him in; Jordans became a distant monastery, a small cell cut off from the rest of the world's aching rooms, and he felt like a crazed monk inside its isolation, a monk riddled with doubt and on fire, thrown down between belief and sexual heresy. He didn't want Oliphant's bright rooms. He couldn't move among artists, wits, scholars, and journalists. He rejected the fashionable homosexual jargon and all the private little communications of the demimonde in which Oliphant took part. Yet, what did he want? In his room, alone, his clothes stripped away, he lay down on his bed, curled himself into a ball, held himself, and wondered. I still want fame, he told himself. With enough fame, the doors open, room to room, and one can walk freely, in and out of the lives of others, even here and there in the dark little corridors of oneself. I must have fame; I must hurry to it. Money, beauty, wit: these were all passages to power and to a more exciting life. But greater than any of these, he knew, was fame, which was bestowed on just a few men in the caprice of history.

Naked and alone in his bed, he let his hands roam his body. Each muscle and bone, each pore and fiber seemed tense and expectant. Everything was in the future. Existence itself was in the future. He felt he couldn't wait—not another day, not another second. Speke felt that he had to earn the right to be sexual and completely alive.

Burton, almost in spite of himself, began thinking about finding a wife. A very odd thought, he realized, for one going off to the fabled delights of Zanzibar, yet his mind seemed to have the mild, irritating fever of matrimonial longing and all this implied: a fine house like Milnes possessed, a proper study with books and papers neatly stacked, regular meals, and in the mornings—every morning—a familiar, desirable, buxom companion who, after acrobatics, would undulate from the bedroom into the kitchen, where tea and toast would complete the rituals.

"Good, you need a wife," MacQueen told him. They were taking a pub lunch together at the Red Lion, its mahogany bar crowded with civil servants, and Burton, having started the conversation with his new friend, wished he hadn't sounded so ordinary.

"It may be that I'm just poor and hungry," he confessed. "And want some order about me."

"You want to convert the fame you're about to achieve into propriety!" MacQueen said. "You want status! And, of course, a convenient cunt."

"True, I want all that," Burton said.

"Well, how about more beer and shepherd's pie?"

"You paying? I'm still hungry!"

"M'boy, you have a fine appetite," MacQueen said, and he slapped another half crown on the bar with a laugh.

It was women Burton wanted—preferably, that midsummer, some demure aristocrat with large breasts—but he sat in his rooms writing. One correspondence was a long, arrogant one with the Foreign Office, urging them to purchase Berbera and the whole coast toward establishing British rule in Suez and the proposed canal territories. Such brash suggestions from a subaltern in the army seemed to amuse the government. He also wrote letters to Lumsden, Steinhauser, his brother and family, and various officials in Bombay, as well as a short memoir entitled "With Beatson's Horse" which, having written, he left in his desk.

Each day's mail brought minor disappointments. Lumsden seemed unable to secure army leaves for them and suggested that they sail to Bombay en route to Zanzibar—which amounted to a three-thousand-mile detour. The reviews of *First Footsteps in East Africa* were less than enthusiastic ("a curious record of a curious enterprise" the editors of the *Athenaeum* wrote), and his royalties were only enough so that he managed to buy a new pair of shoes.

One of his letters he addressed to Louisa Segraves, a woman he had known when his family lived in Boulogne. He remembered that their flirtation had once been promising, that she had money in her family, and that her breasts were enormous.

After long days of writing Burton wanted seductions. Between his favorite brothel in Soho, where no seductions were necessary, and the homes of his new acquaintances, such as Milnes and MacQueen, where none were possible, he found London's night life unrewarding. He had scant money for prostitutes, he decided, and no enthusiasm for the wives of friends.

But, at last, Louisa, married and living in London, wrote a reply. She would walk with him, she said, in the Botanical Gardens.

"How have you been?" he asked her, as they strolled along. His new shoes, far more stylish than his army boots, made his feet throb. The fringed edge of her parasol dipped and fluttered in his direction, so that he had to dodge and smile as they walked.

"You're the one who does exciting things," she said coyly. "You tell me about *your* adventures, and don't leave out the naughty parts." He tried to measure her tone and meaning, but his thoughts flew away. Was her husband unsatisfactory? Would he open that brocade vest, later on, and pillow himself on those wonderful breasts? Was his imagination running wild?

They talked about their families and all that had happened since the time they were neighbors in France. Louisa, he noticed, had a bit of ice in her voice and posture; she might be the sort, he mused, who would open her bodice, spread her legs, and gaze off with bemused distraction during the act. Each time she spoke and he could steal a look at her, his blood pounded in his veins; he very much wanted to throw her down among the tulips and iris.

As he struggled for control, they strolled around a turn in the walkway and met, on the other side of some shrubbery, Louisa's cousin and a friend. Introductions were made. Isabel Arundell, the cousin, who had an even smaller waist and breasts even more generous than Louisa's, stood looking up at Burton as if he might be a god. The afternoon sun formed a nimbus in her hair, and her perfume blent with the flowers; all Burton's excitements seemed to transfer to her. As luck had it, she was holding a book—which allowed him to recover his voice by asking what she was reading.

"It's Disraeli's *Tancred.*" She sighed. "The book of my heart!"

"Of all novels," he said in reply, "I wish I had written that one myself." He only half meant this, but his words seemed to have a sublime impact on Isabel. The novel was about a young Englishman's romantic journey in the Near East. Its author, now a rising star in Parliament, had based it on his own travels—during which, like Burton, he had lived among the Bedouins and had taken a fancy to Arab clothes and philosophy. Burton envied Disraeli and had always discounted the Jew's literary achievements, but now, oddly, suddenly, he changed his mind.

"You must explain the deeper meanings in this novel for me," Isabel continued, as her friend and cousin struggled to enter the conversation.

"I'd be happy to," Burton said with full literary confidence. "Do you come here often?"

"Every day from eleven to one," Isabel said, being precise. "It's so much nicer than staying in the hot rooms at this season."

The four of them stood in the walkway, so that other visitors had to stroll around them. They received a few stares, but neither Isabel nor Burton were about to move. Louisa tried to make pleasant comments, but found herself talking to the friend.

"We've met before, you know," Isabel told him. "In Boulogne. Years ago. You probably don't remember me."

"Oh yes, I think I do remember," Burton lied. She was not particularly beautiful except for her figure, yet her effect stunned him. He watched the rise and fall of that magnificent bosom as she spoke, and he knew that she could detect the direction of his gaze, but he couldn't help himself.

"Louisa and I were walking on the ramparts," she went on, reminding him of their previous meeting. "We looked at each other. You looked so— intense! I've never forgotten your eyes! And you scrawled a message on the wall, asking if you could speak to me, and I scrawled an answer, saying no, telling you how angry my mother would be."

"Hmm, yes," he said, not remembering at all.

"And you were at a fencing tournament that season and easily defeated everyone—including that group of conceited French Hussars."

"Isabel, dear," Louisa said, trying to invade the dialogue.

"You recall quite a bit," Burton said, flashing his smile. "This must have been—hmm, more than five years ago."

"I have more to tell you, but can't tell you now," Isabel said. "Very much more to tell you. I've never forgotten you."

"I do recall the ramparts around the old city," Burton said vaguely.

"The English families in Boulogne called you Ruffian Dick, did you know that?" she asked with a laugh. "They wanted nothing to do with you!"

"I have heard that name before," he admitted.

"Isabel, dear, how are your mother and father?" Louisa insisted.

"And you had a strange little friend with you, a doctor with a red beard," Isabel went on.

"Steinhauser!" Burton said. "You must have taken great note of me and my friends back in those days! Yes, he's my old friend, who visited me in Boulogne! We're going off to Zanzibar together in just a few weeks!"

"You had a brother with a bad reputation, too," Isabel said, laughing.

"You know all about me!"

"She even has newspaper clippings," the friend interjected. "Of your travels to Mecca, your exploits in Berbera, and your letters to *The Times!*"

Burton was staring deep into Isabel's eyes as Louisa took his arm and tugged him gently away.

"You remember, don't you, Louisa?" Isabel asked. "We met Richard on the ramparts at Boulogne! He had those ferocious mustaches!"

"No, I don't recall, dear, but I do remember how your mother fussed when you talked about men," Louisa said, pulling Burton along.

"Pleasant meeting you." Burton nodded to the friend, then returned his gaze to Isabel.

"When I was a girl in Romany," Isabel said, raising her voice as they parted, "a gypsy woman made a horoscope for me. You were in it!"

Burton controlled his impulse to send Louisa on her way. The friend placed a hand over her lips and giggled.

"Goodbye for now," he said, his feet inside those new shoes aching. Clearly, this girl adored him, and he longed to stay.

For a short distance, he and Louisa strolled in silence. Twice he looked back toward Isabel and the friend, until they were out of sight.

"Your cousin is charming," he finally murmured to Louisa, who was too angry to look at him. "Just think. That little schoolgirl of Boulogne is all grown up."

"Ugh," Louisa said, disgusted with him.

He looked beyond the entrance gate, hoping to see a carriage waiting. Louisa, he felt, should be home with her husband, and he should get back home himself, take off his shoes, and consider this sudden turn of events.

The next day he was back at the Botanical Gardens. He sat on a bench just before eleven o'clock composing poetry—which, he knew, was a little affected, but somehow appropriate. Isabel came strolling by almost on the hour. She wore a white lace blouse, a wide-brimmed hat, and a peculiar smile.

"Poetry!" She sighed, sitting beside him. "I've read almost everything you've ever written, you know, and everything written about you!"

"You have?"

They turned toward each other, her breast pressed against his arm, and she kept to a singular subject: his life and work. He told her about his army leave, the proposed trip in search of the Nile, books he hoped to write, important friends, and all his career plans.

"You said you had something to tell me," he reminded her.

"Yes, the gypsy," she confided. "Years ago I met a fortune-teller named Hagar Burton—in fact, she was from a tribe in Romany who bore that name! She told me that I would travel, see the world, and that I would bear the name of their tribe. It was a profound moment. I don't believe in the supernatural, but I remembered that prophecy, of course, when I saw you on the ramparts and asked someone your name. In Boulogne, my family wanted nothing to do with you or your brother. But I seemed destined to know you. When you came home wounded from Somaliland, I wanted to send you a note, but didn't. Then you were off to the Crimea, so I tried to volunteer to serve as a nurse with Florence Nightingale. I felt that fate would bring us together in the war. But fate waited until yesterday."

"I can't believe all this," he managed.

"It's true, every word. But there's more," she said. "Two months ago at Ascot my family and I went down for the races, and there was the old gypsy again—after all these years! She asked me if I were named Burton yet! When I said no, she answered that I should have patience, that things would happen very soon!"

"I want to hold you," he said, gazing down at the rise and fall of her breathing.

"What shall we do?" she asked, looking up at him with wonder and awe.

He wanted to suggest the obvious: they could go to his rooms. But this was Isabel Arundell of the noted Catholic family. Her godfather was Lord Arundell of Wardour. They were reputed to have a country house in Essex, nannies and carriages, holidays and servants, livestock and farmlands. This was marrying material, he knew, and although she might consent to throwing up her petticoats atop his desk, a little self-discipline was in order.

"We'll continue to meet here every day," he said, thinking quickly. "Then I'll meet your family. Prepare the way for me." For a moment, he became dizzy with the press of her breasts against his arm and the soft, honeyed odor of her body close to his.

The Arundell house in Montagu Place was less than Burton hoped, but there was a pleasant, shabby gentility about it: the furniture and rugs were expensive but old, the rooms were solidly middle-class if somewhat worn. Apart from the older sister, Blanche, there were a number of other brothers and sisters whose names Burton quickly heard and forgot. Everyone called Isabel by the nickname Puss. The father was short, stocky, energetic, and quickly dismayed by the way Burton entered, began talking, and seemed to own the place. The mother's eyes narrowed with suspicion and distrust.

Burton's tactic was to be expansive.

"Mine is the vagabond life," he announced, hardly impressing the mother. "But it will lead to the service of the Empire in exotic cities. And I don't mean to live in tents. I mean to have charge of consulates. To set up libraries, if possible. The study of languages and customs, for instance, is important to any people who declare themselves rulers or traders in the world scene."

The sister, Blanche, who had heard so much about Burton from Isabel for so many years, sat wide-eyed, with her teacup almost sliding off her lap.

"Hargghh," the father said, clearing his throat. "Will you do some hunting on your African caravan?"

"One of my companions is a noted hunter," Burton said. He walked around the room, stepping over footstools as he talked, so that the family had to follow his theatrical moves. "But animals are sleek, fine things to me. Part of the geography, you see? I wouldn't take an animal any more than I'd endeavor to steal a mountain."

"I'm fond of hunting myself," the father announced.

"Fine sport," Burton added, covering himself. "Brings out a man's skill and daring under certain perilous circumstances. Ever shot a lion?"

"No, just partridge," Mr. Arundell admitted.

When his writing was mentioned, Burton pointed out that he intended to write novels, books of poetry, travel volumes, encyclopedias, scientific monographs, and significant translations from the Arabic and various sub-Sahara dialects. When his London activities were mentioned, he brought up the names of Monckton Milnes and James MacQueen. When his army career was mentioned, he spoke of General Beatson and James Grant Lumsden. And, at other times, when left alone to his conversational designs, he dropped hints about his superiority in fencing, falconry, military politics, cultural anthropology, literary criticism, map making, bareback riding, and disguise. The mother was appalled at his ego. The father winced only when his guest spoke of a vast plan for purchasing the coasts along the Red Sea, taming the Berbera tribes, digging the Suez Canal, and establishing the realm in the Mideast. But Burton detected the slight wince and added, "I discussed this plan with several people when we were out at Lord Houghton's estate with Palmy a few weeks ago."

Offered cakes, Burton nervously took one, smiled, and pushed it whole into his mouth. Then he drank off his tea in a single swallow.

Isabel and Blanche, hoping not to miss anything, never blinked.

"And what about your religion?" the mother asked.

"Any thinking person regards the world's faiths as a series of symbolic complexities," he answered, evading only slightly. "I have seen a man raised from the dead in India. I have kissed the holy stone in the Kaaba in Mecca. I have read the Bible and all the holy books in their original languages. And, as for my own spiritual progress, I'm working on it."

The mother made an odd noise in her throat.

Later, as he left, he quoted them lines from some exotic poet. "The meetings of this world are in the street of separation," he said, bowing to kiss the hands of the women. "And truly said the poet that the drought of friendly union is ever followed by the bitter waters of parting."

"Nice meeting you, Captain!" one of the younger sisters called from the recesses of the house.

When the door closed behind him, Isabel announced firmly that this would be her husband.

"He is the only man I would *never* consent to your marrying!" said Mrs. Arundell. "I would rather see you in your coffin!"

"I'll see him every day until he leaves on this wonderful trip for the crown," Isabel said.

"You'll *not* see him! I'll destroy any message he sends to the house! You didn't meet him properly! His prospects are dismal! He preens! He's notorious with women! He's *disgusting!*"

"And he's all Isabel's talked about for six years," Blanche put in.

"I'm twenty-five years old," Isabel stated. "We can argue, but I'll do as I wish! If you won't give my hand in marriage, I'm perfectly capable of giving it myself! And we're talking about a man renowned in scientific circles, a favorite among the journalists, and welcome among the best families in the city!"

"Well, he's not Catholic!" her mother persisted.

"I'll work on that—as he says he's working on it himself!"

"He has very broad shoulders," Blanche added.

"I was wondering about that," Mr. Arundell commented. "I suppose he lifts weights and has himself an exercise program."

"Really!" Mrs. Arundell said. "He's insufferable! Suez Canal! Poetry!"

"All the men I know—except you, Father—are effeminate!" Isabel told them. "I look upon them as members of my own sex! But not Richard. If I were a man, I'd want to *be* Richard Burton, but as I'm a woman, I'll be his wife. I don't have a single doubt!"

"He *is* masculine," Mr. Arundell said to his wife.

"He's a rake, a braggart, and an actor," Isabel's mother said, and she walked out of the room with her head in the air.

Isabel, Blanche, and their father exchanged a look and a sigh.

"He's coming back tomorrow evening," Isabel told them. "Not only do

I want you to welcome him, Father, I want Cardinal Wiseman here for dinner. We might as well get started right."

"I'll see what I can do," Mr. Arundell said, and he gave her a faint smile.

Burton found that permissions for both Speke and Steinhauser weren't easily acquired, so decided that they would sail to Cairo, sail down the Red Sea to Aden, pick up the doctor, then proceed to Bombay, where they could confront the bureaucracy of the East India Company and secure the necessary leaves from the army and civil service. Apart from a flurry of correspondence on these matters, he also wrote to his brother, his editors, and Louisa Segraves—whom he had decided to contact in person, once again, should his courtship of Isabel Arundell not work out.

He also spent most of his days reading the novels of Disraeli and the writings of Ptolemy. The famous Alexandrine, he decided, was just recording rumor and had no idea where the fabled lakes of central Africa might be.

"If we marry," he told her, "I think we should eventually get the consulate in Damascus. If you could give up civilization, would you go with me?"

Isabel seemed unable to answer. They had spent another awkward evening at the Arundell house, this time with Cardinal Wiseman, whom Isabel had persuaded to give Burton papers recommending him to Catholic missions anywhere he might find them. Her parents, weakened in their complaints against Burton by this ploy, had seemed neutral all evening. Now, Burton and Isabel stood by the gate, half hidden in the leafy folds of a gardenia bush; he held her waist in both his hands, bringing her forward against him, and lifting her breasts slightly with his thumbs. He was bold, but she didn't care—and in her excitement she struggled to reply to his proposal.

"I've thought about you every day for six years, since I saw you at Boulogne on the ramparts," she said, finding her breathing difficult. Her gasps brought her warm breath against his lips. "I've prayed for you every day, morning and night. I've followed every little movement of your career. I've read every word you ever wrote, and I would rather have a crust and a tent with you than be queen of all the world."

"We'll have to keep our engagement secret," he said, backing off a little now that he was caught.

"Yes, I suppose that's better," she said, tracing a finger lightly over the scar on his cheek.

"Better because I'll be going away," he said. "And, by the way, I don't fancy tearful goodbyes. When I'm ready, I go."

Mindful that her mother might appear any moment at the front door, she pressed herself against him. He held her breasts and waist as her head swooned against his coat. "Oh, Richard," she sighed, barely audible.

And then the strangest sensation overtook him: his hands relayed the knowledge that she was modestly fat. He had always thought that she was slim in the waist and exceedingly buxom elsewhere, yet now, his proposal made, his blood racing, the powerful odor of gardenia and her breath besetting him, she seemed—how and why did he notice this?—plump.

He kissed her, but her face seemed rotund.

"I want to show you the gypsy's horoscope," she breathed against him. "And this: I want you to have it." She produced a medal on a gold chain with a likeness of the Virgin engraved on it; it was still warm from her own body when he took it, held it up in the glint of the gas lamp from the porch, and inspected it. He knew that she really loved him, that she had loved him all those miraculous years, yet he felt bombarded by odd misgivings: she had no dowry and only that past family history, he might be killed in Africa, she was definitely fatter than he had noticed, her mother was a shrew, sex was out of the question, it all seemed both supernatural and silly.

"Are you out there, Isabel?" her sister Blanche called.

"Yes, coming," Isabel replied, as she drew his head down and kissed him again.

"I have something to give you, too," he told her. "A poem."

"Give it to me at the theater," she said. "You are still accompanying us, aren't you?"

"Yes, the theater," he said absently.

That night he went home and dashed off a note to Speke. He knew of a ship ready for sailing at Southampton, he told his colleague. If ready, Speke was to come to London at once.

Having written the note, he walked down into Piccadilly to post it in the central mailbox. It was after midnight and the streets were bare. His courtship of Isabel Arundell had scarcely begun, and his destinies, it seemed, were suddenly both multiple and perilous. His parents, after all, were both now dead; his brother was going back to Ceylon, and his sister was busy with her own family; he had no one of his own beyond Isabel and wanted her, yet could a man such as himself combat loneliness—or was this just a given part of the wanderer's life?

He strolled back toward his rooms, went in, and made some last revisions on his poem. He wasn't good at verse, but the addiction persisted; besides, melancholy or not, he couldn't afford booze, so he labored at these lines.

> I wore thine image, Fame,
> Within a heart well fit to be thy shrine;
> Others a thousand boons may gain—
> One wish was mine:

The hope to gain one smile,
To dwell one moment cradled on thy breast,
Then close my eyes, bid life farewell,
      And take my rest!

And now I see a glorious hand
Beckon me out of dark despair,
Hear a glorious voice command,
      "Up, bravely dare!

"And if to leave a deeper trace
On earth to thee, Time, Fate, deny,
Drown vain regrets, and have the grace
      Silent to die."

She pointed to a grisly land,
Where all breathes death—earth, sea and air;
Her glorious accents sound once more,
      "Go meet me there."

Mine ear will hear no other sound,
No other thought my heart will know.
Is it a sin? "O, pardon Lord!
      Thou mad'st me so!"

A bit weak and vague in the fourth stanza, he decided, but he read it over, shrugged, then folded two copies—the original and the revised—into separate envelopes. One he would give to Isabel with his farewell note, and the other, just in case matters took another course, he decided, he would give to Louisa Segraves.

On an evening in late October, Isabel went with her family to a performance of *Faust* at the Winter Gardens. Burton had promised to join them, but didn't actually have a seat, so that Isabel understood the promise was only half meant. Even so, she hoped to see him and at one point thought she spied him across the audience. Then, toward the end of the performance, she grew anxious and felt feverish. Her parents hurried her home, put her to bed, but during the night she had a dream that he appeared, embraced her, and said goodbye. "I've gone," he told her in the dream, "but I will come again—I shall be back in less than three years. I am your destiny." Then he placed a letter on her bedside table, saying, "This is for your sister—not for you."

Getting up and throwing a shawl around herself, Isabel went into Blanche's bedroom. "Richard has gone to Africa and I won't see him for three years!" she burst out, tears running down her face.

"Nonsense," Blanche said, holding her and consoling her. "He told you that he would probably see you tomorrow!"

Isabel wouldn't be consoled, though, and sat up all night in Blanche's room, the shawl around her, her tears flowing. At eight o'clock the postman arrived with the morning mail, and there it was: a note to Blanche from Burton, asking her to break the news that he had gone.

"There's something magical about him," Isabel cried to her sister. "And something deeply mystical about our love!"

"Don't worry," Blanche assured her. "He'll come back for you!"

Out at sea, Burton leaned against the ship's rail, gazed off at the horizon, and felt marvelous. He didn't think about Isabel, lack of funds, the troublesome detour to Bombay, or his sulking companion, Speke, who acted as if this great expedition were getting off to a tardy and bothersome start. Burton was thinking only of Africa.

The source of the Nile had eluded its searchers for five thousand years. Arab traders had spoken of the great Sea of Ujiji. Ancient cartographers had drawn crude maps that had included a vast series of lakes—whose actual locations and dimensions were still unknown. Native lore was extravagant: beyond the high country were the Mountains of the Moon, inland seas, surging rivers, and waterfalls. And more: primitive kingdoms, swarming armies, naked women, ivory, unknown beasts, gold mines, human sacrifices, primeval jungles, languages that were the original tongue of men, dreams from which civilization was born, ages from which the present age was only a mere shadow and dim reminder. Gazing out to sea, Burton felt truly free for the first time in his life; unless man ever journeyed to the distant planets, no man ever again would have such a mission as this. A whole continent awaited.

1857–1859

—)0(—

*The Great Journey
and the Betrayal*

At CAIRO THE SMOOTH, YELLOW WATERS OF THE NILE WERE OVERHUNG WITH white mist at the harbor of Bulak. Along the far shore towering sycamores lined the banks, and beyond, pieces of broken columns adorned the desert sand.

Speke looked at all of it with curiosity, but mild impatience. He felt exhausted, already, by their days at sea, and wanted to get into the city and make arrangements for the next leg of the voyage toward Aden. Burton, though, as Speke could already detect, would be in no hurry. He stood on the dock idly chatting with workers as gear was slowly loaded into a carriage for the trip by road into the city; he seemed not the least interested in giving orders, hurrying the porters, making plans, or paying attention to details.

Eventually, they rode into the city streets: jugglers, priests of all religions, acrobats, peddlers, beggars, veiled women, naked slaves, soldiers in various uniforms, old scholars, snake handlers, children, goat tenders, businessmen wearing the fez, prostitutes with their naked breasts exposed, cripples, dervishes, magicians, eunuchs, coffee sellers banging on their brass pots, flower girls, blind men, musicians with their instruments, everyone yelling and talking, singing or pleading. Cairo was loud and boisterous, so that Burton and Speke had to yell at one another as they sat in the open carriage en route to the British officers' club where they would stay.

"There's nothing but sex here," Burton was yelling. "Take your choice! Some fine courtesans who'll cost you a month's pay, the slaves, wives, the old whores out at the aqueducts, and even small boys out around the pyramids who will jack you off for just a few pennies!"

Speke pretended he didn't hear all this.

"You'll get used to it," Burton assured him.

They passed hundreds of beggars, their hands stretched out as they bawled for alms. The hot air rising off the city streets seemed to burn the lungs.

Burton was a favorite among the officers at the consulate and club, yet never abused his popularity, Speke saw, by bragging or by leading the conversation around to his exploits or accomplishments. In all, Speke felt proud to be in Burton's company, except for one thing: Burton regarded him more and more as a mere junior officer. In Aden and Berbera, Speke had not officially been part of Burton's entourage, but here he was an attendant, recognized in introductions, then quickly ignored. Before, he had been independent. Here, although their ranks were the same, Burton was leader of the expedition, the center of attention, and usually seemed not to notice Speke at all.

They had a few slight words over a directive that was presented to Burton at the consulate.

"Here, read this," Burton said with a smile, passing the letter to Speke.

The army had ordered Burton back to London, where he was requested to testify at the trial of another of Beatson's officers in the ongoing affair of the Bashi Bazouks. "It's another wretched court-martial!" Burton sighed.

"It's a signed order," Speke noted, looking alarmed.

"But badly worded," Burton pointed out, taking the letter once more and inspecting it. "I'm *requested* to testify. Bad choice of phrase, that, because if I'm requested, I can refuse—and do." He tore the letter in half.

"We could both get into trouble for that," Speke told him.

"We can always go out of our way to step in camel dung," Burton said. "Far better to keep our eyes on the horizon and not look for such little piles of it."

At a consulate dinner there were hundreds of Egyptian magistrates, minor bureaucrats, stiffly uniformed officers, and assorted women. Burton found himself more inebriated than he had intended to be, so that he forgot names as they were pronounced and spent his time giving lewd stares to every wife and daughter present. Speke stood rigid as a birch rod, never sipping from the glass of champagne that turned warm in his fingers, never seeming to blink.

On a very hot afternoon they went to the baths. These were old, tiled vaults near the mosque of Ibn Tulun with its slender minaret.

"For half a crown we get a masseur, a pipe of good tobacco, a cup of coffee, our sheet and towel," Burton explained. "From the bath boys, you get whatever you want. They'll rub you down with oil. You can get masturbation or fellatio. The sodomy in these places comes with the soap."

They had just given their clothes to an attendant and were walking along a corridor of damp, blue, lacquered stones as Burton revealed all this.

"Do you take part in all the pleasures of the bath?" Speke asked, trying to be as nonchalant as possible.

"Actually, no," Burton said. "But I enjoy everyone's enthusiasms."

Burton hadn't bothered to wrap himself; his hairy body, muscular and compact, had a physical insolence about it as they walked down that corridor of shiny stones. A smirk altered the corners of his mouth as his thick arms and penis swung free. Speke stole glances at him; he seemed indifferent, dangerous, beautiful, and somehow unapproachable.

In the pool, Speke let his thoughts and limbs float. The vast, echoing room was divided into numerous small pools separated by low tile walls. A shaft of sunlight pierced through the window above their heads, and from the street outside came the throaty, gargling sound of camels and the cooing of pigeons.

"Damn, I have grits of sand in my teeth," Burton sighed, sinking into the tepid water.

A boy came with long waterpipes: the *sheeshehs* from Mecca. Speke declined, but Burton, who never declined anything to eat, drink, or smoke, rested the pipe on the side of the pool, submerged himself to his neck, and took a deep breath of the acrid tobacco smoke. The boy was slender, about fourteen, with bony knees. As Burton smoked, Speke watched the boy and found that his attention was returned.

"Did you notice the color of the fields around Cairo?" Burton asked, holding the pipe near his mouth. "Black as a Nubian! And you know where it comes from, don't you? Have you thought about it?"

"No, not really," Speke said. He was nervous and inattentive as the bath boy sauntered off.

"From high up on fertile mountainsides thousands of miles away," Burton mused. "For ages and ages that black soil has washed down the Nile into this valley! Before the pharaohs and caliphs. And we'll find those mountains, Jack, by God, I know we will."

"I'm confident we will," Speke said absently.

"We should probably have a large boat with us," Burton went on, thinking aloud. "Something to ferry us across those big inland seas. Devil of a problem, of course, to take such a boat up-country with us from Zanzibar."

"Sorry, a boat?" Speke asked, obviously not keeping up.

"Just talking to myself," Burton said, sucking on the pipe. "Ah, here comes our boy with a tray."

Smiling, the bath boy squatted alongside the pool. "English, I bring you tea," he said, serving Speke. "And for you, sir, coffee!"

"Who do you think I am?" Burton asked the boy. "I'm English, too!"

The boy grinned and shook his head, as if this could not be believed.

"He must think I'm a tenor in an Italian opera company," Burton told Speke, laughing out loud. "Coffee! Well, I say!"

Speke, withdrawn and watching them, seemed amused, yet oddly ill at ease. Detecting this, Burton soon finished his coffee and pipe, pulled himself out of the water, and strolled off. He made his way toward the masseur's table, nodding and reciting the Moslem greeting as he passed a bench filled with a group of fat Egyptian businessmen.

The bath boy looked openly at Speke. "You want me to touch you, English?" he inquired. For a long time, Speke said nothing; the fluttering wings of the pigeons filled the window above them in that hot slant of afternoon light.

"What exactly do you mean?" he finally asked the boy.

"Rub with oil. You want?"

"No," Speke finally answered, yet the uncertainty in his voice prompted the boy to linger. From the top of the low tile wall the boy selected a brightly colored bottle of oil as if he meant to ask again, but as he did so the bottle's thick, bulb-shaped glass stopper came loose, fell, bounced on the tile, and without breaking fell into the bath. The two of them watched it settle toward the bottom, drifting down, catching the sun's rays until it came to rest.

"Very good for you, English," the boy said gently. "Very fine and very good for you." The young attendant, reassuring Speke, was aware of how tentative and nervous his client felt.

"Please," Speke replied, "go away."

After the boy had gone, Speke pulled himself out of the pool and sat on its edge, dangling his thin white legs in the water. He closed his eyes and listened to the echoes reverberating around him: watersounds, camels, pigeons, voices, the rattle of coffee cups, and there, far off yet distinct, Burton's laughter.

They joined a merchant caravan that took them overland to Suez, where they boarded a sailing barge on the Red Sea.

At night they floated beneath Orion's Belt. By day, the sky looked like hard enamel, and they lay in the scant shadows of the deck, ropes and rigging above them, the sail full, the sun draining their strength away. They passed mud houses, palm groves, immense wastelands of sand. They saw a dead camel being eaten by jackals, the Arabs sitting around their night fires singing monotonous songs, flights of dove, white dogs with their muzzles caked with dried blood, storks along the shoreline, slave boats, and the gaudy sunsets that turned the desert into silhouette.

With a strong breeze they reached Aden in good time. Burton leaped off the quay and hurried up a back street toward the little office of his friend. The doctor was just closing the door, going toward the garrison for lunch.

"You! You with the red beard!" Burton called to him.

"Dick Burton!" Steinhauser said, and the two of them embraced.

They were still standing there in the narrow street laughing and talking when Speke approached, shook hands stiffly with Steinhauser, employed his usual formalities, and calmed them.

"There's cholera along the coast, so I can't go with you," Steinhauser told them at dinner on the verandah of the old hotel. "Besides, you're just going to Bombay to ask permission for our leaves. How would it look if I went with you, then learned that our splendid Company doesn't want me in Africa?"

"Lumsden is a good friend," Burton assured him. "We'll get our permissions."

"I'll join you in Zanzibar, if you send word that my leave is official," Steinhauser said. "Meanwhile, I'll stay on duty here. I'm the only doctor around, and if cholera got inside the garrison, it would be worse than a slaughter. I just can't risk this detour to Bombay."

"We'll miss you on the voyage," Burton said. "But, meanwhile, you can brush up on your Swahili."

"Brush up? I don't know a bit of the language!"

"Then, damn, scholar, get out your books!"

"What about you, Speke? Know any Swahili?" the doctor asked.

"Barely know a bit of English," Speke admitted. It was the first self-effacing statement either Burton or Steinhauser had ever heard Speke utter, and, exaggeration or not, they laughed.

"See here," the doctor told Speke. "Dick and I have a prejudice against rotters tromping around the colonies never knowing what's up!" He laughed as he said this, having forgotten Speke's problems with the Wadi Nogal, the guide, and the interpreter. But it was too late. Offended, Speke paid elaborate attention to his food. Burton turned in his chair and gazed out at the calm evening sea.

Shortly afterward Speke rose from the table and announced that he would go pay a visit to the garrison commander.

"Good, give him my respects, Jack, and tell him that if there are duties we can perform for him in Bombay we'll be only too glad," Burton said.

"You might want to stroll over with me," Speke suggested. "After all, you're head of our expedition."

"No, you take care of protocol—I do appreciate it," Burton answered. "Besides, I'm already scheduled for this evening."

Speke tried a smile, nodded toward Steinhauser, and said good evening. When he was gone, Burton and the doctor sat turning their glasses of cognac in their fingers. Out on Steamer Point, the torches of the lighthouse were being lit and were mirrored in the sea below the rocks.

"Why in the world did you ask Speke to accompany you to Zanzibar?" Steinhauser finally asked. "He's such a petulant chap. Touchy. And very easily slighted."

"It's simple. I felt I owed him something for his wounds."

"Well, I don't fancy his company," the doctor said.

"You and I will get on very well," Burton said. At this point, the woman in the coral necklace made her appearance, accompanied by a small, black, angry-looking Ethiopian who wore a long, curved dagger in a jeweled scabbard.

"My captain," she said, smiling, her voice filled with that sensual and languid stupor that Burton remembered so well. He got up from his chair, grinned, pulled the corners of his mustache, and offered a slight bow.

"Dearest," he said, greeting her. Then, to Steinhauser: "Who's our new friend here?"

"That, I believe, is the new owner of the hotel, madame's secretary of appointments, our genial host, and top pimp in Aden," the doctor said with a wink.

"Have you been practicing your English like a good girl?" Burton asked her in the Somali language.

"For you," she replied cleverly, "I practice only French."

With a sweeping gesture, he gathered up her hand and kissed it. The Ethiopian sensed a night of wonder and profit in all this extravagance.

India: the delicate minarets and glaring whitewash of Bombay, the odors of curry, British tea and white uniforms, religions and intrigues.

James Grant Lumsden met them at the dock with three young sepoys who stood at rigid attention with their sabers on their shoulders, a turbaned child with a bright-orange umbrella, and an elephant draped in brocade and spangles.

"Bit of a show," Lumsden said, shaking Burton's hand. "I admit it. But I figure you're not easily impressed, so there you are!" He looked like a jolly music-hall entertainer in a white suit and yellow ascot; in the withering noonday sun he shed not a single drop of perspiration—and seemed to have no inclination to do so. He was tall, grey, distinguished, and ruled everything with a light touch, but with clear authority. On seeing him that first time, Speke understood that Burton had chosen the right course; there was no use writing letters and asking permissions from London when a man like Lumsden prevailed in the omnipotent East India Company.

"I take it we have permission to go to Zanzibar?" Burton asked.

"My dear Dick, I have whole reams of written permissions for you," Lumsden said. "I also have a schedule of parties, a new brass chronometer, several bags of beads and trinkets, bolts of cloth, medicines, a special pillow, and a Union Jack!"

Lumsden housed them in the small, unoccupied palace of a rajah who was off touring. For the first time, Speke viewed the Company from the inside; he was no mere lieutenant posted to obscurity in some vast, vague colonial network; he was in Bombay, in the company of a man who was a senior official in the Company's council. He felt patriotic and important.

"Do you realize how important our mission to find the Nile is?" he suddenly asked Burton that evening as they were shaving for dinner.

"Why, Jack, yes, I think I do," Burton answered, scraping his neck.

"We could open up a whole new continent to trade! We could do for Africa what we've done for India!"

"And what's that, Jack?"

"Well. We've brought in technology and organization. Everything was anarchy and civil strife and religious wars before we came, wasn't it?"

"Everything still is now. And, really, Jack, you do understand we're taking things *out* of India, don't you? All the tea, all the gold, all the art, those sorts of things?"

"We brought in a productive civilization—and, therefore, a superior one," Speke argued. "The Indians themselves like it. We have thousands of them —sepoys—in our army. Getting good wages. I think we've been very humane to a poor people in a very chaotic land."

"I'm just not as sure of our superiority as you," Burton said, moving his mouth to one side as he traced the line of his mustache with the razor.

"I shall be sure of our superiority until I die," Speke said.

"Then, good, Jack, good," Burton said out of the corner of his mouth.

Somehow frustrated, Speke went outside on the terrace. Below, the garden was a cascade of lilies and roses.

The Company had started with small trading posts in Surat, Bombay, Madras, and Calcutta, Speke knew, and had grown to power by displacing the old Moguls one by one; with British military victories in the Sind and in the Punjab and over the Sikhs in two recent wars it had secured its dominance. The arrangement was obviously beneficial to England, making it powerful and rich in Europe, and there was certainly some rascality in it all, but these primitive natives had benefits, too.

Speke stepped back inside the room, where Burton busied himself with the buttons on his borrowed suit of evening dress.

"Damn, wish this was my suit of clothes," Burton mumbled, turning his profile toward a full-length mirror.

"Our whole expedition to Africa is for the crown and its interests," Speke began again. "If we open up Africa by discovering the Nile source, we'll be as famous as Clive here in India! We'll be national heroes! You know this as well as I do—and you're proud to be going!"

"Please, come now, don't accuse me of being patriotic," Burton teased him.

Speke sat down on the edge of the bed. Burton's humor was usually employed, he felt, to hide the man's true feelings—especially about serious subjects. But Burton also used his irony and wit to keep others in their place, so there Speke sat like a bewildered schoolboy.

Before he could protest again, though, Burton clapped him on the shoulder and suggested they go down to dinner.

Most of the members of the Company's Bombay Council dined with them that evening. Everyone raised toasts, and Speke was asked to say a few words. He stood up at the table, spoke well, and his impact on the audience of officials, Burton noted, was unusually favorable.

"There is no single England," he said, his formal tone serving him to advantage. "It has many shapes on many continents, spanning the world and linking mankind in new systems of communication and distribution of goods.

It combats poverty and ignorance wherever it goes. It upholds Christian dignity and fair play. And it is ever strong—wherever there are gathered such good and strong men as you."

The Council loved him. As he sat down to their applause, Burton leaned over, grinned, and whispered, "Christian dignity! Damn, Jack, bloody wonderful!"

At cigars and coffee, Lord Elphinstone, who seemed completely won over to the expedition, announced that a sloop of war, the fastest ship presently in the Bombay harbor, would be theirs for their journey to Zanzibar. After this, the talk turned political and grave. Lumsden tried to give Burton an appraisal of the Indian situation, pointing out that the Governor-General had annexed yet another Indian territory, the Kingdom of Oudh, from which more than two thirds of the sepoys serving the British army had come.

"We've annexed damn near the whole country," Lumsden pointed out. "But now we've given the sepoys cause for unrest. We've taken their homeland. I wouldn't be surprised if there's mutiny."

"If so, we'll certainly handle it," Lord Elphinstone grunted. He was a tough old dodderer who winked at all his listeners, giving everyone a feeling of being a special insider.

"Yes, but there are many officers' wives and company wives out here now," Lumsden went on. "We're terribly extended in an unsettled land."

"In a report I wrote some years ago, I mentioned this myself," Burton suddenly added. His remark seemed pompous, and Lord Elphinstone gave him a glaring look. Seeing that there might be disagreement, Lumsden soon suggested that they stroll to the harbor for an inspection of the sloop that had been so generously provided.

"Har!" someone said from the back of the room, and they all agreed to this good idea.

Servants soon arrived with torches to light their way along the cobbled maze of streets that led toward the harbor. The night air was pleasant; fireflies sent out soft pulses of light among the stars.

They passed the harbor bazaar, closed and covered with canvas until morning, beggars sleeping in its shadows amidst pieces of rotted fruit and the litter of the day's commerce. In the lighted rooms above the streets, people laughed and celebrated. Wind chimes sounded on the breeze.

"Your friend Speke made quite an impression," Lumsden told Burton as they walked along. "He's the sort who appeals to old boys like his Lordship. They invariably regard him as a son."

"Think so?" Burton asked. "And how do they regard me?"

"I'm not sure." Lumsden laughed. "But probably as a rapist who might soon climb atop their daughters!"

As they walked on, the streets evolved into a wide path leading to the harbor. The odor of salt air blent with the smell of the torches. Trudging on, Burton thought about his friend's remark, and for the first time it occurred to him that Speke might possess ability at public persuasion.

On December 2, 1856, they sailed for Zanzibar.

Burton entertained himself at sea with a packet of letters that had arrived at the last minute in Bombay—mostly from Isabel—and with newspapers, books, magazines, and assorted reading materials, including Galton's *Art of Travel* and Prichard's *Natural History of Man*.

From the newspapers and magazines he learned that Jenny Lind was singing in London; emigration to America continued at a high rate; the Atlantic underwater telegraph cable was being manufactured at the Gutta Percha Company, London, and would be 2,500 miles long; Charles Dickens was reading from his works, returning to the stage after a year at work on a new novel; child labor in the workhouses continued; traffic problems caused by the new, oversized omnibuses disturbed the Leicester Square area; a sea serpent was sighted off the Spanish coast; the construction of a subway under the Thames was being discussed.

When the sloop had been at sea for a week and the interesting news had been read, he tried various essays in the literary journals. There was one on the Oxford Movement concerned with the resurgence of the Roman faith, Newman, and the worship—this was what he made of it—of theology instead of Jesus. Another article outlined Dr. Arnold's theory of education at Rugby School: character, the headmaster asserted, was still more important than brains. That fallacy, Burton told Speke, was at the root of what was wrong with England.

Speke considered disagreeing, but wasn't sure how.

Then, essays and heavier intellectual materials exhausted, Burton turned to one or two fashion magazines stuck in the pile. He read the advertisements for Pears Soap, looked at the sketches by DuMaurier, and learned that the popular colors of the season were Marron Claire, Garnet, Lucine, and Raisin d'Espagne—whatever colors those were.

"Don't you want to read any of this?" he asked Speke.

"No," his companion replied.

As the sloop made its way into the harbor at Zanzibar, the squat little cannon outside the British consulate fired a salute. Both Speke and Burton broke into wide smiles.

From a distance, the island looked dazzling: bright coralline walls glinting in the sun, tall palms, red tile roofs, the lapping dark-blue sea. Along the parkway that embraced the seawall, colorful parasols and stately black carriages moved in slow concert. Viewed from the deck of the sloop, the famous kingdom with its ancient fort and sultan's palace boldly facing the leeward side of the island looked like a paradise: nature and civilization perfectly blent.

As the boat came into the harbor, though, the travelers could look down a stretch of beach at a grisly sight: several dogs were at their dinner, and the meal consisted of a black body—or parts of a body—that had washed up on the afternoon tide. While still at sea with their ships of slaves, the Arabs often threw overboard all their sick and feeble captives in order to avoid the required tax levied on each head entering the sultan's harbor. The dogs were eating one of these castoffs.

Up close, Zanzibar had a ghostly feel.

"I don't like consorting with the Arabs," Speke remarked as the sloop was brought to its place in the harbor. As he said it, they looked across a promenade at the Sultan's palace, which loomed before them.

Burton had explained the necessity of accommodating to Arab ways on the expedition, but Speke had stubbornly wished that they could work solely with the British consulate. By the time of the docking, Burton was less exasperated by Speke's continuing irritations than just merely amused. Consorting with the Arabs was absolutely required—and piety didn't much matter.

Again, the little cannon sent up its loud salute.

"I'm anxious to meet the consul," Speke went on.

"Yes, of course, so am I," Burton answered, but with much greater interest he studied the Sultan's palace, which faced the quay. He speculated about its harem. He wondered if the Sultan served good food and if there might be a cask or two of French wine in these parts that hadn't spoiled in the heat.

There was little use arguing with Speke, who had a conventional view of Arab slaving. Burton meant to use his knowledge of Arab customs to full advantage. He had been to Mecca, could claim himself a convert to Islam and therefore a very special Englishman, and actually had many natural sympathies with the restrained, masculine, occasionally violent ways of the desert race. And Zanzibar, after all, was Arabic: their culture, their fortress, and their market for the Arab slave caravans that originated in the Sahara and followed ancient paths down through the middle of Africa to this strategic island thirty miles off the mainland. The Sultan Sayyid Said had come down from the Gulf of Oman to establish his palace and fort and to rule the entire East African coast from it. He had died in 1855 and now, at the time of Burton's and Speke's arrival, his son, Majid, ruled in his place.

Those slave paths down through central Africa were what Burton intended to follow northward toward the rumored lakes and the source of the Nile. So he wouldn't go into unexplored, impenetrable wilderness, but along an established Arab route. To the north five hundred miles lay the Arab settlement called Kazeh, and beyond, according to all sources of information, lay the vast inland seas.

No use explaining the necessities again to Speke, he decided. Surely things would eventually become apparent.

"H'lo! How'd you like my gun?" a disheveled officer called from the quay.

"Very effective!" Speke called back, excited to see a British uniform—if somewhat untidy and definitely not regulation—among all the blacks swarming around the ship's ropes and gangplank.

This was Lieutenant Colonel Atkins Hamerton with his genial, smiling Irish face.

"Put the torch to the old gun myself!" he called to them as they descended from the ship and took his outstretched hand. The handshake with Burton turned into an embrace, and Hamerton said, "Dick Burton, damn! I've read all about you—and here you are! I've been looking forward to this!"

"I hope you can lend us some help," Burton said, flattered and smiling.

"Help you, by Jesus, of course! Your whole effort's a great tonic for me! The attempt to find the Nile—well, say, I take it as a personal charge. But I might as well tell you straight off that I'm dying of cancer—and have my bouts of malaria while I'm waiting for the bloody end of it! But I intend to live long enough to see you two explorers on your way! My pleasure and duty!"

Touched by this short speech, Burton clasped Hamerton's arms in his. Yet Speke, in spite of himself, withdrew. This was a Burton admirer, once again, and a poor devil, true, but not really an army type he could count on—just another rogue, in fact, like Steinhauser or Burton himself.

On Christmas Day the consul himself prepared dinner for his small garrison of thirty men, Burton, Speke, and another twenty invited residents—most of the white population—on the island. The pudding, baked well in advance and hung in a cool corner of the warehouse, was a great success—most of its ingredients having been ordered from England eight months before this occasion. Boxes of cigars, casks of port, bottles of sherry, and trays of sweets were offered after dinner; the old songs were sung and the men lingered at the consulate house longer than usual on such a holiday before finally sneaking away to the Afrika House—the officers' club—or the local brothels.

The consulate was a big rectangular box adorned with green shuttered windows. It consisted of a maze of rooms, an inner courtyard that featured a date palm tree, offices trimmed in mahogany, interior balconies overhung with ferns, checkerboard tiles, heavy wicker furniture, and darkly lacquered trunks and wardrobes. Attached to the main house were storerooms, kitchens, stables, servants' rooms, and the small service courtyard that opened directly onto the beach, so that boats could be pulled up on the sand and unloaded directly into the house.

High ceilings kept the rooms modestly cool, and Burton began his usual daily habits in an inviting room upstairs overlooking the beach. A steady breeze whipped through his room, so he had to weight his loose papers with seashells and books.

Hamerton promised that the Sultan would soon invite Burton to the palace. At last the invitation came, and Burton received it with high expectations; in his best fantasies he wanted to be set loose in a harem.

"Of course, this harem consists solely of my wives," the young Sultan said to him, disappointing him. "I am devout, and like my father before me, I keep no others. But ours is an island filled with beauty. Most of your officers and men keep Abyssinian women, do they not?"

"Yes, this is so. Eminence, do not worry over my needs."

"Let me suggest that you travel out the west road," Majid said. "As you go toward Mangapwani Beach, you will see a corridor of mangrove trees. That will be Marahubi Palace, occupied by my cousin. You could perhaps stroll his gardens."

"The garden I hope to stroll," Burton said, "is a soft, mossy hill with a trench of fire."

"Truly, you are a poet," the Sultan said, smiling.

Majid was about forty, slender, and confident. As he talked he moved his silk robes to and fro, revealing his thin hands, a golden braid of rope around his waist, the pendant on his shoulders and neck; his movements were slow and deliberate, demonstrating his calm.

They had kebabs of goat meat for lunch.

"Tell me why you seek the Sea of Ujiji?" the Sultan asked. He wore an earnest look, as if he couldn't fathom such a strenuous undertaking. "There is nothing on the slave trails except ignorant savages. In my opinion, the large kingdoms are only rumors. If there had been gold, it would have made its way to Zanzibar—along with the ivory—in the time of my father."

"In your world, rich families are always so," Burton explained. "The poor are usually always the poor. In my country, though, a modest man may dare to achieve a great deal."

"With the English, achievement is sometimes a wearisome process," the Sultan pointed out.

"Truly," Burton answered. "Even those who have achieved are required to accomplish more."

"Who requires all this activity?"

"We require it of ourselves," Burton lamented with a smile.

Before the midday rest they were served sweetmeats, biscuits, and sherbet. Afterward, they took glasses of lemonade and strolled the upper verandahs of the palace, where jasmine, roses, and bougainvillea surrounded them. In a courtyard below, there were two runaway slaves shackled to a shady tree; they looked up into Burton's eyes as he gazed down.

"Do you have any advice for my journey?" Burton asked.

"Take a cannon," Majid said thoughtfully. "A noisy fieldpiece. You won't have anything to shoot with it, but you can frighten away the wild men."

"Anything else, Eminence?"

Majid moved his garments with soft deliberation. "I believe you should visit me here in the palace each day before you leave," he said. "We must have long talks. You are a man of poetry and daring. Do you also know history and theology?"

"Only a little of each," Burton replied.

"Yes, I thought so. You are much more than my informants told me," Majid said, smiling.

The Sultan's informants, who were neither subtle nor secretive, followed Speke everywhere he went. At last, they joined him on his long strolls around town as guides. They were courteous, eager to answer all his questions, and flagrant pickpockets and thieves. They stole the gloves stuck in his belt, the gilt tassle that hung down from his sword knot, and, once, his shoes, which he had left outside a prayer stall. He demanded all these items back, of course, and they were returned to him—except for the gilt tassle, which he never saw again.

The four islands within sight of the harbor, they told him, were called Bawe, Snake, Grave, and Prisoner. Bawe was a stop for local fishermen, and the others were named for what they contained.

The houses were of coral rag, an easily workable material, and none of the thick walls followed straight lines anywhere in town. To Speke, everything looked somehow improper; Burton argued that the town and island had the charm of Italy with its villas and that the houses with their long, narrow rooms opened to the sea breeze had a pleasing simplicity.

Speke's daily walks, though, took him by ditches filled with human waste and those grim odors of the harbor; inevitably, he ended up at the slave market, too, where he was overcome with pity and disgust. He stood watching the groups—usually eighteen or twenty—as they were brought out for inspection; the men's muscles and the women's vaginas were always given an elaborate and disgusting study by the buyers. Speke would stand there on the fringe of the crowd watching the proceedings from the shade of a wall, while the Sultan's men watched him. Then he would stroll back toward the consulate in silence, his head down, fetid puddles underfoot. The sea made its way into the streets of the town at times and seemed to leave a residue of despair.

A giant lifeboat of rusted metal that had washed ashore years ago and had become a relic of the beach was appropriated by Burton. He had it cut into seven sections weighing forty pounds each, then outfitted for sailing on the lakes—if found.

"You intend to carry that monster up-country, put it together again, and go sailing?" Hamerton asked, repressing a grin.

"A perfect craft," Burton said. "Indestructible."

He named it *Louisa* after Mrs. Segraves. It was her soft white hull, not Isabel's, which seemed to be in his thoughts.

One day Burton decided that they would go to Mombasa.

"This will be a trial journey up the coast," he explained. "We'll visit that missionary, Rebmann, who devised that absurd map, remember?"

"I could do some shooting along the way," Speke said.

"It's a famous Arab port. And we can give the *Louisa* a test and see if she floats."

The next day Burton went into a flurry of preparation, hiring men, arranging for a large dhow, gathering supplies, and consulting with Hamerton and the Sultan's representatives. Speke looked on in wonder, which was all he could do since he didn't speak any of the languages. From what he could detect, Burton made very hurried plans and hired the worst sorts of men.

The chief guide was Said bin Selim, a timid, nervous, fragile sort who told Burton frankly that he did not like hunger, thirst, long hikes, fatigue, or loss of sleep. He was an Arab half-caste, recommended by no one, yet he somehow became head man. Two Portuguese boys from Goa, who had come over from Bombay on the sloop with Burton and Speke, begged to be included, so Burton agreed—although they seemed childish and absentminded. The two boys, Valentino and Caetano, were placed in charge of the porters, who immediately began to instruct their masters in how to load the dhow. The dhow, called the *Riami*, with a huge yellow sail, would tow the *Louisa*—which resembled a pile of scrap metal, Speke thought, designed to impede progress at sea.

Before they could put off, the monsoon rains began.

"I thought you meant to find yourself a woman or two here in Zanzibar," Hamerton told Burton, hoping to persuade him to stay.

"As a matter of fact, I've been studying illnesses on the island," Burton said. "It's discouraging. Everyone has fever. There's leprosy, elephantiasis, syphilis, ulcers, abscesses, cholera, and diarrhea. But there's so much gonorrhea, the natives and Arabs don't even consider it a disease!"

"So you're going to be a cowardly lover?"

"In a manner of speaking, yes."

"Why not wait until the rains slacken? It would put my mind at ease."

"No, my friend, we're off to Mombasa. And if our missionary is only half right, perhaps there's a way to the inland seas from there."

"Are you properly armed?" Hamerton asked.

"With a pistol and half a case of Warburg Drops!" Burton said, and the two of them shook hands.

The monsoon rains blew up with greater force than they had calculated, so instead of a pleasant sail to observe the coastline, they huddled on the bare deck of the dhow sheltering themselves from the torrents. As the sail whipped against the wind, Burton covered his notes with his body and Speke tried to keep his ammunition dry. Beneath a heavy tarpaulin they sweated profusely in the steamy heat, but outside it they nearly drowned. While the two Portuguese boys spent their time vomiting at the rail, Said bin Selim led the porters in prayer. The old Zanzibari fisherman who sat at the tiller, though, never changed expression, so that Burton felt mildly confident that the boat wouldn't end up on the rocks.

By nightfall, wet through, they stopped at Pemba Island. The men, Burton noted, kept a curious form of watch that night: they sat up singing around the fire until about ten o'clock, then lay back and fell asleep.

The next day they walked around the island as the rains temporarily ended. It had an old fort, crude settlements, poor crops, and a look of desolation. Its business was conducted by Banyans who had settled there with the early Portuguese visitors. Cocoas and cloves occupied the indolent dock workers, and Burton, who was interested in finding a suitable woman, saw none who interested him; in fact, the population looked and behaved as if they were ill, and he recorded in his notes a guess that most of the population very likely suffered from venereal or urinary infections.

That afternoon, as great pavilions of rain clouds built up for another downpour, they walked back along the beach toward their dhow. Speke was armed and ready, hoping to see a leopard—of which the island had a large number—when an antelope, a pregnant female, strolled out of the jungle just ahead of their party. With a quick aim, Speke fired and knocked her down. As the men cheered, though, she sprang to her feet and made her way back into the thick foliage that bordered the beach.

"Come on," Speke told the porters. "I know I hit her. Let's go!"

Reluctant to chase off into the bush, the men hesitated, so that Speke had to utter a few furious words—none of which the porters could comprehend apart from his expression and tone—to persuade them to follow.

They picked up a trail of bright beads of blood, followed along a path, and entered the dry bed of a stream, where Speke found her dying. Then, seeing she was pregnant, he pulled out his knife, slit her open, cut the womb, and found the fetus. The porters were aghast: this was bad juju. But Speke, casual as any Somerset farm boy, his arms bloody up to his elbows, tore the fetus out and showed it to the men. He said something else that they didn't understand, then finally made it clear that the large carcass should be carried to the boat.

Burton waited on the beach during all this, sitting on a boulder and making notes on some of the flora he had recognized.

"Good!" he shouted when Speke and the men reappeared. "We'll have a roast tonight!" But then he saw Speke, bloody and smiling, holding the dripping fetus in one hand and his rifle in the other. For a scant instant, Burton told himself: ah, see this, we've never had Speke in such a mood.

"It's the fetus," Speke explained, seeing the wonder in Burton's face. "Best food there is!" The porters, coming out of the jungle bearing the dead antelope, looked at Speke as though he were an apparition: sweating, bloody, smiling, holding up that oddly colored fetus like a trophy. They stood nearby, gaping at this tall, wild-eyed Englishman, when Speke brought the thing to his mouth and bit into it.

"Damn," Burton said, in spite of himself.

Speke had to talk with his mouth full of raw meat. Said bin Selim seemed frozen in place, and the porters, their heads filled with all the primitive animisms about which their fathers had warned them, looked on with terror.

" 'Sgood," Speke insisted.

"You always do this?" Burton managed, folding up his notes and getting to his feet. In spite of all, he watched his companion as if the man were possessed.

"Done it before," Speke admitted. His face, arms, teeth, fingers, and clothes were now wet with gore. "Same as eating rare beefsteak, old chap. Have some?"

"Thanks, no," Burton said. Then, seeing the dumbstruck porters, he ordered them onto the dhow. They dropped the antelope, though, and refused to carry it aboard.

"What's wrong with them?" Speke asked, genuinely uncertain.

"It's what you've done," Burton explained. "They think you've tampered with the soul of the animal."

"Which animal? The one I shot?"

"No, the one you're chewing on," Burton said.

The coastal current took them quickly toward Mombasa, but as soon as they set sail again the rains resumed. Somewhere beyond Pemba Island in blinding sheets of water, the *Louisa* came loose from her tie and was lost. Afraid that the dhow might be blown against the rocks, Burton ordered them to shore. As they reached the mainland wet and tired, again the monsoon eased, the rains stopped, and the sun appeared.

The sea remained rough and windy, though, so that Burton suggested hiking along the coast to Mombasa from where they were. "We can leave the dhow here and come back for it," he said. "By my estimation we've got a two- or three-day march."

"Fine," Speke replied. "I can do some shooting."

Along the way, the thick-trunked baobab trees were in new leaf. Wild mangoes and pineapples were everywhere. They kept to the coastal paths and beaches, but then the country became arid, dry and sandy, with the jungles receding toward a series of low hills to the north. On the second day Burton spotted what seemed some interesting ruins, so they detoured toward them. At high tide two streams encircled the ruins, transforming them into an island; they were made of coralline and overgrown with creeper vines. From a distance they had looked impressive, but up close they were rotting away and some nearby villagers used them as goat pens.

On that windy hillside beside the ruins they had a commanding view of the sea and surrounding countryside. They could also hear the keening voices of women at a funeral farther on, so they pressed inland another mile.

Beyond the burial ground where the women mourned, market day was being conducted at a village. They watched tribes coming in from the bush: Masai, Swahili, Wasegeju, and others, the men bringing in their meager crops and quantities of ivory tusks, which they hoped to trade for beads, cotton, salt, thread, needles, dried fish, knives, and hatchets from Zanzibar. Wearing only strings of colored beads, the women walked in undulating nakedness. As they moved around the village center, Burton gave them such careful attention that he failed to make notes.

Speke, because he could talk in none of the languages, could only watch and listen. He did ask Burton to inquire if there was good hunting to be found, and Burton reported to him that "the warriors tell me there are monkeys, antelope, leopards, and only an occasional lion. There's possibly hippo farther on—at the river pools."

"Splendid, hippo!" Speke said.

Burton didn't bother to ask his companion why he would want to shoot a hippo, which was just an oversized pig.

The Masai especially interested Burton. This was the nomadic, pastoral tribe that had reputedly blocked the way inland up at Mombasa, closing all the trails and murdering strangers, but at this coastal market its members seemed docile and pleasant. Their cows were scrawny, their men were grim, but the women had a peculiar gaiety and sexiness.

On their last evening in the village the drums and bassoons of hard blackwood began, and all the tribes started to dance. From the spot on the hillside where Burton sat on a patch of soft grass, he could see the moonlight shimmering on the distant sea, those shadowy ruins, and dozens of naked girls moving around the village fires; the girls' eyes were modestly downcast, but their loins rolled in perfect time with the sensual drumbeat. It was all too beautiful and almost more than Burton could stand; he knew that he preferred to be in Africa more than anyplace else on earth, that here his senses filled up.

After this the porters began to complain and threatened to quit. They had expected a leisurely boat ride along the coast, but were packing through jungles and arid stretches with an Englishman who stopped to observe ruins, villages, tribes, and natural phenomena—and who desecrated everything by taking notes.

A series of villages now: each chief wanted brass or gunpowder or brandy and seemed happy to exchange any member of his village for these items. It was a hard lesson for both Burton and Speke to see the enthusiasms for slavery even among the blacks themselves; the Arab slavers provided the market, but most of the actual dirty work of slaving—capturing, chaining, imprisoning in crude stockades—was done by natives to members of their own tribe or to their traditional tribal enemies. At one village, the old chief, wanting tobacco, offered the choice of his wives or children.

Set back from a strip of white beach in a cluster of boulders and palm trees was a small fort, one of the Sultan's outposts that ostensibly guarded miles of coast and proclaimed it the domain of Zanzibar. The fort was occupied by a few scraggly soldiers—askaris—among whom was a small, wiry, odd-faced creature who called himself Sidi Bombay. He had a flat cranium, teeth that had been honed into sharp points, and a countenance that looked as though it had been mashed down into a bag of wrinkles.

He wanted to quit the army of the Sultan, he said, and join Burton.

"Yes, I work like a horse, but seldom for love of my masters," he admitted with a grin that revealed those sharp little teeth. "It is duty, instead, to my belly!"

Burton interviewed him beside a barricade of stones surrounding a rusted cannon. The monsoon wind had returned and the sky threatened rain. They were speaking in Swahili, so that Burton only barely followed the humor in Sidi Bombay's statement.

"I understand that you are an escaped slave who works in the army of the Sultan," Burton said, trying to get the rhythm of the language correct.

"When I was a boy, I escaped on the mainland," Sidi Bombay answered in Arabic. "It is well known that all slaves are blindfolded on the coast and shipped to Zanzibar without seeing where they are, so although very young I knew that I had to escape on the trail. I did this. For some years I worked for a Banyan who taught me many things. Then I became a soldier and learned the shape of the coast. I know many villages and their wicked chiefs."

"Will you be faithful to us?" Burton asked in Arabic.

"The sound of coins is the sound of freedom," Sidi Bombay replied in a dialect of Hindustani. "If paid, yes, I will be very loyal!"

"You seem small. Are you strong enough?" Burton inquired in his own more formal Hindi form of address.

"I am strong," Sidi Bombay answered, again in Swahili. "But some say that I am fit to be more than a mere porter. I have languages and can serve as interpreter. My great fault is cooking. Food prepared by Bombay, I think, is always thrown to the donkeys."

Pleased with this little man, Burton took him to Speke.

"Don't you know a few words of Hindustani?" he asked Speke. "If so, here's someone else you can converse with!"

"I know a few words in the northern dialects," Speke said. He and Sidi Bombay practiced greetings in this foreign tongue and found that they did, indeed, seem to understand each other.

As the rains resumed, then, they started their march along the coast toward Mombasa again. Sidi Bombay, whose bowed, thin legs seemed tireless, walked at the head of the column close to Burton's side. Immediately, he began to dominate Said bin Selim and to usurp his leadership, which was never strong and never without complaint.

As the party reached the outskirts of Mombasa, the natives ran alongside their march, calling, "What news?" and "Ho, Europeans!" After a stretch of beach they were within sight of the old Portuguese fort and the harbor. The harbor was reputed to be the best on the coast, and this afternoon it was filled with naked girls who called and waved. Burton felt inclined to tell Speke something, yet didn't: his dreams, lately, he wanted to confess, had been filled with these black beauties, not Isabel or Louisa or any of the proper London types.

Until late in the day they stayed near the harbor, objects of considerable speculation and discussion among those who came to encircle them and watch. Burton ordered his art supplies brought out. He made sketches of the harbor, fort, town, and surrounding landscape, and as he did so the natives bent toward him, smiling, hoping to be models. Speke and Sidi Bombay went into the bazaar and brought back fresh casks of water, oranges, and dried beef for a late lunch.

Eventually, the Wali, or Governor, came to greet them. He was a short, fat Arab who smoked a cheroot.

"How far is the mission?" Burton asked him.

"There, in the hills."

"And what lies beyond the hills?"

"Alas, sir, *nyika*," the Wali said. Only wilderness.

Before sundown they started out for the hills, a low, maritime range called the Rabai, where Rebmann's mission stood. As they walked out of Mombasa and the arid region of low vegetation and thorn toward the mountains, the air cooled and a lush greenery began.

Again, local gossips ran alongside them, calling to the porters, "Ho! Don't let the white man lead you into the land of the Masai! Stop at the mission! Go no farther!" The porters grew genuinely afraid, but Sidi Bombay told them that the Mombasa Mission Station was favored by God, so that no harm would come to them.

After three miles they reached the foothills and came in sight of the German mission: a low, vine-covered, flat-roofed series of structures that had the general appearance of a cattle pen. Rebmann himself stood there to greet them, looking very severe in his long black smock and square hat.

Burton greeted him and handed him a packet of letters, including some official introductions. Speke seemed unable to deal with this strange, gaunt man; he made a movement of his torso that resembled, all at once, a salute, a bow, and a partial wave of the hand. They were ushered inside, where a great urn of hot tea was presented to them in the semidarkness; in spite of their weariness and the sweat on their bodies, they drank it and tried to smile.

At supper, later, they listened to the missionary talk. "I'm the last of ten of us out here," he said in his heavy German accent. "The others went home with various ailments. I remain."

"Commendable," Burton managed, eating his rice and goat's meat. He had a difficult time with religious types and knew soon enough that he would with Rebmann.

Most of the conversation naturally dealt with the presence of the inland lakes and possible routes over the Masai plains to the north.

"I just can't believe it's an impassable route," Burton stated. "I know these situations. One murder of one pilgrim and some minor official or government agency closes a perfectly good road for years. I've seen it in Asia. And I was told in Somaliland that I'd never reach Harar, but I did."

"Yes, you can go, of course, but no porters will hire on," Rebmann said. "Famine has made the Masai renegades desperate. You could be killed for a pinch of salt or the buttons on your shirt. You have to understand. Their children are dying in their arms from hunger. They would ask no help from you, just murder you and take whatever you have. No porters or guides in Mombasa would go two miles beyond this station."

They ate in silence for a minute. Flies buzzed in the room, but the air grew cool with the arrival of evening. Above their heads the long mangrove rafters, heavily polished and gleaming, reflected the lamplight.

"But the lake is there?" Speke asked.

"Oh, yes, it's there," Rebmann assured them. "So many natives have seen it. In all these years, I've heard about it from slaves, traders, everyone who has come down over the Masai Plain."

"How big?" Speke ventured. "How large do they say it is?"

"I must tell you," Rebmann said, "that exaggeration is part of the folklore, part of the family, part of their stories of wars and hunts. But in concerns of geography, no. Why should they exaggerate the size of a mountain? Why should they elaborate on stones and trees? They see no reason for exaggeration in these matters. When we were marching toward Kilimanjaro, we considered it an exaggeration: a gigantic mountain covered with snow! Near the equator! In the middle of Africa! But it was more majestic than our imaginations. When the cloud lifted off it one day, our hearts pounded."

"How big is the lake, do you think?" Speke repeated.

"As big as the Caspian Sea," Rebmann answered.

He waited dramatically for his words to take effect. Slowly, Burton took out his long-stemmed pipe, pressed in some tobacco, and lit it.

"What matters, of course, is the elevation," Burton said. "Is it truly a high lake and the possible source of the Nile?"

"From here the climb onto the Masai Plain is constant," the missionary said. "From the higher elevations you can always see a blue line of mountains in the distance—many, many. I think you can easily assume that the great nyanza —the lake—lies among those mountains."

"You had no boiling thermometer when you were on your trip to Kilimanjaro?" Burton asked, blowing a tiny puff of smoke.

"No," Rebmann said. "And I know how skeptical the geographical organizations have been concerning our map. I never claimed to be a cartographer either. If our map is in grave error, the lake is still there—and immense."

"You've done a great service to geography, I'm sure," Burton told him.

"I'm a man of God," Rebmann stated. "Your letter asked if I would consider going with you over the Masai Plain. Not unless this were a mission for Christ. I'm not interested in either geography or personal fame otherwise."

"Yes, quite," Burton said, puffing at his pipe.

"I would never have gone to Mecca in disguise as you did," Rebmann went on, pressing the point. "They are the infidels, not we. I could only have gone among them as a Christian."

His piety was so complete and so silly that Burton saw no reason to be offended. "Hmm," Burton answered, chewing at his pipe stem. Speke looked from one to the other, as if observing a tennis match.

"So far the only real light on this continent has come from the missions," he went on. "Our schools, clinics, and churches, don't you see? I would not go north again for nations or commerce or mention in the newspapers."

"Yes, I see that," Burton replied patiently.

"And what of your own religion?" Rebmann asked. "Would you go for God? Would you join *me*, if asked, on a journey to open up the great soul of this place?"

"On our way here," Burton replied, "we heard the wailing of some women in a lonely valley. They were at an obscure village burial ground— mourning their dead and trying to break the spell of the nameless dread that comes to all men."

"Yes, what is your point?"

"There is soul and religion already present in this place to the north," Burton said as calmly as possible. "Such things have been here for thousands of years. And religion, I contend, is actually a matter of geography. Where one is raised, there is his religion."

"And one is as good as another?" Rebmann inquired, fearing the inevitable agnostic pose.

"I don't know," Burton said. "But I have seen most of them. I've been in Asia, here, and in the sweet Lutheran valleys of Germany."

"And you fail to see the superiority of Christianity over the heathen religions?" Rebmann kept on.

"On an intellectual basis, I see merit in every religion—and foolishness," Burton said. "On a personal basis, my soul is my own and not for discussion."

"I think you consider yourself a scholar who is above faith," Rebmann said. The missionary suddenly had a tight, mean smile, which made Speke so uncomfortable that he burrowed into his own silence.

"I do believe in the search for knowledge," Burton admitted.

"Then, simply, if that is all you believe, you are damned," Rebmann said, his smile altering into a grimace.

"Like any searcher, I take a great deal on faith," Burton said evenly. "I think your lake—for which you have been criticized and maligned and laughed at—and whatever its proportion or latitude—is there. And I am willing to risk my life to find it."

Rebmann slowly gained control over himself. "Yes, true," he managed, and his theological grimace eased, once again, and became the face of a man trying to act as host. "I suggest, please, that we sleep on the roof tonight. It is very pleasant underneath the stars."

"Fine idea," Speke said, relieved.

Wrapped in blankets, then, they settled themselves on the flat mud roof of the mission that night, a canopy of stars and planets wheeling above them. Conversation remained light. Rebmann apologized for having no coffee or liquor, but the situation of the outpost was clear: it was at the edge of civilization, at best, four miles from Mombasa, where one could purchase the amenities, a pathetic satellite on the fringe of the Masai Plain. "You've been very kind," Burton assured the missionary.

Burton dreamt of the Eesa girl, his rooms in St. James Square, and, finally, of those scattered human limbs on the beach at Zanzibar. With this last dream he woke up, pulled himself into a sitting position, and listened to the night. His restlessness, which at first he had imagined to be sexual in nature, seemed altogether more profound.

Speke woke up in the middle of the night, too. He saw Burton sitting there wrapped in his blanket, glaring back at the darkness like an animal at bay. Curling himself into his favorite position, Speke tried for sleep again, but the effort seemed to require more patience and concentration than he possessed. At last, a series of vignettes ran before his eyes—dreams or daydreams: he saw his brother William calling to him from behind a stone wall in a field where they hunted together, the family drinking lemonade in that gazebo at Jordans, and, at last, himself—naked and alone, steam rising around him, walking down that corridor of blue-lacquered stones in the bath house at Cairo, a corridor that never ended, toward someone or something, indistinguishable, in the far distance.

Almost as soon as they started back from Mombasa and left the dry, arid country, Burton came down with fever. It was mild, but his Warburg Drops did him no good and his weakness caused them to stop early that day.

Speke seemed mildly cheerful that his leader had fallen ill while he felt so strong. "Think you can make it?" he asked Burton. "I suppose we can rig a stretcher for you."

"No, I'll make it to the dhow," Burton assured him.

Burton lay in the thick shade of a mango tree, his head propped up on his case of art materials. He didn't want to admit to Speke that he felt he couldn't move again.

"What do you think of Rebmann?" Speke asked.

Burton wanted only to close his eyes and say nothing. He knew that he suffered malaria and that he had quinine in his kit, but little was known about dosage or the real curative powers of the medicine.

"Rebmann," he said, as if he just barely remembered. He was on the edge of delirium. "There is a man who has arranged to be unsuccessful in life."

"The great nyanza is there, though, isn't it?" Speke said, smiling down on his leader. "Are you awake? Would you like tea?"

No reply. Burton seemed to have retreated behind his mustaches.

That night Speke pitched a tent, fixed his lantern, and set himself the task of inspecting the new brass chronometer. Everything about it seemed important: shape, design, and size—about as large as a man's fist. Sidi Bombay was especially awed by it and reached out a tentative finger, once, to touch it gently. Yet Speke had difficulty from the beginning trying to see how this timepiece fit into the business of geography and exploration. While Burton slept, Speke admired it, though, and read through an instruction manual; in the end he could only determine that he had in his hands a very sturdy and precise clock.

Toward midnight, he blew out his lantern and went to sleep. In another hour the porters began to cry out, first one, then another, in a series of sharp wails. As Speke got up, Sidi Bombay arrived to address him in the rough Hindustani that they had devised between themselves.

"Insects!" Sidi Bombay hissed. "We must go! I wake up Captain Burton!"

Their camp was being overrun by a column of bulldog ants. Even as he hurried to gather up his tent and gear, Speke was bitten on the leg; it felt like a long, hot needle entering the flesh, and he heard himself cry out, "Ah!"

Said bin Selim and the two Portuguese boys ran around in circles, frightening the porters. Every man swatted at his ankles, shouted obscenities, and seemed unable to think because the ground beneath him was alive with ants.

"The loads!" Speke shouted at them. "Pick up your loads!"

No one could be sure of the column's width—it could have been twenty yards across or one mile—but Sidi Bombay, with Burton astride his back, headed for a nearby stream, and Speke encouraged others to follow. In the darkness, a porter went down, screamed, got to his feet, and went down again.

They reached the stream, stumbled through it, and located each other in the darkness of the other side. Burton, weak and disoriented, managed to keep on his feet while Speke, Sidi Bombay, and Said bin Selim counted the loads.

"Anyone lost?" Speke asked in a loud voice.

"Medicine," Sidi Bombay replied. "Medicine needed badly." The men were bitten, but safe.

"We're not far from a stretch of beach," Burton said when gear and men had been reassembled. "Let's get to it and walk. I feel better, and I believe we can make several miles if we use the darkness."

They walked all the rest of that night, then, and until noon the next day when the porters, complaining and threatening to quit, demanded a stop. Burton's Warburg Drops had done him little good, so he was ready.

Only after a meal did Speke realize that he had left the expensive chronometer behind.

"It was sitting on a log inside my tent," he explained to Burton. "In the confusion, I forgot it. How many miles do you think we've marched?"

"I will return and fetch it," Sidi Bombay interrupted.

"We must keep going," Burton said. "You'll never catch up with us."

"Oh, yes," Sidi Bombay assured him. "This will be a very beneficial thing for me to do. The ants will be gone! I will do this!" As he spoke, he prepared a bag of dried meat and fruit. Clearly, he intended for this service to establish him as a permanent addition to the explorers' work.

"If we reach the dhow and you haven't returned, we will wait only one day," Speke warned him.

Sidi Bombay only grinned, and within minutes his thin, bowed legs had carried him off. Speke estimated that it would require a trip of about fifteen miles to retrieve the chronometer and wondered if they would ever see him again.

"Oh, I think we will," Burton said.

That evening they reached a series of swampy rivulets where a small stream trickled down to the sea. Up in the jungle at a distance of half a mile were some hippo pools, according to Said bin Selim, and a large congregation of the beasts.

Speke made an elaborate show of unpacking his carbine, fastening the stock in place, loading, and firing a practice round out to sea. The porters applauded in anticipation. Then everyone except Burton and Caetano went off in a long single file toward the pools, marching quietly over the soft, elastic ground of the swamp. Giant lily pads floated on the velveteen scum of the pools, and in the midst of lilies, bullfrogs, water sprites, algae, and birds, Speke saw his first hippo—mostly submerged, its eyes just above the scummy surface. Without much hesitation or ceremony, he aimed and fired a bullet into its head just behind its ear.

The hippo turned the pool into a boiling churn of brown water, but seemed unable to hide itself. When it exposed most of itself, Speke fired again. The pool began filling with blood. For a moment it seemed that a hidden pump deep in the bowels of the swamp would fill the pool to overflowing; the birds fled in shrieks, and that velveteen scum turned soft red. Then the hippo disappeared in a final splash, as if it had burrowed down beyond the shallows in its fat embarrassment of death. Speke and the porters stood there regarding the discolored pool in stunned silence.

Meanwhile, Caetano walked out into the surf, soaked Burton's shirt in cool salt water, and came back to the bamboo shade where he placed it around the captain's shoulders. Burton heard the commotion at the hippo pools, but paid it little attention. His fever had weakened him so much that he could only lie there, enjoy the shade, and go over his list of Swahili verbs.

Three porters quit and disappeared when they were ordered to become bearers for Burton's stretcher.

"Either find us willing workers or carry the stretcher yourself," Speke told Said bin Selim. The chief guide apologized for what he called "these lazy coastal niggers," but admitted there was nothing he could do.

The group made little progress toward the dhow, so that in the evening Sidi Bombay arrived with the chronometer. Only after returning to camp did he sit down to eat his dried meat and fruit.

The next day they also recovered the *Louisa*. The natives who delivered her to a small lagoon wanted an immediate reward—either brass wire or cotton. When Burton gave them the preferred wire, they became very friendly and invited everyone to their nearby village. When they mentioned that they had slave girls for sale, Burton agreed to go inspect the merchandise.

Their village sat on a hill, so that its thatched domes resembled the exposed brown vertebrae of some prehistoric beast. Fires filled the air with soft wisps of smoke as the evening dance began.

The slave girls were fat, sullen, and busy picking lice out of each other's hair. Even so, Burton found the energy to get off his stretcher and tease them, saying, "Wouldn't you like to try a white man in trousers?"

They said in unison that they had no interest at all.

At the dance, there was a long discussion concerning the exact whereabouts of the hippo Speke had shot. The warriors of the village wanted to go drag it out of the swamp, cut it up, and eat it. In spite of the growing frenzy of the dance, Burton's fever weighed him down; he lay down on his stretcher, closed his eyes, and wondered if he had the strength to reach the dhow on his feet. Speke's smile, he thought, had seemed to say to him all day: I am stronger than you, I am on my feet and you are not, I am walking to the dhow.

Walking was a silly thought, of course, with good strong porters who could bear him along, but it came into his head nevertheless.

The next morning they decided to paddle the *Louisa* along the coast to the anchored dhow, and this proved to be a very satisfactory idea except that four more porters quit over the prospect of actually having to row the big iron boat. By midafternoon they were out in the sea breezes, so that Burton, although his skin had yellowed, felt stronger and talkative.

Speke had to endure a number of the captain's theories, such as:

—smoked glass could be developed into eyeglasses that would be beneficial to the eyes while out in bright sunlight.
—the saber, far from being a useless weapon, should be developed by the army for use in guerrilla warfare and other close-quarter situations.
—malaria was probably caused by the bite of the mosquito, and a plan should be introduced for draining the world's swamps and ridding mankind of the breeding ground of this pesky insect.
—pornography, if properly introduced to the reading public, would have a beneficial result on mental illness and the nervous disorders caused by sexual repression.

By the time they reached the dhow, Burton had finally exhausted himself with his burst of intellectual enthusiasms. His stretcher was placed on the deck of the dhow, and Burton, sound asleep, never woke up.

At the same time, Speke began to feel weak.

"Sidi Bombay," he called, but before he could be reached, his knees gave way and he sank down. That night he entered into delirium.

On their return to Zanzibar, Hamerton assigned servants to them and personally nursed them through the worst of their fever attacks.

"In my opinion, this little bout with the fever will make us immune," Burton said. "We'll be able to go on our principal journey without this curse."

"Not much medical precedent in that theory," Hamerton told him. "Everybody out here gets the fever. Stays in the blood, and comes back on a chap, too."

As Burton improved with his return to Zanzibar, Speke seemed to get worse. From Burton's room, where Hamerton frequently came to sit and talk, they could sometimes hear Speke talking in his sleep, his voice carrying across the inner courtyard. Hamerton brought books to Burton, made lists of items he believed they should take with them into the interior, and rightfully insisted that his guest should take large doses of quinine—and not just Warburg Drops.

The two became good friends. Burton felt that Hamerton had a life-loving spirit about him and was a man dying without great sadness or rancor.

"I wanted to be a great success in the diplomatic service," Hamerton admitted to him one evening. They were drinking banana beer and looking out to sea. "I was out here in the tropics to make my mark. Then I realized they were leaving me here—and that others in London were getting the choice appointments elsewhere. It was a bad moment for me. I felt stupid—finding out that my ambitions were mere dreams. But somehow my bitterness stopped and I found that Zanzibar, good liquor, women, nature, my own little evolutions were all marvels, really, and that life is a hell of a lot more than one's silly career."

"Hmm, yes," Burton replied.

"Take Speke. He's out here so that he can successfully return to England. And you. I'd say you're not so much that way—you enjoy the days of your life."

"Make no mistake," Burton said. "I want my success. But, true, I like where I am when I'm there."

As they sipped at their beer, Speke's moans penetrated the corridors between them. He called a name over and over, but they couldn't make it out.

"Poor, poor devil," Hamerton said of him, and his meaning was slightly ambiguous.

In the mornings, as his strength returned, Burton walked across that wide intersection of cobbled streets to the island post office. Usually, Isabel's chatty letters awaited him, brimming with romance and loyalty, so that, at times, he had misgivings about tearing them open and reading them. She considered their engagement holy and absolute; he considered life tenuous.

One morning the mail brought him four of her letters, but two others of some significance. The note from Steinhauser reported that the good doctor had failed to board a ship from Aden to Zanzibar, had started overland on the Somali coast toward Mombasa, but had fallen ill. He wouldn't be coming at all—and, in fact, expected to take a year recovering. The other letter was an official instruction from the Bombay office asking Burton to explore the region for copal —a gum resin—and the trees that produced it; copal was used in making paints and varnishes and had become so rare that the Bombay officials had become interested in its increased market price.

Burton walked back to the consulate, where Speke was having tea and cleaning his rifles.

"Have some news. We're going on another short excursion along the mainland," Burton informed him. "Looking for a tree called the *Valeria Indica*. Here, read this from the Bombay council."

"We've been here weeks!" Speke protested, taking the letter. "When are we going for the Nile?"

"And Steinhauser is ill, so isn't coming," Burton added. "That makes you second in command."

"Really? Sorry to hear that," Speke said, not sounding sorry at all. He turned his attention to the correspondence from Bombay, Burton felt, with what seemed a sudden new authority and enthusiasm.

Over and over they heard the story of the fate of M. Maizan, a French officer who was tied to a tree in the feared Ugogo district. A savage began to cut off the poor man's head with a knife that proved to be too dull for the task. So halfway through the gruesome business the savage stopped his work, got out his stone, and honed the edge of the knife as the horrified victim looked on. Then, everything proper, the job was finished.

This story, which they heard from locals and consulate guards alike, was always accompanied by fierce laughter. Africa's humor was always bloodthirsty; dread and death always turned into farce.

At Marahubi Palace, each day, the Sultan's cousin set loose his wives and concubines to walk naked in his large, elaborate garden. At dusk, he walked among them to choose his companion for the night.

The garden sat at the end of a shady corridor of immense mangrove trees and featured a bubbling green fountain, soft grass, tailored hedges, and the caressing breezes of the nearby sea.

Burton's invitation came one lazy Sunday afternoon, and so he arranged for the consul's carriage to deliver him to the gates. With his expectations high, he sat down on an embroidered hassock beside the robed and jeweled cousin in a cool inner courtyard of the palace.

After all the greetings, formalities, compliments, and small talk had ended, the cousin smiled and said, "I have for you a very pleasant woman."

"Very kind," Burton replied, hoping, actually, for a stroll in the garden himself. "I was just wondering if it might be possible . . ." He paused, trying to select a tactful phrase.

"Yes, my new friend?"

"Eminence, I was just hoping for . . ." Another awkward pause.

"Something more?" the cousin persisted.

"Uh, yes," Burton managed. The cousin's face wore a look of puzzlement, as if he certainly wanted to be creative as well as generous in his guest's behalf.

"Very well, I have it!" the cousin finally said. "*Two* women! This would please you, would it not?"

Burton regretfully surrendered his fantasy of strolling through a buffet-style offering of many females, and answered, "Yes, two would be plentiful."

At dusk, then, Burton strolled down from the gardens, followed a footpath through some tall lemon grass, and with two women entered an isolated cove, where a white sandy beach met the soft green surf. One of the women, the one originally designated for him, was a beautiful doe-eyed creature, slender and long in the waist, who spoke in a husky whisper. The other seemed to be a typical Arab concubine: fattish, broad-faced, gap-toothed, with a thin waist, but immense buttocks and thighs. Burton cursed himself for his gluttony. Yet, determined not to offend his host, he led them both along the warm sands of the beach.

As they strolled, they began to undress each other. Burton paused to unclasp the brooch adorning the cloak of his doe-eyed beauty, and when the garment fell away the woman's full breasts stood up and her rib cage revealed a delicate and seductive architecture. At the same time, the fat one roughly pulled down Burton's trousers, almost tripping him.

Naked, they walked in the surf. He was unashamedly aroused, but they all smiled at each other awkwardly and went along picking up seashells as dusk began to deepen into night. Eventually, they settled into a bower beneath the gnarled branches of a dead tree. Their hands began to roam and caress each other, they smiled and made cooing sounds. The legs of the doe-eyed beauty seemed slack and inviting, but the fat one seemed to possess the eye of a referee.

"I wonder," Burton suggested, clearing his voice and speaking in formal Arabic, "if you might bring us some wine and food?"

A momentary confusion entered the fat one's expression, but the two women consulted one another with a glance, nodded, and she agreed to leave on the errand.

When she was gone, Burton tried to concentrate his energies, but the doe-eyed beauty insisted on a preliminary kiss.

"In the European style," she requested.

Burton bent her backward, parted her lips with his, and kissed her long and deep. When they had finished, her face was filled with astonishment, and she breathed in her sensuous whisper, "Oh, please, Allah, *again!*" It pleased him to excite her so much; gathering a handful of her long, dark tresses, he pulled her down again and felt her swoon against him. Then he began wrestling her into position for a consummation, but she tore away from him, rose to her feet, and began pacing back and forth beside the bower.

"What's the matter?" he asked, frustrated.

"I am hot and confused," she said. "I think I love you."

Proud to have such a profound effect on her, yet desperate to have her, he pleaded with her to come lie down.

"I was once a favorite in this palace," she told him, still pacing. Her body —what he could see of it—seemed lovely in the darkness. "But now that I have found you, I want you to take me away. Say you will. I will make for you a drawing of the palace and show you how to find my room."

"Please," he begged her. "Don't be agitated! Come and lie down!" He didn't want to hear her history or troubles or long-range desires.

Suddenly, she sprang at him. Her lips sought his, but her attack was so impulsive that she managed only to kick up a spray of white sand and to knock off one of the low branches of the dead tree.

"You must take me from here!" she breathed in his ear, pressing her breasts against him, and he was willing to grant her anything when the fat one reappeared. She dropped down beside them, breathless, her arms filled with bottles of raki, loaves of bread, and a powerfully smelly cheese. She looked as though she had sprinted from the beach to the palace and back.

Their sandy bed was now littered with groceries for a picnic. The doe-eyed beauty ate and drank heartily, but with labored breathing, as if Burton's presence was too exciting for her to bear. The fat one ate with a grin that conveyed, clearly, that she felt her turn had arrived. Burton, in spite of himself, worried over the age-old venereal question: Should one take risks? Was there a hygiene problem here? Taking a bottle of raki with him, he got up and walked to the surf, where he scrubbed his genitals in salt water—for the sake of precaution.

When he returned to the dead tree, though, the two women were arguing, calling each other a variety of names in Arabic, Swahili, and dialects Burton didn't know. The fat one tapped a finger on her forehead to indicate to Burton that his doe-eyed beauty was crazy.

"Please, be calm," Burton asked them.

"I love you and want to live in London," the doe-eyed beauty said. "Come to the palace tomorrow and I will go away with you!"

As the fat one continued to insult the doe-eyed beauty, she popped bits of cheese into her mouth. They circled each other like wrestlers, glaring.

"Behave yourselves," Burton pleaded.

But they kept on until he sat down on the sand some twenty feet from the bower. As they reviled each other, circling and cursing, the moon came up and illumined the sea and countryside. Drinking the bottle of raki in the moonglow and listening to the women's strident voices, Burton became suddenly tired and forlorn; he thought of the coy dancers on the way to Harar, women he had known in India, and he tried to be philosophical and amused at life's caprice.

After a while he got up and walked out to the main road, which led to town, their voices following him, rising and falling, until he was far away. From the beach to town was a three-mile walk, but the raki had numbed his sexual longing so he didn't care.

In the old Stone Town of Zanzibar there was a Banyan named Ramji, who wanted to rent slaves to Burton and Speke. The rental price was so high, though, that Burton suggested—in partial jest—an alternative.

"For that amount of money we can go to the slave market, purchase our own slaves, take them with us, then later set them free," he said.

"You can't be serious," Speke replied, his piety again ready for display. When Burton saw how offended his companion was, he kept on.

"Think how they'll work for us! We'll give them wages, then make them free men! Damn, it would be very economical and humane!"

"We'll have to get by with Said bin Selim's porters," Speke said with real irritation. "What if someone in England heard we'd considered buying slaves?"

"Well, we wouldn't tell them," Burton went on, trying not to laugh. "And, after all, Speke, everyone expects us to go native down here!"

"Really, I hope you're teasing!" Speke said haughtily, having no idea that Burton actually was. "Slaves!"

At times it seemed that Speke was taking notes on his leader, trying to observe anything and everything that might be useful against him in a report, but Burton kept busy, paid little notice to the young captain except for a daily inquiry about Speke's health, and never socialized with him in the evenings—keeping Hamerton's company instead.

They did have one brief conversation about copal, which almost became an argument. "You do know what copal is, don't you?" Burton asked him.

"Yes, I read the literature sent out from Bombay. Gum, resin, the stuff that comes out of that peculiar tree, isn't it?" Speke said.

"Not exactly. It's the tree gum that gathers on the tree's roots and becomes fossilized. One has to dig in the ground for it."

Corrected, Speke exploded, "Then you keep your notes on this damned trip we're about to take and I'll take mine!"

"It really isn't a matter of taking notes," Burton said evenly—and with a definite superiority.

"This is just another delay, as far as I'm concerned, and a stupid waste of time," Speke said, his voice raised.

They stood in the doorway of Burton's consulate room. A young subaltern, passing by, gave them a frightened glance.

"Should we find copal along the coast, we might become bloody rich," Burton pointed out. "We might become more famous and more appreciated by our mercenary little country, too, than if we actually discover the Nile!"

Their voices echoed through the interior courtyards. Hamerton, sitting at his desk downstairs, called out to them to stop bickering.

"I read all that material on copal," Speke repeated. "I know what that damned tree looks like, and I'll keep my own notes! But I'll wager we don't see such a tree anywhere on this trip!"

Suddenly, Burton laughed. "Probably true," he admitted. "But we have to take a look."

"And just remember: I fully understand the principle of digging for copal," Speke said again, making it abundantly clear that he didn't.

They set out for the mainland south of Zanzibar with Sidi Bombay, Said bin Selim and his dispirited porters, and the hired slaves Burton called the Sons of Ramji. Their dhow took advantage of a fair wind and made sight of the coast in less than five hours.

En route, Burton continued to study Swahili and Speke sulked.

Their plan was to inspect the jungle while out at sea, sailing close enough to detect the presence of the essential tree. But when the tide was out, a mile of shallows and mud flats kept the dhow from sailing close to shore. At the end of that first day, then, they rowed to shore in canoes and spent the night in a village where Said bin Selim had relatives. Beyond, they were told, lay hostile inland villages where cannibalism was still very much in fashion.

At the village that night Burton spoke with Bori, the chief, as they ate a dinner of fish and corn mush.

"Where do you trade?" Burton asked him.

"There is a market at another village eight days' march," the chief said. "Or we watch for boats like yours from Zanzibar. Between here and the market village our enemies live, so we go there not much."

"I noticed cotton and maize. Do you have other crops? And do you dig copal? What do you trade?"

"Copal is difficult to dig, and there are not many trees. Transport is difficult. When my people have grain to eat, they will not dig copal. We make only a little cloth with our cotton. When we are very poor, we make war. We take slaves from our enemies, sell them, and buy what we need."

"What lies to the south? Are there trees for digging copal? Ivory?"

"Only swamp with many mangrove creeks. South, it is all the same."

"How does a man become rich and powerful like you?" Burton persisted, trying some flattery.

"With many wives and slaves a man is rich."

"What of the Arabs?" Burton asked. "Are they friends or enemies?"

"Oh, friends!" Bori replied. "They keep the price for slaves high."

"Perhaps your people would dig copal," Burton suggested, "if the price was very good, so that a man could become rich digging."

The chief looked at him blankly.

"One day," Burton said, "a man's value here might be determined by his labor, not by his price on the slave market."

Again, the chief gazed on his guest with no understanding whatsoever.

Burton related this exchange to Speke, who was dutifully disgusted.

The next morning they ventured into the swamp, walking for six miles in search of the *Valeria Indica* and finding, at last, two specimens where the local natives had in the past dug copal. When Burton asked his porters to dig below the roots, though, they cursed and refused. When he offered double wages for the day, they calmed themselves, but still didn't start working.

"We will stay in the swamp until the digging is accomplished," Sidi Bombay told the porters. "There are snakes, crocodiles, and cannibals here. Captain Burton has his pistol, so he is not afraid. The rest of you should keep your knives ready."

The porters grumbled, complained, but still did not dig.

"When we start for the Nile," Speke said, "let's not take Said bin Selim and his men. We need porters who will work."

"Our problems are just beginning, I fear," Burton said, making a bed for himself at the base of the tree. "We'll get little work out of any of these people."

As the day wore on, Burton, Speke, and Sidi Bombay had a lunch of dates and dried fish, offering none to either Said bin Selim or his porters. Everyone sat around in the humid shade of the swamp saying nothing. Then, at last, two porters began digging into the damp clay around the roots of the trees, so that Burton and Speke—taking separate notes—had their first look at copal.

"What will you report to the Company?" Speke inquired. "That we found two trees?"

"We'll take the dhow south tomorrow," Burton said hopefully. "There might be whole forests of such trees."

The next morning they sailed, but there was just a jungle landscape stretching along the coast: those same mud flats, meadows of lemon grass, fields of giant fern, clusters of palm trees, small beaches, and, occasionally, a few huts of thatch and wattle with a few timid Waswahili standing around.

After two days, dark monsoon clouds gathered on the horizon, and they turned back toward Zanzibar.

"We leave for the lakes immediately," Burton said. "There's no time to waste! As soon as we get back to Zanzibar, Jack, get our stores together and estimate how many loads and porters we'll need!"

They were suddenly hurrying to find the Nile; after six months in Zanzibar and what seemed to Speke two doubtful expeditions, Burton appeared to be in a frenzy to begin. He had idled away weeks studying and reading; he had dallied with women; he had been drunk with Hamerton; he had managed to get himself and others sick with fever; he had made endless notes, as if Zanzibar and the coastal region had been their objective; he had never seemed decisive and now he wanted to hurry.

As Speke prepared the loads for the porters, Burton hired men—again, it seemed to Speke, in a spendthrift and rather thoughtless manner.

The Sultan provided thirteen askaris and ten gunbearers under the command of a preening black who wore a monocle and armed himself until he resembled a clanking mobile fortress of pistols, knives, sabers, and scatterguns. He was Jemadar Mallok, called the Jemadar by his men, and in dealing with Burton he demanded payment on all his debts and property mortgages.

"How much do you owe?" Burton asked.

"Five hundred pounds sterling," he answered. "And our sultan will want you to pay it. His wish is that I alone should command his askaris."

"Hmm, I see. In order to get the sultan's free soldiers, I must pay off the debts of his Jemadar?"

"Are you not here in Zanzibar to spend British pounds?"

"That may be our principal function," Burton admitted, and he accepted the terms—which immediately transformed the overbearing Jemadar into a mild executive to whom the askaris paid little attention and wouldn't obey.

Burton went to the banyan, Ramji, to hire on once again ten of the leased slaves, and during this transaction he overheard Ramji discussing the trip with a customs inspector. The two men addressed each other in a Hindi dialect, having no idea that Burton would understand them.

"Will he ever reach the lake?" Ramji asked.

"Of course not," the customs inspector replied. "Who is he that he should pass unharmed through the country of the Ugogo?"

"Don't worry," Burton interrupted in the dialect, startling the two men. "I'll bring your rented slaves back safely."

After agreeing to pay a high price for the Sons of Ramji, Burton once again hired Said bin Selim and his men, none of whom seemed yet inclined to work or even to stop complaining. Speke was aghast at both Burton's willingness to hire these indolent locals and at the price. Apart from these enlistees, there were Valentino and Caetano, the Goanese valets; Sidi Bombay; thirty-six porters who had been hired on the mainland and were waiting; five donkey drivers; and a personal servant for the Jemadar.

At the last minute Burton had to go back to Ramji and ask for more porters, but the Banyan said no more men were available. "You can leave a number of loads here in Zanzibar," he said. "I'll have them sent up-country later on."

Burton thought this over and decided there was nothing else to do. "All right, but I'm going to tell both Hamerton and the Sultan that you've promised this."

"You can trust me. The loads will catch up with you," Ramji said.

Speke, meanwhile, counted out the stores and divided the ever increasing loads. They had bags of beads, bolts of cloth, coils of brass wire, staples and tea, a box of cigars, 60 bottles of brandy, 7 canisters of snuff, Warburg Drops, 4 loads of ordnance, 140 pounds of gunpowder and 2 years' supply of bullets, 2 tents, table and chairs, 70 pounds of nails and a toolbox, clothing, fish hooks, matches, umbrellas, lanterns, the Union Jack, 2 chronometers, a lever watch, 2 prismatic compasses, a pocket thermometer, 2 boiling thermometers, a telescope, a sundial, a pocket pedometer, a rain gauge, an evaporating dish, 2 sextants, a mountain barometer, measuring tapes, a box of mathematical instruments, writing materials, books, almanacs, volumes on surveying and navigation, and a table of the stars.

Sultan Majid provided his own luxurious corvette, so that they could travel over to the mainland in comfort; Burton paid him a last visit to thank him for the courtesy.

They sat in a domed room built on the roof of the palace. Gauze curtains moved softly in the morning breeze, and the Sultan touched his cloak here and there, as before, but there was an uneasiness about him now, as if he touched himself to affirm his own presence. Burton asked him what was the matter.

"Oh, politics." He sighed. "There are those on the island who imagine that I'm not as willful as my father. They intend to test me."

"If you need my sword in your service—" Burton offered.

"No, it's good that you're leaving. I fear some bad times. But I can cope with any difficulty."

"We plan to find the Nile, then travel up the great river to Cairo," Burton said. "It may be years, Eminence, before I see you again."

The Sultan pulled back his sleeves and reached out to Burton, taking both hands in his. "You will find your peril and I will find mine," Majid said. "But Allah will give us both a long reign."

That night Burton was at the consulate preparing his personal gear and found Hamerton, pale and gaunt, dressing himself for the journey. He had items of clothing, pith helmets and turbans, epaulets and braid spread out in his bedroom, and tried on various combinations—looking, somehow, always out of uniform and disheveled.

"Yes, I'm traveling over to the mainland with you," he said.

"Sure you're well enough?" Burton asked, genuinely alarmed at how the consul looked.

"Actually, I'm not at all well enough," Hamerton answered. "But I'm going. Because I believe, Dick, when I close my eyes and listen, I can hear the sound of the camel bell."

It was an old Arab expression meaning that death seemed near.

Hamerton sat on the edge of his desk trying on a pith helmet and admiring himself in a hand mirror. Burton couldn't help thinking how good it would have been to keep the consul's company on the journey—especially since Steinhauser, who was also older, wiser, and a fine linguist, couldn't make it.

They brought out a bottle of Irish whiskey, blew out the lamps, and sat talking in the cool darkness of Hamerton's room beside the open windows. Far off in the night was the sound of crows: something had stirred them, so their cawing echoed across the waterfront. Curiously, there were no gulls on the island, just crows; like everything else, blackness.

"Oh, Christ Jesus, what a life!" Hamerton sighed after he was drunk. "I suppose everything comes to him who waits—among other things, death!" And before Burton could respond to this morbidity, the consul began to laugh.

The next morning they sailed for the mainland in the Sultan's corvette. Native porters came out with chairs and litters to carry each man through the soft surf and across the mud flats to the palm groves near Bagamoyo, the site of some forlorn greystone ruins and the settlement where slaves were herded together from arriving caravans, then shackled and blindfolded for their journey over to Zanzibar. The area was a moaning confusion; neither Burton nor Speke could distinguish their porters from the hundreds of slaves and free blacks who wandered around. Only Sidi Bombay seemed to have initiative; he threatened the indolent porters into exertion, moving from one argument to another, but loads were picked up, put back down, cursed, and abandoned. As Speke strolled around displaying his pistol, rubbing its barrel gently against his cheek to discourage theft, the Sons of Ramji and the local porters complained and wailed about the size of their loads—each one being about equal in size and weighing close to fifty pounds. Hamerton sat on a litter saying goodbye to everyone, preparing to return to the boat, looking exhausted yet brave. Said bin Selim looked lost. The Jemadar, seeming not to know what to do, beat a donkey standing in the road.

Burton stood beside some Arab slavers who sipped tea from gourds as they crouched beneath a giant eucalyptus tree; their white robes were dappled with sunlight filtering through the branches of the tree, but their hems and sandaled feet were caked with dark mud. After opening courtesies and greetings, one of them asked Burton if, as leader of this dangerous expedition, he possessed *baraka*. It was the Arab word for personal power—charisma or strength of soul.

"Naturally," he told them, never changing his expression. As he stood there above them, he gave them a view of his profile as he opened a tin of

Warburg Drops and slipped one onto his tongue. The Arabs nodded among themselves.

The Jemadar went on beating the stubborn donkey with a bamboo rod, but the animal only brayed and continued to block the path. "Please, can't we get moving?" Speke called above all the noise, but the Jemadar only stared at him as if to say, See, I'm doing my duty as fast as I can.

Burton went over to shake hands with Hamerton.

"You forgot that bloody iron boat of yours," the consul said, managing a weary grin.

"No, I'm leaving the *Louisa* with you," Burton responded. "If there's a lake up north, surely some native will lend us a canoe."

"Logical, very logical," the consul said, pumping Burton's hand.

"If I were logical, I would have stayed in London," Burton said, and they grasped each other's arms in farewell. The consul seemed to stiffen himself into a mildly formal and official last display.

"This is it, then," he told Burton. "Goodbye."

"Goodbye, sir," Burton answered, as the consul sat down in his chair, waved, and was carried off. Hamerton called to Speke and others, but the noise prevented his being heard, and soon he was out of sight on the jungle path.

During the remainder of the afternoon, fights and arguments continually broke out over the matter of the size of the loads. Speke put away his pistol, turned sullen, and seemed to surrender to the caravan's disorganization, while Burton contented himself with being the center of attention. Two local chiefs arrived to pay homage; dancers from one tribe, their arms and ankles bound in wire, their bare breasts and bodies bouncing with their gyrations, provided entertainment; and a black buffoon—everybody's favorite—stood on his fuzzy head and mimicked animal noises until Burton gave him a coin.

That night Speke had the porters raise his tent, then he went inside and sat cross-legged in the darkness. Delay and more delay: Would this whole trip become another postponement of his ambitions, as India, Berbera, the war, and the rest of his life had been? He couldn't bear it. He sat there listening to the incessant giggling of women, donkeys, and slaves, the laughter of the Arabs, and the clang of cooking pots. Later that night he heard Burton and Sidi Bombay discussing prospects for the next day. "Oh, no, no, I don't think we'll start tomorrow," Burton remarked casually. "Not tomorrow. Perhaps the next day."

That night the first of the monsoon rains began, and their camp was soon awash with mud. During the night, too, as thunder sounded and as Speke lay listening to the torrent, he thought he heard the guns of the corvette sounding. A deep thudding: a last, distant, melancholy note of farewell.

At four o'clock on the afternoon of the next day, the caravan gathered itself together and managed a march of thirty minutes to the next village. On arrival, every porter dropped his load, resumed arguing, and loudly complained of fatigue. Within the hour the cooking pots were boiling—it was like a monstrous picnic with supplies dwindling fast—and quantities of *bangi* were being smoked. Burton seemed as enthusiastic for the narcotic as he usually was for women; porters, askaris, hired slaves—everyone seemed to possess a waterpipe, suitable gourd, hookah, corn cob, cigarette paper, or other means of inhaling the stuff.

Speke's disgust was complete.

The next morning the path was blocked by a huge, insolent Wazaramo tribesman who demanded "dash"—a bribe or sufficient toll fee. He stood with his thick black arms crossed, and no one dared confront him, so that Burton was sent for. The warrior was at least six and half feet tall, said little, and clearly expected to arrest the whole caravan.

After fifteen minutes Burton was located and brought face to face with the apparition, as Said bin Selim, the heavily armed *askaris*, porters, and others looked on. "Who are you?" Burton asked, but the giant said nothing in reply. So, pivoting quickly, Burton slapped the man hard, jerking the tribesman's head to one side, causing his eyes to bulge, and starting a trickle of blood from one corner of the mouth. Then, as Burton stepped forward again, perhaps to deliver another blow, the unarmed giant meekly stepped aside.

"Pick up your loads," Burton told the porters.

"Very, very bad," the Jemadar warned, shaking his head. "Now there will be a battle, and we will all be slain."

"Keep the men moving," Burton said. "If there's a skirmish, I'll do the fighting for everyone."

"My askaris are brave enough," the Jemadar replied, sensing an insult.

"Your soldiers behave like women," Burton snapped at him. "As for you, I imagine you will always be first at the banquet and last at the brawl."

The Jemadar puffed up with indignation—although he was only partially sure of what Burton had said—but let matters drop because, clearly, he decided, the leader was in the mood to strike blows rather than argue.

That night everyone seemed afraid. There were distant drums. A hyena was reported near camp. But the greatest unrest was in the camp itself, with porters and the Sons of Ramji arguing among themselves over the weights of the loads, over dangers up-country, over duties and rations. At last, a knife was drawn. Burton stepped in front of a fire so all could see him, raised a fist in the air, and shouted for quiet, but the bickering continued—and the threats—until in the middle of the night, a light drizzle falling, thirteen coastal porters got up and deserted.

The next day on the path, a delegation of tribesmen from a nearby village appeared to ask Burton, "Are you warlike? Who are you? Do you come to kill us?"

"No," Burton assured them. "We come to give you beads and cloth in exchange for meat and ghee. We only make war among ourselves."

In the mornings, shrouds of monsoon mists hung over the jungles where they marched. By the afternoons these had burned away, so that the coastal sun was on their backs and their lungs filled with the steamy, thick vapors of decay. In the evenings, the rains came: pounding torrents followed by lingering, cold drizzles. So, alternately, the men shivered, then gasped for breath as they marched and perspired, then made camp in downpours—surrendering any hope of keeping themselves dry through the nights.

Food supplies continued to dwindle, but around the main trail hunting was poor, as if the animals had long ago learned to stay off in the bush. Sharp, wet blades of spear grass encompassed the paths that intersected the main trail, so that out there, hunting, lost in the maze of grass and unable to see, a man's impulse was to climb a tree or to search out a hill so that he could get his bearings. Giant fern, thorn trees, razorlike grasses, fetid pools, screaming birds, the odors of primeval rot: nature was in revolt, conspiring against their passage.

Burton sent a slave back toward a village they had passed to buy grain, if possible, from natives the slave claimed to be his cousins. The porters were weaving traps for birds and mice. Speke had been hunting, but unsuccessfully, and he returned from an hour's search to say, "Sorry, but I think my fever's coming back."

"Better lie down, then," Burton snapped at him. "If you can't do the shooting, I suppose I'll take over that duty, too."

This infuriated Speke, but he was growing too weak to reply.

That night the porters and the askaris again broke into petulant arguing. While Burton tried to settle matters, a slave ran off, carrying a bolt of cloth and the Jemadar's pistol with him. As Burton tried to organize a small party to go and find the slave, sheets of rain swept over the camp, putting out the fires and drenching everyone, so that Burton was left in the middle of a muddy clearing, turning like a slow dervish, talking to no one.

The next morning two donkeys had died—one of them, apparently, drowned in a tiny stream filled with water during the torrent.

The slave who had gone for grain returned with a sixty-pound bag— which was considered too little. The Jemadar, still angry because his pistol had been stolen by another slave, beat the young man with a cane rod, giving him six hard lashes before Burton interrupted. Another howling argument ensued.

"You must beat the slaves!" the Jemadar instructed the leader.

"What I will do," Burton shouted, "is shoot anyone who creates a distur-bance!"

He took the slave back toward his tent, sat him down, and applied salve to one particularly nasty welt. Sidi Bombay, meanwhile, tried to get the caravan moving.

"I have a message for you," the slave said, as Burton dabbed on the salve.

"A message?"

"Yes, there was a runner back at the village where I bought the grain. He was from the Sultan's boat. When he learned I was coming back to this caravan, he gave me the message to spare himself work."

"Yes, I see," Burton said, finishing his duty as doctor.

"Your friend has died," the slave said. "The English."

"Hamerton?" Burton asked.

"The English," repeated the slave, his eyes sad because he understood the gravity of his news.

For a while after the slave had gone Burton sat in the tent. The consul, he estimated, must have died soon after going back to the corvette, and Speke's mention of hearing the ship's guns must have been significant—a signal. As he sat there with his head in his hands, porters began taking down the tent over his head, so that he had to call out.

"Oh, sorry," Said bin Selim apologized.

Burton disengaged himself from the folds of the tent, stood in the mud with the heavy mists around him, and tried to gather his thoughts.

That day they crossed the same yellow stream nine times. Once, they forded it by crawling across a crude bridge of fallen trees and creeper vines, the men handing each other their loads, the donkeys, being driven across where the water was too deep, washing downstream and having to be found later.

Caetano dropped Burton's elephant rifle—a French weapon with fancy metal carvings—and it was lost in the muddy swirl.

Speke had to be passed across in a litter.

The monsoon continued, rains pelting them.

A war party of young Wazaramo blacks, their spears tipped with poison, their faces expectant and hopeful, appeared on the path. Burton made his first substantial payment, giving them cloth and beads.

On a small hill, Burton could see the soft blue line of distant mountains, but Speke was unconscious, so couldn't share the sight. At the end of the day, Sidi Bombay came to Burton with a packet of matches that wouldn't strike.

"All are like this, no good," he said. "So tonight we have no fire and no food again."

Burton lay on the muddy ground of his tent, one arm propped on a load of writing materials—all the books and papers soggy like cheap cloth, everything rotting away with moisture.

"We have German phosphors and some good English wax lucifers," Burton said. "Look through the loads and you'll find matches."

"We searched already," Sidi Bombay answered.

Outside, a raw mist was turning into a cold, steady drizzle, but Burton and Sidi Bombay went searching again through the loads while the porters huddled together underneath the trees. Burton found Speke's rifle and a supply of gunpowder. He knew that he should venture out into the bush and hunt for food, but he was too exhausted and, besides, he felt certain the gunpowder wouldn't ignite either. They couldn't find dry matches. On his way back to his tent, Burton heard Speke talking in his delirium.

Before the night was over, another donkey died, and the askaris cut it up and ate it—refusing to share with the porters or the Sons of Ramji. Another loud argument began and lasted until dawn, but Burton fell asleep and heard nothing.

For two days they stayed in the same camp while everyone suffered fever or yellowjack. Burton's malaria began with a series of fevered nightmares in which he saw haglike women with animal parts growing from their bodies. After a time, weak and uncaring, he languished in his tent, and he remembered his boyhood with Edward—how they followed their asthmatic father, the colonel, through Italy and France, how they disposed of countless tutors, how they were so unruly, at times, that the family's only solution was to move to yet another city.

That dismal winter in Pisa. Edward liked the violin, but the *maestro* screamed at Richard, whom he called insolent, full of sour notes, and an arch-beast, so that Richard broke the violin over the man's head. He had been ten years old that year—which made Edward seven.

In Sienna the boys bought a brace of dueling pistols, saving their money and borrowing from their sister and mother. To their disgust, the colonel made them return them to the shop.

In Rome they found the Palatine Hill unexcavated and the Colosseum a wreck. The Forum was overgrown with weed and bramble and filled with cats. A fever held the city in its grip, and everything seemed worn out.

In Naples, the colonel took another fit of his frequent scientific fantasies. He made a substance that he insisted was soap and made the boys wash with it. There, the whole family became obsessed with chess. And there they met Cavalli, the old fencing master, a leading exponent of the old Neapolitan school. They adored the old man, and Richard wished above all else that he could grow those sloping mustaches. He excelled at fencing, though, and philosophized with Cavalli about how to incorporate the whole French and Italian schools of swordsmanship. It was at Naples, too, that the cholera epidemic excited the boys. They

129

arranged with one of the servants to put on shabby clothes and to make the nightly rounds with one of the dead carts, helping to pick up bodies and dispose of them. Just outside the city, pits had been dug for the infected corpses, with openings just large enough for bodies to be slipped inside. Richard and Edward stuffed the black and rigid corpses into these fleshpots and saw, looking down into the holes, the lambent blue flame that glowed on the putrid flesh in those festering heaps.

"You did *what?*" their mother demanded of them when this was known.

"Fascinating," Richard told her, being offhanded and scientific about the incident. Edward allowed that they had seen the ghostly spirits of the dead leaving the bodies in those holes.

They left Naples, when the boys again saved their allowances, went to a nearby brothel, and sampled the goods. This was not so appalling, the colonel felt, but a correspondence ensued between Richard, the fifteen-year-old romantic poet, and the whores—who replied to his poems and notes with numerous written debaucheries, which the mother found tied in ribbon among Richard's things.

They moved to Provence, where the local Frenchmen spat where they walked on the streets; then they moved on to Pau, a little village at the foot of the Pyrenees. There were a garrison and numerous bars there, where the boys did their best to impress the soldiers and *contrabandistas* who smuggled through the mountain paths. Richard had his first drunk. Although he picked up the local dialect—a combination of French, Spanish, and Provençal—he talked only about women, strong drink, and swordsmanship, so the mother insisted that they move back to Pisa.

There, in a house on the south side of the Arno, the boys fell in love with sisters: Caterina and Antonia Pini. They threatened DuPre, their tutor for a number of years, so that he became genuinely afraid of them. They took up with drunken medical students, shot off pistols in the streets, learned and practiced yodeling, experimented with eating and smoking opium, and excelled only at fencing.

"Too much," the colonel finally said to them. "You will go to university in England. You will become gentlemen. You will not see each other again—because you are bad for each other! I forbid you to see each other—or even to write letters—until your education is finished! If all works out, perhaps you'll become clergymen. I've been thinking that perhaps—"

The boys broke into laughter.

In the autumn of 1840 they were forcibly separated. Richard entered Trinity College, Oxford. It was the year of Victoria's marriage to Albert and a time when young men, except for young Burton in his drooping mustaches, were clean shaven and conservative. He knew several languages and dialects, but was deficient in Latin and Greek. He couldn't recite the Apostle's Creed. Having been raised on French and Italian cuisine, he regarded English food as preposterous. His days were spent with Archibald McLaren, a master swordsman, a minor poet, and a major whiskey drinker. And in nearby Bagley Wood, young Burton met some gypsies who saw in his dark eyes that he was perhaps one of their own, so tolerated his affection for one of their daughters, Selina.

"You're too bold," she told him. "You stand too close. You breathe on me. You're not like the others."

"Who wants to be like the other students?" he asked. "Come on, let's go down to the glade by the river."

On a moss-covered boulder Selina, refusing to take off her clothes, pulled up her skirts to let him have his way. Stripping himself naked, he felt like a god of the forest, and standing between her legs, his muscles taut, his hands around her waist, their dark gazes blent, he entered her. When he had spent himself, he told her, "Now it's your turn. I don't want a woman simply satisfying me. I want you to come, too." Her eyes flared. He was on her again, backing his offer with renewed energy. Selina, of course, was in love soon afterward. She had never met a student who professed any interest in either feminine physiology or psychology.

In class, Richard tended to make speeches. He spoke Latin in the Italian manner, refusing to accept English pronunciations.

"Yes, Mr. Burton, in Chaucer's day, true, the Italian inflections were favored," the don told him. "But, later, to emphasize the breach with Rome, Protestant pronunciations became the accepted form."

"But Latin is spoken here as nowhere else in the world!" Burton argued.

"Yes, perhaps, but we think of ourselves as a quite well-established school."

"Unearned reputation," he snorted in reply. "There aren't even classes in Arabic here! The British Empire contains the largest Moslem population in the world, but Arabic isn't taught at Britain's finest university! Ridiculous!"

"Please," the don asked coldly, hoping order could be restored.

"There aren't even courses in the original languages of the British Isles! No Gaelic, no Welsh, no Cornish! Lots of posing and mispronunciations instead!"

Rebuttal was difficult for his instructors—especially in his linguistic studies, where he was so unusually gifted.

He let it be known that he hated Oxford. He and McLaren took up playing whist in their rooms. Burton became a heavy smoker. And he wrote to Edward, who was needed, he claimed, to execute the more elaborate pranks.

Lying there in his fever, years later, with Edward off in India someplace, their service together in the Crimea now a faraway dream, Burton supposed that if their father had allowed them to stay together, they might have finished their education at those snotty colleges; they might have become barristers or editors —anything except clergymen—and might have avoided the army for lives more productive. As it happened, he was expelled from Oxford for staying out of class and attending the local races, which had been specifically forbidden. At a hearing that resulted from his infraction, he lectured the dons.

"Trust begets trust," he told them. "You must treat us like young men, not naughty little schoolboys. And, after all, going to the racecourse isn't exactly moral turpitude!"

"You always make it quite clear that you dislike school, anything proper or orderly, and anything that smacks of justice and the common good," one of the dons scolded him. They stood in a room filled with afternoon light that slanted through stained glass, as if, Burton thought, he had been called before God himself on hallowed ground. The dons wore their usual gowns and sneers.

"This was such a petty offense," he protested, waving his hand.

"Oh? Then what should your punishment be?"

"I suppose I should be rusticated. I should suffer your outrage. Perhaps I should be birched."

"Well, you are going to be sent down," the don told him. "We want no more of you. You're finished here."

"Good," he replied. "I'm sure you'll take care to see that my father's money on deposit is returned to him."

The implication infuriated the dons, who started to leave, but Burton, bowing low, stalked out of the room ahead of them. That evening, his things packed, he hired an oxcart and slowly rode it over the gardens surrounding the Trinity College walkways on his way out. Its wheels crushed all the newly planted flowers. The next day he showed up at his aunt's house in London, where he and Edward celebrated their reunion by getting drunk. They also convinced the aunt that an expensive party should be financed for all their friends, so invited everyone they knew for a lavish weekend—including a pair of gay ladies who worked their trade on Regent Street. The party cost more than £100 and became, so far as the colonel was concerned, the last straw. Although arrangements were no longer official or easy, he purchased Richard a commission in the Honourable East India Company and began plans for Edward to follow suit.

"I want you to learn restraint, regimentation, and duty," he told his sons. "And I want you each to learn these things, by God, halfway around the world and far from my sight!"

While the brothers waited in London for their next departure, Burton went every day to Angelo's fencing salon and soon became the drinking companion of Duncan Forbes, a huge Scot who played chess brilliantly, taught languages at King's College, and agreed to teach his new young friend Hindustani.

It was June, 1842, when Edward accompanied Ensign Richard Burton to Gravesend, where the barque *John Knox* was bound for India. There was no sadness—only their usual extravagant display. Both of them smoked long-stemmed opium pipes. Burton was dressed as a dandy and officer in an elaborate white outfit, sword and pistol dangling from his belt, and a big white bull terrier straining at the leash in his hand. Packed among his six trunks were saddles, swords, rifles, pistols, dozens of uniforms charged to his father's accounts at the best tailor shops, hundreds of books and grammar texts, and a wig. Declaring that Indian weather was beastly hot, he had completely shaved his head, and the wig, he announced, was for formal occasions. Standing there on the dock, he looked extraordinary: young, bald, heavily mustached, dressed in gleaming white, heavily armed, leading his dog on a leash.

"You look damned splendid," Edward told him.

"Yes, I think I probably do," he agreed. "But I do wish you were going with me, Edward, so we could ride into battle together—at the brothels and pubs."

"I love you, brother," Edward suddenly blurted out.

Touched by the crack in Edward's voice, Burton moved forward and held him in his arms. Years of foolhardy, devilish, happy, and ghastly adventures passed his memory. He loved no one in the world so much as Edward, and this parting was exquisitely brutal. He turned and walked up the gangplank, his bull terrier barking a hoarse reply to the sound of the ship's whistle.

Lying in the stinking mud of his tent, fevered and restless, these memories of Edward seemed to help revive him. After hours of sleep, Burton lay there, hands propped behind his head, thinking about the joys of good companionship; he wished Speke were more like Edward. Speke could maintain his aloofness even in sickness, staying in his tent, never complaining, never asking anything, never giving anything. Aloofness was a bore—especially when practiced amidst life's frailties. Yet, good comrades and dear brothers were never really lost, he told himself; memory is an art. Time retains all things. Edward is still with me, he mused, and the thought brought a smile.

On the morning of the next day a runner arrived from Zungomero, a large trading stop along the path—their first major station. The runner announced that food supplies were good at the station, so everyone made a concerted effort to rise, load, and continue. Speke rode a donkey. Burton began at the head of the caravan, but kept stopping to rest, so that by afternoon he was a mile behind, with only Sidi Bombay to protect him and keep him company.

The path began to climb into the hill country. They passed occasional rice swamps, cane fields, haycocks, and little villages of grass-and-mud huts that resembled English cow houses. The wet ground seemed made out of putrid elastic. As the distant hills became more defined, the men could also see a number of kudu, elephant, rhino, and mongoose.

The local black women, naked and thin, lined the path at times, begging for food, beads, or wire.

Speke fainted and fell off his donkey, badly bruising his arm.

Burton estimated that in eighteen days they had walked 118 miles, with the altitude increasing at a rate of four feet per mile.

Near Zungomero, natives came out to meet the porters and askaris, bringing *bangi* and pombe beer. By the time the men arrived at the settlement, they were exhausted, sick, drunk, or giddy with narcotic.

Soldiers, slavers, ivory traders, and bands of desperate raiders occupied Zungomero. The raiders—slaves, escaped criminals, and men from the remnants of smaller, less warlike tribes—were armed with muskets, sabers, bows, spears, and knobsticks. They preyed on the tiny villages of sometimes only four or five hovels, frequently taking the wives and children, slaughtering the animals, eating the crops out of the fields, and sometimes even breaking up the hovels themselves for firewood. They were a surly, vicious bunch, but clearly didn't want to test the white men with all their armed guards. Besides, the caravan was already depleted, except for a few useless instruments.

Speke lay in his tent, still too weak to move.

"This is an evil place," Burton told him, kneeling beside him. "We'll move on as quickly as possible." But they stayed on, trying to gather food: scrawny fowls, papayas, limes, plantains, coconuts, pombe beer, everything at high prices. There was no milk, no meat except those few thin birds, no staples.

The askaris, made bold when they finally decided the raiders were afraid of them, stole a goat and ate it. They also made advances on the women, one of whom cried that she had been raped.

Burton spent most of his waking hours with the few Omani Arabs, who were courteous enough to lend him additional porters to replace those who had run off.

"What about the Sea of Ujiji?" he asked them.

Yes, they had heard of it. No, they hadn't seen it.

Again, the raw winds and rains came. Burton, like everyone else, wanted only to sleep, so he stayed in his mud hut with a roof that leaked; the floor was a sheet of mud. One morning he took blankets, covered Speke, who was alternately shivering with cold and burning with sweaty fever, and then found Sidi Bombay and Mabruki lying by the cold, wet ashes of a fire, he placed the extra blankets over them and for this luxury they thanked him profusely, but began to lie in their blankets all day long, never stirring or working.

In the midst of plunderers, slavers, rascals, and criminals, a slave appeared before Burton one afternoon with something wrapped in shiny, large leaves: a golden watch lost by Said bin Selim. Burton was astounded that it was returned.

"Bad juju for me," the slave who found it said. "The object belongs to somebody else."

That night Burton recorded the incident in his notes. Among the dregs of humanity, he wrote, where there was no religion, little else except savagery and misery, little sparks of kindness flickered.

On August 7, the caravan moved out of Zungomero: the weather vile, the men still feverish, the great mangrove jungle imprisoning them. Large rats stood up on the soggy ground to watch them pass. Slowly, they ascended: a steep climb, two days of it, everyone barely able to go on, until they found a small abandoned village at the top of the escarpment and threw themselves down in exhaustion.

They had reached the beginning of the highlands.

When they awoke the mountain air had revived them, and as if by magic their fever had diminished and every man was stronger.

"It seems I slept for days," Speke said. "I lost weight. Look, my trousers are too large." He wore those canvas trousers his mother had ordered, but had to tie them at the waist with a piece of rope.

"You did sleep for days, I remember," Burton replied. "Almost the whole time we were in Zungomero, so count yourself lucky. Our food is low. Half our donkeys have died. We have some new porters. I don't even know if we've spoken about all this."

"It's pleasant up here."

"Very. And I estimate we'll climb higher. The inland seas must be in great mountain bowls, as I see it, where rains gather."

"I'm still weak, but I'll soon do some hunting," Speke said. "This morning I saw flights of dove and raven. There must be some game."

"Fine, but don't exert yourself too much," Burton warned. "The settlement of Kazeh is still four hundred miles north. Our destination is beyond—how far no one seems to know."

They walked through a bright landscape of solitary tamarinds, leafy mimosa, calabash, and euphorbia. The grass was silky, wafting in the cool breeze, and they saw monkeys scampering across the path and watching them from available branches. The sound of field crickets was all around them.

But the men were strong enough to argue among themselves again. On the second night, no knives were drawn but threats came from everywhere. Some of the new porters deserted, taking loads of beans and fruit with them.

Speke left in advance of the caravan the next morning, hoping to find game on the path. They passed near a small village that day, its inhabitants all disfigured and dying of smallpox: their bodies made of sores, their eyes pouring pus, their breathing rapid and desperate. Later on, they found Speke, who had seen nothing to shoot except small birds, and who sat exhausted in the path, his fever on him again, so that two porters had to carry him to his pallet. During the night Speke got up, dizzy and hungry, and staggered around camp looking for food and water. Somehow he had one of the boiling-point thermometers with him and dropped it, breaking it. Two others had already been found broken in their cartons and another was missing, so Burton, in spite of himself, snapped at him.

"What are you *doing?*"

"I was studying it. I need to familiarize myself with the instruments," Speke said, and he seemed so tired and confused that for a moment Burton expected him to break into tears. "They're very difficult for me."

"Yes, all right, go back to your bed. Someone will get you what you need. You can't just stagger about."

Burton's own fever was still with him, but remained mild and bothered him only after a day's travel when he was too exhausted to oversee the making of camp, to read, or to eat his supper. At that point he could only lie down, stare out at the whirling stars, and succumb to those fierce nightly dreams that fever created. As a result, the camp was always unruly. The Jemadar and his askaris bullied the porters, stole food and objects from the loads, smoked opium and *bangi,* and stayed up so late that they slept half of the next day.

In the mornings, though, invigorated by rest and the crisp morning air of the plateau, Burton felt his best. He made his diary entries from the previous day, took breakfast, and concerned himself with the breaking of camp.

"I've noticed how the porters' loads have shrunk," he told the Jemadar. "And at the same time, the loads carried by your men seem to have trebled. So I propose that half your loads should be inserted into the porters' packets. Let's do it this morning, shall we?"

"We shall not open our baggage," the Jemadar stated, and the slur in his voice made clear that the effects of opium were still with him. Burton knew that he should let matters drop, but went on.

"I don't want to look in your belongings," Burton said. "I want to redistribute the loads. Your men are carrying too much."

"Hamerton is dead!" the Jemadar shouted. "You have no support in Zanzibar anymore! You are nothing!"

The askaris gathered to watch the spectacle. One of them, furious in his support of his leader, took off his shirt and threw it on the ground—a gesture that Burton found only amusing.

"Besides, you are starving us!" the Jemadar went on. His monocle fell from his eye, and his hands shook with excitement. "You give us no food and no respect!"

"All of you eat shit," Burton told the Jemadar. The insult brought a loud gasp from the askaris, and the Jemadar clapped his hand to his dagger, forbidding Burton to repeat the words.

"Shit," Burton said, using the word boldly. "You eat it! Shit!" Fearless, Burton walked in a circle, staring at each askari. They were dumbstruck. At the edge of the argument, Speke slowly made his way into position so that, if necessary, he could use his pistol, but a look from Burton assured him that everything was under control. The Jemadar, faced with strength, whirled on the timid Said bin Selim and let out a string of curses. Then he marched away with his men—including Said bin Selim—for a conference conducted loudly at a distance of about thirty feet.

Sidi Bombay, also armed, joined Speke.

"Shit! Shit eaters!" Burton yelled after them, taunting them.

Eventually, Said bin Selim was sent back to Burton to state that in future each askari should receive one sheep each day and four measures of cloth instead of the promised one. Negotiations were carried on at the top of the voice, so that all could hear.

"One sheep each day! These are men who in Zanzibar probably ate meat once every year on the Eed!" Burton shouted. "Tell them to eat more shit! And tell them they agreed to take one cloth and one dollar each day! I offer no more!"

"If refused, they will sleep this night at the nearest village and return to Zanzibar tomorrow!" Said bin Selim cried out.

"Tell them to depart, then, and tell them shit is their food and bed!" Burton called toward the knot of men surrounding the drugged and furious Jemadar.

"That man should be shot," came a voice from among the askaris.

"And tell them to walk easy with me," Burton shouted. "If a man attacks me, I will quickly kill him without thought. And for one surly glance I will gladly cut off a man's balls and hang them for decoration on the hilt of my sword!"

Suddenly, the Jemadar and his askaris were truly frightened of Burton's swaggering rage. They continued to mutter threats, but slowly dispersed. Soon the caravan resumed its journey and by nightfall there had been constant complaint, but no further incident.

"Shall we post a watch tonight?" Speke asked. "Sidi Bombay says he'll stay awake, if you wish, so no one will get stabbed in his sleep."

"No, the brave askaris are calming themselves with *bangi* again," Burton noted. "So you get your sleep, and I'll have no trouble getting mine."

The next morning the Jemadar and two others came forward as the donkeys were being loaded. Behaving like fools, nodding and smiling, they took Burton's hands as the Jemadar began his plea. "Give us a paper to cover our shame, so we may return home," he asked. "Please, master, you have neglected our needs. We want to leave your service with honor."

Burton smirked and refused to answer. Instead, he mounted a donkey and rode away, leaving them to talk among themselves. After a while the caravan began moving and the humiliated askaris joined in. By noon they were talking and laughing as if nothing had happened.

That night hyenas tore open the flanks of two donkeys. The braying screams continued until daylight, when the animals were found standing, still alive, in pools of their own blood. At the same time, two porters were brought to Burton—who determined that they definitely had smallpox.

"You must stay beside the path," Burton told them, speaking in Swahili. With this pronouncement, their doom sealed, they both began to weep. "We will give you rations of food and cloth, so you can eat and trade." The porters were pleading, but Burton moved on.

As the caravan departed, the other porters claimed that the appearance of hyenas was bad juju. Speke argued with them that this only meant other game was in the vicinity. Later that day antelope and zebra appeared for the first time, so that Speke had to hunt for only an hour before his bearers returned with fresh meat.

As they moved toward the Myombo River, they saw signs of a more peaceful highland life: huts surrounded by scraggly gardens, men burning off patches of land for farming, animals grazing, the sky filled with birds. As they approached the river, tsetse flies announced themselves, inflicting a few sharp bites. That night they banked up their fires around the river.

"It was an awful sight, Jack, seeing those men and animals sitting in their little circle beside the road as we left them," Burton said, staring out through the branches of a thorn tree at the night.

"You had to do it," Speke assured him.

"If I get the pox, you must leave me. I'll leave you. I've heard it can spread like wildfire through a caravan."

"What about the fever?" Speke asked. "Could we die of it?"

"I won't give in to fever," Burton said.

"Well, no, neither will I. But after my hunt this afternoon my legs began to shake so hard that I couldn't stand."

"We must rest at night and ride the donkeys while they last. But let's not give in. Not to fever. If we stay resolute, damn it, we'll outlast it."

"What's your greatest fear, then, Dick? Suppose we don't die. What's your greatest fear after that? Do you worry we'll fail?"

"I worry about the bloody instruments," Burton said. "I still believe we'll find the Sea of Ujiji. By God, I do. But what if we don't have the proper measuring instruments? The big chronometer is broken. We're keeping time by a sixpenny sundial! Our boiling-point thermometers: three out of four broken. If we find our Nile source, but our instruments won't tell us anything, fine geographers we'll be!"

"I've been trying to repair the chronometer."

"I could comprehend my death," Burton said. "But I don't know if I could tolerate some monstrous irony like that."

"I worry we won't be successful," Speke said. "I worry over it more than anything else. And there are so many ways to fail."

After this conversation they gave the pedometer to Sidi Bombay. Impressed at his new status in possessing such a wonderful machine that measured how far he walked, he immediately lengthened his stride—which, of course, betrayed an instrument set for a normal stride of thirty inches.

For a whole day the little man bounced along, his thin legs vaulting ahead, his sharpened teeth gleaming in a smile, until Speke had to request that he stop. On this occasion they examined the pedometer and found it broken.

"I did not drop it," Sidi Bombay said, defending himself before being accused.

"Perhaps it never worked," Burton added.

Yet they were disheartened. That afternoon when the caravan stopped, they spread out all their instruments, finding another chronometer—shiny brass made by the good English firm of Parkinson and Frodsham—only to discover that its glass was broken and its second hand lost.

Burton finally created his own navigational workshop, lecturing to a mildly interested group consisting of Sidi Bombay, Speke, Caetano, and Mabruki as he did so. "The only means of ascertaining longitude is by finding the difference between local and Greenwich times and then converting the difference into space," he said to that gathering of faces that encircled him. As he talked, he split a four-ounce rifle ball, inserted a string into it, then hammered the halves back together. He fastened the string—measuring 39 inches from its point of suspension to the center of the weight—to a file, then lashed the file to the branch of a tree. Then he took the sextant, one of their few unbroken instruments, and measured the altitude from the horizon of the evening star, which had just made its appearance. "From this reading we get local time," he went on. "Then we can discover Greenwich time by taking the distance between this star and one of the planets or the moon. Our crude little pendulum will tick off the seconds for us!"

Burton looked up, smiling with satisfaction. Only Speke remained in his audience and, clearly, understood nothing.

For a while they traveled in a region untouched by slavers. There were a few scrawny cattle, farms, tobacco, and sweetgum trees. As they went along they easily bought provisions, even goats and sheep, but a raw south wind blew up and their fevers gradually returned, weakening them and shortening their days.

They also saw the first outcroppings of giant boulders: clusters here, there, and on the near horizon, like sentries guarding a holy path. Burton sketched one group of boulders, and their daily conversations invariably turned to those phenomena.

"Like a series of Stonehenges, aren't they?" Burton remarked. "Except nature's arrangements. Wonderful!"

One night as they made camp beneath the moonlit shadows of one of those outcroppings, Speke confessed to an eerie feeling. No native village was built anywhere near the boulders, they noticed, although the rocks provided an obvious fortress and benefits. Neither children, cattle, nor wild animals seemed to wander close. Yet they couldn't find out from the natives if any particular juju was associated with the markers.

"We'll find out later," Burton finally said. "Surely there's some secret to discover."

As Speke again grew weak with fever, he hated himself for it.

He liked to think of his robust shooting expeditions into the Himalayas, hiking at a steady pace in the thin mountain air, the old matchlock over his shoulder.

He usually went with either Edmund Smyth or Jim Grant, both of them penniless young officers and eager hunters like himself, but his most memorable trips were made in solitude. He ranged far up into Tibet, once, and frequently entered that labyrinth of high trails and hidden villages so that he had to find his way out. His commanding officer, William Gomm, indulged him in these trips; in turn, he usually brought back wild pheasant, figs, or berries for the colonel's table.

More than once he walked due north from the smelly Ganges toward the peaks of Annapurna. The mountains lay in heavy shrouds of monsoon cloud, revealing themselves only occasionally in bursts of sunlight; the air thinned out and a landscape of gorges and rockslides began. Then that maze of trade paths and tiny, wet side trails: patches of snow all around, meadows of grey shale, edelweiss, giant fern, pine trees wrapped in bougainvillea, giant cotton trees and oaks, luminous springs, piles of prayer stones, rope bridges, booming streams, mists, and waterfalls.

He hunted the wolf, the fox, the wild sheep, the cheetah; in the late afternoons he would usually kill a pheasant for his dinner. Yet in spite of the plentiful game, hunting was always a struggle, as if he suffered a desperate sport, as if he had to find and shoot everything in the mountains and passes, and the peace of samsara, the peace of soul that eased the pain of the world, was not his. He had little tolerance for the beguiling relaxations of the Buddhist and Hindu mentalities; he was a British officer, always, and felt his driven duty in his bones. He wanted danger, exhaustion, accomplishment; then, if possible, trophies and honors.

At first he hired Sherpa guides, but later he went alone. They were a sullen lot, he felt, who demanded wages he couldn't pay and seemed to mock him. So he walked, ate, and slept alone, talking to no one; in his solitude he watched the thin wisps of smoke from his fire, ate the unleavened bread, cursed the inactive nights and longed for more strenuous days; if the desperation was a kind of karma, let it be, he told himself, and he pushed at his limits.

Jim Grant, when he accompanied Speke, was a good companion: quiet, hard-working, and filled with deference for the more experienced hunter. Late in August one year they were both relieved of barracks and parade duty to make another trip into the mountains. Within sight of the great cloud that was Annapurna, they pitched their camp in a high meadow at about ten thousand feet; the air was thin and gusty and that night a storm blew in, covering them with snow, so that they rolled their blankets together and slept in each other's arms. Speke nestled his face in Grant's soft beard, and in the morning, stirring themselves, brewing tea and preparing to move on, neither of them spoke of it. On another day, Grant stripped and bathed in a mountain stream. He had a round, seemingly unmuscled body that, nevertheless, always seemed tirelessly capable at any task or exercise; his hair and beard were soft brown, and his gaze, deep and dark, flashed with intelligence. As he bathed that morning, he saw Speke watching him. Later, they were both uneasy. Speke, worried that his curse had been detected or guessed at, became sour-tempered.

"Damn, you've got to cook more food!" he snapped at Grant.

"Sorry, here, take mine. I've had plenty."

"I drink no spirits, I smoke nothing, but I eat heavily. Especially when I'm hunting! And I don't want *your* food! I want more of my own to start!"

In the end, Speke went on his journeys alone. On that long effort into Tibet, he entered a trance of silence and strength: up and up, on and on, willful, and almost inebriated of the climb and that maze of mountains. By the last days, he felt sure that some important kill awaited him: he would get one of the big rams or perhaps even a snow leopard, he decided. Something was up there.

The last village was like all the others: mud huts, goats, wide-eyed children, odors of spicy foods, pariah dogs, fires banked with stones, the women in their red wraps, the shrine, bags of grain and water jars on the roofs. He found a little tea house overlooking a ravine and paid for a table in the corner, where he slept the night. In the morning the old woman brought him tea and a strip of dried meat for breakfast.

By noon he had ascended into the high pass where thousands of hailstones lay unmelted. A carpet of glistening ice balls: they cracked underfoot and gave him a feeling that he had entered another dimension—the land of death itself. Was it the country, he wondered, all travelers truly wanted to visit?

Soon he was in the crevice of the mountain: a series of narrow paths surrounded by rock walls that gave him a dizzying sense of claustrophobia. He could see nothing except the next curve in the path; hard, wet stone all around, and above his head just a thin opening revealing a cold and unreachable sky. Then he felt it: something was stalking him. A big cat, perhaps, but something pitiless and deadly. For a moment he stopped and listened to the driving thump of his own heartbeat and his labored breath. A coldness at his center: colder than the rock beneath his fingers. Impulsively, he leaned his rifle against the wall of stone and went on without it; the path narrowed into a tunnel, so that his shoulders scraped its sides. Something knew his presence, something cold and terrible. He covered his eyes with his hands and allowed the walls to guide him forward on the path; blind and fumbling his way along, his mouth dry with fear, he would not look ahead.

He went on like this—hands over his eyes, unarmed, terrified—until the rock walls narrowed so he couldn't pass. Now he waited for the painful, final blow. He waited in his own cold darkness, but nothing happened. At last, his body drained of nerve, he backed out. He found his rifle and hurried away.

He had seen it: the land where there is only a blank numbness of spirit. He had visited this place before in Somerset, in his barracks, in those moments of the kill when his aim had been true, in the silences of himself. Now he had been to the top of the world in a maze of cloud and rock to see it once again: the final, bleak solitude. If he had samsara or karma, he knew, this was it.

For two days the caravan waited as Speke's fever boiled over into loud hallucinations in which he called out names and gritted his teeth in fright. Then he managed to sit on his donkey once again, so Sidi Bombay could lead him along the path.

That day they came across an entire caravan that had died: Arab masters, their slaves, animals, porters, everyone. Skeletons of slaves with their necks still linked by rope lay like a grisly bracelet of bone alongside the path; beneath the soft folds of the Arab cloaks, meanwhile, thousands of ants were at their meal.

"Pox!" the porters whispered among themselves as they hurried by.

Speke turned his eyes away. His dreams were bad enough.

It was September in the highlands now, as they passed through a series of more prosperous native villages. In the giant oaks and sycamores tribesmen had hung beehive logs, mud packed into each end, and the caravan bought the tasty honey from these hives and ate it with butter and milk from the farms.

One day the caravan joined its camp with a small Arab caravan on its way down to Zanzibar. The Arab leader was Isa bin Hijj, an ivory trader whom Speke ignored and whom Burton found warm, intelligent, and gentlemanly.

"True, you are approaching the feared land of Ugogo," the merchant told them. "But we had no trouble passing through. There is drought, so prices are high. But war or attack, no, I don't think so."

"The porters and askaris talk of nothing else," Burton said.

"I predict that you'll easily pass through Ugogo and arrive at Unyanyembe. In the last famine, tribes from everywhere came to live together at Unyanyembe. It became a trading center and outside it, on a hill, is the Arab settlement we call Kazeh."

"And beyond that? Have you seen the inland seas?"

"When I was a boy I came across the desert in a caravan. We traveled for two years. Once, we passed a great body of water—called simply nyanza, or lake, by the natives. But I'm not sure where this was. Now, I go between Kazeh and Zanzibar with my ivory. I've heard stories, but no one travels north from Kazeh. I suppose there are lakes, yes, many miles north."

The merchant was in need of trading goods and food because many of his porters had deserted, and those who remained were needed to transport his ivory. Burton agreed to sell him a few bolts of cloth, a bag of beads, and some coils of wire.

"When you arrive at Kazeh, you will stay in my empty house," Isa bin Hijj affirmed. "My friend Snay bin Amir, who is very rich, will attend your needs while you rest. I suggest you stay several months and recover your health before attempting to travel north to the lakes."

"You are very kind," Burton said.

That night Isa bin Hijj called together Said bin Selim, the Jemadar, Sidi Bombay, and the leaders of the porters in order to curse and shame them.

"You are lazy!" he told them. "If you were in my caravan, I would have you whipped! Each night you should make fires, draw water, and build fences around your camp! You should see to the comfort of your masters—who are very sick with fever! But you look only to yourselves! You live and behave like pigs!"

The men only grumbled in reply.

After this, the merchant began a series of trades with the askaris and porters, including one doubtful transaction: he sold two women into Burton's caravan. Speke considered this an outrage, but since he spoke no Arabic could complain only to Burton. As quickly as the two women became properties of their new and eager masters, disruptions began—and Burton seemed to become interested in observing sexual nature running rampant, although his fever kept him from entering the intrigues. One woman, Zawada, was calm, indifferent, and a bit sullen. The other, however, was named Don't Know and was clearly a match for the big, strong porter who bought her. That night they fought so that nobody in camp could sleep. Their copulations were dogfights. And, by morning, Don't Know had given her new master a number of rivals.

"This is ridiculous," Speke told Burton as they prepared to leave camp the next morning.

"Yes, it certainly is."

Speke stiffened himself and presented a piece of paper. "A list of needed medicines," he said. "We'll die of our fever if we don't get more quinine. Perhaps your Arab friend will arrange to send some up from Zanzibar."

"Good, thank you," Burton said. "Yes, I'll write him a check on the Bombay bank. I believe we can trust him to send medicines."

"And the mail, too," Speke said, his mouth beginning to quiver. He seemed about to faint or weep—Burton couldn't tell which. "I'd like some mail. I've been thinking about my family. I'd like—" His voice broke.

"Yes, Jack, of course," Burton said. "The mail, too. I'll have him see to it."

Soon after this they began their ascent of the narrow, rocky path of the Ruhebo Mountains, which preceded the land of Ugogo. The path was so steep that neither Burton nor Speke could ride their donkeys; delay followed delay, and the climb became torture. When Speke passed out, falling in the chalky dust, Burton ordered the porters to rig a hammock, but they refused. "God damn you! Pick up this man, or I'll shoot you!" he bellowed, but their fatigue was so complete that they could defy his strongest threats. For a moment, everything reeled. Burton stood beside the fallen Speke, calling for help. A donkey slid down the path, fell, and broke its leg. As it did so, a bag of shiny red and blue beads showered everywhere, as if some insane celebration had begun. At last, Sidi Bombay and Mabruki grabbed Speke up, supported him, and endeavored to climb.

The climb took six hours. At the top, Speke seemed in a coma: his eyes watery and glazed, his tongue dry, his lips trying to form words, his fever raging. Burton felt sure that death was near.

They assembled their camp in a pine grove at an altitude of 5,700 feet in a breeze that was suddenly cold. Their fever and fatigue made them argumentative and lent a kind of desperation to every movement. Their water supply was low. Burton announced that they would stay two nights on the summit, but porters and askaris shouted at him, saying they intended to go on. Speke, clearly, couldn't be moved, but Burton felt disoriented, too weak and exhausted to argue.

"We know our duty and we will move on!" the Jemadar stated, pointing a finger toward the heavens. "We will not be stopped!" His testimony seemed ludicrous and illogical, so that Burton, without answering, fell down on his bedding, half covered himself, and closed his eyes.

That night Speke, delirious, sat up in his blankets and waved his pistol as he jabbered nonsense. Burton, burning with his own fever, got up and wrenched the weapon away from his companion. In the heavy, dark mist falling around them, Burton could see that many of the porters had already left camp and that others were tying their loads and preparing to depart.

"Wait! Don't go!" he called to everyone, but each man was just a shadow, misty and silent, and the caravan was obviously on the move. The next morning Sidi Bombay and Mabruki again carried Speke in a hammock while Burton shuffled alongside it; late afternoon had arrived before the four of them caught up with the others.

They arrived during a battle.
Swords flashed, curses were spat out, cudgels waved in the air.
Sidi Bombay's eyes were wide with fright, but Burton's assessment prevailed: yes, there were warriors from some tribe and, yes, the askaris had their

swords drawn and, yes, there was considerable noise, but all was well. Without so much as drawing his weapons, Burton lengthened his stride and walked into camp, demanding in a loud voice that he needed water, Warburg Drops, his bedding, lantern, and books.

Several Wakhutu warriors, spears pumping, screamed and pointed. They were frightfully painted, so the askaris were afraid of them; but on the other hand, the askaris rattled with rifles, sabers, daggers, and cudgels, so the natives were equally afraid of them.

Speke was brought in, unconscious, and placed beside his tent, which had not yet been raised.

Burton, without looking directly at the fray, overheard its principal arguments: the warriors wanted to keep the porters who might suffer smallpox out of their village; someone had a quantity of liquor that was not being shared; someone else had stolen a brass pot; someone else had offended a woman of the tribe.

"Please," Burton called to them. He said this with royal indifference.

It disappointed everyone that the fracas would not have a judge who would seek out injustice, reward the innocent, punish the guilty, and provide an audience. Before long all their arguments ended and the caravan collapsed into silence. Soon everyone was asleep and the night was filled with restless and profound snoring.

They rested for one day and two nights, while Speke emerged from his stupor. Burton drank half a bottle of brandy during this pause, which made him violently dizzy, but after a few hours he actually felt stronger and joined the men at the main campfire. Usually the local tribesmen would squat at the outskirts of the camp at night, out there in the darkness beyond the flickering fires, as the porters ate and the white men spoke their curious words. When camp was struck and everyone left the next morning, the tribesmen would usually come looking for scraps of food, bits of string, empty cartridges, anything. But on this night *bangi* was smoked and some Wasagara tribesmen, bolder than usual and talkative, sat with the strangers and exchanged stories and legends.

One man told of a giant hole many miles wide—a crater, Burton decided —filled with all the creatures of the earth and containing a lake adorned with thousands of flamingos. Near this place, the tribesman went on, was the mountain where God lived, the tree where man was born, and a hole in the sky.

Another tribesman, who had seemed more than mildly interested in Don't Know and the other woman of the caravan, told of a tall, long-legged blond woman who ruled an army of fierce warriors. It was well known, he said, that she was the most beautiful woman in the world.

There were men in these parts who became leopards after dark, said another. This assertion was argued not because others thought it untrue, but because they knew the Leopard Men lived elsewhere—near their home villages.

Burton mentioned King Solomon's Mines.

His grandfather told him of a mountain so high, said another, that its snows reflected starlight.

There is a bird of many colors that lures men from their homes, Sidi Bombay added with a smile. A man will follow this bird forever without catching it.

On the downslope of the mountain valley they could see the wide Ugogo Plain: scrubby bush, scorched grass, withered cane stubbles, the beginnings of a raw, barren country. Speke's pace was slow and wobbly on the descending trail, and he spoke to no one. Burton felt well enough to worry over the supplies and spoke to Said bin Selim about them.

"I made a check of the loads this morning and I estimate we've used up a year's supply of trading goods in only three months," he said.

"At Unyanyembe we will be joined by an escort of twenty-two porters —the ones you left in Zanzibar," Said bin Selim said with perfect Arab confidence. "Allah is all-knowing. The caravan *will* come."

Burton found such fatalism infectious and ceased to worry.

In the next days they met a series of village chiefs who demanded extravagant *honga*, or tribute, for the passage of the caravan, but Burton found himself being generous. One chief demanded six porter-loads, but settled for twenty cloths, thirty strings of coral beads, six feet of red broadcloth, and a coil of brass wire.

Both Burton and Speke began to recover slightly each day from their last bouts of fever, and all went well until a porter was attacked by a swarm of bees. He ran screaming off the trail, and later that day, when he was found and brought back to the caravan, which had traveled several miles, it was learned that he had lost his load in fleeing the attack. Even then there wasn't much concern until Burton learned what the load contained.

"All the books and writing supplies?"

"Yes, master, sorry," the porter whimpered, expecting a flogging. "I ran into a ravine, trying to escape the bees. As you can see, I have many stings. My eyes, see, are slits. I ran looking for water, dropping my load. But the streams were all dry. Then my eyes were blinded and—"

"Yes, yes," Burton said, and he felt a deep depression coming on. As the porter whined and explained, Burton walked off to his tent. He sat by himself for two hours as twilight turned into darkness, then he smoked some *bangi*, drank some brandy, swallowed a Warburg Drop, and went to sleep.

Speke, in his tent, thought of Oliphant.

It must be grand to live in the full glare of daylight like Lowry, he felt, where one's curses and vices are mere ornaments on one's accomplishments. No one would ever be concerned that Lowry drank too much, waved his handkerchief too much, boasted of his travels, gazed on everything with contempt, or used his wit to do injury. He was, after all, modestly rich. And he was a gifted writer and correspondent who was invited to the best homes and knew everyone.

I would like to go to Paris with Lowry, Speke told himself. I would like us to be seen laughing together on the boulevards. Or I would like Lowry to come into a restaurant—no, some late-night cabaret—and a curtain would draw back on the stage and I would be there, posing, say, in one of those classical tableaux with my muscles displayed, my body flexed, my hair illuminated in spotlight. Why not? And afterward I would like us to drink absinthe while he said amusing things, making everyone laugh while I kept my silence, looking very handsome, very muscled and strong.

In the sunny glare of such a life, Speke decided, one's vices are hardly noticeable eccentricities.

The Greek isles. That swim to the boat.

If I were in London and had this terrible fever, I would invent some idle, comic remark about it.

After days of tiresome marching across the Ugogo Plain, the caravan stopped at the Ziwa, a shallow pool and dirty oasis, where more tribute was paid to various tribal representatives who appeared every hour. Food from the villages was plentiful once the *honga* was paid, but the men became restless, quarrelsome, and unpleasant as the stop lasted for four days.

Speke, Burton noted, hardly acknowledged anyone's presence, as if he had completely drawn into himself. Said bin Selim and his porters were fighting. Then, from the south, a large Arab caravan appeared, led by Said Mohammed: several female slaves and concubines, pillows, poultry in wicker cages, medicines, numerous *fundi*, or managing men, healthy male slaves, colored tents, pipes.

They also had in their possession Burton's load of writing materials and books, which they had found near the main path. He was overjoyed and made a speech of thanks that seemed to amuse—and tire—the Arab leader.

That night as they ate and shared the fire, Said Mohammed, who was a thin, ascetic man with a goatee, suggested that they join their caravans. "It will help you crossing the desert," he said. "We know the places to stop. I have traded many times with all these chiefs."

"Delighted," Burton said, and his gaze moved toward the small night fires where a dozen female blacks, some of them with magnificent undulations, sat talking among themselves. He was definitely feeling stronger. And since the comforts of this caravan were so obvious, he meant to partake of them.

After the caravans joined, Burton discovered that Said Mohammed and his colleagues reached the villages first, always claimed the superior places to pitch their tents, and consistently made the most advantageous trades. Even so, having company was a relief. Speke remained ill-humored about everything. Was it the Arabs and their slaves? The sexual activity? The lack of organization in the journey? Just his illness? Burton was tired of guessing, so gladly spent his evenings with the Arabs. Said Mohammed's brother, as it turned out, was married to the daughter of Fundikira, Sultan of Unyanyembe, too, so this lent their travel a nearly official status.

The Wagogo natives, Burton found, were lively and more inquisitive than others they had passed. One old man had been to Zanzibar and actually knew a few sentences of Hindustani. One chief asked about *uzungu*: the land of the white man near the edge of the world.

"Is it true," he asked Burton, "that there are beads underground in your land?"

"No, the white man has machines for making beads," Burton explained. "Machines. Like the rifle."

The old chief wore an uncomprehending stare, yet asked another question. "And there at the edge of the world: what does the white man see over the edge? Only more stars?"

"Yes, more stars," Burton said. "Nothing else."

The askaris, the Sons of Ramji, the porters, Said bin Selim, the Jemadar, and Sidi Bombay all feared the Wagogo and expected bloodshed every moment. But Said Mohammed told Burton, "Have no fear. The warriors in these parts have an inflated reputation. Perhaps one hundred years ago they murdered some poor Warori, who live to the southwest. This victory is still celebrated in their songs. Legend has become myth. Now the Wagogo are bullies—they even believe in their power. But they have no recent victories, and in my opinion they are lacking in true courage."

Deep in Ugogo territory they met the most powerful of the chiefs, Magomba. He had little interest in another Arab caravan, but asked to gaze on Burton and Speke. When the caravan stopped near his village and the white men lingered too long to suit him, he came in person to stand before Burton's tent: a black, wrinkled elder with corkscrews of grey hair. He wore a greasy loincloth and his body was covered with an oily sheen. He spat his foul tobacco everywhere.

"You will give me five cloths," he commanded Burton.

"Indeed, yes, I will be happy to do so," Burton said, smiling.

"With names!"

"What?"

"Each cloth shall be different and shall have a name!"

"Yes, of course," Burton replied, and he presented Magomba with a few measures of imprecisely named cloth: calico, paisley, plaid, rainbow, and polka dot. This last cloth, he claimed, was named after a famous white man's dance, the polka, which was performed in regions where snow covered the ground, women wore wooden shoes, and wine was plentiful.

Magomba spat and smiled. He seemed extremely impressed.

As the next days passed, Burton entered only sparse notes in his diary. These, he hoped, he would eventually convert into an engaging travel book. He would write it, he decided, in France—sitting on the terrace of a villa, say, as the Mediterranean glistened in the distance. Among his notes in this mid-October period he wrote:

—Speke down with fever again. Sitting all day under a calabash tree.

—large down caravan arrives led by Abdullah bin Nasib, who gives us a goat and some measures of fine Unyanyembe rice.

—a labyrinth of elephant tracks in the soft red earth.

—another chief, Maguru, is "sitting upon *pombe*" his ministers announce, so cannot visit with us. In short, he is too drunk.

—tzetse, swarms of bees, and gadflies.

—a rough, thorny, waterless jungle. Many deserters now. Only five donkeys still alive of the thirty we brought from the coast and bought at Zungomero.

—into the land of Uyanzi, leaving Ugogo. Everyone fighting over loads. A great desert and elephant ground, now, called Mgunda Mk'hali, or, by the Arabs, the Fiery Field. Eight days march across this expanse. More of those curious outcroppings of rock.

—several boxes of ammunition and all our bullet moulds are lost.

—another day's trek and the earth begins to darken. Red clay turning into black soil once more.

—everyone's strength ebbing back. Tonight, around the fires and in the shadows beyond, a number of loud copulations.

—last day of October, 1857. We pass a series of dirty villages as we enter the district of Unyamwezi. Children run alongside us, calling out. Speke off on his first hunting expedition in many days, walking into a nearby swamp where he shoots a fine ruddy goose.

"Your head porter tells me that none of his men will follow you toward the Sea of Ujiji," Said Mohammed told Burton.

"Said bin Selim is weary. Everyone will rest at Kazeh, then go north to the Sea of Ujiji," Burton replied with confidence. They sat on cushions beside the fire, having finished a dinner of goose and rice. Burton drank brandy, while the Arab sucked at his water pipe.

"The Sea of Ujiji lies *west* of Kazeh," said the Arab. "Due west through a miserable swamp where there are no trails. No one goes there."

"There is no great sea north of Kazeh?"

"Perhaps. I've heard stories of one. But Ujiji lies west."

Burton went to Speke's tent with this bit of news before retiring for the night. Speke was lying on his bedding, arms behind his head, staring out at nothing. The sextant and an overripe banana lay beside him.

"Well, our orders from the Royal Geographical Society plainly state that we should investigate the Sea of Ujiji," Speke reminded his leader.

"Quite so. Ujiji was the only name known in London or Cairo. But there must be two or more inland seas."

"To put a fine point on it, our orders declare that we should investigate Ujiji, then, if possible, other inland lakes or seas. Correct?"

"Yes, but we've always thought Ujiji sits north of Kazeh," Burton said. "But there's no way of judging an unmapped interior. One must go and find out. And, by the way, Mohammed says the porters won't go with us. He's heard them grumbling about a mutiny."

"They should be lashed," Speke said. "The whole caravan needs discipline."

"Of a military sort, you mean?"

"Precisely."

"My experience is that military discipline is a great comedy in Africa," Burton stated. "As it goes, our porters have deserted almost daily—two more this week. Personally, I believe that if we had shown any real severity they would have stolen everything and departed long ago."

"Your Arab friends whip their porters," Speke said.

"Their porters are slaves. Perhaps our useless porters and askaris should get their pay docked. They've already stolen much more than we agreed to give them in cloth and beads. I can't see that we owe them their dollar a day."

"I'm for giving them lashes," Speke repeated.

"Go ahead. I'm too tired for such exercise myself," Burton said, and he gave his companion a tight smile and started out of the tent.

"You seem much too tired to conduct the business of a caravan," Speke said, having the last word.

The caravan, having passed through the thick Kigwa forest, moved alongside a series of rice fields in the Unyanyembe district and arrived at the Arab settlement of Kazeh. As they entered the settlement, the men, dressed in their finest clothes, sounded horns and fired off rifles while, in turn, the native women called out the familiar African lulliloo and the children lined their path to smile and wave. All around were tiny lush farms crisscrossed by rivulets of sweet water and a countryside marked by low hills, soft grass, and immense mango trees. Beyond the native village lay the Arab settlement: familiar plaster buildings and architecture, enclosed courtyards surrounded by thick walls, studded Zanzibar doors, lawns planted with flowers and adorned with crude stone benches. Burton saw a cluster of Arabs and gave them the Moslem salutation.

Among them was the leader of Kazeh: Snay bin Amir, a Harisi Arab, who accepted Burton's letters from Zanzibar.

"On the path we met Isa bin Hijj, who generously offered his house here in Kazeh," Burton added.

"I will provide a much larger and better house," Snay bin Amir said, folding the packet of letters into his tunic. He was a man of obvious ceremony, each gesture conducted in an impressively slow movement. "I will also send your caravan two goats and two bullocks. We also have limes, vegetables, coffee, and a few of the amenities I'm sure you'll enjoy. Our settlement is yours. After our feast this evening, you will see that we are determined to surpass all others in every generosity."

Burton glanced at Speke, who seemed relieved, yet not impressed.

"We do not wish to burden you, sire," Burton replied, being very impressed himself.

"No burden. It will be my pleasure to spend each evening with you," Snay bin Amir said, smiling. "You have much to learn. But so do I. The soul of life in these parts is conversation, so I intend for us to enjoy one another."

Speke and Burton were shown to an impressively large house standing beside two mango trees. The water well was in a grove of palm trees. Around the inner courtyard of the house were kitchens, storage rooms, and servants' quarters. Heavy mahogany beams crossed the ceilings of the inner rooms, and thick walls cooled the air; across the front of the house was a wide verandah supported by pillars, and there, on an assortment of pillows, woven mats, and rugs, all conversations, meals, prayers, and business were conducted.

"Dirt floors," Speke noted, viewing his quarters. "There's probably vermin."

"We'll fix that," Burton replied, and after their Arab hosts had departed to prepare the night's feast, he ordered Sidi Bombay to set off piles of gunpowder in each room so that it would be smoked and purged. After this, the house was swept and loads were delivered—all valuables being stacked in the living quarters for safekeeping. Burton walked around with a look of contentment; he liked the prospect of staying with Snay bin Amir, recovering, reading, and conversing about the next leg of the journey. Speke, of course, was already anxious to leave, but his fever lingered and the bivouac was as necessary for him as for Burton.

Snay bin Amir's house was set inside a maze of garden walls. Essentially a fortress, it wore a deceptive landscape of flowers, shrubs, and cascades of vine.

That night Speke fell asleep before the main courses were served. Since he spoke neither Arabic nor Swahili, he couldn't share the conversation, and after devouring a single holcus biscuit and sipping some tea, he lay back and closed his eyes while Burton and Snay bin Amir discussed the trip to Ujiji.

"You must let me help," the Arab said. "Our rainy season will come very soon, so the swamps west of here will be difficult. You will have no paths. Few villages. But you can manage if you heed good advice."

They sat on pillows between two overflowing ferns eating omelets, pilaf, goat's meat, plantains, sweet potatoes, cucumbers, onions, and *firni*—a kind of rice pudding—from plates of engraved Indian brass. Two veiled women, both concubines, served their food, including additional onions at the end of the meal, which Snay bin Amir said was beneficial to one's general health.

"Health is the great worry here," he said. "If a man is immune from sickness two successive months, he can truly boast. No one enjoys robust health. Death lurks in insect bites, pricks on the fingers, and small catastrophes. You will learn to eat only twice each day, for instance, and never in the evenings, except on such special occasions as this. I have heard that we are approximately twenty marches from the Sea of Ujiji. You should make the journey in twenty-five days, but take care of your body. It is your real enemy."

"Is there another sea to the north?" Burton asked.

"Yes, probably. But I know only rumors and stories and exaggerations."

"No caravans come here from that direction?"

"In the old days, yes. Caravans began in the land of our fathers, crossed the desert, and came heavily armed into these districts to take slaves. But now we have settled here. The chiefs sell us their enemies or their own people. There is no need for dangerous desert crossings. If my companions want to enter the trade, they sail to Zanzibar and we arrange for them to have a house here with us. Slaves and ivory are transported, then, only between here and the coast."

"So you have no idea how far the northern nyanza might be?"

"No, but I know of a black kingdom to the north stronger than any caravan. Its lord is Mutesa. Some of his exiled people have migrated here. They speak of his gold, his armies, and blood sacrifices. I believe them."

"And have you heard of the Mountains of the Moon?"

"Again, only rumor. No Arab of the true faith, you understand, has ever brought us reliable word. I should certainly like to see mountains covered with snow."

"You must teach me all you know about these parts," Burton said.

"We will dine together every day and talk," replied Snay bin Amir. "And if I may say this without offense, you require help with your caravan. This afternoon we gave your porters and askaris other vacant houses. With your generous allowance they can buy goats, sheep, and fowl—luxuries they never enjoyed at Zanzibar. Yet, they are an ungrateful lot. They complain that both you, their master, and we, their hosts, are meager and stingy."

"Their stupidity and greed is without question," Burton answered. "Allow me to—hmm, how shall I say? To properly arrange matters."

"Thy threats are undoubtedly fearsome," Burton said, smiling. "But their laziness and ingratitude is also a fearsome thing to behold."

West of Kazeh lay the village of Unyanyembe, and westward beyond that was a glade of wild mimosa, low thorn trees, and shady mango where the slaves were kept. They were far enough from the Arab settlement so that no one could hear their moans, smell their waste, or witness their daily agonies. Around the valley was a low, thick fence of thorn and bramble patrolled by armed servants who were, in turn, watched over by Arab sentries. Inside that thorny fence, or *boma*, were dozens of lean-to huts made of sticks and tattered cloth; crowded among the huts were cooking fires, ditches filled with feces and buzzing flies; hundreds of blacks moved in a daze of infirmity.

Speke walked over to a hillside overlooking the *boma* and gazed down into this human cattle pen.

Afterward, he was so angry that he couldn't speak to either Burton or Snay bin Amir. Arab slavers, he felt, were barbaric creatures who practiced a veneer of religious and social manners. Burton, who seemed to be enjoying all the Arab amenities in Kazeh, was somehow even worse. Speke found he could in no way accommodate himself to it all.

On the verandah of their house two women prepared dinner for Burton, setting up a small charcoal brazier and cooking a dish of finely shredded roast beef—called *bokoboko* in Kiswahili—and then serving him as he lay on a stack of pillows inside his room. Burton shifted himself on the pillows, drank brandy, studied more verb conjugations, and watched the movements of the women as they worked. After dinner a crude little orchestra assembled itself: two drummers, a lute player, and a gnarled hunchback who produced sounds from an old biscuit tin that had been converted into an instrument with the attachment of two tightly strung wires.

After a few minutes of music the youngest of the cooks went into Burton's room and closed the door. Speke had emerged from his room by this time to observe the source of the noise.

"The cook," he said to one of the drummers. "I want my supper now." He spoke in English, so there was no communication except his authoritative tone. The drummer shrugged and continued pounding away; his eyes rolled back in his head, and he smiled as if in ecstasy. Speke addressed the hunchback, enunciating carefully—yet without the least communication. In frustration, he pointed toward Burton's closed door, repeating, "Supper! My *supper!*"

The little black hunchback, confused as to the nature of the command, began acting out what he supposed Speke wanted to know. His deformed body began a swaying dance punctuated by obscene bumps. His fist formed a version of the penis, growing and swelling as his dance became more specific; his legs parted, his hips rolled, and he lowered himself, slowly and rhythmically, onto his little fist. As Speke looked on, the hunchback accomplished an elaborate pantomime of a particular copulation. Clearly, the concubine in Burton's room was skilled in a dance in which she impaled herself on the erect male member. The musicians howled with laughter when Speke said, "No, eat; I want to *eat!*" and pointed into his gaping mouth, which caused them to howl even harder. At last, Speke understood, but he was not amused.

Long after he retired, feeling hungry and peculiarly foolish, Speke listened to the crude music. The little black hunchback was still out there on the verandah, having created and established a successful comedy routine, bumping and thrusting in his dance.

As the days passed, Burton studied the history of this curious Arab slave encampment in the middle of the wilderness.

During a famine once, long ago, tribes from all over East Africa had migrated here because of the abundance of mango trees—which provided food. *Unyanyembe* meant Place of Many Mangoes. The tribe of this region, he learned, was the Wanyamyenze—from the same basic root word. But there were other tribes who had come here, including a remnant of the coastal Watusi. From these people came the other name for the place, *Kazeh.* During that terrible drought and famine, Burton learned, the Watusi women and children had journeyed here; then, later, their chief and warrior husbands had followed. On the occasion of the men's arrival, the Watusi women had lined up, clapped their hands, and chanted, "Kazeh! Kazeh!"—their greeting for returning hunters or great heroes. The word eventually became associated with the Arab settlement not far from the village. As more and more distant tribes arrived during this time of famine, smaller villages and camps grew up, such as Tabora, meaning potato, which was a village of mixed tribes to the south along the Kwihara road.

Fundikira, the chief of the entire region, was a salaried employee of Snay bin Amir. The day Burton went over to pay him a visit and to deliver a present of tobacco, the old man squatted on the ground, his bony knees sticking up, his penis dragging in the dust. He had been playing a game of *bao,* and beside his crusty feet were the familiar rows of holes dug in the earth and filled with worn pebbles.

The chief spoke in lists and sequences, as if reciting items in numbers increased the intelligence of a conversation.

He recited the names of all the Unyanyembe chiefs before him. He named a number of trees, including the wild poinsettia, the candelabrum, and the beautiful *nsongoma*, whose leaves were used in making dye for cloth. He named many things that cursed a man throughout his days: a talkative woman, a mosquito, diarrhea, death in a place far distant from home. But the sequence that Burton found most curious concerned how a lion eats a man.

"When a lion kills a man," Fundikira said, his eyes glazed as he peered off into the distance, "he will eat, in order, the buttocks, the backs of the thighs, the flesh of the upper arms, and then, sometimes, as a final delicacy, the face and tongue."

That evening the rains came, and Burton sat by himself before his little charcoal brazier on the porch of his house. In an hour or so, he would get up and walk through the mud to Snay bin Amir's, where they would drink brandy, tell stories, and recite Scripture to one another, but for the present he felt alone, poetic, and oddly sad. Life devours a man, too, he was thinking, and it eats, in order, his muscles and strength, his restless heart, and, then, as a last delicacy, his brain. The brain lasts longest, though: it gathers its lists, it pulses with a last dim light, it knows almost more than it wants to know, then flickers and goes out.

The porters and askaris, according to the Jemadar, would not travel on to the Sea of Ujiji. A year had passed, he claimed, and the men should be paid and permitted to return to their homes in Zanzibar.

"We've been gone seven months, not a year," Burton argued with him. "And you won't get paid a penny unless you continue."

"Besides, the lakes are not there."

"You know bloody well the lakes are there."

"If the men aren't paid, they'll desert you," the Jemadar asserted.

"Will they? And will they go without money or food on the return trip? And will they face their shame?"

The argument went on for days while Speke counted the stores. Supplies were low, so Speke worried a great deal. He spoke sharply to natives and Arabs alike (they understood only his dour expression), and when he was completely frustrated he went hunting. It was a cold, rainy summer. At the end of each day's hunt Speke came back to their verandah, his hair in blond ringlets over his eyes.

When neither Burton nor Speke seemed able to organize the caravan to Ujiji, Snay bin Amir took charge. He lectured the porters on their duty and cursed them for wasting food and ammunition; he put his own slaves to work stringing beads for trading—a chore Burton's porters considered too demeaning; and when porters couldn't be hired, Snay bin Amir arranged for additional supplies to be sent along later, when they arrived from the coast.

"But *will* they arrive?" Speke demanded of Burton.

"My companion is agitated," Burton told Snay bin Amir.

"If supplies fail to arrive," the Arab said, "I'll make up a small relief column. And, by the way, would you like a few women? I can spare some."

"I feel my fever coming back," Burton said. "So, no, thank you, I don't suppose a woman will do me much good."

"The swamps are chilly," Snay bin Amir argued. "I say you should pillow yourself on a nice hot breast."

The day came when Speke took charge of half of the caravan and began the journey westward toward Ujiji. He had been out hunting every day, getting his stride back, and felt much stronger and more ready than Burton to go; he also felt irritated by Burton's delays, uneven health, and prolonged enjoyment of Kazeh and its women. Finally, when Speke insisted on departing, he had his way—Burton agreeing to catch up.

Speke took command of half the caravan, then, barked orders—which Sidi Bombay translated and softened as he relayed them along to the porters—and got underway in the early afternoon. "Never fear," he told Burton, somehow more jolly in command than in his usual secondary role.

"I don't worry at all, Jack," Burton told him. "See you shortly."

"I hope your fever's better," Speke said, but in a tone suggesting the opposite, as if he hoped Burton wouldn't quite be able to follow.

That night Burton decided on following immediately and sent word to Snay bin Amir that they should have a last dinner together.

At dark he went over to Snay's house for an early pipe and they became sentimental. For weeks now they had shared the pipe, maps, women, meals, jokes, theologies, and dozens of stories, but their prospects of seeing each other again were poor, especially if Burton did succeed in finding the source of the Nile, so that he could trace it northward toward Egypt and home.

They ate a small meal, drank some brandy, and passed the pipe back and forth again. A sweet vapor hung above the cushions where they reclined, and from the window came the sounds of that endless, cold summer drizzle.

"Friendship is such an oddity," Burton mused. "Why is it that you and I were such trusting friends from the beginning?"

"Oh, a certain humor and cynicism," the Arab offered. "Truly, I don't know. It is true, though: some men are compatible."

"Pity, but Speke and I aren't," Burton said.

"A true pity," Snay agreed. "You put your life into the hands of a man who talks little, worries much, angers easily, and has no humor whatsoever."

"My life is in my own hands," Burton assured him.

They took deep inhalations from the pipe.

"Ah, me, I shall miss thee." Snay sighed. "And I fear you will be the victim of many temperamental fates: your friend, the swamps, the weather, your health, and perhaps a number of Allah's whimsies."

"I'll take great care," Burton promised.

Heavy rains prevented Speke and the main body of the caravan from advancing, so that Burton and his party easily caught up with them at Yombo, a muddy little settlement where the natives stood in the downpour asking for tobacco and the Arabs, again, offered everything they had.

"Beyond this point is the *msene*," their Arab host explained to them. "It's a rather pleasant plain. But then you will reach the swamps. The rest of your journey to Ujiji—well, hmm, I think you will consider coming back here to my house many times."

In a bothersome drizzle the next morning they started out in small groups, each one more sullen than the last. By evening, though, they had reached a flat land of huge palmyras and sycamores whose leaves rattled gently in a cooling breeze. Scattered huts, like bird's nests, lay around the countryside.

On Christmas Day of 1857, then, they came to the house of another Arab who called himself the Simba. He was a muscled man with a nagging cough who lived apart from others in this westward outpost, who seemed indifferent to slaving or money, less refined, yet as gracious as any of their other hosts. His *tembe* was constructed out of those hardwoods from the plain, notched and put together so that it resembled an American fort built to withstand an attack by feathered Indians. The Simba provided meat, honey, and milk for their Christmas feast, and Burton, assuming the role of holiday cook, prepared a sirloin of beef.

"You seem emotional about Christmas," the Simba remarked, watching Speke's eyes.

"I'm emotional about sirloin of beef," Speke replied, and they laughed until the big Arab began coughing and had to sit holding his head.

After the meal Burton and the host smoked a little *bangi* and they talked about their childhood holiday memories. Speke talked about Jordans at length, and the Simba, who understood English, nodded his head, coughed, smoked the pipe, and gave his young guest every attention. Toward the end of the evening they talked about the task ahead.

"Gather as many bags of rice as possible from our land here," the Simba told them. "There is no more westward. The water is also no good. And if you have a bit of fever, count on it to grow worse."

"I take it our prospects are poor," Burton said, sucking on the pipe with a grin.

"Exceedingly," the Simba said. "Why would you want a map of Ujiji anyway?"

Burton explained that the maps of Africa were notoriously wrong. Then he gave the Simba a short introduction to the life and work of Jonathan Swift and quoted the poet's famous lines:

So Geographers in Afric-Maps
With Savage-Pictures fill their Gaps;
And o'er unhabitable Downs
Place Elephants for want of Towns.

"True, I have seen many stupid maps," the Simba said, laughing and coughing out a wisp of smoke.

"At the Sea of Ujiji," Burton asked, "is there a river at the north? Our great puzzle is whether a mighty river might flow out of the lake."

"I have seen a number of warriors, traders, mercenaries, and lost souls in my days at this village," the Simba replied. "They come and go. Some even went in the direction of Ujiji, though I never saw any of them again. I've talked to slaves and migrants who claimed to have seen the great water, but their stories bear little resemblance to one another. As I understand it, the journey is long and the result is no prize—a shoreline swarming with mosquitoes and strewn with dead fish. But who am I? A man who lives alone at the edge of a wilderness. So what do I know?"

"Why do you live out here?" Speke asked. "Why do you live apart from Kazeh and Yombo and the men of your race?"

The Simba smiled and coughed. "Every day I prefer several copulations," he answered. "It is my habit and I won't change."

Burton returned the Arab's smile. "But, surely, there are enough women among the slaves and concubines of Kazeh," he suggested.

"No, not really. My vice is that I lust after all available women. I get into trouble with husbands. Snay bin Amir cursed me for taking his favorite woman. I was falsely accused of raping one of Fundikira's daughters. My appetites are shameful. So I am in my own exile—trying to be satisfied with what is here."

"What is your usual number of copulations each day?" Burton inquired, his tone raised to a sort of scholarly detachment.

"Nine times daily," The Simba answered, laughing and coughing once more at the same time. "Preferably with nine different companions. Allah, please, continue thy benevolence! With the balance of my time I eat and pray. Sometimes, if my legs are strong enough, I walk outside—once around my *tembe.*"

Burton and the Arab shared a loud laugh. Speke, as if embarrassed by this subject again, kept his silence.

The maze of the swamp.

Each day the paths disappeared in an undergrowth of weed and bramble. Above, the indigo sky breathed down in humid vapors during the nights; one sweated through sleep, dreaming of vines, plumes, reeds, cacti, thorn, and endless stalks of wiry grass.

Porters began to disappear, and even Selim's own son became one of the deserters, leaving word that he had decided to find his way back to Kazeh.

When the rains started again, Sidi Bombay was missing.

"Have you seen him?" Burton asked the Jemadar.

"I believe he has fled," the Jemadar said haughtily, as if this were to be expected.

"Not Bombay," Burton answered, and he went looking for him in a tiny village of three huts in a stand of bamboo beside an overflowing stream.

He called among the huts, but received no answer.

"Hello!" Burton shouted, but the inhabitants had gone, leaving the area to the noisy, disheveled caravan. A few feet from the doorway of each hut the embers of a village fire hissed at the falling rain. Burton heard the sound of his own voice, as empty and as distant as a stranger's.

He looked inside the first of the huts at the meager remnants of life there: broken clay pots, soiled mats, an old Zanzibar trunk with its studs rusted and its buckle-type fastener broken.

At the next hut he peered in, trying to accustom his eyes to the dimness when a shadowy movement caught his attention. Seconds later he recognized the shape crouched and covered in a corner.

"Come on, my man," he beckoned, helping Sidi Bombay to his feet.

Wet and chilled, they trudged back through the tall grass toward the caravan. Neither of them spoke, though Burton assumed without asking questions that his servant had meant to hide until the rest of them had moved on. In the silence between them was a forgiveness Sidi Bombay appreciated.

The two Portuguese boys, Valentino and Cactano, could quickly form a lookout stance, the little Caetano jumping up on his companion's broader shoulders and peering out over as much of the marshland as he could possibly see. On occasion, they found trees tall enough to use as sentry stations, but Valentino, who did the climbing, gave often inaccurate views of what he surveyed. They tried to find proper spots along the rivers and streams for crossing, to avoid bogs, to keep their direction straight, but they were frequently lost in the crisscrossing paths and in a labyrinth of stagnant streams doubling back on themselves.

In the day there was rain. At night, a chilled wind kept them shivering. Their bedding was constantly wet, and Burton's writing materials and books turned into a mildewed pulp.

Sidi Bombay, penitent, slept at the opening to Burton's tent. The two Portuguese boys, Burton noted, had joined Speke in his tent during the nights.

Inside Speke's damp tent there were elaborate instructions—worked out in pantomime and a few words of English—on sleeping arrangements.

"Each evening," he explained to them, gesturing broadly, "you will spread our mat just so. We will wrap ourselves in these two blankets. Do not touch the sides of the tent or water will ooze in. If you are quiet and make preparations to suit me, you may sleep here with me. No smoking. No talking either."

The two boys nodded and smiled, comprehending some of these rules.

Speke took off his rough canvas pants—and spread these out carefully atop the blankets. The Portuguese boys observed his ritual and followed suit, so that all three of them slept naked from the waist down. Under the blankets, the boys giggled—undoubtedly happy with being out of the wetness—so that Speke had to shush them.

"Please," he said, when they tossed around too much.

Outside, the others were huddled around the fires. The Jemadar slept beneath the folding table. Mabruki, the slave, could burrow down in the ashes of a fire, so that everyone wondered why he didn't burn up. In the morning, he would rise up white and warm, letting the inevitable first shower wash his naked body clean before he dressed.

Speke slept fitfully with Caetano and Valentino. Once, he thought he heard them whispering. Another time he was sure they were quietly and gently fondling each other, so swatted at them with the back of his hand.

During their second night together Caetano suddenly rolled over, and his small, stiff penis pressed against Speke's bare thigh. Already awake, Speke held his breath, waited for further movement, and found that he couldn't possibly sleep. The object was definitely there, hard and soft and very annoying.

At the first light of day when Speke got up to find his trousers, Caetano stirred himself and got out from underneath the blankets, too. There it was: stiff and unruly. Yet the diminutive servant paid no attention to Speke's interest in the matter. Standing inside the tent and brushing out his hair with his fingers, Caetano yawned, stretched, and hung his own muslin pants on that stiff little member as if it were simply a convenient peg. After a moment, he removed his pants, slipped them on, then went outside to splash some water on his face.

After a march of several hours, Burton felt his fever returning. His legs gave way, so he sat down in the wet grass alongside the path and called for help until Speke came to his aid.

"My jackboots," he begged. "Pull them off."

Speke tried, but the boots seemed stuck.

"My legs are swelling. And they feel like they're on fire," Burton groaned.

"Shall I cut the boots with my knife?"

"No, they're my best walking boots. Pull hard. Do it!"

Speke took a firm grip, yanked hard until a boot came off, then saw that Burton had passed out from the pain.

By evening Burton was rolling in misery, unable to control his moaning, suffering chills and fever and clawing at his aching legs. Sidi Bombay boiled water and applied hot wrappings, but the treatment had no effect. Speke gave his patient a large quantity of quinine, but felt, somehow, that this was neither yellow jack nor malaria, but something far more exotic and deadly. The legs had swollen to twice their normal size, and more than anything else Burton seemed to need a heavy sedative.

"Jack, I think I'm going to die," he said, sweat pouring into his eyes. The campfire flickered around them. Burton's cries and writhings while lying outside his tent, were witnessed by all the porters and askaris who strolled by. Nobody gave him much chance.

"You must get through the night," Speke told him. "If you can't walk, we'll get you a litter. We'll carry you to Ujiji, if necessary."

Burton managed a smile, but had no hope. The leg muscles were tightly contracted and numbness had set in. This is the final agony, he told himself, and in his delirium he began to review his life and fate in a series of desperate emotions: he loved dear Speke who hovered above him, nursing him; he felt the poignant loss of Hamerton, and he missed both Edward and Steinhauser, wondering if he would ever see those great souls again; he regretted having not fucked Louisa Segraves and Isabel Arundell; he worried that his poetry would be mocked and laughed at; he saw himself with Milnes drinking sherry and discussing the history of the nude in the graphic arts; he saw Lumsden, good fellow, as he stood at the dock in Bombay with that elephant bedecked in brocade and spangles; he saw the faces of Arabs, those he had forgotten on the journey to Mecca; he heard Stroyan's hearty laughter; he envisioned the breasts and thighs of women he had known, yet the whore who breathed on him, now, he knew, was the hag of death.

The next morning his paralysis and contractions seemed permanent. Speke, using Sidi Bombay as interpreter, argued with Said bin Sclim about rigging a hammock and using porters to carry Burton.

"It would take too many men—six or eight. And who would carry their loads, which they would have to put down in order to carry this cripple?"

"Tell this man I demand help," Speke ordered Sidi Bombay.

The message was delivered, but Said bin Selim seemed unmoved. "Besides, for this extra duty my men would require two bolts of cloth each day," he said. "This caravan cannot support such an expense."

"You were hired on to *work!*" Speke shouted, and his face was so red that his words required no interpreter.

In the end, Speke took a small party of men and went off searching for additional porters among the nearby villages.

Meanwhile, singularly and in groups, the members of the caravan stopped by Burton's tent to inspect the swollen legs. There followed considerable discussion, analysis, and diagnosis. His malady was defined, at times, as malaria, green monkey fever, rickets, the vapors, yellow jack, swamp dampness, or, more eloquently, as the Curse Brought Down Upon Demons and Invaders by the Spirits of the Rivers.

At last came a caravan guard, Fundi, who had been placed on duty in the service of Burton by Snay bin Amir. He touched the legs, shook his head, yet seemed absolutely sure what was wrong and what would happen. "You will suffer much pain, but will walk again in ten days," he told Burton. "This comes from eating poison mushrooms. I myself have been afflicted, and so have my sons. You will have pain, but will make a fine recovery."

"But I haven't eaten any mushrooms," Burton protested.

"It matters not. You have the same affliction," Fundi asserted.

Somehow, Burton believed this man, so in spite of his pain decided that the ordeal would soon be finished.

Speke did secure six bearers from a nearby village that had recently been burned and razed by Wawende and Watuta raiders. Huts had been set afire, women raped, children driven off into the bush, and these men were the survivors, who badly needed money and weapons so that they could begin again. Around their village, Speke reported, the raiders had fixed skulls atop tall stakes, so that the area was cursed and could not be inhabited again.

It was now toward the middle of January 1858.

Burton was carried forward in a rigged hammock, but after two days of such heavy work in the fetid mud of the swamp the bearers deserted, never asking for the six cloths they had been promised for their labors.

As they approached some of the violent, warring tribes, Speke and Valentino were stricken with terrible inflammations of their eyes.

Burton was being carried forward by Mabruki, Sidi Bombay, Fundi, Caetano, and two porters. Propped up in his hammock, he tried to take a few geographical measurements with the remainder of the instruments as they went along, but the process was nearly impossible. He did manage to determine that they were in a high, cold, oddly mountainous swamp, very much like a seaside marsh, yet by his gauges and thermometers almost three thousand feet high. As Speke rode alongside the hammock on his donkey, Burton told him this.

"It's a primeval place," he said. "A swamp at the top of the world. One expects to see dinosaurs!"

"Dick, my eyes," Speke replied, his head held curiously high.

"Are they worse?"

"I see only a milky whiteness. Nothing else. A few dark shapes. Valentino says he's the same. The Jemadar is leading him by a rope. We're blind."

Burton stopped the bearers and had Speke sit down on the path. He examined his companion's eyes, noting the inflamed iris and retina.

"You see nothing?" he asked.

"Just a misty veil. Don't leave me. I can sit on my donkey. I can ride."

"Don't worry, friend. I'm with you."

"I had this as a boy," Speke said. "Ophthalmia. It kept me from my books, so was the reason I had to forgo schooling and take an army commission when I was just a young man. My mother treated it with various salves and washes, but nothing worked. I've never had it this badly, though."

"Easy," Burton urged him. "Keep calm. You'll ride with us. I know the inflammation will go away soon."

He gave Speke the last of the Warburg Drops.

"It's awful being blind," Speke said. "I feel such a failure."

"Nonsense. Sit on your donkey and continue to hold your head high."

"I can see better that way—more shadows and movements—although I can't really make out objects or people."

"Yes, but you look proud. Carry your rifle so that it's in easy view. We're coming into Wavinza territory, and we don't want them to know we're without the services of our best shot."

Speke managed a smile and took his place on the back of his donkey.

That evening they rode into a populous valley ruled by the Sultan of Uvinza, Lord of the Malagarazi River. A herd of elephant grazed in the distance. The Sultan strutted and boasted, yet the fact that Burton didn't rise from his hammock seemed to impress him.

"I am lord of the ferry, and no one crosses the river without paying," the Sultan shouted.

"Yes, naturally," Burton said evenly, his hand on his pistol.

"I demand one hundred cloths, one hundred bracelets of wire, and as many bracelets of coral beads!"

"And we shall have your sweet potatoes, the good millet I see growing in your fields, and honey from the logs in your trees," Burton replied.

"Your companion stands by his donkey," the Sultan sneered. "I think he is blind."

"He does suffer troubles. But his temperament is unfortunate because of his affliction, and he is quick to anger," Burton announced. "As for your demands, you may have forty cloths, the coral bracelets, and six coils of wire."

"I am lord of this valley and this great river!" the Sultan shouted, giving his warriors a knowing smirk.

"You must not provoke me to stand on my feet," Burton answered.

The Jemadar, Said bin Selim, and the askaris sucked in their collective breaths. For a moment the Sultan of Uvinza glared at the invaders of his domain, then his shoulders fell in a heavy sigh.

"We have food and you have payment," he conceded, sweeping up his bark-cloth tunic and walking away. "Something will be agreed on."

Afterward, the Jemadar was worried and full of warnings. "They will attack us in the night if you don't pay properly," he told Burton. "You must not be meager with a great and powerful chief!"

"He's lucky I didn't shoot him," Burton said. "Tomorrow we cross the river. These tribes are all alike—full of bluff and an overblown sense of their courage. If you ask me, there's not one true warrior in all Africa."

The Jemadar looked away and fell silent.

Following the river after crossing under the supervision of the Sultan, the caravan made its way through a red clay country filled with bats, crocodiles, mosquitoes, and a cold, dewy mist. Both Speke and Burton improved, and on the tenth day, just as predicted, Burton gave up his hammock and managed to sit on a donkey once more. They traded among the scattered villages and during early February discovered in the distance a blue line of mountains—which they took to be part of their objective, since they imagined the great inland lake to be nestled in hills.

"And how do you imagine the settlement at Ujiji?" Speke asked. "As great as Zanzibar?"

"Just as large—perhaps more exotic," Burton said. "We know many slaves come from the place. Yes, as great as Zanzibar."

On the morning of February 13, there were many problems. Caetano was ill—and had stopped on the trail the day before, refusing to come forward unless a donkey was sent for him to ride. Burton's bedding had been lost in crossing a stream, and he had slept on a bare mat spread over the damp ground in his tent, so his weakened legs ached. Speke's vision was still poor, and in climbing a stony hill covered with thorn bushes his donkey suddenly cried out and died beneath him; as it fell it tossed him aside, and he landed heavily on his shoulder.

"Are you all right?" Burton asked, hurrying to him.

Speke was in a fury, kicking the dead animal until its nose bled and striking out at anyone who tried to console him. He neither cursed nor cried out, yet seemed so completely out of his head that Burton walked away.

While the commotion continued around Speke's dead mount, Burton and Sidi Bombay struggled up to the summit of the hill; Burton's steps were agony, and he leaned against his frail little companion so that, once, they almost tumbled back on the path. "If I die helping you," Bombay joked, "please don't kick me."

At the top of the path, ahead of the whole caravan, they overlooked a valley of thick jungle; beyond, a streak of shimmering sunlight glistened from the trees.

"What's that streak of light below?" Burton asked.

"I am of the opinion," said Sidi Bombay, covering his eyes and gazing into the distance, "that it is *the* water."

Burton's heart sank. He moved a few more steps and saw that they gazed on a puny body of water. Had he risked his life and health for this? Damn all Arabs and exaggerations. Damn all folly.

"We'll have to turn back," he said. "I don't think the elevation's high enough. And it's not enough—it's too small."

But Sidi Bombay had run along the top of the hill's summit. "Sir!" he called. "Oh, sir!"

Burton went toward him and began to see that they gazed on a mere inlet. A wonder lay beyond: an immense lake stretching northward toward the horizon, an inland sea. A true wonder. Tears of relief filled Burton's eyes.

Speke and Burton immediately dressed in better clothes. Although he couldn't see anything of the distant water except its faint glare, Speke replaced his shirt torn in the fall from the donkey and tried to make himself more presentable and imposing; Burton strapped on his saber and put on a fresh tunic. With as much ceremony as they could muster, they led the caravan down the zigzag path from the hills toward the lake.

As they advanced, Burton described the look and dimensions of their discovery. Emerald trees and a yellow beach close to the water, he said. He saw mountains on the opposite shore, he told Speke, at a distance of perhaps thirty miles. The lake appeared blue and deep, with actual whitecaps out from shore. It looked as though it possibly went on northward for hundreds of miles, he suggested, until it transformed itself into the Nile.

"Oh, God, my eyes!" Speke complained.

By that afternoon runners had come out from Ujiji to greet them. Rifles were fired in salute, spears were raised, drums sounded. Burton sent out word that he would pay handsomely for guides, canoes, information, and fresh milk.

Sitting on his new mount, Speke could only listen as Burton bellowed commands and exclaimed about the lake. He felt an utter fool, and the milky daylight of his vision depressed him. Everyone shouted and laughed. And Said bin Selim had the impudence to announce to everyone, "See, just as I foretold! I have brought them to this great prize!"

After walking down the long hillside path, Burton became weak. By this time they had come into a lush tropical jungle filled with fern and flowers. A number of local natives had appeared, anxious to accompany them toward Ujiji, but Burton suddenly called out, "Camp! Make camp here! We go on tomorrow!"

The men grumbled, wanting to press on and enjoy a celebration in the town, but their feeble commanders held them back.

After dark, though, an even larger welcoming party arrived from the lake settlement: six sturdy whores, a dozen porters bearing gourds of pombe, a derelict who served as the group's comedian, and a local entrepreneur who wanted to light torches and have a look at the caravan's cloth and beads. Soon a loud party began and all complaints died down.

The next morning they all filed into Ujiji: a muddy, shit-smeared little lakeside port of dirty huts swarming with flies and mosquitoes. The shoreline was strewn with rotting fish and broken nets, as if the fishermen had abandoned their work years ago; everything was grey with slime, as if goats, trees, children, huts, and everything had recently surfaced from a bog. Burton felt that he might fade into this drab pastel of mud himself, never to be found again.

"Our tents are pitched," he told Speke. "Which gives us the best abodes in Ujiji—the cleanest, certainly, with the strongest walls."

"That bad?" Speke replied.

"Lucky you can't see much."

"I can smell, though. Awful."

"It's not at all like Zanzibar," Burton said with a sigh.

That afternoon Burton looked up and found a squat, smiling, hideously black little creature standing inside his tent. The creature was fat and resplendent in his beads and nakedness, but Burton's legs still ached terribly, and he was in no mood to have his nap interrupted.

"Out!" Burton commanded him, pointing to the tent flap.

The man attempted a smile.

"Out!" Burton shouted, and his visitor turned and ran.

Later in the day Burton learned that this was Kannena, the chief of Ujiji, and began to worry over his offense. He ordered the Jemadar and Said bin Selim to prepare elaborate gifts of cloth and beads and to arrange a proper meeting. His aides took this opportunity to tell him that the askaris demanded to be paid immediately.

"They want to buy slaves for themselves," Said bin Selim pointed out.

"Payment is made after a job is finished," Burton said.

"The bazaar here at Ujiji offers cheap prices," the Jemadar said, adjusting his monocle and drawing himself up to his full height. "You must pay now or the men will desert you!"

With these two following him, Burton went out for a short inspection of the bazaar. It consisted of a plot of higher ground, cleared of grass and shaded by a crooked tree; there, hundreds of blacks shouted, drummed, blew trumpets, and bargained at the tops of their voices. Fights broke out. Some ivory and a few frightened slaves were hawked by dealers, but most of the articles for sale were goats, poultry, fish, coarse yarns, and palm wine. Two or three Arab merchants who looked as though they had been at this dreary site for years nodded as Burton edged through the crowd. He walked with the support of a knotty cane, limping badly and shaking his head at the squalor.

"Is this all?" he finally asked an old Arab who stood near the tree.

"Certainly not." The old man laughed. "We have cockroaches, termites, mosquitoes, spiders, crickets, scorpions, ants, ticks, and thousands of unnamed bugs." He and Burton shared a smile at the hopelessness of the place. "Actually,

if you're interested in slaves, there is a large *tembe* where numbers of them are kept. As for ivory, there is little. Few of our warriors want to take on the elephant in order to get it."

Burton went back to Speke's tent, where his companion sat cross-legged staring out at nothing. He told what he had seen, but Speke was uninterested in the demands of the askaris, the bazaar, the affront to the chief, or anything else except finding canoes and going off toward an investigation of the lake and the river at its northern shore.

"There's no sense going until you can see better," Burton said.

"My vision is definitely improving. We have to get out of here!"

"We will recover ourselves. I have to speak with the chief. Matters need tending. I don't see any of the large canoes we hoped to find along the beaches, so I'll try to locate some. Have patience."

"You are such a bloody, bloody idiot!" Speke screamed at him, rising to his feet. "You like it here! You want to whore and drink! Don't think I don't understand you!"

Furious, Burton walked out.

The meeting with Chief Kannena went poorly. Burton took an abundance of gifts, but his announcement that he was no trader and that he had no interest in the slave market made a negative impression.

"I tax the head of each slave who leaves Ujiji," the chief explained with no lack of exasperation. "Yours is the largest caravan in many moons. If you do not trade, I will be embarrassed. I will be forced to tax you anyway."

"That would be an unfortunate effort," Burton said coldly.

Their words were translated by those same dirty Arab traders who had been at the bazaar beneath that crooked tree. Burton could tell little of what was being said in the Wajiji tongue, but assumed that his Arab interpreters had no interest in helping him. He asked about longboats—canoes that held more than thirty men and were reputedly used to navigate the lake. No response. He inquired about the river reputed to be at the northernmost point of the great water. No response. His hosts wanted to talk only about slaves and cloth.

With matters unsettled and mildly threatening, he went back to his tent. His legs throbbed and he felt a heavy exhaustion, so he determined to get out his writing materials and to make as many notes on the people, lake, customs, and geography as possible. In spite of Speke or Kannena or the pitiful world of Ujiji, he decided, he would attend to work.

After a few days Speke, more sullen than ever, began to see more clearly, so strolled along the edges of the lake. His melancholy was so fierce that Burton remembered Speke's remark back in Aden when they first met about wanting to come to Africa to die.

Burton worked at his notes.

The lake was called Tanganyika by the Wajiji and other surrounding tribes. It meant "meeting place of the waters."

The Wajiji were an insolent people, even their children. No civilities, no sign of family affection, no morals. The norm was drunkenness. Every man was beardless, having tweezed out each whisker from his face. Rudeness was common, and a Wajiji native would ridicule a stranger asking directions or do a mock imitation of a stranger's speech and manner before his face.

The fish of the lake, caught in various reed traps, were inedible by European standards. The region had little rice and poor vegetables, and these were overpriced.

Burton wanted to record everything about the flora of the region, but after a few days he could neither write nor think. He took long naps, and his only serious confrontation was with the Jemadar and his askaris when they once again demanded cloth and beads. "Yes, all right," Burton conceded, and so he and Sidi Bombay distributed payment to the guards, who immediately bought women and pombe with their shares.

One morning Speke appeared inside Burton's tent. "I've heard of an Arab across the lake who owns a dhow," he said. "With your permission, I want to go after it. We could use a ship of some size if we mean to explore the whole lake."

"Yes, go. I'm glad to be rid of you."

"I don't want to disturb your rest, of course, by insisting that we proceed with the business of the expedition."

"Oh, Jack, you're such an ass. I wish you luck, but go on."

Free from Burton, Speke imagined he would feel wonderful, yet didn't. His eye problem remained worse than he let on, and as soon as he gathered cloth and beads for his journey, the monsoon rains began, throwing him into terrible and lonely depression. He had pictured himself being rowed across a sunny water, making a shrewd negotiation for a ruddy good ship, giving orders himself for a change, and feeling cheerfully important, but it was now clear that he would be exposed to the elements, half blind, in need of Burton's bravado, and, in all, physically miserable—while Burton remained in his tent with books, candles, whores, palm wine, and the solitude of real recuperation.

By the time a canoe was found and he had picked his companions for the trip—two porters, Caetano, and Sidi Bombay—he had second thoughts. But too late: he had made his move, and pride kept him from returning to Burton and announcing any reconsideration.

The lake was a misty vapor, like a dream. Although he wore virtually all his clothing, Speke shivered. His ophthalmia—if it was that—had caused a curious distortion of his face, so that he had to chew and speak out of the side

of his mouth. Caetano had a lingering fever and curled into sleep in the bottom of the canoe. Only Sidi Bombay, smiling so that his honed teeth glistened like sharp little fangs, seemed to have any spirit about him.

After several days of relentless rain, Burton popped open his umbrella and paid another visit to Kannena, who was displeased that Speke had gone off—in search of better food prices, the chief thought, or canoes at a bargain.

"It is very cold and damp," Burton conveyed to the chief through one of the Arab translators. "I have brought you this six-foot length of scarlet broadcloth, which will undoubtedly improve your nasty humor."

The Arab relayed only a bit of this. Burton, with a flourish, placed the scarlet cloth across the chief's shoulders.

"The chief likes his gift," the Arab told Burton. "But wants more coils of wire, many measures of cloth, and, above all else, rifles."

"Tell him I will make a payment of valuable *honga* in due time," Burton answered. "Also, say that I have needs of my own. I want two young women sent to my tent—to attend my bodily aches and tensions."

As the interpreter began explaining all this and as the chatty Kannena replied, listened, added rebuttals, and asked questions of the Arab, Burton popped up his umbrella and strolled back to his tent. The mud of Ujiji ran like an open sore.

Moving from island to island across the rainy lake, Speke took ten days to find anyone who resembled an Arab who might own a dhow.

"No, no, I have no boat," explained an old Arab to Bombay, when he finally understood the question put to him.

"Is there anyone who has a large boat?" Speke inquired.

Only canoes, Bombay reported.

"Do you know of anyone who has seen the river at the top of the lake?"

Yes, he himself has been near such a river and has felt its waters pull him northward, Bombay reported.

"Then such a river exists and flows *out* of the lake?" Speke persisted.

Yes, this is so, Bombay relayed. Yes, out of the lake.

Speke felt elated, but fretted that a sufficient number of canoes would never be found. This western shore of the lake certainly had little: a few more bird-nest huts, this senile Arab, fishbones, and mud. Plainly, African journeys were a series of false leads, dashed hopes, exaggerations, and poor information, and as one went deeper and deeper into its interior, the means to finish a task or to complete an investigation always vanished.

That evening they started back across the lake, but a monsoon gale forced them ashore on a small island. Speke managed to erect his tent, but several stakes broke loose, and he had to hold on to its center pole so high winds wouldn't carry it away. Sidi Bombay, Caetano, and the porters huddled underneath the overturned canoe during the storm. Rain lashed the island for hours, so that, once, Speke fell asleep, dropping the pole and getting soaked in the ordeal. After midnight he finally secured his tent, then lit a candle inside it in order to rearrange his gear.

Hundreds of black beetles began crawling in toward the light.

For a few minutes he tried to brush them out and fasten the flap, but they managed to get inside. Around the tent the ground crawled with them—flooded out of their holes by the storm.

Deeply exhausted, Speke stretched out on his mat, determined to ignore them, and with beetles moving in his hair and underneath his clothes he fell asleep. He woke up several times, batting at them, but his dreams took him under again and again, so that it was hours later, when one of them burrowed into his ear, that he finally became fully awake.

It was eating its way deep into his ear. He could hear its legs and jaws working, but couldn't get it out. His efforts only resulted in pushing it farther in, too, so that he went outside and called Sidi Bombay.

No response. He went down to the canoe, heaved it off the sleeping forms of his men, and shouted at them, but in their sleepy states they only half understood.

"My ear! Help me!" he screamed at Sidi Bombay, who was on his feet in the confusion. The men were wet through and cold—and Caetano and the porters stayed wrapped in a knot of arms and legs on the mud.

Back in the tent Sidi Bombay produced his stubby pipe, which he only occasionally used for *bangi*, and found a dry match. He blew smoke into Speke's ear in an effort to drive the beetle back out, but this was tedious, didn't work, and Speke became angry.

"Fool!" he said, and he staggered outside the tent, holding a hand over his ear, slapping at his head with his other fist, and reeling around in the first daylight like a madman. By that time the others had come up from the canoe to witness his agony. Caetano tried to run to Speke, hold his master, and comfort him, but Speke pushed him away.

The beetle was eating through the tympanum. Speke could hear its painful gnawing and felt as though his head might split open.

Sidi Bombay heated some butter and they tried pouring it into the ear, but the beetle was too far inside, digging away, and Speke threw himself on the ground, rolled over in the mud, and shouted a long, protracted, "Ahhhhhh!"

Then he took out his penknife. While the men looked on in horror, he probed his ear until the little knife almost disappeared inside his head; blood oozed out and down his cheek; his eyes turned upward in a frenzy of pain.

"Please," Sidi Bombay implored him. "Please."

But Speke kept on until he dropped to his knees, sighing, "There, I think I killed it." These were the last words he said for days, for his cheek and jaw began to draw up, closing his mouth, all his muscles tightening. He knew that he was deaf in the ear. And his suffering was a humiliation, too: his men were watching as he butchered himself, he could not keep his cries to himself, and eyes, mouth, ears, his whole look and physical demeanor was wounded and gone. He wished he could die, for he felt less than a man; a true cripple, a pathetic waste.

On the trip back across the lake, moving slowly from islands to campsites on small bays as the rains constantly harassed them, Speke's facial paralysis grew worse, so that he could only feed himself on liquids through one corner of his mouth. His hearing was gone in the ear and his eyes seemed unable to make a full recovery, everything remaining drenched in milky cloudiness.

Bits of the beetle's legs and wings came out of his ear, occasionally, along with the constant trickle of blood and pus. And, once, sitting in the canoe, blowing his nose into his handkerchief, a definite whistling noise sounded from the ear. The porters and Caetano broke out in laughter. When Speke blew his nose a second time and the whistling sounded sharply again, they beat on each other in their hilarity.

Their trip across the lake, when they finally reached Ujiji, had taken twenty-five days.

"You've failed again, the same as at the Wadi Nogal," Burton told him when they met. "Except this time you acted on mere rumor—on your own initiative. I'm sorry about your physical shape. You look bloody terrible. Half dead, if you want to know. But this was due to your impatience and moodiness. I'm not surprised at your failure. In fact, I'm surprised you didn't get eaten by cannibals or crocodiles. You must learn to risk yourself for better things than rumors or gossip."

Speke could only glare. His mouth tightened, and his reddened face, drawn up and shaking with anger, distorted his eyes.

"I've arranged for two large canoes—one sixty feet long, the other forty feet—and I've hired the porters for our trip north on the lake. The rains will soon stop, I think, and I look forward to a rather pleasant float. Word is that the tribes up there are hostile and won't even trade, but we'll see."

Speke continued to glare.

"I've heard various stories about the river at the head of the lake—usually, that it flows *out* of Tanganyika, which would make it a prize worth all our risks. I've also sent a messenger back to Snay bin Amir, asking him to forward any supplies. And, oh, yes, we have a very good interpreter—a new boy named Sayfu, who knows the languages of the lake people and especially those at Uvira to the north."

Speke made a low noise in his throat.

"So we'll put your failure behind us once again," Burton went on. "The canoes are ready. When you've mended yourself and rested, we'll be off. We're waiting on you alone."

Not wanting to be dismissed, Speke dismissed himself.

When he was gone, Burton's two girls arrived for the afternoon treatment. They were both slender black reeds, thirteen and fourteen years old, young but hardly virginal, with their hair in pintails and their shoulders decorated with raised welts, cut into crude patterns. As Burton undressed, one of them opened the bottle of palm oil while the other fluffed the pillows on his cot.

They massaged his still swollen legs, each one taking a leg as her special project; they rubbed in the palm oil, softly, in long strokes, stopping to let their thin fingers play between his toes at one end of their work, then gliding up to his genitals, where their fingers often met. During Speke's absence, Burton had taught them their skills, so that now they were both very deft and very proud of themselves; they used an abundance of oil, feeling and watching his muscles respond. When their massage became sexual, they mixed his emission with the palm oil, insisting that this was probably beneficial. More often they worked on his legs while he read or made notes; meanwhile, the sturdy Mabruki guarded the entrance to the tent, standing there with his giant arms crossed like some Nubian eunuch at a palace.

During Speke's trip across the lake, Burton had received almost constant attention from the girls, had slept long hours, had eaten quantities of *sushi* and broiled fish, had worked at his notes, and had conversed little with either his own or Kannena's men, so felt rested for what lay ahead.

He watched Speke strolling beside the lake at night. The candor of moonlight on the ripples of the lake. A man who seemed devoured with his pain and moodiness.

Burton wondered if his companion imagined himself to be engaged in analysis and contemplation. The true intellectual, of course, was an actionist. The written page, the sword, the body of a woman, the jungle latitudes: these were the far fields. And energy, not just some meager pensiveness, defined a man.

Their two long canoes were loaded with instruments, weapons, palm wine, salt, cloth, and beads, but also with Kannena himself, half his court, most of his relatives, assorted friends, and various black tourists who seemed interested in viewing the northernmost reaches of the lake. Burton inserted his Union Jack —the one given to him by Lumsden—on the bow of the larger vessel, and with a clang of iron, the sounding of horns, considerable singing and howling, they set off. Speke, his face badly distorted and swollen with pain, said nothing to anyone.

Every hour they stopped while the blacks loaded their pipes and took deep inhalations of *bangi*. Afterward, they rowed with reduced energies, but some degree of levity; they howled a melancholy singsong as they put in, day by day, at Ubwari, Wafanya, Mzimu, and numerous other dirty little villages along the way. At each stop, Kannena demanded daily payments of additional cloth and beads— and intimidated local leaders, who hoped to trade with these newcomers themselves. The result was that packages and loads more or less traded positions in the canoes, while the villagers along the shore received no benefits from the visits.

At each stop, they also heard the same stories.

"Beware the angry Wavira," they were told. "They will not trade with you. They are cannibals. They do not want you in their land."

At the village of Mtuwwa, three young sons of the Sultan Maruta, whose domain bordered the land of the Wavira tribe, came into camp. Although Kannena disdained these young ambassadors, Burton and Sidi Bombay sat down with them and the interpreter, Sayfu, and asked them questions.

"Yes," they said, "there is a river in the land of the Wavira."

"Does this river have a name?" Burton inquired.

"The Rusizi," replied the older of the sons, whose face was a patchwork of raised decorative cuts.

"And which way does this river flow? Into the lake or out of it?" Burton quickly asked.

"Oh, *into* the lake," said the older son.

"You have seen this yourself?"

"Many times. It brings the lake a fish my father prefers to eat."

Burton's spirits began to sink. He asked the question twice more, once to each of the other sons, each of whom confirmed the story. "We have heard a very different report," he protested. "Everyone in Ujiji says the river flows *out* of Tanganyika." He knew, somehow, that he was hoping beyond hope, for these young men seemed intelligent and certain.

"On the far side of the lake, my other master asked the old Arab this same question," Sidi Bombay interjected. "But I believe my master misunderstood the old Arab's reply and heard only what he wished to hear."

"We have come a long way for this bad news," Burton said to the sons.

"The course of the river is certain," the older son assured him. "And the Wavira tribe is truly angry, so my brothers and I will escort you and give you protection to our father's *tembe.*"

"Are you afraid of going on toward the Wavira?" Burton asked Bombay.

"Wild birds hate tame birds," Sidi Bombay answered, speaking in a curious, hushed tone.

They reached Uvira on the edge of hostile territory after almost a month's travel on May 6, 1858. This was the last trading outpost, a muddy hovel where a female slave could be bought for half a British crown.

The men were terrified. Sayfu would not leave the beach to bargain for milk in the village. Mabruki, who was clearly the largest and strongest of all the men, became highly nervous and kept staring with fear into the thicket beyond the settlement. Kannena asserted that his men would not venture on, although he himself was unafraid.

Although Speke's vision and general health had considerably improved, Burton now suffered from an ulcerated tongue so that he could hardly eat or talk. Just as Speke had fed himself on broth for weeks after the beetle attack, Burton was now obliged to take only liquids into his swollen, painful mouth. And because he felt bad and couldn't converse, he took little interest in discussing plans or deciding what they would do next.

"Does the river flow *into* or *out* of the lake?" Sidi Bombay asked everyone, taking over the roles as interpreter and leader.

Replies were all consistent: the river flowed into Tanganyika. And everyone's warnings about cannibals increased to hysteria.

The rains began again, too. Burton, his tongue swollen and useless, hunched under the folds of his mackintosh, making a small tent of its waterproof fabric. He seemed to like it in there, shutting out Kannena, the foul weather, Speke, and all responsibilities.

Once, during a downpour, Sidi Bombay approached the mackintosh and squatted beside it. "Sir, are you inside there?" he asked.

"Of course," Burton managed, his painful tongue distorting his reply.

"Good," Bombay said, then waited. Rain drenched his bony knees, which were near his odd little face in this squatting position. "There was some argument," he continued, "that you were magic and were no longer with us."

For nine days the rains continued, and Kannena's advisers and the local chief agreed that a new monsoon season had begun. Ten miles from actually seeing the Rusizi, Burton ordered the party back to Ujiji. Speke concurred, agreeing that the river was undoubtedly a confluent of the lake, that trouble with the warring tribe seemed likely, and that the weather was too foul.

Burton wrote in his notes:

It is characteristic of African travel that the explorer may be
arrested at the very bourne of his journey, on the very threshold
of success, by a single stage, as effectually as if all the waves of the
Atlantic or the sands of Arabia lay between.

The return trip to Ujiji was marked by some violent drunkenness at one of the villages where they stopped. Kannena and a local chief got into an argument, and threats were made.

A drunk struck someone with a club.

Kannena's warriors rowed themselves out into the lake to await the result of the chaos.

Valentino, terrified and impulsive, grabbed Burton's big Colt pistol and fired into the argumentative crowd, wounding one of Kannena's friends.

Daggers were drawn and numerous ultimatums were delivered.

Burton ended the fracas by paying Kannena extra for the insulting gunshot wound—which had passed through the friend's shoulder.

"Tedious," Burton said of the fracas the next morning. "Let's paddle on."

Back at Ujiji fifteen porters from Snay bin Amir had arrived with packets of goods and the first mail Burton and Speke had seen in eleven months.

Burton learned that a mutiny had occurred in India, just as Lumsden had predicted and as he had feared, in which sepoys serving the British army had murdered a number of Englishmen and had seen, in turn, hundreds of their own killed and hanged.

Letters were sparse. Speke received none. Burton had only official word of Hamerton's death, a note from Snay bin Amir stating that he was holding additional goods and awaiting orders from Burton on how to dispose of them, and nothing from Isabel, who had inundated him with mail during the first months of his absence. He decided that she was probably married and that he should definitely forget her.

The goods brought by the porters were inferior: the cheapest cotton cloths and almost worthless white beads. Burton knew that the merchants of Zanzibar had unloaded their worst wares on a caravan never expected to be seen again.

Burton and Speke agreed to return first to Kazeh, then to Zanzibar.

"We could visit the nyanza due north of Kazeh," Speke suggested. "If there is a lake there, and if we have the goods to search it out, we ought to."

"Goods are the problem. Our stores are depleted. These items from the coast are worthless. Let's go back to Kazeh, recover ourselves, and decide then."

"Our orders were to go to Ujiji, then, if we had time, to explore the northern lake," Speke reminded him.

"Yes, Jack, but we might not even have the materiel for a return march to Kazeh. These are a base people, who would never help us out if we ran out of trading goods. Our beads and cloth are like water in the desert: we can only go so far, then we have to get back on the remaining supply."

"I understand that," Speke conceded.

"My measurement of the altitude of Lake Tanganyika is eighteen hundred feet," Burton went on. "By my calculations, that's not enough altitude for the lake to actually be the source of the Nile. But my theory is that Tanganyika is part of an immense basin of mountain lakes that feeds the Nile. I'm sure there's a northern lake that is part of this system—just as I'm sure the Rusizi flows *into* this lake, as all reports finally agreed. But we can't go forever. Most of our instruments won't work. Our trading goods are gone, and these new things won't much help. Tell the truth, I don't even know if I can walk back to Kazeh —let alone to go in search of another lake."

"I feel fit myself," Speke said.

"Yes, all right. But you do agree that we should go back, if we can?"

"Quite," Speke said.

They gathered the caravan together quickly and left Ujiji by a northern route reputed to be easier than the paths through the swamp. Monsoon rains swept them along, but the way did seem easier; Burton hired additional porters who carried him in a hammock while Speke rode a donkey. They stayed at separate ends of the column, contented to be apart during the long, annoying daylight hours.

Slaves bought by members of the caravan complicated the march. The Jemadar, his monocle intact, but nervous and suspicious that his six new slaves might try to escape, finally woke up one morning to find all of them gone. He raved, wept, cursed his fate, cursed Burton, and carried on until Burton threatened to leave him behind on the trail. One of the porters from Unyanyembe fell behind the caravan because the young slave girl he had bought for himself had developed sore feet and couldn't keep up. The next day the porter caught up without her.

Sidi Bombay came to Burton with news that the porter had murdered his slave girl. "Cut off her head," Bombay reported. "So that no one else might enjoy her."

Burton tended not to believe the story, but when he saw Mabruki abusing a small boy, perhaps ten years old, he interfered. The boy was another newly bought slave whom Mabruki had regarded as a clever pet during the first days of the march, but lately the boy had suffered a great deal from slaps and kicks. Burton went to Mabruki and took the boy out of his care.

"I'm giving this child to Sidi Bombay," he told Mabruki, who had a look of sadness more than anger behind his eyes. "Kindly don't bother any of us about the matter again. You have forfeited your privilege and your slave."

Mabruki offered no argument.

In such a matter, Burton always moved quickly and without any seeming fear—which brought comments from Bombay, the Jemadar, Said bin Selim, and all the askaris and porters. Out on caravan, few men would deal with such a brute as Mabruki. Any slight could be avenged with a bullet or knife in the back. The mercurial temperament of primitive men always required reckoning—the same as the wild and dangerous nature of the land around them—yet Burton moved with a supreme and arrogant confidence, they admitted among themselves, and seemed willing to put his life on the line in such confrontations.

The new, unexplored trail is harder because it is mysterious; the same path, on the way home, rushes by. They reached the swollen Malagarazi River on June 4. That morning they felt a slight earthquake, which Burton recorded in his notes and which the men took to be a bad omen.

The ferryman at the river extracted large payments of oil, beads, and cloth, and when Said bin Selim and the Jemadar argued with his fees he left them stranded on a little sandbar, brown water cascading around them, until they became more agreeable. Speke traded beads and several cooking pots for a pig. On the rest of their journey toward Unyanyembe and the hospitality of Snay bin Amir, once more, they enjoyed good trading for food. At their old house in Kazeh—newly plastered and made ready for their arrival—they sat down with their Arab host for a meal of omelets, ghee, curried fowl, giblets, and manioc boiled in the cream of the ground nut. Other packets, trading goods, and letters awaited them—still nothing of personal mail for Speke, and nothing from Isabel for Burton.

It was now June 20, and Speke wanted to prepare immediately to head north to the other lake.

"If your legs aren't strong enough, Dick, I can go alone," Speke announced. They were dining with Snay bin Amir, who gave Burton a glance.

"It's not my health so much," Burton told him. "We haven't enough trading goods. Our instruments are virtually gone. I just don't see how we can do it."

"Other goods will probably arrive from the coast," Speke argued. "We can do it, if we want. I can do it by myself."

"We'll stay here a few days and discuss it," Burton allowed.

"Very good advice," Snay bin Amir said, raising his glass in a toast. "Stay and recover your strength. Decide later."

That evening before bed Burton was writing in his notes when another earth tremor sent a little black viper of ink down the page. So strange. He put no stock in omens, yet this corner of the earth they wanted to explore seemed to complain against being known.

As Speke tried to begin preparations for a trip to the nyanza to the north he and Burton never crossed each other directly, but opinions and arguments were exchanged.

"There just aren't enough beads and cloth," Burton said. "We didn't even have enough to explore the southern end of Tanganyika."

"I can take a small caravan," Speke insisted.

Neither Said bin Selim and his porters nor the Jemadar and his askaris would consider going on another trip without payment in advance. In frustration, Speke argued with them, threatened them, then turned to Sidi Bombay for support.

"I require a payment of cloth before the journey, too," he told Speke.

"Do you want him to make this journey without you?" Snay bin Amir finally asked Burton. "If so, he probably has enough trading goods—counting the inferior ones that just arrived. I believe you will receive more from the coast, as you hope and expect. If not, I can lend you goods for your return to Zanzibar later on."

"I'd be happy to be rid of him," Burton admitted.

"Then let him go."

"If he failed, it would just be another of his failures." Burton sighed.

They sat on pillows in the sunshine outside the Arab's house, enjoying a bright day after the rains had ceased. Beyond, in a field of *bangi* plants growing wild, a woman balanced her washing on her head.

"What if he succeeded?" Snay bin Amir asked. "You are the leader of the expedition, is this not so, and credit for any accomplishment would be yours?"

"Yes, but what success could he have? If he finds another lake, he will have no instruments, no language, no information except what he learns third hand. Besides, he has a tendency to abuse himself physically instead of getting any job done."

"He might even get himself eaten by cannibals!" the Arab said, laughing.

"He'd make a sour morsel," Burton said.

With the aid of Snay bin Amir, Speke assembled his small caravan and appointed Sidi Bombay next in command and chief interpreter. Only a few porters agreed to go along—most of them Snay's men and slaves. Said bin Selim, Mabruki, the Jemadar, both Valentino and Caetano, and other key members of the larger caravan decided to stay in Kazeh with Burton.

Early on the morning of July 9, 1858, Speke left Kazeh without saying farewell. He was beyond ceremony with Burton or the slavers. The dew was heavy on the grass and the morning was especially invigorating, and not long out of the settlement they found those giant, monolithic rocks rising up once again.

The free highlands.

Speke was glad to be rid of Burton and all the man stood for. Burton was a dabbler, a poet, a gregarious scholar who seemed to lack any single-mindedness of purpose or dedication to goals. He would stay at Kazeh and whore, Speke knew, and he would consume himself with notes, conversations, the pipe, a dollop of brandy, this theory, that gossip. If the man had talent or energy, Speke felt, these were spread too thin; he was capable at times of preening and appearing strong, yet was finally weak-willed. If I'm less smart in many matters, even so I'm no fool, Speke could tell himself as he took his long strides across those thorny grasslands. Perhaps I'm simpler, but I'll achieve more; I won't smoke, drink, practice sex, scribble notes, keep the company of slavers, or pretend I'm a scientist or theologian. I'm keen for accomplishment and real fame. I want the Nile. Let Dick Burton twist his mustaches in fancy drawing rooms or low-life bars hoping to impress his audiences with his escapades. I'll have knighthood. I'll have true celebrity.

Two days out of Kazeh the men got drunk and remained all day at a village. Speke fretted and considered threatening them, but hated getting off to such a bad start, so waited for them to sober up.

In the late afternoons Speke practiced his drawings and watercolors, improving each day while Sidi Bombay and the porters stood around and watched. He wore a pair of grey-tinted French spectacles while painting—eyeglasses that he had never allowed Burton to see—and the porters became fascinated with these, bending in front of him and peering into his face in order to catch glimpses of themselves. Their camps were overrun by ticks these first days out, so the men scratched, patted kerosene on their bodies, and complained; but Speke at his drawing pad, his colored glasses down over his nose, worked with seeming indifference.

"I taught myself painting in India," he told Sidi Bombay. "There were places up in the Himalayas few men have ever seen where I made likenesses of the landscape."

"Burton himself makes pictures with his pen," Sidi Bombay remarked innocently.

"Yes, but poor drawings indeed," Speke replied. "And kindly do me a favor on this trip: don't speak his name."

The little caravan met a column of Wasukuma who were carrying ivory, the long tusks over their shoulders. As the two groups passed each other on the trail in a small gorge filled with thornbushes, the porters on each side lowered their heads and butted at each other.

Speke stepped off into the brush and drew his pistol.

The butting continued. One man fell into the dust to avoid being struck by a tusk that came at him like a lance.

As Speke cocked his pistol and imagined the worst about to happen, all the men broke into laughter.

"This is the custom on the narrow trails," Sidi Bombay explained, when, at last, he himself understood.

By this time the Sukuma warriors and porters had dropped their loads and had sat down among Speke's men to share a few gourds of pombe.

Every day they walked five or six hours in the cool air and sunshine. Speke shot a number of partridges, so the camp had good meat.

At the village of Ukini he was ushered into the presence of two albinos —considered to be sacred creatures. They were both fat young men with idiotic grins, their skin a pinkish, freckled neutral.

At night, Speke tied his donkey to the tent stakes and soon after supper curled himself into his usual sleeping position on the cold, hard mats inside his shelter. There, before he went to sleep, he recounted all of Burton's offenses.

The man was physically beautiful, of course, and he remembered how, at Aden, at the first, he had admired those soft lips beneath the heavy mustache, how he could have kissed them. But now, so much later, only a litany of the man's faults seemed to remain.

The next region along their way was ruled over by a stumpy little black woman, about sixty years of age, called the Sultana Ungugu.

She and Speke sat down across from each other in the midday sun for a conference meal of corn mush and beef strips. Her eyes, he noted, were bald of brows or lashes.

Soon she had moved closer, so that she could touch him. Her fingers began to trace over his shoes, trousers, waistcoat, buttons, and coat.

"She says you are wonderful," Sidi Bombay explained. "She says your fingers look very soft, like a child's, and she expresses the wish to touch them."

"Give her permission," Speke answered.

The Sultana grinned as she fumbled Speke's hands with her own. Then she ran her fingers through Speke's hair, feeling its soft texture and marveling aloud at her court, an entourage of nine warriors and fat maidens who squatted in a circle around them. Everyone smiled and sighed in reply.

"She says your hair is like the mane of the lion," Sidi Bombay said, interpreting her syllables.

"Tell her this pleases me. And ask if she believes me to be as strong as the lion and able to reach my goal."

"She will pay you this fine compliment if you ask her," Sidi Bombay answered without any guile of his own.

"Ask her anyway," Speke persisted.

Walking, Speke guarded a secret.

Snay bin Amir had given him a map of the northern lake, which the Arabs called Ukerewe, and without Burton's knowledge Speke had forwarded this simple drawing with a letter to Dr. Norton Shaw, the secretary of the Royal Geographical Society. That same group of porters who had brought them their last goods from the coast were now en route back to Zanzibar with the crude map and Speke's first personal correspondence to the Society.

In the letter to Shaw, Speke had written of Burton, "He is always ill; he won't sit in the dew, and he has a decided objection to the sun. Meanwhile, I am off to the Ukerewe lake to see if accounts of it are true." So he had begun to undermine his senior officer by corresponding separately and by making clear that Burton merely languished in Kazeh while he was ready to achieve the goals of the Society. By including Snay bin Amir's crude map, he had even established that the Arabs entrusted significant documents to him.

The longitude of this Ukerewe lake, he knew, was favorable; it seemed to align itself with the Nile in Egypt.

I might have only a few instruments and very few trading goods left, Speke told himself. But he won't be able to refute anything I assert. He is in Kazeh with his pen in one hand and his prick in the other. I am the true captain now.

At Snay bin Amir's rambling house, Burton met representatives of various tribes and attempted to compile a vocabulary and grammar. It was painstaking work, especially with the chief of the Wapoka, who sat on the Arab's cotton and satin pillows discoloring them with his body grease.

"Listen, O brother!" Burton intoned. "In the tongue of the shores—in Kiswahili—we say one, two, three, four, five!" He counted out these numbers on his fingers, so the chief would understand that he wanted the names of the numbers.

"*Hu! Hu!*" the chief exclaimed. "We say fingers, too!"

"No, by no means, that's not it," Burton went on. "This white man wants to know how you speak the names of the numbers!"

"One, two, three *what?* Goats or women?" the chief argued.

"No, by no means. The numbers themselves: one, two, three in your own tongue! In the tongue of the Wapoka!"

"*Hi! Hi!* What wants the white man with the Wapoka?"

Speke and the little caravan entered a series of marshes crisscrossed with small creeks, which he hoped were the beginnings of a swamp that formed the southern extremity of another giant lake. If they were close, this march would have been far easier than the trip to Ujiji with Burton; the weather had been splendid; none of the men had been ill; the days had been a series of brisk walks.

Each morning, now, feeling destiny at his sleeve, Speke was the first man awake in camp, calling the others to get up and move.

Those huge boulders were everywhere. They seemed to guard the inland sea like sentinels.

On the morning of August 3, 1858, they moved along a corridor of immense stones until they were in a canyon of forbidding grey rock, with hundreds of strange waterbirds wheeling in the sky overhead. The men suspected that they were near their goal because of the birds, but the stones themselves seemed to announce the nearness of the lake to Speke. Toward noontime Speke and Sidi Bombay ascended a low hill, hoping for a better look to the north, and there it was: the lake with its silvery waters stretching off toward what seemed like an endless horizon.

As the men caught up, cheers began to sound, and Sidi Bombay embraced each porter as he arrived at the top of the hill. Gourds of pombe and pipes of *bangi* began to appear as Speke, giddy with laughter, loaded a scattergun with shot.

He knew that he had discovered the great reservoir of the Nile.

A low-flying florican turned too close to the hill. When the gun roared and the bird fell, the men marveled and sent up a loud cheer. It was a moment of pure exhilaration for Speke—and he had celebrated.

With their supply of beads and cloth low, Speke estimated that they could explore the lake for only about three days, so after staying the first night at a lakeside village, he and the men started out. The villagers at the lake were fishermen, but their canoes were flimsy and Speke hoped to find larger ones for exploration out on the water.

The view of Tanganyika had been a better one, but this was his alone. He decided that this great nyanza was extensive, filled with many bays and inlets, and from what he saw this seemed so. One couldn't see hills on any distant shore, so Speke supposed that he was looking eighty or a hundred miles from the low hills above these southern marshes.

"Yes, that far," an old chief confirmed. He was an ancient creature with withered hands, as if he had stayed too long in the waters of the lake. "Eighty or one hundred miles across!"

"And how far to the north?" Speke asked, using Sidi Bombay as interpreter. The old chieftain, who spoke Arabic, threw out his arm and snapped his brittle fingers in exasperation, as if nobody could possibly know the answer to this profound question.

"Probably," he told them, "to the end of the world."

Later that day, walking the edges of the lake, following those enormous boulders which, now, embraced the shoreline and appeared several hundred yards into the lake itself, they found an Arab settler, a man who had been a slaver in his earlier years, but who had taken a dumpy native wife.

"I have lived north on the lake," he informed them.

"Is there a boat? We want to go around the lake," Speke had Bombay tell the Arab.

"No one goes around the lake," the dumpy black woman answered. When she grinned she displayed rows of broken teeth. "It is far too big! With storms!"

Unable to set sail on the lake or to take soundings, Speke did take several thermometer readings, which told him the same thing: the lake's altitude was almost two thousand feet above Tanganyika's. This excited him. But he also knew that at latitude 5 degrees north the Nile was almost two thousand feet below the level where they now stood. How could this be so? There must be great waterfalls to the north, he decided, and swampy marshes in a complex river system that had kept travelers from coming up the Nile in ancient times.

Over and over he took thermometer readings, getting the same results, and growing more elated each time.

In the evenings he sat outside his tent and talked with Sidi Bombay.

"That hill on which we stood I'll name Somerset," he told Sidi Bombay. "And that creek we passed today I'll call Jordans Nullah—after my family's estate. The lake itself will be the Victoria Nyanza. What do you think of these names?"

"Very fine English names," Sidi Bombay replied, managing to say the right thing. He kept one hand in the air, slapping mosquitoes occasionally as they landed on his wiry body.

Before bedtime that night Speke took yet another thermometer reading and found it the same.

He couldn't sleep, so walked down through the village toward the lapping shore. Bulrushes rustled in the late breeze, and he wondered, in one of his few moments of idle speculation, if these water reeds were perhaps native to this region and if, somehow, their seeds had been washed down the Nile toward Egypt and had taken root there thousands of years ago when Moses, the lonely, abandoned child, had been placed in them for safekeeping.

The next day Speke and his group trudged around the edges of the lake trying to get better views of its broad expanse.

They met some natives who spoke a language Sidi Bombay couldn't fathom. They asked about a body of land—perhaps a peninsula or isthmus—and were told by another native who spoke Arabic that this was an island called Ukerewe.

"Is not the whole lake called this?" Sidi Bombay asked.

The man didn't know. The lake, he suggested, was simply referred to as nyanza—the lake.

Although Speke lacked precise instruments, better information, boats, and trading goods, he still felt certain. That afternoon he went hunting, shooting a number of partridge and giving them to the porters for an evening roast, and he felt dizzy with success.

Again that night Speke couldn't sleep. This was his prize, and he pondered how to keep it for himself alone. The right words, the right tactics—I must be forthright, he told himself, and unmovable.

Burton, he reminded himself, isn't even truly English. He's lived in

Corsica or someplace. Italy and France. And looks it. That's why he's so good with foreign languages and ideas. He'll have no part in this."

Before dawn, he struck his tent and called to the men. "Let's turn back," he said to them. "Back to Kazeh! Come on!" At first the men grumbled, but they began to pack. Mosquitoes bothered them, and they weren't unhappy to move out.

Two days before Speke's little caravan returned to Kazeh, Burton heard that they were on their way. Snay bin Amir had been worried about rumors of wars in the north, so the news was welcomed.

On August 24, Speke and his men were only eighteen miles from Kazeh, so got up at midnight and began the last march, arriving at the settlement for breakfast. Burton went out to meet them and threw his arms around Speke, who was stiff, but managed a smile.

"Good luck?" Burton asked.

"Yes, let me tell you at breakfast," Speke answered. "Allow me to take off my boots and wash."

Caetano, Mabruki, and dozens of women prepared the pillows, brazier, food, and drink on the verandah of the house. By nine o'clock they sat together eating, and for the first minutes of the meal Speke said nothing, just pushed food into his mouth. He thanked Burton for passing him ghee and bread, and his tone, somehow, achieved that deep hostility of English politeness.

"I found the lake," he said, at last. "And I'm completely convinced that it's the principal feeder of the Nile. In a way, I know this is just assertion without proof, but I did take a number of thermometer readings, and I know I'm right. I also want to make clear that this is my discovery."

Burton sat silent, not knowing what to say. The implication that what had happened wasn't a victory for the expedition, but only a personal one for Speke, took him by surprise.

"Well, I'm happy, Jack, that you've had a personal success," he managed.

"The thermometer readings put the altitude of the lake at about thirty-six hundred feet," Speke said. "I know I'm right. This is the main source of the Nile."

"What evidence do you have apart from thermometer readings?"

"The word of Arabs who have lived around the lake all their lives. I place the upper reaches of the lake at, oh, four or five degrees north latitude."

Burton ate a fig, then drank some tea.

"Twenty years ago, my dear Jack," he said finally, "an Egyptian expedition sent by the late Mohammed Ali Pasha reached three degrees twenty-two minutes north latitude. If what you say is true, they would have sailed fifty miles out into the nyanza. And the Egyptians never even heard of a lake, Jack! Never even *heard* of a lake!"

"Well, that's my information," Speke said.

Burton drank off his tea, watching his companion. Speke still ate heartily.

"You don't speak Arabic," Burton went on. "How did you talk with these Arabs? Did you use Bombay as interpreter? You know that he has only a poor smattering of a single dialect of Arabic himself. Are you sure that you didn't misunderstand?"

"I know I'm right about this! That's all I can say! I *know.*"

"In what way, Jack? In the mystic sense?"

"If you wish," Speke said.

"I'm not being critical, Jack, just skeptical. I hope you can see that."

"I can see that you stayed here in comfort. I can see that I'm the one who troubled to go find the largest lake any of us will ever imagine—a real inland sea. And it's my discovery. If that's an assertion I'm making without full proof, I'm happy to make it. I'll do so, in fact, with the Royal Society."

Speke finished his meal as neither of them spoke. Burton found it impossible to say anything else, so gazed out at a herd of goats wandering beside the well. After a few minutes, Speke drank off his tea and heaved a sigh.

"I suggest that we prepare for another trip together," Speke said. "We'll go to the nyanza together. This time, since I know the way, I'll be the leader of the expedition."

"No, the monsoon rains begin here in September," Burton said. "We're out of goods, and our health still isn't the best. Let's go back to Zanzibar, back home, get some more money, and make a return trip. Our army leaves have almost expired, so that's the thing to do."

"I suppose you want to claim the discovery for yourself," Speke blurted out. For another minute they glared at each other, saying nothing.

"That's not it at all," Burton said coldly. "Perhaps we should speak no more of this business of having found the Nile source."

"But I did find it," Speke said, rising from the pillows.

"By mutual agreement, we must say no more."

Speke made a sound in his throat.

"My legs are still badly swollen," Burton said, trying to alter the topic. "I can see you still have eye trouble, and I've worried over the condition of your ear. With the monsoon rains coming, we must stick together. The path back to Zanzibar is that same arduous path. It's going to be terrible."

"We can rig another hammock for you, I suppose," Speke said.

"Yes, I think we'll have to. And I think our fever will come back. We must stick close."

"Of course," Speke said, and his voice was as sharp as the edge of a sword.

Preparations began as Burton hired back all the disgruntled porters and askaris, telling them that they would be assigned bundles for the return trip and that they would be expected to follow orders. Snay bin Amir helped with everything, providing goats, beef, cloth, and beads from his personal stores.

A hammock was rigged for Burton and all available donkeys were purchased, so that Speke could ride.

Only once did they get back on the subject of the lake, and that resulted in a violent argument. Speke mentioned that he had named the lake Victoria and had given British names to other landmarks.

"Indigenous African places should not have European names," Burton said flatly. "I strongly object to that practice."

Furious about being rebuked again, Speke replied, "You can't afford objections to anything that happens now! You made your choices earlier!"

Burton's legs were still badly swollen, especially at the knees, and he felt justified, still, in having allowed Speke to go north without him. Yet he began to see that he had lost a vital chance. Life had few golden moments, as he had often said himself. This one, perhaps, had escaped him. Yet he hoped for the best: time would heal all scars, he felt, and these animosities and vanities would pass away—especially on the hard trail back.

At their last meal in Kazeh, Speke lasted only an hour at Snay's house, taking a few bites of food, then making his apologies for the night.

He seemed to be drawing into himself again.

Burton remained to have a long dinner with his host and a number of Arabs who came to pay their last respects. Their meats and vegetables were served on porcelain plates set in straw mats; afterward, they drank cups of farewell punch and smoked cigars.

"You are true sheikhs," Burton said, toasting them. "Praise Allah for good men."

Speke lingered in the darkness outside his bedroom before trying to sleep. The smell of the first monsoon rains was already in the air, and he could hear, far off, the singing moans of the slaves, still imprisoned in that thorn *boma,* still complaining against the night. Other sounds came to him, too: the sudden, soft laughter of the men still at dinner, a bird's wild cry somewhere in the bush, a whole cacophony of lunatic noises that he didn't want to hear.

Arguments, fights, threats, and an inspired laziness began the journey as each porter sought ways to carry less, demand more, and do nothing.

Speke stayed in his tent, so Burton followed suit; every evening, then, was punctuated with quarrels and brawls. By the time they had left Unyanyembe with its mangoes and soft grasses, loads were being lost along the path and the men were showing their knives in heated exchanges.

One night sharp cries came from Speke's tent, and when they continued Sidi Bombay went to see what was wrong. "Ah! Ah!" Speke called out, and when Bombay tried to shake him from his sleep, he couldn't. Speke's brow burned with fever, so Burton was summoned.

Hour after hour Speke emerged from hallucinations, then drifted back into them once again. "My legs!" he said, his eyes wide. "I saw leopards and tigers harnessed with iron hooks dragging me over the ground by my legs! Look, see these cramps! Oh, God! It's hideous pain, Dick!"

Soon the whole camp was awake with his screaming. Several porters came to the opening in his tent to watch, but he barked like a dog and scared them off.

"Demons!" he yelled out. "They're stripping the tendons out of my legs! See, long bloody tendons! I won't be able to walk! Look at this!"

Sidi Bombay brought herbal tea, which Speke spat upon the ground. His mouth chopped and barked, so that Burton thought the seizure was hydrophobia.

"We must stop," Sidi Bombay told Burton. "We can't march on." He seemed on the verge of tears as he watched Speke.

"Of course, we'll stop," Burton assured him.

The next day in a lucid moment Speke called for pen and paper so that he could write a farewell letter to his family.

"I'm dying," he told Burton. "And I've got to say goodbye."

Burton held Speke in his arms, helping to guide his hand as he attempted to compose a letter that was never finished. For half a day, Speke's fevered body rested against Burton's as they stayed on the mats and pillows inside the tent. Once Speke woke up angry, turning his face to Burton's and lashing out. "I'll never forgive you for taking my diary and notes on the Somali coast! You had no right!"

"Steady, Jack, rest yourself," Burton soothed him.

But the wild fever wouldn't go away. Speke moved in and out of a shallow sleep, tortured by nightmares, until Burton considered turning back to Kazeh. Then he firmly decided against it. Speke is going to die, he told himself. We can go on. He won't last through this.

Although his vivid nightmares ebbed away, Speke was too weak to travel, so they halted several days while Burton attempted to rig an additional hammock and to convince some of the porters that they should become bearers. None of the porters would agree to this heavier task, though, and instead fought among themselves, arguing about duties and trying for lighter loads.

Sidi Bombay went to a nearby village of a dozen huts hoping to purchase help, but only four men would work.

"They say they will carry the white man thirty miles, but that is all," Bombay told Burton. "For this they want three cloths each."

Two of Burton's own porters, overhearing this bribery, began to laugh.

"What are you laughing at?" Burton shouted at them.

When they continued to laugh, they saw too late that Burton was coming at them. He seized the largest of the two, spun him around, and smashed a fist into the man's mouth, so that blood flew everywhere. The whole camp silenced itself.

"Come here, you!" Burton called to the other one, who backed off. "Bend yourself over this man's back! You, stay where you are! Bend over!" As the fallen man tried to rise, Burton kicked him down again. Everyone gathered at a discreet distance to watch. "You bend down! Do it, I tell you! Sidi Bombay, go fetch my sword!"

As the man on the ground spat out bits of enamel and clots of blood, Burton grabbed the other porter's ear, twisting him down with a curse. "God damn you, get down there!" Burton's eyes flared with such intensity that the crowd eased back, forming a larger circle.

Seeing Bombay bring the sword in its scabbard, the fallen man pleaded that his head should not be cut off.

Burton used the hard leather scabbard itself, though, and delivered a blow that raised a long, red welt across the man's neck and shoulder.

"There are over one hundred and fifty of us in this caravan!" Burton shouted so that everyone could hear. "And all of you *will* carry your loads!" He delivered another blow, well aimed, across the length of the man's back. "And you *will* care for the sick!" Another blow, so heavy that the man grunted with pain. "And you *will* keep me from flogging anyone again!" Another blow, harder yet.

He told the two offenders to change places.

"Oh, master!" came the plea from the man on bottom. "My wounded mouth!"

"Never mind your mouth! Get on top now and take your punishment!"

Afterward when Burton returned to his tent, his hands were shaking and his swollen legs wobbled beneath him. He drank brandy and tried to calm himself, thinking, God, I've had to lose my temper again with them. But it's necessary. I've got to be supremely in charge.

"Sorry I'm still sick," Speke said, looking up from his pallet.

"I'm sorry, too, Jack, and have bad news. I just can't arrange hammocks for us. There aren't any bearers at prices we can pay, so you'll have to manage to sit your donkey. Tell me when you can do it."

"I'll soon be fit," Speke said.

"Don't worry yourself. We have time—always lots of that."

"Please don't leave me, no matter what we've said in the past."

"No, of course not," Burton replied.

In early December as they entered the Ugogo Plain, they met a caravan of Mombasa Indians who brought them newspapers and a packet of letters.

Speke wanted any sort of mail, but again received nothing. Burton badly wanted to hear from Edward, but instead found a stiff little note of greetings from Captain Rigby, Hamerton's replacement at Zanzibar, and an official wigging from the British government in reply to his suggestion that England should strengthen its position in the Red Sea, Suez, and the Indian Ocean.

"What did they say?" Speke asked, looking over Burton's shoulder at the correspondence.

"They told me I'm a presumptuous young officer. They paid no attention to my advice, just judged everything on the basis of my rank."

Burton angrily folded the letter, noticing that Speke seemed quietly pleased that the authorities had been so haughty.

That night Burton opened a sheath of Bombay newspapers and discovered that there had been a massacre in India. All the Christians at Jidda had been murdered while the British army had been powerless.

"See, here we are! In the same packet of mail! India and everything in the Mideast is going to be a catastrophe!"

"I really know nothing of politics in India," Speke said, not accepting the newspaper Burton thrust at him.

"You were there! You talked with Lumsden! You heard those old farts at dinner! What is it you *do* know?"

"I know what I know, nothing more," Speke answered.

"Spoken, Jack, like a woman," Burton said, going to his tent.

In his tent, Burton paced around before finally settling down to read the small columns of those old newspapers by the single candle. He couldn't help thinking of Edward; he also wished he had married Isabel, so that her heavy breasts might pillow his homecoming. Above all, he was exhausted with Speke's idiocies.

Toward midnight, when everyone in camp slept, Said bin Selim began to wail. He weaved his way among the smoldering fires, kicking up dust and ashes, crying in distress because in that same packet of mail he had received a note saying that he was considered dead in Zanzibar, so that his brother had taken over his wife and all his worldly possessions. Men shouted at him to go to sleep, but he kept on until morning. Sleepless and hysterical, he began shouting at everyone to get up before dawn, to pack and to get on the path home, to make every effort to get to the coast as quickly as possible.

The trip back across the Ugogo Plain took three weeks.

Not only did the monsoon rains begin, but all around them the tribes warred with one another; they passed village after village that had been razed, huts burned, and all the inhabitants gone, debris and signs of life washed away in rivulets of mud.

On Christmas day Sidi Bombay bought a fat capon at a nearby village, which Speke and Burton shared for dinner. Burton learned that the villagers also had six goats for sale, so offered to buy these for the porters and askaris, but the men of the caravan were too lazy, too fevered, or too gone on *bangi* to walk back to the little settlement and collect their feast.

Speke, alone in his tent, the rains pounding down and shutting out all other sounds and all sense of time or place, tried painting by candlelight, but gave up the effort. He tried drinking, but liquor sickened him. Long hours of sleep were his only solace. He felt that he would burst open with what he couldn't say to Burton and couldn't wait to tell the world.

In their separate tents, seldom speaking from day to day, they spent the hours from dark until dawn in isolation. Burton made notes on archery, witchcraft, weaving, pipes, sexual customs, medicine, and the local geographies. He also wrote at length about slavery, noting that there needed to be commerce in Zanzibar that would make slavery unnecessary. As he had said so often, he wrote, "Men must be valuable by their labor, not by their sale." As he wrote, he drank heavily, reducing the supply of brandy, pombe, alcoholic medicines, or whatever was available to him. One night, drunk, he consumed the ink with which he wrote; his lip and chin beneath his mustache looked like a deep, dark hole.

As if moving through a sea of mud, they reached Zungomero again—still infested with raiding parties, sullen mercenaries, and men as desperate as the rats that fed on everything. Having descended from the highlands again, their fevers ebbed back into their bones; the humid squalor drained them; scratches became open wounds; they stayed wet and cold.

The porters and askaris were still restless and testy, but afraid to cause much commotion because of the dozens of killers who camped around them. Said bin Selim did try to take advantage of the raw climate and Burton's uncomfortable fever in order to demand additional pay for himself and his men.

"Pay us all that you owe right now, or we won't proceed to Zanzibar," he finally argued.

"I'll pay you at Zanzibar, as we agreed," Burton answered, and he gave the timid foreman a mean, even stare, ending further discussion.

Another Arab caravan arrived at Zungomero shortly after they did. Two huge men—arms as thick as Burton's swollen legs—ruled the caravan: an Arab named Rashid and an ebony-dark Swahili called Mohammed. Burton kept the company of these men in the evenings, but Speke, as usual, spoke none of the Arabic, had no sympathy for the company of slavers, and seemed not to care for their geographical findings.

The slavers had left the coast six months previously, had gone due west, and had found another lake—the Nyasa—below Tanganyika.

"A very large lake," Rashid informed the Englishmen. "With a river linking it to Tanganyika."

"Do you think there is a whole system of lakes—linked up by rivers—in this part of the continent?" Burton asked them.

"Oh yes, definitely," the Swahili said.

"Even so, such a system isn't the Nile basin," Speke said to Burton.

"What more did you see and do?" Burton asked the slavers as a courtesy.

"Bless Allah, very little," Rashid said, accepting the pipe Burton offered. "We took eight hundred slaves, sold some, lost some. And then misfortune occurred. We camped one night in a dry riverbed, but the monsoon rains had begun in the mountains, so that a flash flood washed away one hundred fifty souls for whom we had paid good coils of wire."

"We also took some ivory," the Swahili giant added.

"Yes, but poor-grade ivory. We have not been favored," Rashid said.

"Woe to anyone who gathers wealth and counts it over thinking that it will perpetuate him," Burton replied, quoting the Koran.

"Truly," the slavers answered in unison.

They left Zungomero in the rain, walked for two days, then fell into their tents for another rest. Fevered and lonely, Burton suffered an overwhelming desire to see Isabel again, to ravish her, and to marry her. With the ink he hadn't consumed, he wrote a poem.

> That brow which rose before my sight
> As on the palmer's holy shrine;
> Those eyes—my life was in their light;
> Those lips my sacramental wine;
> That voice whose flow was wont to seem
> The music of an exile's dream.

He was a wretched poet and knew it. And this was one of his worst efforts, but if he ever made Zanzibar, he decided, he would post it to his love. At that moment, he remembered Isabel's waist as tiny and her breasts as immense.

He dreamed of meeting and having solid literary conversations with real poets. There was daffy Tennyson—at least he knew his brother. Once, some years ago in Rome, he had met a strange man named Guiseppe Belli, who read his poems in the bars of the city, never published them, and contented himself with being adored by peasants and literate drunkards. Belli wrote overtly sexual sonnets, which Burton somehow wished he had written. His own work, he knew, seemed set in high-minded granite, even confessions of love such as this ode to Isabel.

Damn words, damn deeds, and damn the man with aching needs.

In late January 1859, the porters began to squeal with delight on sighting the first mango tree, a sign that the coast was near. The next day they saw lime, coconut, and pineapple growing wild.

At the coastal village of Konduchi the men fired off guns and heard, in reply, the low drums and the high lulliloo of the native women who greeted them. That night at the feast celebrating their arrival, the Jemadar appeared before Burton to say goodbye.

"My village is on this side of Zanzibar Island, and I have arranged a canoe," he explained, and as he spoke thick tears formed in his eyes. He took off his monocle and rubbed away the tears with his fist. "So I shall say farewell. We have seen wonders. Our adventures are legend. Our strength will be known, and you will show a fine map of our travels!"

"Yes, yes, I suppose so," Burton told him. This was the rascal I could have killed, he was thinking; who never worked, who never fought, who complained at every step and threatened at every stop.

The Jemadar wept and kissed Burton's extended sleeve. This excess of emotion, Burton knew, was self-serving; the Jemadar depended on Burton's endorsement if he ever expected to be given charge of a group of askaris again.

"We have tamed the mighty Ugogo," the Jemadar went on, his rhetoric aglow. "We have found the mother of all the waters!"

"Yes, thank you. Now you'd better be off," Burton replied.

The next day Burton sent word to Zanzibar asking for a ship, and he and Speke met with a local Arab, a peg-legged man who seemed to be the nominal head of that little settlement of thatch huts and Arab houses. The man dug holes in the muddy earth with the tip of his wooden leg as they conversed.

"A bad political situation over at Zanzibar," he told them. "Sultan Majid has hired mercenaries. The town is filled with knives, and I believe the new British commander supports first the Sultan and then the other side."

"Perhaps it will all blow over before we get there," Burton said. "As a matter of fact, I believe we'll linger here on the coast for a while as we wait for our ship. I've thought about exploring the mouth of the Rufiji River."

They were speaking English, so Speke became alarmed at this announcement. "Stay here?" he asked, incredulous. "Let's get on with things!"

"You are always in a hurry. And for what?"

"There is considerable cholera along the coast—in almost every village," the Arab said, pawing at the ground. The earth was like sponge in places and made soft sucking sounds underfoot.

"See there, sickness," Speke interjected. "We can't stay here."

"But we must. A ship will take time. I won't be rowed back to Zanzibar like some meager porter. We'll want to make an entrance on our return."

Speke looked aghast.

"There may be a ship leaving Zanzibar for Aden," he argued. "If we wait around here, we might miss it."

"We're staying at Konduchi awhile," Burton said firmly.

Soon Speke understood: women.

Burton began his daily habits at Konduchi as if, once again, he courted the whores at Aden or Zayla. In the mornings he rose late, sipped coffee and ate fruit, then made sketches and jotted down his eternal notes. At midafternoon he ordered their large meal, then afterward napped for hours. At dark, he drank and invited women into his tent—native girls, a lanky Watusi who plied her trade along the coast, and an Oriental named May Wu. She had a subtle body, rather slender except for the hips. But when she copulated—and the sounds of their lovemaking, at times, echoed from his tent long hours into the night—she sounded like a bellows.

"How much are you paying your women?" Speke asked him one afternoon.

They had said little to each other since making camp within sight of the sea. A grove of palm framed their view of the lapping shore. Across the muddy road a young black hacked his way through a green sapling with the bare blade of an Omani saber, and Burton watched this labor with fascination. Not answering Speke's question, he sighed. "Have you noticed, Jack, that they don't even jag their knives into saws here in Africa? It's unbelievable. Surely, someday, some Daedalus will come teach them a few mechanical simplicities."

Silence fell between them until Speke persisted. "If you're paying your women with our last coils of wire, I thought I should know," he said.

They walked over to a nearby fishing cove, where Burton intended to arrange for a dhow that could take them south to Kilwa.

"Why there?" Speke asked, unable to fathom this additional delay.

"Because of the poet Camoëns," Burton explained. "Da Gama's explorations at Kilwa were immortalized in the finest Portuguese verse—surely you know that? How can we visit East Africa and not see Kilwa?"

"I'm no poet or scholar," Speke protested. "Let's get back to Zanzibar and home!"

"We want our mission to be thorough."

"Whatever you're doing, you're too late for thoroughness." Speke laughed.

But they found the dhow and sailed along the coast, swept by an east wind that brought heavy morning showers, then sunshine and cool evenings. Cholera cursed every village, so they didn't put ashore. Speke rode out their journey with his arms around the mast, as if he meant to pull it down, as if he could hardly bear the agony of this detour.

He and Burton had little to say, but once Speke mentioned that he had known Rigby, the new consul and military commander at Zanzibar, while in India. "He's a good sort," he told Burton. "I know he'll help us with a speedy return home."

Burton had seen cholera in Italy as a boy—staring down into those morbid fleshpots with his brother Edward—and in India, too, traveling the southern provinces, but nothing compared to what he found at Kilwa. The air itself stank of rotting death. Corpses had been thrown into the bay, and the bodies at the edge of the shore were mottled—brown and ghastly white—and the women's puffed and swollen breasts bobbing in the shallows looked like pickled, scalded pig's meat. Limbs were scattered in all directions, and squadrons of birds picked at the deadly carrion.

Beyond the beach, the town was virtually deserted—emptied by death. A few workers dragged bodies to the bay, as if they meant to pollute the ocean itself with the land's carnage. Columns of stinking smoke rose above the huts, and a doleful silence held everything.

"I'm going ashore," Burton told the crew.

"You can't mean it," Speke protested. "You'll bring the epidemic back aboard the boat with you when you return!"

"I want to ask about the Rufiji River," Burton explained. "I want to know if it's open for commerce and if there's copal trading going on. I might visit the ruins nearby. And I want to collect some of those skulls lying about on the beach."

"Whatever for?" Speke asked.

"For the museum of the Royal College of Surgeons," Burton said. "We're not out here on holiday, you know. Let's worry about the geography and a few commercial and scientific matters!"

A dinghy took Burton almost to shore, where he walked through the shallows, stepping over those piled-up corpses and severed limbs, to reach the town's beach. He spent only a few hours at Kilwa, learning that the river was another festered mouth of death, that all trade had stopped everywhere, that no one knew or cared if the Rufiji became part of the huge Zambesi river system. In the late afternoon he strolled out to the ruins—which were not particularly impressive. Yet he felt the obligatory melancholy, the deep drum of time. He could feel his fever rising, and with it a definite depression; a somber dreaminess.

He hired two listless workers to find skulls and they collected, in all, two dozen, roping them together in a large, grisly bracelet.

Back onboard the dhow, he dropped the skulls near the bow of the boat. Although Speke stood at his position at the mast, the rest of the crew cowered at the stern, as far away from those evil, vacant bones as they could stand. Their fear amused Burton, but Speke's mouth drew straight in anger.

"When we get to Zanzibar, boil those skulls," Burton told Sidi Bombay. "When they're clean, we'll parcel them up and send them to London."

Sidi Bombay looked out to sea, as if this had certainly never been said.

The cannon in the harbor at Zanzibar boomed at their return, and hundreds of well-wishers met them at the quay. Rigby's garrison turned out in clean white uniforms, saluting and smiling, so that Speke commented favorably on the difference between this arrival and the casual greeting given them before by Hamerton, whose uniform was always soiled and wrinkled and who smelled of Irish whiskey and cloves.

"Speke!" Rigby said, grabbing the hand of his former acquaintance. Then he turned and pumped Burton's hand, too, saying, "Yes, yes, I remember you from the Gujarati language examination! You took first and I took second— scarcely one point apart in the final score!" Burton didn't recall it that way, but smiled with relief that Rigby seemed so effusive.

The town was in chaos, so that the Sultan sent only a messenger to the quay to inform Burton that he hoped to see them soon. From Musqat, the Sultan's elder brother planned to invade the island, so fortifications were being built. Cholera also plagued the town, and the death rate, Rigby told them, was 250 a day.

Speke was whisked away to the consulate and given a room next to Rigby's, but Burton took rooms at Afrika House. There he looked at his swollen legs with despair and sprawled across his bed in the high reaches of the old house, listening to the sounds of the city drift across the rooftops.

"Can I get you anything?" an orderly asked.

"No, nothing," Burton said, covering his eyes with his arm.

"Are you all right, sir?"

"I have fever. Is there anything to read in this place? I don't want to leave my rooms unless the Sultan sends for me."

"There are a few saucy French novels in the sergeant-major's care," the orderly reported.

"Bring me those. And a bottle of brandy."

"You'll want me to bring your meals, too," the orderly said, sensing the mood. "And writing materials. I know you're a fine writer, sir, and in a day or so, when you've rested, you'll want pen and paper."

Burton gave the young man a smile and closed his eyes. The depression that had come to him at Kilwa now encompassed him.

Speke dressed in a clean uniform, buttoned himself up, and dined with Rigby that evening.

"The consulate looks spick-and-span," he told his host.

"I think you can say military matters have been set straight," Rigby said.

Speke ate several portions of roast pig, washing down his heavy meal with glasses of raw goat's milk. In a short time the conversation came around to Burton.

"I'm sure he considers himself a personal favorite of the Sultan's," Rigby announced, "so I don't want him on the island for very long. He'll muck about in politics here and get us all in hot water, if I know him. He's a troublemaker. Always has been. I'm not even sure that he's English. Did you ever look him hard in the eyes?"

"I've had the thought myself," Speke admitted.

"How'd you ever stand him?"

"He was definitely an impediment. I discovered the source of the Nile by myself while he stayed behind with some whores in an Arab slave camp."

"You found it? You know absolutely that you found it?"

"An immense lake that I've christened Victoria. Huge. I know the Nile flows out of the north end, so I've got to come back with another expedition when Burton's out of the way."

"He's a dreadful egotist," Rigby said, drinking off his wine and shaking his head with disgust. "Talented, perhaps, yes, but no one in India could bear him."

"I'm not very ready with my pen, you know," Speke said. "If we go back to London together, Burton will write his reports and his books and steal my victory in this and I'll be powerless. He's done it to me before. He blows his trumpet loudly. He has high-placed friends, and I have none. It sickens me to think about what's coming."

Rigby sat in thought and poured himself another glass of wine. He was a small, thin man, clean shaven, with a mouth that moved and twitched before words actually came out. His dress was impeccable—a compliment to his belief, as he told Speke, that a career officer could never hope to be a general if his neatness wasn't prominent.

Their table was on the wide balcony facing the sea. Flies buzzed over their food, and a large crow—one of the island's biggest and blackest—perched on the railing not far from Rigby's shoulder.

"I want to take you into my confidence concerning Burton," Rigby said, looking out at the water. "He left a package here, which he expected Hamerton to mail to your Royal Geographical Society. It was a manuscript on Zanzibar: I found it waiting for me when I took over. Mostly it concerns anthropological matters, but there were some nasty criticisms of the government implied in it. I mailed it to the Bombay office for inspection by army officials."

"Good procedure," Speke said. "But why tell me?"

"When Burton was in India he was asked to write a report on Indian civilian customs, for use by officers out on the frontier. It was a filthy document, as it turned out, concerned with sodomy and sex—almost exclusively. Almost got him drummed out of the army. All of us heard about it."

"Sodomy?"

"He has peculiar tastes, if you ask me. But whatever, he dislikes the army and anything that restricts his individualistic style. Of course he'll steal your fame. He'll turn your achievement to his own advantage in every way he can."

"I dread what's coming." Speke sighed.

"Let me help," Rigby offered. "Surely a man like that will take enough rope to hang himself. The way he preens and holds his nose! Let me tell you, if he tries to undermine my authority with the Sultan, I'll have his balls. Let him step wrong anywhere and I'll ruin him."

"Frankly, I'm of a mixed mind about him. By the way, what do they call you?"

"Call me Christopher, that will do."

"Of mixed mind, as I say. He has courage. He nursed me through fever and delirium. But I won't have him take what's mine."

"No, of course not."

"I'm just a simple farm boy. That's the truth. And I really don't know what's best to do."

"You certainly eat like a farm boy," Rigby noted. "Look, leave things to me. You need an ally. I'm very glad we've had this little talk."

"Thanks," Speke said. "And, by the way, call me Jack."

Said bin Selim and various porters soon dropped by Afrika House, looking for Burton and more pay. Hamerton, they claimed, had promised them bonuses.

"I was to receive one thousand dollars and a gold watch!" Said bin Selim told Burton. They met in the street outside the club with young officers leaning out of windows above them listening to their disagreement, a coffee vendor hawking his drink beside them as he banged two metal cups together—all irritations Burton didn't need.

"You've stolen enough and worked hardly any," Burton told the leader of the porters. "You'll get no more."

Said bin Selim glared and spat, but not in Burton's direction, because he was wisely afraid of the man. But at a safe distance down the street as he went his way he sent up a barrage of curses.

The £1000 provided by the Foreign Office had been long spent, and Burton did feel obliged to pay some of the porters who had worked hard, so he wrote drafts for £1400 from his personal accounts. Although he hated to discuss finances with Speke, he went to him.

"Yes, when we get back to London I'll settle with you," Speke promised, so Burton let the matter drop. Money matters made Speke touchy.

That evening Speke told Rigby about Burton's conflict with Said bin Selim and the porters.

"Burton's probably a poor manager—men like him always are," Rigby said. "Besides, he identifies himself with Arabs, so probably thinks blacks are animals and not worthy of pay. But one must treat porters fairly, or future caravans will be ruined in these parts."

"You know, I suppose, that Burton actually became a Moslem on his famous trip to Mecca?" Speke asked. "Kissed the holy stone. Brags about it."

"That does it. He joined a race of slavers, don't you see? Hates niggers. And that sort of hatred contributes to ruined commerce hereabouts."

"Quite," Speke agreed.

"If we looked at matters, we'd probably find that he's robbing the government as well as overspending and managing poorly. And don't believe him when he says he's paying out his own money to those porters! He detests their kind. Don't believe him for a minute!"

Rigby's grudge against Burton was pure. And unfair as it was, Speke knew it could prove useful.

When Burton was finally invited to dine with the Sultan Sayyid Majid, he found a troubled man, beset by intrigues, but also fretful deep inside himself. "You will perhaps understand this because you are a man of knowledge and theology," the Sultan said. "Something inside me withers. I feel it, but know it not."

They sat on an open verandah, Burton drinking cognac and the Sultan sipping a tepid tea after the meal; beyond, the windless sea was like glass, and the muffled noises of the distant city comforted the evening.

It was a curious conversation, Burton acting as priest, while the Sultan worried over his soul. They tended to speak in mythical stories, aphorisms, and allusions.

"In Oman, the country of my fathers, there was once an argument over who was the rightful successor to the Prophet Muhammad. In the war that grew from this argument, my forefather lost and set sail as an exile with his six sons from Shiraz. He and his sons settled this coast, each one taking a fortress: Mombasa, Pemba, Zanzibar, Kilwa, and all the rest. But my forefather had a terrible dream, which came to him almost every night of his life: he saw a rat

with an iron muzzle eating at the wall of his castle. He knew that he was cursed by Allah, that his exile was probably just, and that his cities—built by him and his sons—were doomed to destruction and ruin."

"Men often dream of death," Burton said. "Because it stands at the end of a man's time, it makes life short and sweet. But it also devours all he builds, all his vanities, and all his works, good or evil."

"The cockroach whirring flits the empty halls," said the Sultan Majid, quoting a poem. "Where nobles gathered, shrill the cricket calls."

"If a man has courage, he still doesn't have everything," Burton mused. "Deep inside is an emptiness. No amount of courage can fight this emptiness. By its nature, it is an unseen nothingness, which can't be found or overcome."

"Yes, this is the thing of which we speak," the Sultan agreed. "I have paid a witch doctor to cast the bones and read my future in them. I talked to a Parsee who gazed into the fire in my behalf. My spirit is with Allah, yet lost."

"While seeking the lakes, I felt the earth tremble," Burton added. "The porters took this as an omen—and, alas, so did I."

"The dream of my forefather has become mine," Majid confessed. "The rat eats through the wall, breathes on me, and I become grey, turn into a rat myself, wear a muzzle of iron, and feed on others."

"Dreams lie to us. They aren't always our friends."

"Madness is a form of wisdom."

"Madness is also just crazy," Burton said, consoling his host.

Sidi Bombay came to Speke one afternoon, asking if he might be permitted to sit in Speke's room upstairs at the consulate.

"Yes, I suppose so. Why do you want to?" Speke asked.

"Burton stays in his bed with women or books," Sidi Bombay explained. "I have gone to the wonders of the inland seas, but have nowhere important to sit during the days!"

That evening Speke returned from a stroll along the beach in order to dress for dinner and found his servant sitting beside the window, hands folded, looking contented and happy.

Captain Ian McFarlane's clipper ship, *Dragon of Salem*, arrived in Zanzibar in the early days of March 1859, bound for Aden.

While Burton arranged passage, Rigby wrote to the officials of the government in Bombay, notifying them that Burton was in process of leaving Zanzibar without having properly paid the porters in his caravan. In addition, he wrote:

> Speke is a right good, jolly, resolute fellow. Burton is not fit to
> hold a candle to him and has done nothing in comparison to what
> Speke has, but Burton will blow his trumpet very loud and get all

the credit of the discoveries. Speke works. Burton lies on his back all day and picks other people's brains.

On the day before the ship sailed, Rigby conferred with Speke a last time. "I've actually thought of going with you to help you, but I couldn't bear Burton's company at sea," he said. "So I want to make sure. Would you say he's hostile to our native porters? Intolerant and brutal?"

"Yes, I'd say so," Speke agreed.

"Then don't worry about who'll get credit for the accomplishments of this expedition. Believe me, Jack, there's great things in store for both of us in London. You're going to be one of the most famous men of your time. I'm going to be promoted general. You'll see. Great things."

They shook hands warmly and laughed.

That last day Burton got drunk with Captain McFarlane.

"I suspect the worst of Rigby," he told the seaman. "I can't prove it, but I suspect he didn't pass along all my correspondence. I suspect he's plotting with Speke to discredit me. They watch me like hawks."

"I'd rather listen to Hamerton puke than listen to Rigby talk," McFarlane admitted with a laugh.

"Here's to Hamerton and here's to gin," Burton replied, raising a toast.

They sat on kegs aboardship, watching Sidi Bombay as he made his way among the dockworkers who loaded stores and baggage. A small hard monkey of a man: that crushed-down face, that smile flashing with sharpened teeth, eyes round and shiny. Slowly, he made the gangplank, then came on deck to stand beside Burton and the captain as they drank. The scent of clove and brine rode the breeze around them as they all grinned at each other.

"Bombay, I have come to admire your ugliness," Burton told him.

"Will you come back?" the little man asked with an uncertain look, as if he wanted to be casual, but couldn't.

"I'll definitely return," Burton said, slurring each syllable. "Because your countenance has become pleasing to me."

Captain McFarlane, who claimed he didn't like to be sober when he steered any vessel out of harbor, raised his glass and peered through it at the sun, seeing a corona of empty thoughts.

"You will go to London Town?" Sidi Bombay persisted.

"Yes, to London. And, eventually, with luck, back here."

"So you will write me a letter?"

Burton regarded Sidi Bombay with such stern, drunken concentration that the little man stiffened, as if undergoing an important military inspection. "Oh, Captain, give me your opinion," Burton said, slurring.

"Yes, adventurer, what is it?"

"What shall we do with a squat, ugly, loyal askari who speaks many tongues and takes up very little space?"

Sidi Bombay brightened as the captain grunted a reply.

"Get your gear. You'll go with us," Burton announced.

Sidi Bombay hurried down the gangplank and ran through the narrow streets to his stall behind the market, where he gathered up all his worldly possessions: his knives, his extra shirt, his rusted saber, and the broken pedometer —still his prize and badge of merit.

As the clipper ship cast off its lines and edged away from the quay, a rough fishing dhow moved in beside it to dock. The great vessel and the small boat passed each other at a distance of only a few feet, so that Burton, standing at the rail with his half-empty bottle of gin, saw the Oriental girl from the mainland, May Wu, looking at him from the deck of the dhow.

Undoubtedly, he knew, she had come to Zanzibar to find him again. Clearly, she could see, he was off to the distant seas. All this was clear in the gaze they shared, yet they said nothing as they passed out of each other's lives— passing so close that they could have whispered farewell.

The monsoon winds still gusted, though the days at sea were dry and sunny: perfect, fast weather for sailing.

Speke, whose ear still throbbed with pain, seemed unusually good-spir-ited. He laughed out loud at the porpoises in the ship's wake and cleaned his rifles while chatting with McFarlane and the crew.

He and Burton never mentioned the Nile. Instead, like old army mates who had found each other again, they told stories about their service, the ironies of the Crimean conflict—Beatson's Horse, the idiocies of command, the bore-dom of Kertch—and their lives with their families. Burton talked about his brother Edward while Speke, in turn, admitted that he had never been close to his brothers because of his long military career.

They inquired about each other's health.

"I've thought about taking some opium because of the pain in my ear," Speke said.

"Why don't you? I'll give you some."

"Oh, I just detest the idea of taking narcotics. My eyes improved without medicine, you know, and my fever's gone. I'm hoping that my ear will stop hurting—though I'm resigned to deafness."

"Look at my legs," Burton said, pulling up his trousers.

"My God," Speke said.

The knees were still badly swollen and discolored. Burton had also lost weight and looked very gaunt, Speke noticed, and wasn't at all the man who had gone up-country to Ujiji. Having accused Burton of laziness, Speke didn't want to linger too long on thoughts that the man might be badly ill, yet there it was: the hollow cheek—accented by that wide scar—and the pall of fever. In spite of himself, Speke felt sorry for Burton. He was past his prime. And strength, now, the strength of youth, was everything.

When they arrived in Aden during the middle of April, these feelings were reinforced by Steinhauser's greeting. The doctor stood in the middle of the crowd at the dock, waving and calling as the ship moved into its slip, but as he saw Burton, his face collapsed in concern.

"Damn me, Dick, you're sick!" he said, as they embraced.

"Just a little fever. I'll soon be fit," Burton answered.

The two old friends talked loudly in that din of noise around the gangplank, laughing and already beginning to tell their stories, before the doctor turned to acknowledge Speke with the first hello. But such lack of courtesy didn't matter to Speke anymore; Burton, beside the hearty Steinhauser, seemed ghostly; his skin had yellowed and his lips drew away from his teeth when he smiled, so that Speke felt a superior pity now, nothing more.

"You'll come to my house," Steinhauser was saying to Burton. "You'll stay with me, so I can look after you!"

"Yes, fine, yes," Burton replied, and the two of them were laughing, their arms around each other's shoulders.

Lawrence Oliphant watched this whole scene.

He stood on the deck of the big steamer in the next slip, looking down on the arrivals, shading himself with an umbrella and trying to call to Speke, though he couldn't be heard.

The ship was the *Furious*, which had just arrived in Aden from a diplomatic mission in the Orient. Oliphant, who had been serving as Lord Elgin's secretary on the trip, was trimmed out, as usual, in top fashion: white morning coat and top hat, silk shirt, and a paisley cravat. He still looked like a Belgravian dandy as he called out, "Speke! My dear Speke!"

Steinhauser and Burton had left the dock when Oliphant, holding the umbrella high, smiling and making his way through the crowd, came toward the gangplank of Captain McFarlane's clipper ship, where Speke directed the porters who stacked his personal baggage.

"I say, Jack!" Oliphant said, finally making himself heard.

"Lowry!"

"So where are you taking all that filthy-looking baggage?"

"To the garrison," Speke said, breaking into a smile.

"No, not at all! See this fancy steamer? I have you a fine stateroom and a friendly face: mine!"

"I can't believe it!" Speke said, but by this time Oliphant held his hand, leading him through the crowd of passengers and dockworkers. Broken sacks of cloves gave everything the aroma of Zanzibar. Nubians with shaved heads and skimpy loincloths lifted bundles for the wives of officers, women with bright parasols and wide-brimmed straw hats.

A young ensign saluted as Oliphant led Speke aboard the *Furious*.

The stateroom was done in inlaid teakwood, brass, silk draperies, and white marble; the early-afternoon sunlight slanted through its portholes, but the room breathed a cool, reclusive air. "It's wonderful, Lowry, really," Speke managed, feeling as though he had entered a palace. He felt acutely aware of his own look and stink and stood there, tentative, waiting, until Oliphant embraced him.

"I missed you," Oliphant whispered, and something in Speke gave way.

They stood just inside the door, which was still partially open, but the deck was empty, all the officers having gone ashore, and the shadows of the room seemed to gather them in. Speke, for a moment, clumsily patted Oliphant's back —a sort of thumping reflex that left prints on his friend's white coat. Then, from some spring down inside him, he began to weep softly.

"Jack, come now, what's the matter?" Oliphant asked, holding the embrace.

"Oh, Lowry, it's my ear," Speke managed. "I'm deaf in it. A terrible thing happened, and I'm half deaf!"

"Ah, good man, there, it's all right," Oliphant said, and he held Speke closer, running his fingers above Speke's collar and touching the bare flesh at the back of Speke's neck, bringing their faces together as he began to stroke the neck, cheek, ear, and hair. "Steady, please, it's all right," he assured him. Speke's legs felt weak, as if both a very old and very new fever were upon him, and he leaned into Oliphant's body, which was stronger than he remembered it, older and stronger, as if he could never let go.

While Burton and Steinhauser had supper at their favorite hotel that evening, Oliphant and Speke dined aboard the steamer with Lord Elgin. The old boy came back from the mainland drunk, got drunker, and retired early, so that the two young men could talk. They sat in a salon on velvet couches, the walls above them hung with maps and Chinese watercolors, as Oliphant smoked a long, curved opium pipe with a jade-and-silver bowl.

"A curious thing happened a few days ago," Oliphant said, taking short puffs at the pipe. "Coming back from China, I had a dream. My father appeared at bedside and called me."

"I remember Sir Anthony quite well," Speke added.

"Yes, and so I got out of bed in my dream, embraced him, and kissed his temple—which was quite cold. At breakfast the next morning I told the other attachés that my father was dead. Odd, the words just popped out of me. Days later, when we reached Ceylon, my father's death was confirmed. It happened, as best as I know, at that same hour when he appeared before me."

"Oh, Lowry, sorry," Speke said.

"I've had a strange two years. We fought off some attackers at the consulate one night. I used a sword well and shot a man in the leg. We've had a very successful diplomatic coup: got a treaty that allows Europeans to navigate on the Yangtze River and to trade. Our forces occupy Canton and, ah, you know: the British are naturally trying to run things properly, what else? But for me, personally, things have changed, too. I think I'm entering my mystic period, Jack, truly. All things have a mystic dimension for me. This matter of my father's death. This coincidence—meeting you on a funny little wharf at the edge of a desert halfway around the world!"

"It is strange," Speke admitted.

"And you've changed, too. Something has happened. Tell me what."

"It's the Nile," Speke said. "It's mine."

The next morning at breakfast Burton heard that Speke was staying aboard the *Furious* with Oliphant and Lord Elgin—and preparing to return to England with them when they sailed in two days.

"You shouldn't go yourself," Steinhauser warned him. "Your legs look awful. You should stay in bed and rest for months."

"Well, I haven't been invited to go with them, have I?" Burton answered.

"No, I suppose not. Is there something wrong between you and Speke, Dick?"

Burton told him how Speke made his trip to the nyanza alone and how they argued. "For all I know, too, he's right," Burton admitted. "He may have found the damned Nile. Certainly, the position of the lake's right. But he hasn't a whit of proof, not a single accurate calculation, not one good reading—just a guess."

"Dick, I fear the worst in this," the doctor said.

"Unfortunately, so do I," Burton told him.

That noon they all gathered in the officer's mess of the garrison. Lord Elgin was there, looking drunk, still, although Oliphant assured everyone that he wasn't. Lord Elgin was a large man with thick muttonchop whiskers and eyes that seemed out of focus, working this way and that, and never quite falling on whoever talked with him. The meal consisted of boiled beef and cabbage, but the English ale was most admired.

Speke confirmed that he would leave on the *Furious*.

"I'll give you our maps and drawings," Burton told him. "And I'll send along a letter to Shaw, the Society's secretary, in the event I'm laid up indefinitely and you decide to report to the Society without me."

"Don't bother about that," Speke said. "Just take care of your health, Dick, and come along as soon as you can."

"I say we're all heroes," Oliphant said, raising a glass of beer.

"Hear, hear," others replied. Steinhauser and the officers raised their glasses while Lord Elgin gazed here and there, trying to think of proper words.

"To men who open up the bowels of closed countries," he finally managed, including diplomacy and exploration in the same rush of breath.

"Bloody right," Steinhauser whispered to Burton. "And you know, don't you, Dick, what lurks on the insides of bowels?"

That evening Burton composed a careful letter to Dr. Norton Shaw, the secretary of the Royal Geographical Society. Without mentioning Rigby or the possibility of intrigue, Burton told Shaw that his lengthy correspondence to the Society about Zanzibar had been misplaced or lost. Then he wrote:

> A fresh attack of fever and general debility will delay me for a short time in the return to England . . . Capt Speke, however, will lay before you his maps and observations and two papers, one a diary of the Tanganyika lake between Ujiji and Karwenge and the other his exploration of the Nyanza Ukerewe or Northern Lake. To this I would respectfully direct the serious attention of the Committee as there are reasons for believing that this lake is the principal feeder of the White Nile.

Having given Speke this official benefit of the doubt, Burton found a bottle of brandy and drank himself unconscious.

Before noon the next day Burton went down to the dock to say goodbye. Lord Elgin made a speech to the commander and officers of the garrison, Oliphant was nowhere to be seen, and Captain Osborne led Burton to the main deck, where Speke sat cleaning his rifles. Speke stood up as Burton approached, and they shook hands stiffly.

A Union Jack and several flags of fair weather flapped in the breeze above their heads. Speke had trimmed his beard and looked handsomely fit.

"Take care," Speke said.

"I shall hurry up, Jack, as soon as I can," Burton replied.

"Goodbye, old fellow," Speke said, then, clearing his throat. He seemed to have prepared a speech and appeared nervous in delivering it. "You may be quite sure that I won't go up to the Royal Geographical Society until you come to the fore and we appear together. Make your mind quite easy about that."

Burton's mouth went dry, yet he managed to answer something. They went on pumping each other's hands in an awkward, curious manner, so that the lie—delivered with Speke's familiar, odd formality—hung between them like a vapor. Burton wished he could believe what had been said, but couldn't; and something in his eyes must have told Speke this, for Speke's mouth twisted into a half smile, half grimace, then he turned and left.

The sound of those flags in the breeze.

These would be the last words, Burton felt, Speke would ever say to him.

Going up toward Suez on the steamer, Speke lay in the deck chairs, letting the sun heal him. He also slept long hours on the navy's white linen and ate the heavy meals and elaborate teatime snacks brought from the galley. He meant to rest his body and thoughts, but all his conversations with Oliphant, all his inner voices kept him confused.

"Burton stole from you in Somaliland and will surely steal whatever fame he can again," Oliphant argued. "He will steal your maps and documents—just as he appropriated your notes in Berbera—because he fancies himself the only writer in the world. He'll steal your discovery, Jack, and so you had better go to Murchison and the government before he can cut the ground under you."

"The trouble is, I have uncertainties about what I found. I need to go back to the nyanza and definitely find the Nile, then follow it to the sea. I need to know absolutely."

"But that's it: *you* should do it. If another expedition is formed, it shouldn't be his."

"I'm a better man than Burton."

"True, Jack, and you must prove it. He is merely a writer who travels —and not a good writer, either. But you are a great explorer. Be sure to mark the difference."

The steamer anchored one day while everyone went ashore to visit a caravan, so that Lord Elgin could set up an elaborate tripod and take photographs. He was in high spirits, jumping this way and that as he pointed with his top hat, trying to arrange group shots that included an unruly string of camels. The camels were finally linked together by a rough strand of rope passed through their nostrils, which made them behave themselves and properly pose.

At night Speke curled up in his bunk, shut his eyes tightly, and tried to sleep. He wished Lowry would come into his room, yet wished he wouldn't. Oliphant behaved discreetly, drinking no liquor and showing little of the old gaiety, but Speke understood: because of the death of his father and that mystic telepathy, Lowry's spirit was engaged in a strange inventory.

During the days when they were apart from Lord Elgin's company, they talked of little else except the Nile.

"Jack, be convinced of this: You can have real fame," Oliphant told him. "Burton has to publish his findings with the journal of the Society. That will take months—a long, tedious, scholarly process. But you have the extraordinary materials. And you can publish anywhere. I suggest *Blackwood's* magazine."

"Why there?"

"For one thing, I know the brothers quite well. I got only fifty pounds for my articles on the Crimean war at *The Times*. After I squabbled with the editors, I switched my allegiance to *Blackwood's*. The brothers are fine chaps who pay small sums, but they publish my every whimsy, and their magazine enjoys real prestige. Look, Jack, you can make money, see your claims on the Nile in print, and tell Dick Burton to go to hell."

"He'll definitely try to steal my materials again," Speke said.

"So save your findings for the press and become famous."

"Mind, I wouldn't want the Society angry at me, if I went to a popular magazine and withheld findings from their journal."

"Let me handle old Murchison of the Society," Oliphant argued. "He badly needs a young, handsome explorer so that his little club can beg funds from the government. He'll welcome all good publicity. And he'll prefer you to Burton. I'll see to it."

They sat on the top deck, wind blowing, sipping lemonade.

"You know, Lowry, that Burton is actually the same as an Arab," Speke said. "He's not truly one of us."

"He certainly doesn't look English," Oliphant agreed.

"And he wasn't fair to our porters on the expedition, didn't pay them."

"Probably thinks all niggers are slaves."

"The women especially. He's a sexual glutton."

"And hates Christianity, I'm told."

"Rigby at Zanzibar put him on official report for mistreating our porters," Speke said.

"That's interesting. I'd press on that point," Oliphant advised.

"The discovery's the important thing," Speke said. "And we want to make sure the glory belongs to England, not to some curious outsider."

"Precisely so," Oliphant answered.

At Suez, while Oliphant arranged overland passage to Cairo so that they could continue their journey to England, Speke wrote to Burton.

The letter arrived in Aden as Burton settled into the familiar ease of life there: Steinhauser with those loaves of bread underneath his arms in the mornings, the long noon lunches at the hotel on Steamer Point, the dancers and whores in the evenings. Although his legs ached, Burton felt well otherwise. He had his books and his cronies: the doctor, End of Time, Sidi Bombay, Al-Hammal, and all those women lying on the pillowed *cafas*.

Yet, doubts ambushed him.

If he had gone back to England after his trip to Mecca, he reminded himself again, he would have been knighted. But he had delayed—fatally—and now delayed again. Not that he could have packed onto that ship with Speke, Lord Elgin, and that little fop, but now, again, he felt he should go.

Then the letter came.

It discussed the trip up the Red Sea, urged him to care for his health, and then added:

> . . . together and only together will we visit the Royal Geographical Society.

He found himself staring at those words, as if to make them real. Surely, he knew, Jack was wrestling with indecisions; or rejecting what he already felt determined to do, for what he had sworn was a lie, a bold one, and there was no mistaking it, said face to face or written down.

"What do you make of it?" he asked Steinhauser, showing him the letter.

"Ah, beware, Dick, something isn't right." The doctor sighed, scratching a bit of tobacco from his beard.

"He protests too damned much, doesn't he?"

"Afraid so. And you'd better follow him to London quickly."

"I'll take the next ship," Burton said.

On May 8, Speke arrived in London and took a modest room at Hatchett's Hotel in Piccadilly. The city smelled like flowers and sounded like hooves and carriages. *The Times* carried comments on Darwin's *On the Origin of Species*, about which loud and troubled sentiments were already being sounded—although, in general, everybody was happy that an Englishman had accomplished something bold and scientific.

Everything seemed propitious.

Speke took off all his clothes and looked at himself naked in the full-length mirror. Quite strong and ready. He bathed and put on lilac water. After he had dressed, he unpacked his maps and his few notes and placed them on a table—beneath the thermometer with which he had measured the altitude at Victoria Nyanza.

He was too excited to eat lunch.

That afternoon—having been in the city for four hours—he went to the offices of Sir Roderick Murchison, president of the Royal Geographical Society at Whitehall Place. Laurence Oliphant joined them at the appointment.

1859–1860

———————)0(———————

Controversy Begins

*B*URTON'S PEOPLE WERE MERELY IRISH—UNDOUBTEDLY, LIKE HIM, PEASANTS, poets, solitaries, and eccentrics. Speke's people out in Somerset were formerly the Especs, present in England at the time of the Domesday Book and known in Normandy as Le Spek or De Espek as early as A.D. 1036. They were landed gentry with fine stone houses surrounding the villages of Dowlish Wake, Bramford Speke, and Ilminster near the city of Taunton. They had been High Sheriffs, Gentlemen of the Privy Chamber, members of Parliament, esteemed rectors, prosperous farmers, and, in all, devoted subjects of the crown and nation.

Murchison could see it no other way.

Burton was the well-known rogue. Speke was the handsome son of a proper family.

"So you went to the northern lake on your own?" Murchison asked that afternoon at Whitehall Place.

"Yes, of course," Speke replied.

"Tell me why you went alone."

"The Society asked us to explore such a lake—after we had visited the Sea of Ujiji. Burton was in no mood to go, though, so I did it myself."

"In no mood? He reported that he was ill."

"Yes, his legs were swollen. But he also claimed that we were short of supplies."

Oliphant sat watching, a smile curling his mouth. Murchison was a heavy man swaddled in woolens, perspiration beading on his forehead, his breath filled with little wheezes. He was clearly no explorer, Oliphant could see; the man could get lost between Mayfair and Knightsbridge. Yet he had become a shrewd leader of his organization. The Royal Geographical Society under his presidency had secured ample funding from the government, had managed to keep the public interested in exotic, far-flung places, and had begun to establish geography and anthropology as bona-fide sciences.

"But you felt the safari to the northern lake could be accomplished?" the old man continued, urging Speke to elaborate.

"And was accomplished—easily," Speke answered. "For that matter, Burton could have come along, too."

"But he fancies Arabs, slaves, and nigger women," Oliphant put in. "You told me as much, Jack, admit it."

"If these were his reasons for staying behind, speak plainly," Murchison said.

"I really don't want to speak against my commander."

"But Sir Roderick needs to know why you acted alone," Oliphant prompted.

"Would you say that Burton was an able leader?" Murchison persisted.

Speke and Oliphant exchanged a telling glance.

"At times he was a very forthright officer," Speke conceded.

"But, of course, he accomplished very little of his assignment," Oliphant added. "At Ujiji he failed to visit the river to the north. There was some question as to whether the river flowed into or out of Lake Tanganyika, isn't this so, Jack?"

"We never saw the important river in question," Speke admitted.

Murchison paced over to the windows, measuring his steps. His little wheeze grew more pronounced. "Would you say that Burton actually impeded the progress of the expedition? Be bold and say what you think."

"Sometimes it would have been much better had I been in charge," Speke allowed. "And, occasionally, because of Burton's various kinds of incapacity, I *was* actually in charge."

"The only real accomplishment of the expedition was the discovery of the great nyanza for which Jack alone was responsible," Oliphant said. "That's the essential point, isn't it?"

Silence between them. Murchison peered out the window. While Speke sat with his hands folded, Oliphant lightly slapped his white gloves against his thigh.

"You must return to Africa and settle all doubts about the Nile," Murchison said finally. "Clearly, you should head the next expedition—unhampered by any want of supply or anyone who would limit you. I'll see that the Society goes along."

"I'm fond of Burton," Speke said. "He made his contributions and he should have his due."

"I'll see that Burton is honored and dismissed," Murchison said. "The important thing now is for you to address the membership of the Society. I want you to tell what's been accomplished. Can you meet with our membership tomorrow?"

"That soon?" Speke asked.

"In my opinion, we should meet before Burton recovers and comes back," Murchison said.

"Good point," Oliphant said. "And I'll help you with the press, Sir Roderick. This should have the widest publicity."

"Good, Lowry, good," Murchison said. "I'll arrange rooms for tomorrow at Burlington House."

"The Society deserves a fine young chap like Jack," Oliphant said, standing and putting on his gloves. "And, after all, the discovery belongs to him alone. I'm glad Burton's not here to mess around in matters. All for the best."

"We must make sure this discovery isn't lost to the glory of England," Murchison said, having the last word.

The hall at Burlington House filled up early as, outside, carriages blocked Savile Row, New Bond Street, and the whole neighborhood. Oliphant, laughing and behaving with all the charm of a host, directed reporters and guests toward favored seats. One young man, climbing up for a seat in the upper window of the hall, knocked out a pane of glass with his elbow and caused a momentary confusion. Coats were draped over the backs of chairs and ties loosened in the humid afternoon. Milnes was absent, but most of the membership of the Society was present including James MacQueen, another of Burton's admirers, who annoyed everyone by puffing at his cigar in the close confines of the room.

Speke, before the introduction, worried that his family hadn't arrived.

"I'm sure they'll be here tonight, my boy," Murchison assured him. "We'll have a good meal and raise a few toasts, never worry."

Speke displayed his notes, maps, and the thermometer with which he had taken readings at Victoria Nyanza. He stood tall, spoke clearly, even smiled once or twice, and looked completely in command.

"In my view," he concluded, "the nyanza is the probable source of the White Nile. And while we had some discussion that Lake Tanganyika—and perhaps other bodies of water in the region—is linked into a system of lakes and rivers that comprise a Nile basin, I personally reject that possibility. I feel the northern lake, which I have had the honor to name after our Queen, is the principal source of the Nile. And I intend to go back with your kind permission and support and to trace the Nile from its main reservoir into Egypt. In fact, gentlemen, I greatly look forward to the long walk across the desert as I prove my theory."

Laughter turned into cheers and applause as Speke sat down.

Oliphant returned to the hotel with Speke, so that they could dress for dinner, and for a time, giddy and excited, they drank a bottle of champagne, slapped each other on the shoulders, laughed, and celebrated the conquest.

"The press is aglow," Oliphant said. "You looked marvelous—so sure of yourself! You're famous!"

"I wish my mother could have been in that hall," Speke said, drinking off his champagne. The wine bubbled into his nostrils and made him sneeze.

"After this we should go to Paris," Oliphant said. "Let the French pin a medal on you!" Speke walked into the bathroom, blew his nose into a towel, and took off his shirt. He was tanned and robust in the midst of that bathroom porcelain. "I wrote a novel set in Paris," Oliphant went on, watching Speke through the open doorway. "I'll bet you didn't even know that I'm a novelist."

"No, I didn't," Speke called.

Oliphant poured himself another glass. "It was a comedy of manners, a silly little novel," he continued. "In those days I knew I'd be a literary champion. Now I want to go to Paris for you—not for anything of my own. I want to parade you around the best salons."

Oliphant waited, expecting Speke to say something, but saw him pick up a bottle of lilac water and smash it against the tiles.

"Jack, what's the matter?"

Rising and going toward the bathroom, Oliphant felt a drunken amusement, but this faded when he saw Speke's distorted face. For a moment Oliphant stood in the doorway watching. Speke hurled a bar of Pear's Soap into the tub, then picked up a fragment of broken glass, cutting his finger, and smashed the fragment into smaller pieces on the floor. Jerking around wildly, his bloody finger sprayed a crimson signature on the walls.

"Burton!" Speke said, his teeth grinding together.

"Yes, never mind—" Oliphant started to comment, but Speke had already changed the subject.

"My family should have been here by now!"

Oliphant stopped to watch. Speke slapped the pull-chain on the toilet, knocking off its handle, which bounced around the little room noisily.

"And not everyone at that meeting believed me, Lowry, so don't think for a moment they did! Members of the Society who didn't believe me! I could feel it! I'd have to be stupid otherwise, wouldn't I?"

"Jack, please."

"Uncertainty, Lowry, don't you see? Uncertainties everywhere!"

"If you're talking about the Nile, you'll go back to Africa and settle matters," Oliphant said, soothing him. "You'll settle all doubts, Jack, because you're the greatest explorer of your day. The very greatest. So calm yourself."

Speke's family, Murchison, Oliphant, and the explorer went to the Cremorne Gardens for dinner. There on the embankment of the Thames, under softly illumined lanterns hanging from the trees, they watched the ebb and flow of the crowds in this popular pleasure garden. Their table sat at a discreet distance from the pagoda where the band played, and they saw the young men from Oxford and Cambridge, fashionably dressed, strolling the walkways with girls on their arms; displays of fireworks went up from a barge anchored in the river; laughter drifted toward them from the various bars situated throughout the park; an entertainer in a checkered suit strolled around yodeling and reproducing the calls of assorted birds; special sherry was consumed and they dined on cold salmon, meat pies, capon, and other delicacies surrounded with brightly colored aspic jellies.

After several glasses of the Cremorne sherry, Speke's brother, William, began to talk about farming, to interrupt Sir Roderick, and to disagree with anything Oliphant said. The mother held Speke's hand beside his plate, the father smiled genially, and William's behavior was overlooked.

Murchison raised a toast in which he spoke of Speke as a son. Oliphant suggested that a portrait of the explorer should be commissioned.

"Perhaps a bronze statue in this or another suitable garden or park," William suggested.

"Mark you, a proper sculpture shouldn't be out of the question," Oliphant replied sharply, fixing the elder brother with a look.

The next days evolved into a series of meetings, public and private, and, in between, Speke and Shaw, the Society's secretary, exchanged a constant flow of notes and messages that confirmed everything was busy and important.

New routes to the nyanza were discussed at several of the meetings: from Mombasa over the Masai Plains, down through the desert from Egypt, westward from Harar or Ethiopia. But Speke observed that he preferred known dangers to new and mysterious ones, so laid plans to go back to Zanzibar and to travel the same familiar slave paths.

Money was frequently discussed. "The journey, done properly, will cost about five thousand pounds," Speke told one of the committees at the Society.

"But you and Burton went for two thousand," Murchison reminded him.

"And we overspent. Both Captain Burton and I are at a loss of hundreds of pounds—and have yet to settle our debts. We were woefully underfinanced."

"You shall have the best transport and gear for this next journey," Murchison promised him. "Nothing will be spared. Never fear."

They met in a room that smelled like a church, heavy ash furniture with brass fittings and dusty rows of books all around them. The committee argued amounts while Speke excused himself and went into the hallway; he knew that he had made a good impression on members of the committee, yet wished that he had come before them with sums and documentation. In spite of their stiff authority and all their talk of scientific method and correct procedure, there was something zany and haphazard in their deliberations. They were amateurs. And so was exploration itself, he mused, standing there in the hallway, leaning against the cool stone of the wall; like art or politics or most other endeavors, there was no formula; committees could play at being experts and authorities, but they were amateurs entirely.

At last Murchison came out into the hallway and announced with pride, "You shall have two thousand and five hundred pounds, Jack. Congratulations."

"Is that all?"

"Without Burton's wasteful extravagance, I'm sure that will be plenty," Murchison said, laughing and wheezing all at once.

Perhaps, Speke decided quickly, this was so. He thought of all the delays, the endless weeks in Zanzibar, the side trips to Mombasa and Kilwa.

He shrugged, shook hands with Murchison, and joined in the laughter.

With Oliphant's encouragement and Murchison's influence, Speke took a room at the East India and United Services Club on St. James Square.

He tried to adjust to his sudden new stature, but a thousand considerations came to mind. Should he let his beard grow? Whom should he contact in order to name the lake officially Victoria? The Queen herself? Would Burton return soon? Would he meet Vice-Admiral Back, Charles Darwin, the Prime Minister? Was Sidi Bombay still with Burton in Aden? What of Rigby? What of Burton's friends Milnes and MacQueen? Was the Nile really there?

One morning Oliphant brought around a cab and they drove over to Paternoster Row to meet the Blackwood brothers, William and Robert, in their editorial offices. The Blackwoods were tall young gentlemen who offered Speke firm handshakes; they seemed like Scots farmers with rough accents, but it was evident to Speke that they were also the intelligent, canny booksellers and editors Oliphant reported them to be.

"Lowry's proposal," said Robert Blackwood, "is that you should publish your comments and notes with us. Of course our magazine would be honored."

"I'm not much of a writer," Speke admitted.

"We'll help you with your material. And I take it you want to publish as quickly as possible."

"Yes, before someone else puts out an inaccurate report," Oliphant said.

"The Society will probably publish some dry, scholarly account," William Blackwood noted. "But our public will want something lively."

"You'll get something a good bit more intelligent and entertaining than anything Burton could concoct," Oliphant said.

"Yes, I would rather die a hundred deaths than see a foreigner take from Britain the honor of this discovery," Speke announced, raising his tone to sudden formality. His words and tone brought a momentary look of confusion to the Blackwoods' faces.

Robert Blackwood tried for clarification. "Are the French or others planning a Nile expedition? Whom do you mean?"

"I mean Burton himself, of course," Speke replied.

"Oh? What nationality is Burton?"

"Irish, Corsican, some Mediterranean type—who knows?"

The brothers kept silent, yet exchanged a glance.

"I'll be busy traveling this summer," Speke went on, his tone still formal. "But I'll write you a first draft and we'll correspond. I seem to have quite a lot to do."

The men shook hands, then Oliphant escorted Speke outside. The noonday crowd around St. Paul's watched a puppet show, ate cones of hokey pokey, and strolled around idly in the warm sunlight.

"How did I do?" Speke asked.

"You impressed them," Oliphant assured him. "And, Jack, they're very powerful men in the scheme of things now. With the printed word on your side, nothing can be against you. You and I will see this whole matter through nicely."

"I had the feeling they might have been skeptical of me."

"Nonsense. Tell you what, I'll manage an invitation to their home in Edinburgh. We'll court them a little. You'll all become great friends."

"Do you mind walking, Lowry? It's a nice day."

"Let's walk until our appetites stop us, then have a big lunch."

They were strolling into Fleet Street. A man with a barrel organ, turning out his music, tipped his cap to Oliphant.

"London's a fine place." Speke sighed.

"It is when you own it," Oliphant answered.

Thirteen days after Speke had returned to England, Burton arrived in London. Pale and tired out, he went to the town house of Monckton Milnes at 16 Upper Brook Street, but found that his friends were on the continent. He stood in the hallway, his canvas luggage at his feet, talking to a butler, who suggested that he should go up and occupy the guest room.

"If you think it would be all right, I will stay," Burton consented. "I'm feeling very weak and tired."

"The master would want you here. I'll take your bags and bring you some broth later."

Upstairs, Burton fell asleep. When he awoke he seemed fevered and his hands trembled.

En route to London, he had read recent newspaper accounts about the noted explorer, John Hanning Speke. He knew everything, yet couldn't decide what to do. He felt somehow too weak—physically and emotionally—for much of a squabble and wanted only to see Isabel. On the way to England and now, too, depressed as he was, he had in mind a singular and definite consolation.

Speke was with Murchison again the next morning when Shaw, the Society's secretary, delivered a note from Burton.

"He plans to convene a meeting of the Society," Murchison told Speke.

"Should I arrange a reception?" Shaw asked.

Murchison thought this over. After a moment he said, "Yes, call a special meeting of the membership for tomorrow afternoon. We'll present Burton the medal and have done with him."

Shaw went out to attend to the meeting, leaving Murchison and Speke temporarily silent.

"I won't attend," Speke said, at last.

"Won't be necessary or appropriate," Murchison said. "This will be a hastily called session—not many members present, I'm sure. We'll dispense with ceremony. I'm sure Burton will take note that we regard him casually."

"He'll take note," Speke agreed.

"Tell me, Jack, there's something I've wanted to ask about Burton. About his sexual curiosity. What do you know about it?"

"He's active enough," Speke said.

"Yes, legendary—or so his friends claim. But that's not precisely what I'm asking. Years ago in India—perhaps you don't know about this—he was asked by his commanding officer to prepare a short report on civilian customs. We needed general as well as military intelligence, you see, and Burton spoke the languages like a native, so was the obvious choice for such research. But his report was about male brothels. Sinister stuff. What I want to know is—well, how far afield are his appetites? Oliphant says he fancies nigger women, but does he fancy anything even more—how shall I say?—unusual?"

"Burton's Karachi report was a scandal, of course," Speke said. "Rigby talked about it with me in Zanzibar. Everyone in the Bengal army knew about it."

"Tell me in confidence. What do you know of his tastes?"

"Burton is a dark, dark man. Take that as you want to," Speke answered.

"I'm shocked," Murchison said. "Deeply shocked, but I suspected as much. And I'm glad I asked you. I don't appreciate gossip, understand, but this does make a definite difference in how he should be regarded."

"Naturally," Speke said. "Glad to be of help."

That afternoon Burton boldly visited the Arundell house and rang the bell. He was partially relieved to find that no one in the family was home, but got an address from the maid where Isabel might be found.

In the cab, riding back toward the West End, he caught sight of his face in the reflections of the window: a gaunt, scarred, suddenly aged face. He looked very little like the dashing young cockbird Isabel had met on the ramparts in Boulogne years ago. He looked very little like a lover—more like some weary Bohemian type, a drunken artist, he thought, or a fretful, unpublished author. He had other doubts, too: Would Isabel receive him? Would they have to talk at length about this sad business with Speke? Would her family still object to him as strongly? He leaned his face against the bumping, swaying image in that glass pane, flesh against cold flesh, against this reflection that was less than himself, yet true.

At the Belgravian house, Isabel found that her friend wasn't at home when she called, so settled herself with a magazine to wait for the friend's return at teatime. The magazine was just a distraction, so she put it aside; her thoughts were only about Richard. She had heard that he was probably due back in London soon, yet she had no notion that he was already there. Opening and closing her fists nervously, she worried over herself. She had lost weight. She had begun to wear a bit more rouge. But was she beautiful enough? Was the time, finally, right?

She heard the maid admit another visitor at the front door, but thought nothing of it. Her hand was at her throat and her thoughts were miles away when the door to the sitting room opened and there he stood.

"Found you," he said.

"Oh, God," she cried, and she ran across the room into his arms.

He closed the door, held her, opened her mouth with his, and began to unbutton her blouse. As he turned and pinned her against the wall, she thought she might faint; their breathing mingled and her crinoline skirt crackled as he pressed against it. He's going to ravish me, she told herself. Right here. Standing up. For a frenzied moment she planned how to assist him; her blouse was undone and he cupped her breasts through the light cotton chemise she wore underneath; her legs melted away, so that her full weight rode in his arms; she could taste his tongue and feel his hardness against her thigh.

"Not here, Richard," she finally gasped.

"Then let's leave," he said.

Then she was crying, tears streaming down her cheeks so that he kissed them away.

"No, oh, no, Richard, I have some terrible news for you," she managed.

"Not now. Let's get out of here."

Blinded by tears, she allowed him to lead her outside. He hailed a cab as he held her.

"Come on, everything's all right," he said. "I've read the damned newspapers."

"Oh, Richard, dearest."

Inside the cab, she found that she was still unbuttoned and wondered for a moment if she had gone into the street so disheveled. But his hands were inside her clothes again and he kissed her neck; pity, adoration, blind lust, endless weeks of longing swam among her tears.

"Oh, please, I have to tell you."

"Say nothing," he begged her. "Here, come to me."

She straddled him. One blind of the carriage was drawn, but the opposite window was wide open, so that Hyde Park's soft trees soon floated into view; she supposed that people on the walkways could see their condition, but she didn't care. Clothed, but crushed against him, she rode his body, tossing back and forth with the movement of the cab, their rhythms caught by the horse's steady hooves as they caressed each other. Once, she glanced up to see if the driver could see them. No, he couldn't. Then she tried to hold Richard's face in her hands, tried to stop his soft assault so that she could speak to him, but only the tears came and her words choked in her throat.

"Stop crying," he commanded her, laughing gently. "Stop it!"

"Oh, Richard, I can't, I can't!"

"Feel me. There, feel me against you."

"I have to tell you."

His hands roamed over her, the crinoline complaining with every stroke. She felt her clothes tearing, but no matter. Her nipples were hard, outlined against her chemise, and he kissed each one, wetting the cloth. Yet she couldn't stop weeping; she had this terrible news for him.

"Oh, please," she asked, trying to undo his hands, but they were underneath her skirt and chemise, now, and she felt his fingers run between her legs, as natural as ever, softly, in that mossy wetness at her center.

"Don't stop me," he asked her, but she cried, "No, no, it isn't this at all, I don't mind this, oh, please." Weeping, she bent and kissed the scar and the hard set of his jaw.

"Oh, dearest, it's Edward. It's your brother," she managed.

They left the cab and walked out onto the green. She buttoned herself clumsily as she went, blurting out the news that had come into her keeping.

"Is he dead? Tell me outright," he asked her, but she couldn't control herself.

"Perhaps worse," she finally answered in a sob.

He heard a bird sing a solitary note from the nearby wood as he waited for her to regain herself. The scent of horse dung from the bridle path blent with the heavy perfume of flowers bordering the walk.

"No one knows what happened," she went on. "Perhaps sunstroke. One report said that he had been badly beaten by thieves. His head. His brain."

He watched her face ever so closely: each spasm of grief, each scalding tear. "Is he still in India?" he asked her. "Am I to go to him?"

"No, he's being sent back here. In his terrible stupor. He's lost. Oh, Richard, dear love, he's lost."

With this, he gave way. His shoulders bumped with sobs as he went over and braced himself against a tree. Seeing him out of control, Isabel dried her eyes and went to him, pressing her cheek against his back and holding him.

"Oh, love, I'm sorry to be the one to tell you," she said evenly.

On the path, the cabby's waiting horse pawed roughly at the earth.

They went to the house on Upper Brook Street, where she told the servants that Burton had a fever and that she was to be left strictly alone to take care of him. He averted his face as he went upstairs.

In the guest room he wept silently, unable to stop. Sitting on the bed beside him, she began to loosen his clothes.

He was thin, very thin, and his skin seemed yellowed. He was hard and muscled, hairy, thick in the chest and biceps, yet somehow slighter than she had imagined. He rolled over, taking the corner of a pillow in his teeth. When she had finished undressing him, she stood and removed her own clothing.

Then she curled against him, and he held her tightly; she stroked his hair, his eyes, his temples. His eyes were open, staring out at nothing; the tears kept flowing. She watched his ordeal, not even thinking of her nakedness, not thinking of being alone with him at last or their first sexual union, just stroking his face as if they might be a married couple, long together, waiting out this brutal hour. It seemed natural that her bare leg was thrown over his and that her breast lay against his shoulder.

His weeping stopped and he gazed off into a distant corner of the room. She watched the rise and fall of his breathing and felt the coil of his body. Many deep pains, she guessed: this great loss, this nagging ill health she knew he must hate, this betrayal by Speke, all the burning memories he must have now. Perhaps he will always be quite beyond me, she told herself; his experiences, intellect, private pain can't ever be fully shared. Yet she wanted to travel with him—in the real world and in his deepest thoughts and feelings—as far as she could go.

She slipped out of bed after a while and smoothed the coverlet over his thin legs. The window was dark. Her parents would fret, she realized, and so she couldn't stay the night, yet now, feeling the coolness of the room on her naked body she became aware, again, of that core of heat he had started within her. At a mirror, she stopped and regarded herself. That soft center where his fingers had gone. His fingers. In the cab.

He called her name in a hoarse whisper.

She turned and went to him slowly, allowing him to watch.

As he reached for her, she said, "No, let me."

She surprised herself with her innovation and natural impulse. This was an uncomplicated affection: her hair falling over him like a tent, his thrusts upward into her body, their blent rhythms.

"Oh," she heard herself say, finally, as if she were telling the room a secret.

They stretched themselves out full length against each other afterward. She wanted her own taste from his mouth; she wanted, if possible, to fuse their veins and pulse; she wanted to pray to him like an idol, to thank him, to call out the syllables of his full name to the servants, wherever in this immense house they might be hiding.

He whispered some hoarse endearment, and she felt as if this had been practiced between them for years. His eyes still pooled with tears. On the sheet beside his leg were two or three drops of blood.

"Please, Richard, again," she whispered in reply.

The next afternoon Burton met with a few members of the Society at a hastily summoned meeting at Whitehall Place. They hadn't bothered to arrange for a large hall, so met in one of their regular sitting rooms: worn chairs, dusty books, the faint odor of mildew in the air.

"This is Murchison's fault," James MacQueen said to Burton before the business began. "No proper hall! No evening session with proper refreshments or cigars! No government officials invited! This is rubbish!"

Burton placed a hand on MacQueen's arm. "Please, never mind," he said.

"You're too sick to care, I suppose, but I consider this a horrible slight. I'm aghast!"

"But the meaning is clear," Burton whispered. "I failed. Speke has all the credit. Personally, I'm of the opinion that he hasn't discovered the Nile source, but one thing is certain: I didn't."

"Speke should be present," MacQueen said. "He should stand by his leader, no matter what he accomplished on his own." The Scotsman's face was bright-red, and his jaw shook with anger. Burton remembered the man only slightly from their meeting at Fryston with Milnes, yet appreciated the support.

"I've got to sit down," Burton said. "My legs are giving way."

"I wish Milnes were here. He'd have faced Murchison down! We'd have a proper ceremony!" MacQueen said, leading Burton to the chairs at the front of the room.

In a short time Murchison stood talking before the group. His voice was a drone and he managed to say little. Burton, dressed too heavily in his same old tweeds, felt uncomfortably hot and drowsy and could only take solace in that every man in the room seemed sleepily inattentive, too.

Murchison wheezed through a review of how the expedition came into being, how funds were approved, all that.

But Burton's thoughts drifted away. He could envision poor Edward strapped into a deck chair, say, on some creaking frigate bound for home. Eyes glazed with nothingness. The mindless sea rolling around the ship. The reward for all far-flung service is an empty homecoming, he felt, and the inevitable nothingness. Vacant, hollow, drab nothingness.

Murchison was talking about Speke. "Seeing that this vast sheet of water extends northwards and knowing that its meridian was nearly that of the main course of the White Nile, Captain Speke naturally concludes that his nyanza may be the chief source of that mighty stream—on the origin of which speculation has been so rife."

No arguments against Speke, no protestations, no logic will matter now, Burton knew. He switched his thoughts to Isabel, the voluptuous curve of her hip and breast, the softness of her mouth.

Murchison wheezes when he talks, he told himself. He wheezes and he's talking about Speke, not about me.

A tapping of raindrops at the high windows. Burton saw MacQueen sitting with his head down, as if in shame.

Murchison urged support for a new expedition led by Speke that would prove out the nyanza as the Nile source. Clearly, all had been decided about a return trip.

"Let us hope that when he is rested the undaunted Speke may receive every encouragement to proceed from Zanzibar to his old station and there to carry out to demonstration the view that he now maintains—that the lake Nyanza is the main source of the Nile," Murchison went on.

All has been settled, Burton realized. The route is set. The time for the next expedition. Its leader. In all probability, the money.

Rain splattered off the windows, now, and the dull greyness of a London twilight seemed to settle on the room.

Murchison referred to the "lake Nyanza" once again—a hopeless redundancy that made Burton about as uncomfortable as anything being done or said. Men who don't know the languages of foreign places: pitiful.

He felt perspiration trickling down his neck underneath his heavy tweed suit. Sweat, rain, tears, great rivers and small; he felt that the earth's waters were surely swallowing him up.

Murchison, true to form, talked for two hours. Only toward the last of his ramble did he mention Burton. In cryptic references, he outlined Burton's qualifications and told why the Society had originally put him in charge of the expedition. The tone was apologetic.

Then Burton stood to receive the medal. Sir Roderick gave it to him in a small velvet box, undisplayed, as if he might be handing him a coin in payment for his services.

Rain pelted the windows as Burton, holding on to the back of his chair for support, addressed the membership: twenty or so bored gentlemen, he estimated, who by this time probably thought him unworthy.

He made his remarks brief and restrained. "Thank you very much for this highest honor which the Society can bestow," he began, trying to manufacture a smile. He paused, trying to think. MacQueen's jaw trembled. Burton patted the chair on which he leaned as if it were a dear friend, a live companion who held him up. "To Captain Speke," he went on, slowly, "are due those geographical results to which you have alluded in such flattering terms. While I undertook the history and ethnography, the languages and the peculiarities of the people, to Captain Speke fell the onerous task of delineating an exact topography and of laying down our positions by astronomical observations."

The audience waited for more. Rain battered the windows.

"Thank you again," Burton said, and he took the little velvet box, never opening it to read the inscription on the medal inside, and sat down.

The membership applauded lightly and MacQueen left the room in shame.

Burton tried another smile, but felt weak and forlorn. He wondered why he had given Speke credit for the more scientific activities, remembering that Speke actually couldn't read the instruments, apart from a simple thermometer.

A few men came up to shake Burton's hand after this, but the group quickly dispersed. Murchison left immediately. One old man complained to Burton that he hadn't brought his umbrella. MacQueen had returned to the room and stood at the back with Shaw, the secretary, both of them looking embarrassed as Burton finally came toward them.

"This was disgraceful," MacQueen said.

"I got the medal because I'm alive and here," Burton answered. "Nothing more. But that's sufficient."

Oliphant accompanied Speke to the family home in Somerset, where neither the parents nor the brothers and sisters knew what to make of their fancy guest.

"Jack, my fellow, you live in a mausoleum!" Oliphant said that first afternoon as they stood on the marble floor below the great winding staircase of the old Georgian mansion.

"Ssh, Lowry, they'll hear you," Speke told him.

"No wonder you go off to India and Africa! One must hear every footfall in this place!"

They laughed like schoolboys.

The family became a little less sensitive when they discovered how Oliphant's humor worked: he was snobbish toward all things, not simply farmers who lived in stiff stone mansions. He also ridiculed affectations that he cultivated for himself: fashionable clothes, Oxford educations, literary ambitions, social rules.

"I'm extremely snobbish about snobbisms," Oliphant said at dinner that first evening. "I mean, one can't go about sniffing the air to ascertain what's fashionable. If one does, he's caught with his nose in the air—which is the least fashionable posture of all."

The next day Ben said of their guest, "I almost like your friend, Jack, and Father and William have only minor reservations."

"Very charitable of you, Ben, thanks," Speke said. "And please remember that Lowry is very helpful to me with my correspondence and contacts."

"If he can assist you in publishing your findings about the Nile," Ben asked, "will you make any money?"

"Hmm, yes, Ben, probably quite a lot."

"Good, the farm needs a few renovations."

"Oh, my money couldn't possibly go to the farm. I'll need genteel clothes like Lowry's. Cravats, top hats, capes, polo collars, that sort of thing."

Ben watched his brother, hoping that this was meant as a joke, but Speke didn't relent and smile. And Oliphant remained a fascination.

In the evenings, alone in Speke's room, they composed letters to Lord Elgin, seeking help in naming the lake Victoria; to the Blackwoods on prospects for a book; to Shaw at the Society on dozens of matters. Oliphant produced a selection of pipes and assorted bags of blent tobaccos, even some opium. The room filled up with so much smoke that Speke fanned it out of the windows with a pillow.

"Now try some of this," he told Speke, laughing as he offered some of the opium.

"The family would die if they knew that substance was in the house," Speke said, coughing. "Especially Ben, who would object on religious grounds."

"A good narcotic is entirely helpful in religious mysticism," Oliphant argued. "Ben should stir some of this into his incessant tea. He'd become known as the visionary of Somerset!"

Their laughter echoed through the house.

When Oliphant decided to return to London, Speke saddled two horses so that they could ride and talk. He asked Oliphant to stay the summer.

"No, I have to go, Jack, sorry. I can't be near you every day like this without touching you."

"Lowry, you mustn't say that."

"I want to do and say as I please with you."

"We can't ever do anything of the sort you mean," Speke said.

"Why not? Because it's illegal?"

"Because there would be knowledge of it—and scandal."

"Can you believe, Jack, that in our modern world men are put into prison for sodomy? Imprisoned because they love and desire each other!"

They rode until they came into the little town of Ilminster with its muddy streets. As their horses slopped along, they suspended their talk until they were safely beyond the town.

"Before the summer's gone I want us to be together," Oliphant said. "Without families, without the army, without the damned Geographical Society."

"Stay here. We'll have—well, some jolly times."

"Picnics with your family? No, thanks. I want to sleep with you in a feather bed."

"Lowry, don't carry on."

"You want it, too, Jack, but you just won't say the words or risk the enjoyment."

"Don't tell me what I want. Don't presume."

"And don't use your formal tone with me."

"Let's not argue, Lowry, please."

"I'm going to London in the morning."

"Why? What will you do there? You can easily stay here longer!"

"When I get to London, I'll eat a French meal. I'll throw away these boots, which are ruined with your thick rural mud. I'll take a long bath in rose water. Then I'll go down to Chelsea, hire myself a fourteen-year-old lad, and violate his tiny pink bumhole."

Speke broke out in embarrassed laughter. "You won't do anything of the sort!"

"Wait and see," Oliphant said. "I'm gone tomorrow. Come up and join me when you can tear yourself away from Mama's bosom."

Burton appeared again at the Arundell household, where Isabel's mother met him with total scorn.

"As far as I'm concerned, you're poor and public," she told him. "You must be nearly forty years old and still a brevet captain in the army. Your name is in the newspapers. You're irreligious. Your affection for Isabel, as anyone can plainly see, is one of convenience whenever you happen to be stopping off in London."

Burton wanted to appear calm and witty in the face of this barrage, but he turned crimson. Had Mrs. Arundell been a man uttering all these venomous truths, he would have closed the offending mouth with his fist. Instead, he permitted Isabel to have a tantrum in his behalf.

"Mother, you won't say those things!" she shouted. "He was just awarded the Society's medal! He's a national treasure!"

"I'm very sorry to hear of your brother's condition," Mrs. Arundell went on, drawing herself up stiffly. "And I understand your health is suffering. I'm sure you need considerable solace, but your hold on Isabel's emotions has been a catastrophe in this house. Far better, I think, for all of us had you been eaten by a crocodile during your exotic flights."

"That fate, madame, was spared me until the present moment," he countered, preparing to leave.

"If you leave, I'm going with you," Isabel told him.

"No! No you will not!" Mrs. Arundell shouted, her voice quivering with rage.

At the iron gate on the street Isabel caught up with him as he stalked away from the confrontation.

"There's only one question," she said. "Where shall we meet? I want to be in your arms."

"We should marry right away," he said. "But that seems out of the question."

"Time will smooth things out. And I'll marry you—with her consent or without it. But for now, where shall we meet?"

His hand gripped the cold iron of the gate, but she laid her fingers gently across his. "I'm still at Upper Brook Street," he told her. "But Milnes and his family will be returning soon. I'll make arrangements elsewhere."

"I'll come to you anywhere."

"But I can't have you going in and out of the Milnes house like some Regent Street tart. I'll find suitable rooms."

"I'm dying for you," she said, and he believed with all his heart that he was dying for her, too.

But was he?

In the next days he tried to set his finances straight and found himself so depressed that he wanted only to see Isabel. Yet there it was: he employed her like medicine, like a gooey salve rubbed into his wounds. He had looked her up first thing when he was ill, numb with the turn of events, in need of some homecoming greeting. But did he love her?

He decided to write a poem, but instead made a set of lists in which he matched reasons for marrying her against reasons not to. On one hand, he ranked her with his little nun in India, that fantastic Eesa girl, and only a half dozen others who practiced complete abandonment and loving skill in the act of copulation; she was also sweet-tempered; she seemed as devoted as a pet; she had intelligence and a soft voice—attributes that weren't usually present simultaneously in a woman. On the other hand, there was her wretched mother; the family truly had no money; she tended to be overly plump; and if they married, he feared, she might have a tendency to seek a religious conversion in him.

Sitting in the guest room, he went over his financial and romantic accounts. When his father died, his part of the family estate had been £16,000, but its annual yield was small, and he feared that he would have to raid the capital in order to pay off debts for his African excursions. He had his puny army salary. There was an occasional trickle of royalties from his books, but nothing substantial; he realized that he should get into print immediately again, if only for the most meager gains; his most widely reprinted book had been *A Complete System of Bayonet Exercise;* but it was a best-seller only in France, where the army had published it without bothering to pay him a fee. His own stingy army had refused to reimburse him for his losses at Berbera.

The desk in this fine guest room was made of polished ebony. He hated the thought of some shabby hotel elsewhere; Isabel deserved more, and for that matter, so did he. Poverty was shit. How could anyone presume to be a writer, an adventurer, or a lover without proper means?

Murchison decided that Speke should be the Society's principal speaker at the annual meeting of the British Association of Science in Aberdeen during the late summer.

The Royal Geographical Society was trying to convince the Association, after all, that geography was a bona-fide scientific study; Speke was popular with the press, handsome, and would make a persuasive presence.

"Stand on the stage before those good doctors and hold your head up," Murchison advised him, when Speke had come back to London. "Surround yourself with chronometers, thermometers, maps, and notes. Tell them how you employed the sextant, all that. You did use a sextant, didn't you?"

"Hmm? Yes, Sir Roderick," he lied. He glanced over at Oliphant, who had taken the best chair in Speke's room there on St. James Square. Oliphant smiled and flicked away imaginary particles of dust with his gloves; clearly, he had arranged Murchison's enthusiasm for Speke at the Aberdeen meeting.

"Will you be going up to Scotland, too, Lowry?" Speke asked.

"Definitely. Consider me your factor. I'll make all arrangements. Take you on tour, too, Jack, if you want. There's money in public speaking."

"Shall I stand under a spotlight with a chronometer in my hands?"

"Yes, something like that. Be dramatic. And especially at Aberdeen, where science, after all, should be very theatrical."

"That's all it ever is," Murchison said. "I would rather attend a convention of poets than a convention of scientists."

"For that observation, Sir Roderick, lunch is on me," Oliphant said.

The dining room at the East India Club that noon provided them with heavy walnut furniture and pasteboard food. Speke ate without complaint, though, and finished off the overcooked roast beef from Oliphant's plate as they discussed a new companion for his next trip to Africa. Speke's first choice was Edmund Smyth, the friend from the Crimean War with whom he had been refused permission to hunt in the Caucasian forests.

"I knew him in India, too," he told Murchison. "He's a good hunter. A fine chap. As I see matters, Smyth and I could shoot enough game to keep our caravan moving if supplies ran out."

"Submit his name to the committee," Murchison said, trying to chew his meal. "But you should have a second choice, too. The committee likes to take an active hand in such decisions."

"There's another chap," Speke said. "Jim Grant. I knew him in India, too, and I believe he's out of the army—living up in Scotland. We hunted together up in Tibet, once, and he might be available."

"Why not me?" Oliphant asked. "I'm plucky."

Murchison wheezed, grunted and laughed all at once.

"Lowry would make a fine companion," Speke said, going on with the suggestion. "Of course we would have to find tailors and hatmakers for our porters and askaris."

After lunch Oliphant kept an appointment with the Blackwood brothers, who had just read the first sample of Speke's writing. Speke wanted to attend the meeting, but Oliphant insisted on acting as agent.

In the offices on Paternoster Row, again, the men sat in silence while Robert Blackwood perused Speke's work a last time. Finally he looked up, trying to summon a phrase.

"Not good?" Oliphant asked.

"Ah, no," Robert Blackwood said. "Terrible."

"Do you suppose, then, that the two of you could possibly edit Speke into existence as an author?"

"A difficult task," Robert said. "He seems to possess an absolutely wooden language. At times, Lowry, it reads—" He stopped, not wanting to insult the friend. The two brothers exchanged their coded glance.

"Consider this," Oliphant said. "An author need not be a writer. And Speke is newsworthy, popular, and marketable, isn't he?"

They sat looking at each other, pondering what to do.

"Speke will make a speech in Scotland in August," Oliphant finally said. "Why don't you invite him to visit your offices in Edinburgh? Become friends and work with him—help him to publish. You'd never forgive yourselves if he published his work with strangers and made thousands of pounds for someone none of us know."

It was a persuasive argument.

"As a matter of fact, we will be at home in Edinburgh in August," William Blackwood allowed. "We could invite him to visit our family."

"I'm sure the children would love hearing his tales from Africa," Robert Blackwood added, and the matter settled itself.

The Surrey County Lunatic Asylum.

Its grounds had been sown with broom and colorful foxglove, but the old stone house itself was surrounded by thick bramble and prickly vines: an unkempt manor with tall, thin windows, barbed and forbidding. The dark wood of the interior hallways reflected little light; a thick cabbage odor hung in the air; moaning voices echoed everywhere, as if the inmates meant to prove their acquaintance with the void.

He was shown to a room over the kitchen where the cabbage smells assaulted his nostrils. The furniture consisted of a thin pallet and a single rocking chair beside the window. Edward was much thinner, and his face seemed to ask a question; the eyes were not glazed, but fixed in this interrogative stare; his hair was long over his ears and he was unshaven. At the corner of his mouth was a little puddle of drool.

Burton sat on the edge of the windowsill, leaning close to his brother and speaking his name. He looked deep into the face, as if behind those questioning eyes there might be a record of how this had happened. Only that unruly spittle at the mouth bothered Burton; it flowed down into the stubble of Edward's beard and hardened there, so Burton wished that he could have a damp cloth to wipe it away.

Seeing Edward like this, he didn't weep. He was through with that. The news itself was the horror, and somehow even this wretched place, sealed with thorn and bramble to keep its lost souls inside, could be understood and tolerated until a more suitable circumstance could be arranged.

"Can you hear me, Edward? It's Dick. Can you hear my voice?"

No sign. Memory flooded Burton's head.

I've saved everything of yours. The long nights in Constantinople. Their shining uniforms. *Damn me, I'm beautiful.*

"I'm thinking of going to France to write my next book," he said, watching the face to see if any glimmer of comprehension appeared. "France is always nice. Good food and sunlight. You'd like it, I think, so I expect I'll find a spot for you. On a hillside near Boulogne, would you like that? I'll have to get together money, you see, so that you'll have proper care—and I'll have a desk and proper materials. In the mornings, we can have coffee together before I begin. On a sunny patio, say, with a view of a valley. How does that sound?"

Their lessons at épée and foil. The death carts at Naples. Their dreaded tutor, DuPre. Their father's scowl as he regarded them together.

"I've got problems, at present, but I'll work them out. I wish it had been you accompanying me from Zanzibar. Damn, I do wish that. And I'm somewhat in love and don't know what to do about that. Perhaps the bottom half of me is in love." He put his head back, laughed, and slapped his knee, as if Edward shared this. "And the army's the same," he went on. "As petty and niggardly as ever, but I don't have to tell you. They won't reimburse me. They won't recognize me. I'm less than I was in the Crimea, Edward, when, by God, I had some mild status with Beatson! I'm nothing now! A brevet captain! Mrs. Arundell pointed it out!"

Afternoon shadows slanted across Edward's odd, questioning gaze. That trickle of drool annoyed Burton greatly.

"They gave me the medal of the Society at a—well, nice enough ceremony. But I'm not going back to Africa, soon, I fear, although that's where I ought to be. Nobody in the Empire knows it as well. No one speaks any of its languages. Sometimes, Edward, I think it might well be my place."

A fine brother. Someone will see your talents in this goddamned land.

Sitting on the sill, leaning close, he told about his legs and fever; he told about throwing those skulls aboard the ship and how the crew cowered at the far end of the deck; he told about Lumsden's elephant, what a sight it was; about that Asian girl, the way she looked at him that last time. Odd bits, stray thoughts, an ambling recollection.

The drool bubbled. It was like a river out of hell flowing from Edward's scrawny body.

"I'm sorry about this temporary room," he said at last. "But we'll remedy that. I'll be back as quickly as I can arrange matters. You hold on. You keep the sound of my voice, Edward, will you do that for me? Remember my voice as I well remember yours. There, I'm on my way now. You wait. I'm leaving, but I promise I'll be back very soon."

He kissed that awful drool from his brother's mouth and went away.

En route to Aberdeen in August, Speke stopped off to visit Jim Grant in Dingwall, the small town above Inverness in Ross-shire. He announced his intended visit in a letter, suggesting that perhaps Grant could arrange a hunt, and when he arrived there were cousins, gamekeepers, neighboring farmers, and assorted friends ready to go off into the hills after deer.

Grant was much the same, pleasant and easy, but Speke disliked the wife. She contrived to remind her husband of chores and petty duties; while she hovered, cooed, smiled, and entertained, she also made her soft demands.

"Just tell me," she said. "If you men plan to be gone tomorrow night, let me know now."

"If the hunting's poor, we may decide to stay another night," Grant explained to her.

Speke didn't care for wives and their small aggressions. Somehow they arranged for the home fires to burn the skin off good men like Grant.

Grant was a gentleman farmer now: his sleeves rolled, his boots soiled, his face reddened by the summer sun. Yet he was something of a barnyard creature, heavily married, and Speke decided early in the visit that he preferred Smyth to Grant as a partner in the next African trip.

They ate a hearty supper that evening, the table crowded with more than a dozen cousins and clansmen who had come to dine and to listen to Speke's African tales—which, he protested, he was not so good at telling. They drank heavily: several strong malts distilled in nearby valleys. And if they detected Speke's usual aloofness, drunkenness and good manners prevented any revelation of it; they clapped him on the shoulder, insisted that he join them in songs, toasted his presence. He would have endured a long evening of bagpipes and reels, he supposed, except that the men became drunk so he retired early, making the excuse that he looked forward to the hunt the next day.

The next morning blew up cool and rainy, but a small army of hunters, richly colored in various tartans, carrying their ancient heavy bore rifles, breathing whiskey and camaraderie, gathered outside Grant's farmhouse. They all started off together, calling each other's names through the mist, and Speke only began to enjoy the hunt when they split off into several smaller groups and his began to make its way more quietly beside the banks of a narrow stream that descended from the hill.

"So when will you go back to Africa?" Grant asked him on the path.

"In a few months. I don't suppose you'd be interested in going with me?"

"Don't know. Perhaps."

Speke didn't know why he asked and said no more about such a possibility as the day went on.

He did think about Grant. The Scot usually has a dark streak of violence in his otherwise placid nature, but Grant seemed to have none of it. He remarked on the beauty of the hills and flora as they walked and seemed endlessly amiable and mild-tempered. Whereas the English conversational style is always slightly contentious, Grant, with his soft brogue, seemed always encouraging, positive, and agreeable—although he made enough of his own points and observations while nodding and smiling at those of others. In fact, Speke felt, here is the very opposite of Burton: a man of even emotion, of deference, self-assured, yet casual and relaxed.

As they climbed into the hills the lochs came one after another, linked by roaring rivers and streams, black water booming down foamy white across the boulders, running black again into dark pools. The hills, which soon enclosed them, had mossy furrows where banks of spongy grasses formed steps up to the stark rock ridges. They quickly saw the prints of deer. In the forests there were rabbits, partridge, wild duck, and—as if they had flown inland for all this beauty —the ever-present gulls. But Speke, as always, was no mere observer. Everyone in the country walked nature paths and appreciated the moss, the wildflowers, the waters; he wasn't one of those sexless little women or men, wrapped in woolens and smelling of sachet or scented tobacco, who became even more passive than usual in the outdoors. It was all a nuisance to him unless he could find a prey; he was here, again, to stalk.

He struggled to say to himself just what he felt. These were farmers, domesticated men; and they brought their domesticity into the woods.

The rain never slackened, and the hunting was poor. By noon they were all soaked wet, having penetrated far into the hills, and a few of the men talked about returning. But the signs were good—droppings here, the sizable print of a stag there—and Speke was determined to stay. If the foul weather kept the deer in their thicket all day, surely, he reasoned, they would move around in the late twilight before settling again for the night.

In the afternoon he was starving. He and Grant sat on a boulder beside a stream and ate hard biscuits, dried meat, and an ear of corn. A steady drizzle fell around them.

"This is a fine glade we're coming to," Grant told him. "I've seen lots of deer passing through it. Why don't you take a stand? I'll circle round it. There's a small loch on the other side. I'll hunt there, and if nothing comes my way soon I'll probably join the others. There's a carriage house on the far end of the loch where everyone gathers—and where I expect most of our mates have already gone."

"They're not much for hunting, are they?" Speke asked, biting one of the biscuits.

"Oh, they shoot a fair amount of game year round. In this sort of weather they'll probably kill only a few bottles, though."

"What's the use of hunting if you mean to fail at it?" Speke said, wiping the rain off his face.

"You're the same old Jack," Grant replied.

The long twilight began soon after this—that strange, lambent dusk that would continue toward ten o'clock at this time of year. Speke knew he wouldn't leave the woods with the rest of the hunting party; he wanted no loud pub scenes. A few hours later, when the drizzle turned into a steady, pounding rain and he knew that everyone had fled, he only turned his collar up, hunched down beside a fallen oak that lay across the small stream, and waited. He listened to the heavy drip and gurgle of water all around him. And the light held: a ghostly, soft, greyish glow that turned all the greens of the forest into shadows. Once, a flash of lightning came, but it was soft, too, and he heard its answering thunder like a dull faraway drum.

In the carriage house, he knew, the cousins and farmers would be staring into the amber warmth of their drinks. Scots and Englishmen were certainly alike in this: they drank and chatted their lives away. They complained of being poor, yet emptied their purses every night, most of them, in thousands of pubs and lounges. They drank in order to talk and talked in order to drink, slapping their coins on the bars, reciting their endless opinions. Life was a topic to them, not an activity; beer, whiskey, and port were the fuels of discussion.

He preferred getting soaked through. The forest sustained its silences. He hated drinking and chatting. He hated wasting money on such idleness. He hated smoke-filled rooms with paltry verbal competitions.

The waters of the glade washed out his thoughts. He was getting cold, and now he didn't want the others to see him struggle in late, wet and shivering, with nothing to show for his trouble. No, let them come and find me, he told himself. Let them worry and search me out—and hear me say that I'm contented out here alone, out of their gaslight glow of drunken talk in some safe, dry, cozy corner. Before long, they'll remember that I'm out here. They'll begin to fret as the twilight ends and darkness comes. But I won't leave. Let them find me tomorrow, if it comes to that.

At that moment he saw the stag.

It filled up the last illumined space along the top of the ridge, turning its head in silhouette against the quickly fading horizon. Speke moved his rifle into position, then stopped. He held his breath. Hunched and cold, beads of water in his whiskers, he admired the size of the animal and waited. It had come over the ridge, so meant either to go along the summit—or to come directly at him. For this scant moment it remained magnificently proud, its antlers high as it sniffed the air.

The sound of water falling and running obliterated any noise that might frighten it. Speke calculated that his position was good; with luck, the stag would come directly down the hillside into his sights.

The lochs and streams reflected a last, pale light now, as if pieces of the sky had fallen about the countryside in melancholy fragments.

Speke kept still. Slowly, the cautious stag came his way.

He raised his rifle into position. His thumb brought the hammer back in an unhurried deliberation. There: the stag moved down toward the stream, heading for the fallen log. Its bearing was nonchalant, as if nothing could possibly be waiting in that wet underbrush. Speke saw its eyes for the first time: pools of intelligent darkness.

Onward it came, right at him. He aimed.

The explosion rocked him back and sat him down in mud.

Twigs seemed to fall from the trees; a cloud of acrid smoke filled up the glade; birds flew up in sprays of ascent; the sound of the rains ended in all the ringing echoes. For a moment, lying on his back, Speke saw nothing. Then he leaped up, beating away the smoke with his arm, staggering forward over the slick stones, until he saw that he had knocked the creature down with a direct hit; he went toward his quarry knowing that he had broken its shoulder and had probably made a clean kill. Blood everywhere. He laughed aloud as he approached and saw it kicking; it was as if the stag worked hard at pumping the last drops of life from itself.

But as he reached it, the stag got to its feet in a rush of effort. It was immense: antlers high above Speke's head, a beast equal to its killer and more. For a moment as he stood there with his rifle unloaded, Speke saw himself being charged, but the stag turned and bounded off, as if it bore no wound. Speke couldn't believe it. He had seen its shoulder torn away; the gaping hole should have destroyed its heart and lungs, yet the stag moved off in liquid grace so that Speke's impulse was to call after it, to say, wait, come back, you can't do that! He found himself running after it.

Suddenly, the game was different. If with its last strength the stag could flee its tormentor, there would be no prize; there would be nothing, for the rains would wash away all traces of its bloody trail on the floor of the damp forest.

He chased it out of the glade into the valley beyond. Night loomed all around him, and he knew that he had to find it. For minutes he ran in the direction it had disappeared, but then he stopped and listened; only the sound of his heavy breath and the endless rain came to his ears.

He saw a bright ruby of its blood on a leaf.

Walking now, already exhausted from his sprint with the heavy rifle, he felt that he had the right direction. Fifty yards, one hundred. He stopped and listened again, fearing that he might have walked by it.

Standing still and listening, he became cold again. His shoulders quivered, and he saw his misty breath before his face. Yet he dared not move just to warm himself; ten paces this way or that, now, and he would be lost in the strange hills without proof of a trophy. Listen: the rains, the gurgling water over the stones, nothing more.

As night fell, he refused to move. He thought, once, that he heard the last death kicks; leaves and branches formed shadowy shapes, so that the forest became a picture puzzle; the stag's outline formed itself in those patterns of mottled hues.

He sat down, dropped his head, pulled up his collar, and settled into a cold sleep. It was a bone-chilling dampness, not unlike the vapors of Zungomero, and he imagined feeling the old fever as he sat there. Hours passed, and he awoke now and then to study the dark woods.

At the first daylight, he got up, stretched, and as he walked a few paces he saw the lifeless form of the stag. He trembled with damp cold—and wished, somehow, that he had found this fine specimen last night; he would have split it open and crawled inside it for warmth; he would have slept in that gory blanket, he thought, and he laughed to himself as he conjured up a vision of Grant and all those farmers finding him there; it would have been the same as on the beach at Pemba, when he bit into that forbidden fetus.

Before dawn he heard gunshots and voices calling him.

They came over the ridge as he pulled his kill toward a sapling where he planned to gut it.

"It's the largest any of the men have ever seen," Grant told him later.

"Really? The very largest?" Speke was excited about the prospect; he very much wanted to be known as the man who had killed the largest stag ever shot in Ross-shire.

They hung it on the sapling to dress it while he told them about his effort to find it in the dark. A cousin passed around a bottle, and Speke took a mouthful, not really liking it, yet feeling more familiar with everyone now that he had made a noteworthy kill.

"I told them last night that you were in the woods to stay," Grant said, laughing. "And I could have wagered and won. I knew you'd get a trophy."

"Has anyone counted the points on the antlers?" Speke asked.

Someone announced that a count had been made: sixteen.

"The largest stag ever—fallen to my rifle! Think of it!" He laughed out loud, and the men laughed with him.

His good mood continued as they trudged home. "I want you to consider the possibility of coming with me on this next trip to Africa," he said to Grant again. "If your wife will let you go."

"I'll think about it," Grant promised.

"Truly, will you? Would you like to go?"

"I think I would, yes," Grant said, being cautious.

"I always have good luck with you on the hunts," Speke said. "You're a charm for me, Jim, you really are."

In Aberdeen, Speke and Murchison disagreed about the presentation.

"It seems to me," Sir Roderick said, "that you should emphasize the total accomplishments of your expedition. Remember that we're trying to impress a gathering of skeptical scientists. We do want to convince them that the principles of cartography and navigation were employed."

"Naturally," Speke said. "But the question of the Nile will come up."

"We don't want controversy to cloud the issue at this particular meeting. They won't be interested in our internal business."

"My discovery of the nyanza and the source of the Nile is our most notable scientific breakthrough," Speke argued. "I can't discuss maps and measuring devices and exclude the obvious."

They strolled along the main street of the town, Murchison trying to light his pipe in the cold wind blowing off the North Sea.

"About the Nile we have your—hmm, enlightened assertion. Little actual proof to show a gathering of scientists."

"Oliphant says they all have the status of alchemists and that there are very few true scientific minds at the meeting," Speke said.

"Lowry is always cynical," Sir Roderick said, wheezing through his pipe and producing a single white puff of smoke. "But, please, hear what I'm suggesting. Concern yourself with methods, Jack, and leave the larger questions alone."

Speke met the delegates in the town's Assembly Hall and gave a solid account of the expedition, its gear, its rough findings, and his hopes for positive geographical proofs on his return trip. When asked about the Nile, he answered boldly about how certain he was. He also announced that under the direction of Laurence Oliphant he would be conducting a tour of cities, lecturing on the Nile search. "Be assured, gentlemen," he said, "that I'll conduct my lectures at the very highest level of scientific reportage."

Oliphant stood in the back of the hall. Because the weather had turned so foul and cold, he wore his new overcoat with its fur collar. It pleased him that Speke managed to complete his entire address without mentioning Burton's name.

That evening Oliphant and Speke dined at the Royal Hotel. Speke told about his hunting trip in Ross-shire, which impressed his companion not very much, and Oliphant seemed enthusiastic about shopping on Princes Street in Edinburgh when they traveled there—an enthusiasm Speke didn't share.

"You know, Lowry, we're not much alike," Speke remarked. "You're city and I'm country. I'm army and you're definitely civilian."

"But we are alike," Oliphant said. "We're both outsiders. You're neither country nor army, if you admit it. You don't fit with your family, as I've seen for myself. You really don't fancy your Royal Geographical Society because you're far too individualistic for committee work. You might even write a book, but you're no scribbler—haven't the temperament for it."

"Yet we're still unlike each other."

"No, not at all. You think about it, Jack, we're the same."

They ate second helpings of trifle with mugs of West Indian coffee.

At ten o'clock they went up to their separate rooms, not looking at each other as they parted. Speke knew that Lowry wanted them together for the night, but he could give no encouraging signal. Propped against his pillows, he read some of his copies of *Blackwood's,* trying to note the wit of the columnists, but he fell asleep with a recent issue opened across his chest.

Toward midnight a knock came at the door, waking him.

"It's Lowry," came the whisper.

"Door's unlocked," Speke called, rousing himself.

Oliphant stood in his nightshirt, his arms around himself. He had the look of a small, forlorn boy who would not come inside without an invitation, yet who stood in the hallway with dire need. "I'm freezing, Jack," he said weakly. "My room's like an iceberg."

Speke couldn't decide what to do or say. "Can't you ask for more blankets?" he suggested feebly.

"Do we continue to bump into each other on the decks of ships and to fall into each other's arms when we get sick?" Oliphant asked, pleading. "Or do we deliberately comfort one another?"

"Lowry, I can't. I don't—"

"And, damn, Jack, my room *is* freezing," Oliphant said, going back to the original petition.

"Please, Lowry," Speke managed.

Oliphant turned and went back to his room. Getting out of bed, Speke went over and closed his door; he leaned against it for a moment, feeling the room's chill.

The next morning he went down to breakfast and found Oliphant sulking. There were two elderly couples at nearby tables, so they kept their voices low.

"Lowry, do understand that I'm not as free as you," he began.

"You're not free from stupid conventions," Oliphant accused him. "You're Mama's good boy. You must win prizes for her."

"I must win some for myself."

"And when you've won enough, will you be free? Will you ever be?"

"Perhaps. Pass the toast," Speke said. "Perhaps I'll eventually be even less shackled by what I am than you are."

"Oh, that's cruel," Oliphant whispered.

"Have patience," Speke told him, spreading some marmalade.

They ate in silence. Somehow, although neither of them acknowledged it or shaped it into words, perhaps because of the reluctance and delay on Speke's part, Speke had taken command of the relationship.

In Edinburgh, Speke went to the offices of the Blackwoods at 45 George Street, where he viewed a map about which he had heard a great deal; the map was a detailed drawing of the Upper Nile. Another of the Blackwood brothers, John, explained how he came to have it.

"It was drawn by John Petherick—with whom you have to meet and correspond," he said. "Petherick was a mining engineer in Wales who went to Egypt to prospect for coal. He took up ivory trading in the Sudan and was eventually appointed consul in Khartoum. He's a big, jolly Welshman—you'll like him. And I knew you'd want to see this wonderful map. On your next trip, you'll undoubtedly follow the course of the river from the lakes until it joins the locations on Petherick's map."

"Yes, the map's a marvel," Speke agreed, admiring the close detail.

"Petherick's undoubtedly the expert on the White Nile in this region," the editor said. "You must write him."

"I shall," Speke said. "In fact, I'm trying to discipline myself to write more. I'm practicing at doing more correspondence. I'm not a natural, you know, but literary circumstances seem to demand it of me."

"We'll help you with your work," Blackwood assured him. "You'll be surprised if I tell you how many great men can't spell."

"Really?" Speke asked, laughing with relief.

"You do your best. Then we'll go over every page. And the public, I know, will be the beneficiary."

Oliphant stayed in a hotel, but Speke moved in with the family at Number 3, Ainslie Place, within walking distance of the editorial offices. There were many children in the house, but Speke's room was high on the fourth floor, and from those rear windows he could view Fife in the distance. The Blackwoods were unlike his own family: they were noisy and full of laughter and mischief. Stewart, one of the young children of the household, teased Speke about the amount of macaroni consumed at dinner.

"Stewart, don't be rude!" the father told his son. "Soldiers eat quite large portions!"

Speke, far from embarrassed, said, "Yes, Stewart, please, I am the Late Bengal Macaroni! I must have my nourishment!"

The children squealed with laughter, and the table talk never returned to normal.

Before leaving Scotland, Speke did begin to write letters, most of them to Rigby in Zanzibar, in which Burton was the object of scorn. Among other remarks he wrote, "I am sure that everybody at Zanzibar knows that I was the leader and Burton the second on the expedition," and "Had I not gone with him he would never have undergone the journey." He told Rigby about the help the Blackwoods had offered, also writing that "the publication of my story in Blackwood's may have the effect of reforming Burton; at any rate it might check his scribbling mania and may save his soul the burden of many lies."

With Oliphant, Speke also began to plan out his lecture series, essential correspondence, and general schedule. They sat in the editorial offices on George Street or in the lounge at Lowry's hotel devising a calendar.

"Jack, you've got to travel to Paris with me," Oliphant said. "Let's fit that into our plans. I mean, after all, the fixtures in the baths at this hotel are made of zinc! The food is mush! I want you to see the best: crepes for luncheon and satin sheets at night!"

"We'll go to Paris one day," Speke promised him. "At the moment, Lowry, I appreciate your help with all I'm doing. I have to choose a companion for the next trip. Letters have to be written. Money arranged."

"I can help you with all this, Jack, so don't leave me out."

"Of course not. I need you."

"You won't do as well without me."

"I know that perfectly well, Lowry. There's no one like you."

Early that autumn, when Speke's articles were being published in *Blackwood's* and he had appeared on the lecture circuit, Burton received a harsh reprimand from the army in Bombay concerning his mistreatment of the porters at Zanzibar and his refusal to pay them properly. The reprimand—Rigby's handiwork, Burton guessed—accused him of racial intolerance, lies, misrepresentations, and possible fraud. After reading it, depression went through him; he walked the streets through Mayfair, Soho, Holborn, along the embankment, then got drunk in a quayside bar with a group of surly Maltese sailors. He remembered buying a round of drinks, but not long afterward found himself in an alley, his wallet gone, the stench of garbage and vomit all around him, his thoughts addled. I must leave the army, he told himself; I mustn't turn to drink; I must stop seeing Isabel in hotels and carriages and make an honorable woman of her. He stood up on these resolutions and fell against a wall, skinning his face; he prayed to Allah, farted, and tried with all his manly strength to focus his gaze.

My ambition. "My ambition," he said aloud to the alley, "is to become consul in Damascus! To visit America! To write a great poem! To—" He stumbled forward through slime adorned with tea dregs. "To walk all the way home without being arrested!" He slid to earth beside the dustbins.

The next day, sick with his excess, Burton took the train north toward Leeds. At Milnes' invitation, he was going to stay at Fryston Hall awhile.

The train had a sickly sway, so that about every fifty miles Burton puked out its windows. Not wanting to impose this spectacle on the occupants of a single compartment, he strolled the length of the train—on wobbly, uncertain legs—and shared his misery with dozens of gentlemen and ladies.

The carriage ride to Ferrybridge made him feel better. At last he was driven down that long corridor of oaks and maples, through the stone gates with their sculptured wheat shocks, alongside the familiar paddocks and stables, and into Milnes' smiling presence. The old boy's pop eyes shone brightly as he grabbed Burton and hugged him.

"God, I've missed you, Dick! By Jesus!" he said, and Burton felt a warm flood of relief, as if he had come into harbor at last.

There were a number of guests present, but, once again, the rambling house and the renovated summer cottage where Burton stayed suited the crowd nicely. Hankey was there, having just smuggled in a new stock of erotic books for the bulging library. The painter Samuel Lawrence and his wife were also present, along with several other married couples, including Dr. and Mrs. James Bird, who liked Burton on first sight, and Mansfield Parkyns, who had sailed up the Nile in 1843, but who had since settled down in Nottinghamshire. Rumor had it that Carlyle would visit before the week ended, and Milnes hoped that Alfred Tennyson might show up, too.

"Dick, I've come into money," Milnes said. "And I mean to turn Fryston —this weedy resort on the River Aire—into a salon! What's life, I say, without conversation? Oh, I have my inheritance at last, my boy, and do I mean to spend it! I'm thinking of building a wing on the house for Tennyson, if he'll come here to write!"

"The house is packed," Burton noted. "You have a good start."

"I've put you in the cottage. You and Hankey are the only bachelors, so you can pull the girls out of the kitchens, if you have charm enough."

The first dinner went well. Burton and Dr. Bird, who had equally pointed good humor, entertained everyone talking about the famous trip to Mecca.

"Tell us, Burton, how do you feel when you kill a man?" the physician asked, leering across the table.

"Oh, jolly, Doctor, how do you?" Burton retorted.

Later that evening Mr. and Mrs. James MacQueen arrived. Burton and MacQueen greeted one another with an embrace, and MacQueen began to talk about Speke's recent behavior, but Burton said, "Please, let's not talk about it now. Let this be a nice weekend!"

During the morning hours, then, while the ladies and a few of the husbands played croquet on the front lawn, Burton, Milnes, Hankey, and Mac-Queen sat under the marquee near the little yellow summer cottage talking and drinking—for Burton his usual brandy and for everyone else gins with tonic. After Burton had recounted a few of the more trying moments in Africa, Hankey told about Milnes' speech before Parliament attacking a proposed anti-obscenity law. "A splendid, funny, very persuasive speech!" Hankey told them. "The law failed to get votes!" MacQueen added that the occasion was important for the concepts of free speech and free publication, and they toasted Milnes as a great liberal defender. "Please, gentlemen, watch your insinuations," Milnes said, smiling. "I'm soon to be a peer!"

Hankey had fallen into greater and greater depravity, Milnes noted.

"He's been collecting statuettes, photos, and books in a devoted mono-mania of corruption! He's utterly hopeless!"

With Hankey present, Burton noted, the conversation usually found its way to sex and its perversities. Hankey was tall, thin, and sallow; he combed his hair so that he looked like De Sade, and was like the philosopher, Burton decided, except for the intellect. He was intrigued by Hankey and his extremity of thought, yet found him distasteful, too. During some of Hankey's more sensational moments he talked of taking two women to a Paris hotel room where they could view a scaffold and make love during a hanging. He also spoke of flagellation. And he asked Burton, once, if on some future expedition into the tropics he might please bring home a human skin—which would make an excellent book jacket.

Burton understood all of this as Hankey's depraved humor—meant as a joke—and tried to appreciate it. This was a world where even the mention of a French novel, in some circles, would be considered an outrage, Burton realized, and where all British thought was mired in pious repression.

"The heresy that really offends my countrymen is sex," Burton told Hankey at one point in the conversation. He stirred his brandy with his finger. "They fancy exotic places, but only if investigated under the auspices of a proper committee. They fancy free thinking, even agnosticism, but only if expressed in a university lecture. But sex is altogether too wild and personal. It's the hideous offense."

"Exactly," Hankey said, turning serious. "Which is why our host puts together this extraordinary library. I smuggle books through customs for him, you know, because even the mere descriptions of sexuality in print are seditious."

"Hear, hear," MacQueen said. "There ought to be—somewhere—a naughty library!" The men laughed.

"In fact, there should be," Burton agreed. "And when I'm old and sexless and can't travel anymore, I want to translate some really blasphemous literature and drop it in the midst of the English countryside—on the fair shelves at Fryston, if no other place!" They all raised their glasses.

When Mrs. Milnes rang the bell for luncheon on the terrace and everyone strolled toward the house, Milnes drew Burton aside. "I want us to talk," he said. "You must tell me your troubles and what you need."

They walked beyond the garden to a forest path surrounded by broom and wildflowers. Milnes, his mouth forming that little round shape, placed an arm over Burton's shoulders in a fatherly gesture.

"I must have time to write my book on the lake regions," Burton said. "And my brother Edward—I told you about his condition. I've got to place him into suitable care. And then Isabel. I've got to find some resolution to my affair with her."

"What about Speke?" Milnes asked quietly.

"Oddly enough, he's no great problem for me. I know he and Rigby talk behind my back. But I can't—and shouldn't—reply to any slander."

"Quite right. Keep your silence for now. Let MacQueen and others in the Society handle Speke. As time goes along, Speke will falter."

"Yes, he probably will. Because he's wrong about the Nile. What will kill Speke is lack of certitude. He wants to be right all the time, but neither life nor the Nile lets a man be right that much."

"About those other matters, then, I can help," Milnes said. "My advice on the woman, of course, is to marry her—the sooner, the better, and no matter how troublesome her family is. Marriage is like a title and money in the bank —a social protection. I also have a possible solution to your brother's situation and your need to find a place to write. I've taken a villa in Boulogne."

"Boulogne? I lived there once, you know."

"Use my villa. Let the servants care for Edward. You write—and get into print as quickly as possible. No use letting Speke have the public to himself!"

"I might well accept the villa for a few months," Burton answered.

"Do accept. I tell you, Dick, it's wonderful being rich. I can collect paintings, books, and famous people—and put them here and there. Never had so much fun in my life!"

They heard the distant sound of the luncheon bell again. As they strolled back toward the house, Burton began to feel a great relief.

Back at Jordans with his family, Speke continued to improve his writing style with a number of letters to Rigby, Petherick, Murchison—and with letters almost daily to the secretary of the Society. He wrote an elaborate support of Edmund Smyth as his possible new companion on the next African trip, saying that "he is a chap who won't go to the devil, full of pluck and straight head foremost . . . a man precisely of my habits, and one entirely after my own heart."

But a committee of the Society rejected Smyth, after which Speke wrote to Shaw, the secretary, saying, "Smyth is feverishly inclined, and I won't have him with me. I am as hard as bricks."

The choice then turned to James Grant.

Speke asked his mother about the possibility of inviting Grant to visit Jordans.

"I think that would be fine," she said. "You can take him hunting. Shall I also invite his wife?"

"No, not the wife. And, Mother, I'd like you to interview Grant, if you will. I respect your judgment."

They sat at the breakfast table, the remains of clotted cream, muffins, and eggs around them. His father and brothers had gone to the fields or to do errands, but Speke, instead of striding out for his early-morning shoot, lingered with a last cup of tea.

"Tell me what you think of an idea of mine," his mother said. "I want to redesign the family coat of arms. Add something to it in your honor. The word *Nile*, I think, and some appropriate symbol."

"Wait until I come back from this next expedition," he said. "All that would be nice, but I might be unsuccessful. We have to trace the river out of the mountains into the desert. There are still what we have to term minor uncertainties in all that." He smiled and took her hand across the table, as she liked him to do.

"You'll be successful," she assured him. She returned his smile and squeezed his fingers.

"And you'd better consult Father—although I know he doesn't care much for family crests and all that," Speke told her.

"Your father and brothers—well, they're not disappointments to me, not at all," she said, sighing as she took a final sip of tea. "I did want your father to stand for Parliament, once, did you know that? But he's so content in the country. Loves horses. And just the look of things—each hedgerow, I sometimes think. And your brothers are good men who love life here, too. But you, Jack: you've become so much, so very much!"

"I count on you in everything," he told her.

"I'll send an invitation to Grant," she said, giving his beard a little tug as she withdrew her hand. "We'll have him down here and see what he's made of!"

Boulogne was expensive—not so forbidding in the winter months, but in the springtime, when Burton expected to be there writing his *Lake Regions of Equatorial Africa*, prices would be excessive. Having Milnes' villa would make the trip feasible, but he needed money for transportation, for Edward, for croissants, for brandy, and for some of life's pleasures in France.

Excursion trains would take the masses in England to cheap resorts like Scarborough or Gravesend; Brighton would be more fashionable, and Folkstone would be wonderfully dull and dignified, but those who had real money for holidays—the peers, the gentry, royalty, men like Milnes—would be traveling to the continent. And the French restaurateurs and hotel keepers would drain every pence and most of the good spirits from such tourists.

As he prepared to go, Burton found that he had to write to Speke about money. It pained him, but the government had asked him to pay what the expedition had overspent—and Speke had agreed to pay half of what was owed.

In his shabby little hotel room on the edge of Soho, Burton carefully composed a letter, beginning with the familiar "Dear Jack." The salutation itself annoyed him, but the letter had to be written. That afternoon, before he posted the letter, Isabel came to visit him and saw it lying on the table beside his bed.

"Good," she said. "I hope the two of you are making up."

"No, not exactly. A business matter," he told her.

Isabel undressed as she talked. "If the two of you want to patch things up, perhaps I could help," she suggested, draping her blouse over the arm of a worn velvet chair. "As it turns out, John Speke and I have a mutual friend— Kitty Dormer, the Countess Dormer! It's a long story. Kitty is older now, but years ago, when she was a raving beauty, she used to be engaged to my father! Somehow she's still friends with all of us, and she told me recently that, once, a Speke had been married to one of the Arundells—one of my own family! We were neighbors! And now Kitty says that if she could help, she'd be all too glad!"

"Come to me," Burton sighed, pulling Isabel to the bed.

"I just hate to see you miserable over that man," she said, allowing him to open her chemise.

"I've been reading Mr. Speke's articles in *Blackwood's*," he told her, running his fingers across her skin. "He's making absurd assertions that he can't prove. If I bide my time, he's going to make a fool of himself. This letter is about money. I believe he's honorable enough to pay his part of our losses on the expedition, but I worry about that."

"You're both honorable men. You should work this out and stay friends."

"So your two families had a marriage once? Interesting. I suppose that makes you cousins, you and Speke."

"Oh, do that again," she said, pressing her hand atop his.

"All you rich English types are incestuously interbred," he whispered. "I don't know why you'd want me in your bed. I'm not even related to you."

"Ah," she said, answering his touch.

"There. How's that? Do I seem like a close cousin?"

"Richard," she asked, kissing him beside his ear, "can't we have an engagement with a proper announcement and ring?"

"I'll do anything for you," he promised.

"Ah, ah," she whispered. Then, recovering herself, "I hate that you'll go off to Boulogne to write! I want you calling at the house! I want to see you every day!"

"There, cousin, there," he said, teasing her.

She laughed, but her eyes were half closed, her lips lay open, and she could say no more.

The villa in Boulogne was damp and cold that winter, yet Burton knew that a number of bright, warm days would occur during the bleakest months, so settled in to work without complaint. Edward, propped in a chair and covered with a blanket, looked like a piece of hapless furniture; the servants, fearing Burton's wrath, though, took good care of the brother, feeding him mush and apple sauce, which he accepted in a series of lazy bites, and cleaning him when he fouled his clothes. His room faced the hills and garden at the rear of the villa; Burton turned the rest of the place into a study, writing on desks, the arms of chairs, kitchen counters, and small tables laden with biscuits and brandy.

Milnes stopped by for a visit while en route to Paris to visit the Goncourt brothers and to stay with the Rothschilds. His library had become his obsession.

"The Rothschilds and Mrs. Milnes want Fryston furnished with Dresden, marble, damask, and Sèvres, with three clocks in every room," Milnes said. "But I just want bookcases." He planned collections in theology, biography, history, memoirs, poetry, and fiction, he told Burton, with a special collection of erotica. "I want a collection as good as anything owned by Monsieur de la Popelinière or other amateurs of the Régence," he said. "Anything you can get me will be appreciated. And I have poor Hankey working overtime smuggling banned books across the channel!"

During the short visit they talked almost entirely of books and Milnes' collection. "I'm also collecting all of De Sade," he told Burton. "Some day, I fear, Fryston will be the only place in England where certain books can be found. And I mean for them to be preserved for high reasons and low: I want to assert the freedom of the press—in which, by God, I truly believe—and, besides, books with a bit of cock and cunt are damned enjoyable!"

Only toward the end of the visit did they mention Speke.

"Have you been keeping up with his writings in *Blackwood's?*" Milnes asked.

"Yes, all rot. I saw his latest. An epic account of Captain Speke's adventures in Somaliland. I was there and don't recall anything he writes about."

"You think he's wrong about the Nile?"

"Yes, very wrong. If we had stuck together in this, ours would have been called the greatest exploration the world has ever known. But Speke will be driven into more and more controversy, you see, because his assertions are without proof. And when he proves out to be wrong, I don't think he can survive the consequences, either. Speke isn't one to stand fault, not even in himself."

When Milnes left the villa, Burton tried to get back to his writing, but found that he was drinking more brandy and working less than usual. A circle of depression and drink began: Edward was there with drool on his lip, Speke was carrying on, Isabel was far away, the rearrangement of English sentences was a bore. The mail brought no solace, either. In long letters—punctuated by phallic exclamation points—Isabel pleaded with him to overlook her mother's behavior and to come courting. In terse, mean little notes the army threatened to cut his pay for all his extended leaves from active duty. And Speke, at last, replied on the matter of the expedition's debt; he stalled, postponed his obligation, and asked if the government couldn't relieve them both of financial responsibility.

Burton read Speke's letter twice, then got drunk for days.

One night he went to Edward's room and helped him out of bed. Supporting his brother under the arms, he staggered out to the patio with him—into the cold winter night beneath a canopy of Gallic stars.

"It's not that I bear Speke a grudge, not even that," he told his brother, who stared out at the dark, empty sky with the same placid innocence. "But mistakes have been made. Needless pain. Misunderstanding. Alienation." He held his brother's thinning body and began to talk about Speke and his lost and distant companions, all of whom became mixed up and confused in the drunken monologue. He realized that he might be talking nonsense, but hoped that by some fraternal magic Edward might comprehend. "Stroyan, for instance, is gone," he said. "Completely gone. I saw his body that night on the sand. And Steinhauser, dear man. I tell you, Jack, time and space and death open up the great chasms. I mean, perhaps Lumsden is gone. Who knows? Perhaps he's dead and buried out there in India! And where's Sidi Bombay, tell me, Jack? Gone back to Zanzibar? Listen, Jack, there are hundreds of these good souls. Men I served with." He realized only vaguely that he confused Edward with Speke in this meandering address.

"And whatever happened to Shamarkay? Do you wonder about him? And for that matter, Jack, you and me?" Burton's brandy came up in a loud belch. "And remember the one who called himself End of Time? Now there's a name for all of us! End of Time!"

Edward shivered in the cold moonlight, so Burton placed both arms around him and held him close. After a while the sky stopped reeling so much and Burton understood that his brother had a chill. They staggered back into the villa together.

"Time, time, bloody time and distance!" he said, covering Edward in coarse blankets. When Edward continued to shake with cold beneath the covers, Burton lay down atop the quivering mound, sheltering it and giving it his boozy heat. The room and bed tilted in different directions, but he held on.

"Oh, Edward, oh, Jack, oh, poor, poor, poor Dick!" he moaned, holding on and feeling that shivering thing beneath him.

A week later Hankey came out from Paris for a visit, bringing his beautiful mistress with him. Burton half hoped that this lovely woman was a gift, yet dreaded the thought that Hankey might want all three of them in bed together. Her presence excited and perplexed him; she was a slender, tall, long-legged creature whose hair, he knew, if she let it fall, might reach the soft curve of her flanks. But Hankey, who insisted on dirty talk every minute, kept a close, jealous watch on her, so that Burton finally knew that nothing was going to happen. This made him more angry than he supposed; Hankey was a vulgar bore, he decided, and a tease.

"Now you get me that human skin," Hankey said, bringing up in jest again a subject Burton felt should be left alone. "Preferably some dark female flesh, remember, and let it be in flayed strips!" he went on, laughing loudly at himself.

"Yes, yes," Burton answered, humoring him. He tried not to look in the direction of the mistress, whose face had become a clever mask.

His guests stayed only two nights, but on the second he heard the woman padding around the villa after everyone had gone to bed and he lay on his pillow deciding if he should get up and move through the darkened rooms himself to locate her. He wanted no complications with Hankey, who behaved like a husband.

The woman was restless for something—possibly for him. He decided to get up and find her. Tying the sash of his robe, he moved down a darkened hallway, stopping twice to listen for her movements. She was definitely there: wandering idly, letting her slender hip bump into the unfamiliar furniture, sliding a silken sandal across a tiled floor. He thought, once, he was close enough to hear her breathing. Then he lost her and stood holding his breath, waiting for another movement. She was in the sitting room, he decided.

For more than a minute he stood in the doorway, until his eyes adjusted to the shadows of the room and he knew she sat at one end of the long couch beside the patio windows. He started to speak, yet hesitated. Slowly, then, he went toward her. Be bold. Sit beside her, not across from her. Sit down so that the thighs press together.

Not a word passed between them as he slid against her. One hand went behind her, taking her waist; he could feel the sharp intake of her breath and the soft, tense, expectant body when he touched her. Their mouths were close, yet they neither kissed nor spoke; seconds, minutes ticked away and he smelled her perfume and felt the warm, uneven breath from her nostrils. Her head tilted downward slightly, as if she pondered what to do, and although he waited for her to raise her lips, he knew she wouldn't. Shall I find her mouth with mine?

Shall I run my free hand, he asked himself, into the folds of that soft peignoir?

Before he could weigh all such possibilities, she moved away from him. Standing above him, she turned as if she might speak. But instead she hurried out of the room, and he was on his feet when he heard the door close at the far end of a hallway. Hankey's room. She'd gone.

It was almost enough. She had let him hold her, and the hot, distant, ambiguous communication was almost enough, yet he stood there in the darkness for a long time—until his feet ached with cold—thinking about it.

The next morning they were gone after an exchange of bright courtesies.

The guests at Jordans during this time were Mr. and Mrs. John Petherick and Jim Grant.

Petherick was jolly, positive, full of plans, and very much the favorite of everyone at the estate. On Sunday in church at the little stone chapel at Dowlish Wake, he fumbled with his hymnal, unable to find his place, until all the children thought he was wonderful. In the usually quiet household, he was loud and demonstrative, banging his pipe on a bowl and saying, "Together, Speke, we'll rip Africa wide open!" Such outbursts almost brought applause from the family. Laughter and excitement filled the kitchens, and Speke's mother gave everyone her best smile.

They had a giant mutton at one meal, and Petherick, who weighed perhaps twenty stone, devoured most of it while they explained their plan.

"He'll ascend the Nile from Khartoum," Speke announced. "He'll make maps and notes for the Society as he goes."

"And take as much ivory trade as I can," Petherick added. "We'll need the money. If I know the Society and the government, we'll get mostly encouragement from them and little else."

"He's right. So he'll gather ivory, too. Then at Gondokoro—the last outpost, far south in the Sudan desert,—there's a small Austrian mission station. He'll leave boats and supplies for us there, and we'll collect them on the way north from the Victoria Nyanza."

"Of course I'll press on, too," Petherick said. "I'll try and reach the lake myself by the old northern route. Possibly we'll run into each other, if we stay on the river. But I know I can get to Gondokoro and leave supplies."

"And I know I can reach the nyanza and follow the river to the supplies," Speke said. "We can't fail."

"What do you think, Jim?" Petherick asked.

"I have a shorter stride than Captain Speke," Grant said. "But I was always able to keep up."

"You certainly were!" Speke said, and everyone laughed.

During the days of their visit Petherick had cheered and encouraged the new undertaking, and Grant, quietly, had been assumed to be the new partner;

he had neither spoken for himself nor insinuated himself, but the mother found him agreeable, Petherick thought the matter settled, and Speke liked Grant very much away from the wife. The visit, then, acquired an unexpected turn: instead of a preliminary interview with a companion and an aide, it became a strategy session.

"The problem, frankly, is still money," Petherick reminded them one evening after supper while everyone sat around the hearth. "My own estimate is that our plan might cost five thousand pounds. I believe I'm being reasonable —even conservative. Recently, our government increased my consulate salary to three hundred a year. So there's always quite a difference in what a man is asked to do and any real support."

"We had to write dozens of letters for a small rise in salary," Mrs. Petherick added.

"Oh, Jack's had his own problems with the Society," the mother said. "We imagine the new trip will cost the family dearly. And Burton—you must hear this—wants Jack to help pay for the wasteful extravagance of the last journey."

"Let's not talk of that," Speke asked her.

"I can never get it in my head that the Nile flows north," said William, the brother, for no apparent reason. "I mean, on the map—well, it looks as though gravity would want to pull a river to the bottom of the page!"

The women roasted chestnuts, and Mrs. Petherick rattled the flat brass pan as if to erase the last remark.

"One thing I want is an impressive man-of-war ship for my return to Zanzibar," Speke said. "I do want enough money to sail into that harbor flying the colors proudly. I've already written the admiralty about it."

"An important point," Grant said to Petherick, "is whether you'll have enough money to buy supplies and to leave them for us at Gondokoro. Or enough money to keep coming south toward us."

"That's why I'll trade ivory," Petherick said. "I've been in that country often, mapped it, know it well. I'll live off the land and, yes, I know I'll manage for all of us." He sucked at his pipe and blew an authoritative ring of smoke— a perfect circle that made its way toward the ceiling.

The next day the men went hunting and shot a few partridge, Speke's father having the best luck. At the end of the afternoon they came back to the house, where tubs of hot water for their baths were prepared in a room behind the scullery; they hung their birds on pegs beside their clothes, bathed quickly because the evening air had turned cold, and wrapped themselves in towels warmed on racks in front of the kitchen stoves. Everyone had a brandy after this except for Speke, who went upstairs to confer with his mother.

"Yes, I like Jim Grant very much," she said. "But don't let him go wandering off on his own. Remember this is your expedition. Keep control."

"Do you like Petherick?" he asked her.

"He's plucky—a positive sort. Yes, I like him. Don't you?"

"Not entirely," Speke admitted.

"I worry that he's only a Welshman with no real family money. But he's brimming with confidence and does know the land. I'd say his experience counts," she offered.

Speke let the matter drop.

He couldn't say exactly what he felt for Petherick—at least not to his mother. In his room writing letters that night, Speke thought, well, Petherick's just too large; he puffs for breath climbing the hills; he uses his girth to bluster and to establish authority. But what is he, really, except an opportunist, using my fame for his own advantage? And he's too married. She's always there at his elbow. And what will he do with her? Take her up the Nile and dress her in shiny boots for the difficulties? Have her brew pots of tea and bake biscuits? Throw his gigantic body atop hers for sexual consolation when he feels frustrated?

Now Jim Grant has good qualities, he told himself, but I'm weary of men settling themselves on a woman's strength; damned if I'll compete for a man's better nature with all the insipid homebodies of the world. I hope Grant knows this is the moment of a lifetime. I hope he finds his soul in Africa and never goes back to being a domesticated squire in Ross-shire.

Of course, time ran short. Petherick did know the South Sudan. Grant would have to do.

He wrote to the Society that night, recommending that both men should be approved—one as his new companion, the other as an associate in the venture. After a few hours' sleep, he sent word downstairs that he would work at his correspondence all day, until supper; he wrote to Rigby, again; to the Black-woods; to Murchison at home. At noon a servant came up to his room with a lunch tray, but he worked on, preferring to keep his own company. The solitude of writing appealed to him, and he thought, yes, very well, I can write books; this withdrawal from small talk I can manage very well indeed.

He took supper in his room, too, and worked through the next day until his mother came upstairs with two letters. She sat across from him in the window cushion watching his face while he read them. Oliphant had written that after a tedious correspondence with various officials in Paris he had secured for Speke the medal of the French Geographical Society. He asked Speke to come up to London so they could celebrate together. The other letter was from Kitty Dormer, the countess about whom the family always managed a good deal of reverent talk, proposing a meeting between Speke and Isabel Arundell on the matter of Dick Burton.

Speke handed both letters to his mother and sat there amused while she read them. Everyone seemed to need his attention and care, even a new prospective wife.

"I admit I'm curious to see her," he told his mother, laughing. "Burton has undoubtedly found himself a rich fiancée, and I'll wager she's frowsy!"

"You think you'll go up to London and see Lowry?" his mother asked, and there was an odd hint of concern in her voice.

"Hmm, yes, I suppose so, but also to serve Kitty Dormer's wishes."

"This is wonderful about the French Society. I'm so proud." She leaned across the window seat and kissed his cheek. "And I hope it won't be unpleasant meeting with this woman."

"Think of it. Dick Burton is sending me a female ambassador."

"When will you go?"

"Oh, as soon as our guests leave. And, mind you, don't fret about Lowry. I know you feel he's too—cosmopolitan. Perhaps not solid enough."

"I said nothing of the sort. He has many accomplishments."

"You think he's unlike me—or any of us here. But, please, I don't belong just to Somerset anymore, either."

"No, you're a man of the world. This award from the French is another clear proof. And I realize that Lowry has worked hard in your behalf."

"But you have apprehensions."

"No, not at all," she insisted.

The Countess Dormer was a little blue woman: blue veins in her wrists, bluish hair, blue eye makeup, even a tiny blue tongue sloshing around in her mouth as she spoke. Speke sat in her parlor in Mayfair unsure of which of the women before him, the countess or Isabel Arundell, was the most ridiculous.

Isabel, he thought, looked like fresh dough about to erupt into a cake: plump and powdered with delicate flour. She sipped tea with them, but looked as though she might grab every cake and biscuit on the dish before them and stuff them all into her mouth at any moment. For a long time through the tedious introductions, he thought he might burst out laughing; then he felt mildly sorry for her.

When the countess finally left them alone together, Isabel cleared her throat. Whatever happens, Speke decided, I'll try not to embarrass her.

"I'm deeply grateful to you for meeting me," Isabel began. "Richard, of course, has no idea that I asked to see you, but I do hope for a reconciliation between you. She jutted out her chin as she spoke—or, rather, both chins. She was so fat and funny that Speke concentrated on the pattern in the Persian rug.

"Sorry," he managed. "I don't know how it all came about."

"Richard is very sentimental and very loyal to the men who serve with him," she said. "I know he must have deep affection for you."

Speke gazed toward his feet and didn't respond.

"After all, the significance of your discoveries together is yet to be evaluated," she continued, going on boldly, although in a soft, small voice. "You're returning to Africa because further investigation is needed. Richard is in France writing his report for the Society. And everything is so inconclusive. It seems awful to have controversy and bitterness at this point."

Speke gathered his breath, waited, then finally said, "Yes, he's writing the report of our expedition. And do you know that the Society asked me to turn over all my personal maps and notes so that he could use them? Naturally, I obliged, but, once again, your fiancé has the benefit of my labor and his own theories."

Isabel picked up a wafer, then returned it to the tray.

"I'm pleased to see you and to acknowledge the wishes of the countess," Speke went on. "And, believe me, I'm sorry to disappoint you, but you must imagine that much is involved which you don't know or understand."

"I do know this must be painful for both of you," she answered softly.

"Dick was so kind to me," he said, rising from his chair. "Nursed me like a woman, taught me such a lot, and I used to be so fond of him. But it would be too difficult to go back now."

"Then you'll stand on that?" she asked. "You'll always so remain?"

"Yes, I'm sorry."

A formal tone had dominated their meeting, but Isabel rose from her chair, went across the room, opened the door to signal to the countess that their interview had ended, then turned back to Speke with a relaxed and cordial smile. She held out her hands to him as he came toward her; there seemed to be a loving warmth about her that touched him, in spite of himself, and she looked at him as if their meeting had been successful and dear to her.

The Countess Dormer appeared, as if on cue, with a smile of her own. "And how has your family liked having a famous son?" she asked, extending her little blue-veined fingers.

"They've treated me the same," he said, laughing. "I think my father would still prefer that I ride into the fields each day with the laborers."

"Yes, I'm sure," she replied, leading him toward the front door.

When he turned and looked back, Isabel Arundell was no longer there.

Although Oliphant wanted him to stay for days, Speke stayed only one night, dining with Lowry alone at the Reform Club where its famous chef, Alexis Soyer, prepared pheasant à la Flamande. Oliphant drank most of the Möet and became emotional about Speke's wanting to return home so quickly.

"I'm trying to arrange a ship, Lowry. Put yourself in my place. I have responsibility for an enormous expedition!"

Oliphant tried to sustain a jaunty, casual look, yet said, "You're ruining my dinner, Jack, with your usual obstinacy."

"Sorry."

Later, they talked about Speke's small profits from the lectures and publications and managed a laugh about how the Blackwood brothers wanted all references to African nakedness deleted from the articles in their magazine. They also talked about Lord Elgin and the efforts to name the nyanza after the queen, the meeting with Isabel, and places Lowry planned to travel while Speke was absent. They returned to the hotel in a more pleasant mood, but Speke announced that he was tired and meant to go directly to his room.

"You really don't care about my feelings at all," Oliphant complained as they stood in the hallway outside his suite.

"Lowry, I promise: we'll go to Paris later. Everything will come to pass. But I'm leaving in a few days and I must get ready."

"This is our last time together!"

"No, that's the point. We'll have many good times. But you know how much is on my mind just now."

"Gad, Jack, you're such a *pain*," Oliphant said, emphasizing that last word so that he sounded, Speke felt, like Sir Anthony.

As they embraced, Speke could feel Lowry's body melting. As they parted, though, his friend held up his head and managed a stiff "Good fellow, Jack, have a fair wind and good luck!" Once more they had retreated from one another into a zone of decorous ceremony, of simple courtesy, and of male custom, which helped to cover their separate anxieties.

"Write me, friend, please, and I'll write to you," Speke answered.

Back at Jordans, Speke waited while everything fell into place.

He read *The Mill on the Floss* during the mornings, and it seemed to him, clearly, that his reading skills—his power both to read more quickly and to retain—had increased in the last year. His enjoyment of the novel indicated that he was over his old malady, his childhood disability. He also continued to keep up his correspondence, and in writing letters he felt that his wit and humor increased, too. He began to feel—oddly—literary. Let Burton take note of a true rival, he decided, and he felt jolly about himself.

A new ship, the steam frigate HMS *Forte*, was provided by the admiralty. Unfortunately, it would sail first to Brazil, then to Zanzibar, so the journey would take additional weeks, but Speke contented himself with the prospect of entering that African harbor with real display.

In the afternoons Speke went out hunting alone, making his usual circle through fields bordered with gorse and covered with the new spring grass. Then he came back to his room to write more letters: to the Blackwoods, to Shaw, and finally to Grant, asking him to come back to Jordans en route to Devonport and the boarding of the ship for the journey.

In the evenings after dinner and conversation with the family he often went up to his mother's room for consultation. Their talk in these last days frequently came around to the debt Burton had requested Speke to honor.

"You've called him a blackguard so often," she reminded him. "But if you imagine that you do actually owe the debt, we'll manage to pay."

He sat across from her at her desk, his chin resting on his knuckles. "There's so little money." He sighed. "There's not enough for the new journey, but if I had plenty, I'd pay Burton just to be rid of him."

"Has he written you again asking for it?"

"Yes," he told her. "And I believe that silly meeting with Miss Arundell was motivated by Burton's financial concern."

"Have his letters been civil? You haven't shown them to me."

"Oh, cordial enough," he said. The salutations of the letters, four in all, had evolved from "Dear Jack" to "Dear Speke" to "Dear Sir" to "Sir:" and the contents of each letter had become more pointed, but Speke couldn't tell his mother all that. Yet now, his ship about to sail, he felt a pressing need for settlement.

"If I'm very honest with myself, I do feel I owe the money," he finally managed to tell her. "I wrote Burton that he should seek restitution from the government, but they won't pay. They won't help Petherick, and they'll scarcely help me."

"Then the family will pay," his mother said firmly. "I'll arrange it through our accounts after the next harvest, if that suits you."

Speke got up and paced the room. The decision tortured him, but at last he said. "Yes, I suppose that would be best." He hated to penalize his family for his endeavors, but saw no other way. "It's just that I detest having to tell father and William about the matter," he said, still pacing.

"They'll understand," his mother assured him.

He came to her side, leaned down, and kissed her good night.

"When you come back from Africa again, you'll be very famous and potentially wealthy," she told him. "We'll celebrate at Taunton. We'll drape the whole town in bunting and have a brass band! And you'll be able to restore any money you require. So go to bed, sleep well, and don't give any of this another thought."

She traced her fingers over his brow and beard as she kissed him.

In his room, though, he couldn't sleep; he kept thinking about Burton, and for some odd reason his emotions began to turn on him. With the debt finally admitted to his mother and resolved, he began recalling his last time with Burton in Aden: the man's gaunt look, the pall of fever, the suspicion in Burton's eyes that last moment together when the flag whipped in the breeze above their heads.

His feelings rose and fell, soaring from one frenzy to another. He wanted to kill the man, yet craved his approval; he hated that arrogant glance, yet wanted him near.

Why tonight? What's happening to me?

He took off his clothes, curled himself into position for sleep, then got up and paced some more. He remembered too vividly that time together in the baths at Cairo; the sway of Burton's genitals, the slope of his shoulders and thighs; he wanted him, suddenly, like a penetration, like a deep, final, pleasureful dagger, like a wound that could bleed away all these extremities of feeling.

He wished that Burton, not Grant, accompanied him on this new venture, and that instead of Oliphant waiting in London with all his attentions it could be Burton there, too; he wished he could see him, give him a check for the money owed, hear his laughter, and see that melodramatic scowl.

At his desk, stricken with what seemed to be a violent indecision, he attempted to compose a letter, yet the words—each bloody scrawl—came out badly. Not saying half of what he felt, he settled for a rigid facsimile of emotion, beginning,

> My Dear Burton,
>   I cannot leave England addressing you so coldly as you have hitherto been corresponding . . .

Not at all what he meant or hoped to say. Burton would just have to read through to all the heartfelt meanings: time to pay debts, to make amends, to settle all differences. Damn words, though: they came out onto the page either foolish or severe. He wanted to say, come on, take this voyage with me—in a subservient role this time, of course, but do join me. But there on the page were only words: hard, again, as metal.

Yet he finished the letter and sealed it up, hoping for the best.

In April, having finished his manuscript, Burton came back to London to deliver the work to Shaw at the Society in Whitehall Place. Lord Ripon had replaced Murchison as president, but nothing else had changed, everyone seeming anxious, still, to ignore Burton. Shaw, the dapper little secretary, tactful and courteous, accepted the large packet of manuscript and promised to keep in touch with both Burton and the editors at the printing house.

"And is there anything else I can do for you?" Shaw asked.

"No, not really," Burton said. "I've written to Speke for the last time about the debt he owes. After this, I want there to be no direct correspondence between him and me. You can help me in this."

"I'll be glad to serve as intermediary," Shaw offered.

Burton was preparing to leave the office when Shaw's voice altered from its usually professional tone and he asked kindly, "Please, are you all right, sir? And your brother? Is he well cared for?"

Burton stopped and smiled. "Thank you, Shaw," he said. "Yes, I'm well. And I've made arrangements in France for my brother's care—at least for the time being."

Burton was dressed in strictly Bohemian attire: a cap pulled over one side of his face, a long woolen scarf trailing him, baggy trousers and an old greatcoat purchased at a fair near Boulogne; he looked like an out-of-work artist and smelled of brandy, wet wool, tobacco, and cheap lotion.

"Your own health is good?" Shaw inquired.

"Oh, I'm still a bit drunk from last night," Burton answered, grinning.

"I want to tell you . . ." Shaw began, then stopped. He came forward with a pencil in his hands.

"Yes?"

"I want to say how very much I admire you," Shaw said, revealing even more sympathy than he perhaps intended.

"Thank you, Shaw, very much, indeed."

Burton went out into the crowded streets and hailed a carriage to take him to the Arundell home. He knew that he looked atrocious, yet something in him prompted him to want to shock them all; he wished for another drink, so that he could properly stink up their drawing room.

Isabel met him at the door, kissed him, and ushered him into her father's presence before disappearing into the rear of the house. The two men shook hands stiffly and forced themselves to smile.

"I'm afraid Isabel's mother won't welcome you," the father said. "We've had a—an upsetting morning awaiting your arrival."

"You wouldn't have a glass of whiskey or brandy?" Burton asked boldly.

"No, afraid not."

Silence fell between them. At last Isabel came back looking distressed, but trying to put on a pleasant face. Burton decided that she had definitely added weight around the hips.

"I'm afraid my mother—" she said, but her voice broke and she couldn't finish. Fluttering a lace handkerchief, she dabbed at her eyes.

"Isabel, I'm going to my hotel," Burton said, pulling at his long mustache and tossing the scarf over his shoulder in a cavalier manner. "You're welcome there. So are you, sir, and so are all your children and Mrs. Arundell."

"Personally, I have nothing against you," the father said, as Isabel began to cry more loudly.

"You know where my hotel room is," Burton said to Isabel, who admitted her guilty knowledge with a nod of her head while her father's eyes widened.

"See here, Burton," the father began.

"Careful what you say to me, sir," Burton interrupted. "If I've been discourteous to you or your family in any way, it was unintentional. But you must not be intentionally rude to me." He fixed the father with a glare, leveling a gaze at him that seemed to threaten violence. "You simply must *not*. I'm in no mood for it. And none of you will be any happier if you cause Isabel and me to become even more impetuous."

"I'll come to you," Isabel said, as Burton turned to leave.

"When you can choose between me and your mother, please do," he said, and he went out the door.

For the next two days Burton spent hours at the Bag o' Nails, a pub not far from Westminster Abbey, where he occupied a back table, wrote letters to the army, to Edward's caretakers, to Milnes, and to publishers and accountants while consuming numerous brandies and sodas. Somehow he didn't want to go to his hotel because Isabel would arrive with explanations and requests; he couldn't go to Upper Brook Street because Milnes and family were at Fryston; he felt displaced in London and this pub was as good as another; he let the liquor fetch his thoughts away and by closing time he was drunk.

"The Mormons in Salt Lake City, Utah, all have several wives," he said, lecturing the patrons on religion and sex in one rambling address. "God told them to do it—and, by God, they obey! And how better off we'd all be with three or four wifeys! A good cook here, a seamstress there, another who plays piano, another—rich, please—to pay the bills!"

"And all frivolous in bed!" someone shouted from the bar.

"Do you know," Burton said, raising a finger in mock authority, "that sex is the driving force of most of the world's religions? In some, like the Hindu faith, it's *o*vert, and in some, like the religion of poor Saint Paul, it's *per*vert, and in others, like the faith of the great Confucius, it's *in*ert!"

"Kindly don't blaspheme in here," the barkeep asked, but his request received a hardy round of laughter from the congregation.

"I'm a true believer, always have been!" Burton shouted, raising his glass. "But a man must go where his faith leads him! Even, yea, unto the great abyss! Verily, into the dark, lost, mossy regions! Where the slime encompasses him! Where his essence becomes one with infinity!"

"Are you talking about what I think?" a nearby drinker inquired.

"Indeed I am! I'm discussing the cave of winds! The dark hole of universal truth!"

"I think I knew that lady me'self!" the drunk replied, and the room erupted in howls.

"To the Mormon faith and all true beliefs! And let us go where our pointers point us!" Burton announced.

Waiting with Grant in Devonport for repairs on their ship, Speke received Burton's last letter. It began,

Sir, I cannot accept your offer concerning me corresponding less coldly. Any other tone would be extremely distasteful to me.

So now Burton's wounded pride would keep them apart forever. Speke sank into his chair in the breakfast room of the Thomas Hotel, let the letter fall beside his plate, and decided that he would read the remainder of it later. His correspondence in the last week had been congratulatory: an official encouragement from the French, cheers from Murchison and Ripon, even a warm letter from Albert, the Prince Consort, wishing him "God Speed." But this ruined so much; it seemed unfair that in such a short, hard life one should lose a friend.

He tried to keep his feelings hidden and under control.

"Is everything all right?" Grant asked him that evening.

"Very bright, Jim. All's well," Speke answered. Yet nothing was. His mood rose and fell like those restless Atlantic waves beyond the harbor.

Isabel agreed to walk with her sister and a friend in those same romantic Botanical Gardens where she and Richard had met. The day was sunny and warm, yet as they went along the paths, Isabel began to feel increasingly distressed. For a time she worried that she was growing ill, then she put her hand over her heart as her eyes filled with tears.

"I'm not going to see Richard for a long time," she said.

"Why, you shall see him tomorrow," said the friend, comforting her.

"No, I shall not. And I don't know what's the matter."

Late that afternoon a messenger brought a note to the Arundell house: Burton was gone. Isabel's mother, feeling not too unhappy with this turn of events, put her stricken daughter to bed.

Both Speke and Burton left England in April 1860.

With Grant as his quiet and steady companion, Speke would seek to prove all his assertions about the Nile.

Burton would go to America and stay drunk for almost a year.

1860 – 1861

————)0(————

*Down the Nile
and Across the Mississippi*

*A*GAIN, A SHIP BEARING SPEKE TOWARD AFRICA WAS TAKING THE LONG WAY around. Instead of traveling to India, this time he was going to South America, and he had forgotten how much he detested the idleness of a sea voyage. While Grant practiced photography, watercoloring, nautical observation, and read books on botany, Speke grew desperate with worry: Would Petherick find funds and be at Gondokoro as promised? Would Burton's new volume throw doubt on any of Speke's own accounts and assertions about the nyanza and the Nile? Would there be good interpreters in Zanzibar, so that their findings this time could be declared certain?

Speke paced the decks and shot some skeet, but his discontent grew worse after the first week.

"I'm staying up again this evening and studying the stars with Captain Turnour," Grant said, excited as ever. "I think you really would enjoy it, if you cared to join us."

"I'll entrust that to you," Speke said. "So study well. We have to be sure this time. No mere theories. There are a lot of geographical complexities, you see, Jim, and it won't do unless we have proof. Come on, let's sketch another map."

They went into the officer's mess, where Speke began to sketch furiously in a school tablet. He seemed crazed and tortured. The cook served them tea from the galley, but Speke scarcely noticed.

"I've decided to write to Shaw at the Society," he explained to Grant. "I've made a decision about the Rusizi River at the top of Lake Tanganyika. We didn't visit it, you see, because Burton was afraid of hostile tribes up there. We heard reports that the river flowed *into* Lake Tanganyika, but now I'm sure it's an effluent—flowing out of the lake—and I intend to tell the Society this."

Grant became confused. "But wouldn't that actually help Burton's theory that all the lakes are linked?"

"I'm tired of Burton!" Speke shouted. "My *own* source told me the river flowed *out* of Tanganyika! I must trust my own findings!"

"But you didn't actually see the river yourself, did you?" Grant asked, blowing on his tea to cool it.

"Suppose the Rusizi is the Nile? Suppose it flows east, somehow, and joins with my nyanza?"

"Your Victoria Nyanza is at a higher elevation, isn't it?"

"My instruments were inadequate. What's worse, Burton's estimates of the altitude of Tanganyika were probably dead wrong! Don't you see? Better to leave our minds open on this, I daresay! It's all very, very complex!"

"Yes, I can see that," Grant admitted.

"So I'm sending the Society this new map! We must all be cautious in this—and, finally, absolutely certain!"

"Then your new map will differ from the one you published in *Black-wood's?*" Grant asked, sipping his tea and keeping his voice level.

"Yes, but we don't know the real truth, do we? We can't be sure!"

"Wouldn't it be better to draw a new map later? I mean, we're just now en route. We're out at sea and need a look at things, don't we?"

"I'm drawing up a new map," Speke insisted. "And I must write and tell Shaw and the members of the Society why this one, the one I created in Africa originally, and the one in my *Blackwood's* article all seem to differ. Everyone must understand that there are definite uncertainties. But you study all your navigational procedures, because we'll require confirmations on these estimates —we'll need all your powers!"

"Yes, quite," Grant replied.

"And I must get it all straight in a book, don't you see? A book very much more persuasive than anything Burton can concoct!"

"I'm sure you will, Jack."

"I'm no mere travel writer like him. I'm an explorer and author. And there's quite a bit of difference there!"

"Yes, absolutely," Grant agreed.

Two South African dignitaries, Sir George Grey, Governor of the Cape Colony, and Admiral Sir Henry Keppel, commander of British naval forces at the Cape, were also aboard the *Forte* with Speke and Grant. They engaged both explorers in games of whist, told stories, kept the meals lively, and forced Speke to relax from all his concerns, at times, and to act a little more lighthearted.

At the island of Madeira they forced Speke to go ashore for a dinner and dance. The stop itself annoyed him—he wanted to get on the way—but he was also reluctant to meet young ladies and to demonstrate his clumsiness on a dance floor.

Sir George insisted, saying, "You know, Jack, all of us are farm boys. But we have to regard these occasions as we would a country dance. We can't be afraid of our shoes, our dance steps, or our manners at table. Let's get on."

Once at the party, Speke seemed to enjoy himself as he gorged at the buffet and consented to a few dances with the young ladies who floated around the floor of the governor's ballroom in taffeta and ribbons. Throughout the evening he was asked to recite African stories, so enjoyed being the center of both male and female attentions. Grant wore a gleaming jacket with medals from the Crimean campaign in bright display.

"Grant, I say, you were a hero!" Sir George said, viewing all those medals. They were surrounded by admiring young women at the punch bowl.

"Ah, I was in the rescue of Lucknow," Grant told his listeners. "But, alas, all my friends received at least this many awards, and some of them were even thoughtless enough to receive medals for personal bravery." The girls fluttered their fans and laughed.

At sea again, though, Speke sank into heavy moods. Grant wondered if such inconsistency would curse their whole trip.

"Don't fret over all these myriad geographical matters," Grant finally said. "It's really quite simple: We go to the nyanza, follow the river that leads out of it, and see if it's the bloody Nile!"

They reached the terrifying calms of the Sargasso Sea: dolphin playing aimlessly among the great clots of seaweed. They saw debris floating by: pieces of a ship's rudder, a sailor's cap, the remnant of what seemed to be a desk with an indolent tortoise riding atop it. Speke became sick with the sight of it; his elation had soured and he felt sure, he told Grant, that if they kept sailing west, they'd fall off the edge of the world into the void.

A room in the Fifth Avenue Hotel in New York cost $2 daily, but Burton thought this heavy expense might be worth it because he could ride one of the first public elevators. He rode up and down several times a day, passing his floor, coming back, getting off and on, holding on to the brass pole in the center of the car.

He had traveled to Canada, then had come down to New York to shop for gear. Most of his luggage consisted of books and medicines; his prize possession was Bartlett's *Dictionary of Americanisms,* which introduced him, of course, to this colorful foreign language based on English. The medicine was straight opium and Warburg Drops. He had also acquired a number of flannel shirts to augment his greatcoat, his tweed shooting jacket, his rubber poncho, and his chocolate-colored umbrella. Among his many books were the American novels *Moby Dick* and *The Scarlet Letter,* the first of which he found astute in its religious observations and the latter in every way unreadable.

"I suppose I'll buy the necessary weapons before I go to Utah," he told an editor, Mr. Sledge, as they sat in a dusty little office on Madison Avenue.

"You want to go to Utah?" Sledge asked. As they talked a young woman with a long, slender waist moved papers from one desk to another, distracting Burton's efforts to discuss his new venture or possibly to sell some of his current volumes to this Yankee literary merchant.

"Uh, quite, yes, Utah: the City of the Saints," Burton managed. "My eccentricity is visiting the holy cities."

"About that," the editor said, leaning forward. "I sorta hoped you'd stay in New York awhile. I could arrange a lecture. You could tell the story of your famous trip to Mecca."

"Mecca and Medina." Burton sighed, watching the girl.

"Oh, let me introduce you to my wife. Katey, this is the famous adventurer Richard Francis Burton. He invaded a holy city in Arabia. If they'd have caught him, they'd have whacked off his head."

Katey Sledge, wife and secretary, took Burton's extended hand and peered deep into his rapt gaze; her full lips formed a single word, which came out in a whispered breath: "Adventurer."

"We could make a lot of money on such a lecture," Sledge continued.

"My room number at the Fifth Avenue Hotel is *nine,*" Burton said, not looking away from young Katey. "Perhaps we could discuss a suitable arrangement."

"I tell you, I'd rent the biggest hall in town and we'd make money."

"Yes, a lecture," Burton said, trying to regain the conversation. "My own countrymen wouldn't think of such a spectacle. I'm a renegade in London." He glanced back toward the wife. "My ways are too wild."

"Not for us," Katey assured him.

"Certainly not for Americans. We admire guts. And maybe you could find some actors wearing those—whatcha call 'ems the Arabs wear."

"Burnooses."

"Yeah, for an illustrated talk. I tell you, Burton, we'd score big."

That afternoon Burton bought a new Colt pistol from a gunsmith on Washington Square. He stopped at a street vendor's and ate a hot dog, then sat in a bar next door to a Chinese laundry drinking brandy and reading the newspapers. Indian wars raged in Nebraska, matters of slavery and the secession of Dixie were of great concern, and a Corps of Engineers had been established to build bridges, to prospect for gold, and to settle the frontier in an orderly manner.

"Now that's American progress for you," Burton said to the barkeeper. "Doing things scientifically! A Corps of Engineers!"

The barkeeper replied with a smirk.

Burton strolled back to his hotel wondering about whores, Indian squaws, octaroons, riverboat ladies, and Mrs. Sledge. He considered a lecture tour as a means of meeting and conquering whole audiences of women, but, though drunk, knew that it would be far easier to trust his charm than to toil for celebrity. In the elevator he balanced himself against the brass pole so that neither his new Colt .45 nor his bottle of brandy would slip and fall from his shooting jacket.

In his room he put on his robe and poured himself another two fingers of brandy. The liquor and the hot dog ached in his stomach, but covered a dull, deeper ache and helped to obliterate his confusion. He didn't know what he felt for Isabel exactly, only that he had to flee. Time will make a fool of Speke, he felt, and space will heal me; if I had stayed I would have bored Milnes with my melancholy and would have insulted Murchison and others; time is solace and in distances, again, I'll have my peace of mind.

A soft knock sounded at the door, and when he opened it he found Katey Sledge's anxious smile awaiting him. On most occasions, he would have pulled her into the room, yet now he could only speak her name.

"When I said I was going out, my husband told me that the shops were closing and that I shouldn't stroll about the streets alone," she began as she walked past Burton into his room.

Burton drank off his brandy in a single swallow.

"I thought you might wish to accompany me. For a short twilight stroll. But of course you're busy. I see you're going over your travel schedules." She spoke haltingly, although her mouth formed a definite sexual pout.

"Let me dress," he said, moving sideways behind the screen that hid the lavatory in his room.

"Please, I don't mean to disturb you."

"But, of course, you do mean to disturb me," he said from behind the screen. He dropped his robe and struggled to find the leg of his trousers.

"Oh? What do you mean by that?"

"I've been studying," he began, but his voice broke like a schoolboy's. He became somehow impatient to change the subject. "I've been studying various routes toward Salt Lake City. I'm contemplating the direct route across the Rockies, as traveled by the Mormons themselves, but I have to get to St. Louis in order to book passage on a stagecoach."

He saw over the screen that she took a seat on his bed. God, he told himself, I don't think I have to recite travel stories in order to command this New World; I could be called Billy Bowlegs before I travel the length of the continent.

"Then there's the southern route via Yuma, Arizona," he went on, speaking more loudly than necessary. "But that way seems arid and troublesome. We'd pass through Apache territory." A button from his new flannel shirt managed to pop off and roll away. This is a continent with natural beauty and rough mystery, he said to himself as he peeked over the top of the screen at her corseted waist. Still buttoning himself, he came out from behind the screen and seated himself in the room's only chair.

"Tell me again what your specialty as an adventurer is," she asked hoarsely, closing and opening her eyes slowly.

"The penetration of forbidden citadels," he said, wishing he hadn't been so bold. "And you? Do you have a specialty of your own?"

"I've met a number of famous authors," she admitted. "But I seldom meet men who actually *do* things."

She had a way of closing her eyes so that for an instant she almost seemed to fall asleep. This movement of her lids approximated total rapture.

"Well, my books are really nothing," he heard himself say. "But you know what the Arabs say: Travel is conquest!" His words seemed silly, and he had no idea what he might utter next.

"I seldom go far from home myself," she replied, being equally illogical.

He poured himself another drink and tried to gather his wits, but only said, "Care for brandy?" Actually, there was not another glass, but she declined.

She's not sitting there wanting booze, he told himself; and if I make a single suggestive overture I know that her stockings might fall down around her ankles and her dress might fly off to the bedpost and fold itself neatly.

"I suppose you've known a considerable number of women," she said, getting to the point. Her eyes dropped in that soft closure.

He tried to think of a reply, something amusing, but his effort was interrupted by another knock at the door.

He counted himself lucky that he was discreetly clothed—especially when the editor called out sharply as if he deserved a reply.

"Burton, open up!"

Katey closed her eyes and made no movement whatsoever, as if she were no longer present in the room. Burton felt that he had become an actor—playing either farce or tragedy—who had only clichés to recite.

"Unlock this damned door!"

"Sir," Burton managed in his best English accent, "I am not alone!"

"That I know well enough! Let me see my wife!"

On his feet, Burton felt infinitely more sober than moments before. He gave Katey a withering glance which, her eyes being tightly shut, she didn't see.

"I'm armed with a new Colt pistol!" Burton shouted through the door. "And if you don't move away, I'll fire it through the paneling and send you off —whoever you may be!" In all, this was a clever speech. Burton, meanwhile, did search for his unloaded weapon as the demands from the hallway ended.

"See here, this is Sledge," said a less resolute voice seconds later—now at some distance down the hallway. "If you don't open up, Burton, I'll be forced to summon hotel clerks and policemen!"

"Sir, you certainly won't intrude without authority!" Burton called back, beginning to gather up his scant wardrobe.

"Then, by God, I'll have it!" Sledge shouted, and Burton could hear him stomp away.

"Has he gone?" Katey whispered, still not opening her eyes.

"You led him to believe you were coming here," Burton accused her as he gathered up his books, umbrella, and poncho.

"Well, you looked at me very openly today in the office," she offered by way of defense. "In fact, you had a wanton stare."

"That's my natural expression," he explained, finding the unloaded pistol and the remainder of his gear. His thoughts were suddenly sober and rational: I'll take that ship for New Orleans tomorrow. Tonight the weather's perfect for sleeping under the stars down at the pier.

"If you're leaving in such a hurry, what will I tell him?" Katey asked.

"My dear, my advice to you is to use the stairs, not the elevator. I know my own way out. Goodbye and good luck with your authors."

He hurried down a back stairway marked for use by bellhops and valets, feeling silly, reminding himself to send the hotel the $4 owed, hoping that nobody would see him, and dropping only *The Scarlet Letter*, which he meant to lose anyway.

Weeks at sea.

On July 4, 1860, Speke's ship sailed into Simon Bay at the Cape. He was still agitated and had begun writing furiously on a book that he hoped to get to press quickly.

"Jack, please, rest yourself," Sir George told him. Grey had continued to act fatherly toward Speke throughout the journey. "As soon as we're at port, I'll approach the Cape Parliament in your behalf. I'm sure they'll decide to help in this venture of yours."

"We need to sail to Zanzibar as soon as possible," Speke replied.

"What you need is money and men," the diplomat said. "So you should attend a few luncheons, practice a broad smile, and bide time for a few days while I explain how important you are."

Speke reluctantly agreed, and in the next few days Lieutenant General Wynyard, commander of the Mounted Rifles, had donated £300 and ten Hottentot volunteers who would accompany the expedition. These were blacks with only a modest amount of soldierly skills, but they would be far better than the lazy askaris who served the last expedition, Speke knew, and he thanked Wynyard and Grey for their help.

So they were in Africa again. Grant began gathering specimens of the flora, pressing leaves and blooms under glass, making drawings, and preparing himself to become the expedition's botanist as well as its navigator. His excitement became contagious, and when Sir George informed them that they were being supplied with another ship, the *Brisk*, a slave-hunting corvette, they were ready to go. At the docks, they began to feel important: uniformed soldiers loaded their gear aboard the corvette, tea was served in the cool shadow of the ship, and a half dozen band members in bright-red coats played a medley of marching tunes.

"You shall have this little brass band on your trip to Zanzibar," Sir George told them. "An additional farewell gift. Perhaps they'll play for the sultan!" The teapot, surrounded by a display of gold spoons, was set in an ebony-handled cozy; a nutty, sweet, mysterious fragrance rode the breeze; the band played softly, in that delicate, restrained manner of a good brass band under control.

"Ay, Jack, we're not in the Highlands!" Grant said, laughing and enjoying the fanfare of the departure.

The *Brisk* hugged the coastline, sailing into many of the larger coves, and on the third day they came upon a small dhow, manned by two surly Arabs, father and son, and their cargo of six manacled slaves. Speke, Grant, and Keppel, who had come along with them, watched from the deck as the captain and his marines towed the dhow between the coral reefs, then set the slaves loose in the jungle. Then, standing on the deck of the Arab vessel, the captain took the slavers' purses, quoted them Her Majesty's wishes and laws in matters of slaving, and sent them off—probably toward more mischief. The six slaves, four men and two women, had scampered off into the bush like rabbits, never looking back at either their Arab tormentors or their rescuers.

As the *Brisk* made its way back out into the deeps, the little brass band played a waltz. Speke's recent depression continued to ebb away; he felt excited as they neared Zanzibar and useful to the crown because of the morning's encounter.

Keppel, the naval commander, was a small man with large ambitions as a hunter.

"I'll find you one of the big four," Speke promised him. "You'll have yourself a nice trophy—elephant, lion, rhino, or water buffalo."

"What about a hippo?" Keppel asked, eager for tonnage.

"Oh, hippo, yes, I shot one once. Damn thing swam down to the bottom of its pool, you see, where we couldn't even watch it die."

Keppel talked incessantly about the navy and its importance in England's status, so Speke was glad when they reached Zanzibar. Rigby greeted the ship with a full regimental presentation: officers with bright sabers held high, men in white uniforms with brass buttons, flags flying. From the ship the brass band played a somber anthem, attracting a large native population to the quay, and Speke waited to disembark, stalling in his cabin until Grant, Keppel, and the captain were all ashore, then coming down the gangplank, young and fit, smiling like a conqueror.

"Dear friend!" Rigby called out, greeting him.

"My good man!"

They stepped forward and gave each other a smart salute. At that moment from somewhere in the maze of the town a call to prayer sounded and the muezzin's voice cracked on the high notes of the holy wail.

In New Orleans, Burton stayed at Eliza Murray's licensed brothel on Dryades Street. Her girls were all French, having been shipped over from an infamous house of correction in Paris as possible wives or companions for colonists, but ending up in the trade of the tenderloin district. Burton found the room cheap, the girls talkative—they admired his command of the French idiom —and the food delicious. Many girls in the district had fled to the gold rush in California, but there were still numerous houses of this sort around, as well as gaming rooms, dance halls, cockfighting pits, cafés, and rooming houses.

Outside the brothel Burton feared for his life. Murder was rampant— bullies on the streets thoroughly ventilating their enemies with razors and Bowie knives every evening. An infested swamp ran through the middle of the district, so disease was the rule. There were flop houses, the girls told him, where sailors always disappeared; jealous boyfriends of various prostitutes toured the French Market looking for fights; there were special clubs where women were caned or beaten with whips or switches; beyond Canal Street duels were fought on the small patches of open ground; in the bars and dance halls the music was a prelude to brawls.

Perhaps because he was so drunk so often, Burton thought, fear crept in, but he definitely felt it: this was a land of brutes, with little rough charm and considerable menace.

He bought a quantity of Patent Improved Metallic Pocketbooks, in which he planned to make notes, and a long, straight dagger—an Arkansas Toothpick —which he secured on his right boot. Then he booked passage on a mule wagon heading north along the river road toward St. Louis.

"Leaving so soon?" Eliza Murray asked him, as his gear was loaded into the wagon one morning before breakfast.

"Madame, you were a kind hostess," he said, taking her hand lightly in his.

"And you're quite an English gent," she said. "And what are you any-how? Some kind of professor?"

"No, just another vagabond with a different accent," he told her, smiling. The driver loaded his case of French brandy.

"Goddammit, you goddamned mules!" the driver then said, addressing his team. Burton stood in the middle of the French Quarter making his first entry in his little notebook, observing that this particular American curse "in these lands changes from its expletive or chrysalis form to an adjectival development." Perhaps, he decided, I am a professor.

They bounced along the river road, the great muddy flow of the Missis-sippi beside them, the way often overhung with mossy trees. The mule skinner handled a bullwhip, and the other companion, a squat little guard who kept one eye closed, was so heavily armed that he could scarcely move: shotgun in hand, rifle strapped to his back, pistols, knives, and belts of ammunition rattling around his waist. Burton offered to share his brandy, but neither of the men liked his liquor, the little guard commenting that "out here, sir, we measure our red-eye by how far a feller can walk after drinkin' it."

Shrugging, Burton drank off that bottle and started another. Writing with a stub of a pencil on rough road, inebriated and bouncing along through the ruts, he recorded that biscuits were called *crackers*, that corn was *maize*, and that certain English expressions, such as "knocked up"—which meant, back in London, to be very fatigued—were not to be uttered in the presence of American ladies. Bumping along, listening to his companions and making notes, he sensed that he traversed a fearsome land, more terrifying, somehow, than deepest Africa;

nearly at flood, the Mississippi seemed more threatening than the Nile; the land swarmed with ugly grasshoppers, and its undergrowth was infested with rattle-snakes and thorny weeds; and here men weren't isolated in little tribes with accountable rituals, but were killing and fighting their way across the continent, moving toward that next ocean in fits of slaughter.

In St. Louis, Burton bought a $25 Hawkin rifle, a small six-shooter as a companion to his big Colt, a silk hat in a box, a pocket sextant, a used and worthless telescope, tea, sugar, cigars, opium, and more brandy. Then he went by train to St. Joseph, Missouri, where he paid $175 for his stagecoach fare.

"Aw, sure, there'll be plenty Indians," a new acquaintance assured him. The man was a federal judge traveling west to accept a new position and could spit a perfectly aimed quantity of tobacco as a kind of exclamation point to every statement.

"If Indians attack, I want to be ready," Burton said.

The other occupants of the stagecoach were a young army officer, Lieu-tenant Dana, his wife, his daughter, and a lawman who was known only as the marshal, a deadly pistol shot, as Burton understood it, who was being sent to some California county to rid it of outlaws. The marshal had little to say, the young officer and his family stayed modestly silent, and the judge had views on everything. The judge also coughed, belched, wheezed, farted, gagged, and seemed to have a full array of sounds.

"What is it you do for a living, Burton?" the judge asked that morning outside the Patee House as they prepared to leave St. Joseph.

"I'm an army officer on leave."

"Then you should know firearms," the marshal said, squinting.

"Well enough," Burton said, and his understatement pleased both men.

They started off through dry creek beds, and after ten miles everyone— except for the lieutenant and his wife and two-year-old daughter, who cowered in one corner of the coach—was sufficiently drunk. Even the driver was drunk. For a few miles they saw houses and farms, then the dense nimbus of the prairie showed itself: an eternal grassland braced by giant blue columns of rain.

Burton, who had felt much at home in India, Arabia, Africa, and the exotic expanse of many another place, felt himself a stranger to this land; its dangers were oddly uncertain, its Indian languages unknown, its size staggering. Yet he wasn't thinking about Speke here—or Isabel or fame or the secondhand life of books or the infuriating British government.

The sickening sway and August heat inside the stagecoach made them dizzy as they watched, bleary-eyed, the flat landscape going by. Fine dust settled over their clothes, and the men continued to wash it down their throats with liquor, while the lieutenant's wife dabbed at her child and husband with a wet cloth. Burton passed out, woke up to view the passing land, passed out again. He wanted to stay drunk; to witness, if possible, a scalping; to hear the coyote's doleful cry; to copulate with an Indian maiden; to find that crazy, holy city on the Salt Lake; to cut away the heartache and disappointment.

In Zanzibar, by odd circumstance, Jim Grant found himself the officer in charge of the consulate, and when a contingent of blacks came to him bringing with them three other frightened blacks in shackles, he wasn't sure what to do.

"These men are prisoners," the sergeant explained.

"I see that," Grant answered with only mild sarcasm. "They're in chains. But what do these other fellows want me to do with them?"

"Sir, it would probably be better to wait till Colonel Rigby and the others come back."

"Yes, I'm sure. But it seems I'm to do something now."

Speke, Rigby, Keppel, and others had gone off hunting, leaving Grant at the consulate. The early formalities had passed: Rigby had given the explorers and Keppel a lavish military dinner at the Afrika House, and Speke had called on the Sultan Majid, presenting him with a gold watch from Her Majesty and trying to converse through an interpreter who was only passable at his job. The Sultan had also annoyed Speke by talking about Burton's fine qualities and by suggesting boldly that the caravan should start across the Masai Plain from Mombasa instead of forming itself at Zanzibar again. What did a mere sultan know, Speke later asked angrily, and how could he presume? After the interview at the palace everything proceeded in Rigby's military style: stores tended by a quartermaster, porters properly hired and instructed, additional barter goods sent ahead for later use, everything written down in signed orders or useful lists.

Now, though, Grant had to understand what was going on—and render some decision. The men in chains looked bored. Their captors, talking wildly, tried to make themselves understood by pantomime and raised voices.

"Find me an interpreter and make haste," Grant finally said, sighing. He felt as he had felt out in India as a new, young officer: confused and painfully uncertain. But now he had the skill to cover up.

The sergeant took an hour to find Sidi Bombay, who, since the arrival of the explorers, had waited for an audience with Speke. Sidi Bombay badly wanted a significant job with the new caravan and since his return to Zanzibar from Aden had been living with two women and two goats down at his old stall near the slave market while the officers decided how to organize their journey. Now, eager to serve, he hurried to the consulate, only to find that the prisoners had been transferred to the local jail. He and Grant, who had never properly met, greeted one another awkwardly: Sidi Bombay extended his hand for a handshake and Grant manufactured an Islamic bow. They walked over toward the jail through that maze of streets with its smell of coffee, urine, cloves, and leather.

"How many languages do you speak?" Grant asked of this strange little man who had filed his teeth into sharp points.

"Not so many as Captain Burton, but more than anyone else in Zanzibar," Bombay answered.

"Did you like Captain Burton?" Grant asked, taking long strides so that Sidi Bombay had to hurry to keep up.

"Sometimes he had a bad temper. But he taught me to love women more. Since I knew him I have found many wives and concubines."

"I thought only a wealthy man could possess many women."

"Yes, but I am poor and have many women. When I came back from Aden, Colonel Rigby did not require my service. The Sultan gave me goats, but would not give me a house. Cloves, slaves, and the other work of the island I will not do because I am a soldier. But I became a friend of women, so made my fortune—a small one, yet here I am."

They reached the jail, which consisted of a wide shadowed hallway off one of the narrow streets opening into a sunny courtyard, where prisoners were kept in the hot sun. In that oversized hallway, leaning with their backs against the cool stones, Sidi Bombay questioned the deputies who had delivered the prisoners. Beyond, out in the sunlight, the chained men smoked a large opium pipe, passing it back and forth, their eyes glazed, perspiration dripping off their crouched and naked bodies; a few scrawny chickens pecked the earth around their small circle, and the glare of light from this odd spectacle caused Grant to look away and to adjust his vision to the faces of the men beside him. The conversation went on and on before Sidi Bombay explained.

"Those criminals murdered an Austrian missionary and his family," Sidi Bombay reported. "The deputies want permission to execute them."

Grant peered into the terrible sheen of that courtyard. He listened, absently, as Sidi Bombay recited more: how the missionary outpost was ransacked, how each family member was butchered, how the murderers were caught. Scotland seemed far away to Grant, and he tried to reconstitute himself again as a British officer in authority.

He watched those chickens, too: long-legged, sleek like runners, and probably monstrously inedible. Sidi Bombay completed his report.

"Yes, certainly, by all means do proceed," Grant heard himself say.

The beheadings were carried out with immediate and eager dispatch. One by one the prisoners were bent over in the yard; they were so heavily doped that they seemed obliging and indifferent to the rough handling the deputies gave them. The little deputy with the saber took off all his clothes for his work. After his first clean stroke the chickens flew around the yard, excited by this sudden movement and the blood; Grant saw one of the remaining prisoners glance up at the birds with something like envy.

Afterward, Grant thanked Sidi Bombay, walked back to the consulate alone, lay down on his bed, closed his eyes, and listened to the sea.

Said bin Selim, anxious to please and making promises that his porters would behave themselves, was once more put in charge of the caravan's loads. He seemed older and less agitated; like everyone else in Zanzibar he had come onto bad times and needed work, and Speke assured him that this journey would be conducted in a military fashion with no nonsense.

The ten Hottentot volunteers would act as askaris for the caravan, and Mabruki, as large and as stupid as ever, was commissioned as sergeant.

A new man, Baraka, became Speke's personal servant and gunbearer. He was young, very vain about his thin nose and European features, and overestimated his somewhat lowly rank in the caravan.

While Rigby and Grant inspected all sextants, compasses, guns, beads, wire, cloth, and food, and divided everything into equal loads for the porters, Speke interviewed Sidi Bombay in his office at the consulate. In a large entry book on Speke's desk—imposing in size and drawing both men's gaze—all expenditures were listed.

"This caravan will have discipline and planning," Spekes said. "Colonel Rigby has sent barter goods ahead to Ugogo. All loads and wages will be equal."

Sidi Bombay stood first on one foot, then the other; he tried to smile and to behave casually.

"Of course we will require your services as interpreter," Speke went on. "Will this be satisfactory to you?"

"Oh, yes, very satisfactory. But—"

"Yes?" Speke said, waiting.

"You know that I am a soldier," Sidi Bombay began, tentatively.

"I'm aware that you served the Sultan."

"Truly, I am small, but a fighting man," Sidi Bombay continued, looking out of the window as he searched for words.

"So, yes, a fighting man," Speke said.

"I believe that I should be put in charge of these Hottentots. They do not know this journey. They have no languages except their own. And I don't think they will fight unless I command them."

Speke waited, staring down at his entry book.

"I have done more harm to enemies with these sharp teeth than any Hottentot soldier has done with a rifle," Sidi Bombay argued, and Speke, although he meant to observe strict business procedure, found himself laughing.

"Very well," he said. "You'll be in charge of the Hottentot volunteers."

"So I should be paid two sums—as soldier and interpreter," Sidi Bombay said, pressing a sudden advantage.

"No, only one salary. But you may have a rank. What rank in the British army would you prefer?"

Sidi Bombay, surprised by this generosity, could only remember the names of two ranks and knew that a title so esteemed as Rigby's was out of the question. In a hesitant tone, he asked, "Captain?"

"All right. Captain Sidi Bombay it is."

Relief and pride swept over Sidi Bombay's face. "Please, I must tell my women and friends," he said, and without asking about his salary he ran downstairs to announce his good fortune.

The next morning they all sailed to Bagamoyo on the coast in the Sultan's corvette. Rigby went along, so Grant and Speke wore uniforms. They were served a picnic by enlisted men on the sunny deck. Grant had two satchels of art and photography supplies, noting that he would concentrate on the flora, mapmaking, pictures, and drawings. Speke would lead the caravan, and together they would shoot enough game, they agreed, to help substantially with the food supply. Their mood was lighthearted and optimistic.

"Jim, this is a very different beginning in comparison to Burton's caravan," Rigby said.

"Yes, you can't imagine," Speke agreed. "Trouble was, Burton never really got going. He had one delay, then another!"

"Burton's great fault," Rigby offered, "was that he talked to the natives too much."

In the picnic basket was curried meat, fruit, and wine. The sails billowed out, driving them toward that thin line of jungle in the distance.

"Yes, far better to attend to ourselves in our own manner," Speke said.

Bouncing along toward Fort Laramie, Burton endeavored to take notes on this vast land, which became more barren as it stretched westward.

He saw Indians in feathers and buckskins; mule trains and covered wagons; young Pony Express riders; a town called Troy—which, he noted, was perhaps the final insult to the memory of the hapless Pergamus; unmarked graves; a chimney rock; stone bluffs and hot arroyos; thousands of fireflies; a prairie-dog village; and immense reaches of eroded brown earth.

They passed rivers called the Kansas, the Little Blue, the Platte.

At an Indian village, the maidens and little girls came out of the tepees laughing. But when the stagecoach driver offered to trade tobacco for a favor the girls put up their hands, fingers closed and thumbs outright, in polite, good-natured refusals.

They slept at little Fort Kearny: a tiny blockhouse of thick timbers surrounded by whiskey shops and tepees. One night they were in a mud house whose walls inside were papered with *Harper's Magazine* and the *New York Illustrated News*. At other stops there were crude shanties with no windows and floors dirtier than the ground outside.

The marshal kept his silence and read *Ivanhoe*.

The lieutenant and his family suffered.

But Burton and the judge bought a keg of local rotgut whiskey for $36 —one part fire and four parts water, with added ingredients including pepper, bitterroot, tobacco, and burnt sugar.

"Damn, damn, damn, this is awful!" the judge yelled, tasting it.

"Yes, I like it, too," Burton answered.

When an hour of sobriety arrived, Burton listed the names of all the Indian tribes that could be remembered by McCarthy, the driver, and the passengers: Pawnee, Cherokee, Kickapoo, that whole confusion of races with their hundreds of designations. His English readers, he knew, would be impressed with the haphazard effort. He also wrote down two suggestions which, he informed the judge, he intended to forward to Washington: (1) that a camel corps similar to General Napier's should be established to deal with the Indian uprisings in Nebraska and the Dakotas and (2) that the world's animals—the yak of Tibet, the llama of South America, the kudu of Africa—should be imported, so that the globe's population could be easily fed off the production from these vast prairies.

Fort Laramie was a proper garrison with stores, log houses, corrals, and soldiers who wore at least parts of their uniforms. Burton, the judge, and the marshal were invited to dine at the commander's table, but the driver, sensing that others might be enjoying themselves, seemed anxious to travel on. The entree was buffalo steak, but the commander's wife prepared vegetables and served home-cooked bread. Burton wanted to converse, but after an hour McCarthy was at the door, kicking dust off his boots, behaving as if the Rocky Mountains might go away if they didn't promptly leave. Burton wanted to discuss the pantheism of the Indian tribes, the disappearances of the great buffalo herds, the complicated language of the Sioux, the art of scalping, the fabled gold in the hills surrounding Denver.

"McCarthy, please, another hour!" he told the driver.

After this, they drank the commander's home brew. Elaborate toasts were concocted and delivered in slurred speeches. Even the marshal, who was not a man overburdened with sentiment, raised a glass in praise of Sir Walter Scott.

As Burton became tipsy he also became filled with his usual, emotional sense of camaraderie. "All men are equal!" he shouted with such a strong conviction that the others at the table seemed amused. Here was a man whom they regarded as having an aristocratic bearing and an Oxford pronunciation making a great deal of an American concept. "All men are equal!" he said, filling and raising a glass. "You are no man's superior and no man is yours!"

In London, Samuel White Baker, who had met Speke on that frigate bound to Aden from India more than six years before, sat down with Murchison and Ripon of the Royal Geographical Society to discuss another exploration into

Africa. Baker still looked like a wrestler—a wealthy one—and he was still ambitious to have a dangerous and important adventure.

"Oddly enough, I do remember Speke," he told the officials. "The boy could become formal in a wink. Tall chap. And a damned good shot. We watched him kill the gulls behind our ship."

The men smoked cigars and drank amontillado. Baker had recently returned to England after profitable years in eastern Europe and Asia Minor, where he had hunted big game and worked toward the construction of the Danube railway. He was notoriously rich, and since the death of his wife, who had always stayed at home with her religion, rumor had it that he had purchased a second wife, a Hungarian woman of extraordinary beauty, at one of the eastern slave markets.

"With Speke and Grant in Africa, we thought you might consider some other exploration for the Society," Sir Roderick said.

"No, no, Africa's my choice," he told them.

"We're also supporting Petherick, you see. There just isn't the money."

"I could investigate Dr. Livingstone's work on the Limpopo River," Baker suggested. "That could be very satisfying."

Ripon said, "No, we feel Dr. Livingstone will eventually make a new exploration."

"Yes, he should have the Limpopo and his work on the Congo to himself," Murchison agreed.

"I see," Baker said. "Africa is neatly divided up. Speke has been given the Nile and Livingstone the Congo?"

"It's all a matter of finances," Sir Roderick said, wheezing.

"I've petitioned the Society for years," Baker told them. "Never got a penny of help. Never had your sanction or encouragement. And both of you know well enough that Speke may never emerge from central Africa. My expedition could help—might even rescue him. And I've only asked for your goodwill and the smallest sum."

The men were not enjoying their cigars or sherry. Outside, a soft brown fog lulled the streets into a late-afternoon silence.

"A sum of one thousand pounds isn't particularly small," Lord Ripon noted, looking out of the window at the thick fog.

"When my wife accompanies me to Africa," Baker said, "she'll probably wear that much around her throat in jewels."

"You intend to go to Africa with or without our support?"

"Gentlemen, I do. And this should give you some mild alarm. What if Dr. Livingstone's health is never recovered, so that he fails to trace out the source of the Congo? What if we never hear of Speke, Grant, or Petherick again? The Society will be remembered for its failure. If I were you, I'd support my request."

"We would gladly support an exploration elsewhere," Sir Roderick said.

"Ah, but there is no place like Africa. I've wanted it all my life. And now I suppose I'll go there. You've been rejecting me all these years, so now I can reject you. I have money. My health is wonderful. I'll travel the Nile, I think, toward Speke's nyanza."

The men stood up, both Murchison and Ripon trying to maintain courtesy. Sir Roderick wheezed, smiled, and asked politely, "You actually intend to travel with your wife, then, Mr. Baker?"

"Yes, I imagine I will. She's a dear—and looks exceptionally good in a trim pair of Wellington boots." He put down his cigar and slipped into his coat, preparing to leave. "And it would give me extreme pleasure to sail up the Nile, as if we were going on a picnic cruise. I think I'd like my journey to stand in sharp contrast to Speke's—with all its military ceremony. And in contrast to the Society's penny pinching." He put on his top hat and smiled, relishing his own toughness now. "Yes, I think we'll take a proper picnic basket, two parasols, and a good deal of money—so that we can bribe and buy what we require. Sounds effective, don't you agree?"

Sir Roderick and Lord Ripon endeavored to be pleasant as they saw him to the door.

The body, Speke decided, forgets its pains and agonies: the spear wounds at Berbera, the fevers with Burton, the pain inside his ear had all been mislaid in the mind's turnings. He felt somehow foolish to have forgotten when the fever came again, when he was so ill that he couldn't raise himself off his cot in that misty heat near Zungomero.

Simzima. All the natives said it: I am not well. And they lie about like rags every evening, too exhausted to eat or to make the fires properly, too sick to care for themselves or one another. The porters had mostly deserted. One of the Hottentots had died, and five others clung to their blankets and burned with fever. All the mules except one had died. The food supply was almost gone because no one had the energy or will to engage the villagers along the path in bargaining. Grant was weak, inclined to say nothing or to do nothing—and Speke saw in his new companion a shadow of his own behavior during that first journey with Burton when he had stayed in his tent trying to fathom a few instruments of navigation, cut off from languages he didn't speak, lonely, confused, and on the edge of desperation.

Only ninety days had passed since the caravan left Zanzibar, but they had made a sojourn, Speke felt, into a province of madness and desolation.

Only Sidi Bombay and Baraka had any spirit left, and they seemed to manufacture it arguing with each other. Said bin Selim was down with a venereal disease, walking and sleeping with hallucination; each day he fell behind the caravan, yet, terrified that he would be left to die on the trail, managed to wander into camp in the evenings, where he would cry out in his sleep at the visions assaulting him.

"Jim, we've got to go hunting tomorrow."

"I can't. You know I can't. And you're worse off than I am, Jack, look at you. We couldn't steady our rifles."

"If we don't hunt, we're going to die," Speke said. They lay side by side in Grant's little tent while a torrential rain hammered the ground and sent rivulets of mud to ooze around their thin bodies.

Grant managed a soft laugh. "You always want to go shooting."

"But we must. The caravan's virtually out of food."

"We'll soon be at Rigby's stores. We'll trade the barter goods for food, as you said we would. We'll make it."

"We passed the village where Rigby sent goods ahead," Speke told him. "That was two days ago. The chief confiscated everything for *hongo*—as a toll for letting us pass through his region."

"Arm the Hottentots and make him give our goods back," Grant suggested.

"The goods are gone. Besides, even if they still existed, Sidi Bombay would have to attack the village alone. It's no good, Jim, we've got to hunt."

As the rains became deafening, Grant—trying to converse, but unable to stop himself—fell asleep. The soft mud flowed into his hair and around his face as he dreamt. From a vast meadow of darkness Speke's voice continued for a while.

"No good. You and I had only an ear of corn with some salt last night," Speke went on. "We're losing strength. But there are guinea fowl and partridge in every field, and we're getting into a region of big game. We must hunt, Jim, don't you see? If we just lie here, we're finished."

The next morning, dripping wet, muddy, and trembling with chills, they forced themselves to rise. They asked for gunbearers, but only Sidi Bombay and Baraka consented to accompany them to a thicket at the bottom of a nearby ravine. Because there were tall trees in the ravine, they knew there must be water to attract larger game.

Grant could not carry his own heavy 12-bore rifle, yet refused Sidi Bombay's offer to do the actual shooting if a suitable target presented itself. Baraka carried Speke's weapon and all the ammunition, complaining loudly that a porter should have been flogged and made to do this menial work.

The ravine's loose gravel betrayed their footfall. Slowly, they eased themselves down toward that stand of thick mimosa and acacia; once, a movement stopped them and they waited, holding their breaths. Speke felt weak and dizzy, yet intrigued with the game.

"You take the first shot," he whispered to Grant.

"No, please, you're the better shot.

"Yes, so I'll back you up. Understand?"

Grant nodded and they went on. At forty yards from the waterhole Baraka and Sidi Bombay passed the loaded weapons to the hunters. Thirty yards. A few more short steps.

Feeding idly on the tender grass at the muddy bottom of the ravine, a big Cape buffalo—a cow—showed herself. She wandered out between two acacia, framed by their yellow bark.

Grant and Speke exchanged a glance. Then Grant heaved the rifle up and fired in one quick movement. Dust and blood seemed to explode from the cow and a small white egret, perched on her shoulder, flapped into the sky. It seemed to Speke a perfect hit, and he knew that the cow's heart and lungs were destroyed as her legs buckled and she went down.

"Ho, Jim!" he shouted in excitement. "Ho! Fine shot!"

They took another step toward the waterhole.

A bull, its horns down, suddenly thundered toward them from the high grass on the other side of the waterhole. Its hooves pounded through the shallow, muddy water, sending up a spray; it was so fearsome and admirable with its great shield of bone and horn lowered that for a moment Speke seemed to see everything: the wet nostrils at the tip of its nose, its eyes like fixed fires, the egrets in flight, the gallery of limbs overhead. The bull vaulted over its dead mate in an oddly graceful jump, then came on.

In the momentary panic, Speke raised his rifle. There was simply no target. Thick horn seemed everywhere—and a shot into that mass of bone would scarcely cause the beast to twitch; its legs were thick and flying; a shot into the nose might turn it away for an instant, but the men would be left standing there unloaded and vulnerable.

Baraka, screaming, broke and ran.

Some of us may die now, Speke thought.

He had always pictured himself in this fix except, in his imagination, a lion, not a buffalo, would charge; he would have one bullet and one chance. Perhaps, with a lion, he would wait until that final leap, catching it with his shot in the last second. But the lion would be a soft, easier target; now, as he began to squeeze the trigger, he could hear each separate beat of the hooves and see only that wall of horn. This shot, he felt, would fail. Death drew a tight string around his heart.

He braced himself and fired.

In the plume of smoke and the confusion afterward he didn't even know what had happened. But Sidi Bombay's hands were extended above his head in applause. Grant, with newfound strength, pumped his heavy rifle in the air one-handed and shouted at the top of his voice. Baraka, far off at the edge of the thicket, danced on one foot and then the other, as if his toes were hot.

Speke's shot had somehow deflected off the horn and had severed the bull's spine. It lay dead at their feet, so that Speke could have reached out and touched its nose with the heel of his boot.

"Jack! Oh, Jack, oh, my word!" Grant said, coming up and grabbing him in a rough embrace.

Speke began to laugh as Grant went on calling his name in praise.

His fever, Speke knew, was gone. The lucky shot had cured it.

As they started across the hot Ugogo Plain some of the porters grumbled with fear, but Speke assured them that the evil spell of this region was broken and that they would pass without incident. He was right: the villages were almost empty, the land shriveled with famine, and the people extended their hands to beg as the caravan passed.

Speke and Grant hunted every day as the caravan moved, the sport driving them on. The large herds were off the path to the north, but many birds were available, and they shot zebra, antelope, and even warthogs. The hunting became an elixir for Speke. He paid little attention to arguments developing between Baraka, Sidi Bombay, and Said bin Selim, although at night, when everyone's sleep was troubled by fever, the trio often became noisy and impossible.

"Just tell me what's wrong," Grant asked Sidi Bombay, who looked angry and forlorn.

"Said bin Selim has sores on his body," he answered. "He plans to quit the caravan, so Baraka says he will be the new governor."

"I'm sure that Captain Speke will decide who heads the caravan, if that occurs," Grant said.

"Speke believes that Baraka is a loyal servant, but he isn't! He is no soldier and no true friend! I should rule the caravan, not him!"

"Yes, all right, but keep quiet in camp," Grant said.

"If I kill Baraka, we will all sleep peacefully."

"Yes, thank you, but in the meantime shut up, please."

As the caravan reached Tabora and Kazeh in late January 1861, only two of the original one hundred porters remained, the others having deserted or died. Grant's fever raged. Heavy rains had flooded all the rivers and streams to the north, too, so that there would clearly be a long stay at the Arab villages.

As they arrived at this valley of sweet water, mangoes, yams, and slave *bomas*, Snay bin Amir prepared to leave with four hundred armed men to chase a renegade chief. The chief, Sera, had imposed a heavy tax on ivory taken from his district and had begun to fight the slavers. Since Snay could not greet Speke, then, Musa Mzuri, another slaver and an opium addict, offered his house to the white men.

"I'm not particularly fond of Snay anyway," Speke told Musa. "He was Burton's friend, not mine."

Sidi Bombay interpreted this sentiment, and Musa laughed loudly, perhaps understanding what had been said, perhaps not.

That evening they dined on curried meats, yams, rice, and fruit. Grant, drowsy with fever, dressed in his kilt and uniform and managed to converse with Musa and the other hosts through Sidi Bombay. They were entertained by a dancer who was much too fat, then by a fakir who played a flute and coaxed a cobra from a basket. The cobra was old with one eye, loose scales, and an inclination to sink back into its cozy basket rather than to sway and stare before the fakir's music.

"Sidi Bombay says the snake's venom has been drained," Grant said, leaning over to Speke during the performance.

"Yes, I suppose so."

"Are you feeling bad, Jack?"

"Naturally I'm feeling bloody awful," Speke answered sharply. "We're back with these miserable Arabs again! Their language, their hot food, and their slaves! And we must beg and bargain with them! Yes, I feel damned bad!"

"Everything will turn out well," Grant said hopefully.

"Optimism is silly," Speke told him. "You should have stayed at home with your wife and cows. You're no good, Jim, in any sort of crisis."

"Please, Jack, you're tired. Otherwise you wouldn't say something like that to me."

The Arabs around the table watched closely.

Speke abruptly got up and walked outside.

He could smell that putrid slave camp off in the distance. Those poor devils slept in their own shit. As he walked around Musa's house, he remembered how he had hated this place with Burton. He wished that some brave chieftain, the one who warred with Snay or another, would plunder this wretched camp; he wished Snay with all his manners would find himself on the end of a spear; he wished that Musa, smoking and popping his little pills of opium, would have his degenerate Arab soul drained out of his body. If Rigby sent fresh supplies as he should, he reasoned, we'll be out of here.

Otherwise, I'm lost. I'm a deaf man. I'm a mere captain. I'll be a footnote in some dusty, half-witted history book.

The stars burned yellow and sickly overhead.

At the dinner table, meanwhile, Grant stood up among the Arab hosts and displayed his kilt. The pattern of the cloth, Sidi Bombay explained, was the design of the Grant tribe back in Scotland.

"The tartan of the clan," Grant said. "Tell them those exact words."

Sidi Bombay complied. The Arabs smiled and drank Grant's health. And even though he felt weak and exhausted, Grant got up and danced a jig, which was much appreciated.

"They want to know why Speke left the dinner," Sidi Bombay finally asked Grant. "What shall I tell them?"

"Say that he has fever, too. Tell them he has moods because of the fever."

Sidi Bombay and Musa discussed this at length. Watching Musa suck on his pipe and talk, Grant finally asked what was being said.

"Musa say: a man's bad weakness is no matter, but if a man is not courteous he gives offense."

"Yes," Grant said. "Tell him I quite agree."

Burton, drunk on whiskey and high on jimsonweed, which he smoked by the handful in his meerschaum pipe, talked about women and wanted, if possible, just one. The desert air had been like a furnace. Buttes and mesas. Graves everywhere. Dry biscuits and flea-infested pallets in the coach houses at night.

"I travel to Salt Lake City out of sexual curiosity!" he told the other passengers of the stagecoach, causing Mrs. Dana to turn away and to cover the ears of her child. "And for theological reasons, of course! According to the Mormons, God didn't say anything against polygamy! Or sex! And that's a town, I'm told, with ten women for every man! And if there's divine justice, by God, I want my ten!"

"Please, sir," young Lieutenant Dana asked.

At one dingy station there was an Irishman with two wives: an arrangement that almost drove Burton mad.

Then one night they arrived at the Green River Station. Three bony Englishwomen operated the establishment: a two-roomed store, kitchen, post office, hotel, wash house, and café. The cook's helper, an obscene-looking Yorkshire female of perhaps thirty years of age, gave off a promising laugh when Burton, staggering, loudly announced, "Tonight I mean to get consoled!"

He did try. Long after midnight he tried to coax her inside a buffalo robe, onto the chopping block in the center of the kitchen, into the chilly desert night. McCarthy, Dana, and the marshal complained of this loud process of seduction, but the judge grunted his encouragement, and all the others lying about on the floor of the station—the other women and various children belonging to them, Indians, a youth riding for the Pony Express—slept soundly throughout Burton's mating calls and desperations. In the hour before dawn he finally ended his pursuit and fell asleep himself beside the stove.

Fifty days in Kazeh.

Grant's fever came and went in cycles: delirium, renewed strength and the promise of recovery, fatigue, another relapse, delirium again.

"Go on without me," he told Speke.

"Sorry, won't do that," Speke replied, holding his companion's hand. "Besides, we're waiting on those supplies from Rigby. There's no going on. Just waiting."

"You know," Grant said, lifting himself on his cot and trying to smile, "I was once told that I was a nice chap, but dull. That I am: sick and very dull indeed. You should go on without me."

"Nonsense," Speke said.

Speke went hunting, attempted to call on the Arabs and to be pleasant, stayed away from the slave *boma*, and tried to keep his many apprehensions to himself. He shot a rhino, telling Grant that it was like an execution. When the weather turned cold and rainy, he stayed outdoors too long one evening and contracted a chest cold. He made attempts to hire more porters in Tabora and surrounding villages.

Finally, Snay bin Amir returned from his little war with the renegades. Speke went to his house with Sidi Bombay as interpreter and at dinner said, "You don't seem the same. You seem—hmm, how shall I say? Desperate. Yes, tell him my exact words, Sidi Bombay."

Uneasy about translating this, Sidi Bombay nevertheless lifted his palms, sighed, and related it to the Arab who, in turn, talked at length in reply. While they conversed in Arabic, Speke ate two dates, placed the seeds on a brass plate, and listened to the soft drizzle beyond the window.

"He does not wish his troubles to be yours," Sidi Bombay said at last. "He also say: So do you seem desperate. But he believes you will see your nyanza once again."

"You are desperate, my friend, because all this in Kazeh will come to an end," Speke said, addressing his Arab host who could not understand. "Your natives rebel. A single chief has become a great foe. And what I believe I see in your face is that all is finished here. You Arabs have lived in this land like vultures, but your day is over. I see it in your eyes tonight."

"I cannot say this to him," Sidi Bombay whispered.

"No," Speke answered, coughing. "No, of course not."

Leaving Grant on his cot, Speke went north seeking porters from Chief Lumeresi, who ruled the neighboring region en route to the lake. Grant agreed to recover his health and to wait for Rigby's supplies, then to march northward and join his commander.

The August weather remained chilly and damp, so Speke's cough worsened. The chief was like so many others, too: he was interested only in gifts and *bongo*, demanding more every day, promising porters, yet detaining Speke and giving him few straight answers or direct aid. Baraka and Sidi Bombay argued with each other, smoked and drank with Lumeresi's warriors, and flirted with the women of the tribe.

"The chief likes none of our gifts and seems angry with me," Sidi Bombay reported to Speke.

"But we've given him everything we can. And how many porters has the chief promised us?"

"Many porters, but some of the men have already run off into the bush because they won't travel with us."

Speke coughed up mucus and spat. "I can't tolerate these delays and endless bargainings," he said. "Damn. I wish Grant would come."

"There will be a dance tonight," Sidi Bombay offered by way of consolation.

"There's always a dance," Speke replied. The women worked in the fields all day and danced for hours every night. They were dark, sturdy, and heavily tattooed. One of them, the chief's favorite, had her breasts tattooed like point lace—as if she had seen, someplace, a photograph of a European woman in a lace gown and had mutilated her body to resemble clothing.

As his cold and coughing continued, Speke slept badly and suffered nightmares. Dreams and terrible fantasies: his skin became serpentine, not his own, his arms and legs were often covered with bleeding sores, his penis was swollen and hideous—flopping out of his trousers for all to see. He also dreamt that he had no ears. And, once, waking up on his cot, his dream of his death continued as he stared wide-eyed into the shadows of his tent: he saw his body torn open and his heart pumping wildly on the ground beside him.

In the daylight, trying to shake these nightmares from his thoughts, he went hunting. But one day, finding some plovers in a marsh surrounding a brackish jungle pool, he witnessed another horror: when they were on the wing and he had raised his gun to shoot them, they seemed to burst into orange flame and disappear.

Another day Baraka and Sidi Bombay got into a fight over a woman. Baraka cursed and kicked dirt at his competitor, but Sidi Bombay pulled a knife and bared his teeth with a snarl. The little man became a live, fearful gargoyle, so that everyone in the village moved back in fright; Baraka, his lips trembling, stopped his invective and could only watch as Sidi Bombay took the woman to his tent. But afterward, standing alone in the middle of the village, Baraka shouted to everyone, "Ho! See! He is as crazy as his master!"

A few days later there was an execution. The lover of a young adultress was tied to the village gatepost while everyone in the tribe came to spit at him and revile him. Speke arrived to witness the final minutes. After the witch doctor smeared the boy's genitals with oil, Chief Lumeresi, wearing his ceremonial garb of feathers and bones, set the oil alight. While the youth screamed, the chief's son and daughter-in-law killed him with spear thrusts: six, seven, eight, until he screamed and moved no more. The body was dragged beyond the gate and left in the bush. There, Speke knew, the birds, animals, and ants would clean away the remains.

Visions of all this invaded his dreams and waking moments for days afterward. He saw those flaming genitals charred and curling.

"This cough!" he shouted one day to Sidi Bombay. "I've got to get well! We must start for the lake! We must start!"

But Sidi Bombay, who had stood beside him seconds before, was no longer there. Speke called for him in vain.

"You're always off in some other part of the village with your women! Where are you? You must come translate for me! Damn you! Whom shall I talk to? Damn you!"

After weeks at Lumeresi's village Speke's fever slowly came back. When he became certain of it, he sat in his tent weeping. At first he knew that he would never reach the Nile, but then he became certain of his death.

When Baraka came to see what was the matter, Speke said, "Quick, fetch me a packing needle! If we don't bleed me, I'll surely die! Hurry!"

With the large, dull needle Baraka brought, Speke clawed at his wrist, trying to open a vein. Baraka became frightened at the sight, but Speke wouldn't allow him to leave. When Speke grabbed him and held him, they both became covered with Speke's blood; meanwhile, Speke swore, wept, and shook his head wildly.

"Do not hold me like this and die!" Baraka screamed. "Your evil spirit will enter my body! I know this! Let go!"

Unable to get the blood flowing properly, Speke stabbed hard at his wrist with the packing needle. He saw raised tattoos on his body and his genitals on fire; he heard himself weeping and speaking, yet in a voice not quite his own. Baraka begged to be released. When Speke had stabbed himself again and again, he passed out—and his servant fled.

In late September, Grant arrived with new supplies, barter goods, gifts, and letters. He tried to cover his shock at seeing Speke, who seemed both in command and, yet, at the next instant, oddly disoriented.

A letter from Rigby reported on the contents of Burton's *Lake Regions of Equatorial Africa*. Speke, it noted, was never mentioned by name. The guess of the northern extremity of the Victoria Nyanza lying at latitude 4 or 5 degrees north was soundly ridiculed, Burton noting, again, that an Egyptian expedition had once penetrated to latitude 3 degrees north without ever having heard of a giant lake. And, finally, Burton had written, according to Rigby, that his "companion" had been arrogant, without language, and incompetent to do anything except hunt.

In the anger caused by reading Rigby's letter, Speke recovered himself and took charge of plans for the caravan to leave Lumeresi's tribe. While Grant and Sidi Bombay organized the porters, Speke wrote long letters to both Rigby and Blackwood about Burton's impudence—and his own plans to publish a book that would fully answer any slur.

Grant prepared notes, gleaned from reports and rumors, about the three great black kingdoms to the north.

Karagwe was the kingdom west of the lake ruled by King Rumanika. Its inhabitants were farmers and fishermen, generally friendly. The king would expect an exchange of worthy gifts.

Buganda lay at the northern edge of the lake. Its ruler, the Kabaka Mutesa, was bloody and powerful—and an unknown factor. Dispatches had been sent by runners asking permission to cross his territory, but bloodshed could occur. The Kabaka ruled Africa's most powerful black domain.

Bunyoro was ruled by King Kamrasi at the north of the lakeshore. About it little was known except that its people were less fearsome than Mutesa's.

In October, with the weather dry and cool, the caravan started out. Both Speke and Grant had shaken their fever, and soon they felt exhilarated by the high, beautiful country around them.

In this same month Petherick and his young wife were on the Nile, making slow progress upstream toward Gondokoro. At one of the great cataracts, where the river's waters turned white over boulders, they camped for three weeks while a portage was conducted. Petherick spent the time writing letters as the British consul at Khartoum and talking to ivory traders who stopped by his camp for a look at the splendid white woman.

Isabel, who had stayed in bed for weeks being doctored for mumps, sore throat, fever, influenza, and delirium, but not for her heartsickness, went to stay with relatives in the country.

Oliphant was in Paris, staying at the Grand Hotel with a new friend, a dapper young aristocrat, John Cowley, who carried his father's riding crop, drank absinthe, and collected both art and models.

Milnes was at Fryston, reading.

Shaw, the secretary of the Society, showed Murchison, Lord Ripon, and the acting chairman Lord Ashburton letters from both Speke and Burton. Speke's letter, which included new and contradictory maps, different from those previously submitted or published, seemed oddly confused. Burton's letter from Salt Lake City, on the other hand, was forthright and jolly.

MY DEAR SHAW, You'll see my whereabouts by the envelope; I reached this place about a week ago, and am living in the odour of sanctity—a pretty strong one it is, too—apostles, prophets, *et hoc genus omne*. In about another week I expect to start for San Fran-

cisco. The road is full of Indians and other scoundrels, but I've had
my hair cropped short so my scalp is not worth having . . .

"What do you make of Burton as a man?" Lord Ripon asked Shaw, after
all of them had read the letter.

"Oh, a definite eccentric."

"And what of Speke?" Murchison asked.

"I think their separate letters speak for themselves."

"Yes, but what exactly do you see? Come, Shaw, I want you to answer."

Dr. Norton Shaw was a thin, bespectacled clerk of a man, who rarely had
an opinion on anything, but who was respected by the Society's membership for
his diligent work and long hours. Yet no man's opinion was valued more by
members of the Society; he knew the daily workings of the group, its finances,
its explorers, and its troubles better than anyone.

"I have my suspicions," he offered.

"Yes, very well, what are they?" Lord Ripon asked, prompting him.

"I have some feeling that Speke is a cad."

"Really?" Murchison asked, wheezing out the word.

"Hmm," Shaw replied, setting his glasses straight on his nose.

The waters of the Great Salt Lake were salty, but, nevertheless, the
human body would not float in them. Burton wrote down this scientific fact in
one of his little pocketbooks. He had other, greater disappointments. Of the
many wives and assorted women of this pious settlement, none was available
unless a man intended to settle down in the valley, to farm, and to join the
faithful. So the wild harems and pleasures of this holy city just weren't there;
the women were calico and gingham servants; the streets were wide and dull;
the most excitement was generated when the elders spoke of plans to build a new
tabernacle.

Burton was identified, though, as the man who had visited Mecca and was
asked by the governor to lecture on his escapade. He declined. But his notoriety
led him to several dinners—stiff, boring, smiling Christians and greasy fried
chicken—at which he received highly formal introductions and little else.
Brigham Young, the prophet, had less severity and more humor in his face than
Burton had imagined. But it was an uninspired city, as if the members of this
crazy sect had invented a religion of boredom.

Anxious to leave, he visited the officers and men at nearby Camp Floyd.
He understood the army talk: Indians, liquor, the stupidity of bureaucrats everywhere, the probability of a civil war.

"My problem, boys, is this: I've got to have a woman. Soon. And I'm
running short of cash, but I'll pay all I have."

The officers and enlisted men were sympathetic, but couldn't help much.

They did introduce him to a wild young girl, Bessie Coe, who had been servicing the men at the fort, but who was on her way back to Sacramento for medical treatment and recuperation from her sexual excesses. She was a pretty thing, but horribly buck-toothed. With any and all her sentences she managed to say, "You bet!" which confused Burton somewhat, although the expression was generally good-natured and positive, he decided, and had probably contributed to her wayward life.

He and Bessie booked passage on the next stagecoach west via Carson City and Virginia City. The other four passengers—four rough types—were so inebriated that they failed to offer their names or occupations. Their baggage consisted mainly of cases of whiskey, and each man wore pistols and kept his rifle handy for fighting Indians en route.

"I'll be broke when I reach California," Burton explained to Bessie as they traveled. "Do you suppose we can locate someone who will cash a check for me?"

"Oh, sure, you bet."

"And I'll also be in need of some good hygienic female companionship. Perhaps you have some girl friends?"

"Hey, you bet."

She was a tough nugget, she said of herself, and pure gold. She laughed at everything and seemed oblivious to discomfort.

At a station house in the mountains, nothing was left except a charred building and corpses left by a band of raiding Indians. Wolves had been at the bodies and a human arm stuck up grotesquely from the snow, but Bessie Coe looked at everything with solemn interest. Beyond this catastrophe the canyons became ominous; a winter chill lurked in the high passes, and they emptied bottle after bottle of their whiskey supply to keep warm. They covered themselves with blankets inside the coach, and Burton placed an arm around Bessie and squeezed her breasts, but she was genuinely ill, sick with sex and sick of it, too, she confided, and she seemed, eventually, like a daughter, hugging his body for warmth, breathing her soft whiskey scent against his neck. Her hands were rough like a dock worker's, and she snored when she slept.

By the time they reached Carson City she had fever and stayed with him in his hotel room while cowboys and miners emptied their pistols in the row of barrooms and brothels comprising the main street. The noisiest city he had ever visited: gunshots, pianos, trombones, boots stomping, mules braying, shovels clanking, girls squealing. He sat in his room watching Bessie sleep. He thought of visiting Vancouver, Yosemite, Los Angeles, and other tourist attractions, yet knew he wouldn't; he grew tired and vaguely wanted to return to England. The girl in the bed—hair tangled, in need of a bath and a friend—reminded him of Edward, Isabel, and all and anyone who might need him, who might want him and believe in him.

They ate biscuits and gravy with eggs, then boarded the stagecoach again for Virginia City. Bessie seemed stronger. Her language, at least, was vile and resolute.

The silver-mining town was made of mud: everything covered with it, so that Burton was reminded of Ujiji. Horses and men made a sucking sound when their hooves and feet walked the streets. "They say all the men here are rich, but, shit, I can't tell it," Bessie said, holding on to Burton's arm as they stood outside the hotel. He agreed. At noon every day a bright, white newspaper was published, and until it turned grey and disappeared into the mire it reported the daily amounts taken from the Virginia City mines, the number of men shot down, and the possibility that Abraham Lincoln would soon be elected—which meant certain war. Burton and Bessie Coe sat at the hotel dining table for hours reading the paper, talking, and drinking coffee. Their table seemed safely away from the muddy brawl outside the window, and occasionally she looked up and smiled at him, so that he felt somehow useful.

In the next days the stagecoach rumbled into California, forded the Sacramento River, and made its way to San Francisco. There, Bessie introduced Burton to her occasional client, a banker named Booker, who knew of Burton and insisted that a public lecture should be arranged.

"You accomplished a wonder!" Booker insisted. "You went to Mecca and Medina and came back alive!"

"Please, sir, I must decline. I need a check cashed and a pillow to lay my head," Burton said.

But Booker took his celebrity to the fashionable Union Club for men, showed him off, and kept insisting on a lecture. Burton had a good dinner, became friendly with Booker's colleagues, and traded a few stories about exploits, but when his check was finally honored and he had £100 to spend, he left their company and joined Bessie. She resided at a brothel near Fisherman's Wharf, an old mustard-colored house with bay windows. Burton impressed the madame, Mrs. Cohoon, with his manners and accent.

"If you're looking for a few days of quiet relaxation, feel at home," she told him.

"Actually, I'm not looking for too much quiet," he said. "I'd like to have the place to myself, though, for, say, three days. So if you'll devise a price, I'll pay for all the girls and services for that period."

"You want the whole house for three days? Well, I don't know. I got my regular customers," she said.

"G'wan, he's a pal of mine," Bessie urged.

"Naturally, I'll require your own personal services, too, if they're available," he said with a flattering wink.

"Well, then, I reckon so," the madame replied, laughing.

"You bet," Bessie added.

The evenings at the mustard-colored house became social occasions at which Mr. Booker, who relished Burton's continued company, brought his friends to drink, to talk, and to await the election results. When Lincoln was elected President and the last toasts were raised, Burton told his new friends that he needed rest and settled in with the girls; they slept late, took long breakfasts in the garden overlooking the bay, went sightseeing, then took naps together before dinner. One afternoon, however, Mr. Booker sent two army officers to escort Burton and Bessie on an inspection tour of the fort's battery. Burton liked the excursion. Wearing a wide-brimmed hat and clutching Burton's arm, Bessie looked small and radiant, and the soldiers treated her with every courtesy.

On his last night at Mrs. Cohoon's house, Bessie asked if she could sleep at his side. "Remember, we can't make love, though," she warned.

"There are a number of ways to make love," he reminded her.

"You bet, but let's just cuddle, okay?"

She slept in the crook of his body. For a while that night her light snore and the soft curve of her flanks kept him awake; he felt her tender weakness and drew on her strength. Eventually, he slept soundly, as if the world could never do him harm.

The next morning she woke him with a long, deep kiss. Her mouth played against his until all his emotions were engaged; her arms held him as if she might never let him go. Then, suddenly, without a word of good-bye, she sprang from his bed and ran from the room.

That afternoon he boarded a shiny new steamer bound for Panama. The ship was called *The Golden Age*.

Speke measured the fattest woman of the tribe.

She was the gigantic, giggling sister-in-law of King Rumanika: 23 inches around the arm, 31 inches around the thigh, and 4 feet 4 inches around the chest. She sucked on a milk pot while Speke circled her with his tape measure.

"See if she'll consent to lie down," Speke asked. "I want to measure her height."

Sidi Bombay conveyed this request, but the sister-in-law just giggled and sucked at her milk pot. The king looked on admiringly as Grant and Baraka tried to keep their faces straight.

It was *krismasi:* Christmas Day. King Rumanika, who measured the beauty of his ladies by their girth, had been a generous host. He required no *hongo*. He had provided additional porters, killed his finest oxen for a banquet, and offered his sons as guides. When Grant had fallen while hunting and had cut his knee, the king had ordered poultices of native medicines and had lent his own personal doctor.

"How tall would you say she is, Jim?" Speke asked.

"Oh, quite tall. I'd say five feet and eight inches."

"Yes, and I'd put her weight at about—hmm, what?"

"Five hundred pounds, if an ounce," Grant said.

"Hmm, yes," Speke agreed, writing this amount in his notebook. "Very well. Enough science for today. Let's have lunch."

They strolled back toward the king's circle of huts, which overlooked a small muddy lake surrounded by tall sycamores. Grant limped badly.

The people of Karagwe, the king's domain, were generally slender—unlike the wives. They lived off the land in this high country, providing for themselves with small vegetable farms and cattle. King Rumanika counted his ancestry from King David and considered himself an Abyssinian. Because of their dark eyes and narrow noses, his people did have the look he claimed.

Beyond the village lay a larger, beautiful lake, which Speke called Little Windemere. Once, on a clear day, standing at the edges of that lake, he and Grant had seen a peak shining in the western sky, and Speke wondered aloud if this could be a peak among the Mountains of the Moon. Yet they hadn't traveled toward the lure; it lay off their course, and they were both anxious to pursue the Nile.

"How's the leg, Jim?"

"Sorry, no better," Grant said, as they sat in the circle around the king's fire.

The king, according to Sidi Bombay, wanted to talk theology. He wanted to know the difference between Christians and Arabs.

"Tell him they have only one book, but we have two," Speke said, and Sidi Bombay, who considered all such talk silliness, laughed and translated this reply for the king.

Grant rolled up his trouser leg and showed his injury to Speke. "Can't get the swelling to go down," he observed. The knee, swollen and misshapen, drew the attention of King Rumanika.

"Mutesa will never let you enter his land with such an illness," the king informed them. Sidi Bombay translated his words. "Many Arabs and Swahilis come to his land with disease. But he kill all of them. His warriors search a man's body to see if it has sores. All men and women have to be perfect for Mutesa."

Grant and Speke discussed the powerful king who ruled over the next territory to the north. "I heard a great deal about him during my last trip," Speke said. "I heard then that he was especially concerned over any spread of venereal disease among his people. And that he was ruthless."

"If I don't get better soon, you should go on without me," Grant offered.

"Wouldn't think of it."

"I can easily catch up, Jack, really. We're already weeks off schedule. Suppose Petherick is waiting for us at Gondokoro. We might arrive late—successful, having found the Nile—yet we might be ill equipped to make the long river voyage to Egypt."

"If we reach Gondokoro, we'll get home," Speke assured him.

"Jack, please, consider going on without me. No telling what will happen. I may get an infection. I could die. And you could wait on me until the expedition failed, don't you see?"

"My friend, we're together in this," Speke replied.

In another week a messenger arrived from Mutesa answering Speke's request to be allowed to enter the land of Buganda. The Kabaka, or king, was greatly excited about seeing white men, according to the messenger, and had liked the gifts sent ahead by Speke's runners. He had sent, in turn, slaves who would serve as guides for the next leg of the journey. Also, the messenger brought other news: another expedition of white men were marching on the nyanza from the north.

That evening Grant and Speke dined on goat's meat and fruit in the king's circle. A soft breeze rattled the sycamores beside the lake.

"I'm going to take your advice and proceed," Speke announced to Grant. "After all, runners can keep us in touch."

"Yes, do go ahead. I'll be along shortly, never fear."

"Suppose that Petherick reached Gondokoro, didn't find us, then decided to continue following the river. Suppose he has the money and means. He might find the lake—and take credit for everything. Or this could be another group—foreigners. We can't risk waiting longer."

Grant touched Speke's arm. "We're behind schedule. You go on."

"I hate going without you," Speke said. "But, of course, I'll stay in Mutesa's land and wait for you. Be assured of that."

"There's really no problem at all," Grant insisted.

The next morning Grant watched the caravan depart. He propped himself on a sturdy staff cut from a tamarind tree, put his weight on his good leg, and waved good-bye. He knew the odds of seeing Speke again and of reaching their goal together were poor; the leg threatened to get worse, and the distance between them, he realized, would soon be filled with peril. But he was a soldier, after all, and under orders.

One of Mutesa's slaves stayed behind to travel with Grant. The man seemed jubilant to be at Rumanika's camp, apparently confident that he would never go back to his old status as a slave in the land of the Kabaka.

Grant waved goodbye to Speke and the others on a bright morning while the grass was heavy with dew.

Those enormous stones marking the way toward the lake.

Speke led the caravan down from the highlands of Karagwe into a swampy plain surrounding the Kitangule River. The last time he had passed this way he had deduced that this could be a western feeder of the nyanza, but now rains had made a bog of the countryside, so he took no instrument readings or soundings. Scouts searched for solid ground, so the caravan could move; mosquitoes and multicolored butterflies swarmed everywhere, and the swamp was alive with hippo, waterbirds, giraffe, and elephant.

He made a few drawings of the area, but the pages of his sketch pad were mildewed and soggy, coming apart, if picked up, like wet leaves.

He knew that he should do something more scientific, yet didn't.

Those immense boulders. They seemed to dare him to look upon their blank and hideous faces.

Burton enjoyed *The Golden Age*. He stayed drunk, discussed women and life with Commodore Watkins, and dined on terrapin soup and deviled crabs à la Baltimore. At Acapulco he stopped drinking cognac and started on muscatel, which caused him to hallucinate that he was the ghost of a Spanish priest, frocked and hooded, come back to haunt this squalid peninsula.

On December 15, 1860, he debarked at Panama, a place smelling of fish and fecal slime. His hotel reminded him of a Parsee slum in Bombay, but he went up to his room, fell on his dirty bed, and slept two days.

He rode the rusted, creaking Panama Railway to Aspinwall, sipping muscatel and smoking a Havana cigar en route. That same evening he boarded a steamer and by morning he sailed Caribbean waters, keeping himself drunk as he stood beside the rail and gazed into the sheen of those tepid waves.

Life's great chance.

Somehow, now, he had to recover his dignity.

The American continent was a land of rough equality and vast material opportunity, yet common. The England toward which he sailed was thick with pompous and false values; it had a shameless class system and was blighted with rules; it was an elaborate, infuriating culture, yet a culture. A man could hide in its rituals; he could wear an expensive worsted coat, a top hat, sport a good Mayfair address, and manage a few comforting pretenses.

At present, he had a ruined gut and a dull wit; he had become a simple tourist; he had achieved a vulgar alcoholism, being one of the oafs standing around the whiskey keg; it was time to recover something, and he hoped that time and luck would grant him one more opportunity to perform with courage.

"By God, I hope so!" he told the lilting sea.

Near Southampton an immense fog bank awaited the ship. He stood on deck with the other passengers listening to the sound of harbor bells, but couldn't see the land; as time went on, the fog, far from lifting, grew worse, so that the bells became muffled and lost. The captain came around to inform everybody that the ship couldn't enter port until all cleared up, so Burton went below, climbed into his berth, and slept. When he awoke, though, the fog was still there.

They put out to sea to avoid collision with other ships coming into port.

For three long days they stayed offshore until the fog seemed to erase both time and space. Once, they heard noises and voices as if the people on land had moved up beside them; ghostly echoes in the grey cloud. Then, eventually, late on the third day, they made their way toward docking.

The messenger sent by Mutesa, Speke finally understood, was a royal officer and ambassador named Maula. As the caravan made its nightly camp in those marshy lands approaching the nyanza, everyone gradually learned more from the man. He told them that Mutesa, upon hearing that white men approached his kingdom, had gone into a frenzy of excitement and had killed a number of slaves in celebration.

Sidi Bombay, who found his job as interpreter difficult, slowly asked questions of Maula.

"He say fifty big men and four hundred small ones killed," Sidi Bombay reported, giving Speke a frightful look.

Speke tossed a branch on the evening campfire. "Oh, I can't believe that," he said, and his response was passed along.

Maula, hearing Speke's reply, only smiled. Then he gave them a short history of Mutesa's bloody reign.

The Kabaka Mutesa had been one of sixty-one sons left after the death of Kabaka Suna. At the time of his father's death, he had not been considered a serious claimant; he was very young, slender, almost feminine, and close to his mother, the dowager queen. But bloody years followed, Maula said, and the borders of Buganda were closed to all outsiders while the internal struggle for power began. In time, most of Mutesa's brothers and enemies were murdered. After another period, Mutesa ruled with his mother and a prime minister named Katikyro, but lately, according to the ambassador, Mutesa ruled alone. His power was fearful; vast ritual massacres, called *kiwendos*, were common. On hearing that he would be visited by white men—which Mutesa considered a supreme compliment to the fame of his kingdom—a *kiwendo* was staged that took the lives of the four hundred and fifty male slaves.

Even so, Maula said that Speke and his caravan should proceed without fear. Mutesa was sending cattle and gifts, so the last days of their journey toward Buganda would be pleasant. He would also show the white men an old trading route across the Masai Plain, an easy road back to Mombasa.

This last news especially interested Speke, who tried to explain its possible significance to Sidi Bombay. "We could possibly find the Nile, yet not have to trace it thousands of miles through the desert to Egypt! We might be able to turn east toward Mombasa and the coast—then go back to England with our prize!"

Sidi Bombay did not understand. Only the terrifying stories of Mutesa's court impressed him. "Please, we must not offend this ruler," he warned.

Speke wished that they had Burton's swaggering presence at this moment, but answered, "Mutesa will be a great help to us, never fear."

Cattle and gifts of food arrived.

The caravan made camp at Maula's village two miles from the western shore of the nyanza, yet Speke made no effort to see the lake, to sketch its shoreline, or to confirm the simple measurement of the lake's level, which he had taken with his thermometer in 1858.

Instead, he seemed distracted. He strolled around the camp and village aimlessly. His feet shuffled through the dust, raising little clouds.

On the morning of their scheduled departure, Maula found that Mutesa's cattle had grazed too far from the village, so that they had to be rounded up before the caravan could depart.

"We must not go toward the Kabaka without his cattle!" Sidi Bombay said, repeating Maula's instructions. "Maula say not to move!"

An elaborate and fearful concern over a few scrawny cattle: Maula, caravan porters, women and boys from the village all went looking for strays. But Speke only shuffled through camp, head down, as if in a stupor. When Baraka offered to feel his leader's brow, Speke said, "No, I have no fever!" and thrust the servant's hand away.

That night the moon was like a hole in the sky: beyond, a bright, clear universe. On this side of the moon, in this time and cosmos, though, the clouds were like scabs; the swamp was a running sore. Lying on his cot, Speke felt an old disorder, the thing he used to experience in school when he couldn't set the words in order on a page. He lay there thinking, yes, yes, now: I am here beside a great lake, but where is it? Where is Said bin Selim? Yes, back in Kazeh with syphilis or worse. And where is Grant? For the life of him, he couldn't recall where his colleague had gone. And who went with him into the mountains long ago, into those icy dreamfields? And which of his brothers wanted to be a rector? And what was the name of that silly iron boat towed behind the dhow? As sleep encroached upon him, he remembered nothing— no matter how hard he tried to set things in order. The moon went on with its wild transit.

At noon the next day Speke drove out his disorientation with impatience. "Strike all tents!" he ordered. "We begin our march!"

Sidi Bombay, afraid that they should wait as Maula ordered, said, "How can we go? We must wait for the stray cattle!"

"Obey my orders and strike the tents!" Speke shouted.

When Sidi Bombay only stood there with his arms folded, Speke summoned two porters and in seconds they began pulling down tent poles everywhere. The large mess tent was crowded with village women who boiled plantains at an open fire, naked children, bundles, strings of gourds, a pet monkey, and brass pots, but Speke jerked down the pole, sending sparks flying and the natives scurrying away.

Sidi Bombay raged at the porters who helped Speke do this. "There's gunpowder in those loads! See! You'll make a fire in the gunpowder! Fools!"

"Don't abuse my men!" Speke shouted.

"The place will blow up!"

"If I choose to blow up my own property, that is my lookout! Do your duty or I'll blow you up, too!"

"Fools! Don't do this! Put out those fires!"

"These men obey me! They're better than you! Don't abuse them!"

"You go crazy! I will not be insulted by a crazy man!"

Moving up close, Speke struck Sidi Bombay hard with his fist. The blow landed high on the little man's cheek, knocking him down, but he sprang up again, pouting and hissing.

Both men squared away at each other. Speke struck again, knocking Sidi Bombay down once more. He rose again, but slowly; blood flowed from between his sharpened teeth and from his split lip as he came and stood defiantly before Speke again. Another blow. This staggered him, yet his pout never altered. Then another blow sent him to his knees. Someone in the crowd of natives and porters laughed, and others joined in.

Sidi Bombay slowly managed to get his feet underneath himself and to stand up. His small hands shook violently, and he could barely focus on that circle of black faces around them. "Now," he told Speke, "I will serve you no more!" With effort he turned and stumbled through the crowd and was gone.

The children who had witnessed this odd comedy laughed and pantomimed the fight, digging at each other's heads with their tiny fists. "Ho! Ho!" they barked at each other, acting out the strange ways of the white man. Meanwhile, the women and porters put out the fires beneath the folds of the mess tent and continued to help Speke to strike camp while bursts of laughter sounded from all around the village.

Before the caravan departed Maula returned with the precious cattle. He was alarmed that Speke was prepared to march and complained to Sidi Bombay that he wasn't ready.

"See what you have caused me with your delays?" Sidi Bombay said, showing his swollen face. "If you want to argue, go talk to the captain!"

While Maula and his slaves gathered their personal belongings and herded their cattle, Sidi Bombay resumed his role in command, distributing loads to porters. By the time the caravan started to move he seemed to have forgotten his vow to quit; he dabbed at his bleeding mouth with a cloth, spat, sulked, but worked on.

"Where would I be?" he asked Baraka, speaking loudly so that everyone who knew the Swahili language could listen. "I would be alone without food or money in a strange place! I would be miles from Zanzibar and my wives! Better to travel with a crazy man who never knows what he is doing! A fool who almost blows us up!"

Since Speke understood none of this, he allowed Sidi Bombay to carry on. Others on the path made no sign that they heard or cared.

"He struck me with his fist because I was insubordinate!" Sidi Bombay announced to everyone. "Yes, I was—and I am a soldier who understands discipline! But then he struck me again and again! You witnessed it! He struck me out of anger! He is angry and crazy, believe me, I know him!"

They marched beside a column of those boulders: long, thick fingers pointing up toward an empty sky.

That night as they made camp Sidi Bombay offered only an occasional curse in Swahili. Rolled in his blanket near the fire, he said in a loud voice, "Too angry and too crazy!" His was the last voice before everyone slept.

The next day the caravan met several of Mutesa's officers and cowherds driving cattle toward King Rumanika as a gift; the Kabaka was grateful that the white man had been sent to him, the officers reported, and meant to show his generosity. They also told how the silk handkerchief that Speke had sent ahead was now worn proudly around Mutesa's head. The powerful Kabaka, they also said, would fast until he gazed upon the white man's face.

"Very good," Speke told the messenger who would run toward Mutesa with news of the caravan's progress. "Tell him we will hurry, so that he will not be in discomfort. Tell him that I regard him as father of the Nile. Say also that I will not be kept waiting like some trader at his gate. And, here, give him this small amount of gunpowder, so that he can see my strength and magic."

In the late afternoon they came within sight of the Kabaka's palace: a series of immense, cone-shaped thatched huts, each perhaps thirty feet in height, set on a hill. Speke turned to Baraka and said, "My God, I've never seen such a sight," but his servant was too awed to reply.

A contingent of officers met the caravan, directing Speke to wait in a small hut near the goat pens at the foot of the hill some quarter of a mile from the palace gates.

"No, this won't do," Speke told them to their dismay. "I must reside inside the gates of the palace, no place else. Otherwise, I must leave." Sidi Bombay apologized to the officers for translating this insolence.

Maula, Speke noticed, was dismissed. He also saw that Maula was physically unlike Mutesa's taller, brown-skinned officers: smaller, blacker, with the pierced ears of the Masai and without the oval eyes of the Waganda.

"They say the Kabaka has a bad temper. He is a god, too. You must be patient until they speak with him," Sidi Bombay said. His face was still swollen, but his services, he knew, were badly needed, and he implored Speke to give deference to the ruler.

"Tell them that I am a prince whose foreign blood could not stand such an indignity as staying here," Speke replied.

The officers finally went off to convey all these sentiments to Mutesa. Darkness and a light drizzle began to fall, so that it became apparent that Speke would not gain entry to the palace before morning. He and his men made camp around the little goat hut. After a dinner of beef and fish, Speke opened several bolts of red broadcloth and brought forward twelve of his men, including Baraka and Sidi Bombay, to wrap them in bright new drapings. From another porter's load Speke took out his army uniform, then laid out his belt, saber, epaulets, and braid.

At midnight he gave each member of his platoon a carbine with bayonet. Then, outside the goat hut, they practiced marching in step—which amused them and at which they were tolerably good—until they retired into the hut, where he addressed them.

"Here, chaps, have a brandy," he told them. "In the morning before we march to the palace, you shall have another. Your scarlet cloaks look jolly. You shall march, as I've shown you, with rifles on your shoulders. You shall hold your heads high and you shall look splendid, understand?"

The men laughed nervously as Sidi Bombay relayed all this. Speke talked with such confidence that they all felt assured.

"Now we shall all sleep," he said, dismissing them. "In the morning we shall meet this fearsome Kabaka and then go forward to the Nile." The men laughed and nodded, asked for another brandy, please, which they didn't receive, then filed outside to sleep rolled in their blankets in the drizzle.

For another hour Speke lay on the floor of his hut staring into the flame of the candle beside him. He would unload and prepare gifts for Mutesa at dawn, he told himself. He thought of Grant. Then he began to fret about himself: he wavered, he knew, between such confidence as he had just displayed with his men and an odd residue of depression and anger.

Yes, I struck Sidi Bombay too many times. Yes, when I stood my ground and killed that charging buffalo that day I was quite alive, quite decisive and open, but at times, damn, there is something very much like boredom taking hold of me. Except it isn't boredom. It's a shadow life: a curious, cold vapor of melancholy I can't shake off. And only extreme moments end it: hunting, physical danger, confrontations.

He peered into the hot center of the flame, then blew it out.

The elusive peace of samsara.

Perhaps it's sex, he said to himself, lying back and closing his eyes. I do need release. If I don't have it soon, I might truly go mad.

I slept with—whom? Did I sleep in the arms, once, of Grant or Burton? Where was it?

Samsara. The bleak solitude of self. The only samsara is death. And, oh, that's really distressing.

The huge thatched palace buildings, like pyramids, sat about a quarter of a mile uphill from the goat hut where Speke and his men gathered to march. When summoned by pages, they organized their parade: Speke in front, his scarlet platoon ten paces behind, then the rest of his porters, led by the Union Jack fluttering atop a staff.

As they started uphill, the natives covered their mouths in astonishment, crying out, "Beautiful! Oh, beautiful!" It was a magnificent audience, which made Speke and his group, for all their display, seem drab. The Waganda wore bark cloaks, antelope skins, turbans, necklaces of tusks and charms, bracelets of shells, beads, wood or ivory, vests of snakeskin or suede.

But Speke and his entourage held up their heads and made steady progress toward the palace, where Mutesa's ministers waited. Since the morning sun was especially hot, Speke and his men were covered with sweat near the end of their climb.

"*Mzungu! Mzungu!*" the ministers shouted, announcing Speke's arrival.

The towering thatched pyramids loomed ahead.

Suddenly, the royal orchestra struck up a melody. Nine-stringed Nubian harps twanged out a solid rhythm. Drums festooned with beadwork picked up the beat, and flutes made an off-key contribution.

The ministers, dressed in bright feathers, beads, tusks, and amulets, parted and gave way so that Speke could see the young Kabaka Mutesa.

As Speke approached, slowing his step, he took out his umbrella with an elaborate, theatrical gesture, then popped it open above his head. The crowd groaned with pleasure. The young king struggled to keep from making a response. He sat on his red blanket on a square platform of tiger-grass reeds. His hair was combed into a high ridge, like a braided crown or cock's comb, and his arms, legs, and fingers were weighted with copper rings, charms, shards of ivory, and amulets on chains. He drank nervously from a brass cup and wiped his mouth with a patch of gold-embroidered silk. Speke's gift, the silk kerchief, was worn around his neck. Around him stood his chiefs of staff, a tall, beautiful female sorcerer, and his wives and sisters. Close by was a separate, symbolic group: a white dog and a woman with a spear and a shield. Leopard skins covered the earth, and ceremonial drums adorned the scene like architectural columns.

Speke sat on an iron stool no more than six paces from the Kabaka, and they studied each other in silence. Faced with the language barrier and the tense uneasiness, Speke opened and closed his umbrella several times; the Kabaka Mutesa allowed a smile to curl his mouth, but his eyes betrayed his absolute astonishment. At last he spoke, but no one could understand.

Sidi Bombay was brought forward and knelt in the dust to serve as interpreter, but his gifts were not enough. The interpreter for the Kabaka couldn't help much either, so Maula—black, fat, covered with perspiration and eager to be available—joined the conversation. A long, arduous palaver. Speke felt rivulets of sweat inside his uniform.

At this point, while the interpreters struggled with each other's words, Mutesa stood up and walked in a circle. His stride was immensely awkward and funny, but Speke dared not laugh. When the Kabaka walked, his rump went up and down and his knees bent and straightened: a ridiculous lope. At last, he sat down again on his throne.

"The great Kabaka wants to know," Sidi Bombay finally managed, "if you have truly seen him?"

Speke considered this request. "Tell him yes," he answered.

The response was quickly relayed. Ministers, wives, officers, and slaves breathed a sigh of relief, but the question was put to Speke again.

"Yes," Speke answered once more. "The white man has seen Mutesa, father of the Nile." This was a highly satisfactory answer, once it had been translated and delivered, which took several minutes.

Sidi Bombay took the opportunity to inquire if anything serious was the matter with the royal person, but learned that the strange style of walking was deliberate. "He imitates the lion," he told Speke.

"Ah, good, very reassuring," Speke replied.

Mutesa bit into a banana, breaking his fast.

At this point, Speke took a gold ring from his own finger and passed it forward. The Kabaka fitted it to his own finger with some difficulty; he was perhaps twenty-five years old, slender, oddly effeminate, with large dark eyes. His head seemed to balance on a thin neck, swaying as if it were too heavy for its pedestal. Very often, as he did when he fitted the ring on his finger, Mutesa would glance at his sorcerer: the tall, black woman with high cheekbones and nearly Grecian features.

The slow, elaborately interpreted conversation continued. Speke was asked if he would like to be shown a route across the Masai Plain that would take him to Mombasa in only four weeks. He pursued this invitation, but further reply was lost in the cacophony of translation.

The Kabaka Mutesa then wanted to know about guns and other gifts. He pointed to the two-grooved Whitworth strapped across Speke's shoulder.

Gifts were passed to Mutesa through the hands of his sorcerer, who touched everything to ensure that it was immune from witchcraft. Out came Speke's presents: a tin box, four silk cloths, the Whitworth rifle, a gold chronometer, a revolver pistol, three rifled carbines, three bayonets, a box of ammunition, bullets, gun caps, a telescope, an iron chair, ten bundles of fine beads, and a set of knives, forks, and spoons.

Something was asked about the iron stool that Speke had brought with him for sitting in the presence of the Kabaka, but both question and reply, again, became lost among the interpreters. Further talk was such a strain, in fact, that the interview began to close. Mutesa squealed with delight over each new gift. Everyone was hot. Sidi Bombay had such difficulty with the languages and shrugged in dismay so often that the rise and fall of his bony shoulders delighted the audience, many of whom mimicked him as they laughed.

After a while the interview ended, with none of the ritual with which it had begun. Courtiers and ministers departed, the white dog was led away, the wives chatted among themselves and went off to their duties.

While Mutesa inspected his gifts, Maula led Speke back down the hill, where lunch was served in his goat hut. Maula explained that a room inside the palace was being prepared, and he and Sidi Bombay finally understood each other on the matter of the iron stool on which Speke had sat.

"The Kabaka wishes that you would sit on the ground like everyone else," Sidi Bombay said. "Please, sir, do this thing."

"It gave him offense?"

"Oh, please, yes. Our lives were in danger for this insult."

By evening, when torches were lit around the Kabaka's tiger-grass throne, Speke was summoned to give a demonstration of fire power. He went back uphill, carrying his umbrella, which had become his magic wand and status symbol.

Four cows were led into the torchlight of the Kabaka's courtyard and Speke was handed the empty Whitworth so that he could dispatch them, but he told Mutesa and his ministers—again, after lengthy exchanges—that such animals could be killed with a much less impressive weapon. Taking his revolver from his belt, he killed the cows with five shots.

Torches were pulled from their posts and paraded about, casting flickering shadows on the wives, ministers, and more than two hundred courtiers who danced about. Mutesa chanted in high falsetto. The statuesque sorceress applauded.

Maula, Sidi Bombay, and a gaggle of other interpreters talked, but Speke understood nothing.

Then Mutesa, smiling, held one of his new carbines aloft. Presenting it to a young page—a boy of about ten years dressed only in a loincloth—the Kabaka spoke a few words that received loud praise. Speke assumed that the boy was a prince being handed a gift. While dancers continued to raise dust in the torchlit courtyard, some attention was paid to cocking and pre-paring the weapon to fire. An officer in a feathered headdress crouched before Speke and pulled feathers out—wide-eyed and excited, as if he had gone mad and tugged at his hair. Another man kept springing into the air and falling flat on his back in a comical pantomime of death. The cows were so many bloody heaps.

When the young page ran from the courtyard, Maula and Sidi Bombay asked the purpose, but a long conversation ensued from which Speke learned nothing.

Then came the shot and the approving roar of the crowd in the outer courtyard located one tier down the hillside.

"What is it?" Speke asked Sidi Bombay for the third time.

"I believe the boy has shot a slave," Sidi Bombay shouted above the crowd's noise. "To show the power of the weapon."

By this time the page returned, holding the rifle high and pumping it with enthusiasm as Mutesa began his falsetto descant once more.

Maula confirmed the event: a slave had been shot dead. The Kabaka Mutesa had displayed the strength of a mere boy of his great tribe.

Incredulous, Speke wanted to see for himself, yet didn't. The deed had been carried out casually: the order, the shot, nobody from the circle of dignitar-ies around Mutesa even bothering to watch. Several officers around the throne pounded on brass drums, sending up an impossible noise. Again, Maula, Sidi Bombay, and the interpreters of the Kabaka engaged in animated talk, but minutes passed before Sidi Bombay came to Speke with a message.

"The Kabaka Mutesa is pleased with his gifts," he reported. "He say this: very pleased and happy you are his prisoner."

The noisy clatter and drumming made it necessary for Speke to lean close to Sidi Bombay and to shout.

"Prisoner? I'm not his prisoner! Did he use that word?"

"He say so. You are his wonderful prisoner, who will stay with him forever and teach the ways of the white man!"

The next day Mutesa surprised Speke by asserting that Grant—in spite of any injury—should be with them at court.

Runners started both south and north to contact Grant and, hopefully, Petherick. As Speke sat at the foot of the throne suffering in the heat, he grew excited with prospects that his colleagues might soon join him—though he worried that Petherick might advance too quickly. The hot day went slowly, every phrase and nuance undergoing translation and interpretation.

Mutesa wore a fez and turned the gold chronometer in his fingers as if its mystery might somehow be fathomed by a caress.

The Waganda studied the bearded white man's every action. Soon they knew him; in turn, he sensed their knowledge and became uneasy.

He wore heavy boots, so his feet couldn't listen to the faint, important rhythms of the ground. His magnificent umbrella was a shield that hid his face, so he obviously didn't wish to be known, perhaps not even by himself. His guns were loud and mighty, yet his long fingers seemed soft like a woman's. His aloof and haughty manner was admirable, yet the Kabaka was equally impressive, and knew the heart of men and the silences of the earth, while the white man seemed to feel or hear little; he was truly remote, like the leopard who roamed the solitary mountain paths.

The women, especially, kept watch. They whispered about the possible size and color of his genitals. While his men enjoyed noisy copulations every hour of the day in huts all around the royal hillside, the white man seemed indifferent. Perhaps, they whispered, he was anxious about the ways of the Waganda—who, in fact, enjoyed copulation above all else. Perhaps he was wounded in the soul. Perhaps he desired young boys, yet he seemed manly and didn't prance or giggle like others in the tribe who showed that preference.

The queen mother, Namasole, lived in a miniature palace resembling her son's a half mile from the royal gates. She summoned Speke because she was ill and required his attentions as a doctor, so when he went to see her he took along his medicine cabinet. Because she knew the language of the Swahili, Baraka went along as interpreter. Beer was served. She lay back on a couch of tiger grass: a fat, smiling, sweating, chocolate-colored woman perhaps forty-five years old, who fluttered her lashes and played the coquette.

She wanted to know what medicines were brought.

"All sorts," Speke answered, opening his little wooden case. "What is madame's complaint?"

She suffered belly pains, insomnia, but most of all a lonely heart. Her husband, the Kabaka Suna, had been dead for six years. Love was scarce.

Drummers and flute players assembled around the couch as Speke opened tiny bottles of camphor, sulfur, soda, calomel, and opium. As the little orchestra began to play, the musicians swayed from one side to another, so that Baraka had to sway with them in the crowded bedroom.

The doctor must examine me, she explained, so I must call ministers to witness his hands on my royal person.

"Yes, good," Speke answered. "Let's have a few more people in here."

Two dour ministers, summoned to duty, occupied the doorway.

One visit would not be enough, Namasole made clear. The white doctor would have to visit each day.

"How does she know I'm a good doctor?" Speke asked.

Because the medicines smelled strong. Because his hands on her pulse made her heart sing.

"I am very flattered and happy," Speke replied. He knew well enough that he had to gain favor with the queen mother, if ever he expected to leave.

Would he look at her tongue? Would he touch her breast?

"Yes, I'll make a complete tour of inspection of this black heap," he told Baraka, who managed to nod and smile in the direction of the queen mother while swaying with the musicians.

The flute players had a distant, faraway, romantic look in their eyes.

Each day, Namasole repeated. My belly is not yet full of you.

Her double meaning was made abundantly clear, but Speke only smiled and pushed a spoonful of calomel and opium into her mouth.

By this time the ministers in the doorway swayed with the rhythms of the drums. The room became excessively hot, so that Speke imagined the beer might boil in the gourds; body odors reeked, and he had to close the bottles of camphor and sulfur or pass out.

After he had touched Namasole's breasts and stomach, he closed his medicine cabinet. She groaned with pleasure and announced that all her maladies were much improved.

The swaying musicians and ministers, though, had shuffled into a dance. They circled the couch of tiger grass, the beat of the music picking up their enthusiasms, so that Baraka had no choice except to join them.

I am charmed by my doctor, the queen mother sighed. Charmed. It is time to celebrate my new health with a dance.

Speke rose to his feet and stood tall in the growing frenzy around him. Ministers and musicians had shed their loincloths and belts of fur; Namasole, her legs wide apart, answered each thrust of the dancers with one of her own. Speke took a deep breath, drew himself up, repressed a smile, and asked Baraka to translate properly. "Although I drag my body away, my heart remains," he intoned. "For I love the queen mother very much." The speech impressed her. Looking down on her, he wondered how much power she retained in the kingdom; surely her status in this miniature palace meant something, and he knew that he badly needed her favor.

A flute player bumped into Speke and apologized.

Backing through the door and waving farewell, Speke retreated.

Two days later while considering a second courtesy call on Namasole, he received from her a perplexing gift: two young Bahima girls aged eleven and thirteen years. Kahala, the youngest, was merely a slender brown child, but Meri, the oldest, was more woman than Speke needed. They were both naked except for a string of beads that they wore around the waist. The gift of the young slaves was obviously meant to break the will of the white man and to coax him into the recreations of the kingdom.

Mutesa insisted on hunting, though he had little interest in sport. His object was to behave like the white man, so he borrowed Speke's trousers, wore the explorer's wide-brimmed hat, summoned an orchestra and some one hundred courtiers, and moved his entourage into the bush and along the banks of jungle streams where, of course, all animals and birds fled before the clatter.

Speke tried to discuss the Masai route toward Mombasa.

"The Masai won't stop our caravan traveling through their land?" he inquired.

The guns of the white man are all-powerful, the Kabaka replied.

At a clearing beside a stream the orchestra played while Mutesa's wives served pombe in gold cups that bore signs of Egyptian origin. While sipping from his cup, Speke saw the sorceress among some trees about thirty paces distant across the stream; she was magnificently naked, leaning against a willow, her hip jutted out, the branches of the tree draped around her like a soft curtain. She watched the hunting party until all eyes seemed drawn to her nakedness; she seemed part of the willow and forest beyond, so that Speke wondered, even as he gazed on her, if she was really there at all.

The little blackamoors slept on mats at the foot of Speke's cot in his new residence of reeds and clay near the Kabaka's palace. Each night and morning he watched them curl themselves into sleep, then stretch themselves awake; the little one had a mound as smooth as pudding, and Meri, who gave him a sultry and direct gaze, had a soft downy tuft and small breasts. In the mornings they combed out his blond hair and beard while other women from Mutesa's household and court came and peeked in the door; then they dressed him and brought him a bowl of fruit, and he allowed all these attentions, but kept his eyes straight and his posture rigid. He meant to be paternal toward them, yet this was difficult in an undertow of gentle fingers and warm breath.

Morning, afternoon, and evening, the same: women.

They stopped at his hut to offer him domestic services, to attempt conversation, to flirt, to make bold suggestions. All offers came in elaborate pantomimes, because Sidi Bombay had disappeared into the village with a harem he had accumulated, and Baraka, the other interpreter, stayed up all night at the dances, so slept through every day and remained unavailable.

Women constantly and everywhere.

The wife of the Kabaka's chief minister came calling, breathing heavily, as if she had to lie with the white man immediately. Speke popped open his umbrella, offered her his arm, and walked her around the edges of the village as if they strolled through a crowded park, a lord with a lady on his arm, for all to see.

One afternoon a delegation of naked dancers appeared: a half dozen paunchy women who practiced their imitations of copulation outside his door. He stood smiling and watching while they held out their swaying breasts and raised a cloud of dust.

At one of the evening banquets he saw the drunken Namasole down on her hands and knees at a trough of banana beer, drinking like a pig. Mutesa, viewing his mother, registered no expression.

On another day's hunting expedition with Mutesa—replete with orchestra, ministers, wives, and jesters—they came to a swollen stream. Speke gallantly offered to assist some of the Kabaka's wives and sisters in fording the little torrent, and when Mutesa understood the intention he laughed and chanted in his high falsetto until everyone in the hunting party joined in. The wives and sisters, Speke learned, were anxious to feel what the white man was like, and in minutes Speke was carrying them piggy-back, one by one, through the foaming water. Lubuga, the Kabaka's favorite wife, insisted on staying atop Speke's back even after crossing the stream, and for a moment the ministers were aghast, watching Mutesa to see if his infamous temper might explode in jealousy, but he only laughed again, as if Speke could do no wrong.

Speke declined invitations to explore the shoreline of the nyanza and to visit its small western islands. Instead, he waited to hear from Grant or Petherick, made only a few sketches, used none of his instruments, and did nothing. During the next weeks; heavy rains fell in the mountains and flooded the lands around the Kabaka's hill.

The month of April knotted Speke's veins and nerves: a tight, helpless anguish. He had no energy for excursions or hunting; he wanted only to set himself free, somehow, yet he seemed unable to think or move, as if he were an exotic plant, not even a man, painfully opening into some dark, unruly flower. He tried thinking of Lowry, of Burton, of home, but couldn't keep his mind on anything outside the village.

The women came and went, padding around his little residence, watching him. He saw the sorceress whispering in Meri's ear as they both looked toward him and nodded. Hens in the yard, cows in the fields; even the Kabaka, with his head tilting this way and that on his thin neck, his falsetto mocking the night, his soft eyes, seemed feminine. Time itself was a womb. Those huge thatched pyramids were like breasts raised to the sky. The flooded swamp around them became fecund, soft, gentle in its murmurings.

Grant, limping around on his ulcerated leg, had the news that he was welcome in Mutesa's court, but could only prepare slowly to make the journey. He worried constantly that he would die, never seeing home again, and in his most solemn moments recalled how the fences and trees of the Highlands bore small strips of wool signature where the sheep had scratched their backs.

The Nile, swollen with seasonal rains, had stopped Petherick's party. Two colleagues were dead and his wife had malaria.

The white man just north of the Kabaka's palace was not Petherick, but a Maltese ivory trader who had also been stopped by torrential rains. He eventually turned around and made his way north once more where, meeting Petherick, he would report that he had never heard of Speke's expedition.

Just before Christmas 1860, Isabel had visited the country estate of some relatives in Yorkshire. She and another twenty houseguests trimmed the tree, sipped rum punch, and encircled the piano for a round of holiday songs. Their sheet music was propped up with a recent edition of *The Times,* and Isabel's gaze fell on a small notice: CAPTAIN R. F. BURTON ARRIVES FROM AMERICA.

She stopped singing and tried to get her breath. Finally, she went to her room and began to pack. After dinner she gave a servant a pound note to hitch up a carriage and to drive nine miles through the snow to the railway station, where arrangements could be made to have a telegram delivered to her. The next morning, when the message arrived calling her away to London, her luggage was ready.

At the Milnes townhouse she learned that Burton had taken his old rooms in St. James, so she hurried through the icy streets toward him. When she knocked at his door, her shoes were soaked; she hadn't slept all night, and her teeth chattered with cold.

Then he opened the door and neither of them could speak. She was in his arms for a long time before he whispered, "You're slender. Very thin."

"It's from worry over you," she breathed against his neck.

"I wrote you two letters—one of them only two weeks ago. Did you get them?"

"No, Mother must have kept them from me."

"Close the door. You're shivering. Come inside."

"My feet are freezing," she said, unbuttoning his shirt. "Let's warm them in bed."

Since her parents thought her to be in Yorkshire and her country relatives thought her back in London with her parents, she and Burton had three days together. At a little restaurant in Jermyn Street he asked her to marry him. They spent long hours in his bed. But their talk lent itself to practical matters and Burton's prospects for a career.

"I'm a soldier out of favor with the army, an adventurer with no place to go, and a man who has done just a few interesting things—discovered an obscure lake in Africa and peeked into some forbidden cities. Everyone has already forgotten me. So our marriage has to be a step toward respectability and career, you see that, don't you?"

"You're a writer, a linguist, and a famous explorer," she answered, encouraging him. "We'll see that everything works out for you."

"Speke attracted Murchison, Rigby, Oliphant, the Blackwoods, and even Prince Albert to his cause," he said, trying to explain to her. "He has the army and the government ensuring his success. I have only you and Milnes. And we've got to score a public success. For one thing, damn, we have to impress your mother."

"I'll arrange for Cardinal Wiseman to perform our ceremony. Please, don't fret, darling. I've waited years, and nothing is going to go badly now." Her determination strengthened him. She was insatiable in bed. All seemed right.

The ceremony took place in the Bavarian Catholic Church, Warwick Street. Burton dashed himself with holy water and made an oversized sign of the cross before repeating the vows. Afterward, they went back to his rooms, where he composed a long letter to her father announcing that the deed was done. That evening they dined with Milnes and his wife, who gave them their most important wedding gift.

"We've arranged for Lord Palmerston to give a party for you newlyweds," Milnes announced with a wink. "That should do the trick. And, later, we want you up at Fryston for an extended visit. I want you to meet Carlyle, young Swinburne, and all my others."

"I don't know how to thank you," Burton said.

"A good marriage is a solid business arrangement and a social plot. I'm sure you know your role, Isabel. And I believe we'll have fun at this—turning our renegade into a gentleman, at last."

In their excitement, Burton and Isabel held hands across the table. Burton laughed out loud, while with her free hand Isabel popped a buttered biscuit into her mouth.

At the Palmerston house in Mayfair, Isabel spent the evening in the company of Lady Palmerston and Lady Russell while the men howled over her husband's stories of the American West. Lord Russell was head of the Foreign Office, so Isabel immediately pressed for a consulship for Richard.

"Few government officials comprehend the advantage Richard has as a linguist," she explained to the women. "He's a master in Arabic. He should have the consulate in Damascus, so that he can help England settle all the disturbances in the Middle East."

"It's wonderful to see a couple so in love," Lady Russell said, taking Isabel's hand.

"I am in love, yes, but also sure of Richard's professional promise," Isabel went on. "No man will ever render greater service to the crown."

Other ladies joined the bride and her group. Milnes' wife added her praise for Burton, calling him a wicked wit.

"Ah, that's good news," Lady Palmerston drawled. "Most applicants to our diplomatic services are dull scribes carrying coin purses and satchels."

The ladies laughed and rearranged their skirts.

"Now, then, my dear," Lady Russell said, patting and stroking Isabel's hand. "I shall do myself and you an honor. Yes, indeed, you should be presented at court on the occasion of your marriage. No doubt of it. And, yes, I'll take you to the Queen. She deserves to see your shining face."

Isabel was overwhelmed. Half an hour later she managed to excuse herself so that she could go to Burton with the news, but he stood in a circle of men in the drawing room expounding on the New York hot dog and the Arkansas Toothpick. For a moment she stood watching and listening to her beautiful husband through the nearly closed door; her happiness was almost an agony. Then, deciding that she shouldn't interrupt, she stepped over to a table of desserts where she found a tray of iced cakes. In her giddy excitement she quickly devoured four of them.

It became a season of social occasions, a string of rituals observed in London houses and at Fryston, where Milnes, as social patron, directed Burton's contacts. In his own rooms with Isabel, Burton kept busy at his desk; he wrote letters, began work on his American book, even managed a few poems. But in the evenings they were always at dinner. They met Carlyle, Kingsley, Buckle, and others. They bought clothes for the occasions. And in the end, somehow, Burton sensed that the wedding itself had been only one of the rituals; he seemed to be practicing a new language, a rapturous small talk belonging to women and London townfolk. On the surface of things, he seemed to fit in; he had stories to tell, yet he could listen, too, and keep his silence while others held the floor; women grew shy in his presence; his laughter seemed infectious.

But he felt drunk and disoriented, as if he still rode in that swaying stagecoach across unknown prairies. A deep, sick, dreadful nausea: nothing was right, nothing, and he knew it.

Every three or four days Isabel dressed in her finest clothes and walked over to the Foreign Office, where she pestered the staff in his behalf. The consul at Damascus was unavailable. Yes, her husband was an African expert. Yes, Lady Russell had insisted that she should keep trying. Yes, anything would do. These morning excursions and the evening dinner parties invigorated her; she was in her brightest time, glowing and talkative, ravenous in bed and aggressive in public, and in contrast he stayed at his desk more and more, retreating into verbs and notations, into the inky smears that took his public thoughts away.

"We've been invited to dine with my parents and family," she said. "Sunday next. I know you and Mother will get along. You will, I know it."

"Fine, I'll try my best."

"The day after we go back to Fryston for a few days. You're sure you can write on the book in the cottage?"

"Yes, certainly, I'll manage."

She seemed not to notice. In the end, Milnes, not Isabel, detected Burton's mood and began staying in London more so that he could cheer his friend. There were bachelor breakfasts and dinners at the Upper Brook Street address, and Burton did seem to come to himself again, especially when he met Algernon Swinburne, an unlikely new friend who was frail, emblazoned with a mop of red hair, only twenty-four years old, and ruthlessly opinionated.

"A man is a giant or nothing," Swinburne said at that first dinner, sitting across from Burton. He jerked his legs and hands about as he spoke. Burton regarded him as a flamboyant undergraduate, yet found himself laughing at almost everything Swinburne uttered. "There are only great poets and extremely minor ones," Swinburne went on. "And the principal duty of the minor poet is to recognize his lack of genius and stop bothering us."

After supper Burton and his new young friend went to a corner of the drawing room, drank a bottle of brandy and smoked cannabis. Swinburne giggled with high energy and pumped his leg while he talked. He had published his undergraduate papers, he confessed, and meant to be a complete literary figure, but needed a recess, at present, for drinking, conversation, and sex.

"You prefer women, do you?" Burton asked, being a little suspicious.

"I definitely have a preference for women, yes, and spend my time up in the flats of some girls in St. John's Wood," Swinburne giggled. "But, of course, I've *tried* men! One must embrace experience! But, in all, I prefer women, especially Italian ones. I would also try any handsome gatepost, a good lap dog, melons, wheels of cheese, or comely bottles."

They talked about French brandies and African *bangi* as they laughed. Milnes, pleased to see Burton's good mood restored, told the other guests to leave them alone.

Swinburne wore a gigantic scarf made of paisley; in his herky-jerky movements he frequently tugged at it, so that his head bobbed forward. He resembled both a puppet and its master, moving himself here and there, flitting from one expression and conversation to another. Burton learned that the young poet considered himself a Bohemian, an admirer of De Sade, a friend of Rossetti and the emotional pre-Raphaelite painters, an artist for art's sake, and an immoralist. Although he was physically different from Burton, he reminded Burton of himself as a young man: filled with panache, curiosity, energy, and raw lust. These were the impetuous virtues, after all, Burton recalled, which had sent him off to Mecca in disguise and had made his reputation—such, he admitted, as it now still existed.

They discussed what Swinburne called *"Le vice anglais."* There were an estimated eighty thousand prostitutes in London, he told Burton, and the husbands and bachelors of Mayfair couldn't be expected to do battle with them all. "Farm boys must be recruited from the country," he insisted, getting drunk. "We need strong lads with ample appendages! Patriotic lads willing to serve. Organize, I say! We can stick together in this!"

As they laughed, Burton waved to Milnes and the others who sat around the dinner table smoking cigars.

They agreed to meet again at Fryston to discuss books. Burton promised to supply Swinburne with the *Kama Sutra,* which the poet hadn't read, as well as his own *First Footsteps in East Africa* with its omitted appendix on female circumcision.

"Do you know old Hankey?" Swinburne asked, getting to his feet and attempting to take a step.

"Yes, and have you met his mistress?" Burton replied.

"No, but heard of her. Ah, Hankey's a nice grotesque, isn't he?"

"Yes, do you like him?"

"Adore him," Swinburne said, steadying himself by holding on to Burton's shoulder. "He promised me an edition of *The Perfumed Garden.* Between the two of you, I suppose I'll catch up on my pornography."

"I'll have to translate these books for you, of course, or else you'll just have to look at the illustrations."

"Translate from the Arabic? Burton, dear man, you're a gift. Can I tell you how much it means to meet you?" They staggered back toward the men at the table, who laughed at their approach. "Here is a god, a bona-fide god!" the young poet told the party, his arm draped around his new friend. "Author, swordsman, traveler! Of course, I'd travel myself if my parents raised my annual allowance!"

The men stood and offered a mock toast to Dick and Algernon. After that a drunken discussion on what should be toasted next began.

"Gentlemen," Burton finally announced, holding his brandy better than most, due to concentrated practice. "Let's be serious here. I have seen the wonders of many a continent. I have noted the achievements of the Empire and its shortcomings. I have studied religions, cunts, geographies, bureaucracies, and principalities, so let me suggest that I know it all, know it all, gentlemen, and come like Lazarus to utter this toast."

"Hear, hear!" the men murmured, growing attentive.

"To the harem system," Burton pronounced, his face solemn and dramatically sad. "And all it could mean."

In a heavy mock silence, the men dutifully drank.

"Lovely," Swinburne said. "I appreciate true sentiment. Your words have caused tears of hope and tenderness to well up in my soul."

Long after midnight Burton made his unsteady walk home. Isabel, propped on pillows in bed with another book by Disraeli and a box of bonbons, was extremely sober, forgiving, and somehow too pleasant.

"Did you have a good evening?" she asked, her question betraying not even a slight hint of wifely sarcasm.

"We talked theology all night," Burton told her.

"Then I'm sure you were the most informative and well read."

"My dear, I cannot fathom life—much less the mystic plateaus."

"You're a humble person deep down, Richard, and I love you for it," she said. "Now come to bed and take your rest."

Burton's shoe hit the floor. He undressed and did as he was told.

One evening he accompanied her to church. Kneeling before the flickering candles, he began to weep. He was thinking of Edward, of Speke, of his own blighted career, and the tears just began to flow. Isabel, beside him, patted him gently on the shoulder.

"I believe you might be experiencing the beginnings of a conversion," she whispered beside his ear.

"Yes," he lied, drying his eyes. "I'm sure that must be it."

A letter arrived from the Foreign Office just as they prepared to travel to Fryston for a long holiday weekend. Burton, through Isabel's efforts and the generosity of Lord Russell, had been awarded the consul's position on the island of Fernando Po.

"Never heard of the place," Burton said, peering into the announcement as if words might be seen between the lines.

"This is wonderful," Isabel said. "Let's look it up on a map!"

They found it in the crook of Africa's curve, a tiny outpost in the Bight of Biafra; to its east lay the Cameroon Mountains and to its north was the old city of Calabar. Isabel tried to put a good face on things.

"I'm sure this is a lovely tropical spot."

"The graveyard of the foreign service, no doubt."

"But we must start someplace, if we're going to have the consulate at Damascus and fulfill your destiny," she said.

He didn't know if he even wanted Damascus anymore. "West Africa is as unknown to me as Lapland," he complained. "I've traveled East Africa, and in my heart I'm an Arab and know the ways of the Sahara and Arabia, but this is silly, don't you see? They've paid no attention to my talents, none at all."

"You'll have a wonderful career," she promised him, and her confidence made it clear that she intended to see to it herself.

The next morning they arrived at Fryston, where Isabel was appalled to meet Swinburne; when she extended her hand, the poet threw back his head, jerked this way and that, kissed her fingers, laughed, and acted the fool. She felt unsure if she should laugh, too, or if this was derision for her.

"You must come here," Swinburne said, leading Burton away. "Come see! This is marvelous stuff!"

They went off to the library, where they remained together for hours. In the meantime, Mrs. Milnes took Isabel for a ride along the river road in a gaily painted little horse cart. Afterward they came back to the house to unpack the Burton's clothes, to take tea, and to examine a book of photographs on specimens at Surrey Gardens. Still, Burton and Swinburne stayed locked up in the library. When they emerged they were mildly drunk and disoriented, but Isabel kept her distaste for the poet to herself.

At dinner that night Milnes talked about his friendship with the late De Tocqueville, after whose country estate in France he had patterned Fryston. This led to a lengthy discussion of friendship in general; Burton smiled and entered the conversation occasionally, but a dull melancholy had returned. He was thinking about exile in Fernando Po.

"Men are great swollen egos who have to test the waters with one another to see if friendship is possible," Milnes suggested.

"No, not at all," Swinburne argued. "There's an electric charge between friends or lovers. It's felt at once."

"Can men and women be friends?" Isabel asked. "Or is friendship reserved woman to woman and man to man?"

Everyone agreed that a sexless, Platonic friendship was virtually impossible—except for Isabel herself, who protested.

"Friendship between man and woman," Swinburne mused. "Isn't it called marriage? Isn't that what's left when the electricity sparks out?"

"Metaphors annoy me," Isabel replied.

Sexual love is a fire, Burton thought to himself. Marriage is the smoke. Yet, even as the thought passed, he looked at Isabel seated beside him, then reached over and took her hand. Her eyes showed her gratitude. With her free hand she forked a morsel of roast beef into her mouth.

Burton, now in the consular service, received a letter informing him that he had been dropped from the rolls of the army. The news came as a blow, so he sent off a flurry of letters to combat the decision, yet there it remained: he would no longer have his meager pay, his pension, and the extended leaves that he had used for his journeys and writings.

"This is Rigby's hand," he told Isabel. "Rigby and Speke! They've taken an active part in this somehow!"

"I'll see what I can do," Isabel offered. "I'll see Lady Russell."

"Other consuls have kept their army commissions! They've singled me out!"

"We have important friends. See Milnes about it."

"No, please, you and Milnes stay out of this! I'm man enough to argue for myself in this rotten situation."

He found himself in offices at Whitehall seeing a thin bureaucrat who was filled with courteous explanations. The man—who tried to disguise his Cockney accent and smiled intolerably—told Burton that the government had decided to divide the army from other foreign services; the East India Company, consulates, civilian business interests, and army sorts had become too mixed up.

"Then my case should have special consideration, don't you see? I'm no doubt the only officer in months who has been assigned consular duty! Why create a new plan that affects only me? Who's behind this?"

"Firm decisions have been made," the little man said, smiling. He seemed pleased with Burton's agony, pleased with himself, pleased to have something officious to pronounce.

They ended up in the street outside the offices, Burton raising his voice, repeating all the arguments while people stopped and listened. Then he heard the echo of his own voice and stopped; he sounded, already, like some quibbling civil servant cheated on a pay packet, and he wanted to tell the bureaucrat that once, out in the desert, he had broken a man's fingers for a minor insult. He wanted to say, see here, I have stored behind my eyes visions no European has seen; I cannot be trifled with.

But he calmed himself and walked away. He followed a narrow close until he came to the river's path, the Thames flowing by with all its implacable silence.

Rigby probably did have a hand in this, he told himself, yet there were more coercive forces by far. The career system: a world of offices, rules, protocol, committees, and alien constraints. He sensed the worst: having qualified himself for a government position through exercising independence, daring, and all the freedoms, he would now be required to surrender these. I have evolved into a clerk and a husband, he told himself. The future was so bleak that his depressions of the last weeks returned with a rush.

Big Ben signaled its dignified admonishment; all the clocks and chimes of the city agreed in their solemn tones; the river beside him seemed fierce.

"I'm going down to Brighton to see my cousin," he told Isabel. "We'll decide about Edward's care. And I just need to keep up with my family."

"Yes, certainly. Shall I go spend a day with my parents?"

"Very good. Cousin Samuel likes a toddy now and again, so I'll probably spend an evening and come home with a headache."

Isabel had a bit of biscuit crumb on her lip when he kissed her goodbye. Carrying a small cloth valise, he walked to the railway station, where he met

Swinburne in the tearoom. They occupied a first-class compartment and shared a bottle of brandy on the train ride to the seaside resort.

On the way they recited their troubles. Burton faced a job and a wife. Swinburne, who had ended his Oxford days without a degree, had persuaded his indignant father that fame and fortune would follow the publication of two of his finished manuscripts, *Rosamond*, and *The Queen Mother*, and that the cost of printing was all that was lacking. As they listed their woes, the bottle's amber contents vanished.

"I've learned that Rigby is now both general and consul at Zanzibar," Burton said. "He holds the highest military and diplomatic positions simultaneously. Because I've been given some mosquito-infested little island, though, the army has terminated me. What's fair, I ask you?"

"Nothing's fair," Swinburne replied. "My father has never liked me. Just because I never fancied sports or chapel services."

They talked not so much to each other as to themselves.

At Brighton they agreed to end their complaints and to stroll around with the crowds at the beach and on the piers. Bathers were building sand castles, watching marionette shows, listening to musical ensembles, and admiring one another. Burton, dressed inappropriately as usual, sauntered along in a sticky woolen suit, the one Isabel had bought for his wedding. Swinburne displayed an enormous scarf, so that with his flaming-red hair he resembled a Christmas package. The diminutive poet trailed Burton by a step, so that together, making their way through the crowd, they drew glances and a few smiles.

Slowly they made their way across the boardwalk into a seedy part of town. They passed a stately house with nine gables, the illegal gambling casino, where baccarat and *trente et quarante* were the rage. At the end of an alley, men in top hats huddled over an enclosure where trained terriers killed rats while loud shouts went up and bets were called out. Then they walked across a barren, sandy dune and came to the brothel, a house of turrets and bay windows on the edge of town. By late afternoon they had settled in their rooms, opened another bottle of brandy, then returned to the sitting room where they pondered their choices among the girls.

"You first, Algernon, by all means," Burton offered, giving the poet first pick, and causing the girls to giggle at the odd name and courtly manners.

"They all look satisfactory," Swinburne announced.

"You don't," one of the bawds answered, and the giggling increased.

"I have not arrived to satisfy you, only myself," he said.

"You'll make me happy enough if you give me to your friend," another girl said, turning the giggling into raucous laughter.

Swinburne chose the slimmest and Burton picked the fattest: Meg and Susie. In a room upstairs, determined to remain a foursome, they finished off the brandy and undressed each other. Swinburne looked like a carrot. The girls duly admired some of Burton's scars. Meg resembled a length of pipe, and Susie was like a large serving of trifle.

Burton slumped on the side of the bed, unable to stop laughing, as the poet wagged his tiny member and chased the girls around the room.

"This isn't going to work out," Burton prophesied.

"Yes, it will, dearie; I'll just give it a pinch," fat Susie said with encouragement, and she withdrew from the chase to do this.

"It's just not there," Burton said. "It's out of the army and won't salute."

"We could have a picnic instead," Meg suggested.

"Fine idea. I'll order something from the kitchen. I'm famished."

Swinburne objected to this change in plan, but the girls decided to attend his needs while Burton placed an order for food. Soon the three of them piled into bed, moaned in unison, and began wrestling; Burton tried to stay amused with their acrobatics, but found himself at the window gazing down into the sandy field that stretched toward the town and beach. Later, when the food arrived, the four of them sat around the edges of the bed, indifferent to their nakedness, eating and drinking.

"Give us a chance, dear fellow, and we'll fix you next," Meg offered.

"Perhaps later," Burton allowed, drinking from a bottle of cheap red wine that fought with the brandy inside him. He was clearly disinclined.

When evening arrived, they were downstairs in a parlor listening to Meg play the piano. By this time Burton had washed down his troubles with two pints of ale.

"Going home," he told Swinburne. "Best to be sick in my own berth."

"You're in no condition," the poet argued.

"There's a late train. I read the schedule. I'm off, dear chap."

He made his way across the field, into town, and somehow found the railway station; steam and noise blew his thoughts away as he struggled to board the late train and to find a seat. A baby in his third-class coach had fouled its diaper. Burton had lost his cloth valise. All around him the lower classes, weary from their tedious fun, pressed against each other, prattled and snored.

After a while he fell asleep, but when he awoke the train had passed his stop, and he staggered down the aisle until he could find the conductor.

"Stop. I must get off," he said.

"We're in open country again, sir, and can't stop."

"Halt the train. I'll be sick on all the passengers and you, if you don't."

In the middle of the night Burton stood at a crossroads—no signposts anywhere. The moon was high, though, and the grassy fields wore a shimmering silver. His nausea rose and fell as he pulled out his pocket compass and tried to fix his position. Near Worthing, he concluded. Very well. Dead reckoning and onward. He started across a pasture, stepped into some fresh dung, but went on without a curse. In time, exhausted, his feet turned down a cobblestoned thoroughfare and he found a crude sign directing him toward London Centre.

Isabel was at home when he arrived.

"Where on earth have you been? You smell awful!"

"Missed my stop on the train. I'm afraid I've dung on my shoes, too."

"I'll draw a nice bath. Here, fetch off those clothes."

"I can't keep up with Cousin Samuel anymore," he said. "Why didn't you go to your family's?"

"I thought you might return tonight," she said, kissing him. "Oh, dear, I'm afraid your trousers are torn."

"Ruined them on a fence." He sighed.

"Richard, this is your wedding suit. Try to be more careful with your clothes, won't you?"

"Indeed I shall," he said, and he closed his eyes and let his head fall back on the chair's threadbare cushion.

That night he dreamt of cataracts and booming waterfalls and awoke, once, when he became lost in the white foam of a narrow gorge. He wondered —odd thought—if he had dreamed Speke's dream; if, somehow, his enemy and companion had seen this magnificent vision in reality. For a long time he sat on the bed, Isabel's warm rump curving beside him, and set his thoughts straight.

At breakfast he appeared in his other suit—an even more unseasonable worsted—and, as consul, addressed his wife.

"Fernando Po is a miserable outpost, but I'll work at it," he said. "For years its administration has passed back and forth between Spain and England. Each country wants it, yet doesn't. Malaria kills off Europeans as quickly as they set foot on the place. The stone-age natives export nothing and do nothing. It's the Foreign Office graveyard, Isabel, so I've decided to go without you. In a few months I might send for you. But, at first, I'll set up office and see what's there."

Her lip was quivering as she watched him eat his toast.

"If you think about everything, you'll agree this is best. I'm forty years old and without means. But we can manage to keep you here until you pack up and follow."

"I'll die without you," she managed, trying to hold up.

"No, you'll be very resolute. You'll keep me advised if some better post turns up. You'll be with your family when you want to be."

"Perhaps I should go back and live with my parents," she whispered, trying to think.

"The move would save rent," he agreed, being more practical than she had ever seen him.

"We've been married only a few weeks," she whispered. Her voice seemed gone. "Will we be apart like this?"

"I'll take you on other assignments with me," he assured her. "The proper assignments where a consulate wife wears silk and entertains. But not this one at this time. It's too grubby and too dangerous."

Although he felt bombarded by indecisions and mixed emotions, he tried to show only strength. Isabel's face contorted, and she shed a tear on the toast, which she promptly ate.

1862-1863

—————————)0(—————————

Success and Exile

SPEKE FOUND THAT HE COULDN'T TAKE HIS EYES OFF THE TWO BAHIMA GIRLS: their liquid movements, the way their thighs fitted into their small buttocks, how their sloping armpits became their new breasts, the sheen of their hair, the cushioned slits of their mouths and vaginas. He awoke each morning to see them entwined in sleep on their mat beside his cot; naked himself now, he watched them over the contours of his own body, framing them in a vision of his own white flesh; if Mutesa still held him captive, the girls held him in deeper captivation, and he hated the thought that Grant might arrive and force them to leave the court. He failed to visit the lake, to make drawings, to take bearings. Instead he fixed his concentration in Meri's wanton postures and in Kahala's boyish movements, so that he became indifferent to everything else. The court-yard with its primitive protocol meant little. Courtiers and ministers came and went in a constant flurry of messages and emotions; chickens made their indolent circles around the huts; the women whispered and laughed; Mutesa's strange falsetto could sometimes be detected above all the bustle; yet Speke sank down in the narcotic of his own consciousness, into a primeval paradise of words he didn't understand, young gazes, soft touchings and gestures, where language wasn't needed, for all communications were plain.

When they awoke they crawled off their mat and into his arms: sleepy children in a warm crush of limbs and breath. Sometimes the three of them sprawled together for the duration of the morning, until hunger or their need for their toilet pried them loose. But then they gave him every attention: comb-ing, washing, caressing, and kissing him. He taught them how to use their hands so that in spite of their own protests he kept their virginity intact; they relieved him, then, with an economy of movement until he could only hear the rise and fall of his own labored breathing in the hut. The first time this happened Meri sprang from his side and ran outdoors; she gave his essence to the sorceress, but in spite of his efforts Speke couldn't learn what they had done with it. Rampant speculations: Did the sorceress somehow take it into her own body? Was it implanted in the earth? Was it displayed for all those wives and sisters who clamored in the courtyard?

Those morning pastimes eventually became day-long appetites; the girls led him down to the stream, where they bathed and cavorted together, as the women, boldly watching, tried for a glimpse of the white man's genitals. Speke became increasingly casual. He stood in the doorway of his hut, at times, like a blond study; his dammed-up emotions came loose in a flood, his modesty swept away.

When Mutesa invited him to hunt hippo on the lake, he made excuses. At last, protesting, he unwrapped his weapons and agreed to leave the girls for a few days, but in his vexed preparations forgot to take either instruments or notebooks.

Maula, who would serve as interpreter for the hunting party, was required to comfort Meri and Kahala. He was clearly embarrassed at Speke's heavy sentiment.

"Tell them I'll be gone two nights at most," Speke insisted.

Maula explained and the girls pouted.

"Tell them I'll miss them very much. Say it."

Maula shrugged, shuffled his feet, and managed to utter the words.

The party headed north along a major stream, stopping almost every hour to drink and to feast. Mutesa clearly had little interest in hunting, only in this mobile jungle revelry.

Speke finally explained to Maula that he intended to go back to his girls, but the little man was appalled. "No, no, Mutesa must see you shoot a bird from the sky! He has heard you do this magic thing! He must see!"

"That's no great bother," Speke replied. "I'll shoot us a bird and we'll trudge back."

The party, though, kept moving until it reached the shores of the lake. Again, the immensity of the nyanza impressed Speke, but everything was a bother. A cold wind had blown up, so Mutesa ordered fires built and tents pitched; cooking pots soon boiled, and dancers and drummers began the evening show. At dusk Speke wanted to walk along the marshy edge of the lake so that he could possibly see a waterbird, but Mutesa and the others were already too drunk to care about the white man and his gun. At dark Speke sat before the fire, wrapped in a blanket, while Mutesa retired to his large tent with his concubines. The evening meal was sparse. Angry at being treated so rudely, Speke complained to Maula, who tried to keep peace.

Shivering with the damp cold, Speke stirred himself early the next morning and made enough noise among the pots and sticks of firewood to rouse the camp. Mutesa appeared outside his tent with a resplendent smile on his face and ordered everyone into canoes; the Kabaka obviously felt wonderful, but Speke's bones ached with fatigue.

The waters of the lake were rough and frightening, so that Mutesa, who tried to remain stoic, soon ordered his men to row for shore again. Speke loaded his weapon with birdshot and waited for his revenge. As they neared the shore a loon flew into view and Speke stood up, causing the large canoe to sway, and fired off a thunderous blast; Mutesa gave a shriek, his men went over the sides into the waves, the bird swooped down in death, and Speke broke into loud laughter at all the disorder. A cloud of acrid smoke hung over the canoe while the oars stuck out in all directions; warriors beat the waves with their fists, trying to gain their footing in the shallow surf, and Mutesa, pointing first at the bird and then at Speke, cried out, "*Hoo! Hoo!*" Maula, who seemed to be swimming for his life, failed to translate the Kabaka's excitement.

That afternoon Speke requested to go back to the court, but the Kabaka refused. After some argument, Speke complained of sickness, so the party broke up, but Mutesa was in a foul mood. They walked for hours, arriving back at the court at midnight, where Speke went to his hut, stripped down, drank a whiskey toddy for his chest cold, and made room in his cot for Kahala and Meri, who covered and warmed him with their limbs.

The mood of the Kabaka Mutesa grew worse.

A girl offered him a bowl of fruit, but displeased him with her manner, so he grabbed up a club and began to beat her. When her head was split open, the women of his court began to wail and beg for mercy for the victim, but the beating continued until she was dragged away.

Speke complained about his food, so his kitchen boy's ears were cut off. The boy, a slender fifteen-year-old, was sent back into Speke's service covered with blood, his gaping wounds cauterized, his eyes wide with pain.

When Speke, outraged, spoke to Maula about it, the interpreter begged him to do and say nothing directly to Mutesa.

"You, your own life," Maula said, exasperated. Speke's welfare was clearly in jeopardy, too.

Neither was the queen mother pleased with Speke. Namasole sent word that she would see the white doctor no more, not even if he sought to call on her. Speke obviously spent far too much time with his girls, so that petty jealousies and antagonisms occupied the court.

His relationships needed improvement, so Grant's arrival helped.

Jim Grant arrived on a litter, accompanied by musket fire, drums, and harps as Speke, coughing into his handkerchief and flanked by the Bahima girls, greeted him. The court was in an uproar, Mutesa crouching and walking like the lion again, and making his falsetto sound.

As Grant was led toward the royal throne, women held out their breasts and danced. The Scotsman hobbled off the litter, came into the presence of the Kabaka, and knelt in the dust.

After a few words were exchanged in the same painful process of translation, Grant snapped his fingers and summoned his art supplies from a porter. With an elaborate flourish of gestures and preparation, he set up his easel and drew a likeness of the Kabaka, which he adorned with watercolor. The portrait, Speke thought, was modestly fair, but the ceremony of its production was ingenious.

"*Hoo!*" his majesty exclaimed, holding the finished portrait aloft for everyone to see.

"Tell the Kabaka that this power of drawing and painting I will teach him," Grant said. The promise brought a shout of joy from the Kabaka, and all his ministers responded by pounding their spears on the earth. Suddenly a dance

323

commenced; wives and sisters, warriors and ministers, courtiers and Mutesa himself bounced to the rhythm of drums.

"You're a brilliant success," Speke called to Grant through the noise and activity.

"Who's that tall woman?" Grant yelled back.

"The sorceress!"

"Who are those girls?"

"My daughters!"

"And how are you?" Grant shouted.

"Well enough, thanks."

"Made any studies of the coastline or lake?"

"No, not yet. Been waiting on you, old chap!"

Namasole, the queen mother, resembling a hippo in heat, danced with her hysterical son. The Bahima girls stood on each side of Speke, hugging his arms, as Grant sat on the ground and tried to comprehend what was going on.

"We've got to get moving," Speke said. "We're already four months late for our rendezvous with Petherick."

Grant, gnawing on a strip of dried beef, his swollen leg propped on cushions, asked hundreds of questions and remarked on everything, but Speke seemed single-minded. For several days Grant had seen little of anyone; Sidi Bombay, Mabruki, Baraka, and Speke himself seemed totally occupied in their separate huts.

"What about the route over the Masai Plain?" Grant asked.

"I've abandoned the plan. We'll go toward Gondokoro, as we agreed to do. How's your leg?"

"Not well, as you see. I can manage, though."

"I've spoken to Mutesa about leaving, but he always breaks off the conversation or changes the subject. For a while I thought I was truly his prisoner, but now I believe he regards us as powerful men of the world—and he'll let us leave when the time comes. Tomorrow I try a new tactic: I'll tell him that I don't want to leave empty-handed and that I want to show off his power and gifts to the white men in the north."

"How will this help?"

"Oh, he's all pride. He'll load us down with gifts, I suspect, and bid us farewell."

"You're still confident, then?"

"I still worry that Petherick or another white man will take the prize first. I heard of a Maltese trader lurking around. The French could decide to send an expedition. And there's yet another king and palace to visit north of the lake: King Kamrasi of Bunyoro. I expect delays. Can you travel except by litter?"

"I'll make it somehow," Grant answered.

Later that day Speke, Maula, and Sidi Bombay went in delegation to Mutesa to discuss the upcoming departure. The Kabaka, disturbed, suggested several reasons for delay—including his unfinished art lessons—but asked, through the interpreters, at last, "So you really intend to go?"

"Yes, Father of the Nile," Speke replied. "We must follow the wondrous river that flows from your nyanza. And you must give us fine gifts, so that your power and generosity may be known by white men everywhere."

Mutesa summoned his ministers. A lengthy discussion followed, during which Speke learned that he and Grant would receive a farewell gift of sixty cows, fourteen goats, ten loads of butter, loads of coffee and tobacco, and one hundred bark cloth *mbugus* to dress the porters. In addition, slaves were provided to carry the loads and a warrior named Budja would serve as guide.

Even during this generous exchange, as amounts of various gifts were discussed, Mutesa kept asking, "So you will leave us now?"

Speke, putting on a sad face, kept answering in the affirmative.

At the end of the day it was known throughout the kingdom that the Kabaka was gravely sad. During the night a doleful drumbeat started; torches were lit around the palace, but neither Speke nor Grant attended the ceremony. To assuage his grief at the departure of his white guests, the Kabaka Mutesa had one of his favorite wives beheaded.

As the caravan formed, Speke and his girls slept together for the last times. A soft hysteria: they sobbed against his chest, whimpering like pups, and because of Mutesa's thoughtless sacrifice of a wife Speke worried that Meri and Kahala might be in danger, too.

He knew he couldn't take them with him, though he wanted to. Grant already suspected the little body servants, and they certainly couldn't travel openly up the Nile and back to England, so had to be abandoned—better here than later on, assuming they wouldn't come to harm. But Speke was unprepared for his own feelings in these last hours: these were his daughters, his lovers, his pulse beat, and he clung to them. They were now the best parts of himself—insane as that seemed—because they had broken his curse; he somehow flowed free because of them, secrets finally washed away, a new freedom possible. And would he stay this way without them? He didn't know, so pressed their bodies against his as if he might memorize their touch.

They gave him the deep kisses he had taught them. Whispering in that language he didn't understand, they spoke their endearments.

On the last morning Maula brought the sorceress, so that Speke could try and ensure the girls' safety after he was gone. The sorceress remained haughty, instructing Maula to tell the white man that her own favors could have been enjoyed.

"I have put my charm on this pair," Speke said, standing tall in his uniform and looking the beautiful sorceress in the eyes. "And my vengeance will befall the one who harms them—even if this should be you or the Kabaka himself."

The sorceress smirked and jutted out a hip, so that Speke worried that she concocted some arrogant argument, but Maula conveyed her message: "The girls will have honor until they are old. They have served a god."

Later, at the foot of the royal hill, Mutesa reviewed the caravan during an hour of profuse thanks and lengthy farewells. Maula and Sidi Bombay took turns shouting translations of the Kabaka's words and promises.

"He shall always wear trousers!"

"He shall kill his enemies only with guns!"

"He shall practice his watercolors!"

"He will welcome other white men as friends!"

With all these declarations, Mutesa kept asking, "So, you are really going?" Speke, in turn, assured the Kabaka this was true.

At the end, the Kabaka raised his arms, sang out his falsetto note, then lowered his voice in a last speech. "Bana, I love you," he said, as Maula quickly translated. "Because you have come so far to see me and have taught me so many things since coming here."

Grant hobbled into place beside Speke at the head of the caravan, both of them surrounded by all their cows and goats. "Damn," he whispered, "we look like herders."

Speke was too emotional to reply. Mutesa had turned and walked back toward the palace in the way of the lion—in those long, silly strides.

As they moved forward into the land of Bunyoro they came to marsh-lands where hundreds of small streams began to flow out of the north end of the lake; these effluents, if they came together in a river, were clearly what they sought, so their excitement began to gather. But they also came to an obvious crossroads, for according to Budja, their guide, they could follow a known path northward from this juncture and reach Kamrasi's palace or follow the marshy edges of the lake in hopes of finding the main current of the river they sought.

"We must split up," Speke finally decided. "If you admit the truth, Jim, you can't easily keep pace. So I want you to head north with the cattle. I'll follow the lake—taking the long way around. But I'll cover twenty miles each day, pressing forward, and meet you at Kamrasi's palace."

"Then I'm not to see the beginnings of the Nile?" Grant asked flatly.

"It's very important to communicate quickly with Petherick," Speke said. "Perhaps he's already with Kamrasi."

"True, but I was hoping to see the river exit from the nyanza."

"But you can't keep a pace of twenty miles a day, can you?"

"No, afraid not. I know you're probably right, but it's a disappointment."

"You'll see a great deal of the Nile, if this is it."

"You know this is the Nile," Grant persisted. "But I travel with the herd."

They sat beside a small campfire outside Grant's tent; the sky above them had ignited with stars and fireflies. Grant's leg was propped on a stump, his trousers split and rolled up to reveal a wound looking no better than it did months ago when first injured. Speke poked at the embers with a stick, not answering Grant's last remark.

"Of course, if this is my assignment, I'll gladly obey," Grant went on.

"It's much for the best. We're months late. What if Petherick and all our supplies are no longer waiting for us at Gondokoro? We must travel all the way to Cairo on the Nile. Our pace now *is* of consequence—and if you go with me around the lake and through the swamps, our journey could take months longer, don't you see?"

"I see," Grant admitted. "All right, good, you don't have to explain it anymore, Jack, really."

The next morning the caravan divided. By late afternoon, as Speke's group made its slow progress through the swamp, they began to hear promises and rumors from the fishermen and villagers. Ahead, they indicated, were the Stones: rocks at a main stream which was the start of a great river.

That same afternoon Grant, usually mild-tempered, became furious with a goat boy whose flock had strayed, causing those with the herds to halt early in the day. Mabruki, following orders, tied the goat boy to a tree, and Grant took off his own belt to administer lashes. To the astonishment of Mabruki and the others, twenty hard lashes were delivered, each one with Grant's full weight behind it, until bloody welts rose on the boy's shoulders and he passed out.

Movement through the marshlands at the upper reaches of the lake was tedious, but Speke felt a rousing new enthusiasm. At night around the campfire he made notes, sketched, and regained some of his old resolution; he felt the confidence of sexual awakening, he knew, and it somehow transferred into all his ambitions, his dreams of public success, his new regard for himself. He knew the White Nile was near—its misty breath on his shoulder in these fetid swamps. He looked forward to standing before the Society again. He could take Lowry in his arms, he felt, and boldly love. He could stroll those hallways and fields at Jordans and be truly home: the accomplished master.

These swamps had a soft mystery: fishermen with long bamboo poles padded over the spongy earth, going to and from their secret pools deep in the jungles beyond the main path; grassy banks and lush trees rose up as ornaments to a beautiful and primeval nature; hippos and crocodiles eyed the caravan from sluggish ponds adorned with water lilies; giant white birds spread their silent wings, gliding on the evening sky.

They passed a devastated village where elephants had run wild. The people had fled, leaving their trampled houses and fires.

The swampy land, at last, converged into a giant stream. Its flow was soft, a mere trickle.

In late July 1862, when Speke and his party reached Usoga, called the Stones, and saw there, forty miles from the Kabaka's palace, a line of low rocks bordering a stream that all the natives claimed to be the beginning of a great river. Shortly after along the path they saw a magnificent and picturesque waterfall: seven hundred yards wide, about ten feet high. In the blue pool below it, hundreds of native fishermen worked their bamboo poles; grassy islets dotted the extended pool with crocodiles, hippos, and herds of hartebeest grunting their calls; fishermen's huts decorated with wildflowers stood everywhere; fish jumped the low falls; everything was like a carefully kept park, the sky overhead whirling with birds.

Excited and remembering his awed feelings for the Himalayas, Speke ordered his men to shave their heads and bathe in this perfect and sacred spot.

"Shave our heads?" Sidi Bombay asked, trying not to be obstinate again.

"Yes, in celebration! Like the Hindu faithful in the sacred Ganges!"

"Sir, the men will not want to do this thing."

"Give them my order. Tell them to enjoy themselves."

They enjoyed themselves, but by disobeying the order and by wandering off to drink wine with the local women of the Wasoga and Waganda fishermen. Speke, meanwhile, paced up and down the banks. The White Nile! All his intuitions had been correct!

He unwrapped all his rifles and scatterguns. While the fishermen in the stream below him cheered each shot, he killed several birds. Then, making an elaborate show of loading his big 12-bore, he took aim at a crocodile sunning itself on the islet in the middle of the stream; the impact of his shot turned the big reptile over in a sudden flip and all the natives saluted with their bamboo poles and shouted encouragements. For hours after his display of firepower, the roar of the waterfall kept his attention. Toward evening he climbed down the rocks, took off his boots, and waded in the shallows. Then, perched on the rocks before this breathtaking landscape, he tried to capture his elations in notes. He wrote down everything that came to mind, including some odd reflections and assertions unlike anything he had ever penned before.

> —what a place for Missionaries! They could never fear starvation, the land is so rich; and if farming were introduced by them, they might have hundreds of pupils.
> —I feel as if I only want a wife and family, garden and yacht, rifle and rod, to make me happy here for life, so charming is the place.

By the next day his enthusiasm still ran high, and he ordered Sidi Bombay to take a search party to find canoes, so that they could float toward Kamrasi's palace. When they had gone on their search, he entered additional notes, deciding that these magnificent low waterfalls should be named after Lord Ripon, the current president of the Society. With Baraka's help he also managed to interview several fishermen and villagers, although he paid little attention, at times, to what they actually said.

"Angry tribes downstream," they warned him.

"Yes, but we have rifles," he replied.

"And other lakes. Many lakes along the way."

"Hmm, but we'll have boats, you see, to row across them."

During the five days in which Sidi Bombay and his men located five boats and brought them back, Speke hunted and rested. Each morning he stretched out naked on the warm elastic grass beside the stream; once, free and unashamed of his thin, muscled body and in view of all the natives fishing and bathing below the banks, he stood up and pissed into his beautiful discovery.

All through the days he let his thoughts soar: Meri, that fat wife of Lumeresi sucking on her milk pot, Lowry, the girls in taffeta at Madeira, Burton, Kahala, bodics and shapes.

He also speculated on Grant's progress. Had he possibly already reached the palace of Kamrasi at Bunyoro? We've already been slower than I estimated, he admitted. Jim could have kept pace. Yet the cattle couldn't have made it through those swamps, so it was undoubtedly better this way. I definitely have a knack for making the right decisions.

When the boats arrived, loads and passengers were fitted in. The fishermen at the falls waved good-bye with their bamboo poles. Speke had given them small quantities of tobacco and had shot crocodile, antelope, and hundreds of birds for them to eat—food that they usually provided for themselves only with difficulty and danger—so they seemed genuinely impressed with the white man and his visit.

"To the center! Find the main channel!" Speke called, as his men poled and rowed the boats from shore.

The stream narrowed into blue swirls. Speke stood up proudly in the bow of the first boat, his rifle cradled in his arms, feeling like the god the sorceress had said he was.

Burton returned to the bottle, stayed drunk, and disliked everything: his month's cruise down to Fernando Po, the noisy crew, the insolent West African Negroes, the abundance of pious European missionaries, the American slavers, and finally his little island itself.

Named after a Portuguese navigator—undoubtedly lost, Burton concluded—the very name of the place, Fernando Po, made him mildly suicidal.

In the one and principal town, called Santa Isabel by the Spaniards and Clarence by the British, Burton's office was a ramshackle bungalow beside a deserted plantation at the edge of the jungle. His desk, files, closets, and the cast-iron safe were all the same: empty. There was no ongoing work, nothing to do, and he wrote in his notes that first day that his outpost was "the very abomination of desolation."

Staggering through those empty, dusty rooms, he talked to the walls and the green depth of the jungle beyond his windows.

"Marriage was a mistake," he stated. The grimy walls and the thousands of leaves and vines made no dispute.

"I missed my great chance, too." No argument.

"And I've come to this!" A silent, profound confirmation from all around. In the next few days he discovered that there was no club, no café, and a general absence of social life so that he could make friends. The cuisine consisted of tainted meat, overripe fruit, and the strong local beverages—palm wines, sweet beers, and rotgut brandies.

"What does one *do* here?" he asked the proprietor at the only hotel, a wrinkled old Spaniard named Amadeo, who kept a seraglio of black women in his upper rooms.

"The only action is mosquitoes and women." The old man sighed. "In order to play the game a little longer than a month, you must naturally take precautions."

"Well, I have Warburg Drops and a flyswatter for mosquitoes," Burton offered.

The hotel keeper sent him three different women in three nights. "Hello," he told the first of his visitors. "Hope you don't mind my untidy little consulate. There's my bed, such as it is. Tell me your price, my dear, but don't tell me your name."

"You are rude! All right, I won't say my name! But my price is expensive —because my body is clean and sacred, God's gift!"

"Sounds like the missionaries have talked up the price of pussy in these parts," Burton said to the walls as he removed his shirt.

"This is my temple and shrine," the woman said. "If you want it, the charge is half a crown."

"Very well, looks good from here."

"You are such a very rude, hateful person!"

After his interludes three nights in a row, he felt heavily depressed. When he learned that a ship was scheduled to depart for the Oil Rivers on the coast, he booked passage. His salvation, he decided, lay in the fact that British ships called at the island with frequency, so that he could travel up and down the West African coastline and avoid the doldrums of his job.

Seven days after his arrival for duty, then, he was aboard HMS *Arrogant* heading toward Lagos through the coastal slave waters. In those thick jungles off the starboard of his ship black chieftains were at war with each other, selling their captured enemies to Arab and American buyers; British gunboats were actively involved in trying to stop this commerce in human flesh; the jungles all around moaned with ghostly pain; ragged ports such as Old Calabar, Bonny and Brass, as well as Lagos itself, swarmed with slave brokers, naval officers, and European palm-oil merchants. Yet Burton had no part in this great morality play. He was a minor official on a lackluster island down the way, and the pain of this knowledge festered in him, anger turned into depression, and depression became a reckless melancholy. He wanted to take his sword and run naked into that steamy jungle, to do something vain and remarkable.

He found himself thinking about his journey to Medina and Mecca. That prank—begun as a whim during one of his leaves from the army years ago—threatened to remain the deed for which he would be remembered.

When the army granted him a year off to study Arabic, he grew a beard to match his mustache, stained his skin with henna, and started out. The robes and disguise looked good, yet he took care: clothes, gestures, even the mind itself had to be right if he meant to keep from being detected and beheaded as an infidel.

In Alexandria, Burton stayed with a Scots merchant named John Thurburn. In a small stucco house on the rear of the walled estate Burton perfected his disguise for the hajj. He read the Koran, went to public baths and Arab coffeehouses, practiced his prayers, and devised a role for himself as combination doctor, dervish, magician, and fakir. Thurburn gave Burton one of his slaves as an aide and servant, a young man named Aga who helped with all the elaborate deceptions. Aga smiled continually, made a fine turtle soup, conversed in Arabic, and helped to secure costumes for the pilgrim. Aga also instructed Burton in the oriental *kayf:* the pleasures of repose in which a man clears the mind and thinks of nothing.

Burton eventually transformed himself into a fakir and pilgrim whom he called Mirza Abdullah, an Afghan who had lived in Rangoon and who spoke Persian, Hindustani, and Arabic—all this to add layers of cover to a complicated disguise in the event anyone grew suspicious. But in the blank rhythms of the desert landscape Mirza Abdullah and Burton blent into one, came apart, and grew together once again in the pure animal existence of *kayf* and disjointed time. Beyond Suez their caravan joined with others, tributaries of Moors, Turks, Tartars, and Indians going toward the holy centers; Burton swayed in the wooden saddle above his camel, witnessed one dry wadi after another, roads of dark lava, oceans of sand, and made his notes and sketches as the pilgrims around him shouted in the night, "*Labbayk!* Here am I!" to remind Allah that they had come all this way for his blessing. Beyond the oasis of Medina they came to

Mecca and gazed on the mystic Kaaba, the Sanctuary, that square windowless building draped with the *kiswa*, an immense black cloth embroidered with inscriptions from the Koran. Inside its walls he saw the Black Stone, the holy of holies, which he decided was probably a piece of a meteorite; he drank from the holy well as he observed the religious delirium of those around him; he listened to a sermon on Mount Arafat, then rented another camel and rode in a pillowed saddle toward the Red Sea port of Jidda where a British consulate awaited. He was the hit of the evening with the English ladies around the dinner table at the consulate. Every European in Jidda listened to stories of his adventure that night and the women—brazenly, over and over again—asked him to open his robe and to show the difference between his normally white skin and the henna stain. They laughed nervously and one of them actually touched him, letting her fingers trail through the hair on his chest.

Since he had abstained from drinking for such a long time while on the hajj, the wine went to his head that evening. "He's famous now! Famous!" the consul kept saying, filling everyone's glasses. But in some corner of himself Burton didn't know if he wanted the experience converted into fame. He was too drunk to think clearly, but something seemed wrong in such a recognition: a burlesque of what now seemed, unmistakably, a serious matter he had gone through.

Now, years later on a ship going toward Lagos, he tried to recollect the hajj, but it was a mere romance lived long ago, an adventure that had become folly, and the adventurer was now a civil servant traveling second class on a grim little vessel steaming toward a pitiful port on the wrong side of a continent.

Lagos, when it finally came into view, looked like the open, wet mouth of a viper.

Such a place made him long for East Africa with its highland breezes, its soft equatorial light, its airy beauty. Here, the jungle pressed on the sea. The harbor was filled with the wastes of nature and men: bales, excrement, crates. Beyond the lagoon lay labyrinthine streets and canals. Swarms of insects sent up a complaining descant of noise. Men slept in black heaps in doorways and on the wharves. Small boats as frail as withered leaves choked the waterfront, each one packed with naked children and women. All Europeans looked trapped, and everyone, native and traveler alike, seemed a stranger here: misplaced drifters in a place cursed by its slaving and dank heat, a place where men had come to make their fortunes in hell.

Burton found a sinister hotel of sagging porches and broken shutters. He needed to hire help for Fernando Po, yet dreaded asking the local and British bureaucrats for help in this. He sat in a bar one afternoon, then, sipping a harsh brandy.

He watched the one single clean white jacket in the bar, a white serving frock worn by a pleasant-looking black man with Semitic features who delivered drinks to the clientele. Burton took satisfaction in that white coat: it was a symbol of respectability in a world of tatters. The servant—who seemed mildly familiar —smiled at all the bar's grubby guests in their crusted work clothes, partial uniforms, and soiled pith helmets, but as he approached Burton his smile altered into recognition.

"Another brandy, sir, or will you continue to take the *kayf?*"

"Aga?" Burton asked, the name coming from nowhere.

"Yes, the same! I knew it was you, sir!"

Thurburn's slave from those days before the hajj in Alexandria. Burton stood and clasped the thin body in his arms. "How can you be here in West Africa?" he asked, laughing.

"I am no longer a slave except to a salary," Aga replied. "I was freed and joined the army. I've traveled far. Now this."

"Do you still make a turtle soup?"

"Oh, yes, for you especially."

"You must come to work for me," Burton said. "Leave this job. Come and live on a tropical island. Bring that white frock with you."

"If only I could." Aga sighed.

"You can. Do it this hour. I need you again."

They traveled together on the river road north of Lagos toward Abeokuta, a center for slaving. Burton wanted to see the country and hoped that the Foreign Office might somehow use him in its resistance to the widespread traffic in flesh. He wanted to fight slavery, he told Aga—because he hated it and because other men with less talent and less capability were using their work against slavery as a moral and political springboard to better positions and career posts. He referred to Rigby as he explained this, but Aga, unsure of all Burton meant, could only listen with sympathy.

The country upriver was lush and dotted with missionary stations. The area was also a virtual war zone: roads and villages choked with refugees who had fled King Gelele of Dahomey and other brutal chieftains who slaughtered or made slaves of their enemies in these parts.

"Why do we want to see this?" Aga asked, looking around at all the suffering.

"I need to tell my government that I've seen the slave coast," Burton explained. "When I write to them offering my services, I must be informed."

Around them was sufficient human suffering: hungry children wailing in the dust of roadside ditches, terrified mothers, disease and death. Burton and Aga rode horseback from village to village, hearing awful stories of the Custom: bloodbath rites over in Dahomey in which hundreds of captured victims were sacrificed.

Burton had only disgust for the missionaries who indulged in songs and Bible stories while this sea of wretched people passed their gates; the ministers fretted over trousers for the naked natives, over tea and *The Times,* over trifles of theology and etiquette while an immense social upheaval reverberated around them. Burton's notes turned to acid: Christians had an infuriating piety and an unerring capacity for irrelevance.

On the way back to Lagos they stopped at a village dance. Burton drank off an entire bottle of brandy, then sprawled out to watch the supple bodies of young girls who gyrated in the fireside shadows. He smiled with drunken contentment, considering himself fortunate to have Aga with him. Life's journeys had given him good companions, he felt: Aga, Sidi Bombay, Al-Hammal, Stroyan, Milnes, Lumsden, Edward, Steinhauser, even Speke, men of both status and servitude, all appreciated. Perhaps, he decided, there are only such fleeting alliances: affinities in which one person serves or pleases another for a short time, then passes on.

They watched the girls dance. One of them rolled her hips in an obscene mimicry of desire, her thumbs slipping inside her cotton skirt, edging it down so that her pubes came into view. The elders grinned, watching their guests to see how they reacted to this display and keeping up the rhythms of their drums. Burton and Aga looked at each other and smiled, too. Could Aga help make Fernando Po bearable? Could anything?

The next day in Lagos as they searched for a ship en route back to Fernando Po, Burton talked to Aga about his frustrations and plans. They were at the docks, where a carnival craziness seemed to exist: naked blacks, women in veils, cattle, a man carrying the mere skeleton frame of an umbrella, a vendor in whose little stall there were only clocks without hands, dozens of disfigured characters without various body parts, clouds of bugs, men in assorted military uniforms, bells and horns, wagons of dung, cooking fires in the middle of the dusty alleyways, whores in open shanties, mountains of garbage.

"I intend to travel the whole coast," Burton explained to Aga.

"But why?" his factotum asked. "It's all like this!"

"On the other side of Africa, men are searching for the Nile—and I'm left out of it. In Egypt and Arabia there is a whole culture whose language and ways I understand—and I'm not there, so that I can be of use. And here along this miserable coast where they've sent me there's a great fight against slavery —and I've been left out, again. It's unfair, too unfair. I'm going to learn everything and become an expert. I must make myself indispensable to the government here in West Africa. I must!"

Aga's face wrinkled in disapproval. As they strolled beside some barrels of palm oil, he said, "When we return to your island we will find ourselves a pleasant house. I will make you a fine herbal tea. You will grow calmer."

"No, Aga, there's much to do."

"Did you not write many books? You should take time, sit and ponder, and set down your thoughts in more books."

"I'm a man of travel," Burton explained. "Always have been. Books don't come out of solitude and contemplation, as some people believe."

"You should calm yourself, this I know."

"Ah, yes, the *kayf:* I did practice it years ago, you know, after you instructed me in it. But, Aga, idleness bores me. I fall asleep when I try to ponder things. And when I wake up I want to move."

They paused beside an American steamer where sailors were throwing out lines and bellowing at each other.

"Perhaps a man should mistrust constant movement," Aga went on. Servant and master seemed to be at the edge of some philosophical point, yet an elusive one.

"When I am old," Burton said, "I want to be placed on a ship which will never put into port and which will go round and round the earth until I die."

Isabel, who did not have an audience with the Queen, tried to keep busy in her husband's behalf. She worked with his editors, bringing out his book on the Mormons and his travels across America. She wrote to various members of his family, who didn't bother to reply to their relative's Catholic and not very rich wife. She wrote to the army, urging them to reinstate him on their rolls. She tried to have a gunboat assigned to Fernando Po—following his suggestion —and went on visiting the Foreign Office where, each week, she was referred by secretaries to other secretaries.

One afternoon her cousin, Louisa Segraves, who hadn't visited since the marriage, came by the Arundell house. The two women sat in the parlor listening to tunes on an oversized music box, sipping tea, and eating cakes dusted with sugar and cinammon.

"Rumor has it that your husband is keeping a seraglio on his little island," Louisa said.

"There are always rumors about Richard," Isabel replied.

"True, ever since I've known him, dear, which is longer than you."

"If he keeps a harem—which I refuse to believe—he has little time for it. He travels constantly. He went to the Cameroons, explored the mountains, and named one of the highest peaks after his dear friend, Milnes, did you know that? He intends to go to Gabon—to try and capture a giant gorilla. And to the mouth of the Congo River. He's involved with trying to stop the slave traffic. He's even writing poetry again. Would you like to see some of it? Some of his best work, I believe."

"Hmm, I've seen his poetry. He wrote some for me, once, you know."

"There's one he just began," Isabel said, ignoring Louisa. "A long philosophical poem called 'The Kasidah.' "

"I have friends who have read his *City of the Saints* about polygamists in Utah. He *is* certainly an author who finds unusual material!"

"You haven't read the book yourself?"

"Actually not. I was hoping you'd find me a copy. I'm told it's most revealing."

"I take it you have an acquaintence who gossips about Richard. Who is this person?"

"Oh, Isabel, we were girls together in Boulogne, remember? I don't want you to be hurt. I do care for your feelings. Everyone in London talks about your husband—constantly."

"If that's so, then you mustn't," Isabel said. "You last and least of all. And especially not to me, Louisa, don't you see? You and I must always defend him."

"Oh, dearest, don't be such an innocent!"

"If you fail to defend him with me, I'll consider you as I do all the others who are jealous and spiteful. I have a virile husband—in a world of tame men and tame, insipid views. Others sit and chat, but Richard has always done things. He writes and they do not. He sees the world and they do not. He is worthy of talk—appreciative or vile, as it may be—but none of those who speak against him has ever done a thing deserving of comment."

"I don't really care for the way you speak to me, Isabel."

"Cousin, dearest, you don't care a whit for me—and you've proved it saying some of these things to me today. I fancy you're envious that I'm in Richard's bed and that you're stuck with only wild speculations about strong, physical love."

Louisa rose to her feet. As she put on her wrap, Isabel ate a cinnamon muffin, calming herself with food.

"The fact is, your husband's not in your bed either, is he? He's halfway to nowhere on an island nobody can remember the name of."

"Give my best to the rest of the family," Isabel said with a dismissive smile.

When Louisa had gone, Isabel felt miserable. A fever stirred inside her, a premonition of illness, and she fretted that she might take sick and die without ever holding Richard in her arms again. The next morning she did have a glowing fever, but dressed and walked to the Foreign Office in Whitehall once again; she looked so pale that she was shown into the office of Sir Austen Henry Layard, a diplomat and archaeologist who had received a number of enthusiastic letters from Burton himself. Layard found himself faced with a wife in tears.

"I beg you, please, bring Richard home," she wept. "I've been very strong for all these months, but I must see him. I can't go on."

Layard excused himself and left Isabel dabbing at her cheeks with his handkerchief. On his desk, an old French clock counted the minutes until he came back.

"I've arranged a four-month leave for your husband," he told her quietly. "The dispatch goes out this afternoon."

Isabel rose to thank Layard, but became dizzy and sat down heavily again. He summoned a cab and walked her down to the courtyard.

"I've been in these offices for weeks," she said, unable to control herself.

"Yes, I know. Please, you must stop it, too."

"I feel humiliated and silly bothering you," she said, holding Layard's sleeve. "But I've had to. I've really had to."

"Yes, quite so. Now go home and care for yourself."

That evening Isabel's mother called a doctor, who diagnosed an attack of diphtheria. Yet Isabel, though ill, surrounded herself in bed with notes and correspondence, writing to Burton and, once more, to the army, to Lady Russell, to her husband's editors. She also concocted a list titled "Rules for My Guidance as a Wife."

I.   Let your husband find in you a companion, friend, and adviser, and *confidante*, that he might miss nothing at home; and let him find in the wife what he and many other men fancy is only to be found in a mistress.

II.   Be a careful nurse when he is ailing.

III.   Make his home snug.

IV.   Improve and educate yourself in every way that he might not become weary of you.

V.   Be prepared to follow him at an hour's notice.

VI.   Do not try to hide your affection for him, but let him see and feel it in every action. Never refuse anything he asks. Keep up the honeymoon romance whether at home or in the desert. Do not make prudish bothers, which only disgust, and are not true modesty.

VII.   Perpetually work up his interests in the world.

VIII.   Never confide your domestic affairs to your female friends.

IX.   Hide his faults from everyone.

X.   Never allow anyone to speak disrespectfully of him before you. Never permit anyone to tell you anything about him, especially of his conduct with other women. Never hurt his feelings by a rude remark or jest. Never answer when he finds fault. Never reproach him when he finds fault. Always keep his heart up when he has made a failure.

XI.   Keep all disagreements for your own room, and never let others find them out.

XII.   Trust him and tell him everything, except another person's secret.

XIII. Do not bother him with religious talk. Be religious yourself and give good example. Pray and procure prayers for him, doing all you can for him without his knowing it.

XIV. Cultivate your own good health and nerves to counteract his naturally melancholy turn.

XV. Never open his letters nor appear inquisitive about anything he does not volunteer to tell you.

XVI. Never interfere between him and his family.

XVII. Keep everything going and let nothing be at a standstill; nothing would weary him like stagnation.

Grant waited twenty-two days at Kamrasi's village in Bunyoro until Speke and his men arrived in their wooden boats. Speke was in high spirits and greeted his colleague with excitement.

Kamrasi and his court gathered for an official greeting. The king was a tall, dour, muscled chieftain who used his spear like a shepherd's crook. There was none of the fancy ritual of Mutesa's court here; in dress and manners Kamrasi and his men were rough warrior types whose village consisted of grey, rude huts of wattle and thatch. At the edge of the river where Grant met the boats was a mountain of sweet yams, and around its perimeters a group of naked, sullen women kept busy culling as they glared at the new white man.

Grant, Speke, and the interpreters went forward to meet Kamrasi, who never altered his expression. He told them that he didn't care for strangers, but that he intended to show kindness to the friends of the Kabaka Mutesa.

"Splendid fellow," Grant whispered to Speke.

Bundles of gifts were unwrapped and displayed: beads, wire, mirrors, cloth, a rifle, a bottle of brandy. Kamrasi frowned over each item, always looking to see what was next.

In the end, the king offered a few gifts of his own: flour, some palm wine, and a bag of salt from a lake west of the village. Efforts at conversation continued only for a short time after the exchange of gifts, then Kamrasi gathered up his new things and retired.

Grant led Speke to an open shed, their camp: a bower of animal skins, bamboo, and clay. While slaves prepared supper, Grant and Speke exchanged news and began deciding what to do next. Speke talked about finding the Nile as it flowed from the nyanza, about the beauties of the Stones, and about the dangers on the river en route to Bunyoro. He also mentioned that he had seen an inlet of another possibly large lake, called Kyoga, which he hadn't explored because of hostile natives. Grant, in turn, reported that his leg was healing, but that they had definite problems with Kamrasi.

"He wants us to stay a very long time."

"We'll be courteous," Speke said. "But we do have to prepare and travel on."

"He wants us to remain until we've eaten all of Mutesa's cattle," Grant explained. "We just can't make him a present of Mutesa's gift to us, you see, but he and his wives and ministers do have a taste for beefsteak. So it's the same as at Mutesa's palace: lots of protocol, lengthy conversations, dances, everything. Sorry."

"What about travel north?" Speke asked.

"The Nile turns westward from here. This salt is from another lake in that direction—perhaps part of the Nile system. But there's also a jungle path leading due north, which bypasses this great westward bend in the river and any other lakes and will get us to Gondokoro in good time. I have a map of this route, and Kamrasi will provide guides. If we travel this path, we could save weeks."

"I'm for it," Speke said. "We're way off schedule now."

"But if we take this overland route—understand this, Jack—we'll not be able to say that we've completely traced out the Nile. And you have critics who would complain at such an oversight."

"There seems to be a series of lakes all along the Nile in these mountains," Speke pointed out. "We can't explore each one in the chain. No one at the Society would expect us to."

"But perhaps we should. If we're taking all this time, perhaps we should work very carefully."

"These are trying conditions," Speke argued. "Perhaps I saw only a small portion of the lake called Kyoga. Perhaps I just traveled a minor fork in the river and missed some significant landmarks. Who can say? It will be years before this region is properly mapped, but our job has been to affirm that we've found the Nile."

"I sketched this map from descriptions and information given to me by Kamrasi's guides. Here, take a look. The lake to the west looks quite large."

Grant opened the folds of a crude map. Flies buzzed around the cooking pot and settled on the edges of the paper.

"Probably inaccurate," Speke said, studying the sketch.

"Very likely so."

"I've made some sketches and I've taken a few altitude readings, but we'll have no real scientific proof of anything when we go back to London," Speke said. "We'll only know the obvious: that we found the Nile and traced it from its source in the nyanza."

"Burton and all his friends will be skeptical. Are you sure that we shouldn't follow the river westward toward this other lake?"

"The shortest way is best now, believe me," Speke replied.

That evening after supper Speke told Sidi Bombay to prepare himself for extraordinary duty. "I'm sending you northward along the jungle path with some of Kamrasi's guides," he explained. "You're my best man and know the most languages. If you reach Petherick, tell him we're coming, then, if possible, return to us. We'll start along the same path when we can."

Sidi Bombay, proud at being given this assignment and forgetting the blows Speke had dealt out, smiled broadly and showed his rows of jagged teeth.

"Remember how I went back alone to find the chronometer?" he asked his commander. "You thought you would never see me again, but you did. And you sent me for boats, so I found those. And now I go to find Petherick. I will tell him that I am a captain, the same as you."

"By all means, yes, do that," Speke agreed.

Stranded again.

Grant watched him closely in the camp at night, trying to understand all of Speke's questions and rambling commentaries.

"Do you know my curse? Did I tell you about it before or did you guess?"

"Your curse, Jack?"

"A sexual calamity. Saying it—just the words themselves—is a terrible thing for me."

Grant said nothing, just poked up the fire and waited for Speke to continue. A light rain had fallen, so the thatch above their heads creaked and dripped. Beyond, the jungle filled with wet noises: droplets oozing down each leaf and thorn, becoming soft veins of water, becoming the river's heavy flow.

"How many days since Sidi Bombay left us?"

"Hmm, tomorrow it will be twelve."

Silence between them. At times, Speke's brooding became a menace; he was a big man, a Nordic giant, Grant felt, who could possibly emerge from those morose depths with a knife or club in his hand.

"Did we hunt today? How many times have we gone hunting since I came here?"

"It was too misty today, Jack, so we didn't hunt. We've only been out a couple of times in the last week."

Again, a lapse: just the rivulets of slow time out there in the jungle.

"I'm not talking about my sexual tastes, not that at all," Speke finally went on. "No, not about preferences. About how I'm dammed up. I feel as though —" He stopped, peering into the fire.

"I don't have to hear any of this," Grant replied. "It might be best if I don't. I can't help you."

"As if my semen might come out as dust. As if I'm another element— so different from others. Not earth or air or water. As if I'm fire: meant to live in the flame and not in any of the normal elements. Don't you see?"

"No, afraid not. We needn't talk about all this, really."

"You heard those sounds out there?"

"What sounds?"

"In the jungle. Soft, wet sounds. And the Nile. That's the river, that low monotone. And the ground makes its little seeping noises. But I'm like none of it. I'm dry as powder. Believe me, I've been baked down into nothing—I'm nothing at all."

"I think you're truly exhausted. You need a good rest. You should sleep around the clock."

"Oh, God, Jim, what a clod you are."

Burton returned to London, but not entirely to Isabel. He spent the Christmas holiday of 1862 with her family, sitting through all the usual sentimentalities: the spangled tree, the opening of gifts, the meals of greasy stuffings, watery puddings, and heavy cakes.

He was mostly in the company of men and alone with his writings. *City of the Saints* had been published, dedicated to Milnes, and although it had received only a mild public response, Burton was already in the midst of an enormous new project soon to become two separate books: *Wanderings in West Africa* and *Abeokuta and the Cameroons*. At daybreak each morning he was scratching out words, sipping coffee, and searching his notes; he worked until noon, then shaved and joined old and new friends at Bertolini's restaurant in Leicester Square.

"Are you off again?" Isabel asked him one noonday.

"Yes, be back this evening."

"We have invitations, remember. What shall I say to Dr. Bird and the others? And are we going up to Fryston as we've been asked to do?"

"Everyone knows I'm writing. They'll understand. And, after all, we've had several social evenings since I've come back on leave."

Isabel's face hardened, then relaxed. "You came in so late last night," she managed. "I worry you're tiring yourself. And then you work more. And come to bed so late."

"Yes, I'm at it early and late," he said, tying his scarf. "And now I'm off to lunch."

"Are you and I going to stay apart during your leave?" she suddenly said, in spite of herself.

"I've been thinking of taking you with me when I return to duty," he said. "Not to Fernando Po. But we could stop at Tenerife in the Canary Islands. A lovely spot. Take ourselves a holiday together."

"Oh, Richard, could we?"

"Yes, I think we should plan on it."

She kissed him goodbye and watched him leave. Standing at the window and observing him, she saw something in his stride: a small sign of that old trouble with his legs, perhaps, some small pain. Yet he held up his head and appeared jaunty, and she watched with pride until he disappeared down the street.

Burton ate veal and spaghetti that noon with a number of friends including James MacQueen. The talk, as conversations had gone for their last meetings, concerned a point in scholarly politics: it would be better for Burton's career if he called himself an anthropologist rather than an explorer. An influential lunch guest was Dr. James Hunt, a medical man by profession but also an amateur scientist, who seemed to understand the esoteric workings of university faculties, scholarly groups, and even the Royal Geographical Society.

"Geography is not exactly a science," Hunt explained. "So your Society, Burton, has a difficult time getting funds from the government and recognition from the British Association—our most esteemed scientific organization. I propose we form our own society. An anthropology club, with a fancy title."

"And we should have a magazine," MacQueen added.

"Oh, definitely. A scholarly journal," Hunt agreed. "We'll ask the government to help sponsor us. And no one is going to reject the proposal. To be against Science would be very much like being against Motherhood these days."

"Good, I'll write for the magazine," Burton said.

They drank Chianti, laughed, and drew up a few by-laws. In a light-hearted manner, they decided they should concentrate on various social characteristics of foreign peoples in exotic lands. Burton offered to contribute articles on sex and physiology.

"Is it true that you lined up some wives in a Moslem village and studied their privates by candlelight?" MacQueen asked him, laughing.

"I have broad scholarly interests," Burton assured him.

The men invented more by-laws, ate more pasta, and decided to become the Anthropological Society of London. Hunt, whose bushy sideburns framed his face, began an impromptu lecture on the cranial bones of the Negro, asserting that a Negro's brain was smaller and inferior to a white man's. He based this opinion on his study of two skulls that he claimed sat on his desk at his office.

After lunch, Burton and MacQueen walked through Soho.

"If you establish yourself as an anthropologist, you'll possibly serve the Geographical Society better than Speke," MacQueen suggested. "They believe that Speke will return victorious and make them all much more respectable in the eyes of the government. But what they badly need—much more than another successful explorer—is to have themselves represented in the British Association of Science. Actually, you're their best man for that. I'll help them see it."

"You hate Speke, don't you?"

"Detest him. I hope he's lost in a bog."

"If Speke does come back, he'll have all his information wrong," Burton said. "He'll have no scientific proofs for the Society, the British Association, or anyone else—just a few stuffed animal specimens, if I know him."

"Mind that you write and think like an anthropologist," MacQueen said. "Believe me, you'll become very useful to men like Murchison."

"I was a soldier once and decided—almost on a whim—to become an explorer. Now I suppose I can decide to become an anthropologist—although, damn, I'm not exactly sure what one is."

At Fryston Hall the Burtons found that Swinburne had moved in.

"I very much like it here," he announced. "The sheets are clean and the books are dirty." He wore a dressing gown whose sash trailed the floors and carried a bottle of brandy and a Persian cat with him wherever he went. Burton brightened when he saw the poet again, but Isabel knew on sight that Swinburne was an alcoholic and an atheist.

"Yes, well, I do think he might be an atheist," Burton told her. "But you'll be relieved to know that he's also a hypocrite about it. I know for a fact that he composes poetry in praise of God—or certainly with a modicum of respect. He'll write in praise of almost anything, naturally: the Empire, nature, men and women, even himself."

"I can't care for Algernon," Isabel said stiffly.

"No, of course not," Burton replied. "So leave him to me."

The dinners were long and elaborate. Milnes, who had favorably reviewed *City of the Saints*, spent his time after the conversational meals reading the manuscripts of Burton's new works while the ladies chatted. The poet and the explorer, who spent considerable time trying to define anthropology and the social sciences, retired to distant rooms.

"Can't say I care for your new works all that much," Milnes suddenly said one evening when he joined Burton and Swinburne beside the fireplace. Sleet fell against the windows, and for a moment as Burton tried to adjust to this remark there was only silence except for that bleak sound. Milnes shook his head slowly, and his mouth made that little round hole. He was quite serious.

"Perhaps I'm writing too quickly," Burton allowed.

"No, you're changing. You're picking up—hmm, drawing-room opinions. You disapprove of other authors, old men who dance, mistakes in history books, Jews, Americans, Irishmen, missionaries, Negroes, the tsetse fly, sharks, and slavery. Sometimes you're amusing. Sometimes I hear the opinions of others in your words. I like the parts best where you tell us about your travels and where you describe the sights and sounds of places we haven't been."

Milnes had never ventured a criticism. For a moment longer neither Burton nor Swinburne could speak.

"Oh, I fancy the author," Swinburne finally said. "When he was young he was eccentric. Now he's growing cranky."

"You've been staying in country houses with Isabel's relatives," Milnes went on.

The truth hurt, but Burton tried to recover. "You're my dear friend and undoubtedly my best critic," Burton said. "I'll never forget living in France and writing in your house."

Milnes, somehow, couldn't stop. "The bit about Irishmen," he continued. "You're Irish yourself—or your father was. The slander is simply fashionable. You should give us your best, Dick, which is always splendid."

Milnes sat on the ottoman between his guests and lit a long, curved opium pipe. An awkward silence fell, but somehow they managed to begin a discussion of narcotics. All three were in favor, so eventually decided to laugh.

Later in his bedroom with Isabel, Burton stood at the window gazing out on a frozen ground.

"Won't you come to bed?" she called from beneath the coverlet.

"Damned English weather," he said. "Who needs four months of leave here? Let's hurry and go away."

"To the Canary Islands? Sounds wonderful," Isabel said. "I want to persuade you to take me to Fernando Po, too."

"Beastly, stupid weather," he muttered to himself. The window where he stood was both access and mirror. He saw the snowy fields outside, the dripping sleet edging down the glass pane, Isabel propped up in bed behind him, the reflection of the satinwood table with its lamp of cameo glass, his own scarred face. Each image blent and stacked itself on the others: layers of airy facade and of realities as real as any could be.

Until their ship sailed, Burton kept up a heavy correspondence and wrote toward the completion of his two new works. In a long passage, he made a case for polygamy again, calling it "the instinctive law of nature." Then he dedicated *Abeokuta and the Cameroons* to "My best Friend, My Wife."

He learned through relatives that Edward's condition was unchanged, so decided not to visit his brother.

Every day at noon he was at Bertolini's with friends.

While in Isabel's company, he kept at his desk. They were at her parents' house these last days, which he deplored, so he sat surrounded by cartons of books and manuscripts, his brandy hidden in a drawer.

"What are you writing now?" she asked him once, knowing that he had finished work on the books.

"My poem," he told her, not looking up.

"Yes, your religious poem. I'm happy about that."

Knowing that his works would never sell enough copies to justify an investment from a legitimate publisher, Burton arranged at those noon meals to have the books printed with his own funds and then brought out under the auspices of the Anthropological Society. He also paid to print an edition of a favorite work, *The Prairie Traveller*, by Captain Randolph B. Marcy of the

United States Army, which he supplied with footnotes and comments about his own trip across America.

Both at the restaurant and alone with Isabel, he endeavored to stay slightly tipsy.

"Do you think I'm a genius?" he asked his wife the day before they sailed. He sipped at the flask hidden in his desk drawer and pulled his cotton robe around his waist. Isabel folded clothes into a trunk.

"A genius? Yes, very much so."

"Even when I'm soused?"

"Hmm, yes, in spite of a very bad habit."

"I think you probably like me better when I'm soused. I'm more in your power. But, of course, not really. The men at Bertolini's think I'm at my best when I'm drunk— much more outlandish and amusing. Perhaps I am."

"I never want you in my power."

"Oh, yes, you do!"

"Don't raise your voice, please, Richard. Listen to me, too: I only want you in the Lord's power."

"Yes, in the grip of your God! That's the very same as in your own grip, don't you see?"

"Please, dear," she said, trying to quiet him.

"It's not your ignorance I detest," he told her. "It's your ignorance of your ignorance."

She immediately turned away and began to cry. After a loud sob left her throat, her mother and father knocked discreetly at the door to ask if anything was wrong.

"Yes, I'm raping and beating her!" Burton shouted through the closed door. "And she seems to be enjoying only half of it!"

"I'm quite all right!" Isabel called out.

"I'm a drunk, irreligious brute!" Burton boomed at them. "And I'm being held prisoner in a tacky little house with worn rugs in the middle of London! Help! Get me out of here! Help, I'm dying!"

They sailed into warmer waters, arrived on Madeira, then went to the island of Tenerife, where Burton found them some dusty rooms at a mountain inn. While he gathered reading and writing material around himself on a sunny patio, Isabel cleaned the rooms, filled the vases with fresh flowers, and tried to contain her excitement at being in a foreign place with her famous husband.

"I want to make love at least twice a day," he told her. "Think you can manage it?"

"I was thinking more on the order of three times daily," she answered.

"We ought to begin," he said. "That's a busy schedule."

The morning sunlight slanted across their bed through the uneven shutters of a window that looked out to sea. He liked Isabel to lie there, naked and open, illumined by those soft stripes; her body was alabaster, heavy, Grecian, and his fingers traced its contours.

They walked the tropical paths hand in hand, stopping in villages where they talked to the native shopkeepers and guides. Burton decided that they should climb the peak of Tenerife, especially when he learned that the ascent hadn't been attempted in the winter months since 1797. Isabel planned various picnic treats for their climb while he bought some local cigars and allowed that those and his flask of brandy would be all he needed.

"This is the very happiest time of my life—this very instant," she said, lying in his arms at night. They could hear the wind in the palm leaves and the faraway hushed whisper of the surf. "And you must relent and allow me to travel on with you to your consulate this time. I know that Aga and I could make your life there much more pleasant."

"That island is nothing like this one," he said. "This is a rather well-established tourist stop. Fernando Po is a little scab of coral."

"I don't care," she said, rolling on top of him.

"We'll talk about it later," he said, closing her mouth with a kiss.

The peak of Tenerife was more formidable than either of them had guessed. From their hillside inn they took the upward path with two guides, starting too late in the day to reach the summit. Their camping gear was inadequate; without cooking utensils they sat around the fire that evening munching on fruit and emptying Burton's brandy supply. The night was cool, so that they all slept in a circle around the little blaze, no blankets between them, and in the morning they devoured their only meal of bread and cheese, hoping to nourish themselves for the strenuous last climb. They started off in darkness, led by the guides with torches, and reached the peak just before sunrise. Isabel gasped for breath. Even in the coolness, their clothes were soaked with perspiration, and the breeze at the summit chilled them quickly.

The sun rose out of the sea.

The guides, both Christians, suggested a prayer service, as this was a Sunday morning, and Isabel happily agreed.

"No, thanks," Burton said. "I'll just have a cigar while the rest of you worship." He struggled to light a match in the breeze, finally succeeded, and blew out a puff of smoke as Isabel and the guides knelt in prayer.

"We pray, too, Almighty God, that the only unbeliever in our little party might one day receive the gift of faith," she intoned, as her husband tossed pebbles into a nearby ravine. In a voice filled with piety and loud enough for him to hear, she also prayed that he might ease his habitual drinking, find happiness in his work, and enjoy success with his writing. In all, it was too much for Burton, who found himself angry.

346

When they came down the mountain that afternoon he hurried ahead, leaving Isabel and the guides to negotiate the rocky path; by the time she reached the inn he had bathed, poured himself a brandy and lemon, and settled down with the copy of *Moby Dick* he had never managed to finish.

"I fell and skinned my knee," she called to him as she entered their suite.

"Hope you're not badly injured," he called back. "Your bath is ready. Use some alcohol on the cut."

After supper they came back to their rooms, undressed, and made love again. He was wild for his own pleasure, she felt, heaving himself into her, yet his very selfishness excited her and she came with him. A great black lion: his hair splayed out, his nostrils wide, his muscled shoulders steady above her as his hips worked.

Afterward he stood at the window watching the moonlight on the sea. An odor of jasmine and decay wafted on the breeze.

"I'm making preparations to leave tomorrow," he said. "You won't be able to join me, Isabel, because I don't intend to stay at home even there. I want to travel down to the mouth of the Congo. Somehow I want to get into the fight against slavery. There's just too much to do."

She sat on the side of the bed tying the sash of her gown. "I have to go with you," she said, her voice cracking. "I must. I beg of you, Richard, please don't send me back to my parents! I'm not myself there!"

"We must take a long view of my career and our marriage."

"Oh, darling, please, do let me go! I'll die if you don't!"

"There will be other consulates."

"I'll do nicely on the island with Aga while you make excursions! I'll make a good home for you. Please." She stood behind him, her arms encircling his waist.

"I don't want you with me," he said.

"I'm not a woman without design or will," she said, coming around to face him. "I'll not have a marriage like this!"

"You'll have the marriage as you can get it!" he said, speaking more loudly and sharply than he had meant.

"You're angry about my prayer on the summit," she said. "Don't be. I'll never offend you with my religion again, I promise! You've known all the world's religions and you're a religion unto yourself, but I'm not! So please don't be angry!" She wept as she argued, her fists bunched tightly underneath her chin. "Oh, Richard, don't cut me off!"

"You'll not go to Fernando Po with me."

She was on her knees before him, embracing his legs.

"Get up," he asked. "Don't do this, Isabel—"

As she crawled after him, following him, not letting go, her injured knee began to bleed. She wept and babbled as he tried to lift her up.

"If I'm going to be cast out, give me your child first! Oh, *please.* Don't abandon me again! You don't know how I feel! You can't!"

She wouldn't let go of his leg, so he couldn't raise her to her feet. She was down there at his bare feet smearing blood on her face, mingling it with her tears.

"Don't do that!" he cried at her. "Now stop it!"

"Oh, God," she wept, and she gathered the blood from her leg and clawed her face with it. In the moonlit room she became an apparition; she was the hag of the abyss, the unearthly crone, and he recoiled from her with pity and with terror.

Sidi Bombay returned from his mission wearing new trousers, a fez, and a broad smile. His five-week journey had taken him to Faloro, a small Nile outpost, and back along the same jungle trail to Speke and Grant. At Faloro he had met two hundred Sudanese porters, who, among other matters, told him that they had been in the area for months awaiting an expedition from the south.

"They're waiting for us!" Speke said. "Where was Petherick? You didn't see Petherick?"

"Their white man was to the west hunting ivory," Sidi Bombay replied. "So they couldn't read the letter you sent. The big man was Mohammed. He say welcome. But he cannot tell if you are the one he wishes to assist."

"Of course we are! And we must go to them!"

That same day Grant arranged to give Kamrasi everything they had: Mutesa's remaining cattle, all trading goods, all items of value with the exception of their rifles and ammunition. The guns, Grant explained, belonged only to the white men—the implication being that if Kamrasi wanted the weapons he had to take them by force.

The next morning they rowed away from Bunyoro and King Kamrasi in a flotilla of large canoes. They found the river swampy, filled with floating islands of papyrus and numerous hippo and crocodiles, but they were glad to be moving once more. Their strength had returned, and they felt determined.

At nearby Karuma Falls they put ashore to take the jungle path northward. Sidi Bombay would be their guide now, having made the journey himself; their loads were light, consisting mostly of food and ammunition, and the dusty path was well marked. Grant still worried that they should possibly stay with the river, tracing it out carefully, and said so.

"By all reports we're missing a great bend to the west—and another lake," he told Speke.

"Yes, but speed is important now. By the time we actually reach Petherick we'll be more than a year late. It's a wonder they're still waiting for us!"

"We do have a map of sorts," Grant said, referring to the drawing made from descriptions provided by Kamrasi's guides.

"Exactly so. A valuable map. And we'll touch the river again to the north and float along it to victory!"

"Assuming it's the same river," Grant replied under his breath.

The path led them out of the jungle onto a plateau of dry grass, where the breeze bore the faint scent of the desert.

At night Speke seemed disoriented again, strolling aimlessly around the perimeters of their camp. He and Grant seldom talked.

During the daytime he hunted as their caravan advanced. His shots were uncanny: antelope on distant hills, birds in flight.

In one of the villages they passed they found a *strego:* an old Arab seer who read fortunes by the movement of sand in a bowl. Speke sat with the old man in a long conference, watching as the Arab moved his finger around in the sand and murmured, "Oh, oh!"

Grant heard Speke reply, "Ah, yes, I thought so," but when he later asked his companion what the *strego* had prophesied, Speke wouldn't say.

Before they reached Faloro they found the river again: a muddy swirl, its rapids filled with brown foam. As they came down its banks they saw a tall black woman bathing naked, her back turned to them, sunlight glinting off the sheen of her skin; she had a narrow waist and small hard buttocks, so the men hooted as they approached. When they came near, she turned around and they saw that her face was horribly pockmarked: every pore pitted, so that her eyes, nose, and mouth were barely visible among the crags and craters.

When she smiled the men turned away and marched another half day before making camp.

After a dry march through several tribal lands, Speke and Grant came to Faloro: mud huts, a few palms along the river, brown grass, a few camels and goats. Guns fired, signaling their approach. At last a Sudanese officer in an obscure uniform ran out, accompanied by men with drums and fifes, to welcome them with a kiss—which both explorers graciously refused. Next came Mohammed, the major domo; he boomed out his welcome, then began to assert his authority by lashing out at his workers with a leather whisk, insulting his aides, and acting the loud fool. Sidi Bombay could convey only a little of what the leader had to say. At one point, talking loudly and wildly, the big man pushed down his workers, pretended to bugger them, beat himself on the chest, and made Grant laugh at the pantomime, but without any comprehension of what it meant.

They went into the outpost, where Speke refused the offer of a vermin-ridden hut and ordered tents pitched. Sidi Bombay tried to extract more than Mohammed's apology that Petherick was not present.

"Yes, we see that. But where is he?" Speke kept asking.

"He rides the same camel with his wife," Sidi Bombay managed.

"Hmm, glad to learn that. But why is he not here?"

A long exchange continued between the Sudanese and the interpreter, with only a few occasional facts surfacing. "These men are not employed by Petherick, but by the Italian," Sidi Bombay offered at one point.

"The Italian?"

"DeBono he is called. He is not here either."

"Yes, very apparent."

"And the consul is a very large man with a wife."

"Indeed Petherick is. Glad to have news of it."

"He only just arrived in this place. Perhaps he is at Gondokoro."

"Gone back to Gondokoro? Can we go there?"

"The consul is on the camel with his wife. He has men with guns. They are trading ivory and slaves in villages to the west."

"Slaves?" Grant put in. "Did he say that?"

Sidi Bombay and the Sudanese talked again. Mohammed gestured, laughed for no reason, and slapped away flies with his whisk.

"Slaves, truly," Sidi Bombay finally said. "The consul is a big man with no money. In order to have money, he finds ivory and slaves."

That evening Speke and Grant dined on mutton, bread, honey, beer, and coffee. They tried to work out the confusions of whom they were with, what had happened to Petherick, and what to do next.

"If we're more than a year late arriving at this spot and Petherick himself only just arrived, he failed us utterly," Speke said. "He didn't keep his word. He could have been responsible for our deaths, do you see that?"

"Yes, I suppose so. Do you believe that he's actually slaving?"

"Somehow I do believe it. This is a desperate place. If he's here without funds, he must probably accumulate ivory and slaves, then sell them—or die himself. I know Mohammed's a fool, but why would he lie?"

"We should certainly see for ourselves in this matter," Grant cautioned.

"I think we do see clearly. If my intuitions are correct, this little army of Sudanese has slaving in mind. Petherick has obviously joined them—and probably has a platoon of these soldiers with him in those villages to the west. But we'll know soon enough."

The next morning the explorers found Mohammed and more than one hundred men preparing to go on an excursion to the southwest. Speke argued that they should all proceed immediately to Gondokoro, but the Sudanese had other plans.

"I could take the remaining Sudanese force and march to Gondokoro," Speke suggested through Sidi Bombay.

The answer came back slowly, once again: the Bari natives to the north are too fierce, so we must all travel together later, Mohammed said. Also, travel on the river beyond Gondokoro was impossible at this time of year. If Petherick was at Gondokoro now, he would be there later.

"We're to wait, then?" Speke asked.

"Yes, wait," Sidi Bombay answered sadly.

Another crazy delay.

Waiting for the Sudanese to return, Speke became decisive about Petherick, who was a man they should never have trusted, he claimed, and who was undoubtedly slaving, as Mohammed declared. "The reason Petherick was never worried about money appears simple," Speke argued. "He knew this stretch of the Nile and knew he could find slaves and sell them! You see what we've gotten ourselves into? Our whole expedition can be discredited by this person!"

"It's all a bit of a poser," Grant admitted. "But let's wait and see."

"Men in these latitudes go mad with power," Speke said. "With their guns they feel they can do anything to the blacks! And there are very few men such as Rigby who mean to stop slavery, very few indeed!"

Among those forlorn huts at the edge of the river the Sudanese soldiers kept a few women. In the evenings the explorers could hear the loud copulations accompanied by shouts of encouragement from those who watched. During the days Speke walked around the settlement and waited out the idle hours. Blue columns of rain appeared far away in the east.

After more than a week Mohammed and his men came back with a dozen young slave girls, ivory, and thirty head of cattle. They had clearly plundered some villages, so Speke's guess seemed confirmed: Petherick had either used or joined these swine.

"Look at those small black girls," Speke said. "You know what's going to happen, don't you?"

"Yes, I know," Grant answered quietly.

"I can't bear staying here. We'll make up a caravan and march toward Gondokoro immediately."

As they put together arms and rations, Mohammed once again argued that hostile tribes were along the way.

"We have rifles!" Speke snapped at him. "What sort of men are you to be afraid of a few naked warriors?" As Sidi Bombay translated, Mohammed shuffled his feet, laughed falsely, shook his head, and rolled his idiotic eyes.

At last the caravan was set: Speke's remaining nineteen men, eleven Sudanese who were anxious to head north, a few loads of the barest camp materials. They started at a quick pace, Grant keeping up without further trouble. Under orders from Speke to make as much noise as possible, the

Sudanese sang an Arabic chant—a harsh, nasal, unmelodious rhythm—so as the caravan passed close to the villages of the Bari natives, no one came out either to greet them or to harass them.

They walked long days, stopping in the evenings to camp. Speke talked only of Petherick, citing him for arriving at Gondokoro later than he had promised, for conspiring with slavers, and for possibly ruining the reputation of the expedition. Grant kept urging caution. "You're very emotional about those poor slave girls Mohammed brought in. Steady yourself."

"I can't abide failure or slavery," Speke replied. "Petherick is abominable."

After four days runners arrived to report that Mohammed had decided to catch up with Speke's small group. Within hours the army of Sudanese arrived with tons of ivory carried by six hundred new slaves. This huge caravan would proceed toward Gondokoro in luxury: goat's milk and ghee, beer, dried beef, pillows, women, torches, and tents.

As they camped together that first night, Speke arranged a conference with the leader.

"I want to know the truth about Petherick," he stated, as Sidi Bombay translated. "Is he an active slaver?"

"Very severe man. Very good slaver," came the reply. Mohammed seemed proud to know such a brutal, effective white man.

"That's all I need to hear," Speke said, satisfied.

The next night they camped within sight of an attractive oasis: palm trees, tufts of green grass, an old well, a few ruined stone huts. Yet no Sudanese would go near it, claiming that it was a haunted spot where ghosts drew men into complete madness. Everyone slept in the brushy countryside, then, looking at this tempting bower; the deep, dreadful moaning of the slaves and the silence of the stars kept company.

Gondokoro on the banks of the Nile: a backwater toilet where rats ate the food in every house, then scurried to the river where, in turn, they were eaten by crocodiles. The inhabitants at the outpost defecated on their own flat roofs. Donkeys, chained slaves, and soldiers wandered the narrow streets.

A British missionary station, a large whitewashed compound, vacant because its pastor had died of dysentery, served as headquarters for Speke and Grant. The servant boys expected the Pethericks to return soon and happily helped store the explorers' gear.

Speke took a walk toward the waterfront, hoping to hear news of Petherick's whereabouts and activities. As he reached the docks, he saw a rotund, bearded white man striding toward him, and for a moment thought this was Petherick. But it wasn't—and as quickly as Speke became confused the stranger became excited, ran forward, grabbed Speke, and hoisted him off his feet in a powerful hug.

"It's you!" the big man bellowed.

"Yes, quite!" Speke managed, the breath squeezed out of him. He liked the greeting, laughed, and began to recognize the man as he gave his name.

"Samuel White Baker! Don't you remember me? On the frigate sailing toward Aden! You shot gulls at the back of the ship! You wanted to visit Africa and shoot a lion!"

"Baker, yes!" Speke returned the embrace, feeling suddenly that in this huge man's grasp he had ended his journey. After this, he felt, all would be easy: a mere excursion north toward home. They stood there in the hot sun pounding each other and laughing.

"I can't believe it's you!" Baker kept saying. "You're not dead!"

"And I can't believe you're here!" Speke answered. "Where's Petherick? Did you come in his place? What goes on?"

They dined in the empty mission that night by candlelight. The servant boys prepared curry and salads, and Mrs. Baker wore a white dress; she looked so young and stunning that both Speke and Grant watched her constantly, even as they talked with her husband.

"Let's see, where to start?" Baker said. "The Prince Consort died. And the American Civil War started. And the Royal Geographical Society has given you its founder's medal—because it imagines you dead!"

They talked excitedly, trying to catch up on news and to assess everything that had happened.

"Don't forget the three Dutch ladies," Mrs. Baker added.

"Oh, yes, there were three ladies from Amsterdam who sailed up the Nile to rescue you," Baker said. "They retired with fever at Khartoum. One was a baroness! Ah, you can't believe all the speculation!"

"What about Petherick?" Speke asked.

"Well, he's somewhere to the west."

"Trading slaves?"

Baker and his wife shared a telling glance. "There's some rumor of that, but we know nothing," Baker said.

"But you have your suspicions?"

"Never met the man. I've only heard rumors. But one thing I can tell you: he has no boats or supplies for you in Gondokoro. If you count on him for aid and transportation downriver, don't."

"Then he has failed us completely," Speke said, his mouth tight. "He has public funds, some money from my own family, the support of the Society—and he was late arriving and nowhere to be found!"

After dinner they retired to the pastor's study, where Grant showed

Baker the map dictated by Kamrasi's guides. They discussed the Nile: its source at the Stones, its series of lakes, possible tributaries, the great westward bend at Bunyoro.

"You didn't trace out the whole river?" Baker asked, learning slowly what had been accomplished.

"Not really," Speke answered.

"Then we could go forward—my wife and I—and possibly share in your prize?" The Bakers looked from Speke to Grant and back again.

"Yes, certainly," Speke agreed. "Give him the map, Jim. Yes, I think he could very well make some valuable contribution after we've sailed for Egypt."

Grant passed the map into Baker's keeping. The big man held it lightly, as if it might disintegrate like a delicate autumn leaf.

"I don't know how to thank you for this," Baker said.

"It may be a perfectly dreadful map," Grant allowed.

"The whole river system is immense," Speke said. "Might take years to trace it out. Everyone can have a piece of the glory, my good man, but we're the first, the very first, you see, and we've jolly well proved what we set out to prove: that the Nile rises in Victoria Nyanza and flows to this known outpost and into the desert."

"Yes, you're indeed the first," Baker agreed.

"Now tell me about Mohammed and Petherick," Speke said, returning to his new obsession. "Do you suppose our consul hired the Sudanese? Or did he just conveniently find them in these parts and make use of them?"

The Bakers looked at one another with some confusion. "I've no idea if there's any connection at all," Baker said, folding the map into his coat. "There was a Maltese trader named DeBono. He and Mohammed had an arrangement, as I understand matters. But, in a sense, Petherick, DeBono, and Mohammed are rival traders. No, I couldn't say at all that Petherick and Mohammed are colleagues."

"Did Mohammed tell you that Petherick was trading slaves?" Mrs. Baker asked quietly. "If so, he might have done it to discredit a white man who was a competitor in ivory trading."

"Yes, that's possible," her husband added.

"I'm convinced Petherick has little interest in his job, in our expedition, or in anything else except his own profits," Speke said.

"Ah, Jack, careful," Grant cautioned.

"My learning doesn't come out of books and idle study like Burton's. And unlike him and others, I can size up men. Believe me. You, for instance, Baker: you're solid stock. I have no second thoughts about helping you toward a little exploration of your own because I'm confident you'll do the crown—and me—great credit. But I never trusted Petherick, not for a minute. And here's the proof of it: he's not here, is he? He's cavorting in the bush someplace."

"I do appreciate your trust of me," Baker replied.

Grant resisted mentioning how everyone seemed to like Petherick when they planned their strategy at Jordans before the expedition.

"I won't use Petherick's help, even if he has some to offer," Speke went on. "Do you have boats I could use, Baker?"

"Yes, of course. While we follow the Nile south, you and Grant can take our boats as far as the cataracts at Khartoum, then send them back for us."

They all agreed.

Filling their glasses with Baker's best port, they went to the courtyard, where the night was starry, beautiful, and smelly. Somewhere across the sewers of the town someone played an off-key tune on some indistinguishable horn.

Three days later Petherick and his wife showed up.

"But I have boats for you!" Petherick said. "You won't use them?"

"Samuel Baker has boats. We've come to an arrangement." Speke was cold and brittle. He only nodded politely to Mrs. Petherick when she entered the mission, brushing the dust off her clothes; she wore a heavy dress, boots, and riding habit; her smile quickly faded when she saw Speke.

"Please, what's wrong?" she asked.

"Nothing, madame," Speke replied.

"Jack, please, we must have dinner and talk about so many things," Petherick stammered. "You will see us this evening?"

"Yes, we'll talk," Speke allowed.

The Bakers made their excuses, Grant made his, so Speke and the Pethericks dined together at a meal filled with awkward silences. When Speke reviewed his travels, his tone was formal and distant.

"You should have pressed on toward us," he told Petherick. "Now I'm afraid the Bakers intend to explore upriver on their own. You obviously had business with Mohammed and the Sudanese that detained you."

"Mohammed and his cutthroats are scum," Petherick said. "I put him in jail in Khartoum, once, and I know and detest his every move in these parts. Did he tell you something about me?"

"He told me you were a brutal slaver, the same as he is."

"That's a lie, of course, if that's what's bothering you!"

"You were not here waiting for us!" Speke said, raising his voice. "And now that you are, you have little to offer."

"Friend, listen to me. The Nile is only passable two months of the year. We had to wait until we could navigate it. Even so, *you* weren't here either. Both of us have suffered for two years, doing everything we can for this moment. You must not listen to insinuations. You mustn't think ill of us."

"I hurried away from Grant—left him alone, poor man, with a swollen leg—so that I could join with you. For months I've thought of nothing except our reunion. I want to keep faith with you now. I want to keep our friendship —which is why I'm here dining with you."

Petherick managed a sip of his wine. His wife seemed frozen in place. "I would die, Jack, if we were not friends."

"It did—annoy me," Speke said, "that you weren't waiting with boats and trading goods in order."

"I'm sorry to have disappointed you. But it's all easily explained, as you see. And you'll remember that I said it would cost five thousand pounds. It has. And I received less than a quarter of that from the Society. The rest I've made up with my own toil and initiative. I've worked tirelessly. Be careful that you don't ruin my reputation and break my heart all at once."

Suddenly Speke stood up and let his serviette fall to the floor. A stony, withdrawn look came into his face, as if he listened to other voices. "I don't know," he stated, in a long, cold drawl, pronouncing each word as if he had practiced a memorized speech. "I find that I don't believe you. And I won't need your boats. I won't need your help. I do not wish to recognize help that comes too late with too little."

Mrs. Petherick stood up, too, with her face trembling in anger. "Oh, Speke," she managed, her voice quavering. "Your heartlessness in this will recoil on you."

"You can't mean it," Petherick said in a hoarse whisper, moving toward the door as Speke prepared to leave the room.

"I understand that you have a quantity of cloth," Speke said, turning at the door.

"Yes, several loads," Petherick said. "We traded our ivory purchases. I have all you'll need for the trip north."

"On second thought, you can help, then," Speke said with a polite aloofness. "I'll use mostly Baker's boats and goods, but we're short of cloth."

He left the Pethericks to discuss their position. Early the next morning they emerged from their bedroom at the mission to find the Bakers loading their camels for a trip to the lakes and the upper reaches of the Nile; Speke and Grant were already at the riverfront, preparing their vessels.

When the moon was good, they often sailed at night. The land around them looked like snow in the brightness.

During the hot days they stopped wherever shade beckoned them. Various ruins appeared along the banks of the Nile: piles of ancient stones often used as latrines by men and camels who passed by. The birds, too, seemed fond of violating the old monuments.

In a hard little village sheltered by a few scrawny palms, Speke saw a mummy's dark wrinkled face. The inhabitants displayed their prize in the open air, standing it against a wall near the town well. Beside it were the long stone troughs where camels were watered, the sandy floor beneath their feet yellowed with piss.

"Effendi! Effendi!" the children cried out at Speke and Grant, holding out their grubby hands for alms.

Then back to the river: the slow days and nights, horizons of low bush country, sand dunes, the brownish grey of the water gliding by.

One day, seeking shade, they stopped on a small island adorned by two palm trees and thick reeds. An Arab sat under the palms playing cards with himself, slapping down the swords and cups of a Tarot deck. He never spoke or acknowledged them during the hours they surrounded him, and when they left he still sat there, marooned without a boat, alone.

As Speke and Grant entered Khartoum, the river widened and filled with small boats, noisy bells and horns, and that ancient and exciting traffic. Whitewashed buildings glistened in the sun.

Speke asked the boat pilot where the Blue Nile from Ethiopia joined their river. "At that last bend," the pilot informed him.

"In that great clump of bulrushes," Grant told Speke. "I suppose we missed it!"

"We should really go have a look at the confluence of the two rivers," Speke said. "But, oh, well, no doubt we're in Khartoum—and there's lots to do!"

Aides at the consulate put them in rooms normally occupied by the Pethericks, and at the consul's desk Speke composed a letter to Norton Shaw at the Society in London.

Inform Sir Roderick Murchison that all is well, that we are in latitude 14°30' upon the Nile, and that the Nile is settled.

Sidi Bombay, Mabruki, and the remaining men of the nineteen faithful who had traveled with the expedition all the way from Zanzibar were given European quarters with pillowed beds. They giggled like schoolgirls in the marbled hallways of the consulate and bathed in its tiled pool—the first time in their lives any of them had ever bathed indoors.

Grant stood at a window with a glass of French wine gazing at a minaret with storks all over it; the birds looked like part of the whitewashed architecture. He stood there until the golden sun of the pharaohs gave everything an orange, soft hue.

After a meal and a long night's sleep, Speke composed a long letter to the Pethericks, thanking them for their hospitality and efforts and wishing them their "health and safety in the far interior." The letter made no mention of his disappointments or hostilities—and he failed to associate this letter with the one

357

he had written to Burton at Suez years before, the reassurance that all was well and the promise that when he returned to England he would say or do nothing harmful.

That second afternoon delegates from other consulates, Moslem leaders, British officers and their wives, merchants and other well-wishers arrived. Speke and Grant, their uniforms washed but wrinkled, stood in a reception line. The meal lasted hours—filled with many flattering toasts—and at midnight Speke went out into the streets alone for a stroll.

A sultry night air hovered in the narrow lanes and corridors. He walked through darkened arcades strewn with straw mats, a cobalt sky visible through overhanging slats and rafters; figures in soft cloaks passed by; an occasional swirl of dust raised itself on a puff of breeze.

Success overwhelmed him, and he felt a godlike elation: nothing could be denied him now, all was his.

A young boy followed and babbled at him as he turned beside the river. The Arabic words were incomprehensible, yet the child drew close and his thin body brushed Speke's arm as he laughed and talked. Clearly, the boy was both offering and asking, and his company became a pleasure.

At last they were in a maze of smelly alleyways, where the twang of some stringed instrument sounded faintly above the rooftops.

"Here, come here," Speke instructed the boy, pulling him forward by his loose gown. He took a close look at the urchin: a smiling, willing, dark face. Then he pressed a British coin into the boy's palm.

"Over here," he ordered, and he leaned against a wall. Pushing the boy's head down, he unbuttoned his trousers and presented himself; the small wet mouth found him.

A cat gave the night its questioning meow. A shuttered window closed above their heads. Feeling the powerful surge deep inside, Speke said to himself, there, all my life, all my life, there, all the days of my life.

After a few days of rest they sailed for Cairo.

The booming cataracts could be heard for miles in the desert silence. They moved forward in a sailing barge; its keel cutting through the water, its sails full, a giant Nubian boatman at the tiller.

At times they rode the Nile's less powerful rapids, but at some of the fiercest cataracts they kept to the banks, the men on shore straining at the ropes, swarms of sand flies and mosquitoes biting them.

Distant pyramids.

They heard of a coming change in the weather and hurried along. A wind was due called *khamsin*—fifty—because once started, it was said to blow for fifty days.

Speke stood in the bow of the barge and addressed the men. "All of you will be given three years' pay," he promised. "We will arrange your return fare to Zanzibar and there, if I can arrange it—and I'm quite sure that I can—a small patch of land shall be awarded to each of you."

Sidi Bombay conferred with the others, then stood up to respond.

"Captain Speke," he said, raising his voice in the wind that swept down the river, "all of us would like to volunteer to go with you again, if ever you decide to cross Africa from east to west—as we think you will surely decide to do! Also, we thank you! Also, I forgive you for striking me so many times when I was insubordinate! Also, when we arrive in Cairo we would like to attend any concert, for we have heard much about European music! Also, if possible we would like our photographs taken at your side!"

Two thousand miles on the other side of Africa, the warship HMS *Torch* carried Burton far from his post at Fernando Po. Like a wayward tourist, looking up officials at every port, he journeyed down the west coast, reached Luanda in Angola, then started northward again until he reached the mouth of the Congo River. Each day he sat in his cabin reporting his whereabouts and opinions to his Foreign Office superiors, never asking if they wanted him to travel, never inquiring if they had ideas of their own about his duties. He pestered them to allow him to join in some meaningful way in the effort to end slavery, but his letters were also filled with scientific posturings, literary views, linguistic points, and notes on native customs.

From Banana Point at the mouth of the Congo he wrote that he had been collecting plant specimens—490 samples—and that he had compiled a crude vocabulary of West African dialects.

He sent Isabel more of "The Kasidah," his long poem. Other letters went to MacQueen, Aga, Milnes, family members, and the custodians at the asylum where Edward remained unchanged.

The Congo brought him a curious melancholy, as if it were part of the Nile, the Niger, the Zambesi, the inland seas, and all of the continent's teasing waters. He stood on the balcony of a hotel on stilts at Banana Point—a rickety structure made of bamboo and ebony—and peered at the river's wide mouth, which was like a sea itself. A watery horizon. Fish leapt below in the shallows; the jungle's thick undergrowth bordered the banks.

An oddly deep sadness: Where am I, he asked himself, and what's this I feel? Wild speculations: Could this amazing river begin, say, in the undiscovered Mountains of the Moon? At some unknown continental divide no white man has ever seen? Could Tanganyika and Speke's nyanza be part of the same basin that provides this river?

He hired guides and started upstream: ten of them in two heavy dugout canoes as a light rain began to fall. By twilight they rowed in a blinding storm, so that Burton shouted for them to make camp beneath some wiry vines on the river's bank.

His clothes were soaked, so he stripped and walked naked in the mud, his pistol drawn and ready in the event animals or natives attacked. The guides watched him with awe: his hair and mustache plastered to his skin, his genitals swinging with each stride, his eyes piercing into everything.

"Hello! Hello, you bitch!" he shouted at the river, but it absorbed his greeting and curse without acknowledgment.

That night they slept with wet blankets over their heads as rain continued to pelt down. One of the guides, at last, disgusted with the discomfort, asked Burton if he should go into the village for fire.

"Fire? Village? What village?" Burton asked.

"The one around the next bend," the guide said, pointing.

They found a river path and walked along it in darkness until they came to a village with cooking pots hissing in the rain; Burton wore only his shoes, trousers, and a pair of braces; he fired off his pistol, waking everyone and scaring a few of his hosts off into the jungle, but that night he slept on a dry mat and ate a warm bowl of fish soup. It was the home village of the timid guide, who only followed the white man's orders when told to put ashore in the cloudburst.

The rain went on, so they turned back to Banana Point. At that rickety hotel—everyone could hear everyone else breathing and moving—Burton received a letter that had followed him from the Foreign Office all along the coast. He had been appointed Her Majesty's Commissioner to Dahomey.

"I say, is there any brandy in this hole?" he shouted at the top of his voice. "Brandy! Whiskey? Champagne?" On the veranda overlooking the river he waved the letter in the faces of other guests: a palm-oil merchant, two cotton planters, a rough old seaman, a correspondent from Belgium, and an American missionary.

Except for the Baptist, everyone else celebrated with the available spirits: two half-filled bottles of gin, a cask of sherry, and the inevitable banana beer. Burton's arm was quickest, so he became intoxicated first.

"Is this a great boost for your career?" the correspondent wanted to know.

"This—I imagine—is a suicide mission," Burton stated. "The king of Dahomey is a ruthless bastard. No one can stop the brute. I'm being sent—no doubt—because . . . I'm growing old and eccentric. Because . . . if he takes my head . . . the Foreign Office will at least know . . . where I'm located thereafter."

"Splendid, congratulations!" said one of the merchants, who possibly didn't understand.

"What precisely are you to do with this cannibal king?" the correspondent asked, grinning in spite of himself.

"The letter—" Burton said, then stopped to think. "The letter doesn't go into details. Yet, I presume that I'll—well, ask him to cease selling his kinsfolk and neighbors into bondage!"

"Then you have a special talent for persuasion?" the correspondent asked.

"Hmm, I've been thinking on this—since the letter fell into my hands more than an hour ago. Numerous delegations have visited . . . the ruler. . . ." He drank off the last of the gin and studied the flow of the river. "Of Dahomey. And many tactics and coercions have been . . . attempted. So my special . . . my very special qualification must be . . . that I'm . . . *dispensable.* Only that. But a job's a job, isn't it? And this is a capital thing for me, yes, a capital thing!"

When he returned to Fernando Po, Burton turned over the details of his new mission to Aga, who skillfully arranged everything.

"We should have a doctor with us," Aga suggested. "One who can cure diseases and win favors for you. I thought perhaps the British navy could provide such a person. And, then, of course, the porters. And I myself will go."

"Yes, good, tend to it all," Burton said with his usual disinterest.

"I can write a letter to the navy. I believe I can compose a very good letter, indeed."

"Fine, write all the letters you wish."

While Aga manufactured various correspondences on the consul's stationery, Burton studied the kingdom of Dahomey. Its ruler, Gelele, had opened war on all his neighbors, had killed missionaries, and had taken thousands of slaves. The French and English officials who competed for power along the Bight of Benin wanted Gelele's ruthlessness ended. The king had recently captured a town, carrying off a number of Christian converts, so the instructions awaiting Burton at the consulate were plain: he was to deliver presents to the ruler, to behave in a friendly manner, and to secure the release of the prisoners, if any of them remained alive. Complicating these orders was a fact of life in Dahomey: they practiced what they called the Customs. Each year this tribe— which boasted, Burton noted, a large force of women warriors—slaughtered huge numbers of its slaves, criminals, and political enemies in a ritual bloodbath.

He showed Aga the letter detailing all this—which bore Lord Russell's signature, he explained, and which fairly dripped with authority.

"I know nothing of European politics," Aga protested. "But I've received an accounting of the gifts we will present to the king. We pick them up in Lagos. Wrapped in special boxes painted with the colors of the Union Jack."

"The presents, yes," Burton said absently, again reading his letter, which had been opened and folded so many times that it resembled a rag.

"One forty-foot circular damask tent with poles," Aga recited. "One richly embossed silver pipe. Silver belts. Silver waiters. One coat of mail with gauntlets."

"Actually, I've heard of these women warriors for years, and I've wanted to visit them," Burton went on, not listening. "But you understand, I'm sure, that while we may enjoy such a spectacle, we cannot expect to live to tell of it."

"We should probably add presents of our own," Aga continued. "Perhaps some of your stock of brandies."

"These probably won't be real Amazons." Burton sighed. "No, they won't be the same mythic maidens who fought with Hercules and Alexander the Great. I shouldn't get my hopes up."

"I've also decided that we need a flag bearer," Aga mused.

"My government probably wants an incident," Burton went on, talking only to himself. "They probably expect me to offend the king and to get myself executed, so they can rush in with indignation and bombard this pest."

"I estimate that our entourage should be, hmm, let's see," Aga said, studying the ceiling above Burton's desk and tapping his forehead with a pencil. "About one hundred strong. Does that sound sufficient, sir?"

"The London tabloids report to the public that in Dahomey there is a lake of blood each year at the Customs," Burton said, not answering Aga's question. "A river and lake of blood on which the killers float canoes! Public loves such patter! But, oh, my, Aga, what have we got ourselves into?"

"You have another item I know King Gelele would appreciate," Aga said, talking only to himself, too. "That calendar with those white women at their bath. Could I include it among the gifts?"

"Yes, anything," Burton agreed.

In Cairo, Speke tried to explain to his men how to form a living tableau.

"We will be on a stage, you see. Photographers will be there. I will stand among you shading my eyes, as if I'm looking for the nyanza. Sidi Bombay, you'll stand beside me. Mabruki, you'll carry a spear. This is an act—a theatrical performance—very much like a ritual dance, you see, except nobody moves—and the audience will applaud."

Mabruki had difficulty comprehending all this, then, when he did, he flatly refused to carry a spear like some stupid villager. Sidi Bombay offered to display the broken chronometer still in his possession.

"These photographs," Sidi Bombay asked, "we will show our wives in Zanzibar?"

"Exactly. But everyone must remain quite still."

The session, held at Shepheard's Hotel, where they stayed, went well, and Sidi Bombay was asked to pose for additional photos; he was the great attraction to many of the lords and ladies, who were amazed that this scrawny little black with sharpened teeth could actually speak English.

Speke also attended a reception at the Viceroy's palace and managed to assemble his group of faithfuls for a concert by the Royal Navy's brass band. Each evening for two weeks brought dinner toasts, awards, speeches, and honors for the heroes. The East India Company agreed to pay off all debts of the expedition, which had exceeded its budget by £1000. The army extended Speke's leave for another year, so that he could meet his social obligations in London. Letters also arrived to confirm that he and Grant would meet the Prince of Wales and speak before the Royal Geographical Society upon their return.

One evening toward midnight they sat in the hotel lounge after another dinner attended by local dignitaries. The windows gave them a view of the desert at night. Grant wore his uniform in impeccable array; since their arrival he had bathed twice daily and had changed into fresh clothes constantly. Now he smoked his briar pipe, held a glass of good Scotch whisky, and radiated calm.

"There's something I want us to discuss," he told Speke. "I intend to travel on to Scotland as soon as possible after we return. Naturally I'll stay with you and support you through all the obligatory ceremonies, but my wife won't be coming down to London, and there's much to do on the farm. I do hope you understand my situation."

"Yes, quite, you're married and busy," Speke replied somewhat coldly.

Grant sucked on his pipe and gazed out the window. "I'll never forget what we've done," he said. "I'll tell my grandchildren, I'm sure, about how we sailed along the coast with the British admiral, how my leg threatened my life, how I taught an African king to watercolor, all of it. And I shall never forget you, Jack, for all you've done for me. Be sure of it."

Speke looked Grant full in the face, trying to see if there was a trace of sarcasm in this testimony. He decided there wasn't any.

"I'm sentimental, you know, about my own," Grant continued. "My clan, my friends, my army colleagues: I never let go, never lose faith in them, no matter what."

"Thank you, Jim," Speke answered, although he seemed uncertain of all Grant might be implying. Was there going to be trouble? Was Grant's pledge of devotion a necessity?

Speke stretched his arms and yawned. "Are you tired?"

"Hmm, very tired," Grant agreed.

"I'll take a short stroll, then go to bed," Speke said, saying good night. He walked through the lounge, crossed the lobby, and went outside, where two cabs, both drivers and horses seemingly asleep, waited beside the gaslight.

"Speak English?" he asked the driver sitting in the first cab.

"Yes, please, thank you, please," the man said, stirring himself.

"There are some baths in the city. I haven't been to them in years, but I believe they're near a large mosque. Can you take me there?"

"The old baths at the mosque of Ibn Tulun?"

"Are they open at this hour? Can you take me?"

"Yes, open," the driver said, giving Speke his seat and moving into position behind his team of old horses.

"At these baths, the bath boys—" Speke paused. "They're quite accommodating."

"Yes, effendi, yes," the driver said, shaking the reins. He knew very well what his client desired. As the cab rattled off into the night, the man was like all cab drivers everywhere: smug in his cynicism.

1863-1864

—)◖(—

The Last Year: Dahomey,
Paris, London, Bath

PICCADILLY WAS CROWDED ON THE DAY SPEKE CAME BEFORE THE SOCIETY at Burlington House. The foreign and British press had turned out, crowds lined the streets, and the hall overflowed, so that those who couldn't get inside sat in the stairwells so they could hear the explorer's words.

Speke took the stage to a rousing ovation. He stood tall, his hands gripping the lectern until his knuckles whitened.

"I've now quite satisfied myself that the White Nile issues from the nyanza which I've proudly named Lake Victoria," he began. "And that Ripon Falls—a magnificent attraction called merely the Stones by natives and now appropriately renamed—is the beginning of the true or parent Nile."

The room reverberated with cheers and applause.

Oliphant, decked out in a top hat and a new silk suit, slapped his white gloves against his thigh, adding to the tumult. As he did so, he saw James MacQueen, who kept a sullen stillness in the demonstration.

Grant, Murchison, Ripon, Shaw, and others sat proudly in chairs behind Speke, who looked somehow older and worn, yet more authoritative than ever. He talked about viewing the Nile's branches, tributaries, and chain of lakes. Soon, though, his tone turned oddly defensive, as if he almost meant to call attention to his strength and formality as a kind of disguise.

Milnes, seated near the stage, exchanged a look with MacQueen.

"I dare and defy anyone to circumvent my Victoria Nyanza by way of disproving any of my statements!" he declared, glaring at his audience. They studied him, in turn, with renewed attention; his eyes had a curious stare, as if he had entered into some vague argument.

"Had I been alone on the first expedition," he said, "I should have settled the Nile in 1859 by traveling directly to Uganda. But my proposal having been negatived by the chief of the expedition, who was sick at the time and tired of the journey, I returned to England!"

In the increased silence of the audience, Speke's separate breaths between sentences could be detected. Milnes' mouth made its little round hole while Oliphant brought his white gloves to his throat.

"I don't wish to say anything against Captain Burton. But I taught him, at his own request, the geographies of the countries we traversed, and since then he has turned my words against me!"

Total silence. Speke struggled with his next phrases, obsessed with Burton now rather than addressing the particulars of his achievement. His digression stunned everyone.

"I have little patience with armchair explorers in bedtime slippers who judge—" He stopped, gripping the lectern, weaving slightly. ". . . who judge geography at a great distance! Or for mere travel writers who, like Captain Burton, toil with theories only!" His voice had that odd resonance: strong, yet as if it might suddenly break into a sob.

Murchison and others twisted in their chairs. Shaw and Grant lowered their faces.

Then Speke seemed to recover. "Naturally I hope to return over and over to Africa," he announced with a smile, as if remembering his confidence. "I look forward to settling the whole continent and opening it to missionaries." As he paused, a light trickle of applause greeted him. "Yes, missionaries," he repeated. "To open the country to God and the Empire!"

Somehow he managed to finish, yet he stood there until Sir Roderick came to his side, raised a hand, and asked if there were any questions from the members of the Society's committee.

For a moment, no response came. Then James MacQueen was on his feet.

"By defying anyone to circumvent the lake," he said, "you call some interesting attention to your own neglect. We take it, then, that you did not travel all the shores of your nyanza?"

"That's quite correct," Speke replied.

"But you assert that the one outlet you found—at the Stones—is the one and true source of the Nile?"

"Yes, and I think all your particular questions will be answered in time in my written reports and forthcoming book," Speke answered.

MacQueen did not sit down. He had a walking cane that he drew to his lips, as if to kiss its silver handle, before continuing. "Yet you saw many tributaries and lakes as you followed your stream?"

"A stream that became the Nile," Speke reminded him, trying a smile.

"But any of those branches *could* be the main or essential stream," MacQueen went on.

The room grew tense. None of the distinguished men behind Speke on the platform raised their gaze toward either participant in this examination.

"I saw the river in the dry season. In the most favorable time of year for estimating the relative perennial values of branches and streams. And I think, once again, if I may say so, your questions will be answered adequately in my written report."

"Since we can't expect to read your report in our Society's journal, I assume we'll find it in *Blackwood's*," MacQueen said sharply.

As the crowd roused itself at this assault, Speke stammered something no one could hear, then added weakly, "I'll publish my general map in the magazine, yes, so that it can receive the widest scrutiny with the public." As the crowd continued to hum, Speke finished by raising his voice above it. "As you'll see later, the map suggests four possible outlets from Lake Victoria, of which Ripon Falls is principal."

"So? *Four* streams? Yet you saw only one and made all your determinations."

Speke again stammered. Murchison stood up.

"Your nyanza must leak like a sieve!" MacQueen said, touching his chin with that silver handle of his cane. "And we'll find out about it in a commercial magazine instead of our scientific journal! Two things could be concluded, sir: that you did poor work and that you're anxious for immediate fame!"

Speke's face turned crimson. Murchison raised a hand, as if to address the participants, but Milnes stood.

"Perhaps we should ask Captain Grant whether or not he considers that he saw the principal feeder stream of the Nile," Milnes said, the room stirring noisily around them all.

"It is not my report to write," Grant said, standing. "I'm sure that—"

"Come, come," MacQueen added. "Surely you have an opinion."

"I was—" Grant began, quickly stopping. His Scots brogue carried to all corners of the room, easing the murmurings. "I was unable to visit Ripon Falls with Captain Speke," he finally said. "My orders were to follow another path into Bunyoro."

"So you were not allowed to share the prize?" MacQueen asked, incredulous.

"I suffered a wound," Grant tried to explain, but his words were lost in the noise of raised voices and chair legs scraping on the floor. Everyone watched the tall blond man at the lectern: his face red with anger, his mouth tight, his large hands gripping the speaker's stand as if he might topple forward on his adversaries.

"I'm sure," Murchison said, his hand in the air. "I'm sure Captain Speke's report will answer all particulars. For now, we are most grateful to have our men back safely—most grateful, indeed!"

The Society's committee members on the platform and in the audience joined each other around Speke and Grant. Oliphant pushed forward in the crowd toward Speke.

MacQueen's loud voice won the attention of those around his chair. "I for one prefer Burton's claim!" he said. "And when all's said and done, I think we'll find the Nile trickles out of Lake Tanganyika!"

"Hear, hear!" someone called.

"Bravo, Speke!" came another voice.

Oliphant drew close to Speke's side, while not far away Ripon and Shaw huddled with Grant.

"How was it, Lowry?" Speke asked. "Was it terrible?"

"Not at all," Oliphant assured him. "You were magnificent."

An old gentleman leaned forward through the wall of bodies, reached out, and touched the celebrity.

"Tomorrow," Speke said, "I meet the Prince of Wales." His eyes had a faraway look.

"Let me get you out of here," Oliphant said, taking Speke's arm.

"This went badly," Speke said. "But tomorrow there's the Prince of Wales, and my family has planned a big celebration in Somerset."

"Yes, Jack, this way," Oliphant said, pulling Speke through a boisterous group of men. At last they found the cloak room, pressed inside, and closed the door. Someone knocked and asked to be let in, but Oliphant paid the request no attention. Instead, he saw Speke's startling expression: a formal taxidermy that covered some deep bewilderment.

"Are you all right?" he asked, clutching Speke's sleeve.

"Yes, fine. Where are we going?"

Oliphant kissed the patch of cheek above Speke's sun-bleached beard as he patted his friend's back. "We're finding ourselves a cab," he said softly. "Everything's quite all right."

In the billiard room of the East India and United Services Club the explorers shook hands and said their farewells.

"Goodbye for now, dear chap, and give my regards to your wife," Speke said, clasping Grant's outstretched hand.

"I'll be ready to return to London, if needed," Grant promised.

"Mind what I say about writing a book. You can make money—enough to recover any losses from this expedition. And I'll see that the Blackwoods help you in the enterprise."

"Perhaps I'll write, perhaps not," Grant allowed. "But if I do, I'll visit the Blackwood brothers in Edinburgh, rest assured of that and thanks."

Across the wide room some players strolled around the tables; the soft clicking sounds of the balls punctuated these last statements.

In their short stay in London they had visited the Prince; the Queen had sent her congratulations; the king of Sardinia had announced that a special commemorative medal should be struck for the explorers; elaborate dinners had occupied them in the evenings.

"If you don't become an author, at least write to me at Jordans," Speke said as they parted.

"I promise I'll write often if you do," Grant said. "You know, Jack, in my corner of the world, correspondence is everything. And I'm hoping—I know this is a vanity—that I could possibly correspond with Dr. Livingstone and some of the others. Now there, I mean, is a great man. And if any reward could come to me out of this trip, I would want it to be of that nature: a communication with men of note. Exchanging ideas and theories, that sort of thing."

"Yes, Livingstone," Speke replied.

They shook hands firmly again, then let go.

Before leaving London for home, Speke met with the Blackwood brothers, who were appalled at the shape of his notes, yet said they were determined to edit them and to publish all the findings quickly. The work, to be entitled

Journal of the Discovery of the Source of the Nile, would have to be carefully revised under their supervision, they told Speke, yet they felt it would make an instant success.

"Revise it as you wish," he told them. "Language is your business."

"You'll have to come up to London frequently," Robert Blackwood advised.

"I'll have constant business here," he assured them. "Lowry's arranging speeches and appearances for me."

Before departing, Speke also took care to write a report on Petherick, which he forwarded to Murchison. In the letter he accused the consul of failing to carry out the duties assigned by the Society and strongly suggested that Petherick was slaving with known villains in Gondokoro. On the basis of the letter, Murchison paid a visit to the club. Speke was with his brothers, Ben and William, who had come up to London to accompany the hero home, but Sir Roderick met with Speke in a small sitting room downstairs. The window was open, so they listened to a bird chirping in a tree outside as they talked.

"Those are quite serious allegations against Petherick, so we must keep matters private until an investigation begins," Sir Roderick told him.

"Hmm, quite, but you'll find out the worst."

The old man listened to the bird for a moment. "You know, we didn't authorize or charge Petherick to wait for you at Gondokoro beyond June of 1862," he said, at last. "You were months late, yet he was there."

"Very ill equipped to help," Speke replied. "So I took Baker's boats and aid instead. And gave him my help in return—the map I spoke to you about."

"If I know Baker, he'll take that map and punch a hole in the continent."

Speke laughed.

"But this matter of Petherick," Sir Roderick said. "I confess to you, Jack, that it's hard to believe. And, if true, it will be impossible to prove. So it's very dangerous talk."

"You've always supported my intuitions," Speke answered. "Trust me in this, too. You'll find very condemning evidence."

"Perhaps, but only perhaps. Our witnesses are thousands of miles away. Even so, we'd be dealing in innuendo. And what do we gain?"

"That man should be stripped of his consulate."

"Do you think so?"

"Absolutely. He's a shame to the nation."

The bird sang a series of high notes, then ceased. Murchison sat weighing what to do, turning his top hat in his fingers.

"If you insist, we'll investigate," he finally said. "But you must abide by the findings of our committee. So you must consider that Petherick could be found guiltless."

"Naturally I'll abide by whatever the Society finds."

"It's not only that simple," Sir Roderick went on, taking some pains to explain the delicacies. "If you bring this charge against Petherick, the Society could end up turning against you—in a time when you very much need it as a friend. You would be forcing it to turn against one of its own members. Careful now and listen: I can't recommend you bother with Petherick."

"You've said in the past that you regard me as a son," Speke reminded him.

"And still say so, but you must heed my fatherly advice!"

"If I'm a son, you'll trust my charges against Petherick!"

They sat looking at each other as Sir Roderick breathed a long, wheezing sigh. "Jack, dear boy, I'm not the explorer you are. But I'm a damned fine administrator and politician. This business with Petherick is not a good course. Don't you see what others could do? If they defeat your wishes in this matter, they could possibly convert their victory into something more: they could injure your whole credibility in the Nile question."

"Men like MacQueen will not intimidate me," Speke said angrily.

"I just want you to see this matter clearly," Sir Roderick urged.

"Don't doubt me," Speke said coldly and evenly, so apparently angry now that Murchison managed a polite smile and stood to leave.

Accompanied by his brothers, Speke went back to Somerset with its rolling hills and vaulting autumnal trees. At the largest town closest to home, Taunton, he found a hero's welcome: bells rang out, well-wishers with flags lined the streets, and a brass band struck up "See the Conquering Hero Comes!" He stood in an open carriage, waving and smiling as he passed beneath arches of flowers and bunting in the streets. This is everything, he told himself. Let William inherit Jordans; let Burton have his languages and sarcasms; let Grant have wife and family; this is raw fame.

At the end of the procession he mounted a newly constructed platform where civic leaders droned out their speeches of welcome. He only half listened, watching the children with garlands of flowers in their hands, and one particularly sour lad who slumped against a hitching post across the street: a rough, gangling farm boy, probably burning for his own place in the world.

Taunton's senior bailiff came forward with two gold vases embossed with Egyptian designs: gifts for the explorer. The band, off cue, began another salute, drowning out the speech of presentation.

"Four thousand!" brother Ben shouted above the music. "I've estimated the crowd at more than four thousand!"

The crowd's cheers continued until Speke rose to make his reply. After the first courtesies and thanks, he explained how he had named his nyanza and many of its features. "I've called the narrow stream feeding the lake at its southern extremity after my family home: Jordans. The beautiful region into which this stream flows I've named Somerset. This is very symbolic in that . . ." He lost the thread of his thoughts. For a moment the crowd wavered before his eyes; faces blurred into abstraction. "It is very symbolic," he concluded.

The crowd smiled, applauded, and brought him back.

"I defy anyone to go there and disprove what I've done!" he blurted out, as the throng around the platform smiled and waited. "No one in my lifetime will ever circumvent the lake to disprove my claims! Claims I know to be true: this is the Nile! It *is!*" Again, light applause sent him in another direction. "My ambition now is to develop Africa's fertile zone, so that it can be opened to settlers and missionaries! Yes, I'll go back to explore the whole of Africa— myself!" Cheers and applause. He caught sight of his brother Ben leaning forward in the carriage, as if he might leap upon the platform to aid in this suddenly difficult address. "Mind you," Speke went on, "I have a number of detractors. Men who believe that my accomplishment with Captain Grant was simply an easy stroll down country lanes. But let me assure you that our dangers were real enough—and that proof of my findings will be published for all to read!"

The crowd now watched him with curiosity. The whole question of proof was of no consequence to those who had lined the streets in order to admire the resolute look in a hero's eyes.

"My colleague and I suffered many severities of nature. We met hostile tribes—and were forced to use our weapons! We even met treachery in the person of John Petherick, the British consul at Khartoum, who not only failed us, but who was probably taking slaves and certainly behaving in the most villainous manner in those faraway regions!"

The crowd seemed stunned.

"Yes, and I'll tell you very much more about such wicked men as Pe- therick and the cannibal kings of central Africa as you read my reports, later!"

Both of his brothers stood up in the nearby carriage, their faces creased with concern.

"But for now, dear friends of home, this great demonstration has quite overpowered me. I leave to see my family. And I only wish I had the words to express the deepest feelings of my heart."

He left the platform to applause, his listeners struck by the sudden shifts and surprises of his speech. The attack on Petherick had been written down by a newspaper reporter. For more than an hour Speke stood in the carriage with his brothers, shaking the hands of those who gathered around to greet him.

At Ashill, on the way to Jordans, two hundred horsemen and another two thousand people escorted them through the hamlet.

That evening at Jordans a supper party for more than one hundred guests was held in marquees set up on the lawn. A fireworks display, band music, and a bonfire celebrated his homecoming. In the master bedroom of the estate house Speke visited his bedridden father.

"We're very proud," his father said, his breathing labored.

Speke took his father's hand and kissed it. When he went outside again where the bonfire illumined the nearby hedgerows and the faces of all the farm workers who had come to witness the festivities, Speke found his mother and brothers whispering and looking in his direction. He immediately went to them, saying, "You're talking about me, aren't you?"

"Oh, Jack," his mother answered, circling her arms around his neck as he resisted her embrace.

"I'm not what you expect, am I? You feel I made a poor speech in Taunton today, isn't that so, William? You think I'm ridiculous."

"I'm glad to have you home again, Jack, and never mind your usual bad mood."

The mother took Speke's hand. "William, you're drunk," she said.

"He's an ass," William said. "Now a famous ass. And perhaps I am a bit drunk, but there you are."

Speke's mother led him away. As they crossed the lawn, nodding and smiling at guests, sparks from the bonfire drifted across the evening sky and the band played another tune. On the rear lawn, by torchlight, children of the guests rode in a decorated donkey cart and ate fresh candied apples.

"Whatever's wrong?" his mother asked as they reached the terrace.

"Everything."

"But what could be? This is all for you! Your father hasn't felt this happy in weeks! Things should be splendid!"

"But they aren't. I made this extraordinary trip, dearest, and I know I'm right in all I've claimed, but I have so little proof! None, really. No proof at all!"

"But who's to deny you?" she asked. "No one can possibly dispute you!"

"Yes, I keep saying that to myself and others, yet I know: there's no real proof, only my word, so everything is personal and so—dependent on how well I'm liked and believed!"

"Then all's well. You're loved and adored—and never mind what William says when he's potted."

He kissed her cheek and smoothed back the hair from her brow. They could hear the delighted voices of the children at play.

In spite of celebration or solace he felt like a child himself, the one sent away from home—first to school, then to the army—who had never done well enough, who made low marks in class and who didn't rise in rank in the war; who didn't marry or accumulate wealth; who didn't mix with proper friends; who didn't find proofs for his greatest claim, so that all this attention was somehow undeserved. Something grew inside his throat like a terrible little vine; even the warmth of his mother's arms increased the strangulation. The next morning he wrote to Oliphant.

Lowry—

I'll soon go to Edinburgh to complete the mss w/ the Blackwoods, but let's be together in London after that. I need you.

Speke

Late in 1863 Burton and his entourage arrived in Dahomey. With him was a lanky naval surgeon, John Cruikshank; a scrawny black Christian calling himself an assistant missionary and wearing the clerical collar who spoke in an unconscious parody of English; and, in charge of the porters, gifts, and all the expedition's details, Aga. As they went through villages toward their destination they witnessed dozens of dances, and Burton consumed bottles of rum or brandy at each one; Aga made a ritual of presenting his employer with a bottle as these affairs began, removing it from the case and holding it out stiffly. Aga also had charge of ninety-nine porters, cooks, interpreters, hammock men, flag carriers, and the fat bodyguards, who were terrified of both Burton and every male in the surrounding bush. Luckily the doctor and the assistant missionary talked constantly to each other about the plight of the poor black villagers, leaving Burton alone with his notes and liquor.

At Abomey, Burton sat under a shade tree waiting for King Gelele to make a first appearance. Aga had set up a rickety card table for his master, so Burton viewed proceedings over the corks of several bottles, sheaths of notes, an inkstand, and a few of the minor gifts. The palace at Abomey was only a collection of fetish huts, scaffoldings, and thatch. In the courtyard a few nobles and ministers gathered, wearing loincloths and strings of beads or bone. The amazon warriors, spears held high, were the ugliest women Burton had ever seen, all fat with large noses and protruding lips pierced with brass rings. The basic decor of the palace and grounds consisted of skulls and bones; these hung from doorways and adorned stakes.

Burton was assigned an interpreter: a little man with a foot-long ceremonial scar. The interpreter explained that he would address only the king's own interpreter, who would then speak to the king, ensuring that nothing offensive would ever reach the king's ears.

"These women are your amazon warriors?" Burton inquired.

"Our women soldiers feared all over Africa!" the little man replied.

"Twenty British charladies armed with broomsticks could demolish the whole lot," Burton snorted, taking another drink. The interpreter sighed, knowing that this was, indeed, a troublesome visitor.

Drummers lined up, preparing for the king's visit.

Across the courtyard a man was lashed to a tree, a Y-shaped forked stick wedged between his tongue and palate so that his mouth opened obscenely. Burton learned that this was a thief awaiting the Customs, soon to be held in honor of the white man's arrival.

A dwarf appeared, riding sidesaddle on a tiny horse, an umbrella over his head as he sucked on a lettuce leaf. Behind him came a monster: a giant black apparition whose naked body was pitted with smallpox scars, so that his flesh resembled a crocodile's.

A woman appeared, one heavy breast bared, leading a leopard cub on a leash. Not far behind her came Gelele's wives: all fat, all bedecked in cotton wraps of flowered designs. Everyone wore the ceremonial tattoo, the three little marks near the hairline beside the eyes.

"The court of King Gelele," said the interpreter, waving his arm proudly at this extravagant display.

"A shit sack," Burton said drunkenly. "And can you translate that for the king?"

"Please, no, I cannot," came the answer.

A frenzy of activity began in the courtyard. A few of the female warriors began to dance with long razors, waving them about and shouting as the drummers beat a quick rhythm and various ministers called out encouragements. Actually, the interpreter explained, they were all cursing their neighbors and rivals, the people of Abeokuta, whom they had sworn to annihilate in an upcoming war. Those plump women with the long razor knives, Burton also learned, were chaste; otherwise, he was told, the army of male and female warriors would surely get itself into a state of disorder.

Soon everyone in the courtyard fell prostrate in the dust, saluting with his head, touching the forehead and cheeks to the ground, kissing the dirt, mumbling and begging in humble obeisance. As King Gelele approached the courtyard, wives and ministers began to throw handfuls of dust over their hair and clothes; Burton found himself thirsty enough to take another drink.

The king was a large man, big in the belly. He arrived beneath a canopy of spinning umbrellas, nodding and grinning, while his slaves anticipated his movements and followed with shade wherever he went. At last he settled himself beneath a verandah of umbrellas, facing Burton and his party. He was normal enough except for his fingernails: long talons with which he probably ate. His peppercorn hair receded; his eyes were hard; he showed some signs of having had smallpox. His clothes: a necklace of bones, bracelets of brass and coral, a simple white cloak, lavishly embroidered slippers of a Moorish design.

The drums beat until he seated himself. He smiled and asked a question, which turned out, after all the translations, to be, "How is the Queen of England?"

"She's doing nicely," Burton answered.

A woman arrived with a platter of skulls. The king puffed on a native pipe of *bangi* while his wives settled around him.

"And how are my visitors of last year?" the king wanted to know, having his interpreter recite several names of various British authorities.

"Oh, getting along well," Burton replied. "And these are my aides: the doctor, the reverend, and my chief sergeant." Aga, receiving this title, squared his shoulders.

Important business commenced: gifts for the king. As Burton announced each gift, Aga brought the porters forward to display the item. But Gelele, after viewing a new silver pipe, silver belts, French perfumes, snuff, cases of liquor and bolts of cloth, seemed not too pleased.

"He has seen a photograph of the English queen's coronation carriage and horses," the interpreter explained. "He hoped for one of those—trimmed in gold."

Burton shrugged and asked if he had seen the calendar picture of the naked white maidens at their bath.

"The tent!" Aga put in, hopefully. "Wait until he sees the tent!"

Soon porters, warriors, amazons, and ministers wrestled with the folds and geometries of the new tent. The king criticized its color, its size and shape, though he admitted liking the ornamental lion affixed to the top of its center pole.

Burton finished off a bottle. Seeing this, the king ordered the platter of skulls brought forward, then selected one to be filled with palm wine for his guest. The grinning skulls piled on the platter and adorning nearby posts watched the white man as the wine was poured. Skulls everywhere: the grotesque measure of Dahomey's wealth and power.

Drunk enough not to care, Burton accepted the skull, raised it high, and sipped from it. "Ah!" King Gelele cried, and his subjects replied, in kind, "Ah! Ah! Ah!" then began to dance.

When the lopsided tent finally occupied most of the courtyard, the corps of amazons pounded their spears into the earth and danced with a frenzy.

"Tell the king that I have words from my government," Burton said to the interpreters during all the commotion.

But Gelele led his court in chants and songs, so failed to listen to the interpreters. Instead he stomped around the dusty courtyard, arms raised, chased by his umbrella boys, who tried to keep him shaded, crying out for the death of his enemies. Thirty minutes of this tirade. Burton asked about the words of their chant and eventually understood them to be

When we go to war we must slay men
And so must Abeokuta be destroyed!

"Very good," Burton kept saying. "But inform His Majesty, please, that I must give him my speech, so I can depart."

"Oh, you cannot leave until the Customs," the interpreter said.

"Hmm, but that's the point," Burton explained. "There must be no killings. This practice must be stopped. Neither can the king take slaves or attack his neighbors, if he means to have the friendship of the British."

The interpreter looked at this emissary with nervous terror. "Please, I cannot say this thing," he managed in a single rush of breath.

"Now tell him immediately!" Burton insisted.

His interpreter moved away, slipping between the dancers to speak with the king's personal translator. They shook their heads as if to say, no, certainly not, we won't tell the king any such thing. As Gelele led the endless chant, both interpreters came to Burton's side.

"You will make your speech to the king after the Customs," they announced.

"No, that won't do," Burton argued. "I have gifts for the king, something to say, then I leave."

"You must stay many days," they informed him.

"Like bloody hell," he said. "And if there are going to be killings, I'll leave immediately. Neither I nor my government can abide such brutality."

The interpreters conferred with one another, then told the white man, "Your own head will be taken if you try to leave. Never dispute the king, who is a god. If he sneezes, you will bend and kiss the ground. If he drinks, you will turn your eyes away. If he commands you to behold the Customs, this you will do."

Harmattan: the deadly hot wind from the north. Dust from the desert came to Dahomey and obliterated every shape: each person, the surrounding jungle, the senses. Burton sat in his clay hut while the dust storm turned his life into a maze.

I must take hold of myself. Not drink so much.

I must love Isabel, who loves me.

I must take notes on these ugly amazons, the Ffon dialect, and that insipid nigger tyrant.

In spite of this wind and waiting, I must not give in.

At the end of the harmattan the Customs began. Talking to his interpreters and in conversations with Aga and the others, Burton learned that the Grand Customs, held only after the death of a king, were the time of a general and widespread slaughter. The seasonal Customs—a time of carnival, narcotics, dances, and yearly craziness—featured lesser carnage. In the upcoming festivities, he was assured, not many heads would be taken, and those who would die would be local Dahoman criminals and just a few wicked slaves.

"*Khwe-ta-nun,*" one of Gelele's ministers explained with a sigh of resignation: the yearly head thing.

As the desert dust settled on the courtyard and village, Burton strolled down to a bamboo pen where those awaiting execution seemed happy enough. About twenty men sat in the sun chatting, their necks bound in a loose rope; they were either drunk or heavily drugged, their eyes glazed and their mouths tilted in silly grins. A wardrobe master went among them distributing calico shirts with crimson patches sewn on the sleeves. Each condemned man was also given a long white nightcap with spirals of blue ribbon trailing it.

By afternoon dancing had commenced and King Gelele was back on the scene. He made a long opening speech, remarking that this was a fine, old, pious custom that his father and grandfather had celebrated before him. The prisoners inside the pen listened with an odd respect and attention.

Gelele then danced with the most beautiful young wife of his harem, his leopard woman, as his subjects applauded and called out flattering remarks. After the dance the king wiped the sweat from his forehead with his finger, spraying it with a jerk over the delighted faces of his wives and ministers.

Burton sat behind the rickety card table with its bottles of trade rum and watched the king's vanities with a fixed smile. When a handmaiden passed the king another pipe of *bangi,* Burton made an elaborate show of taking out a cigar and lighting it.

The courtyard, meanwhile, still mostly filled with that lopsided tent, overflowed with ritual and curiosity. A cluster of six naked wives danced around the king. Flags and umbrellas moved in the breeze as Gelele distributed coral necklaces to his women and pink cloths to his ministers. Shouts of flattery and homage sounded from everyone, while from every hut and nearby lean-to dozens of objects were brought into the courtyard to be admired and blessed: stools, old muskets, knives, war clubs, hats, broken mirrors, tattered umbrellas, and crude jewelery.

A shabby, sad barbarism, Burton thought, as he took a drink and blew cigar smoke into the air. This was second-rate ritual made important by the fact that doomed men witnessed it.

Another hour passed before Gelele slid off his throne and came toward Burton and his group. He wanted them to dance.

"No, but thank you," Burton said, maintaining a smile. "Tell the king that I am a warrior, not a dancer."

The interpreters spoke with the king. Smiles became rigid and tight.

"The doctor will dance," the king's interpreter announced.

Burton began to make excuses for Cruikshank, but the doctor put up his hand in protest and said, "Yes, I'll try something." Glancing at Burton with frightened reassurance, he added, "We must. Don't you see?"

As the drummers began a rhythmic pounding, the doctor performed a clumsy jig. Although his timing was awful, the king laughed loudly, pointed at him, and applauded. When the jig was ended, Gelele responded with a stomping dance of his own, raising dust and calling for encouragement from his subjects. His own interpreter, who wore a Moslem skullcap, clasped his hands together and rolled his eyes in an ecstasy of reverence. Others yelled out, "*Ka! Ka!*" and pumped their spears and umbrellas into the air.

When the king's dance was finished, the drums continued to pound and all eyes turned to Burton. It was clearly his turn, and the king's sweating face with its grim little smile made this obvious announcement.

Cruikshank, terrified, gave Burton a hapless look.

Burton emptied a bottle of rum. Dizzy and angry, he stalked out into the center of the courtyard. Although the drums continued to roll, king and subjects fell silent as the white man drew out his saber from its sheath; it was a long, slow, somehow profound gesture, and as the blade glinted in the sunlight Burton managed to make it oddly menacing.

Then he danced. He attempted a version of a Hindu sword dance, turning, flashing the blade, jumping over the saber and passing it between his legs. He was too drunk, but kept at it. When he stumbled, the king's subjects—partially out of relief now that the menace had vanished—laughed aloud. In one awkward pass, he ripped his trousers. Then he finished abruptly, raising his arms as his audience became hysterical; the king jumped up and down while the amazons aimed three old muskets at the sky and fired off salutes.

A successful fool, Burton told himself.

"Say to the king that I now want to speak about the Customs," he told the interpreter, replacing the saber in its sheath.

"Later—after the Customs—you will have your words with the king."

"My words are important now! Say this to him!"

"No, not now," the interpreter said, ending the matter.

"Then I'm retiring to my hut."

"You may go," the interpreter replied, raising his chin arrogantly and touching his little cap. "But stay inside tonight. Anyone found outside tonight will lose his head."

As Burton left, Aga, the doctor, and the assistant minister hurriedly fell in behind him.

Alone later, sitting in his hut, Burton hated himself for what he felt: a low, base, drunken fear. This was a land of brutal whimsy. He felt he didn't know its language or mood—or, for that matter, no longer knew himself.

That night so long ago: he had stepped outside his tent into the dark, saber in hand, near the beach at Berbera. Herne and Speke beside him. Stroyan lying there, his body filled with spears.

No man is permanently brave.

One day a man charges the enemy, the next day he cowers in the bunker, too paralyzed with fright to move a muscle.

That lance that passed through my face, leaving this scar: I couldn't bear it now, not again. I'm too old.

Courage may sometimes be public, but it is always truly private.

What now? Do I accept the bitter, restrained, boring life of husbands and minor officials who merely tend to responsibility? Duty requires tenacity, not courage; most men plod faithfully—which, at times, is rather admirable—but is that what I do now?

In the morning he strolled toward the pen where the prisoners were kept. A man was hanged upside down from a stake, his head and genitals cut off.

In spite of himself, Burton examined the body closely. Observing the amount of blood caked in the dust on the ground and the absence of blood on the corpse, he determined that the poor man had been strung up by the feet, then beheaded, then had lost his genitals as a kind of grisly afterthought. He studied the body in a detached way until its horror seemed commonplace.

Farther along the path he saw two heads impaled on stakes. The expressions on the faces: a soft, easy sleep.

Less than a dozen prisoners remained in the barricade. Still drunk and dazed, still wearing their nooses, they ate fruit and chatted, as if they had nothing better to do on such a sunny morning in the outdoors.

Back at his hut, sitting cross-legged on the earthen floor, Burton passed a few hours writing letters to Isabel, Milnes, and Lord Russell.

Then he sat musing. Courage, he knew, was often just stupid bravado.

He knew that he must deliver the message to King Gelele, but it could be rendered with polite disclaimers and apologies. On the other hand, it could be threatening, bold, or candid to the point of insult.

His musing became a series of random memories.

Inside those reddish stucco walls of the Amir's courtyard in Harar: I refused to hand over my pistol and dagger to the guards, who could have killed me on the spot for this insolence. Or that inept mercenary in Zayla: he could have killed me with a lucky thrust. Or that day with Lord Stratford: I called an incompetent idiot by his true name. Or in India: I wrote the truth in my report and suffered from it. Or that Wazaramo giant who stood in our path: I slapped his face. Or Beatson: I stood by him, bless him. Fevers and wounds: I've cursed them all and never whimpered.

And what now? I should probably never leave Africa.

If the lion stands still, if it stands on its hillside and surveys its domain, if it no longer hunts or roams, the tiniest insects begin to eat it alive; they invade its mane; they gnaw into its tendons; they reduce and devour.

Gelele stripped down to his satin shorts, satin with yellow flowers on them, and performed a marathon of thirty-two dances.

Afterward, sitting on his throne, sweating and grinning, he threw out cowries to his warriors—male and female—who fought for them in the soft, fine dust of the courtyard. Their scuffling and wrestling pleased the king, who laughed loudly and pointed at various contestants with his fingernails. Burton stood nearby, having told the interpreters that he wished to speak with the king, once more, about prisoners and ritual murders.

"The king wishes to know if you would care to join our sport," the interpreters asked him. "If you do this, you could then ask his mercy for some of the prisoners."

"Tell the great swine I'll be one of his piglets," Burton said, unbuttoning his shirt.

The crowd murmured, pleased to see so much white skin exposed and anticipating blood. Standing near the new, lopsided tent, a man wrapped his hand with cloth; he had been severely bitten by one of the enthusiasts.

The king, babbling to everyone, threw out another handful of cowries and watched the fray resume. Burton knocked down one attacker with a thrust of his shoulder; an amazon threw a clumsy punch, but he ducked; another warrior kicked at him, missed, and fell down. Dust rose like a cloud while everyone screamed.

The cowries—used as currency by the Dahomans—were everywhere on the ground, so Burton decided to clear a space around himself. Using a modified boxing style, he cocked his right fist and knocked a man down. Another appeared, but went down hard with a solid punch, too. In all their fat, muscled ignorance they had never witnessed the least of boxing skills, so he began to appear strong. A clever warrior came toward him, feinted, moved closer, bobbed, weaved, feinted once more, then caught a solid right cross to the nose and mouth, which sent out a spray of blood. A hefty female came at Burton with her claws, but he bashed her, too.

Soon he was alone in a ten-foot circle of his own, where he picked up the cowries one by one, glaring at his opponents, who seemed suddenly reluctant and disinclined. A last, lone attacker appeared: a broad-shouldered female, hard and shiny black, naked except for a necklace of chain and bone. Her cheeks puffed out as she grunted, "*Ho! Ho!*" She crouched as she approached, so that her fat breasts hung down; her crotch was woolly and colored with dust.

Burton moved to her unexpectedly and drove his fist into her stomach. When she fell to her knees and bent over, she tried to pick up a cowrie, but he stepped on her fingers and ground them into the earth until she cried out. He started to hit her again, to destroy her face, but she looked up at him and he decided against it; instead, he merely glowered at her until she crawled backward out of his circle.

He tossed the cowries at the foot of the earthen throne.

Gelele's interpreters shouted out their king's words: "This is a fine strong Englishman who dances and fights well!" Everyone applauded once more, and a group of young heralds who had lined up behind the king cried out in unison, "*Oyez! Oyez!*"

The king strolled over to some of the prisoners who were tied with their necklace of rope, spoke to them, laughed amiably, and came back to Burton. The interpreters suggested that Burton might wish to beg for the lives of these wretches. Burton buttoned his shirt with hands swollen and bleeding.

"Only kings can show mercy," he told Gelele, speaking slowly and cleverly. "I'm sure that you will show your power through generosity—as you show it by shedding blood."

Gelele had four of the prisoners kneel and kiss the ground. He put a foot on each man's neck, in turn, and pardoned them.

"There were Christian captives recently," Burton said, hoping to keep the king's attention. "May I beg for their release, too?" His words were quickly relayed to Gelele, who, Burton suspected, actually knew a bit of English.

"I know those of whom you speak. They are dead," Gelele replied.

"The Customs are an affront to all white men who trade in this land," Burton went on, his blood pounding in his veins. His words, as best as he could tell, were being translated.

"Criminals are put to death in your land," Gelele answered. "As for the others, this is a religious matter. My father's soul required servants and slaves after death, and so does my own. You will not worry about our religion."

"The taking of slaves must end, too."

"You have many complaints. And here you are without a fine golden carriage or white horses such as your own queen enjoys! I have requested this gift of you and your chiefs, but none of you try to please me!"

"First, slaving must stop."

"We will soon attack Abeokuta!" Gelele said, raising his voice to the loud rhetoric of a politician. "We will burn this puny kingdom and take many slaves!" His subjects roared their approval with every syllable. "The slaves will be fortunate! Many others we will kill!"

"My government has great warships," Burton went on. "They will stop all of the slave trade in coastal waters." The interpreters spoke to Gelele, perhaps passing on some of these irritating remarks.

"We shall also burn the city of Ouidah!" the king shouted. "We shall destroy all the villages! Our enemies will tremble!" The throng rattled spears, fired off muskets, raised and twirled umbrellas and, led by the heralds, called out, "*Oyez!*"

Burton saw that any further argument was futile and noticed, too, that the faces of his companions had turned to frightened stone. The interpreters smirked, as if they had known all along that such a plea from the white man was stupid.

The interpreter with the long ceremonial scar came to his side and said, "Tonight is the Evil Night again. You will sleep in your bed and not walk about."

Burton never slept. The night filled up with screams, so he stretched out on his mat of woven straw, drank a whole bottle of rum, and tried to trick his thoughts away. At least one of Gelele's arguments, he decided, was fairly potent. In this year of grace in lovely England four murderers had been hanged upon the same gibbet before 100,000 gaping souls at Liverpool; five pirates had also been strung up before an enthusiastic crowd at Newgate, a crowd filled with children, picnic baskets, and ladies in silken finery; hanging had become such a popular sport for spectators that an age of Hanging Mondays had been established, rivaling the weekly cricket matches in attendance.

He stared into the black neck of his bottle.

The next morning he learned that the amazons—in a separate compound not far away from his hut—had tortured and killed perhaps forty women victims during the night. All the prisoners in the pen had been slaughtered.

"There are bodies hanging all over the village," Aga told him. "Do you wish to see for yourself and take notes?"

"No, not at all," Burton answered, sleepy and drunk. "Pack up and prepare to leave."

"Is our mission accomplished?"

"Aga, dear heart, we've accomplished nothing. I managed to utter a few agitated words, but the king either didn't hear them or decided against killing us for the irritation. Now it's time to go."

Before noon they formed their caravan and received permission to leave from Gelele, who was weary from his night's exercise and didn't show himself. They paid their respects to ministers, wives, interpreters, and warriors, then marched out of Dahomey.

When they reached the sea, Burton stripped off his clothes and waded into salty surf. Aga made a rack of himself, holding out his arms and splaying open each finger, so that Burton's clothes could be draped and hung there. He watched the consul bathe slowly, cleansing and sobering himself. Burton sat in the sunlight afterward, so Aga crouched beside him to talk.

"Will you go to England now?" the servant asked him softly.

"I don't know," Burton answered. His voice seemed far away and hoarse, as if all his energy had drained away. "No, I'll go to Fernando Po. I'll drink about two hundred palm toddies, then I'll—hmm, take another small excursion."

"Sir, I believe you conducted your mission quite well," Aga said, speaking in Arabic. "The sands are large and a footprint is small, but you walked with strength."

"I took a journey in a sandstorm," Burton replied in the same language. "And in the harmattan there are no traces."

Isabel popped into the Foreign Office again, seeing about her husband's prospects. Her weight, which rose and fell with Burton's absences, was down again: she looked gaunt, buxom, and, Lord Russell thought, very beautiful. When such a pale bloom was in her cheeks he found that he had difficulty resisting her demands.

"Have you read Speke's book?" he asked her.

"No, have you?" she answered. Lord Russell seemed trim and buoyant. There was a brass penholder agleam on his desk and a painting by Delaroche catching the morning light from the narrow window.

"I think your husband will be very interested in the reception of the report. Rumor has it that David Livingstone has swung to Richard's defense."

"Dr. Livingstone?"

"None other. And of course there's MacQueen and the others at the Royal Geographical Society—always set to defend Richard's interests."

"This is wonderful news," she said. "Does Richard know?"

"I haven't written to him, but you certainly should. By the way, he completed his assignment in Dahomey, and we've received word that he's back at his consulate."

"Lord Russell, he *must* have a better assignment. You promised me."

"Tell him when you write that he performed his mission to my utmost and entire satisfaction, will you?"

"You could write him yourself."

"Actually, I can't. I'm most grateful for his services, but we have certain indelicate balances along the slave coast. His work will have to remain unofficial —for which he'll have to accept my unofficial thanks."

"My husband is wasted in Fernando Po," Isabel said with her usual determination.

"Yes, you've told me so—and I believe it."

"And if he doesn't get a better post, I'm afraid I'll not see him. I can't live with my family any longer. I want to be at Richard's side."

"In a few weeks we'll bring him home for another leave," Lord Russell promised. "In my opinion he'll be needed here because of the Speke controversy

—which threatens to be very embarrassing for his old colleague. And, yes, Isabel, I'll try to arrange something else when another consulate opens up. These matters take time."

"He has such *talents!*" she insisted.

"Your Richard—we all know this quite well—should be our roving ambassador to barbarians," Lord Russell told her. "But, please, Isabel, rest easy. We'll eventually find a new position for him." He took her arm and ushered her out of his office again, watching the soft rise and fall of her anxious bosom.

"Seems Speke is becoming a Christian," Dr. Livingstone said.

"What's that, sir?" MacQueen asked.

"Speke. Christian."

David Livingstone, who was everybody's favorite missionary, had a heavy Scots brogue, a nasal tone, and a speech impediment that rendered him almost impossible to understand. James MacQueen, a Scot himself, had less trouble than most of the great man's admirers.

Wrapped in their woolens and scarves, trying to keep warm in the chilly old rooms of the Geographical Society, they had occupied themselves with much of the committee work during the winter months.

"Gives talks to Bible groups," Dr. Livingstone went on.

"That's because he's lost credibility as an explorer," MacQueen was quick to point out. "His agent, Mr. Oliphant, can't book him properly as an expert on geographical matters, can he? I mean, after all, he didn't truly trace out the Nile! If he wants a public platform, he has to be a Christian, doesn't he?"

Dr. Livingstone always declined to address public meetings himself. In private conversations he seemed intelligent and persuasive when his opinions could be deciphered, and in an odd way his impediment and his general physical appearance lent him a nearly saintly air. His hands were large and rough like ancient tablets of stone; he had a long nose, gentle eyes, a stern mouth, and resembled a trustworthy and ordinary—yet fatherly—farmer. Everyone sought his advice, and when his speaking style could be fathomed, the advice he gave was usually followed.

"Mind you, I'm pleased Speke is a Christian," the doctor told MacQueen. They stood at a table in the Society's map room, rubbing their hands together for warmth as they waited for Norton Shaw, the secretary, and Sir Roderick Murchison, whose wheeze could be heard from a distant room.

"Aren't you a bit suspicious of his new evangelical zeal?" MacQueen asked. "His maps don't agree. His book is rot. Don't you see that he's attempting to beguile the public with a newfound morality?"

MacQueen had been attempting to mold Dr. Livingstone's opinions for weeks and had done so with modest success.

"Well, I do intend to sort out Africa myself," the doctor allowed.

"Beg pardon? What's that?"

"Sort it out. Africa. Needs accurate maps, you see. I don't think Speke has much of it right."

"And he certainly didn't allow our countryman, Grant, to see anything! There's no proof they were on the same river in Uganda and at Gondokoro! Yet Speke puts Grant conveniently aside and continues to make assertions—the same as when he came back after the trip with Burton!"

"One has to know a bit of hydrography," Dr. Livingstone said, mangling that last word. "Speke does seem quite innocent. Quite."

"Or a clever liar," MacQueen noted.

Shaw came into the room, pushing his glasses up on his nose as he placed a stack of correspondence on the table. Murchison came directly to the point.

"Whatever we're to make of Speke's maps or publications, we have one certainty: he means to ruin Petherick. As you know, Dr. Livingstone, our council meets soon on the matter, but I'm glad we could all come together today —despite the chill—to reflect. I think our deliberations will have final influence, if I may say so, on what the council decides to do."

Shaw passed a letter to Dr. Livingstone. "Here's Speke's request that an official inquiry should be held concerning Petherick's role in the expedition," he said.

Dr. Livingstone grumbled something no one understood.

"Yes, what's that?" Murchison asked.

"Said I've always liked Petherick well enough."

"Fine chap," MacQueen added, prompting everyone.

Dr. Livingstone stood up straight, rattled the letter in his huge hands, and read Speke's words.

I have the honour to request you will solicit the President and Council of the Society to institute an enquiry into what Mr Consul Petherick has done with money entrusted to him for the purpose of aiding my late expedition; and also to ascertain what steps he took to render me assistance . . .

"He accuses Petherick of not helping him and of misusing funds," the doctor said.

"Speke has always turned against those who have helped him," MacQueen said. "First Burton, then Grant, Petherick, and the Society that sponsored him. And now, as he did with Burton, he covers up his betrayal with slander."

"I'm afraid I have some added news on the subject, too," Murchison said, thrusting his hands into his pockets for warmth. "Speke's allegations against Petherick reached the Foreign Office some time ago. Petherick has just been relieved of his consulate at Khartoum."

"Merely on the basis of Speke's accusations?" MacQueen asked, raising his voice.

"Hmm, afraid so. Entirely on that basis."

Dr. Livingstone strolled over to the large globe, which sat in its frame in the middle of the room. He twirled it absently with his thick forefinger until all its continents blurred in spinning movement.

"Why does Speke do this?" he asked. "Why would he turn on his colleagues?"

MacQueen, who managed to understand, repeated the questions for Shaw and Murchison. Sir Roderick could only shake his head and shrug, but the doctor answered his own question.

"He must believe that Africa is a prize small enough for one man," he said, sighing. "It isn't. I know it isn't." He turned and came back to the table facing the others. "Are you satisfied that Petherick didn't spend the Society's money foolishly?" he asked Shaw.

"The consul put his own resources into his trip to Gondokoro," Shaw replied. "He spent, if I estimate correctly, far more of his own money than the Society provided him."

Dr. Livingstone looked at each man. He knew that he was a judge among judges: venerable, expert, and so completely influential that the council of the Society would rule following his opinion. "If we express dissatisfaction with Petherick over how he spent funds, we might leave him open to legal prosecution," he said, speaking slowly so that he could be understood. "We shouldn't take our lead from the Foreign Office. Petherick is one of our own fellows. My feeling is that we should stand by him. My hunch is that some personal matter exists between him and Speke—something that shouldn't be of concern to us."

MacQueen, blowing into his cupped hands, covered a smile.

"We're not dealing with some petty point of politics here," the doctor concluded. "We're dealing with a man's whole career and life."

"Understood, then?" Murchison asked the others.

"I'll see that the other members of the council have Dr. Livingstone's opinion in this," Shaw said.

They went out into the foyer where they found their topcoats. MacQueen picked up his cane and pressed its silver handle to his cheek. "In time," he told Dr. Livingstone, "I hope the whole story of Speke's behavior with Burton comes into the open, too. I'd like you to meet Burton and judge for yourself in that matter."

"Didn't Burton once think of crossing Africa from Harar and the east coast?" the doctor asked.

"Hmm, yes, think so."

"Perhaps I'll cross east to west. Perhaps I'll solve the Nile and the Congo and the Mountains of the Moon all at once. Or perhaps dozens of us will solve these things over dozens of years. It's an obsession, you know."

"What's that, sir?"

"Obsession. Africa. I should be content to run a simple mission: Bible verses and bandages. But where are the fabled mountains? And where do all the rivers go?"

"Sorry, didn't catch all that," MacQueen said.

"Mountains! Rivers!" Dr. Livingstone rasped, slightly annoyed, as usual, to be repeating so much.

Each day's mail brought complications, so that Speke took to the fields at Jordans as often as possible, shooting as many quail and partridge as daylight and ammunition allowed. He preferred the older, antique guns in the household, particularly a Lancaster breech-loader with silver filigree and a handsomely carved stock. He hunted alone every day, although once that winter a cousin, George Fuller, came over from Neston Park, near Bath.

Fuller was a tall, thin, blond sportsman, as tireless as Speke on a day's hunt, who shot without much talk or bother. He had a special knack for cleaning birds: he could press his thumbs into the underside of their breasts, gutting, skinning, and presenting the breast meat whole in a single, deft movement. Speke remarked that his cousin liked the mutilation of birds more than any actual shooting. When each day's hunt ended, then, he left Fuller with the gamekeeper and cook when he went upstairs to his room at the estate.

His dresser and desk were stacked and cluttered with papers. Oliphant's latest letter urged him to go away to Paris. Beside it, the reviews of *Journal of the Discovery of the Source of the Nile* were neatly piled up, each newspaper clipping and each journal containing criticisms. An issue of *The Times*, also neatly folded atop the dresser, told of how Samuel White Baker had discovered and named Lake Albert, the announcement crediting Speke with having supplied an accurate map for this accomplishment and also accusing him, implicitly, of not having thoroughly explored the region himself. On the desk were more papers and notes: the beginnings of his Somali diary, which the Blackwoods had also promised to publish.

Speke curled onto his bed in his hunting clothes, smelling faintly of blood and leather, looking at all those papers. He hated printed pages: words cold and written down, words and more words. He wanted mobility and vigor apart from such little black headstones spread on pages. I'm no writer, he told himself there on the pillow; I'm no feeble wordsmith; I have no rebuttals or arguments or fine points to make.

Grant, embarrassed at all the criticisms, had fled to the continent for an extended holiday. The public, swayed by the criticisms, had stopped buying the book. A few geographers—among them Livingstone—had commented that they actually favored Burton's ghastly theory that all the lakes of the region were linked in a Nile basin. Sickening.

He lay on the bed, his knees drawn up, going over each criticism of his book, one after another in turn, as he did every day. The reviewers had said that

—the latitudes for the nyanza and for parts of the Nile were wrong
—having gone overland to Gondokoro and failing to properly trace out the river from the Stones, there was no way of telling if the explorers had been on the same river
—all maps, as well as a preposterous Hindu sketch which had been included, were oddly inaccurate and contradictory
—the lake could not possibly flow out in four directions, then reconstitute itself as the Nile
—all river levels were wrong and in one particular stretch the explorers had managed to assert that the river flowed uphill for ninety miles
—Grant was cheated from actually viewing the source of the river at the nyanza
—the explorers failed to take note of the Blue Nile as it joined with the White Nile at Khartoum, yet another indication of their casual regard for good observation and for scientific documentation

Pages of deadly words.

Speke buried his face beneath his arm, trying to sleep, curling up like one of those cold partridges in his cousin's hunting pouch to await the last violence when its breast would be squeezed out. Except words would do the work: the razored barbs of tiny nouns and verbs.

He heard Fuller calling him.

At the window he looked down onto the rear lawn where his cousin stood, bloody hands held out, a smile on his face there in the last twilight.

"I say, time for a beer! Come down to the kitchen with us!"

"Yes, I'm coming down soon," Speke called back.

He changed clothes in the lingering dusk of his room, then went down the circular staircase into the main hallway. A fire crackled in the drawing room. Cousin and brothers laughed together. Before he went in with them, though, he found the day's new mail lying in the pearly seashell on the mahogany table near the door.

More words. Perhaps other reviews. With dread, he stopped, thumbed through the unopened letters, and found one from Murchison at the Society.

The council had met on the Petherick matter and had found no wrongdoing. It had described as unjust the allegation that the consul had been guilty of abetting, much less participating in, slavery, and had accepted Petherick's report of his Nile efforts and his meeting with Speke with complete satisfaction.

Speke folded the letter into his pocket and joined the others.

"Dear me, what's ailing you?" his cousin asked.

"Nothing at all," Speke answered.

That night after supper he went back to his room, stripped naked, and covered himself on his bed with his blanket and smelly hunting clothes. He relieved himself in a muffled fury, then, afterward, his thoughts flying away, he lay very still, waiting, as the warm fluid turned cold and dry on his stomach and thigh.

I'm not so vain about my looks, he decided, but I wouldn't shoot myself in the head, so that my face would be blown away. I wouldn't have the casket closed because of a disfigurement—because Mother would want to kiss my cheek a last time and couldn't bear it otherwise. No, I'd definitely shoot for the heart. And I believe—yes, I'm sure this is right—that the impact would render me unconscious immediately. So there would be no real pain: just a pinpoint instant, then the black sleep.

But, naturally, I would use a gun. I couldn't consider anything else, certainly not hanging or poison or any of that. Or drowning, especially, no, I'd hate that. Too much time waiting for death by drowning, too many last floating doubts.

Definitely a firearm, that's my way.

At the London home of the Marquess Townshend at Number 6, Grosvenor Place, Speke addressed an indifferent social gathering on the evils of the slave trade, the need for missionaries, and the opportunities for British trade in central Africa.

"They aren't listening to him," Oliphant said to young Lord Cowley as they stood just beyond the drawing room where the explorer talked. "There's not more than twenty of them—a dismal turnout—and they're not paying attention."

"He's saying the same boring things everyone hears in church." Cowley sighèd. "They want to hear how he fucked the savages."

Cowley was thin and handsome, with a cruel mouth. Wearing a silk suit and drinking Pernod, he tried to look bored and superior. Speke had difficulty with him—never sure, exactly, how the three of them were meant to get on together—although Oliphant referred to Cowley as a worldly, dear, brash slut of a boy and tried to make the best of it all. Oliphant had also explained that their interests were somewhat separate: Cowley liked the simple life, gambling and sex, while Oliphant had become interested in the complexities of the occult.

"Poor Speke," Oliphant whispered, standing outside the drawing room. "I'm afraid he's had to stoop to moral causes."

"Because he blundered in Africa," Cowley was quick to add.

"Cowley, dear heart, not so loud."

Later in the evening they watched Speke turn his good ear to several guests, making an effort to smile and converse. Then they saw him move to the buffet and gorge himself on salads and cakes as the gentlemen and ladies made their excuses and departed.

"Does he always stuff himself like that?" Cowley asked.

"Hmm, usually."

"He's quite a large sort. Does he fart in bed?"

"Wouldn't you like to know?" Oliphant answered, and they broke into laughter.

At midnight they went to a Turkish café in Soho, where Lord Cowley made lewd remarks and grabbed a passing waiter's pantaloons. Speke, disappointed at the small number of wealthy patrons who had come to listen to him, felt morose. "A terrible evening," he kept saying.

"No, not so bad," Oliphant assured him. "We'll go to Paris and forget it."

"Perhaps I will go to Paris," Speke said. "But I'll have to make a short trip home again."

"I say, look at this moussaka!" Cowley said. "I'm famished!" The waiter served hot portions, poured wine, and tried to ignore the young lord's hand on his leg. Speke allowed himself a full portion and began eating again.

"We'll stand you up at some official receptions in Paris," Oliphant went on. "Stay at the Grand Hotel. Gamble and eat. Attend a séance."

"And keep our pricks at attention," Cowley added with his mouth filled.

"A séance, really?" Speke asked.

"Remember how I foresaw my father's death? Remember, how at Aden I talked so much about mysticism and coincidence? Kismet, believe me, is real, and I want you to see this side of me: this serious, thoughtful side."

"If you like."

"But I hope we don't scurry from one séance to another this time," Cowley said, breaking a loaf of bread and stuffing a crust into his mouth. "That's dreary stuff: holding hands and pondering the infinite! Paris isn't that! It's cocks, cunts, and croissants!"

"You're impossible!" Oliphant said, laughing. "Isn't he too impossible?"

Speke felt that Lowry laughed much too long and too loudly, so he paid elaborate attention to his food once again.

Back at Jordans, Speke told his mother that he meant to stay the summer in Paris. She came to his room while he packed his new suit of evening clothes, a straw hat, and a seasonable if somewhat unfashionable attire for the boulevards.

"I may have to confer with the Blackwoods, but there's not much business to attend to," he told her. "The Society wants me to appear at Bath in September—for the British Association—so I'll probably come back for that. But I may as well take a holiday now."

"What sort of young man is Lord Cowley?" she asked.

"Oh, a jolly type—a bit fluff-headed."

"And you'll be seeing the French authorities?"

"Who can tell? They might commission another African trip for me! Lowry's arranging interviews and receptions, isn't that nice?"

His mother sat on his bed, her hands folded, smiling, and trying to say what she meant in a precise, tactful way. "Do you think your association with Lowry is—the right thing—the most important sort of work, I mean—that you could be doing just now?"

"What do you mean?" he asked, folding a shirt into his valise.

"Well, it would seem you'd be with Sir Roderick—or Livingstone—or some of the others."

"Livingstone has turned against me. His views on the Nile are similar to Burton's. Because he wishes to be known, if you ask me, as a great explorer—the one who finally solves everything. Mere missionary work isn't enough for the esteemed doctor."

"But wouldn't you need to be in meetings and conferences with all the other explorers who—"

"All of us have theories, only theories, don't you see? Never mind that mine's correct! Never mind that I was there!"

"But should you be going off with Lowry? Don't you see? William feels that Laurence Oliphant is just too—"

"My brother William is an idle country squire," Speke said a little more sharply than he had meant. "All my life I've been cursed with elder brothers—who do little—making authoritative judgments! William, Burton, Petherick, even Grant! I'm weary of the lot of them! I don't mean to be vainglorious, but they've done *nothing*, they think *nothing*, they know *nothing*, and they *are nothing!* William is—"

"Jack, please, don't raise your voice."

"William has his place assured: he has my home, Jordans, the place I love, without having done a thing to earn it, while I was sent off to India to struggle for myself! He's pompous as hell and jealous of me. And very ill informed about my affairs, so that he questions my business with Lowry! When I'm finished with all this, Mother, I swear, I'm going back to India, so that I don't have all this harping about my ears!"

"You don't mean that," she said, trying to soothe him. "Your fame and place is here at home and in London."

"No, not really. Perhaps India, perhaps Africa again. In the darkest, darkest corner of the earth, that I know!"

Isabel went to Liverpool to meet her husband's ship.

She was wan and beautiful that summer, thin in the waist from having shed so much weight in yearning and worry. Soft hollows appeared in her cheeks, and her eyes looked deep and sensuous; her hair fell over her shoulders like an inviting blond tent. Burton stood at the ship's rail waving, surrounded by his luggage and ten cartons of notes and manuscripts. He seemed older, gaunt, tired, yet happy to be home—especially as he watched her. She paced back and forth on the pier; her undulations in the soft cotton dress she wore inflamed him.

At the Regent Hotel they threw off their clothes. He knelt beside her on the bed, opened her legs and kissed her. Her body pillowed his face; her sounds encouraged him as he brought her to climax over and over, then he mounted her and drained himself and lay beside her.

"I'm impotent with everyone except you," he told her.

"You've had other women since our marriage?"

"Yes, yet not really. Nothing was ever consummated. And I'll never have another. I don't know when it happened, Isabel, but I'm bound to you."

She stared at the ceiling and tried to assess this new knowledge, which was a confirmation of her worst suspicions, a disappointment and yet, at the same time, an elation filled with hope.

"It's neither guilt nor a sense of duty," he mused, lying beside her. "It's just a strange bond, very strange, indeed, for me."

"We were meant for this," she finally managed. "I've known it since the gypsy's prophecy. Since the first time I saw you on that wall at Boulogne. Since before time itself, it seems."

"I can't quite explain it," he said in a voice filled with wonder.

"I do know we'll never be apart again," she said, staring out into the room. Tears filled her eyes; he had been untrue, yet here he was, true once more. "You'll not go back to Fernando Po. I'll see to it. You'll have a position worthy of you, and we'll be together always."

"I just can't say what's happened," he repeated. "It's so damned curious."

During that summer MacQueen published a series of attacks on Speke in the *Morning Advertiser* and arranged for Burton to meet David Livingstone so that a final effort could be made to discredit Speke's assertions about the Nile. Because General Rigby, known to be Speke's ally, had been appointed to the council of the Royal Geographical Society and because Murchison tried to remain neutral in the controversy, a breakfast meeting was arranged at Milnes' house in Upper Brook Street.

"Now, mind you, Dick, Livingstone doesn't like you or approve of you," MacQueen warned Burton before the breakfast. "But he wants to prove Speke wrong about the Nile, so that central Africa is left unsettled. I know our good doctor is as ambitious as the rest of you when geography's at stake."

"Why doesn't he like me?" Burton asked.

"Because you're a heathen."

"That's intolerant. I suppose he likes only nigger heathens?"

"Don't use that word with him. And be pleasant. If Livingstone stays our friend in this, Speke will be very embarrassed."

At the meal they dined on omelets and jam while Milnes, their host, led them through their initial introductions and small talk. Then they turned to a first item of business: the program for the next meeting of the British Association for the Advancement of Science, to be held in Bath in September.

"Murchison actually wants both you and Speke on the program—perhaps in a debate," MacQueen informed Burton.

"No, no, can't do that."

"But you must attend the meeting," Milnes pointed out. "Our organization needs funds and prestige. Speke is known to the public, but he's suspect as a scientific explorer. You could come as an anthropologist, if you like, and read a scholarly paper, but you must be there."

"Actually, the Nile must be settled," Dr. Livingstone added, chewing on his bread and jam and muffling his words. "A debate would probably be best."

"Sorry, sir, you said what?" Burton asked.

"Nile. Debate. Settle it."

"Speke is an inept cad," MacQueen said. "And I believe his next attempt to explain himself in public will end his career, so that good men like you two can return to Africa and give us proper maps. But, really, Dick, you must be at the meeting in Bath—for the general good of the Society."

"We must all attend," Dr. Livingstone agreed, wiping his chin. "Naturally I won't be making an address, but I'll definitely go."

"What's that you say?" Milnes inquired.

"He says he'll be at Bath himself," MacQueen translated. "And now, I think we should discuss a strategy for dealing with Speke's claims. Let me begin this way: I feel both Dr. Livingstone and Dick Burton have similar views on how Tanganyika and not Speke's nyanza is the true source of the Nile."

"I've drawn some maps, and I've tried to prepare a cogent view," Burton said. "First off, I believe Speke's nyanza is actually a series of many lakes. I also now believe that Lake Tanganyika is at a higher altitude than I originally thought. And, finally, I've decided that the Rusizi River at the north end of Tanganyika actually flows *out* of the lake—and is then linked to a basin of mountain streams, rivers, and lakes. The last lake in this chain, perhaps, is Baker's newly found Lake Albert, which becomes the Nile."

The others at breakfast sat in silence, pondering these sudden announcements and looking around at each other.

"Possible," Dr. Livingstone conceded.

"But, Dick, you have always stuck by two geographical certainties which you're now abandoning: the altitude of Lake Tanganyika and the direction of a river at its north end," Milnes said.

"We had poor instruments at Ujiji," Burton argued. "And, as for the Rusizi, neither Arabs, native guides, nor cannibal kings ever agreed."

"But, Dick, please, you mustn't change your basic findings—the whole of your observations at Lake Tanganyika—just so that you can manufacture a strong argument against Speke," Milnes warned.

"I'm not changing my story, just refining it," Burton said.

"Speke is intolerable," MacQueen added. "He requires strong rebuttal."

For a moment longer the men sat in silence. Burton poured coffee for everyone and offered them cigars.

"My own explorations," Dr. Livingstone stated, "have always been in the region south of your Lake Tanganyika, as you know—along the Zambesi River, around Lake Ngami, and a number of other secondary rivers which I've thought may be the sources of the Congo. But, yes, let me say outright: Speke is a poor geographer, and I disagree with his findings. I've walked more than nine thousand miles in Africa, and I believe I understand the great central watershed. Everything's quite confusing, but on the whole I'd say Burton here is correct."

MacQueen gladly repeated all this for Burton and Milnes.

"Well, I agree that things are confusing." Milnes sighed. "Here, let me have one of those cigars."

Dr. Livingstone leaned across the table to inspect the scar on Burton's cheek. He couldn't help reaching out a finger and touching it.

"Got that in Arabia, did you?"

"No, in Berbera," Burton said, blowing out a smoke ring. "It's one of quite a few scars, believe me."

"I heard you were stuck with a lance," the doctor said admiringly.

"In one cheek and out the other," Burton replied. "Pulled the damned thing out myself. I fancy there isn't a nastier scar anywhere."

"So? You think not?" Dr. Livingstone said, and he stood up beside the table, took off his coat, unfastened his tie, and began unbuttoning his shirt. "Laddy, I have something to show you!"

"It's well known that Dr. Livingstone was once mauled by a lion," Milnes put in, grinning.

The doctor had a broad chest covered with grey hair and a flat, muscled belly, but his left shoulder sagged pitifully, and the flesh on his upper arm and chest was all scar tissue.

"If my lion hadn't just fed, it would have eaten all of me instead of just my shoulder," the doctor boasted. "But I wasn't much of a dessert!" He turned around twice, so that the full extent of his wound could be appreciated.

"Look at this," Burton said, dropping his trousers. "Nice scar on my thigh, too."

Not to be outdone, Dr. Livingstone unbuttoned his tweed britches. "A scorpion bit me on the arse," he said. "Left a nasty hole and scar you've got to see."

Milnes and MacQueen puffed at their cigars as Burton asked the doctor to repeat himself. "Scorpion! See here!"

"By God, that is a bit of a hole," Burton agreed, inspecting the damaged backside. "Did you sit on the bugger?"

"Squashed him dead, but his sting almost killed me, too!"

The men laughed out loud as Mrs. Milnes swept into the room without warning to clear away their dishes. Dr. Livingstone tried to fumble his clothes into place, but Burton stood his ground with his trousers around his ankles. His cotton shorts were pale blue.

"Offhand, I'd say all of you are discussing Africa this morning," Mrs. Milnes remarked, and they didn't know what she meant, exactly, or how she imagined what she saw, but they laughed all the harder, even Dr. Livingstone, who stood in a crouch, red in the face, with his clothes bunched in front of his body.

Burton and Swinburne went to a music hall.

The little poet had promise, but fame had still eluded him that summer. He had lived with Rossetti, corresponded with Victor Hugo, traveled on the continent with his favorite cousin Mary Gordon, whored in London, stayed long periods at Fryston, and started a work called *Atalanta*, which he claimed would be his masterpiece.

"And what have you done?" he asked.

"Very important tasks," Burton said. "I collected three thousand African proverbs in various dialects. And botanical specimens. And wrote scholarly papers on racial characteristics. And I fear I've had a sexual alteration, I really fear so."

"Dickie, my friend, have you been sampling boys?"

"No, not at all, but I believe a form of monogamy has set in."

"Damn me, that's alarming. You listen to me: domestic sex is a narcotic. I've seen good men get on it—and they're done for." Burton smiled, but the poet seemed gravely serious.

They occupied a corner of a long table of ladies and gentlemen at The Oxford—which featured pease pudding, trotters, and solemn ensembles of violinists. Both poet and explorer wore battered top hats and had the shabby, intellectual look they prized; Swinburne also wore his enormous bow tie, while Burton had on a plaid cape and the bone necklace from Dahomey.

"Now you have always been mobile and wild," Swinburne continued, his pointed little face creased with worry. "But all women are Circe. And they summon you—listen to me, Dick, I'm serious—"

"I hear you."

"They summon you to the magic ecstasy of the cunt, but that's not what you get. Instead of erotic experience, you get the soft chains of the nest. You're wrapped round with pastries and doilies, the sweet breath of children, and the sorcery of comfort!"

"Algernon, you're wonderful tonight!"

"I'm not being wonderful, you idiot."

"Of course you are. Want some oysters? They look nice for a shilling, don't they?"

"I became concerned about you on our little trip down to Brighton," Swinburne went on. "You said you were worried about your wife and job. You couldn't have fun. Now you tell me you love Isabel—and the next thing—don't you see this?—you'll consider your bureaucratic chores clever and important! You'll punch time clocks, wear proper vests, and carry umbrellas! You'll even begin to like English food!"

"I'm not some primitive warrior," Burton replied. "I'm usually dry as dust. I write books and lie about on pillows."

"Like all adventurers, you take repose, and perhaps you even have a bit of a feminine side, a truly sensitive self—the same as I do," Swinburne argued, drinking off his Chablis. "But you mustn't give in to it, my man! You're a poet, yes, but a superbly bad one—too masculine and undisciplined. And when you talk fondly of home and hearth you make me dreadfully nervous!"

"Perhaps I'm getting old," Burton allowed, cracking open an oyster. "Fighting, fucking, and roaming around was good for me once, but a man tires eventually and likes a spot of tea."

"Oh, Dick, please, I beg you," Swinburne said, taking his friend's arm across the table. "Be true to yourself and keep to the horizon! You need to— for yourself, but also for all of us who gather ourselves together in such insipid places as this."

"What are you saying?"

"Each tame little village must have its hunter and warrior far afield in order to be itself! Don't you see that?"

"You're drunk!" Burton laughed.

"I'm being a lucid genius! Listen to me! Go back to Africa and lose all this! Bed down in bone and the primeval slime! Do it!"

Burton began another reply, but Swinburne broke his wineglass against the edge of the table, bringing it down sharply until only its jagged stem remained in his hand. Then he cut his palm with a quick, melodramatic stroke, letting the blood flow; a woman sitting nearby, dressed in satin veloutine, gasped and held her throat.

"What are you doing?" Burton asked casually.

Swinburne then slapped both of his own cheeks and his forehead, blotching his face with gore. He appeared calm, but resolute.

"I'm adding an exclamation point, so you'll remember what I say."

"Well, I'll certainly remember because you look ridiculous," Burton said, smiling. "Now sit down and have a glance at the menu."

The poet, disgusted, took his place again.

"How hungry are you?" Burton asked.

"I'm very hungry. Do they serve anything substantial?"

"I'd try the old steak and kidney," Burton suggested. "With a potato baked in its jacket. You look pale, as if you've not been eating enough."

Paris: little shops, bistros, hotel terraces, boulevards, the sounds of tinkling wineglasses and brittle talk floating on the summer air, everything civilized and somehow wrong. Speke grew restless, which annoyed his companions, yet such a place had tamed itself into catastrophe: people lived out their lives buying things, concocting stylish opinions and apparel, eating too much, and attending events that were like mirrors turned to face other mirrors.

His own situation seemed wrong, too. Lord Cowley, like a boy who hadn't learned to behave toward a man of reputation, was both awkwardly respectful and casually arrogant. In one moment he would make clear that they had come to Paris only for Speke's career and that he was happy to be in the company of such an accomplished figure, then in the next moment he would do or say something to indicate that only he and Oliphant mattered, that as lovers and confidants their interests excluded Speke altogether.

In the hotel suite Cowley constantly walked through the sitting room, going to and from the bath, trailing a towel and exposed; his flanks and thighs were slender and hard, and his prick was like a fist, stubby and insolent in the mat of dark hair. He and Oliphant shared a small bedroom overlooking the avenue; the sitting room with its high, bright windows lay between it and the larger, ornate bedroom where Speke corrected the proofs of his Somali book.

Immediately after their arrival Oliphant arranged a meeting with the officials of the French Geographical Society. They met in stuffy, humid rooms in St. Germain, where their hosts were polite and cool.

"So. You will return to Africa?" a gentleman in a monocle asked.

"Yes, I hope so, and I should be happy and honored to take along any of your explorers or mapmakers who might wish to accompany me."

"Our explorers naturally have plans of their own. And plans, I presume you know, about Africa."

"When I make my official report to our Royal Society, I'll see that you and your explorers have a copy with the appropriate maps," Speke promised.

"Ah, yes, thank you. But do you not publish all your findings in the British commercial magazines?" the man asked, taking off his monocle and smiling.

"The reason for that," Oliphant explained, "is that the public in England is very keen on geography. And Speke is a national hero. No one wanted to wait for his report to be published in an obscure journal."

"Yes, I'm sure," the Frenchman replied.

Clearly, the interview had come to an end. Speke stood up and shook hands stiffly with his hosts. The official with the monocle managed to click his heels together lightly.

In a letter from Rigby came the news that Petherick had returned to London and had sued Speke for malicious slander.

Speke read the letter, folded it, then went out into the hallway and stood, dazed, until Oliphant came out of the suite to find him.

"Must have taken the wrong door," Speke offered.

"Are you ill, Jack? Come back inside."

Speke, holding his deaf ear as if some deep throbbing had begun, allowed himself to be led back into the sitting room.

"I'll just go to bed and sleep a few hours," he said.

"What happened? Is there bad news from home?"

Before reaching the door to his bedroom, Speke turned. His mouth was tight with anger. "It's that goddamned Burton," he said.

"Has he said something more against you?"

"We should settle it with our fists! How simple it would all be if I could just smash his bloody face!"

Lord Cowley, wearing an open silk dressing gown and nothing more, came smiling into their presence.

"Is that letter from Burton?" Oliphant persisted. "What's wrong?"

"If ever I see him again, believe me, I'll kick him hard! He has poisoned my life, Lowry, with a deadly, virulent poison!"

Speke slammed the door as he left the room.

"Dear me," Cowley said. "How can you put up with such a petulant ass?"

"Shut up," Oliphant replied.

The séance was held in an apartment between St. Sulpice and the Luxembourg Gardens, around a huge oval table where the clients extended their hands, palms upward, and followed the instructions of Auber, the turbaned medium, who was Oliphant's favorite. Lord Cowley had gone off alone to the Follies because such proceedings bored him, he claimed, although Oliphant accused him of being afraid. Speke was still in his bad mood, but went along. His hands appeared to be the largest spread open on the table; the ladies were from Austria and America; there were a baron and assorted others, a dozen in all, so that Auber made thirteen.

"Each of you will have independent experiences tonight," the medium explained. "You will see the dead. You will also experience certain phenomena together. I will speak in voices not my own—and tell amazing things about certain ones of you: knowledge coming through me from the spirit world."

Auber was a tiny man, perhaps a dwarf, although perfectly proportioned. With dark skin and blue eyes, he resembled a miniature caliph; his voice was impressively deep. Speke remained skeptical, but felt amused by the ominous little drama and was especially intrigued to see how gullible and excited Oliphant seemed to be.

In the center of the table sat a crystal bowl surrounded by thirteen glowing candles. As the séance began, all candles except for the one nearest Auber went out—although Speke felt no gust of wind. Auber's voice then changed into a woman's; she said that her name was Villette and that she brought word from the spirit world about a ring lost by someone at the table, a ring now worn on the hand of an enemy of the person who had lost it. Then the voice became a child's, that of a boy named Falón, who announced that his death should no longer be mourned; at this the Austrian woman wept, so that Auber had to tell her to keep her palms upright on the table.

Speke watched Oliphant's face through all this: a fearsome rapture in the soft candle glow.

Then a large dog padded through the room, a silent Great Dane, which circled among the guests. "The dog of death has arrived," Auber told them. "His ghost belongs to this house, don't worry. He will touch and sniff at all of us, perhaps, but make no movement." At that moment Speke felt the animal brush his leg beneath the table.

Auber's voice became an old man's. In a hoarse, aged whisper he told of things to come to various guests at the table: a sea journey, a sum of money found in an old hiding place, a valuable Chinese vase that would be broken, someone's death in an obscure war far away, a meeting with a mystic who would live in New York City, the death of a grandchild.

Speke felt a chill. As Auber's candle went out and the room fell into darkness, everyone's index finger was sharply pricked. Then candles were once more lighted and each guest found a bright bead of blood on his finger.

"Mingle your blood in this," Auber said, passing the crystal bowl. The baron trembled violently while the Austrian woman dabbed at her eyes with a silk handkerchief.

"I have the Chinese vase," the American woman remarked.

"My ring was stolen and now I know by whom," someone else said.

Auber seemed cheerful as he collected droplets of blood in the crystal bowl. "The dog behaved curiously this evening," he said. "Usually he sniffs at all of us, but tonight, no. Did you see how he left the room, vanishing through that wall?"

"He touched my leg," Speke offered, squeezing out his blood into the bowl.

"No, not tonight. He touched no one," Auber replied.

After the séance Oliphant and Speke made the long stroll into the Latin Quarter. They found a café on the boulevard and talked about the spirit world, immortality, and the mystic arts.

"Conventional religion can't contain my beliefs," Oliphant announced. "I know that I have special powers and that I'm in communication with others who do, too."

"Or you're following another fad," Speke suggested. "Every lady in the West End has visions and studies the Tarot deck nowadays."

"Believe me, Jack, I'm definitely a mystic."

"Auber was impressive, but everything could have been a trick. It was all so melodramatic. Everyone, I mean, takes sea journeys. Many people lose their rings. And besides, Lowry, you're as materialistic as anyone I know. You've always much preferred fashion, travel, and good wine."

"No longer," Oliphant contended.

Silence fell between them; they listened to the familiar café noises.

"Did you see that dog at the table?" Speke finally inquired.

"Yes," Oliphant replied, his feelings obviously hurt.

"It did touch me," Speke said.

"If you would open yourself to certain universal realities and refrain from being such a cold prig, you would be so much better off." Oliphant sighed, resuming his dining.

But now Speke was angry and didn't respond.

During the night a storm blew up, rattling Speke's bedroom window with sheets of wind and rain; a clap of thunder woke him and he saw Oliphant in his room, standing beside the bed in his dressing gown.

"Lowry?" he asked sleepily.

"I do apologize," Oliphant whispered as a shimmering pulse of lightning illumined his face. "You must know, Jack, that I would never deliberately hurt you."

"Sit here beside me," Speke offered, patting the coverlet.

But Oliphant dropped his gown to the floor and quickly moved underneath the bedclothes into Speke's arms; his movement was so suddenly natural, like a child scurrying to its parent during a storm, that Speke didn't resist.

They lay there listening to thunder booming across the rooftops. Speke dared not move or think; Lowry's steady breath warmed his shoulder as the hours passed; if Lowry had made any further overture, Speke would have rejected it, yet he wanted this close silence, this heartbeat darkness until the rain and thunder ended.

"Don't go to Bath," Oliphant advised. "If Burton is there, you'll just cause yourself pain! Why go over old ground?"

"I owe this to the Society," Speke said. "Perhaps Burton won't go and face me."

It was late August 1864, and Murchison had written once more requesting Speke's presence at the British Association meeting, suggesting again that Speke could appear on the same platform with Burton to discuss the Nile questions. Since Speke had finally turned in a meager report on his expedition to the Royal Geographical Society—one so thin that Sir Roderick had to publish an apologetic footnote referring readers to articles in *Blackwood's*—and since Speke felt guilty for this, he had agreed to attend the meeting. It remained unclear if Burton meant to be there, too.

At the end of the month they sailed from France across a rough channel. Cowley and Speke became seasick, spending their time at the rail, but Oliphant ate pork pie, drank beer, and ignored them.

Rigby joined them at the East India and United Services Club, where they entertained a number of young officers during an afternoon at the bar and told stories about Burton.

"You've heard the tale from New York, haven't you?" Rigby wanted to know. "A Yankee editor caught Burton outright! Found him with the wife in a hotel! Story is, Burton had to scamper out a window—yellow and on the run as usual!"

In the ensuing laughter Speke told about the fight at Berbera. "They tied me to stakes," he related. "And where was my friend and commander? He ran off to the beach! He was wounded, I grant you, but he left me to be killed by the renegades! Luckily, I broke loose and fought my own fight!"

"What a complete bumhole," Cowley put in, looking over the young officers crowded around the bar.

Rigby was decked out in uniform and medals. The young officers carefully watched their general's face, taking their cues on when to laugh and when to nod in somber agreement. Several toasts were raised to both the explorer and the British commandant who had conquered slavery at Zanzibar.

At one point Rigby draped an arm around Speke and shouted, "To the conquerer of the Nile!"

Speke's confidence soared as the young men cheered. "Actually, I do hope to see Burton at that meeting—acting cocky and trying to defend his ludicrous ideas!" he shouted at Oliphant above the noise.

The heat of summer lasted into September.

One steamy afternoon Burton and Isabel strolled down Oxford Street gazing into shop windows. Burton's coat was off, his tie hung loose, and his mustache sagged with perspiration. Isabel, the armpits of her taffeta dress dark with perspiration, too, clasped her husband's arm and smiled. A busker with a mandolin played a merry song to a young girl selling oranges from a crate.

"Is that Richard Burton among the shops and boutiques?" a voice asked.

"Hello, Oliphant," Burton answered flatly, turning around.

"Miserable heat, isn't it?" Oliphant said, brushing imaginary dust from his neatly tailored suit. He wore a plaid vest and a starched lancer collar that held his head at an arrogant tilt. "I suppose it will be hot at Bath, too, won't it, or will you be attending the big scientific meeting?"

"I've been invited as an anthropologist."

"Hmm, very appropriate. Good afternoon, madame."

Isabel nodded only slightly.

"Of course, I was invited to debate with Speke. But I don't suppose he intends to share his findings with the scientific community," Burton said.

"Oh, he'll be there. Too bad the two of you aren't debating. He said that if you appeared on the platform with him he'd kick you."

"Speke said that?"

"Absolutely. Frankly, Burton, I believe he's quite weary of you."

"If he said that, then by God he shall have his chance to kick me! That settles it, and I shall go to Bath!" Rivulets of new perspiration edged along Burton's reddened scar.

"I suppose I could arrange the formalities of a debate with Murchison and the others," Oliphant offered.

"Yes, do that. I'm sure you'll arrange things quite well. Did you arrange to find me here in the middle of Oxford Street today?"

"Oh, my, no, Burton, I'm searching for a new topper—something jaunty. Fact is, you could use a new hat yourself. Want to shop with me?"

Burton was almost too angry to decline, but managed.

Again at Bath the weather was stifling, but delegates to the Association meeting asserted their authority over it by wearing their usual woolens, stiff collars, and ties. Arriving that weekend before the session opened, doctors, chemists, physicists, and hundreds from various sciences strolled beside the soft waters of the Avon, viewed the ruins and took the waters at the old Roman baths, and toured the cathedral, which dominated the town. Burton was the only anthropologist. He was scheduled to debate Speke on Nile matters, but had also prepared a paper on customs in Dahomey if the event failed to materialize. Isabel was at his side: pale, smiling, already plump again since his homecoming, and charming to Livingstone, Milnes, Shaw, Murchison, MacQueen, and all the others with whom the Burtons stopped to talk. The old cobblestone streets gave off an atmosphere of a fashionable county fair: gentlemen in top hats, ladies and children, busy shops, serious topics, everything lighthearted yet wonderfully important.

Oliphant was the gadfly, engaging everyone in the town's bars and tea shops as he advanced Speke's cause, but Speke himself refused to stay in a hotel. He was at Neston Park some eight miles away with his cousin George Fuller.

"I presumed you came here to answer your critics at the big scientific meeting, cousin, but I believe you've just come to hunt," Fuller said.

"Just to hunt, most definitely," Speke replied. "I hope to take a short carriage ride into town and to dispose of my detractors in a single afternoon."

The Fuller mansion far exceeded Speke's expectations, sitting in gardens where peacock and swan made their noises, where flowers still bloomed and a heavy, sweet fragrance scented the air. It seemed far away from the crowds and demands of the meeting.

Speke's greatest worry about the debate was that he could only repeat his published claims, whereas others could prepare elaborate refutations; he was also disappointed that Grant wouldn't be there and that Livingstone would be against him. He felt that a hostile, intellectual, authoritarian group awaited him at Bath, and he wished that he could send his part in the debate by messenger.

His thoughts gave way to oddities.

The body of little Meri: profound as the curvature of the earth.

My nyanza is a dream, a vague mist.

"Damn me, this is hot weather!" said Davis the gamekeeper.

"Intolerable," Speke agreed, and his mind filled with fragments of memory.

That fountain of blood in the hippo pool.

"Will you hunt tomorrow, sir, or be at your meeting?" Davis asked. He was a short, wiry man, with a tiny pinfeather stuck to the pocket of his hunting jacket like a badge.

"I have to be seen at the opening session, but I'm not on the program, so I'll hunt. I'll be here tomorrow afternoon."

"There's good birds and plenty of 'em," Davis remarked.

"Yes, I'm sure."

I must hunt tomorrow. Men like Burton are within time, of time, a friend of time, and idleness is their victory over it; but time is my enemy; if nothing is accomplished in a day, time has beaten me.

"Ready for today's shoot, then, sir?"

"Hmm, of course. Let's go," Speke replied absently, and they started through a field toward Lentz Green, where Fuller ran the hunting dogs.

No proof, Speke thought. At heaven's gate with no coin in my pocket. The day's heat kept them at a slow pace, so that they seemed to be measuring each step across the grassy field. After a while they heard the dogs barking.

Jim Grant. Those piercing dark eyes of his: he knew how wrong I was, he really did know, I suppose, and now he won't come here to be with me.

The heat grew worse.

Isabel, on Burton's arm, kept her fan fluttering while her husband, sweating profusely, occasionally leaned over to find a bit of its breeze. All the men kept their coats on, their ties knotted, and their expressions severe as they assembled for the opening ceremonies.

"Do you see him anywhere?" Burton asked, leaning toward Isabel.

"Not yet," she answered, nodding and smiling at those who passed.

The hospital corridors were jammed with delegates. Burton and Isabel passed rooms where patients looked out at all the commotion with tepid curiosity from their sickbeds.

The Mineral Water Hospital at Bath, used in the old days as a healing spa and now staffed with doctors and nurses who struggled toward a more scientific and broader clinical practice—including new techniques in bleeding and restrictive diets—was the site of the Association's meeting this year. The building wore a Georgian facade and contained lecture halls and assembly rooms where delegates in the various sciences could gather. The debate between Burton and Speke, a featured program arranged by Murchison and Oliphant, was scheduled for the second day, but now, at noon, everyone came together for the first session. News of the debate had received comment in *The Times*. Every member of the Geographical Society's council had arrived, and Sir Roderick, having brought this year's meeting wide notice through the debate, had also been chosen as chairman for the opening ceremonies.

"Good seeing you," Dr. Livingstone said, meeting the Burtons in the corridor. He seemed rigid and mildly indifferent.

MacQueen waved hello with his silver-handled cane.

As Livingstone moved away in the company of a talkative man in a clerical collar, Burton asked Isabel, "Did he strike you odd?"

"Don't worry. You know he supports your view."

"He seemed unfriendly," Burton said.

Near the doorway to the main hall the Burtons stopped to greet Shaw, who kept pushing his glasses up on his nose as if the crowd might jostle them off. Everyone kept looking at Burton, keeping watch on the day's celebrity and giving him encouraging smiles.

Then, suddenly, Speke was there, standing taller than anyone, his beard dark with perspiration as he and Burton saw each other for the first time in five years. He looked ages older, with a sad desperation glazing his eyes; out of place, too, Burton thought, like some confused farmer dressed in woolens, wandering among strangers, awkward and lost. He almost greeted Burton, then didn't; instead, he glanced toward the platform and moved toward his seat. He had deliberately turned his face to stone, but it had fixed itself in an expression of pain. Burton, in spite of everything, felt a rush of pity.

"Did you see the look in his eyes?" Burton asked. "Did you see?"

Isabel clutched her husband's arm and led him toward the platform, but Burton could only watch his adversary. He recalled those words spoken in sickness: *Please don't leave me no matter what we've said in the past.*

Livingstone had God in Africa, he found himself thinking, but Speke and I only had each other. *Demons: they're stripping the tendons out of my legs!*

Burton looked keen and magnificent, Speke decided, and far healthier and more confident than when they last said good-bye in Aden. Even the dowdy Isabel looked tolerably good.

The situation was impossible. This man—for all his shortcomings—was a capable linguist and public speaker, and Speke could only recall his own fumbling efforts at the Society, at Taunton, and at the home of the Marquess. He consoled himself with the thought that years ago he had delivered that rousing dinner address in Bombay, impressing all those East India Company officials, Lumsden, and even Burton himself. Yet now, failure was apparent: he felt it in himself and saw it in the room. Livingstone sat comfortably beside MacQueen; Monckton Milnes sat beside Lord Ripon; and poor Lowry, resplendent in his new autumn finery and trying to manufacture an arrogant little stare, sat alone.

I've published in *Blackwood's,* accused Petherick, and have no proof, so I've lost favor with the Society. No proof, just my claim.

Murchison, speaking at length in swollen phrases, managed to say that he had a very high regard for scientific endeavors. Meanwhile, the delegates squirmed in their chairs, fanning themselves and loosening their collars. Burton looked overheated, but confident; his broad shoulders squared.

Speke closed his eyes and saw a landscape: an outcropping of boulders adorned with euphorbia trees and surrounded by an endless horizon of scrubby brush, smoke rising from a distant point to signal, somewhere, far off, a human existence.

The platform on which they sat was crowded, and there were so many in the audience without chairs that when Speke stood up and made his way along an aisle a man asked, "I say, I'd like your seat! Will you be coming back?"

"I hope not," Speke replied, and made his way through the audience as Sir Roderick droned on. In the corridor outside the meeting room: a strong antiseptic smell.

The cousin's livery boy waited with the horses and rig in the street outside the hospital. "Finished already, sir?" he asked.

"Let's get along," Speke answered, and they turned the rig toward the bridge and the road to Neston Park.

"Nice day for hunting," the boy offered, snapping the reins.

"Mind the ruts and don't talk," Speke replied.

The rolling countryside, still in its late summer bloom, became a green mirage. Sorry, he told the meadows as they passed; truly sorry, deeply sorry, he repeated, as if the land itself had to forgive him. He wanted to burrow into its valleys, into the bewildering forests, into the mossy ground among the cold roots, down into the atonement of the earth. He wished that he could plant himself, like a seed.

I'm definitely drying up now, he felt, and I'm sorry for everything; because of my curse; because I'm no good at reading instruments; because I'm not a fine, brave son; not a witty speaker; not a good writer; not devout enough; because I remember only a few hazy latitudes and have no proofs or maps; because I feel the incertitude of space; because I cannot love Burton, Grant, Lowry, William, or a thousand others; because I'm weary in this balmy heat of the autumn sun; because where I've walked my bootprints vanish.

"What's that, sir?" the boy asked.

Speke didn't answer. The livery boy gave him a sidelong, fearful glance as the rig boomed across a wooden bridge.

In an hour they came into his cousin's estate: stone barns, houses and walls, and a few high, grassy hills where the sky opened up into wide vistas of the Wiltshire countryside. At the barn behind the mansion Davis, the game-keeper, came out to greet them, but after seeing Speke's face and exchanging a look with the livery boy said little. Tied nearby, a pair of eager pointers barked and strained at their tethers, ready for the field, as George Fuller emerged from the barn.

"Cousin!" he called. "You look worn out! Sure you want to hunt?"

"Absolutely," Speke said.

"We've heard the birds calling all day, haven't we, Davis?"

"Yes, sir, there's birds," the gamekeeper agreed.

"And I say I'll drop more of them today than you, Jack—for once," Fuller said, laughing.

"I'll change clothes in the barn," Speke said, managing a smile.

When he walked away the master and his workers busied themselves with guns, dogs, and game bags. "He should have stayed with us today instead of bothering with those stuffy scholars in Bath," Fuller said, explaining matters to no one in particular.

The barn smelled of dung and rot. Speke pushed his legs into his favorite britches, the old ones sewn for him from mariner's canvas.

Mother, I love you. Father, I never knew you well.

I could have shot a lion, he told himself, buttoning his flannel vest as he stared into those overhead rafters. I could have stayed in Africa, perhaps, as a hunter, eccentric and solitary, with a native wife and a sunburned nose. It could have all gone differently, but now I'm into arguments and proofs and this green England, my grave.

With easy strides they started across the first field, the dogs panting around them in circles. A south wind sent tremors through the tall grass and the sun seemed to glare down at him, causing his thoughts to burn and explode.

Those wounds on my body: they were like sweet sexual doors, each one. Pain is like orgasm, a crossing over.

The dogs began their patterns, running low and sniffing, making quick turns ahead of the men. Speke, Fuller, and Davis spread out until they were more than fifty yards apart.

As the lead dog went on point, Davis closed toward him, waited, circled slightly so that the birds might fly toward Speke, then took another step in order to flush them out. They came up with a loud flutter. Davis fired, dropping one, then, as a single came toward Speke, he raised his gun—the old Lancaster breech-loader—and pulled the trigger. A miss. He fired the other barrel and watched the bird fold its wings as it came to earth. Davis waved and sent a dog in search of the kill.

The low stone walls. The wide blue sky.

Let my name be in history. Let proofs be found. Sorry, deeply sorry.

They followed a tattered hedgerow as it rose into a high field. Fuller was more than two hundred yards away, now, and walking at an angle, as if he were lost or meant to leave them. Davis and the dogs were busy marking birds ahead as Speke reloaded his weapon. His face began to twist in pain, as if by some sad magic it were being deformed; he didn't know if he would weep, only that his visage was being distorted, only that the field was going out of focus and that his mouth was being pulled down by some deep ravage. He felt a passionate emptiness.

Sorry everyone.

He stepped up on a low stone wall. His eye caught the shiny hieroglyph of a snail's path on the rock: a tiny river of slime.

He held the barrel of the gun close to his side in a cold embrace. Neither Fuller nor Davis were watching; the sky wheeled and shimmered.

When they heard the shot, both Fuller and Davis turned and saw their guest standing on the wall; he paused there, weaving slightly, then fell face forward into the field. They started running toward him.

The wound had torn open his left side at his heart. As Fuller turned him over, Speke opened his eyes, looked up, and in a feeble whisper said, "Please, don't move me."

"We'll fetch the surgeon," Fuller said, giving the gamekeeper a hopeless stare as blood pulsed from the wound and seeped into the ground. "I'm going for Doctor Snow," he said to Davis. "Keep watch. I'm on my way."

As Fuller ran off, the gamekeeper knelt and watched Speke's face as it took its painful sleep. The dogs arrived and sat in a circle, panting and waiting until the familiar and mysterious end had come.

Burton waited on the platform the next morning as the audience stirred uncomfortably and wondered at the delay. At the far end of the assembly room behind a closed door Murchison had called a hurried meeting between Dr. Livingstone, Shaw, and other Society members. Isabel stood with her husband as he waited, a sheaf of papers in his hands, anxious to know what was going on. Above them, a fly buzzed against the window.

At last Murchison came down the aisle, going up to Burton and asking, "Are you prepared to give your lecture on Dahomey?"

"I have my notes with me," Burton answered.

"Then I'll ask you to present your materials because there won't be a debate this morning," Murchison said. "I have an announcement about Speke."

Before Burton could ask anything else, Murchison had moved up to the lectern and looked out on the audience as it settled into silence.

"John Hanning Speke was killed yesterday afternoon in a hunting accident on his cousin's estate," Sir Roderick told the group. "Since we will not have the scheduled debate, Richard Burton has graciously consented to read a lecture on the ethnology of Dahomey."

The audience gasped and stirred. Burton sank into a chair; Isabel sat down quickly beside him and took his hands in hers.

At the rear of the room Dr. Livingstone surveyed the confusion, watching several delegates and visitors rise to leave the assembly, including Oliphant, who without expression, his head held high, walked down the aisle, only to be jostled aside by a lanky reporter for *The Times* who ran past. Milnes stood in front of his chair, his eyes riveted on Burton, who tried to bring himself under control.

All voices and movement ended as Burton slowly rose from his chair and went to the lectern. After a pause, he worked his mouth, trying to speak. His audience grew still and waited.

"Dahomey lies along the slave coast in western Africa," he managed. "I was asked to go there—" He stopped, his eyes fixed on Dr. Livingstone, who stood at the back of the room, his head bent as if in prayer.

"I can't go on," Burton said, his voice breaking. He turned to Isabel, who rushed to her husband as the audience erupted in noise and movement, everyone filing out, shouts being exchanged.

The hospital corridors rang with loud speculations. Many delegates assumed that Speke had killed himself, unable to face Burton, yet there were contrary and insistent reports: a hunting accident, nothing more, purely accidental. Word passed from the livery boy who had come with the news to doctors to various Association officials to those who knew Speke. Details were stated and repeated: no suicide note, an old gun without a trigger guard, climbing over a wall, just an unfortunate mistake. But how could Speke, the careful and experienced hunter, make such an error, others asked, and on the eve of such embarrassment as he was sure to receive from Burton?

"Shot in the heart? Unlikely, unless on purpose," MacQueen responded.

"Isabel, take Dick out of here as quickly as possible," Milnes said, putting his arms around his friends.

"I'm all right," Burton argued. "The controversy's settled now."

"But it isn't," Milnes said. "The charitable are going to say that Speke shot himself. The uncharitable are going to say that you shot him."

Others arrived, jamming the hallways. A mass of delegates collided with another mass going in the opposite direction, so that Burton was turned and pushed backward like a grain between millstones. He reached out for Isabel's hand, but they were momentarily separated from each other.

The lanky reporter was surrounded by delegates, everyone talking at once. Shaw stood against the wall of the corridor, his index finger in front of his face, holding his glasses in place.

Burton reached the stairway, where Laurence Oliphant seemed to await him. There was nothing of the dandy about Oliphant now; his tie hung loose, his hair was disheveled, and he had been crying.

"I'll tell you what will become of you now," Oliphant began, as if picking up in the midst of a conversation and replying to a question he had not actually been asked. "You'll have yourself a few minor government posts. You'll scrawl on paper. You'll smile the official smile. You'll fret over biscuits and casual remarks. And you'll be a wanderer—a petty little diplomatic wanderer—checking into hotels and minding clocks and schedules."

Burton only stared, unable to reply.

"He truly loved you," Oliphant went on, his voice quavering. "And you could have written a small page together. Perhaps it would've been wrong—the latitudes inaccurate and the maps crude—but, damn, the effort and the intention could have been so bold and generous!"

Isabel arrived, and although she didn't hear she became instantly furious to see her husband being scolded.

"Get away from us," she hissed. "You won't say anything to Richard! If anyone caused this, you did!"

Oliphant looked shaken. He turned and fled downstairs.

"Was he blaming you?" she wanted to know. "Did he insult you?"

Clasping his arm, she guided him slowly down the stairway toward the door to the street. Someone dashed by, taking the steps two at a time, and all around them shouts echoed through the building.

She repeated her question, asking what Oliphant had said. Burton could only shake his head. "He's right," he answered. "Right in all he told me. It will all happen just that way, as sure as sure."

In the following weeks Burton published *The Nile Basin*, which kept all arguments alive, although he asserted that he would say no more about Speke. The book, which contained the material Burton had prepared for the debate and which also included MacQueen's libelous attack on Speke himself, was called tasteless by most reviewers. *Blackwood's* called Burton an unscrupulous and jealous rival.

In response he drank quantities of brandy, argued with Isabel, belittled his critics, and tried to shock everyone with his atheism, opinions on sex, and bad manners.

"You're drunk, Jemmy," Isabel told him.

"Goddammit, don't call me that!"

"We're not invited to the Milnes' house anymore! No one wants to see you! The other night you told that horrid lie about cutting a man in half with your sword! At the dinner table!"

"The time before that I farted at table! Besides, I said I tried to cut a man in half, but didn't succeed! Didn't get through the last bit of skin, so he just toppled over sideways!"

"Oh, ghastly! I can't talk with you!"

"Please don't, then! You're standing at my desk, so I can't work! You're in my light! You smell like a bad flower! Go away!"

He worked long hours, not letting Isabel see his work. From her bedroom she could hear the sounds of his pen scratching on paper and the occasional rattle of bottle and glass as he stopped to take a drink. She suspected that he worked at his poetry, perhaps his long work, *The Kasidah*, but he wouldn't talk to her about it.

Meanwhile, she went back to the Foreign Office in his behalf, imploring them to give him a new and more worthy consulate. On an afternoon in early December she came to his study, pulled up a chair, and folded her hands on his desk as he glared at her.

"We have a new position," she announced. "With a fine house and gardens—and very important duties, I think, for both of us. You've been appointed consul in Brazil."

He tried to control his face. "Brazil?" he asked, flatly. "In South America, you mean?"

"Yes, that Brazil."

He put down his pen and covered his papers, so that she couldn't see his work. "I do know a bit of the Portuguese language," he admitted, trying to stay calm. "But my principal languages are English, Arabic, French, Spanish, German, Hindustani, and various African dialects. So I take it that you've persuaded Lord Russell to misuse me again?"

"The consulate in São Paulo is the only thing available," Isabel said. "It's not Damascus, no, but we must live. And you must do an agreeable job, so that you can eventually have what you want."

"You're a fool," he told her, and she began to cry. "Do you think you have to lace my boots, find my jobs, and fluff my pillow for me?"

"We must take care of each other," she wept. "We must, Jemmy. That's what marriage is."

"Goddamn you," he said, pushing back from his desk and looking around his cluttered study. "This house is a tomb."

"Oh, please, don't say that."

"A tomb," he said. "And you're the caretaker of the dead."

When she ran out of the room crying, he rose from his desk and attacked his makeshift bookshelves, sending volumes flying across the floor. He smashed a bowl of tiny seashells and broke a pot plant—one weary, shriveled strand of ivy—and kicked a chair into the wall.

In the early days of December, 1864, with the winter doldrums set in, London's streets windy and icy, and the Burtons preparing to leave for the new consulate, a message arrived from a well-known sculptor, Edgar Papworth, asking if Burton might drop around to his studio in Kensington.

"Another invitation," Isabel said, showing her husband the letter. "But, really, we have so much to do this week. Your anthropological society dinner. Tickets and baggage. Shall I send regrets?"

"Hmm, no, Papworth's got a reputation," Burton said. "I'd like to meet him, I think. Besides, I've been considering having a portrait done. He probably wants to do a bust of me. Let's stop around. Bit of vanity, but why not?"

The sculptor's studio was in Church Walk, situated above a bookshop in a little beehive of rooms, none of which was heated. A modest amount of warm air drifted up the stairwell from a kitchen at the rear of the downstairs shop, where the bookseller cooked pots of soup for himself and his tenant. Papworth was fat, bearded, and covered with clay dust, so that when he shook Burton's hand he left a fine coat of dust on his guest's fingers.

"Yes, I've seen your work," Burton said, trying to make conversation as he ducked through a low doorway into the first of the sculptor's rooms. Isabel, smiling, tried to keep from touching things.

"Seen my work? Where?" the sculptor wanted to know.

"All about," Burton lied, not able to think of any place.

"My work's mostly in private collections. A few homes in Mayfair and Paris. You probably spotted a bust here or there," said the artist, being helpful as he led the Burtons into another room.

"I expect that's why you wanted to see me?" Burton asked. "To talk about doing a bust?"

"No, not really," Papworth said. "It's this: the object at your feet."

Burton looked down to the floor and saw Speke's death mask. For a moment his nerves began to sing. A dull, grey likeness, but there it was: the eyes closed, but unmistakable.

"Where did you get this?" he asked in a whisper. Isabel came around to her husband's side, looked down, and gasped.

"His family sent it up to me," Papworth said, casually. "This happens sometimes. I wasn't even asked my price. But the thing is, I can't really get it right. Here, let me explain." He picked up the mask, inspected it, turned it, and placed it on a workbench.

"No, it isn't correct," Burton whispered.

"I never saw him in life," the sculptor went on. "And what happens in death is—well, some distortion. And the eyes are closed, so there's that odd effect. People seldom see us with our eyes shut. So I was wondering if you could make any suggestions. You knew him intimately. I hope it isn't traumatic for either of you."

Burton stood over the bench, gazing down into the mask, thinking about the long, sentimental, troubled poem he had been composing at the privacy of his desk. He wanted to say everything about Speke in that poem, everything about friendship, tasks, losses, the things men do and suffer, yet the poem, like so much else, had turned into fumbling pain; like this mask, words were facsimiles—and, therefore, lies.

"He was just a colleague of my husband's," Isabel told Papworth. "And, also, years passed until they saw each other recently—and then only for a brief moment."

Burton was relieved to hear Isabel taking up the conversation. He couldn't answer; his voice was gone except as he told himself, I will never see Speke again. Or, for that matter, Africa—the real Africa. He touched the clay mask with his thumb, making a small indentation. Or for that matter, myself. I won't see myself ever again, not ever.

"There, what did you do?" the sculptor asked, coming over to see. "Is that it? Did he look like that?"

Isabel touched her husband's shoulder and leaned in. The clay face had altered into Speke's familiar formality: something slightly haughty in the mouth.

"Yes," she said, "that's it. That's Speke."

Burton felt his body trembling and worried that he might weep, that his tears might fall into the clay in some melodramatic last display. He still couldn't speak, and Isabel, sensing this, gripped his arm and laced her fingers in his.

"I believe my husband is quite moved," she told the sculptor. "You'll excuse us, won't you?"

414

"By all means, madame, and thank you both," the little man said, and he showed them back through that series of tiny rooms toward the stairway, where the odor of noonday soup rose up in a warm draft.

Burton allowed Isabel to lead him downstairs.

Shadows, lies, facsimiles: so much of life was secondhand, weighed down with arguments and explanations. If we stop moving and try to explain anything, he knew, we truly die; if we pause to make maps or poems, if we take our gaze off the shimmering horizon for an instant, we're surely lost; if we abandon the path in order to reflect or to plot our silly course, we go into exile. And so now my exile begins, he told himself; I am led by a woman, Algernon, and fixed at a desk like a burned-out star in a dead orbit. My life is over.

Oh, Speke.

Oh, Africa.

Afterword

JOHN HANNING SPEKE was correct about Lake Victoria being the principal source of the Nile, and his last revised measurements of both the lake and river altitudes were essentially accurate. A simple obelisk of red granite in Kensington Gardens, London, bears on its west face the cryptic inscription:

'IN MEMORY OF

SPEKE

VICTORIA NYANZA

AND THE NILE 1864'

RICHARD FRANCIS BURTON served as British consul in São Paulo, Brazil, 1864–69, where he was often drunk and where, once, he disappeared during an excursion in the Andes, staying out of touch with his wife and all government officials for months; in Damascus, 1869–71, where his side trips for anthropological research led to suspicions of political intrigue so that he was removed from office by Rashid Pasha and the British ambassador; and in Trieste, 1872–75, where he took occasional trips, but where he also concentrated more than ever on a career of extensive writing. He wrote and translated, in all, forty-seven volumes. His most distinguished literary translations were the *Lusiads* of Camoëns, the sixteenth-century Portuguese poet, and *The Arabian Nights*, a translation of sixteen volumes for which Burton was awarded the Knight Commander of St. Michael and St. George in 1887. Even so, the British press often referred to Burton as "the forgotten Englishman." He began to be known as an eccentric in both London and Trieste, often showing up with Isabel at social functions dressed in outlandish Arab robes or addressing religious groups with a humor and skepticism that were never fashionable. He continued to study general anthropology, sexual mores, and erotic literature; after the publication of *The Arabian Nights* he worked at length on translations of a number of erotic classics, including the

Kama Sutra of Vatsyayana and *The Perfumed Garden of Sheik Nefzauoi*. Among his notes was extensive research on farting. His best-known original work, the long meditative poem entitled "The Kasidah," contains his reflections on faith, morality, death, and freedom. After his spree in Brazil, he and Isabel were never seen apart in public. He suffered badly from gout, lumbago, and the bad legs that had first given him pain during the trip to Ujiji, but when he applied for an early retirement at age sixty-five, the British Foreign Office refused him. In later life he met and became friends with Henry Morton Stanley, who had sailed around the shores of Lake Victoria, proving that Speke, not Burton, had been right about the one true source of the Nile. But it was only after Burton's death in 1890 that Stanley finally proved how Lake Tanganyika overflowed in the wet season into a western watershed, so that by finding this lake Burton and Speke had discovered not the source of the Nile but the beginnings of the River Congo.

LAURENCE (LOWRY) OLIPHANT went to America in 1865 as the disciple of Thomas Lake Harris, a mystic who managed to acquire the entire personal fortune of his follower. Oliphant returned penniless to London, where he soon married for money, often boasting, later, that he had never slept with his wife.

ISABEL BURTON, hoping to preserve and secure her husband's reputation, burned all his unpublished notes and forty-one unpublished manuscripts on the night of his death, including the complete translation of *The Perfumed Garden*.

MONCKTON MILNES (LORD HOUGHTON) lost his great personal library in a fire that destroyed Fryston in 1876. As Palmerston's political strength declined, Milnes lost his attractiveness in many social and cultural circles. He was a benefactor to many young poets and artists, however, and a firm supporter of Burton throughout his life.

JOHN PETHERICK's career ended due to Speke's accusations.

SELIM AGA, Burton's servant in Fernando Po, was killed in the Grebo War in Liberia, where he fought as a mercenary in 1875.

GENERAL RIGBY retired famous as the man who set free the slaves at Zanzibar.

EDWARD BURTON never recovered from his coma and died in the Surrey County Lunatic Asylum.

JAMES GRANT stayed in retirement in Dingwall, Scotland. He published *A Walk Across Africa*, dedicating the book to Speke's memory and saying nothing but good of his colleague ever after.

KING GELELE OF DAHOMEY was killed shortly after Burton's visit. The kingdom of Dahomey was burned to the ground, and most of its inhabitants were murdered by the forces of Abeokuta.

SNAY BIN AMIR OF KAZEH was killed in a skirmish with the warriors of the renegade tribal chieftain, Sera, who refused slavery for his people and who successfully fought the influence of the Arabs in central Africa.

SAMUEL WHITE BAKER was the explorer who is given full credit for the discovery and naming of Lake Albert.

JOHN STEINHAUSER died of cholera while serving as a volunteer physician in one of the many epidemics near Aden.

THE SULTAN MAJJID ruled Zanzibar under diminished powers and British control until his death by natural causes.

SIR RODERICK MURCHISON continued to be a force in the Royal Geographical Society until his death. After Speke's death, Murchison changed his stance once again, blaming Burton for the tragedy, and enlisting the subscription that led to the erection of the monument to Speke in London.

WILLIAM SPEKE was arrested for murder by London detectives not long after his brother's death, but no official charges were ever filed. The incident provided another occasion for numerous sarcasms about the Speke family in the London press. William died without heirs, leaving the family estate to Benjamin, the rector at Dowlish Wake, near Jordans, where John Hanning lies buried.

DR. DAVID LIVINGSTONE returned to Africa obsessed with a view that somehow the watershed to the west of Lake Tanganyika was the Nile source. He searched for years for the "four fountains" that he believed would give rise to the Zambesi, Lualaba, Nile, and Congo rivers, and long after Stanley found him and left him he continued his quest. Burton, commenting on Livingstone's death, noted that "there is a time to leave the Dark Continent. And that is when the *idée fixe* begins to develop itself. Madness comes from Africa. . . ."

ALGERNON CHARLES SWINBURNE became the most famous of the late romantic poets. Of Isabel's burning of Burton's notes, manuscripts, and translations, he remarked, "Of course she has fouled Richard Burton's memory like a harpy." Among his poems in the volume *Astrophel* is the elegy, "On the Death of Richard Burton."

SIDI BOMBAY traveled with Burton, Speke, Livingstone, and Stanley on all of their major explorations. He became the only man in the nineteenth century to cross Africa from both south to north and east to west.